IN THE SHADOW
OF KINGS
A TIME OF DRAGONS: BOOK TWO

PHILIP C. QUAINTRELL

Cover Illustration by Chris McGrath
Book design by BodiDog Design
Edited by Anthony Wright

ISBN: 978-1-916610-36-1 (hardback)
ASIN: B0D4W5KPNR (ebook)

Published by Quaintrell Publishings

For Amy. I mean, who else am I really writing for...

ALSO BY PHILIP C. QUAINTRELL

THE ECHOES SAGA: (9 Book Series)

1. Rise of the Ranger

2. Empire of Dirt

3. Relic of the Gods

4. The Fall of Neverdark

5. Kingdom of Bones

6. Age of the King

7. The Knights of Erador

8. Last of the Dragorn

9. A Clash of Fates

THE RANGER ARCHIVES: (3 Book Series)

1. Court of Assassins

2. Blood and Coin

3. A Dance of Fang and Claw

A TIME OF DRAGONS:

1. Once There Were Heroes

2. In The Shadow of Kings

THE TERRAN CYCLE: (4 Book Series)

1. Intrinsic

2. Tempest

3. Heretic

4. Legacy

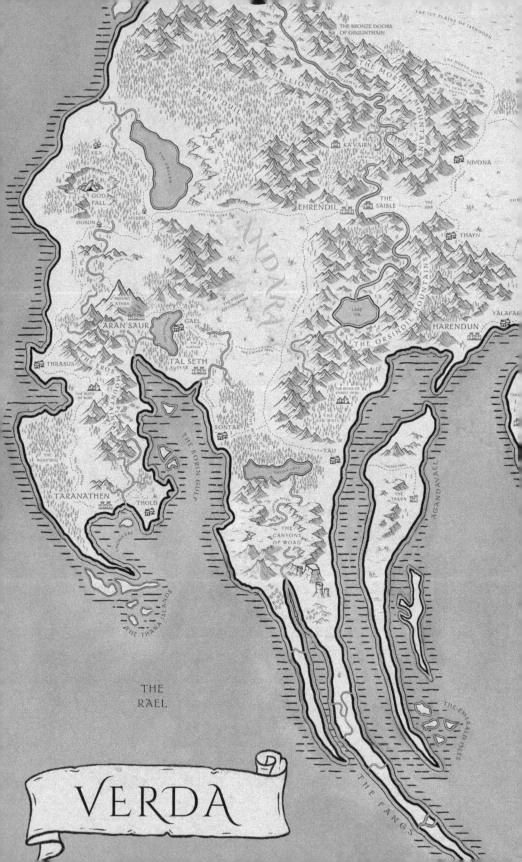

THE BRONZE DOORS
OF ORGUNTHAIN

THE ICE PLAINS OF ISENDORN

THE MOR'HITH MOUNTAINS

THE HELLION MOUNTAINS

FAERN'DUIL

KA'VAIRN

NIVONA

EHRENDIL

THE SAIBLE

THAYN

ANDARA

KILN

GOD FALL

DOSUN

MYRIH

THE ICE LORD

THE FIELDS OF THORIOR

MOUNT ATHAN

ARAN'SAUR

GAEL

LARA IVA

THE ORSINDIL MOUNTAINS

HARENDUN

YALAFAR

THRASUS

TAL SETH

THE RUINS OF KHAEL UNEI

SONTAR

TAU

THE AGAD'DUIL

TARANATHEN

THOLD

THE BORIN GULF

THESEN ISLE

AGANDAVAEL

THE CANYONS OF WOAD

THE TRIDEN

THE RAEL

THE THARA ISLANDS

THE EMERALD ISLES

THE FANGS

VERDA

DRAMATIS PERSONAE

Abel Set-Sedaas
Weaver

Androma
Ex Dragon Rider

Aphrandhor
Wizard

Baelon Vos
Dragonlord

Cob
ranger

Daijen Saeth
Vahlken

Edris Etragon
King of Erador

Galahart
Spymaster of Erador

Gallien Pendain
Smuggler

Garganafan
Dragon/Bonded to Kassanda

Grarfath
Dwarven Smith/The Hammerhold

Handuin
First Vahlken - deceased

Ilithranda
Vahlken

Joran
Half Andaren/Half Human

Kassanda Grey
Dragon Rider

Kitrana Voden
Nimean

Kovun
Vahlken - deceased

Melios
Weaver

Naelin
Vahlken - deceased

Qeledred Isari Arad
Emperor of Andara, the forty-first of his name, of House Lhoris.

Slait
Vahlken

Soveana
Weaver

Soyra
Vahlken - deceased

Tovun
Vahlken Initiate - deceased in present timeline

The Valtorak
Master of Ka'vairn

Yamnomora
Dwarf

Yendi
Vahlken - deceased

PROLOGUE

Death washed over the battlefield. It did not walk as a man nor crawl as a beast but, instead, blew like the breeze, disturbing pools of blood and scattering grains of sand as it rolled over the living. Its ethereal reach extended to grant mercy to the dying and make martyrs of the heroes. It cared little for their banners, the sigils of men as meaningless as the very wars they declared.

While the doomed succumbed to their fate, there was one who remained ever beyond that cold touch. His golden cuirass bore the mark of the dragons, a new breed of creature that had proved themselves the mightiest of allies to the Free Peoples of Verda. His helm had been knocked from his head and his shield left strewn amongst the dead in his wake. Absent both, he bore wounds that tried to slow him, to bring him down to the filth and the blood.

Forged through war, however, *Skara* was nothing if not defiant in the face of death.

Deep purple was his cloak—a humble gift from the people of Qalanqath after his victory in those scorched lands. It fanned out behind him now, lifted high by his daring leap. Where once he might have crashed into his foes with naught but courage, he now landed in their midst with the skills of a warrior, the skills of a *Dragon Rider*.

His sword, a weapon worthy of legend, cut through The Deceiver's minions—the *Husks*—with terrifying ease. What foul creations they were: demons conjured from a world between worlds. Absent their host, the walking beasts were brittle, as fine as parchment, but the enemy had unleashed them upon the realm, consuming villages, towns, and even cities to build his abominable army. Encasing the bodies of their prey, the Husks were killing machines that could only be brought down with fire.

Fortunately for the Free Peoples of Verda, fire was on their side.

Orvax shadowed the battle, his hulking form offering a brief reprieve from the downpour as he glided overhead. His silver scales, wet from the rain, gleamed in the light of his flames, the jet of fire spat from his jaws. Swaths of Husks were torched before ballista bolts drove the dragon away, each tipped with an explosive alchemical concoctions. Still, it had given Gelakor enough time to leap from Orvax's saddle and bring his axe to bear.

It was with a touch of magic that he impacted the battlefield, scattering his foes in every direction. He felled one beast after another, his axe hacking and chopping at his enemies with great precision. Taking their arms and legs where he could, Gelakor left the Husks writhing on the ground, their need to fight still burning in their corrupted veins.

"Where've you been?" Skara demanded.

Gelakor offered a grin that was all too casual for a battlefield. "At least *I* brought a dragon!"

Skara didn't need to reply with a quip of his own—Gelakor already knew that Skara's dragon was fighting in the southern lands, keeping the last Leviathan from interfering with their final assault on the enemy. Thinking of his immortal companion, whose voice was too distant to hear in his mind, was enough to give the Rider momentary pause. Distracted, his sword was batted aside, exposing his cuirass to a painful blow before a boot slammed into his chest.

Taken from his feet, Skara groaned as he rolled left then right to avoid the incoming attacks. He kicked out, taking the left knee of the nearest Husk and bringing it down beside him. Rolling again, he evaded the sword of a second minion, its blade ploughing into its companion instead.

A whistle of steel preceded Gelakor's axe, the weapon finding its end in the skull of the second Husk. The axe vanished immediately, returning to its master's grip, before the Rider launched it again and again, knocking the Husk back step by step until Skara could rise.

Round came the Dragon Rider's sword. The steel edge cut through the night air, and the raindrops sizzled as they made contact with the glyphs and fine shards that burned bright orange down the weapon's fuller. Brighter still was the Husk that tasted that biting edge, its body reduced to sparks and ash. Skara continued to pivot round until he was able to drop to one knee and plunge the tip of his sword into the Husk he had brought down with a kick. So too did the wretch burn up, its ashes scattered with explosive force.

Skara looked down at the scorch mark left on the ground. There had been a time when he saw the men and women behind their grotesque features, they who had been bound by dark magic to dwell behind the eyes of monsters. That time had long past, put behind him by endless campaigns to free Verda from the grip of evil. Those who served *him*, whose name so few dared to breathe, were little more than fodder now—people twisted into creatures to protect their woeful master.

Hounded by the screams of his fellow man and pressed upon by the roars of his enemies, Skara pushed on with a rallying cry on his lips. Like him, a smith, those who fought for the Free Peoples were no more than simple farmers, merchants, laymen—ordinary folk—who had been forced into the life of the warrior. With skills not just gained but *earned*, they battled with fury to reach their commanders.

"On me!" Skara bellowed, his sword slicing through the air to point at the obsidian palace. "Stay on my side," he instructed

Gelakor alone, their close proximity required to power their weapons.

Together with what remained of their army, they punctured the dark legions like a deadly spear. Skara's sword was the tip of that spear, his every swing bringing an end to their monstrous foes. Easily found by the glowing purple glyphs inlaid about the axehead, Gelakor displayed his fortitude, a distinct feature that had initiated his bond with Orvax.

Gelakor's might and courage were accompanied by Skara's unbridled wrath and recklessness. Where Gelakor fought for his countrymen and their right to freedom, Skara fought for those he had lost. The names of his sons and wife were seared into his heart, a burning wound that refused to fade.

Over the plated helms of his enemies, he looked upon the black palace. His vengeance could be found inside, and he was damned if he wasn't taking it before the dawn.

The Dragon Rider met an incoming blade with his own, melting the steel mid-swing before shoulder-barging the Husk to create enough space to backhand the fiend with his pommel. A downward stroke soon followed and the Husk was sliced down the middle, its two halves disintegrating in a flurry of sparks.

The ground shook.

It would have been easy to believe that Orvax or perhaps the hulking Brigabhor had landed on the battlefield, daring the ballistas and catapults to find them. But Skara glimpsed both dragons in the sky—flashes of silver and gold—each harassing the palace's defensive walls.

"Skara..."

Following Gelakor's voice, he was soon looking at the jagged outline of an Ice Troll. It was one of the many abominations that had been brought forth from the dark depths to wreak havoc on Verda's green earth. At nearly twenty feet tall, its body was coated in natural armour, a crystal-like substance that gave the appearance of ice. The face and palms remained the only locations absent the sharp and terribly dense crystal, making such beasts notoriously difficult to kill.

Dragging chains from its wrists and neck, the Ice Troll waded in, sweeping its deadly arms into the men of Verda. It shattered bone and armour alike, making a ruin of its crystalline skin with the hot red of human blood. With a war cry, Gelakor launched his axe at the monster. It struck the jagged features about its face, missing his mark by inches. He threw again and again, succeeding in no more than attracting the creature.

Skara danced about his Rider companion, keeping the Husks at bay with elegant arcs of his sword. "Bring it down!" he cried.

It was no use. For all of Gelakor's skill, the Ice Troll was too erratic and its vulnerable face too small a target. So close was it now that Skara had to battle the rain in his eyes to look up at it. The roar it let loose drowned out the fighting and snarling Husks, a dreaded sound that had accompanied so many into death.

There came a flash of brilliant blue, a hue so vibrant it could only be magic. The Ice Troll reeled as its head, a beastly-looking thing sunken into its chest, was unceremoniously ported from its body. In the same instant, its decapitated head appeared at Skara's feet.

There was a hammer lodged in its face.

Striding towards them as if a great battle wasn't raging, Qif's towering presence parted Skara and Gelakor, allowing her to plant one boot on the Troll's head. Chunks of crystal broke away when the third Dragon Rider yanked her hammer free.

"The palace doors have been destroyed!" Qif reported, the three Riders gliding through each other's manoeuvres to slay Husk after Husk. "Brigabhor has glimpsed the interior!"

Skara found Gelakor's blue eyes, their colour exaggerated in the light of a Husk succumbing to sparks and ash. There was no misunderstanding Qif's meaning—if Brigabhor had seen the interior, then so too had his Rider. With the hammer, she could now port all three of them inside the palace. United, the three could finally face their true enemy together, a feat that had eluded them throughout the war.

Their combined might would be his end, an end to the war, to the suffering and brutal oppression that had chained and choked the people of Verda for so long.

And yet...

Skara could not—would not—allow any other to rob him of his vengeance. That most vile of all living things would be extinguished by him, no other. His desire to kill, to bathe in the blood of the one who had murdered his family, drove out the logic of facing their enemy as a trio. It was the dragon in him—a source of confidence bordering on arrogance—that failed to ask the question of whether he even *could* defeat the wretch alone. He only knew that he *would* face him—and that he would have satisfaction.

Springing from the chestplate of a charging Husk, Skara reached out with one hand and used Qif's muscled shoulder to pivot and come down on another fiend. It made no difference to Qif, her powerful frame more than capable of supporting Skara's familiar fighting style. But what she failed to realise in that brief and chaotic moment was that Skara had touched her quite deliberately.

With the vambrace on his right forearm, Skara was able to reach inside his fellow Rider's mind and see, smell, hear, and even touch everything and anything she had ever interacted with, including her dragon, Brigabhor. After years of honing his use of the bracer, Skara cut through the plethora of memories and interactions until he found the image shared between dragon and Rider.

While it seemed the world had come to a stop, Skara absorbed the memory of the palace's interior—however slight it was.

Upon landing, his sword cleaved through the intended beast with ease, and the mayhem of battle crashed back into his senses. He didn't hesitate—he couldn't, lest Qif note the fine red shards glowing on the bracer's surface and discern his intentions. With one hand, Skara gripped the haft of The Anther and deftly twisted it from her grasp while he himself spun around. His purple cloak dazed her and partially concealed his actions from Gelakor, giving him just enough time to raise the hammer and slam it into the ground.

"No!" Qif cried, but it was too late.

Being not only a weapon of his design but also his creation, Skara ported just beyond the threshold of the blasted palace doors with no ill effect. How many times had it nearly paralysed him before he'd learned to harmonise with The Anther? Now it was an instrument of death in his grip.

The Husks—incapable of displaying or feeling surprise—rushed him from the dark corners of the antechamber. With sword and hammer he obliterated some while sending others high into the sky, porting them from the palace into the very storm that swirled over the battlefield.

Alone, his breath ragged and clothes dripping rainwater, the Dragon Rider laid his old eyes on the thick iron doors that stood tall in the far wall. He didn't need to see to know that his enemy was on the other side, sitting idly while thousands died for his deranged ideology.

Determined to see an end to it all, the Dragon Rider squared his shoulders and strode towards his destiny, towards his vengeance.

The doors refused to budge.

"Coward!" he spat.

Orange light rolled through the air as he positioned his sword and plunged it into one of the doors. The magic within the weapon made short work of the metal, as if an iron rod had been driven through butter. The Dragon Rider took no care in carving out a hole large enough to permit him entry, nor did he temper the magic he poured into his thrusting jab of the hammer. The Anther's head struck the interior of his work and cast pieces of the door far into the next chamber.

"BARAD-AGIN!" he roared, naming the fiend who had unleashed the Leviathans upon the realm.

How grand that chamber could have been, a hall fit for one who might rule over the entire realm. Yet it had fallen into ruin, its splendour neglected while its master focused on the dark worlds that lay beyond understanding.

And damn if it didn't stink of death, a putrid rot that assaulted Skara's nose.

The vaulted ceiling was masked in shadow, though great cobwebs stretched out of the darkness, bridging the gaps between the pillars. Skara could hear faint scurrying and distant hissing, but he turned his attention away from the creatures that dwelled so high. He, instead, took in the debris that littered the vast spaces between the pillars. There was evidence everywhere of Barad-Agin's insidious nature. Bodies—corpses all—were scattered throughout and strapped down. Some even floated without restraint. Every one of them looked to have suffered in death, victims of experimental magic.

Parchments, old and new, were piled high in the corners, the scrawl of magic upon them all. Alchemical processes were taking place on tabletops that had been squeezed into any available gaps. Liquids of every colour bubbled or swirled while steam rose from half a dozen cauldrons. Some of it was familiar to Skara, but so much of it was new magic. *Blood magic.*

Was there anything more seductive? Its potential was seemingly limitless, if frighteningly costly.

Pausing by a table of scrolls and weighty tomes, Skara flipped the cover of one and rifled through the delicate pages. He stopped at a page that detailed the process of binding different creatures together, allowing one to use the characteristics of the other. There were also drawings inside that revealed these experiments had escalated to binding humans with animals as well—what nightmares they were.

Inevitably, his gaze was drawn to the throne that sat upon a large dais. There he sat.

Barad-Agin. The Deceiver to those who had known him. Earthbreaker to those who had suffered him. Blood-drinker to those who had borne witness to the monster he had become.

His true name was that of a shiver that ran up one's spine, or the cool touch of dread that plied one's veins. Shrouded and hooded in black robes, his very person seemed to suck in the shadows about him, as if his entire form was an absence of life and matter. He was evil personified. If only Skara had seen it sooner.

Barad-Agin's voice came from everywhere, gripping the

Dragon Rider by his very bones. "Skara... You've got old," he remarked, though the rim of his voluminous hood continued to hide his eyes.

Skara considered his appearance, all too aware that time had impacted him before bonding with his dragon. Even so, his body was a testament to a hard life of violence, his muscles well-defined and skin still taut. Only his face and hair betrayed his age, the latter having lost its colour and now trimmed into a long braided mohawk.

"I'm *immortal*," the Rider corrected.

"Then you are *forever* old," Barad-Agin replied, a touch of amusement in his ancient voice.

Skara tilted his head, his suspicions growing. "I've come for your head, conjurer."

Barad-Agin gave a rasping laugh that echoed off every wall. "You've come to kill me?" He laughed again. "I'm not sure I'm even *alive*," came the quiet, if disturbing, response.

The Dragon Rider narrowed his eyes on the robed figure sitting before him. "You are defeated," he declared. "Your Leviathans have been chased to the ends of the earth. Your army is on *fire*. And you, *Barad-Agin*, are not what you seem."

Spinning away from the throne, Skara raised his sword high. His will alone was enough to trigger the magic within and further ignite the glyphs etched into the steel. In that moment, it was as if the sun itself had dawned inside the great chamber, banishing the shadows. And any notion that Barad-Agin was resting upon the throne.

A monstrous shriek met that light, and the real Barad-Agin recoiled from the sword, taken away on his eight arachnid legs. What a horror he had made of himself, his body twisted, broken, and reformed into something between man and spider. So much of him was shrouded in dark and tattered robes, though it did nothing to conceal his unnatural form as he scurried up and behind one of the pillars, his nature always seeking the shadows.

Skara dimmed the glyphs slightly. He glanced back at the

throne, seeing now in the light that the fingers extending from the sleeves were those of a long-dead corpse.

"This is Dawnbreaker," the Rider announced, hefting the sword with pride. "I didn't have a chance to introduce you to each other the last time we quarrelled."

Barad-Agin clung to the highest part of the pillar, his humanoid torso peering out to reveal his hooded head. "Your understanding of magic has deepened since the days you called me *master*. A pity you have used it to sow chaos."

The accusation nearly choked Skara. "You are blinded by the power you have amassed," he told the fiend. "The chaos that wracks our world was ushered in by *you*. By your thirst for *dominion*."

The fiend edged out from behind the pillar, his claw-like hands carving lines down the stone. "Of course you don't understand," he rasped. "That's why you abandoned me, why you rebelled against me. To think you had such potential. Your harmony with magic made you the greatest of my apprentices. But your *naivety* made you the very worst of them."

"You see sense in it, do you?" Skara questioned, his fury bubbling over. "You see the justice in murdering *thousands*?" he spat. "Tell me, what didn't I understand about you butchering my family? How did that serve the great plan? Did my childrens' screams bring the peace you thought it would? Did spilling my wife's blood build the paradise you've dreamed of?"

It was with horrifying speed that Barad-Agin descended back to the floor, his pointed legs extending to find every surface before sending a shockwave through the stone. He stood as tall as the doors Skara had sundered, his eyes—all *four* of them—glistening as he loomed over Dawnbreaker.

"The violence and death that has rippled across our fair realm can be laid at *your* feet, Dragon Rider. There is only war because *you* instigate it at every turn. Had you let me build my *paradise*, you and your family would be living in it by now. That's all I've ever tried to do," he insisted earnestly. "Do you think peace and security just happen? I have seen what happens when the world is left to get on with it. When it's left to the murderers and the rapists to crown themselves kings. That's a world where the weak become no more than *things*." Barad-Agin brought his face down towards Skara. "Without *fear*, there is only *suffering*."

The Rider didn't shy away from that grotesque amalgamation. "I am not afraid of you," he said boldly.

"And how you have suffered for it," the vile wizard remarked.

Skara's family flashed before his eyes, their slaughtered bodies ragged and bloody. Dawnbreaker cut through the air and came to rest at Barad-Agin's throat, its bright hue revealing featureless black eyes and oily, mottled skin. His rage had nearly won out, an unsatisfying end given that his sword would disintegrate the wretch. The world, Skara knew, needed to see him dead if it was to move on.

A wicked smile split the creature's face, offering a glimpse at Barad-Agin's fangs. "You will see the truth of it soon enough, my old friend. As you say, I am defeated. Whether you want it or not, the *Free Peoples of Verda* will thrust you upon the throne. Then you will see. Then you will *understand*. The only thing they need saving from is themselves. You can't do that with freedom. You need *monsters*. You need *darkness*. Magic can offer you that and so much more." The beast chuckled inside his hood. "Your time will come."

Skara plunged Dawnbreaker into the stone, leaving it to stand sentinel beside him, while his other hand squeezed the haft of The Anther. "*Your* time is at an end."

PART ONE

1

FUTURE'S END

Through ancient halls and cold stone, Joran had been brought to the heart of Drakanan. His neck craned to take in the slab of wall that stood before him, a seeming end to the chamber in which Kassanda had come to a stop. The flickering flames from surrounding torches revealed the relief carved into the centre of that stone, a single motif stretching from wall to wall.

Dragons!

Three of them there were, their wings fanned and claws bared as they battled an enormous monster born from nightmare.

It was a fantastical, if unbelievable, moment spoiled by the grief that gripped Joran's heart.

Gallien was dead.

Despite the smuggler's uncanny ability to defy the odds, he could not have survived the Andaren forces swarming The Ruins of Gelakor.

There was a part of Joran that tried to protect himself from the pain of it, a part that told him Gallien wasn't his real father. It was inevitably quashed by a lifetime of memories. Gallien had raised him, protected him, taught him everything he knew, and even trusted the boy with his *real* name.

Gallien was his father. And now his father was gone.

The memory was fresh, being no more than two days old. *"Go,"* Gallien had urged. *"Live now. Fight for us later."*

Then Oaken, his mother's Aegre, had launched into the sky, parting them forever. His being there, in the heart of Drakanan, seemed so trivial now. Unchallenged, the Andaren army was pressing south into Erador. The war he was meant to be stopping was raging and had already claimed those he loved. What could he possibly do now that would make any difference?

"Maybe you didn't hear me," Joran suggested, his voice projected at Kassanda as he blinked tears from his eyes. "The Andarens have breached our borders. An entire army marches south through The Giant's Throat."

Kassanda didn't even look at him, her face cast up at the motif as the torchlight bounced off her dark, tattooed scalp.

"I heard you," she replied in her commanding voice. "It falls to others of my order. I have remained here for a single purpose."

The Rider finally turned to lay eyes on him, her serious expression preceding the gravity of her words.

"I am to train the one who will bring about a time of dragons, the one who will end the war."

Joran swallowed the lump in his throat. "But there'll be nothing for me to fight for if you don't go out there and stop them," he argued.

"As I said," she repeated calmly, "it falls to others of my order."

"Androma says there's barely enough of you to guard the coast," he countered obstinately.

"And she is right," Kassanda snapped, turning fully on the young man. "Do you know why?" she demanded fiercely. "Because this war hasn't just robbed us of precious lives, it's also fractured us. The Dragon Riders are a shadow of their former selves."

An intimidating figure, Kassanda was made all the more imposing when she stepped towards him.

"But the end has been seen, and not just *any* end. A time of dragons and Riders offers a glimmer of hope for Verda's future. You haven't walked through enough darkness to know the value of real *hope*."

Kassanda sighed and retreated from him. "I must play my part to see it through."

Joran's mind couldn't help but return to his meeting with Gala-hart, the king's spymaster, in the boathouse on the outskirts of Valgala.

"The future you're talking about is only a possibility," he told the Rider, paraphrasing the spymaster's words where the Helm of Ahnir was concerned. "By acting on it, we might be undoing it. What if we're supposed to go out there and stop the Andarens? What if staying here is the wrong choice?"

"Depending on what happens next," Kassanda said, "those questions are irrelevant."

Joran frowned at the cryptic response, but he held his tongue and watched as the Dragon Rider raised her hand towards the large motif. Her fingers flexed, as if strained, before the wall itself began to respond. To the sound of grinding stone, four columns in the relief descended into the floor, robbing the motif of so much imagery. In their place was a doorway.

A musty odour reached out of the chamber beyond, out of the pitch black. Joran didn't dare advance, his heart racing now. Only minutes ago, he had avoided a fiery death when surrounded by wild dragons, and so the feeling of impending doom still clung to him. Was there a dragon waiting for him inside that darkness? It was enough to make him forget about the Andaren army and focus on the singular reason for his being in Drakanan.

He was to bond with a dragon.

"It has been a hundred or more years since this door was opened." Kassanda's voice seemed diminished, as though taken by the shadows that lay in wait.

"What's in there?" Joran's voice was quieter still.

The Dragon Rider stared into the abyss before turning to look at him. "Hope."

With that, Kassanda strode into the chamber, her sandy cloak the last of her to be seen. Joran more than hesitated—he stepped back.

"Go," Gallien urged again from recent memory. "Become everything they say you will."

With the courage his father had instilled in him, Joran passed over the threshold and entered the darkness. He did so only to be assaulted by the light, as torch after torch came to life, their flames revealing a wide chamber that rose up in tiers. His violet eyes—his mother's eyes—adjusted to the change in luminosity with immediate effect, bringing into focus the natural rock that formed the walls and jagged ceiling.

That was not all his eyes discovered.

Of the numerous tiers carved out of the sloping rock, only one was occupied. The single row's inhabitants—of which there were only six—sat neatly inside their own smooth impression.

"Dragon eggs," Joran muttered to himself.

Though their tones were muted, each egg possessed its own colour. Even the scales that coated their exterior were varied enough to make each distinct in its own right. It was utter curiosity that saw Joran press on, taking the steps that led up to the second tier.

The eggs appeared so ornate, as if they had been carved from the rock and painted as no more than decoration. Joran retracted his hand before he could touch the closest one, its surface a muddy red colour.

"There are so few of them," he remarked, taking in the hundreds of empty impressions. When no reply came from Kassanda, he turned around to find her.

The Dragon Rider was simply watching him, and intently so, her head tilting from one side to the other.

"What is it?" he queried.

Kassanda looked from Joran to the dormant eggs and back.

"What?" he echoed, feeling increasingly disturbed by the examination.

"These are the only dragon eggs we have left; every one of them gifted to us by their mothers."

Joran absorbed the knowledge, failing to see how it had anything to do with why she was looking at him with such concern.

"How do I bond with one?" he asked, glancing at the six eggs again.

Kassanda paused. "It would have begun the moment you shared the same air. But you feel nothing," she stated as a matter of fact. "That much I can see."

It seemed physically impossible, yet Joran felt his insides plummet into unknown depths. "What do you mean?"

Kassanda's jaw firmed up in the face of disappointment, her shoulders squared beneath pauldrons of bone-white dragon scales. "You are not the one."

2

BURIED MEMORY

0 Years Ago...

4

Daijen's warm breath spoiled the frigid air and washed over the dragon egg gripped in his hands. Examining the scales caught in the light of Androma's orb, he marvelled at the dark purple and faintest flecks of gold. It was beautiful.

He had read countless volumes about dragons, factual tomes that recorded any and all observations and interactions with them. He had seen them in the flesh, even played his part in slaying one, and knew them to be exquisite creatures, each a well of knowledge and wisdom. Never had he seen one of their eggs, nor even a drawing.

It felt a profound moment, he—a Vahlken—holding a dragon egg. But it was more than that, he realised, the truth of it dawning on him. While it felt like no more than an object, it housed life inside—*immortal life*. Concealed within was a real dragon, their dormant existence awaiting perfect conditions before hatching. Awaiting their *Rider*.

A sigh of frustration broke his reverie, turning the Vahlken back to his companion. Androma dumped her satchel on the ground and removed a water skin, leaving the satchel's flap open. Her back pressed against the ancient wall, she gulped the water and used a handful to wash the dirt from around her mouth and push back her blonde hair.

"There *must* be a door we can use," she concluded.

Daijen looked to the other side of the room, where it felt natural for there to be a door facing the dais he was standing on. Instead, he found a wall, the slabs of stones notably different in size to those that made up the chamber.

"I think it was bricked up," he said absently, his voice dry and catching. His attention wandered briefly over the skeleton lying in the middle of the room, long dead after having been sealed inside.

Sealed inside with the *egg*.

Inevitably, he was drawn back to the dusty relic in his hands, a relic that had been birthed by a dragon and left ceremoniously upon an altar inside a chamber it seemed no one was intended to find.

"Bricked up?" Androma echoed, her exasperation tinted with curiosity. "A cell, perhaps, for our friend over there," she suggested, gesturing loosely in the direction of the skeleton. "Either way, we will have to climb out the way we came in," she reasoned, her right hand sliding over the wall in search of the jagged hole they had fallen through.

Daijen's eyes pierced the gloom and scrutinised the jagged hole they had tumbled through in their escape from the mutated hag— a curator, she had called herself. Beyond the hole, he could see the ascending slope that would take them back up to the corridor and from there, they could easily retrace their steps to find the others in their party.

"You have a good memory, yes?"

Androma's question required an extra second to process. "I do," he answered, a hint of curiosity in his voice.

"Take another look at this before we leave," the blind Rider instructed, her hand reaching out to tap the stone wall beside her.

Daijen glanced at the painted mural that had long begun to fade, his sharp eyes taking in the golden figure that stood before a dark army, opposed by six dragons. He was sure to note the seventh dragon, its image depicted as falling into a pool of darkness. He had looked at it in detail once already. That was enough.

"Androma..." he called softly, his gaze having returned to the egg in his hands.

His next words were robbed of him, along with his footing.

The sudden quake ripped through the chamber, if not the pyramid itself, drowning out the Vahlken's words with the cracking of stone. Along with the slabs that came loose from the low ceiling, Daijen fell face-first, thrown from the dais. He landed atop Androma's satchel and felt the egg leave his grasp but never heard it land amidst the impact of raining debris and the Rider's yell of surprise.

His first attempt to rise was quashed by a chunk of stone that landed squarely on his back. Silk of the Weavers, hidden beneath his leather cuirass, saved his spine from injury, but the weight was still enough to slam him into the floor.

"Daijen?" the Rider cried.

The Vahlken groaned as he pushed himself up to his hands and knees, his fingers feeling the leather strap of Androma's satchel. His cloak of bear fur had never felt so heavy. Spitting blood from a cut lip, Daijen managed to find his feet—only to be threatened by more crumbling rock. He dived aside and avoided the slab before it could crush him. Coughing through the clouds of dust, the Vahlken managed to call out for Androma.

"I'm here!" she replied.

Daijen looked to the ceiling above her—an almighty crack was running wild across the stone.

"Look out!"

The Vahlken launched himself at the Rider and took her by the waist. Together they hit the floor and rolled, narrowly evading the heavy debris.

"What's happening?" Androma groaned as the Vahlken threw the strap of the satchel over her head and shoulder.

Daijen ignored the question and looked around furiously, his sharp eyes scrutinising every patch of floor that remained.

Where was it?

Where was the egg?

There was no time, however, to suffer the great disappointment he felt. It was move or die.

"This way," Daijen directed, seeing the jagged gap in the wall and ceiling where they might ascend to safety.

Partially dragging Androma by the arm, he eventually began to shove her through the gap and instructed her to start climbing. With one foot of his own resting on the lip of the broken wall, the Vahlken looked back at the imposing chamber, desperate to lay eyes on the dragon egg. It had felt important, sat there upon a pedestal, sealed up from the world and in the heart of a Skaramangian stronghold.

Now it was lost for eternity.

The ceiling buckled all the more, urging Daijen to abandon his search and begin his climb. Their return to the corridor above was arduous, the sloping vacuum between floors interrupted by large rocks and sharp stones. Still, both were warriors of exceptional class and not to be defeated.

Daijen entered the corridor after Androma, who had birthed another orb of light upon reaching the hewn stone. The Vahlken subconsciously ran his hands around his belt, making certain his scimitar and atori short-sword were still clipped to him.

"Can you see it?" she hissed.

Daijen looked down the corridor, aware that the Rider was referring to the mutated hag that had pursued them. He saw no sign of the monster, though he spotted the scorch marks on the floor where it had succumbed to Androma's flames.

"No," he answered. "I see claw marks in the stone, as if it was dragged out."

"Aphrandhor," the Rider determined.

Daijen agreed, unable to imagine anything but magic capable

of dragging the fiend out of a narrow corridor. He was about to agree with her assessment when he noted Androma leaning against the wall, one hand gripped around the hilt of the silvyr sword on her hip. She looked exhausted.

"Are you wounded?" he asked instead.

"No," she assured him. "Just... a little out of breath." It seemed to pain her to admit as much. "We haven't all bathed in Handuin's soup," she quipped, her hand gliding along the wall as she walked away.

Daijen watched her move off for a moment, wondering if he was observing the effects of losing her bond with Maegar. Without that natural bond—a bond of magic—she was becoming more... *human.*

The Vahlken hesitated to follow her, his attention shifting back to the hole they had previously fallen down. Pitch blackness awaited him, the same pitch blackness that had claimed the egg. A sense of failure gripped him then, bringing his shoulders down.

Following the corridor back the way they had come, Daijen noted the scorch marks that blackened the floor and walls in places, remnants of the mutated fiend that had hounded them and suffered Androma's burning magic. Beyond them, they finally reached the door they had been hurled through and returned to the cavernous chamber that dominated so much of the Skaramangian pyramid.

Daijen stopped in his tracks, his gaze rising. It was vastly different to the chamber they had left.

"There you are!" Aphrandhor exclaimed, the wizard hurrying over to intercept Androma.

"Daijen." Ilithranda's voice had a sense of urgency to it.

"Where've ye two been?" Yamnomora barked. "Ye left all the fightin' to us!"

Indeed, the companions were surrounded by the twisted and monstrous corpses of the curators, many of which were licked by The Green Leaf's flames. Off to one side, Mordrith was yanking her hammer out of a nightmarish skull and wiping the gore across the stone.

Daijen ignored them all, *his* question far more pressing. "Where did it go?"

Like him, the others turned to look at the vast and empty space where there should have been a colossal pillar of stone. It had housed hundreds of skeletons, each one as ordinary—if mysterious—as the next. So precious were they that the curator had been enraged upon learning that Yamnomora had touched one, seemingly desecrating their holy sanctum. Their *tomb*.

"It dropped into the floor," Ilithranda reported.

"Didn' ye feel it?" Yamnomora threw her hand out, gesturing at the rubble and debris that had been torn from the surrounding walls.

Daijen looked at Androma, as if to share in the revelation of what had caused the ancient chamber to implode without warning, but she hadn't the eyes to see him. "We felt it," he said ominously, his thoughts lingering on the dragon egg.

"It must be a safety measure," Mordrith reasoned, her boot running over the slight lip between the floor and what had been the top of the circular pillar.

"Hell o' a safety measure," Yamnomora remarked. "Nearly brought the whole damn place down."

"Human ingenuity," Mordrith muttered with ridicule.

Daijen walked over to the lip, noting that the intricate pattern carved into the top of the pillar was now the floor. "Is there no way to raise it?" he asked, crouching to intrude his fingers through the slight gap in the stone.

"There must be," Yamnomora replied. "But yer guess is as good as mine," she added, her head turning to take in the enormity of the pyramid's interior.

"Someone must have triggered the mechanism," Ilithranda pointed out.

"Well, it certainly wasn't one of them," the wizard concluded, his staff sweeping over the littered corpses.

A distant and indeterminable sound echoed through the pyramid.

As one, they turned their attention to the shadows that sat outside of the glowing orb and flickering flames.

"We are not alone," Daijen surmised, his voice low.

"How many more can there be?" Yamnomora complained.

"Quiet," Ilithranda hissed, her head tilted to one side.

Daijen was listening too, his acute sense of hearing hard at work to pull out the subtlest of noises amidst heavy breathing and flickering flames.

Padding feet.

The dying ends of a distant whisper.

A pained groan.

"More are coming," he snapped, his gaze whipping up towards the darkness that shrouded so much of the chamber.

Aphrandhor thrust his staff high and released a white-hot flare that penetrated the thick shadows. Daijen's jaw clamped shut, his teeth clenched.

It was raining monsters.

They poured out of alcoves in the surrounding walls, their pincered limbs gripping the stone as they scurried down towards the companions. Each one had an unnatural shriek and roar of its own, creating a cacophony of descending terror.

"How many?" Androma demanded, her silvyr blade tasting the air again.

"Too many," The Green Leaf grumbled.

"There ain' too many for me girls," Yamnomora said eagerly, hefting her two axes.

Her bravado wasn't shared by her fellow dwarf. "All o' ye," Mordrith commanded, "on me. Now!"

Mordrith's strategy became clear to all but Aphrandhor, who had yet to see the true power of The Anther. "Closer," the dwarf bade the wizard.

"We can't leave yet," Ilithranda insisted. "We need to know what this place is."

"It's a tomb," Mordrith reminded the Vahlken. "An' it'll be ours if we don' get out."

There was no stopping the dwarf, her well-muscled arm

reaching high to see The Anther primed. As it fell, hurtling towards the stone at her feet, so too did the mutated monsters touch down, their grotesque features snarling and spitting.

Only a second passed while that hammer thundered through the air, a second in which Daijen remained braced, his scimitar and atori short-sword having sprung free upon sighting the fiends. For no more than a flash, the shadows were banished when steel struck stone. The monsters reeled as two points in reality were exchanged before their black eyes.

Their surroundings changed in an instant. A cold wind washed over Daijen's face and hands, though he certainly didn't register the sensation as uncomfortable. His eyes were drawn to the sea of stars that reigned over the sky and the crescent moon that hung between them. Before him was the glassy obelisk—the very top of the pyramid that protruded above the ground.

Mordrith had ported them back to the surface.

The Vahlken's attention snapped back to his companions at the sound of vomiting. Both Aphrandhor and Androma were doubled over, hacking and sputtering as they spoiled the hard ground.

Yamnomora slung an axe over one shoulder. "Ye get used to it," she told them with some amusement. "Bludgeon!" she exclaimed upon sighting the distant Warhog.

The great beast of a mount heard its master's call and came rushing over, bringing with it an intense odour Daijen was sure he would never be rid of.

"Ye two must 'ave strong constitutions," Mordrith commented, her dark eyes washing over the Vahlken pair.

"We should not have abandoned our course." Ilithranda's sharp tone cut through the night.

"A thank ye will suffice," Mordrith bit back.

Their argument spiralled, but their every word felt distant to Daijen. His attention had wandered and taken him to the edge of the deep hole not far from where they had ported. He looked down into the darkness, past the contraptions, chains, and ropes that allowed the platform to rise and fall through the shaft. The

Vahlken didn't know what he was expecting to see. There was nothing save the darkness at the bottom of that pit.

A familiar, if piercing, squawk turned Daijen's eyes skyward. However grim his time had been inside the pyramid, the sight of Valyra brought a welcome smile to his face. She was the definition of freedom and an ever-present display of the strength every Vahlken had at their disposal.

Her four legs, each bearing an array of deadly talons, set down on the earth, bringing the Aegre's face and armoured beak into view. Those yellow eyes had a way of holding Daijen, of reminding him that their bond was beyond that of animal and master. They were companions bound by the same magic that flowed through their veins, by the magic of Handuin.

They were mutants together.

Valyra dipped her enormous head, allowing Daijen to run his hand over the feathers between her eyes. The wind rushed over them both as Oaken glided down to meet the base of the pyramid. The Aegre's presence was enough to bring any bickering to an end, even putting the dwarves into a temporary retreat and giving The Green Leaf and the Rider enough time to recover from the apparent side effects of The Anther.

"What power," Aphrandhor rasped, his hands still leaning on his knees while his gaze remained fixed on the hammer. "Can you go..." The wizard paused, retching naught but air. "Can you go anywhere? What are its limits?"

Beside him, Androma managed to stand up straight and shrug off her satchel. "Where are we?"

"Outside the pyramid," Ilithranda informed her.

The Green Leaf took a deep breath and straightened up. "The impact," he continued, his questions seemingly endless. "It is necessary? You can't port without striking the weapon?"

Mordrith twisted the hammer in her hand, adjusting her grip on the haft. "We shouldn' linger," the dwarf warned, ignoring the man's blast of questions. "Those beasties might take up the hunt. An' who knows what other horrors this island is home to."

"You're so eager to leave." Ilithranda's tone was as barbed as her words—she wasn't one to leave a fight unfinished. "*You* came to us, remember? *You* wanted our help making sense of this place. Well, we're here."

"Ye saw how many there were," Mordrith countered fiercely. "Even a Vahlken and a Dragon Rider couldn' survive that."

"You mean a *dwarf* couldn't survive that," Ilithranda retorted.

Yamnomora took offence on behalf of Mordrith and stepped threateningly towards the Vahlken. Ilithranda didn't so much as twitch, but the same could not be said of Oaken. The Aegre bristled, his head extending to arch over the top of his companion and look down on Yamnomora. The dwarf deserved some credit, for she didn't cower from the overbearing creature capable of cutting her in half with a snap of his beak. Yet she didn't advance either.

"Daijen?"

The Vahlken heard his name, just as he had heard the heated exchange. It took his distracted mind an extra second to realise it was Androma who had called him and a moment longer to understand her tone. The Rider was wondering why he had yet to intercede, curious as to why he was entirely absent.

"What is it?" Androma queried, her curiosity turning to suspicion with the lack of any reply.

Daijen felt all eyes fall on him, dragging his attention away from Valyra and the cavernous shaft beside him. The Vahlken looked back at his companions, an eclectic group thrown together by a shared enemy. He met those expectant gazes a little lost for words, unsure how to articulate what he had found and subsequently lost in the buried chamber.

"This is a place of evil," he eventually announced. "It clings to the stone. Whatever else it is to the Skaramangians, I think it is a prison."

A ripple of confusion washed over the group. "A prison?" Androma questioned. "We found naught but the dead."

"In the chamber below—where we fell..." His words faded, but there was no other way to say it. "I found a dragon egg."

Of them all, only Androma moved, her steps bringing her closer to the Vahlken. "You found an... an *egg*?"

"What chamber is this?" Mordrith asked.

"The place is a ruin," Daijen answered, his words rushed. "We fell through a hole in the dark and landed in a room below the pillar. It had been bricked up, as if to seal all inside."

"You found a dragon egg?" Androma repeated, her voice hoarse. "Where is it now?" she demanded, her sightless eyes moving over Daijen.

The Vahlken swallowed, his shame now sitting wholly in his chest. "I lost it," he confessed.

The Rider's features creased into disbelief. "You *lost* it? You mean, you were actually holding it? How could you..." Androma ceased her line of questioning when the truth dawned on her.

"When the pillar descended," Daijen continued, voicing her revelation, "the chamber collapsed on itself. The egg was thrown from my hand." He looked solely at Androma. "I'm so sorry. I know the eggs are—"

"You know nothing," Androma informed him, her response cutting through his own. The Rider slowly turned to face the pyramid she couldn't see, though it seemed she could feel its presence, as if its malevolence was tangible. "It must have been ancient, trapped in there for eons."

"Why would anyone trap a dragon's egg?" Mordrith enquired.

"Because dragons are the real enemy the Skaramangians fear," Ilithranda reported.

"Then why not simply destroy it?" Yamnomora posed.

"Dragon eggs are near indestructible," Aphrandhor explained. "Even silvyr cannot split their shell. Indeed, the *simple* solution would be to imprison them where none could ever hope to bond with a Rider."

"Now it is truly lost," Androma lamented.

"I'm sorry," Daijen reiterated, and earnestly so.

The Rider's head twitched towards him, whipping matted blonde hair across her face. Her mouth opened and clamped shut, her likely biting words subdued while she calmed her thoughts.

"That egg was always to be lost," she said. "Be it sealed in that chamber or buried with it when the pillar descended. It's only by chance that we know it ever existed. It still begs the question of why *that* egg," the Rider went on, her investigative mind supplanting her grief. "Whatever their ancient war with the dragons, the Skaramangians went to great lengths to imprison that particular egg."

"Did you find anything else down there?" Ilithranda asked.

When Androma gave no reply, Daijen described the mural he'd seen on the wall, detailing the Riders and their dragons as they went to war against the dark army and their golden leader.

"You saw Riders?" Ilithranda stepped away from Oaken. "Not just dragons?"

Daijen recalled the mural with perfect clarity. "There were Riders astride all but one of the dragons, yes."

"Then the Skaramangians weren't just at war with dragons," Ilithranda pointed out, a look of epiphany about her. "They were at war with *Riders*. There must be some record of that," the Vahlken deduced, her words aimed at Androma.

"I have read every book, tome, and scroll in Drakanan," Androma informed them. "There is no mention of the Skaramangians, nor any dark army and a *golden man*."

"How can that be?" Ilithranda questioned. "Surely this was a significant event—a *victory,* even."

Androma was pacing now, unaware of the traces of sick that marred her well-fitted scale mail. "It must have been in the earliest days of the order," she reasoned. "Perhaps before there even *was* an order."

Yamnomora sighed and let one of her axes *thud* into the ground. "Another dead end then," she complained. "A lost egg that changes *nothin'* an' a pretty paintin' that explains *nothin'*. So glad we made the trip," she added dryly, scuffing her wide boots as she stepped away from the group.

All turned to the unusual scraping sound that came from the dwarf's feet. Daijen could see the ring of broken stone and disturbed earth where The Anther had merged two places in reality, bringing some of the ancient flooring from within the pyramid to settle under the stars. What they had heard, however, was bone being kicked across that stone. Daijen recognised it as the same skeletal leg and foot that Yamnomora had yanked out of an alcove inside the pillar.

"What is it?" Androma asked, her hand come to rest upon the hilt of her sword.

At last, a glimmer of hope ran through Daijen. "Aphrandhor," he said, addressing the wizard still new to him. "I think this calls for your unique *touch*."

3
THE TRUTH WILL OUT

It was with a defiant roar that Gallien launched his axe. Gold, silver, and bronze were made one as it cut through the air, its image to find acuity again upon impact. Its sleek edges and sloping curves—a blend of true artistry and craftsmanship—were splattered with the red blood of an Andaren. The soldier dropped to his knees, bewildered and confused by the weapon that had penetrated his cuirass, sundering the broken circle and sunburst of House Lhoris.

Before the Andaren could fall face-first into death, the axe dematerialised, vanishing from his chest. It appeared instantaneously in Gallien's waiting grip, and not a moment too soon. The smuggler raised the weapon and deflected a sweeping scimitar intended for his throat. He was forced then to swing in the opposite direction and block the blade of another soldier.

It was certainly more thuggish than the techniques his training had instilled in him, but the shoulder barge he countered with was enough to push the Andaren back. With a degree of space now, Gallien went on the attack, swinging and hacking. The soldier went down under his barrage, never to rise again. The smuggler pivoted and backhanded the other, the blade of the axe slicing neatly through his enemy's face and ending his existence.

More were upon him, though with every Andaren he put down, it seemed the smuggler in him faded to nothing. Even the long-dead soldier in him rose and fell away. It was something else that put fire in his veins, that saw him fight with abandon. He darted recklessly from foe to foe, challenging those who had centuries on him.

It was *fury*.

His life had been upturned the moment he met Androma, and now it had been shattered by her again, for she had sent Joran away. For two days he had been without the boy and, for two days, Gallien had felt himself unravelling. Lack of rest and sleep had their part to play, each robbed of him by the Andarens' relentless pursuit, but it was that great absence that enraged him.

That was not all. For two days he had felt the wizard's gaze upon him.

"You're not Gallien Drakalis," he had said accusingly.

They hadn't had the time to talk about it since, but the words had hounded the smuggler, sure that his true name had been discovered by a Jainus wizard.

And so he fought hard, as if he could forge a new path with the edge of his axe. Indeed, the Andaren party that had taken up the hunt was almost eradicated. They had attacked at dusk and fell upon steel, silvyr, and magic, weapons all, and wielded by those who knew how best to use them.

Cob flew through the air, his blue shoulder cloak and matching battle skirt taken by the wind about him. His bow twanged once, twice, each arrow taking a life. He rolled across the rocky earth and emerged swinging his scimitar of Draven bone. Somewhere between a fight and a dance, he brought his opponents down with brutal efficiency.

Similar in style, Kitrana Voden's fluid movements made it all the harder for the Andarens to keep up with her. Her legs swept out and low, taking soldiers from their feet before she twisted her hips and caught others across the jaw. Wielding no weapon of her own, the Nimean swung Gallien's sword as if it were an extension of her flexible body.

Both warriors were contrasted by the dwarf named Yamnomora. There was nothing graceful or elegant about her style. Like a butcher, she laid into the Andaren ranks, relieving them of life and limb. Her red hair, swept back and high by numerous braids, was just as spattered with blood as her face— and what a face she made. Her snarl was permanent, her teeth always bared, her brow furrowed to knot her wild eyebrows.

Behind her always was her fellow dwarf, Grarfath. The group had exchanged next to no words while fleeing for two days, but it was known that he was a smith. It was all the more obvious now that he wasn't a warrior. He fought with a pair of small hammers taken from his overly large backpack, and while he utilised them both to deadly effect, he remained in Yamnomora's shadow.

Gallien ducked under an incoming scimitar that would have claimed his life before straightening and continuing his charge. It was as if he knew where the attacks would come from, his muscle memory accustomed to every form of combat. He left that one Andaren behind to be cleaved in two by Andioma and her blade of silvyr.

The old Rider had been increasingly slow since her battle with Slait, her injuries yet to be taken stock of. Added to that, she had endured the waking hours as they all had, a fact that exhausted her all the more.

As another fell to Gallien's savagery, his mind a canvas of endless red, the last two of the Andaren hunting party gave their all. At their end, they were met by magic. It was with a limp that Aphrandhor placed himself in their path, but it was with a *boom* that he slammed his staff into the stone between them. Their bodies failed to withstand the force of his spell, their bones breaking at obscene angles as they were thrown back in a shower of debris. Just the once did the wizard run his staff along the length of his sword, Yalaqin, and with it, he extinguished the flames that had danced upon the steel.

He looked even more fatigued than Androma, his aged knees

slowly buckling beneath him. Cob was there to support him while he caught his breath. Brilliantly white was the long beard that poured out of his green hood and down to his laden belt, though it had lost its thick and velvety appearance in the days since they had bid Joran farewell. Despite Androma having centuries on them all, The Green Leaf was still the oldest where his body was concerned.

In the absence of anyone left to kill, Gallien's fury began to dim, his rage slowly churning to grief and loss as he considered the distance between him and Joran. Without that fire in his veins, his own levels of exhaustion seized him, quickly bringing him down to his knees and then onto the cold stone itself.

Beside him, Androma plunged her sword into the ground, the silvyr penetrating enough to keep the weapon standing on its own. Like the smuggler, she crumpled bit by bit until she joined him on the ground.

"We cannot linger 'ere," Yamnomora told them all, yanking her axe clear of an Andaren's torso. "Pick 'em clean, an' be quick abou' it. We take what we can use an' move on before they've the sense to send any more."

"*I* would have us linger a moment longer," Gallien replied, exhausted.

"Yamnomora," the smith pleaded.

"Away with ye," she groaned. The dwarf's ire was slow to cool and the smith looked to have been feeling the burn of it since they'd fled the ruins.

Gallien rolled his head the other way—he didn't care about dwarf business. He didn't even care about weapons of power or invading armies. At that very moment, no one was trying to kill him. He just needed sleep.

Only the sight of Kitrana kept his eyes open. Not far away, the Nimean was seated on the hard ground, her hood naturally drawn to dim the sunlight. Her jet-black hair escaped its confines and fell over her extraordinary attire—a skin-tight, all-in-one piece that stopped just below her knees, revealing her bare feet.

"I still can't believe you're alive," he uttered.

Kit was slow to face him. "As soon as I have enough of this *dry air* in my lungs, Drakalis, I'm coming for my pound of flesh."

It was an ominous response, but it had been coming for two days now. It changed nothing though. If he could go back and do it again, Gallien would still have given Joran her broken sword—its power had been one of the few things that actually kept the boy safe during the battle.

Gallien just about registered the footsteps advancing towards him, though he knew from the confident strides that it could be none other than Cob. The sound of the ranger's straining bow was enough to bring the smuggler's energy reserves to the surface. Flat out on his back, Gallien looked back and up, where an upside-down Kedradi was now aiming an arrow at his head.

Androma's head twitched at the sound. "Cob?"

"Deceit is a tool of the Skaramangians," stated the ranger, a sentinel of strength among the group. "I will not suffer it a moment longer."

Gallien considered the brief rest they had enjoyed the previous day. He had noted the tight knot made up of ranger, wizard, and Dragon Rider. They had said nothing at the time, the enemy on their heels, but it had been obvious what topic had held their attention. That damned wizard had his *name*.

"He is no threat to us," Androma insisted, finding the strength to rise.

Without taking his eyes off the smuggler, the Kedradi replied, "Trust no one. Suspect everyone."

"Not this time," the old Rider said determinedly. "Not *him*. He has more than proved himself an ally."

"He has proved himself a *liar*," Cob pointed out.

Kitrana gave a mirthless laugh. "Sounds like they have you all figured out, Drakalis."

The ranger drew his bowstring a notch tighter. "He is not *Drakalis*."

Kit's big blue eyes narrowed on the smuggler. "What's he talking about?"

"Stay out o' this," Yamnomora warned, bringing one of her axes to rest before the Nimean's throat.

Gallien rolled over and slowly rose to his feet as Androma walked into view, her sandy cloak caught by the wind skipping over the top of the ravine. The old Rider's head was tilted to one side, as if she was taking in the scene by hearing alone.

"Cob," she said gently.

The ranger didn't budge, his aim remaining solely on Gallien's face.

"You can kill him from a distance," she reminded. "Give the man some space."

Without a hint of emotion, Cob stepped back and relinquished a notch of tension in the bowstring.

Gallien took no such measure, the axe remaining firmly in his grip.

Defying his injured leg, The Green Leaf stood proudly beside Androma, his staff held out in one hand while the other gripped Yalaqin's hilt on his belt. "You are not who you claim to be," he declared.

"Unlike you, *wizard*, I don't hide from what I am," Gallien retorted. "Tell me: were you wearing the robes of the Jainus when you killed my father? Were you sworn to their oaths when you took that bracer off his corpse?"

"What do you know about the bracer?" Androma cut in before they could descend into arguing.

The smuggler swallowed the rest of his tirade and glanced at the vambrace on Aphrandhor's right forearm. "I know it was my father's. I know he was wearing it the last time I saw him." He turned murderous eyes on the wizard once more. "And I know he wouldn't give it up without a damned good fight."

"It's a weapon of power," Androma announced evenly.

A flurry of emotions flickered across Gallien's expression. "What are you talking about?"

"Like the axe," Aphrandhor explained, "or The Anther and the broken sword. Along with the Helm of Ahnir, they are all parts of the same collection. All weapons of power."

Gallien pictured his father wearing it, a man of eccentricity and passion but always a man of desperate needs who survived off of luck more than anything else. He hadn't wielded a weapon of power, even unknowingly.

"Horseshit," the smuggler eventually replied.

"You shouldn't have touched me," Aphrandhor countered.

That had been the moment, Gallien recalled. When he had aided the wizard after his fall.

"What does it do?" he asked, not entirely sure he wanted to hear the answer.

"It allows the user to observe people or objects outside of time," The Green Leaf told him, an unhelpful explanation as far as the simple smuggler was concerned. "I can see where you've been, who and what you've come into contact with. I can even absorb your memories and emotions."

"If you've seen in here," Gallien said, placing one finger to his temple, "then you know I'm no threat."

"You lied about who you are," Cob interjected.

"You're not special," the smuggler informed him gruffly. "I haven't gone by my real name since I was numbered amongst the king's men. Which *he* should know, apparently," he added, pointing the axe at Aphrandhor. "I've never lied about who *I am*— only my name."

"Names can carry great import," the wizard remarked. "But there is more than just your name that troubles me."

Gallien could hardly be bothered with the conversation, especially since they were all so tired and cold, their weapons still dripping with Andaren blood. "Such as?" he asked anyway.

The Green Leaf limped a little closer. "I have looked into the lives of many a man and laid bare their deeds. The effect is amplified when in the presence of another weapon of power," he explained, eyeing the glowing axe in Gallien's hand. "I should have been able to view every aspect of your life. Yet," he continued at length, "your memories are those of a broken mirror. Worse: no one piece fits with another. I could make no sense of them, save for one word."

"Your *name*," Androma finished.

Gallien let his true name echo through his mind, the sound of which had passed solely between him and Joran for the last sixteen years. It was, perhaps, the only thing he had ever given the boy—the only thing that would last.

Gallien gestured at the arrow still nocked in Cob's bow as he addressed the wizard. "Do you threaten the lives of everyone whose mind you can't read?"

"First, I would hear you say it: your true name. If only so we might start again, as it were."

"*You* say it," Gallien spat. "You're the one poking around in people's lives and taking things that don't belong to you."

The wizard gripped his staff a little closer, his chin raised. "*Gallien Pendain*."

The name snapped out of The Green Leaf's mouth. It had been some time since the smuggler had heard his true name in its entirety. It felt wrong. Dangerous, even. It was all the more disturbing to hear it spoken by a wizard.

Gallien spared Kitrana a glance. Of them all, the Nimean had known him the longest, though not so long—nor so well—to know that Drakalis wasn't his given name. There was no sense of hurt in Kitrana's expression, only confusion.

Of course, Gallien thought. She was all business when it came to that broken sword, and he had come between them.

Androma ran her hand down Cob's arm until she discovered the bow, her touch enough to make the Kedradi sling the weapon over one shoulder.

Off to the side, Kitrana pushed the blade of Yamnomora's axe away and rose to her feet. "Put your axe to my throat again," the Nimean said, looking down at the dwarf, "and I'll make you eat it."

"Poor axe," Grarfath muttered, the first words the smith had produced in a while.

"Your name," Androma began, ignoring the exchange altogether. "It is Gallien *Pendain*?"

His jaw tensed, as if the muscles therein barred him from answering. "Yes," was his inevitable answer.

"Yet you do not go by this name," Cob pointed out, suspicion brimming behind his dark eyes.

"Does stating the bloody obvious come with being a ranger?" Gallien scoffed. "Or is that just specific to you?"

The Kedradi didn't rise to it. "Explain yourself," he commanded.

Androma flexed the bony fingers of her left hand—a call for calmer heads. "Does Joran know?"

The smuggler could feel his defences doubling with the sound of Joran's name. "What does that matter?"

"Answer the question," Cob ordered, instigating another raised hand from the old Rider.

"Yes," Gallien answered forcefully. "He knows."

The smuggler looked away, wondering if he had made a mistake all those years ago when he had confided in the boy— worse, when he had given him the option to adopt the name.

"And Joran goes by this name?" Androma probed.

Gallien took a much-needed breath. "Yes," he stated flatly. "Am I missing something?" he asked, turning the question around on them.

"It is *we* who have missed something," Cob stated bluntly. "Your deceit, coupled with your *unreadable mind,* makes you a troubling ally."

"Yes," Gallien replied, exasperated, "I use a different name; I always have. I'm a smuggler. It comes with the territory. I could do with retiring Drakalis, if I'm honest," he added as an afterthought.

"He's lying," Aphrandhor said.

Gallien's eyes flicked to the wizard, his gaze boring into the older man.

"Your life is broken, fragmented, yes, but I saw enough to know you're lying. You hold the name Pendain closely. It matters to you. It's not just another alias. It's your... *family* name."

The smuggler said nothing for a time, his mind racing to find a workaround.

"Screw you," he said eventually, a familiar response from his repertoire. "I don't owe you the truth. I don't owe any of you the truth. Not even you," he added, shooting Kitrana a look.

Androma nodded along before breathing a sigh. "You're right, Gallien. Though the concealment of your name was a point of concern, the name itself means more to us. To us *all*."

Gallien's eyes narrowed in suspicion. "You've heard my name before?"

"Oh yes," Androma confirmed. "We first heard the name *Pendain* some decades ago..."

4

ONLY THE DEAD REMEMBER

0 Years Ago...

4

Daijen watched the wizard remove the vambrace from his pack, his eyes keen to take in every facet of the relic. It was more silver than anything else, with details of bronze and gold between the intricate pattern of copper, all of which surrounded the raised teardrop that sat atop the forearm, a feature that lent the piece of armour a bulky appearance.

"What's that on the inside?" Ilithranda asked, her question beating Daijen's by a heartbeat.

Aphrandhor angled the vambrace so he could see inside, where he too noted the flecks and shards of glowing red. "Fascinating," he whispered.

Daijen crouched beside The Green Leaf. "Has it ever done that before?"

"Not to my knowledge," he replied. "The Anther—bring it closer."

Mordrith removed it from her back and approached the wizard. Her eyes grew wide in the blue light that began to swell from within the metal, its runes and fine shards aglow.

"What's this abou'?" she demanded, her harsh dwarven tongue butchering the melodic flow of the Andaren language.

"What's happening?" Androma questioned.

"They're both reacting to each other," the wizard said excitedly. "This confirms my theory."

"What theory?" Daijen probed.

"He believes they're all connected," Androma informed them.

"They *are* connected," Aphrandhor stated. "All the weapons of power," he went on, "the hammer, bracer, helm, and whatever else there might be—they're all from the same suit of armour."

"Your Elderlings theory?" Ilithranda queried sceptically, naming the beings Aphrandhor believed to be the pyramid's architects.

"The first people," the wizard replied eagerly. "An earlier civilisation, lost to time. Their magic still remains a mystery to us all," he added, indicating the bracer in his hands.

"The first people who you believe to be *humans*," Daijen went on, picking up the thread from their first conversation.

The Green Leaf shrugged. "As I said, I have seen but shards of what was. I have likely seen humans because the relics I have interacted with hail from human culture. I've not spent much time in Andara. It's very possible humans made the weapons of power."

Mordrith hefted the glowing hammer in her hands. "Don' count *us* out. Our people 'ave no love for magic, but if it's shaped around steel, ye can bet these Elderlings will 'ave sought out the dwarves o' Morthil."

The wizard offered her a warm grin. "I have seen enough to know that we all share the *same* past. I believe all of our ancestors lived in something of a melting pot before Verda's map was cut with such hard lines."

Yamnomora snorted brashly. "I'm fallin' asleep over 'ere. Who cares who made *what* an' *when*? We came 'ere to hurt the Skaramangians. Or 'ave ye forgotten there's a war goin' on out there?

Touch the bloody bone already an' tell us why they protect this wretched place."

"I suppose it wouldn't hurt to stay on task," Aphrandhor muttered as he slipped his arm inside the bracer, concealing its red glow.

Daijen assumed his full height and stepped back, giving the wizard some space. He spared a moment to exchange looks with Ilithranda, the two quite capable of interpreting the other's emotions with no more than their eyes. It seemed both were feeling the same sense of unease. They remained trapped in a web of their enemy's making, and until they found their way through, the war would rage as the Skaramangians saw fit.

Until their dark end was realised.

Aphrandhor grasped the leg bone and sucked down a hard breath. For just a moment, he looked a man drowning, his face upturned as if in search of the surface, his mouth ajar.

Then it was over.

The wizard let go of the bone and fell back, working furiously to control his breathing. Appearing somewhat fatigued, he sat on the ground and wasted no time in removing the bracer, though he was sure to replace it in his bag rather than leave it sitting idly.

"Green Leaf?" Androma could only direct her concern in his general direction.

"I'm alright," he assured, still catching his breath. "It can be a... taxing experience," he explained to the others. "The older something is, the more memory it carries. My very *mortal* mind can only interpret so much."

Daijen recalled the wizard reading Androma—a Rider of some four hundred years—earlier that day, yet he had absorbed her memories and experiences with general ease.

"How old *is* it?" he had to ask.

Aphrandhor licked his lips. "It's impossible to say. So much of its memory is just lying in that tomb," he continued, looking at the glassy black pyramid. "I felt whole centuries of nothingness in the dark. A great absence."

"And before that?" Androma probed. "When that leg was used by the living."

The Green Leaf looked away, his expression knotted in focus. "Forgive me. I'm trying to separate his memories from my own. It all felt so real. So *whole*. It's normally just fragments, but I saw so much. If I had held onto it for any longer, I fear his life and mine would have become entangled. I wouldn't have known where he ended and I began."

"Take a moment if you must," Androma offered.

"What did you see?" Daijen pressed, impatient for answers. "Who was he?"

Aphrandhor shook his head, perplexed. "That's just it. He was nobody. No," he said, correcting himself. "He was just an ordinary man. A farmer." The wizard tilted his head and closed his eyes while the memories of another man played out inside his mind. "He lived in the shadow of Mount Kaliban, in Erador." His mouth opened, as if his lips had been parted by revelation.

"What did you see?" Daijen asked.

"He saw the Giants lay the great stones of The Tower of Jain."

Mordrith let The Anther drop to the ground, severing the wizard's reverie. "Why is that significant?"

"Because it tells me when he was *alive*. Morvoren, the first of the Jainus, used magic to tame the Giants of The Spine. He had them build The Tower of Jain."

Ilithranda ignored Oaken's attempts to get affection from her, his armoured beak nudging her arm. "When was this?"

"Eight hundred years ago." It was Daijen who answered, his years of reading every book in Ka'vairn's library paying off.

"Jus' brilliant," Yamnomora complained. "We assaulted a Skaramangian stronghold an' risked death for the leg o' an eight-hundred-year-old human *farmer*."

Mordrith crouched to better inspect the ancient bone. "Why would the Skaramangians be interested in the bones o' a long dead farmer?"

Androma was shaking her head. "I'm starting to wonder if there's naught but questions here. We need *answers*."

Daijen held all the information in his mind, and easily so thanks to Handuin's mutations. He considered the facts as an investigator, as a Vahlken. "It is no tomb," he began, reciting the curator's words exactly as she had delivered them, "for there are no dead here. Only *memories*."

"What are you getting at?" the old Rider demanded.

"Straws," Yamnomora interjected. "Because that's all we 'ave."

"That's what she said," Daijen reminded them, ignoring the dwarf altogether.

"This is where he will remember who he is," Ilithranda added, her memory just as sharp as his.

"Who is *he*?" Androma asked, voicing the new question that plagued them all.

"She mentioned *The Eldan* when referring to their leaders," Ilithranda pointed out.

"She insinuated that The Eldan and the master cleric were one and the same," Daijen chipped in, his mind reliving the conversation with the curator.

Androma shook her head again. "She also stated that their leaders were not entombed in the pillar. Our *friend* here is testament to that," she added, gesturing at the ground where the farmer's remains lay.

"I'll be takin' no mind o' the mad," Yamnomora insisted. "That old hag was wet in the brain, an' that's before she became a monster."

"*Only memories*," Aphrandhor mumbled, though it seemed the wizard was more oblivious than ignorant where the dwarf's remarks were concerned. "What use are memories if only the dead remember them?"

Something about The Green Leaf's phrasing resonated with Daijen. "No," he uttered, his eyes drawn to the wizard's bag. "What use are memories if you can't *read* them?"

His question brought the attention of them all upon Aphrandhor.

"They need the bracer," Ilithranda concluded. "We should not have brought it here."

"The Skaramangians had me an' me kin searchin' for The Anther for years," Mordrith replied. "An' they knew abou' the helm ye lot keep in Aran'saur. It's no leap to assume they know abou' the bracer too."

"But to what end?" Androma questioned, the group's collective frustration audible in her voice. "Even if they acquired the bracer, what use are the memories of ordinary farmers? Who else do they have down there? Merchants? Tanners?"

"They must be important to whoever *he* is," Daijen reasoned, his thoughts returning to the mysterious man the curator had spoken of so reverently.

Ilithranda's gaze drew distant as she called on her memory. "The old woman. She wondered if he was among us."

"Only *he* would know to find this place," Daijen interjected, using the curator's exact words. "It makes no sense," he growled, his feet set to pacing. "Everything we've ever gleaned from the Skaramangians suggests they're seeking a way to bring back the Dark Ones. There's never been word of an individual, not even this *Eldan*."

"Perhaps," Androma theorised, "*he* is the only one who knows how to bring back the Dark Ones."

"But *who* is he?" Daijen snapped, his emotions fraught after losing the dragon egg—a fact he refused to acknowledge in that moment. "Why do they believe he's *lost*?"

"There is no *he*," Yamnomora groaned. "That old hag—the lot o' 'em—'ave been driven mad down there in the dark. It's more likely she were referrin' to some Skaramangian fella who comes along an' dumps food an' water at their door."

"Yamnomora's right," Mordrith agreed. "We can' be takin' the word o' those suckin' on the teats o' Andaren magic. There's naught but madness down there."

Aphrandhor tried to rise to his full height and failed, staggering one way then the next before acquiring his balance. He was sickly pale for a human, and his brow was beaded with sweat despite the frigid air.

"There is more at work here than we can understand," he said, his voice ragged. "The Skaramangians are too meticulous, too *calculating* to be storing dead farmers for no reason. I'd wager our enemy do not wish us to pursue this given their regard for this place. More so, they will not want us working *together* to uncover their secrets. This is to be our true strength."

"That I can agree with," Mordrith said firmly, shrugging her shoulder to shake off Yamnomora's warning hand. "The answers are out there. With more o' us askin' questions, we're likely goin' to unravel the truth faster an' bring these buggers into the light. The faster we do that, the faster I can get back to me family."

"The faster *everyone* can get back to their families," Daijen commented, his thoughts spared for the thousands of humans and Andarens who had died on needless battlefields.

"How, then, are we to pursue this?" Androma queried. "We can ignore the ramblings of the old hag, but we cannot ignore the fact that this pyramid holds Skaramangian secrets. It would take an army to clear this place of monsters. How are we *six* to conquer it?"

"It's possible the answers we seek lie with a particular skeleton," Ilithranda posed. "Rather than conquer it, perhaps we have only to infiltrate it." The Vahlken looked at the hammer in Mordrith's hand. "We have The Anther. We can port in and take another before the monsters attack."

Yamnomora hefted both of her axes and sniffed with dramatic effect. "Looks like we're goin' back into the belly o' the beast." There was just a hint of enthusiasm in her tone.

"We can't go back in there," Mordrith counselled her, though the dwarf spared the Vahlken a glance.

"The wizard needs more bones, aye? So let's go get some."

"We don' even know how to raise the pillar," Mordrith pointed out. "It wouldn' be nearly as quick as she's makin' out. Pokin' around in the dark an' surrounded by monsters is the win our enemy need. Use *this* first," she insisted, one stubby finger pressed into her right temple.

"This is where all of our efforts have led," Ilithranda stated, resuming her previous argument with the dwarf. "We cannot run from it now."

"All our efforts?" Mordrith spat back. "Ye're forgettin' the part where *we* told ye abou' this place. It were *our* efforts that uncovered this hole in the ground. Not yers! An' I've never run from a thing in me life, lass. If ye want to throw yer life away an' be done with this war then jump right in." The dwarf stuck a thumb in her chest. "I'm in it till the end. That means beatin' 'em at their own game an' bein' smart abou' it."

Ilithranda opened her mouth to bite back.

"Wait," Daijen bade her, his hand rising to instil calm. He had heard their every word but as if from a distance, his mind working on the problem from another angle.

"What is it, Daijen?" Androma asked.

"We risk much returning to that chamber. Perhaps too much," he began, meeting Ilithranda's eyes. "The vambrace changes everything. We can now seek answers elsewhere."

"What are you getting at?" Ilithranda asked, clearly annoyed with him.

"We need something old—*ancient*—that's been handled by Skaramangians, by their *inner circle*."

Aphrandhor's blank expression cracked. "You know of such a thing?"

Daijen looked to Ilithranda. Her face dropped, betraying her sudden understanding.

"The Valtorak will *not* agree to this," she told him with unshakable confidence.

"What are you talking about?" The Green Leaf's words came out as one.

Looking past the wizard for a moment, Daijen responded to his Vahlken companion. "It's either that or go down there," he argued, his startling blue eyes glancing at the earth under their boots.

"We can handle them," Ilithranda asserted, always the warrior who had survived countless campaigns.

"At what cost?" Daijen countered reasonably. He said no more, not wishing to offend those present by verbalising the good chance that they wouldn't return from another excursion inside the pyramid. "This *is* our true strength," he intoned, using Aphrandhor's words now. "If we don't need to compromise that strength, then we shouldn't."

"What are ye talkin' abou'?" Mordrith grumbled.

With no further protest from Ilithranda, Daijen turned to the dwarf and the others. "We need to go to Ka'vairn."

The wizard's eyes grew large, his blond eyebrows rising into his brow. "Ka'vairn? The Vahlken fortress?"

Daijen was on the cusp of unravelling his train of thought when he noticed a degree of distress flash across Mordrith's face. The dwarf was already lowering herself into a crouch, one hand reaching out to press against the hard ground.

"What's wrong?" he asked.

"The earth is speakin' to me," she replied cryptically.

Ilithranda expressed her scepticism with a single eyebrow. "The earth is speaking to you? And what's it saying, exactly?"

"I feel it too," Yamnomora said, scanning the ground around them.

Mordrith looked up at them all, fear in her eyes. "They're comin'."

Daijen wasn't about to doubt the acute senses of his dwarven companions, freeing his scimitar and atori blade from their place on his belt before Mordrith stood up. Indeed, his own senses, mutated beyond the norm, registered the slight vibration in the ground and acknowledged the rising sound emerging from the shaft. The Vahlken naturally looked for Valyra, who was a little distance away, having wandered off to investigate the area.

The Aegre squawked and Oaken with her, their arching talons clawing at the ground. Oaken flapped his wings and dipped his head to present Ilithranda with an opportunity to ascend her saddle, but chaos was upon them.

Monsters were upon them.

They scurried out of the shaft, their sharp and misshapen limbs having found purchase in the walls. Their cacophonous shrieks drowned out the Aegres, their *thudding* pincers bringing them ever closer. Valyra waded in, her left wing hurling two of the beasts back into the shaft. Another fell under her talons, its mutated body torn to shreds.

Blinded by their hunt for the companions, one of the creatures ignored her presence altogether and tried to race past. Valyra's armoured beak snapped at it, severing its body in two. Yet while the Aegre's armour and chainmail were coated in blood, her efforts weren't enough to stem the flow.

It was always in those few precious seconds before battle that Daijen was struck by clarity. It was with this certainty that he knew where he was supposed to be—where he *needed* to be. Pressed upon by their savage enemy, he was most needed on that line between them and those at his back.

"Go!" he urged Mordrith, his command no more than a bark.

The dwarf didn't hesitate, though she did pause to drag Aphrandhor a little closer. The two of them, along with Yamnomora and Bludgeon, were taken from the scene in a blinding flash. Daijen didn't witness their departure, his flat-out charge taking him in the opposite direction.

Skidding on his knees, the Vahlken whipped out his scimitar and slashed one of the fiends across the midriff, where its once human waist had been reduced to little more than a spine. Emerging at speed, he deflected the pincer of one with his short-sword while rounding his foot about to deliver a kick to another. He concluded the manoeuvre with a pivoting backhand with his scimitar, claiming two lives in one stroke.

"Get Androma out of here!" he bellowed.

Without her sight, the Rider's skill in battle was for naught when pressed against a flood of enemies that fought like wild animals. They would inevitably overwhelm her, attacking from angles she couldn't hope to defend.

Perhaps foreseeing the same outcome for the Rider, Ilithranda snatched Androma by the wrist and roughly guided her to Oaken's side. Daijen missed their mounting, his vision blocked by the scurrying mass, but he witnessed the Aegre's swift ascent, his mighty wings barraging the small horde.

"Daijen!" Ilithranda yelled as Oaken launched them into the night's sky.

The Vahlken's mind slipped into a frenzy only battle could bring about. One by one, the trappings of his life, the people, and the experiences he had gained fell away. What remained was a warrior, an extension of Death put on the earth to send any and all into the Black Abyss. His steel sang that ancient song as it cut and sliced through life. His muscles pushed themselves to their mutated limits, seeing him flip, twist, and dance around his enemies.

Only Valyra reminded him who he was.

The Aegre crashed into the monsters closing in on him. She ripped them to pieces with seeming ease, diminishing his efforts with a display only an apex predator could give. Released from his battle reverie, Daijen sheathed his weapons and nimbly climbed up onto his saddle, careful to keep moving in time with Valyra's erratic actions.

The Aegre squawked, the only warning Daijen received before she flapped her wings and left the monsters clawing at the air beneath them. They soared into the night, abandoning the glassy pyramid to those that scurried in the moon's cool light.

What hell had they uncovered?

5
NOT TO BE SPOKEN

J oran chased after Kassanda, his hastened steps echoing off every wall in the depths of Drakanan. With a handful of words, the Dragon Rider had hollowed out his destiny. He couldn't believe it, *refused* to, even.

"You're wrong," he stated upon catching up with her. "I have to be the one."

"You don't *have* to be," Kassanda told him. "Point of fact: you're not the one. If you were, the bond would have been established in the egg chamber."

Despite having no knowledge of the bonding process, Joran was furiously trying to come up with reasons why that might still be the case. "What if you're wrong?" he tried again. "It might have already begun—maybe we didn't give it enough time."

Kassanda stopped at a junction and pivoted to face the young man, the light of a nearby torch dancing in the dark of her eyes. "I have witnessed the bonding many times and gone through it myself. You, Joran, have not bonded with any of those eggs and, as I said, they are the only ones we have."

With that, the Rider spun on her heel and continued her journey through the halls.

Joran's disappointment was being fanned into righteous flame, turning him to anger. "You don't understand," he began again, quick to take up pursuit. "I have to be the one. I've been hunted all my life—*all my life!*" he echoed, throwing his hands up. "The Skaramangians sent assassins after me—a *Vahlken* after me! The King of Erador sent his spymaster after me. The prophecy! It has been seen!" he said adamantly, using Androma's own words. "*A warrior of both worlds will bring about a time of dragons.*"

"Not a prophecy," Kassanda responded evenly, her gaze never wandering from the path ahead. "And I know what was seen."

His frustration reaching new heights, Joran struggled to find the right words to fight back with. "It's the future—that's prophecy."

"It's *a* future," the Rider specified. "*Not* a prophecy."

Joran's reply was delayed while he took in the large chamber they entered. It had a curved ceiling fixed with enormous candelabras that added candlelight to the torches that flickered on the walls. The room itself was lined with four long tables and benches, though only the head of a single table looked to have been occupied in some time. There he saw a lone cup and plate, the dull tin plate littered with crumbs, while a handful of scrolls sat idly on the tabletop.

"Just give me more time with the eggs," he pleaded. "My bond must be different."

Kassanda stopped again, her stony expression cracking just enough to display irritation. "What has she been saying to you? I can hear Androma behind your words." She stepped uncomfortably close to Joran. "Never allow others to inform you of who you are. If their words don't bring you down you risk them inflating your self-belief. You think you're the one because others have said as much. You think you're this warrior of two worlds because it's been seen by the doomed. You think you must have a different bond—a *special* bond—with your dragon. And why wouldn't you?" she asked rhetorically, bemused. "You're *the one* after all."

With every statement, Joran felt that much smaller, that much more insignificant.

"The relationship between every dragon and their Rider is special," Kassanda admitted, her tone more under control. "But the *bond* is always the same. You just don't have one," she stated, delivering her words as she would a blow.

Joran remained where he stood, his feet rooted into the stone while he watched the Rider make for the door on the other side of the tables.

"I have to have a bond," he uttered, his thoughts spiralling as he dwelled on Gallien and the others—their lives given for him, for his glorious fate.

Kassanda halted before passing through the door, her sandy cloak billowing aside as she whirled on him.

"You're not entitled to an egg," she said sternly. "A bond with a dragon is *earned*. Being the son of a great warrior, even a Vahlken, does not warrant you the title of Dragon Rider. You're just *Joran*." Kassanda turned to depart, pausing only to gesture at the kitchen built into the wall on her left. "Eat. Drink. Gather what supplies you need for your journey home."

"I have no home," he complained as the Rider walked off into the shadows. "I have no people!" he ranted, his fists balling. "I lost everything to be here!"

Indeed, he was *just* Joran—so named by his mother, the first person he ever lost.

Not *just*, he thought.

He wasn't *just* Joran.

He had Gallien's name—his *father's* name. Perhaps it was the only thing he had of him now. It was a fact that sparked his grief again and boiled his blood, setting his heart to racing.

He slammed his fists onto the nearest table, wishing he had the strength to flip it over. Instead, he managed no more than to disturb the plate and cup placed on the end.

"I'm *Joran Pendain*!" he yelled at the shadows. "I thought that was supposed to mean *something*!"

It *had* to mean something... or it had all been for nothing.

The sound of Kassanda's boots preceded her return, her tattooed scalp catching the torchlight. Her approach was slow and measured as she homed in on the boy. The Rider seemed to be looking right through him, her brow knotting into tight muscle.

"What did you say?"

Joran worked to get his breathing under control. "It has to mean something," he repeated, if not rasped. "They all died getting me here. That couldn't have been for nothing."

Kassanda came to a stop in front of him, her eyes wandering up and down as she looked at him with disturbing revelation.

"Your name," she whispered, her aura of confidence shaken. "Your name is Joran... *Pendain*."

Joran swallowed and arched his head back, confused by her sudden and intense interest. "Yes," he confirmed.

Kassanda blinked her glassy eyes. "When I demanded your name outside, you failed to mention that," she replied, almost accusingly.

Joran could feel his defences rising, bristling even. "It's my name to give as I wish."

The Rider took another step towards him. "Who gave you that name? Andromâ?"

It seemed a strange thing to ask, and Joran didn't shy away from expressing his confusion. "My father gave it to me."

Kassanda narrowed her eyes. "The soldier?"

Joran had already made to respond, but her own response caught him off guard. "Soldier?" he asked, his face dropping. "You know who my real father is?"

The Dragon Rider looked to be recalculating her approach and stepped back. "The smuggler, then," she deduced. "The one Andromâ entrusted you to as a babe. *He* gave you that name?"

Joran waved his hand through the air as if to scrub away her line of questions. "You said *soldier*. Was my father a soldier?"

Kassanda looked equally irritated by the divergent branch in their conversation. "Only your mother knew who he was, and she told no one. Not even Andromâ."

"But you said *soldier*," he reminded her with a touch of desperation.

"Because he was," she finally admitted. "There ends the extent of my knowledge on the matter."

It was more than he had ever known about his real father. All at once, it seemed too much and not enough. His mother was an Andaren Vahlken, and his father was a human soldier in the Eradoran army. Was he still in the army? Had he died like so many others in the war, his body left to litter some distant battlefield? Would he know him if he saw him? These and so many more questions immediately plagued the young man. Thanks to his pointed ears, violet eyes, and shockingly white hair, he had always focused on his mother's heritage.

It occurred to him then that he might even have met his father and never known it. He could have served him in one of the many taverns they had worked in or passed him in the street, Joran's vision hampered by his ever-present hood. He could have been one of the rowdy drunks Gallien had ejected—a man not worth meeting.

Noting Kassanda's faraway look, Joran grounded himself in the present. "What about—"

His question was silenced by the Rider, her hand and dragon-scaled bracer cutting through the air. "Eat. Drink. You will sleep here tonight—I will prepare a room."

Joran felt almost dazed by the turn of events. "I thought I was to gather supplies?"

"And now you're staying here."

Once again, Kassanda turned on her heel and strode out of the chamber.

Joran sighed, his hand coming to rest on the hilt of the broken sword on his belt. He had no idea what had just transpired, but it left him with a sinking feeling in his gut. Perhaps Gallien had been right: their name was not to be spoken.

6

AN IMPERIAL INVITATION

0 Years Ago...

4

Haunted by all that he had seen and lost in the Skaramangian tomb, the walls of Ka'vairn were a welcome sight as Valyra broke through the clouds. The valley lay sprawled beneath them, tucked between The Hellion and Morthil Mountains. The Dain'duil dominated that valley, a dark carpet of pine trees whose eastern border was kept in check by the snaking Nheremyn River.

Daijen's icy blue eyes tracked up the slopes of The Hellion Mountains in the west and sought out the only place he could call home. The ancient fortress stood defiantly on its protrusion from the mountain stone.

How familiar it was. How comforting, despite the pain and heartache the Vahlken had endured during his many years inside its walls. The spires and towers—damaged from sieges never recorded by Andaren historians—remained encased inside abandoned scaffolding while the walls around them slowly crumbled.

Yet it would not release its grip on the Hellion stone. Ka'vairn itself was a symbol of Vahlken resilience, if not of their very oath to protect the people of the realm. It also doubled as a vault, Daijen knew, and not just for the countless gems and coins the order had amassed over the centuries. The real treasure it guarded lay deep in its heart, where every Vahlken was born again.

Side by side with Oaken, Valyra glided the rest of the way, bringing them below the snowcapped mountaintops. Daijen soon spotted Aramis within the courtyard, the old Aegre resting in his usual spot in the corner. It was the figure standing beside Aramis that set Daijen's heart to a faster pace.

Valyra and Oaken flapped their wings as one, slowing their descent while their legs reached out for the courtyard. The storm they created blew out The Valtorak's cloak of victory, a fur that had once belonged to a black bear, as Ilithranda's had. That bear was centuries dead, Daijen had decided, never quite sure how old Ka'vairn's current master actually was.

The Valtorak also stood attired in his Vahlken armour, the tanned leather concealing the silk of the Weavers beneath. His scimitar and atori blade hung from his belt, and, as always, he held a tall and curving staff of smooth wood. While the staff was a familiar sight, Daijen could only recall a handful of times he had seen The Valtorak wearing his armour and weapons.

He was an unnerving sight.

The Vahlken jumped down from his saddle with ease while Ilithranda assisted Androma. Daijen's attention wandered beyond them, his gaze scrutinising the ramparts and windows for any sign of his other companions or even Tovun—Ka'vairn's only initiate.

"They're inside," The Valtorak announced by way of greeting.

It never failed to impress Daijen how well his master was able to read him. "When did they arrive?" he asked, wondering if The Anther had shaved off the days it had taken the Aegres to make the journey.

"Last night," The Valtorak answered, his golden eyes washing over Ilithranda and the Dragon Rider before he turned for the main keep. Seeing the pinch in Daijen's brow, the master elaborated.

"Apparently the dwarf was unable to port the distance between here and Nareene. They required several rests along the way."

Daijen absorbed the knowledge as they passed over the threshold and entered the keep's lofty hallway. The musty smell brought with it a lifetime of memories. It seemed so many of them involved him being thrown around by Slait. Even now, he walked over a patch of stone where the exiled Vahlken had once beaten him to the floor, breaking his nose in the process. Seeing the staircase to his left, Daijen recalled the time Slait had shoved him from the top, sending him tumbling down the hard steps.

Behind the pain and blood that marred his memories, there were good times. Every day he had followed his nose, the scent of Laif's cooking drawing him in from afar. Arm wrestling with Soyra for the last dumpling in the main hall. Training side by side with Ilithranda, the most unlikely of friends who had become a sister to him.

The Valtorak turned away from the main hall and made for the staircase, surprising Daijen.

"Where are they?"

"They required a room," the master replied curtly.

Daijen imagined an exhausted Mordrith porting into the keep after days of repeatedly using The Anther. Rather than voice any such concern, though, he spared The Valtorak's attire a curious glance.

"I alone hold the rank of Vahlken in your absence," The Valtorak replied, noting Daijen's glance. "Ka'vairn's security and Tovun's training both fall to me. The armour is prudent."

It was effective in Daijen's opinion. It always lent The Valtorak an air of command, if not a dangerous edge. It showed signs of numerous repairs, scars earned in the war and from a time before the Skaramangians set Verda on fire. There remained slivers here and there where the bronze of the Weaver's silk could be seen.

"Perhaps," The Valtorak continued, "even necessary, given the *wizard* you've invited into our home."

Daijen employed a notch of the stoicism Kastiek had instilled in all those he trained and maintained his marble-like expression. "He was an unexpected addition to our party," he explained.

"He bears the mark of the *Jainus* upon his left wrist," The Valtorak countered, never one to miss a detail—one that Daijen had apparently overlooked. "They are not to be trusted."

"He no longer walks that path," Androma interrupted, gaining Daijen an unimpressed look from his master. "He witnessed their corruption first hand," the Rider went on, her arm hooked into Ilithranda's. "It was Aphrandhor who brought the Skaramangians to my attention."

"Be that as it may, I am ill at ease with the number of foreigners inside my walls. They compromise the security of this fortress."

"Yet you still permitted them entry," Androma pointed out. "Perhaps you *do* see the advantages to an alliance," she added coyly.

The Valtorak came to a stop, if only so his golden eyes could roam over the Dragon Rider with derision before falling on the two Vahlken. "I have been informed of your findings on Nareene. When you're finished with your... *council*, come to my office. Both of you."

No further directions were required after The Valtorak's departure. The dwarven speech exchanged between Mordrith and Yamnomora was brash and loud, as if every word in their language collided with the next rather than following one after the other. Then there was the smell. The dwarves possessed an odour unlike any creature Daijen had ever met, a combination of sweat, spices, and freshly forged steel.

Daijen was first to enter the room—a simple rectangle with naught but a single cot, table and chair. The afternoon light spilled in through the tall but narrow window, the beam of dust leading the Vahlken's gaze to the cot—to the wizard. Pale and clammy, Aphrandhor was lying under a blanket, his blond hair matted with water from the cloth in Mordrith's hand. Yamnomora was on the other side of the room, her chunky fingers inspecting The Anther's glowing runes.

"What happened?" Daijen asked urgently.

Mordrith dabbed Aphrandhor's brow before returning the cloth to a bowl of water. "He got worse with every day," the dwarf informed them.

"Aphrandhor?" Androma's concern forced Ilithranda to guide the Rider to his side.

Daijen deliberately glanced at The Anther propped up between Yamnomora's knees. "Have you seen this before?"

"This ain' the hammer," Mordrith told him confidently.

"How can you be sure?" Ilithranda queried, leaving Androma to sit beside the wizard.

"The Anther don' make ye rabbit on abou' farmin' pigs an' growin' potatoes," Mordrith specified. "By the second day, he started talkin' to folk that weren' even there. I was hopin' *she'd* have the answer to this."

It took Androma a moment to realise the *she* Mordrith was referring to was her. "Only once have I seen this before," the Rider uttered.

"What happened last time?" Daijen asked.

"He forgot he was wearing the bracer," Androma began. "He touched..." Her words faded as her hands knotted into fists. "He touched *Maegar*," she finally managed, her dragon's name a source of great pain. "Four centuries of life rushed through his mind. Without a dragon bond, the human mind doesn't have the capacity to hold so much memory. It overwhelmed him. He slept for a day and a half."

"You have just as many centuries," Daijen pointed out. "He was able to read you on Nareene."

"He didn't touch me by mistake. Aphrandhor knew to look at my most recent memories."

Mordrith placed the wet cloth in Androma's hand. "How was he when he woke up?"

"He couldn't remember his name for an hour or two," the Rider reported while dabbing his brow. "It took about a week, but his mind eventually let go of most of what he had gleaned through Maegar. It was as if the weight of it all created a hole. A hole in which he lost some of himself as well. He says much of his childhood is gone now. It was another month before he could name all the colours again," she added as an afterthought.

"The older something is," Daijen recalled, "the more memory it contains and the harder it is for him."

Androma was nodding along. "He has learned to focus it to a degree, but he still has much to learn about the bracer."

The Rider's words led Daijen to the table, where the vambrace sat beside the wizard's bag.

A thought most dangerous occurred to the Vahlken then.

The bracer clearly required an individual with infinite capacity where their memory was concerned. Daijen knew he fitted such a description, his mind capable of walking though the halls of time to relive crystal-clear memories at his leisure.

Shouldn't he wield such a weapon?

Yet, like Mordrith had with The Anther, it was an unmistakable truth that Aphrandhor had claimed the vambrace as his own, as his responsibility. Daijen, however, was unable to deny the logical conclusion: the bracer would kill the wizard. It seemed all the more inevitable when contemplating the plan that had brought them back to Ka'vairn.

"So," Yamnomora began, her tone as callous as her words, "what's our next move? Why 'ave ye had us return to this sorry excuse for a keep?"

Lost in his own machinations for a moment, Daijen required an extra second to process the dwarf's questions, if not register the fact that he had crossed the room to stand over the wizard's bag. Somewhat exhausted by the dwarf's attitude already, Daijen considered The Valtorak's need of them and decided it was more pressing.

"Androma will fill you in," he stated, the Rider having been enlightened during their journey west. "Our presence is requested elsewhere," he then informed the others, pivoting swiftly so his cloak fanned out beside him.

Ilithranda paused in Daijen's wake. "Make sure she has something to eat and drink," the Vahlken commanded, her words aimed at the dwarves while her gaze rested solely on Androma.

"I'm not a child," the Dragon Rider replied, her tone clipped.

Daijen's ears were pricked as he left the room, expecting some sharp, if not clever, retort from Ilithranda. There came no such reply, however, the Vahlken simply content to look at the dwarves, her expectation etched into her expression.

In the hall outside, Daijen gave Ilithranda a look of his own, conveying his curiosity where her silence was concerned. There came no relief from that silence, prompting Daijen to pry.

"You have formed a good bond with Androma," he observed as they crossed from one side of the fortress to the other. "It doesn't seem that long ago you would have brought your sword against her," he continued in the absence of any reply.

"There would be no honour in fighting her now," Ilithranda finally answered.

Daijen interpreted her words as no more than a shield to conceal her true feelings on the matter. "You have been a good friend in her time of grief," he went on, probing from another angle.

"Her grief has hardly begun," Ilithranda told him, and miserably so. "I was there in her time of anger when the sting of loss is so great it threatens your own life. Androma alone has to carry her grief now."

Daijen conjured a memory of the west wing, where Androma's *anger* had decimated so much of the keep's interior. Still, Ilithranda's defences remained curiously high as she avoided speaking about the bond she had formed with the Rider.

"You speak of such loss as if acquainted," he remarked, sure that in all their decades together, he had never heard mention of anything even close to what Androma was going through.

Ilithranda quickened her pace just enough to beat him to the spiral staircase that led up to The Valtorak's office. "You don't have to investigate *everything*, Daijen. Some things *can* be left to the past."

As had been the case many years ago, upon meeting the illegitimate princess of House Lhoris, Daijen was left with naught but his burning thirst for knowledge regarding his sister's past life.

Knowing that to say more would spark an argument between them, Daijen followed behind her in silence, the quietude only broken by The Valtorak's invitation to enter his office.

The chamber was just as familiar to Daijen as Ka'vairn's exterior walls, each unchanging with the passage of time. The overspilling bookshelves were filled beyond their designed capacity, with tomes and scrolls stacked upon themselves wherever there was space. Dotted between were candles that threatened to burn the entire office to the ground should one catch a piece of parchment. The domed ceiling loomed high overhead, its painted imagery long having faded from beauty.

Then there was the master of Ka'vairn. The Valtorak was, perhaps, as timeless as his office and the walls around it. He sat behind his desk, a figure of stone. Only the web of lines around his eyes betrayed his advanced age or, indeed, the fact that he was alive and not to be mistaken for a statue.

"I wasn't expecting you to leave your new *friends* so quickly," the master commented, his gaze never straying from the parchment laid out before him.

"Master," Daijen greeted, bowing his head in unison with Ilithranda. "You seemed... *disturbed.*"

"A great *many* things disturb me, Daijen Saeth. Mysterious dragon eggs, humans bred for the sole purpose of safeguarding long-dead farmers, and—let us not forget—the arrival of a Jainus-trained wizard." Daijen made to speak but wasn't nearly quick enough. "Added to all of that, *two* weapons of power are in play. One is wielded by a young human wholly out of his depth and the other by a dwarven miner whose personal history is steeped in Skaramangian lore."

"Neither is our enemy," Daijen assured him, drained by the repetitive argument.

"That is not my point," The Valtorak said plainly. "You think your alliance with them gives you an advantage, but it only hinders you. Were you to see things clearly, you would have taken the hammer and bracer and used them against the enemy by now."

"We *did*," Daijen countered, his temper flaring—he knew he

needed to sleep, and soon, before the days continued to rack up. "You said you were informed," he went on. "You know then that we assaulted The Tomb."

"*Assaulted?*" The Valtorak almost barked out a laugh. "Dwarves don't mince their words. I know *exactly* what transpired on that island. You were *allowed* to infiltrate that pyramid, where you then *blundered* into an ambush without your Aegres." The master rose to his feet, forcing his chair back. "Adding to such a miserable start, you discovered *nothing* that advances our place in the war. Ultimately, you *fled* before being overwhelmed." The Valtorak rounded his desk and looked Daijen dead in the eyes. "Kastiek taught you better than that. You insult his memory with your ineptitude just as you insult my intelligence with your choice of words."

Again, Daijen opened his mouth to deliver his version of events only to be silenced by the master.

"You fail to realise that the only thing of any value is that vambrace. You should have returned from Nareene with *that* as your trophy. The Anther too," he added ominously.

"You would have taken what is theirs and left them to die?" Ilithranda questioned, inserting herself with barbed enthusiasm. "There is no honour in that."

"Does it honour those now doomed to die in this war because you failed to act?" The Valtorak countered, his words a surgical strike as he whirled on Ilithranda. "With the bracer, we could uncover our enemy's secrets and, with the hammer, bring ruin upon them. Now we must rely on others, on those who do not have the strength of Handuin flowing through their veins. There is a reason it is left to us to wage war with the Skaramangians, or do you both need reminding that the Vahlken were forged body and mind for that very purpose? We alone have the power to shoulder that burden. It *cannot* be left to others."

"There aren't enough of us left to *shoulder that burden*," Daijen blurted, his voice ragged with righteous anger. "Or do *you* need reminding of our dwindling numbers?"

"Do not speak to *me* of our losses," The Valtorak replied threateningly. "You think because your strategy is new it will prove potent? What must I do to make you see such folly? Must I list the dead, the Vahlken who have already given their lives? I could name them all, though we might perish under the weight of time before I finish."

Daijen rose to the argument with vigour. "I know some of the names on that list. One day," he promised, "it will be my honour to join them. Until then, I'm going to fight this war how I see fit." Daijen stepped within inches of The Valtorak. "And while you have been sitting idly behind these walls, I have *seen* what's out there. What we're up against. If there's one thing I've learned of our enemy, it's that they're *smarter* than us. More *cunning*. More *deadly*. They set us against the Dragon Riders and effectively ended the threat of us both with one move. What have *we* done? It isn't enough to just keep throwing ourselves at them."

The master reduced the gap between them all the more. "All you're doing is throwing *their* lives at the enemy," The Valtorak specified, nodding at the door behind them. "What will you do when they die fighting in this war? Seek out new dwarves and wizards to replace them? A new Dragon Rider, perhaps? You're just going to get them killed, Daijen. We and we alone were *made* for this war."

Daijen was shaking his head, wondering if the master could ever be made to see sense. "If we don't make alliances, we're going to fade into legend," he said simply. "What use are we to the people of Andara if we're just words in a book?"

Something in The Valtorak deflated at that. "You are *both* fools if you think salvation for the realm can be found in dwarves and wizards," he announced coldly. "Heed my counsel: your alliance is doomed."

"You've been here for too long," Daijen said, his tone earnest now. "You can't see the enemy from inside this valley. Your counsel is outdated."

The Valtorak took a breath and broke eye contact. "Very well," he said, moving away. "Like a child, you must learn your own way. Fall if you must. But know this: when *you* fall, *they* will fall with you. Perhaps, when their blood is on your hands, you will listen to me."

"It won't come to that," Daijen insisted. "We have a plan," he explained, embellishing the truth somewhat.

"Ah, yes," The Valtorak replied lazily, assuming his chair once more. "The reason for your return. The dwarves were none the wiser. Tell me then, what does one do after fleeing the enemy with such haste?"

Daijen clamped his jaw shut, taking just a moment to centre himself and maintain his calm tone of voice. "We find the resting place of the Dark Ones and destroy whatever remains before the Skaramangians can revive them." Saying it so plainly made it sound ridiculous, bordering on idiotic. Yet there it was: his plan. His *only* plan.

"Why didn't I think of that?" the master replied mockingly. "I'm assuming you're about to tell me this eight-hundred-year-old farmer happened to have a Dark One buried in his barn."

"No," Daijen replied with every ounce of patience he had left. "As far as we can tell, the skeletons inside The Tomb hold no significant regard."

"None that you can *discern*," The Valtorak pointed out. "I suppose fighting your way out of an ambush and fleeing for your lives has a way of skewing one's perspective."

Daijen glanced at Ilithranda, who looked to be sharing his frustration. "As you said," he began again, "the only thing of value we brought back was the bracer. *I* will use it," he declared, drawing frowns from both The Valtorak and Ilithranda.

"You?" Ilithranda blurted.

"On what?" The Valtorak demanded.

Ilithranda's audible doubt in him wounded Daijen's pride, aggravating old scars that urged the Vahlken to prove himself all the more. "The bone," he answered.

The master's brow pinched in confusion, a mere flash compared to the hard revelation that held his expression. "Out of the question."

Daijen leaned forward against the desk. "It's ancient," he said eagerly, picturing the black bone resting in the chamber with the perilous, if not unstable, pits of Handuin. "We've all seen it," he went on, talking quickly now. "The glyphs etched into the bone. You never talk about it and there's no mention of it in any of our records. That bone belonged to *Ahnir*. Handuin took it when he fled the Warlocks in God Fall."

"That *bone*," the master eventually replied, "is off limits to you. It is to be handled by Valtoraks alone."

"I'm not going to *handle* it," Daijen argued. "I just need to touch it."

"Is that so wise?" Ilithranda questioned, reinserting herself into the conversation. "You've seen Aphrandhor."

"Yes," The Valtorak agreed. "The wizard touched an eight-hundred-year-old skeleton. What remains of Ahnir is *significantly* older."

Daijen's growing frustration slowed his ability to articulate himself. How could they not see the providence?

"You might never wake up," Ilithranda uttered, her hand gripping his arm.

Daijen turned swiftly to the master of Ka'vairn, the obvious hypocrite in the room. "*You* said we were to use these weapons."

"And *you* disagreed," The Valtorak pointed out.

"I disagreed that we should use them at the expense of our allies' lives!" he spat. "I'm suggesting *I* use the bracer because we were clearly meant to."

The Valtorak raised an immaculate eyebrow. "Meant to?"

"Our memories are perfect," Daijen explained. "We can relive every detail of our life—our *centuries* of life. A Vahlken could use the bracer without succumbing to the weight of memory. It's almost as if we were meant to use it."

The Valtorak narrowed his eyes. "You believe the *divine* is at work?" he asked incredulously.

Daijen didn't answer immediately, well aware of his master's lack of faith. Indeed, his own was adrift, knocked by so much knowledge. He felt the hands of the gods at work, yet the very bone he sought was believed to be that of Ahnir, the god who had seen

The End. The same god who had left them his helm, a guide to take Andara into an uncertain future.

Ahnir was also a *dead* god. It seemed a conundrum that Daijen's wavering faith could hardly contend with.

"This is common ground," he said instead, changing tack. "You believe we alone should use the weapons of power. In this instance, I am in agreement. We already possess the bone, so no lives need be risked in seeking out another relic. More important- ly," he added, "we possess a relic we know has been handled by Skaramangians, by the very warlocks at the heart of their order. Imagine what we might glean," he offered temptingly. "We could look back to the very beginning."

"The beginning of *time,* perhaps?" The Valtorak queried— another jibe at Daijen's faith.

"The beginning of the Skaramangians," Daijen replied seriously.

There it was. He had, at last, used the right combination of words to slip through the master's armour. The Valtorak's gaze wandered while his mind churned, contemplating an advantage that came at the expense of losing the argument.

"No."

It was Ilithranda who had spoken, turning all eyes on her.

"You're not using the bracer until Aphrandhor wakes up. Until we know for certain that he has survived," she continued, preventing Daijen from responding, "there's not a chance I'm letting you touch something that might be *thousands* of years old. If anything, you should practice like he has. Start small and—"

"There's no time to start small," Daijen said, speaking over her. "You saw what I saw in that pyramid. We have *no idea* what the Skaramangians are really doing, only that it's rooted in such dark- ness that we cannot comprehend it. They're ten steps ahead of us, and that's if we're even on the same map!" he exclaimed. "We have the key to unlocking their oldest secrets. Why are we still discussing this?"

Quite naturally, their attention fell back on The Valtorak. "Ilithranda is right," he said, if reluctantly. "We don't know enough about this bracer or its consequences. Touching that bone could unravel you, Daijen. This order cannot suffer more losses."

Daijen's expression fell into outrage. "Am I the only one who—"

The Valtorak slid a piece of parchment across his desk, his fingers twisting the missive so Daijen could see clearly the wax seal. That seal was enough to halt Daijen's rant and secure his attention, for there was but one who possessed the ring that could make that impression.

"What is that?" Ilithranda demanded, spotting the seal for herself.

"An imperial request disguised as an invitation," The Valtorak reported. "We have been *summoned*."

Daijen stretched out the parchment, revealing more of its elegant calligraphy. "By whom?" he asked absently, though he already knew the answer from the seal itself.

"Emperor Qeledred signed this himself," the master informed needlessly. "You're going to Aran'saur. To the *imperial palace*."

7
WILD

Joran awoke with a start, his dreams having churned and darkened, bringing him back to that ledge upon the precipice of The Ruins of Gelakor. He had, again, watched Gallien and the others fall away as Oaken took to the sky. How vividly he saw the swarming Andarens, their weapons bristling.

He imagined Gallien falling to those weapons, his body torn asunder by Andaren steel. He would have died fighting, that much he knew. It was little comfort. Dead was dead. That meant he was gone forever.

A cold and numbing sensation settled over him. The feeling of being utterly alone in the world threatened to overwhelm him in that windowless room. Gallien wouldn't have let him dwell, he knew. The smuggler would have had him up on his feet and on the move.

Wiping the sweat from his brow, Joran cautiously abandoned his room and retraced his steps to the kitchen and stores. With no sign of Kassanda and no way of locating her in the maze of corridors, he helped himself to breakfast. He sat there for some time afterwards, wondering where the Rider was.

There had been no instruction following the previous command to eat and sleep. Indeed, there was no way of even knowing what time of day it was from inside the rocky fortress. He assumed dawn was cresting the world somewhere, but he had been awoken by dreams rather than his natural rise.

Deciding he couldn't stay in that room any longer, Joran set his feet to exploring. Though it was disturbing to begin with, he soon acclimated to the torches that sprang to life upon approach. Some would go on and on, revealing endless hallways, while others exposed doorways that offered boundless exploration.

Catching the feel of a breeze, he followed the cool air, a path that took him up spiralling staircases and, once, to a lever-operated platform that saw him slowly rise against a counterweight. He had no idea how high up he was now—his only hope was that the breeze was leading him to the outside world and not deeper into the cliffs.

Unable to pass a set of double doors—his curiosity piqued—Joran temporarily strayed from the cool air and entered the sealed chamber. As with everywhere else, the torches fixed to the walls were sparked by some unseen spell, filling the room with firelight.

A domed ceiling pulled his gaze up, where he looked in wonder at the imagery painted across the smooth stone. Seven Dragon Riders looked down on him from astride their dragons, each holding their weapon aloft, evoking some great victory as they soared through the heavens. Deciding he would come back another time to take in the detail of the large concave mural, Joran turned his attention to the purpose of the chamber.

It was a training room, of that he had no doubt. Dummies stood dotted about the edges, their padding slashed or battered. The centre of the room was occupied by a square dais that offered naught but empty space—a sparring area, perhaps. Joran's mouth slowly fell open as he took in the chamber walls, where there was no end of weaponry with which to spar.

His violet eyes roamed over battle axes, tridents, spears, and all manner of swords. There were even two-handed hammers slotted in between, an unwieldy and inelegant weapon in his opinion. Still, there seemed to be enough weapons to arm a battalion.

Joran's thoughts naturally landed on the broken sword tucked into his belt. He was most anxious to discover that he had forgotten it, the weapon left in his room. He chastised himself, blaming his fatigue, grief, and uncertainty about his future and Drakanan as a whole. Also, he knew, possessing a weapon was new to him, and it didn't readily occur to him that he should have one strapped to his hip at all times.

None of his excuses were good enough, he decided, for the broken sword was so much more than that. The sobering thought turned him away from the training room and set him to tracking the breeze once more.

A sheen of sweat coated his brow by the time he had climbed several more sets of steps. The higher he ascended, the more he was forced to remove torches from their brackets and use the flames to burn his way through entire walls of cobwebs.

The sound of rhythmic clattering found him before he saw the faint light of sunrise. The breeze had brought him to a set of partially shattered doors, one of which had been caught by the funnelled wind and was banging into the wall. Up ahead, the dim light rising over the horizon revealed the enormous tunnel that ran out into the open world.

Unlike the rest of Drakanan, the tunnel looked to have been burrowed rather than deliberately hewn by crafting hands. Every thing from the floor up to the jagged ceiling was natural rock, though there were areas where the stone protruded, concealing some of the floor ahead. Hindering his vision all the more were mounds of earth here and there, great piles of dirt that could only have been deposited in the tunnel.

Enjoying the cool air washing over his face, Joran was drawn towards the distant dawn. As far back as he was, he could see no land beyond the tunnel, the sun rising amidst hazy clouds and a halo of fading stars.

Along with that breeze came a foul odour, a pungent stench

that had failed to breach Drakanan's halls but certainly reigned over the tunnel. Progressing as he was, the boy soon discovered that the smell was coming from the large piles of earth. Pausing by the first heap, a closer inspection informed him it wasn't dirt at all.

His nose felt all the more offended, taking him back a step. The excrement, he realised, could only have come from the dragons he had encountered upon arriving at Drakanan. Every one of them had emerged from the pitted holes bored into the towering walls of the horseshoe canyon. Thinking back on that particular view, Joran was amazed to realise that he had ascended so high.

Thereafter, he chose his steps with more care, giving the piles of dung a wide berth. He continued onwards, seeking that edge and the incredible. As the sun pierced some of the cloud cover, a ray of early light bathed the tunnel, creating stark shadows. The contrast was such that he nearly missed the skeletons on the floor.

Crouching by the first, Joran investigated the bones scattered about his feet. He determined them to have once belonged to a cow or, perhaps, a bison. And they weren't alone. From where he stood to the very end of the tunnel, the floor was littered with dead animals, new and old, scorched and gnawed.

After only one more step, rounding a knot of rock that sloped out of the wall, he saw the last of the tunnel's inhabitants. Joran froze. His heart leaped in his chest.

Eggs.

Three of them.

They sat nestled amongst the bones. They would have appeared as no more than rocks were it not for the sun revealing the green, red, and blue of their scaled outer shells. This had to be it, he knew. It seemed only right that his dragon would be kin to the wild ones, a striking detail that would only add to their fore-seen legend. It would set him apart from all other Riders, who had only ever bonded with eggs given to the order by their mothers.

He approached them with haste, his knees bending to bring him closer to the eggs. Had the bonding already begun? Was he feeling any different? Which of the three was to be his? Joran closed his eyes, wondering if the sensation would become more obvious.

He felt something.

Warmth. It washed over him, briefly banishing the frigid air. Opening his eyes, Joran half expected to see one of the eggs cracking and a peering dragon head.

How wrong he was.

Severe shock and unbridled fear caused Joran to throw himself back and begin crawling away from the eggs on his elbows. Red eyes pursued him as deadly claws stepped over the eggs to close the gap. The dragon that had exhaled its hot breath was no larger than a pony, but its bared fangs bristled inside a strong jaw, and its sharp claws were each as long as his fingers.

The dragon advanced at a stalking pace, its head dipped to reveal a spine of flat, bony protrusions. It opened its mouth and let loose a sound somewhere between a roar and shriek, giving Joran a clear view of the two glands that sat behind the fangs. They pulsed but the once and spat two jets of clear liquid.

Fire was birthed inside the tunnel.

Joran yelled and rolled aside, yet he wasn't quick enough to avoid the flames that now clung to his dark cloak. He panicked and writhed in a bid to be free of the fire, but the flames would not relent, forcing him to unclip the fabric altogether and throw it away.

The dragon had moved. It now looked down at him from one of the piles of excrement. Those red eyes, slitted by a line of pure black, bored into him, making him feel no more than prey. Without warning, the dragon sprang, its claws splayed to grip his flesh. It was, perhaps, his mother's enhanced reflexes that saw him react better this time, allowing him to dash out of the way.

For all his speed, however, he could not compete with an adolescent dragon. It turned on him with wicked speed and raked one of its claws across his chest. Joran cried out in pain and tripped over a rock. His shoulders and back absorbed most of the impact, saving him from a head injury that would have dazed him and ensured his death. Still, he was on the ground again and at the mercy of a wild dragon.

A low rumbling sound caused Joran to lift his head, his gaze landing on the young dragon as it stepped between his legs. Saliva oozed from between sharp teeth and over its maw. Whether from being bitten or burned, he was to die in that tunnel.

And he would have succumbed to that grim end, had a far greater predator not invaded the tunnel at speed.

Oaken squawked, the Aegre capable of making a noise that swelled within the tunnel and hurt the ears. The young dragon should have fled in Oaken's shadow, but foolish youth flooded its veins as it instead gave another shriek and attempted to drag its claws down the Aegre's feathered neck.

With one leg, Oaken pinned the dragon beneath its four talons. The helpless creature squirmed, its tail thrashing to no avail while the intimidating Aegre looked down on it with piercing yellow eyes.

"No!" Kassanda yelled, her voice projecting from the back of the tunnel.

Everything happened at once.

Pitch blackness descended, as if the sun had been snatched from the heavens. Oaken squawked in the dark, his tone one of great surprise rather than the aggression he had previously declared. Joran felt the young dragon scramble over his legs before he jumped to his feet, where Kassanda's hand gripped him by the shoulder and yanked him back.

When the sun, at last, found its way back into the tunnel, Joran saw the truth of what had happened. Oaken was being dragged towards the outside world, his talons scoring deep grooves in the stone.

Garganafan had arrived.

The hulking dragon pulled the Aegre from the tunnel with a single set of claws. The moment Oaken was over the lip and under the sky, he flapped his wings in Garganafan's face and launched himself out of sight. The bone-white dragon chased him off with an ear-shattering roar before beating his bat-like wings and taking off in pursuit.

That still left Joran and Kassanda with a young and volatile dragon. Seeing it from a different angle now, the adolescent's deep orange scales were brought to life in the rising light. Like Garganafan, it walked the line between being beautiful and terrifying.

Kassanda planted a hand on his chest, pushing him back towards Drakanan's interior. The Rider didn't see the pain it caused Joran, her fingers having pressed into the claw marks that had torn through his skin.

"Stay back," she warned him, drawing her exquisite blade.

Joran couldn't help but display his confusion when Kassanda flipped upside down and drove it into the stone, where she then abandoned it. Now defenceless, the Rider approached the young dragon with her hands held out and knees slightly bent.

"She's scared," Kassanda said, her back to Joran. "Any sudden movements will set off her instincts, so be still," she added, briefly glancing at him over one shoulder.

The dragon snapped its jaw in her direction, its red eyes shifting between the two of them. As it had with Joran, the adolescent leaped without warning, bringing four sets claws and an open maw down on Kassanda. When there seemed only inches between them, the Rider proved she was anything but defenceless.

Having turned her body sideways, Kassanda threw up her right arm and balled her fist as if she were presenting the dragon with a shield. Indeed she was, only the shield could only be seen when both came together. The subsequent flash was brilliant and radiated a multitude of colours as it not only deflected the incoming dragon's attack but launched the creature back, sending it reeling across the tunnel.

"How did you do that?" Joran blurted, his young eyes still bewildered by the sight of magic.

"She isn't the only one with instincts," Kassanda replied, advancing on the dragon at a walking pace. "Go!" she commanded the creature, waving her hands at the head of the tunnel. "Go! Find your mother!"

The dragon growled and exploded from its low crouch. Again, Kassanda threw up her arm and repelled the creature with a flaring shield. This time, however, she added a deliberate touch of magic to hammer home her command and flicked her wrist, presenting the palm of her hand. A wave of invisible energy ran through the tunnel, picking up bones and debris before crashing into the adolescent.

Being that much closer to the mouth of the tunnel, when the dragon recovered from its tumble, it gave the pair one final look until sense saw the creature take flight.

Kassanda's shoulders sagged, and her clean scalp dipped towards her chest. "She could have killed you," she said, turning to face the boy. That was when the three eggs caught her eye, and she gave him a sidelong glance. "You cannot be foolish enough to try and bond with a wild egg."

"I didn't come looking for them," he insisted. "I was looking for *you*."

"Up here?" the Rider questioned incredulously.

"I might have got... *distracted* somewhere along the way," he admitted.

"You don't wander the halls of Drakanan like some babe lost in the woods," she remarked firmly. Her eyes fell over his chest and the dark fabric plastered to his skin. "You're wounded," she observed. "Come with me," the Rider commanded before he could speak.

Joran made to follow but paused when Kassanda hung back, the Rider making time to retrieve the three eggs.

"What will you do with them?" he asked, imagining her adding them to the egg chamber.

"Place them beyond Drakanan's borders, where the mother can reclaim them without fear of Garganafan."

Those were the last words Kassanda spoke for some time, their descent back into Drakanan's interior one of silence. Silence and *pain*, for Joran felt the sting of the dragon's claws keenly now. It felt like an age before they returned to the living areas of the keep, where Kassanda had the boy sit on a chair before a giant wall of carved relief.

Joran waited as patiently as he could while she prepared some cloths, a bowl of water, and what looked to be a jar of grey paste. As he did, his attention wandered over the relief carved out of the stone wall, its shadows dancing in the flickering light.

"What is that?" he asked, trying to make sense of the men and women kneeling before a man.

"Take off your shirt," the Rider said, her hands busy soaking one of the cloths.

There was something about Kassanda's voice that left no room for discussion, so he removed his shirt. It made him wince, the physical act pulling at the torn skin.

"You're lucky," she commented, squeezing the excess water from the cloth. "A few inches higher and she would have opened your throat."

"Lucky," he echoed dryly. "That's me," he added with the sarcastic charm Gallien had instilled in him.

The boy's easy smile fell away the moment Kassanda began to clean the wounds. He closed his eyes and groaned and hissed, his hands knotted into tight balls that paled his knuckles. The pain aside, Joran was impressed with the Rider's delicate touch, dabbing rather than wiping. She seemed the heavy-handed sort, and he had expected the pain to be tenfold.

"*That*," Kassanda began, her dark eyes flitting to the relief and back, "depicts a significant moment in the history of the Dragon Riders. It was over a millennium ago."

"What's so—"

Joran's mouth suddenly clamped shut while he tried to cope with the pain. He looked down at the three raking lines of red to see Kassanda applying the grey paste. "What is that?" he asked through gritted teeth.

"Andaren magic," came her unexpected answer.

"*Andaren* magic?" he repeated. "I thought you had... *dragon* magic."

"Andaren healing magic is more practical," the Rider informed him, her attention narrowing on a particular area of his chest. "It's slower," she continued, "but guaranteed to work. All other forms of healing magic have proved to be... unstable—for *both* participants."

Joran groaned, feeling the paste fill the grooves. "So," he said, hoping to be distracted, "*why* is that so significant?"

Kassanda used the damp cloth again and cleaned the skin between the gashes, removing the excess paste. "That is the king of Erador. Or it *was*. The Etragon bloodline is a long one. You're looking at the day the Dragon Riders took their oath and bowed to the king. From then on, we were sworn to serve the throne."

The Rider stood up and let the dirty cloth fall from her grip and splash in the bowl of water. "Don't pick it. The paste will harden and fall off in its own time." Picking up his shirt for him, she noted the rips and blood that marred it. "You will need new clothes," she commented. "And your cloak?" she queried, giving him a once over.

"It... caught fire." He felt all the more naive confessing as much.

"A new cloak, then," Kassanda concluded. "Follow me."

It was in silence again—though with considerably less pain—that Joran traversed a plethora of corridors and halls in the Rider's wake. They passed through the eating area and into a chamber just as vast as the one that had been equipped with weapons and dummies, though the ceiling was far from grand, housing no more than a series of candelabras—all of which came to life, as did the surrounding torches as they entered.

"What is this place?" Joran was compelled to ask.

Looking around, he noted a pair of looms, several workstations, shelves upon shelves of tools, and even a forge. Like the training area, there were lifeless figures standing about, only these appeared to be mannequins attired in various pieces of armour. In the far righthand corner, Joran's keen eyes spotted racks of sandy-coloured cloaks and steel-tipped boots.

"This is... *was* the armourer's workshop," Kassanda explained.

"Should a Rider join the ranks, they would come here to build their armour."

Joran marvelled at Kassanda's black armour, a form-fitting suit of dark plate that appeared to be layered over small scales of bone-white. "You build it yourself?"

"In time. As your dragon grows, it will shed scales. You will want to collect them while they're young and the scales are small. Traditionally, the armourer would assist you in this, but it's essential that every Rider be capable of making repairs and adjustments on their own."

Joran made a point of looking around. "Where is the armourer?"

The Rider said nothing for a time, her gaze having settled on the distant forge. "He honoured his oath to the throne of Erador," she said simply. "And he was killed for it."

The answer was obvious to Joran. "Baelon," he named, drawing Kassanda's attention.

"Androma told you about him," she reasoned, nodding solemnly. "Over here," she added, cutting Joran off before he could elaborate.

From within a small alcove of shelves, the Rider removed and then presented him with a new shirt and trousers. Moving along the rack of cloaks, Kassanda's fingers brushed through them until she pulled free the one she had been looking for. Holding it to his shoulder, they could both see that the cloak stopped half an inch from the floor.

"Here," she said, offering it to him. "You're not supposed to be presented with this until *after* bonding with an egg but, given your circumstances, you'll *freeze*. It's only going to get colder. You may look through the boots and see what fits. Those look like they've seen more than a few miles," the Rider pointed out, her critical gaze running over his feet.

As Kassanda began to walk away, Joran feared he would lose her the moment she departed the room.

"Wait," he demanded, abandoning the row of boots for the time being. "Yesterday you told me to leave, that I wasn't the *one*.

Then you learned my name and changed your mind. Now, without a bond, you're giving me clothes that belong on a Dragon Rider. Why? Why am I still here? I know it has something to do with my name. Before that I meant nothing to you."

The Rider stopped beside a mannequin and slowly turned to face him. "What did Androma tell you of your fate?"

"That it was seen through the Helm of Ahnir."

"*What* was seen through the helm of Ahnir?" she asked specifically.

Joran hesitated. "That a warrior of both worlds would bring about a time of dragons."

Kassanda was nodding along as she rounded the partially armoured mannequin.

"When all those thousands gave their lives to see through the Helm," she began, "there were many who described the one who would bring about a time of dragons. Some saw a man. Some saw a woman. All were half-Andaren, half-human. But there was only one among the doomed who offered... a *name*."

Joran looked down at the cloak in his hands, feeling the rough fabric between his fingers, as he put it together. "*My* name."

"*Pendain*," Kassanda confirmed. "The one who raised you. The smuggler. Did he have any children? Siblings?"

"Gallien never had children," Joran answered, wondering where this line of questioning had come from. "His brother died before I was born."

"Then it would seem," the Rider replied at length, "that you *are* the one, for I have never known a smuggler display anything *close* to the heart of a dragon."

Joran took umbrage with that "Gallien had more honour than any man I've ever met." That was a lie, he knew, but the boy refused to say a bad word about the man who had raised him. "He would have made the very best of Riders. Not that it matters now," he added, shoulders sagging.

Kassanda tilted her head, scrutinising him all the more. "I thought you would be elated. There is a future in which you have been *named* the saviour of dragonkind, if not the entire realm. Isn't that why you're here? Or, perhaps," the Rider mused critically, "you were just in search of some excitement, and the truth of it terrifies you now."

Joran's gaze snapped to her. "I was born in the middle of a siege, to a Vahlken, before being whisked from one country to the next. I've spent my entire life out-running Padoshi thugs and Skaramangian assassins. I've had enough *excitement*," he said venomously.

"An Andaren died declaring your name," Kassanda went on, not one to be fazed by mere tone. "That means there is a future in which you might accomplish all that you hoped for."

"A future where I'm supposed to bond with an egg," he pointed out, his frustration lacing every syllable.

"Your egg is sitting in that chamber beneath us," the Rider stated matter-of-factly. "The reason you haven't bonded with it is simple: you do not have the heart of a dragon."

Joran shrugged, unsure how to argue against something he didn't fully understand. "If that's true, then how can one of those eggs be meant for me?"

"No one is *born* with the heart of a dragon. It is earned through deeds, through our actions. Even in their eggs, the dragons can see into our hearts and see that which matters most—a reflection of *themselves*."

Joran considered everything that had brought him to that egg chamber. "I've crossed Andaren soldiers and outrun Skaramangian assassins. I even escaped the spymaster's men. I've survived The Dawn Sword twice now! Hells, I've even flown on an Aegre. What else must I do?"

Kassanda slowly closed the gap between them. "You've fled, outpaced, escaped... *survived*. You have spent your entire life running away. To have the heart of a dragon, you must stand up to your foes. Be *defiant* in the face of death. Only then will you be worthy." The Rider stepped back and gestured at their surroundings. "You have arrived too early. This is the problem with knowing any future. We interfere. We try and make it happen. As a result, we change it. It could be years before you're supposed to come to Drakanan. Either way, you're not ready."

Joran made to speak but held onto his words as the Rider began to walk away. "Wait," he finally called after her. "What am I supposed to do now? Do I still have to leave?"

Kassanda stopped before the doors. "No," she replied flatly. "If events really are unfolding in the wrong order, we will adapt. First, you train. *Then* you bond."

Joran looked at her in disbelief. "I'm to train *without* a dragon?"

"You've spent your whole life learning how to run, how to hide. I'm going to train you so you don't have to do either of those things ever again." She gestured to the doors. "Shall we begin?"

8

ONLY FORWARDS

0 Years Ago...

4

Daijen's eyes scanned the missive for a second time, unable to reconcile the words with his picture-perfect memory. "The Ankala," he said, naming the ancient tradition.

"Kastiek and I attended the last one while you were receiving your armour from The Weavers. As I cannot leave Tovun to his own training, the two of you will attend."

Ilithranda was shaking her head. "That was only twenty years ago," she pointed out. "The Ankala is every twenty-*five* years."

Daijen indicated the parchment in his hand. "It's been brought forward in an effort to bring the war to an end sooner—*to reduce the loss of Andaren life*," he quoted. "We don't have time for this."

"Actually," The Valtorak replied coolly, "you *do* have time. Until we know for certain that the wizard has survived, I will not permit you access to the pits."

Daijen's counter-argument was on the tip of his tongue when

The Valtorak continued. "Regardless, we do not refuse invitations from the emperor. You *are* going."

"I thought the Vahlken were outside imperial law," Daijen reminded him.

"It is *because* we exist on the outside that we accept any and all invitations to look behind the curtain. We know the Skaramangians operate on the highest levels within the palace—perhaps even within the imperial family. Those are echelons we do not have access to. This is an opportunity to uncover secrets *without* the threat of losing our minds."

It wasn't without the threat of losing their *lives*, Daijen thought. Aran'saur was a viper's nest of politicking and religious law that was most concentrated inside the imperial palace. How many Skaramangian eyes would be on them from the moment they landed in the city? They would be walking targets.

Still, Daijen couldn't deny his hunger to always know more about—if not see—the capital of his country, a splendour by all accounts.

"I'm not going," Ilithranda declared firmly. "I swore I would never go back to that city and I meant it."

"The oaths you took before the pits died with your previous life," The Valtorak told her just as firmly. "You were reborn a Vahlken. There remains nothing of the emperor in you—not even your blood." When Ilithranda looked to renew her argument, the master of Ka'vairn doubled down. "It is unwise for any Vahlken, even myself, to enter that city alone. The Ankala will be testing enough without the threat of assassination. You must guard each other as much as yourselves."

"Then we won't go," Ilithranda stated with an air of victory, as if she had discovered the perfect solution.

It was with a knowing look that The Valtorak's golden eyes shifted to Daijen. The master knew, it seemed, that his words had sunk in.

"Everything we do carries with it the threat of death," Daijen said. "At least this threat brings with it an opportunity—"

"I know what we stand to gain," Ilithranda cut in. "It's not fear of death that keeps me from that city."

"Then what?" Daijen asked. "With this," he went on, gesturing at the invitation, "we can walk right into the throne room. You heard what the curator said," he reminded him, trying to appeal to the investigator that their training had instilled in them both. "The Eldan and the master cleric are one and the same. We can walk *right* up to him."

The Valtorak leaned forward in his chair. "The Eldan?" he enquired, a detail Mordrith must have missed out, if not forgotten.

"The curator named The Eldan as one of their leaders, if not *the* leader. She also spoke of how The Eldan is never given a proper burial because their funeral is always a public affair."

"Because they're also the master cleric," The Valtorak concluded, his tone enough to relay how troubling that fact was.

"Exactly," Daijen confirmed.

"That would explain much of their great influence," The Valtorak noted, speaking to himself somewhat. "The emperor must be seen to abide by the words of the Arkalon more than most. There are none better than the master cleric to embody those words. Or *enforce* them," he added ominously.

The Valtorak looked to a particular row of books on his right. Daijen recognised his master's expression, one that he often wore himself when recalling from deep memory.

"What is it?" he had to ask.

The considerably older Andaren remained eerily still for another moment, his mind elsewhere—another time even. "I have come across that name before," he eventually revealed.

"Where?" Ilithranda was quick to ask, brow furrowed.

"In a rather droll book concerning ancient dialects," he answered, gesturing at a book with dark red binding.

Daijen walked over to it and removed the book from its slot, turning it over to see the cover. "Linguistics, Dialects, and Allogpraphy," he read, the title failing to grab him.

"As far as I am aware, this is the last of its kind," The Valtorak said. "It was recommended to me by *my* Valtorak. An uninspiring read for sure, but you would benefit from its knowledge. After all, our Skaramangian foes date back to a time when our earliest languages were the common tongue."

The Valtorak took the book from Daijen and with great care turned to the relevant page.

"There," he said, spinning the book around on his desk, one finger pointing to the word in question.

"Eldan," Daijen pronounced.

"Apprentice?" Ilithranda queried, reading the translation.

The Valtorak sat back in his chair. "Curious, isn't it? The Skaramangian leader being called apprentice, not *master*."

It only added to the growing list of questions Daijen needed answering where his enemy were concerned, a fact that urged him on.

"I will wait until Aphrandhor wakes up before using the bracer," Daijen agreed, his words aimed at his sister. "But I will not reside behind these walls and simply *wait*. Not while our foe extends their shadow." The Vahlken raised his chin a notch. "I would rather have you by my side, but I *am* going to Aran'saur," he said with conviction.

Ilithranda maintained her defiant demeanour, if for only a moment longer. "Damn you, Daijen Saeth."

————

Piece by piece, Daijen diligently relieved Valyra of her armour, chainmail, and stored weapons. Before leaving for Aran'saur, he would ensure the various plates and saddle were cleaned and any repairs made. He set it all aside, preferring to watch Valyra take off and soar as she was meant to, free of the Vahlken trappings.

Like any Aegre, she was a creature of awe-inspiring beauty that existed hand in hand with the promise of death. The fact that Valyra was an apex predator was never far from Daijen's mind. It was something he would forever respect, lest he suffer the price.

And so he let her be, free to enjoy her time as she pleased. He entered the main keep as Valyra disappeared over The Dain'duil, the cool moon shining upon the ancient stone. After storing his slaiken blade and sundries, there came no hesitation from the Vahlken. He had decided on his course of action before even arriving at Ka'vairn. He would see it through.

Unseen and unheard, Daijen put the Hall of Handuin behind him and accessed the tunnels that descended into Ka'vairn's depths and those of The Hellion Mountains. His destination was unavoidable, the terminus of the plummeting path leading to a singular location.

The birthplace of every Vahlken.

The way was barred by a circular door of heavy iron, its black face embellished with the large four-pronged talon of an Aegre. It had been a long time since he had laid eyes on it, decades even. He retained all the memories of his previous life, and so he recalled a younger, more naive, and certainly shorter Daijen arriving at the door alongside Ilithranda and Elivar. He recalled seeing it again after his transformation, though the door had then appeared smaller and less intimidating.

Now, forbidden from entering, it seemed he was looking at it through those younger eyes once more. One did not easily cross The Valtorak. It wouldn't matter, he told himself. Once he touched a piece of Ahnir he would return to the master with knowledge previously unattainable. It would absolve him of the crime, if not see his future opinions elevated in those golden eyes.

Before attempting to heave it open, Daijen reached around his waist, his fingers exploring the folds of his voluminous cloak. There, hanging from his belt, he found what he needed.

He held the vambrace up in two hands.

He had surreptitiously claimed the piece of armour earlier that day while Yamnomora questioned their next move. Daijen knew he was no thief, but he would accept any title if it helped him bring an end to the war.

And so he reached for the handle.

"Don't," came the short, sharp command.

Daijen turned around, the bracer still held in one hand.

"Ilithranda," he intoned, chastising himself—his excitement and apprehension distracting him.

"You think I don't know you?" she remarked. "Be thankful it's *me* standing here and not The Valtorak. He would not use words to turn you back."

"Is that what you're here to do—turn me back? There is only forwards, Ilithranda. We leave for Aran'saur tomorrow. Wouldn't you rather go there with more than just questions? Think what we might learn from Ahnir. It could give us a starting point. A new lead. That might make all the difference when we're surrounded by enemies."

"It might," Ilithranda agreed. "Or it might put you to sleep until you die from dehydration. What then? We miss the opportunity to get behind enemy lines *and* we lose another Vahlken. You're not going in there," she asserted, stepping towards him with one hand gripping her scimitar.

Daijen considered meeting her threat with one of his own, though a moment of clarity reminded him that it would get them nowhere. They had fought and sparred over the years and proven again and again that they were too evenly matched.

It was with a display of his gifted strength that Daijen used a single arm to open the rounded door. So smooth and swift was his response that Ilithranda had taken no more than a step before the door was fully ajar. She froze, an end brought to her intended intervention before it had even begun.

Daijen understood the moment he looked into the chamber beyond.

The Valtorak stood sentinel amidst the glistening stalagmites, his long, curved staff held to one side.

Daijen wished to stand defiant, an image of the warrior born that Ilithranda so easily embodied. Yet he could but deflate in the gaze of his master. "Don't do this," he pleaded.

"I gave you a command."

The Valtorak's stark response ignited something in Daijen, a petulance he knew he should have outgrown by now. "I'm trying to fight a war," he growled, his own words fanning the flame inside him. "It's my life to risk."

"You gave your life to this order," the master informed him.

"Yes," Daijen agreed. "To the order. Not to *you*. You're not the Vahlken. We were made to bring an end to the Skaramangian threat." He pointed at the alcove on the right, where Ahnir's femur bone rested horizontally. "That's what I'm going to do."

"What you're going to do," The Valtorak replied calmly, "is return to your room. *Sleep*. Tomorrow, you fly for Aran'saur."

Daijen glanced at the lip of the doorway as one foot came up to rest on it.

"If you enter this chamber," The Valtorak warned, "I will see you to your room myself. Though you might not wish to present yourself to the emperor so wounded."

It was the warrior—the *killer*—Kastiek had trained that scrutinised the old Andaren before him. Daijen saw a Vahlken who hadn't tasted real combat in years, perhaps centuries. In recent times, his only sparring partner had been an initiate. The conclusion was obvious: The Valtorak was rusty at best. No match at all.

"If you won't fight this war," Daijen said, "then I will."

He stepped inside the cavern, his fists balled into weapons.

The Valtorak snapped to life like a coiled snake. The pain he inflicted was momentary, a flash of burning sensory input before the world faded to a black so heavy it encompassed every facet of Daijen's mind.

When next he opened his cool blue eyes, the Vahlken was looking up at the ceiling in his room. Streaming through the narrow window was the unmistakable light of a new dawn, its golden hue capturing the dust in the air. As always, Daijen awoke with a sense of consciousness that suggested he had never been asleep, yet he rose with an undeniable ache in his head. It throbbed, in fact, slowing him just enough that he was forced to prop himself up with one hand.

Sat on the edge of his cot, he noted the bloody rags left in a bowl on the floor. He blinked hard, forcing his impeccable memory to catch up. He recalled stepping inside the cavern and the light from the pits dancing across the stalactites. He could picture the blackened bone to the right, resting in its alcove.

Then he saw The Valtorak move.

There came nothing after that, leading him to where he was in his room. With a tentative finger, he inspected the site of his pain and found the source in his left eyebrow. There was a gash cutting through the white hairs and intruding on his brow. Seeing the blood splattered across his cuirass—*his* blood—Daijen deduced that Ilithranda had cleaned him up while he was unconscious.

When in his long life had he felt more the fool? It seemed unlikely he had even landed a blow, his opponent that much his superior. Finding his feet, it soon became obvious that his injury was more than superficial. His right hand reached out for the wall, preventing him from succumbing to the dizziness that assaulted his sense of balance.

"You're going to have to shake it off," Ilithranda announced from his doorway.

Daijen made the mistake of whipping his head around. Not only had he been so dazed as to miss his door being ajar, but his acute senses had failed to register Ilithranda's approach. Damned if the old man didn't have a hard swing.

Keeping his eyes closed while he reorientated himself, Daijen thanked his would-be sister for bringing him to his bed.

"Oh, I had nothing to do with it," Ilithranda informed him, a note of amusement in her voice. "The Valtorak is a man of his word. He dragged you by the ankle. It wasn't pretty. I imagine most of what you're feeling is the number of steps you hit."

Now that he thought about it, there was a constant ache in the back of his head. "I see," he grumbled. "You seem amused by it all."

"Not at all," Ilithranda replied, and most unconvincingly. "But your irritating logic is forcing me back to that *cesspit* of a city, so..." She grinned, revealing the extent of her pleasure. "Yes, I suppose I am amused. Now come along. I've informed the others of our departure, but it's a three-day flight to Aran'saur, and you still need to ready Valyra."

Daijen was dreading the day ahead. Actually, he was dreading his next encounter with The Valtorak.

Thanks to Handuin's magic, the Vahlken's senses were almost back to normal by the time he reached the courtyard. A light rain had settled over the morning, grey clouds hiding the glorious sunrise now. Still, the feel of the rain on his skin was intoxicating. He remembered a time before his transformation when Laif had brought him onto one of the balconies to bask in the pouring rain.

Every drop was electrifying. There had been a time, in those early days after his rebirth, when it had been overwhelming—a sensory overload. Decades on, and he could enjoy it, even when it was naught but a drizzle.

Over the next couple of hours, Daijen cleaned all of Valyra's armour, sheets of chainmail, and saddle before applying them all. The Aegre sat patiently, almost regally. It was as if she knew she was a warrior being suited for battle. The last piece to fit was the plated beak that overlapped her own. The steel sloped down as her beak did, only the armour was tipped with silvyr, enhancing her bite.

The Aegre squawked once—a note of satisfaction. Daijen grinned and ran his hand affectionately across her brown feathers.

"We're going into a different kind of battle," he uttered, drawing her yellow eyes down to him. "The enemy will not be so obvious."

"In Aran'saur," came The Valtorak's steely voice, "you must assume *everyone* is the enemy. It's the only way to survive that city."

Daijen turned away from Valyra and dared to meet the master's gaze. Unlike Daijen, The Valtorak stood without a scratch on him. He approached from the keep's entrance, his staff in step beside him, while young Tovun remained at the threshold.

They met eye to eye, yet Ka'vairn's master possessed an authoritative air that seemed to lend him extra height. Daijen didn't speak, deciding that his words and actions of late had been somewhat brash. And so the two Vahlken stood in silence, the tension building until Ilithranda entered Daijen's peripheral vision. Her arrival broke the spell between them, and The Valtorak began a slow walk along Valyra's length.

"A fine Aegre," he complimented. "As strong as mountain stone and swifter than the wind. Do you know what sets her apart from other animals?"

Daijen could have listed a plethora of attributes he believed Valyra possessed that other animals were lacking, including other Aegres. But he decided to keep such a response to himself, sensing this was more of a speech than a real question.

"Valyra *knows* she is strong. She *knows* she is swift. There is no doubt in her mind that she is a predator. She does not question it, and, more importantly, she feels no need to *prove* it." The Valtorak finished his examination of the Aegre and turned his sights on Daijen once more. "Can the same be said of you?"

The Vahlken took a breath, ensuring his reply was evenly measured. "I am aware of my capabilities, master."

"Yet you believe others are not aware," The Valtorak countered. "I have watched you for decades," the master went on, preventing Daijen from defending himself. "Your need to prove yourself dishonours Valyra—she chose you, Daijen. She deemed you worthy of her. It is your duty to live up to that, to know *who you are*."

Daijen tensed his jaw, if only to stop himself from responding harshly. The pain in his brow was still very present. "I'm not trying to prove myself," he managed. "I only seek an end to the war. I'm sorry if that pushes me beyond the parameters of this order, but if we don't adapt, then the Skaramangians have already won. I will not live in the shadow of the Dark Ones," he proclaimed, finding his feet in the new argument.

The Valtorak said nothing for a time, his head tilted to scrutinise Daijen from a different angle. "You are not the Vahlken Handuin intended. Your appointment here seemed a cruel twist of fate. A messenger guard," he muttered, evidently still perplexed so many years later. "But, I will concede... you are, perhaps, the Vahlken we *need*."

Daijen could feel his defences melting away while his next line of argument stumbled over the favour shown by The Valtorak. It was as disarming as it was unexpected.

"But I would still caution you," the master said, raising Daijen's guard again. "Know *who* you are—*what* you are. Until then, it is not the shadow of the Dark Ones you live in but the shadow of your former self. It is *his* need to prove himself that will be *your* undoing," he intoned, one finger pressing on Daijen's cuirass.

With all the humility Daijen could muster, he bowed his head. "I will endeavour to be better, master."

The Valtorak tutted with amusement. "Even now, you still have far to go, Daijen Saeth." He took in the cool air and turned his face up to the light rain, if briefly. "As with all of your past transgressions," he continued, adopting again the tone of the master and the teacher, "I will overlook last night's foolishness. Though I disagree with these unorthodox alliances, I do agree with your plan concerning Ahnir. You have my word. Upon your return, I will *consider* your access to the bone."

"*If* the wizard survives," Ilithranda interjected.

The Valtorak regarded her. "I will look over him myself. There are tonics and balms known only to Andarens that might aid his recovery."

Daijen managed a smile, though it was a temporary one. "That is generous of you, master."

"I know," The Valtorak quipped, turning to leave. "One last thing," he added, pivoting on his heel and looking at the pair. "Do not linger in Aran'saur. Following a lead to your own demise will *prove* nothing. *Worse*," he specified, his attention falling solely on Daijen, "it will prove me right. Bear witness to the Ankala, learn what you can—*if* you can. Then depart. Understood?"

"Yes, master," the Vahlken answered in unison.

Daijen was already seated in his saddle by the time The Valtorak had returned to the keep's interior. As always, mounting Valyra invigorated him, filling him with a sense of power while grounding him in duty. How hard he had fought to call an Aegre his companion—to call himself a Vahlken.

He could feel it creeping in. The pride. It went beyond the satisfaction of his accomplishments. He felt the whole world needed to know that he had risen from the lowest ranks to that of a legendary warrior.

You still have far to go, he thought, echoing The Valtorak's words.

Movement drew Daijen's gaze high. There, braced against one of the exterior rails, was Androma. The Dragon Rider couldn't see them—couldn't see *him*—looking at her. He had known her with Maegar beside her all too briefly. Yet the difference in her was staggering. He hoped, in time, that she would become more than the shell she was now.

His thoughts naturally wandered back to the dragon egg he had lost. Another encounter that had been all too brief. He was deeply saddened to think that none would ever come to call the dragon within their companion. That it was doomed to dormancy under tons of stone and dirt for all time.

Daijen added the loss of the egg to his recent string of failures. While their excursion to The Tomb had born some new leads it had been as unsuccessful as it was embarrassing. It was unbecoming of any Vahlken to flee, he knew. Then there was his plan to read the bone beneath the keep...

His pride tried to convince him that he would have accomplished more alone, without those around him standing in his way. Even The Valtorak's words made sense to him then—that his allies would hold him back, if only through his fear of them dying.

The Vahlken shut his eyes, scrunching his brow into a tight knot. He banished the thoughts and focused on his duty. There was only forwards, a path that would now take him to Andara's capital. He would need all his wits to survive such a place—a city that threatened to devour him, pride and all.

9

BOUND FOR MADNESS

It seemed a long night to Gallien, the stars having slowly passed overhead to the sound of their crackling fire. Perhaps it had been Androma's words that slowed his perception of the passing world. After all, it wasn't every day one learned that their family name had been voiced in a foreign land, given to a dying man by the helm of a god, and received by the ears of the emperor of Andara.

Either way, Gallien didn't need the wizard's bracer to know the truth when he heard it. At least now, he thought, he had heard the *whole* truth, however disturbing it was.

"He really is the *one*," was his conclusion, his words spoken as the first rays of light topped the mountains about them.

"Yes," Androma replied, her hard exterior revealing something of a crack—a note of hope, perhaps.

"Why didn't you say this earlier?" The smuggler thought of their time on the river, when Androma and Aphrandhor had revealed so much of their motivation to find Joran.

The old Rider twisted her lips, delaying her response. "Because I truly believed that the son of Ilithranda was the one we were looking for, yet he did not bear the name Pendain. I thought..." She trailed off, stumbling over her reasoning.

"You thought it would weaken your argument," he said for her.

"Yes," she confessed.

"So," Gallien summed up, his anger quick to rise, "even though Joran didn't have the name in your eyes, you were still going to force him down a path that would put his life in danger?"

"I knew he was the one—"

"No you didn't!" the smuggler raged. "You didn't *know*. You *hoped*."

"It doesn't matter now," Andromo replied calmly. "He *is* Joran Pendain. That means he's right where he needs to be."

"You're reckless," he accused, one finger jabbing at the air.

"Do you think you win wars by being prudent?" Andromo countered. "It is the recklessness of the few that paves the way for the many. It's left to us to make the hard decisions. It's left to us to make the sacrifices. I have already sacrificed..."

The old Rider cut herself off and took a breath.

"The facts are simple, Gallien. Joran *will* bring about a time of dragons. We've been in this war long enough to know that is the single biggest threat to the Skaramangians and their plans for this world. But Joran has years ahead of him—*years*. He will have to train, and his dragon with him. Until that time, it is up to us to slow the enemy down."

"I don't have to do anything," Gallien asserted, drinking from one of the skins they they had taken from the dead Andarens.

"You wield a weapon of power," she pointed out. "That alone burdens you with responsibility."

"Then take it," he said, tossing the axe beside the fire.

It was Cob, however, who reached out and took the weapon. The ranger was barely able to heft the axe, however, before it vanished from his hand and returned to Gallien's.

Hearing the subtle yet distinct suck of air as the weapon moved from one place to another, Andromo quickly deduced what had transpired.

"You see? You're in this fight. More importantly, we're still fighting for Joran," she explained. "His future isn't set in stone—there are forces working to see their own destiny fulfilled. It's up to us to give him the time he needs."

Gallien's lips parted to give his final word on the matter, but before he could, the air was filled with another sound, distant but distinct.

Horns.

Andaren horns.

The smuggler turned his attention to the rocky plateau to the south. The Green Leaf—who had remained on his feet, determined to strengthen his injured leg—was already making for the peak, where The Giant's Throat came to an abrupt end.

Forgetting their heated conversation for the moment, Gallien made for those billowing green robes, navigating the uneven stone as he ascended the slight rise. The smuggler had seen many things during his time, especially while fighting under the king's banner on both sides of The Drifting Sea, but seeing an entire army was always sure to grip him by the bones.

The Andarens had pushed through the ravine, putting most of The Giant's Throat behind them. Their numbers filled the valley floor with a carpet of bronze and white, their ranks only interrupted by enormous war machines. Their horns blasted rhythmically now, building to a crescendo as they approached...

Gallien looked out on the vista south of The Throat. Like everyone in Erador, the smuggler had heard of The Silver Trees of Akmar but never seen them with his own eyes. The forest lay sprawled beneath him like something out of a dream. The morning light pierced the clouds in the east as if the heavens themselves demanded a view of the land known as Akmar. Flocks of birds flew over the glistening trees, their flight taking them ever southwards, away from the invading battalions.

Standing on the precipice, the canopy of silver robbed Gallien of any fear that he might fall. He could but take it in, forcing his mind to accept that the silver leaves and branches were real in their defiance of nature's laws.

Gallien tore his eyes from the dreamscape and looked at

Aphrandhor. The wizard didn't appear to be suffering from the same reverie. In fact, the old man wasn't even looking at the army below. His grey eyes were cast out over the entire view, as if the distant and empty sky held more concern than an Andaren invasion.

How broken he looked. Gallien hadn't noticed it before, when his blood had been boiling from threats and omissions. He saw it now. The wizard looked to have aged a decade in the last two days, a decade the smuggler wouldn't have afforded him.

"They've advanced quicker than I thought they would," Yamnomora commented. "Damned light on their feet, eh?"

Cob came to stand beside Gallien, having left Androma standing further back, where the ledge offered no threat. "Where are the Jainus?"

He took the question right out of Gallien's mouth, who had heard Aphrandhor's assurances that the wizards would meet the army to defend the forest.

The ranger was heard, apparently, for his question was met by a great disturbance within the silver trees.

The smuggler crouched on the rocky lip, his eyes narrowed on the forest below. "What in the hells is that?"

The canopy was moving.

As if jostled by something truly massive, the trees bristled from the heart of the forest to its northern edge, where the leading Andarens were amassed. Gallien's face dropped when a boulder the size of a large wagon was launched from within the forest. It cleared the canopy and sailed north before succumbing to gravity once more.

The subsequent *thud* echoed throughout the ravine, shortly followed by cries of outrage from the Andarens—from those who had survived the substantial missile, at least. The dozen who had been standing where it landed were now no more than a collective red smear, their war at an end.

A salvo of boulders followed the first, each bursting forth from the silver canopy, hurled by unseen forces. The Andarens were quick to retaliate, their catapults and ballistas releasing their payloads before the next wave of boulders crashed into their ranks.

An order was given, though the words were indecipherable from atop the ravine. Still, it was clear the order had been to advance, for the Andarens began their charge both on foot and horseback.

Only then were the Jainus's defences revealed for what they truly were.

Three Giants exploded from the northern tree line, each swinging clubs that could have been battering rams. Their meaty necks were bound in iron rings, and their wrists bore manacles that dragged broad chains over the ground. Gallien didn't need to see the face of any Andaren to know that they were surprised by the beasts. Their ranks burst apart, the soldiers scattering to flee from the enormous monsters.

Gallien winced. The first swing of each Giant was catastrophic, sending dozens of Andarens into the air, their bodies utterly broken. Those bloodied clubs came back into the fray, sweeping backhand through the army before massive lumbering feet followed in their devastating wake.

The ballistas were quickly reorganised, their angle of attack brought down. The lead Giant fell first, its protruding chest caved in by the missile's impact. The creature made hardly a sound, the air forced from its lungs as it fell back, a slack arm clipping one of its kin. That second Giant stumbled, its misshapen expression creasing all the more in its attempt to regain some balance.

The arrows that bombarded it were no more than splinters, but to be struck by so many was an assault the Giant could not ignore. The subsequent roar died on its lips, the monster too busy shielding its bulbous eyes. It managed one last backswing, crushing four soldiers against the ravine wall, before a ballista bolt slammed into its thick neck.

The last of the trio faced Andaren magic—perhaps the worst fate of them all.

Gallien tried to locate the clerics amongst the ranks, but it was impossible for his human eyes to discern them. The Giant's gruesome death was far easier to spot. High and low, spheres of glass shattered against its tough skin, reducing it to steaming, sloughy mud that oozed and dripped from muscle and bone. The Giant cried out in agony, its pain enough to drive it back towards the silver trees.

The last of their alchemical magic assaulted the ground beneath the creature. The explosion was brief and relatively contained, creating a circumference no wider than the Giant. The hard earth that had rested in the ground for millennia bubbled and churned until the pressure exploded like a geyser. The dark, molten earth consumed most of the Giant in that instant, and, like the others, it fell to the ravine floor with a resounding *thud*.

All the while, unseen Giants continued to hurl rocks and boulders from the forest and the Andaren catapults launched missile after missile. Two of the Andarens' projectiles had been set ablaze, each rising into the air above the trees like a dawning sun. It seemed the Jainus themselves put their magic to work, for both missiles were extinguished mid-flight, and a third was blown to powder and debris above the canopy.

Imminently, the Andaren army would penetrate The Silver Trees of Akmar. Furthermore, it was inevitable that they would breach the heart of the forest and take the god bones for themselves.

"How in the hells are we supposed to get in the middle of that?" Gallien muttered, rising to his full height.

"If we had The Anther," Yamnomora grumbled, shooting Grarfath a scowl that could give Andaren magic a run for its money, "we could get down there no problem. Then I'd show ye how we get in the middle o' it."

"We must offer aid to the Jainus," Cob suggested. "We have to get those bones out of the forest."

"They would never accept our help," Androma pointed out. "They put their faith in magic, not steel. Besides, those bones are the lifeblood of their entire order. They wouldn't trust strangers anywhere near them."

"Bones?" Kitrana interjected, hearing the only word that could possibly cajole her memory.

Gallien was quick with his expression, communicating to the Nimean that she was not to pursue the topic. The bones they had found together in Harendun were to be used when it most benefitted the smuggler. When Kit replied with a questioning look, he responded with a subtle shake of the head. Given her bristling attitude towards him, he was amazed to see her drop it there and then.

"We have to do something," Cob insisted. "The Skaramangians already possess two of the skeletons."

"And soon they will possess three," The Green Leaf declared, though his voice was weak.

"Aphrandhor?" Androma intoned.

"Gallien is right," the wizard explained, relying heavily on his staff to keep him upright. "You're *all* right," he added. "We must do something, yet it is infeasible that we few can halt an Andaren army. The Jainus will do what they can, and the king's men with them—should they arrive in time. Either way, they *will* acquire those bones. We have to accept that the enemy's power will increase tenfold thereafter, that they will be that much closer to unleashing the Dark Ones upon the realm once more."

"I will not accept that," the ranger stated.

"Nor I," Yamnomora put in.

"But you must," Aphrandhor told them, turning his back on the invasion below. "Accord them this victory so that we might plan for our own." He clapped a bony hand on the Kedradi's shoulder. "A victory to end it all."

Cob was shaking his head. "What victory is there to be had if the Skaramangians have the magic of *three* gods?"

Rather than answer the ranger immediately, The Green Leaf let his grey eyes fall upon Gallien. How burdened the wizard looked. It was as if his flowing white beard had lost some of its life while the creases in his face had deepened all the more.

"We must follow the road to madness," he finally muttered, his words little more than a whisper.

"Aphrandhor?" Androma asked.

The Green Leaf hesitated, wiping some of the inexplicable sweat from his brow. "It has been hidden," he whispered.

"Hidden?" Androma pressed. "Green Leaf... what possesses you?"

"What power it must hold," he mused, his eyes flaring.

Cob stepped in and placed a hand to the wizard's chest.

Cajoled from his spiralling reverie, Aphrandhor picked up his own thread. "If we are to defeat the Dark Ones as our predecessors did," he managed, displaying an ounce of his former self, "then we must harness the very same weapons they wielded. While we do not possess them all, it seems clear to me now that there are weapons of power we know nothing about."

"What have you seen, Green Leaf?" Androma asked.

"*He* has seen it," the wizard declared, pointing a crooked finger at the smuggler.

"He's losing his mind," Gallien remarked.

"Lost," Aphrandhor muttered, repeating the word three times before revelation brought some life back to his eyes. "Yes—lost! The answer is lost to your mind. *Taken.* There is only one who knows of it. Only one who can put the weapon in our hands."

Gallien was shaking his head, wondering why they were still listening to the broken wizard. "Who?" he asked with a shrug.

The Green Leaf's focus sharpened on the smuggler. "Your *father*, Gallien."

10

ARAN'SAUR

0 Years Ago...

4

For three days, the realm of Andara had passed beneath Valyra, as if the Aegre was frozen beneath the clouds and the land of mountains, sweeping forests, and great plains had slipped away like the currents of a river.

How beautiful it all was.

Though the land in the west was no different to that in the east, Daijen couldn't help but feel the difference here on the peaceful side of The Gap. Having spent most of his life in the east, where The Saible spat out battalion after battalion, the Vahlken had known only war in his home country.

Then again, everything felt peaceful when viewing the world from the heavens.

Having kept The Eros Mountains on their right and The Fields of Ithornor on their left, the two Vahlken had journeyed ever southward, following the eastern curve of the mountains until they were soaring over The Ilin'duil. The forest surrounded The Nevereen, a majestic lake that appeared as a single pane of glass set into the land. If that wasn't a marker to inform them how close to the capital they were, then Mount Athan certainly was.

Daijen was awed the very moment they cleared the nearest line of mountains and saw that which stood colossal against all others. His lips parted, and his eyes refused to blink even against the wind, for he had to take in every facet of the extraordinary mountain. He had, of course, heard of Mount Athan and seen it depicted in paintings and drawings throughout his life, but he had never seen it with his own eyes. It defied everything he knew about the world and how nature had moulded it.

Though its peak was concealed by the clouds that rolled in from the west, the bulk of the mountain shone like a god upon the earth. From its roots in the ground to that unseen top, Mount Athan was entirely enclosed in a bluish crystal. To the Vahlken's knowledge, no one had ever discovered a way to break through the glassy exterior—not even with magic.

And why would they, he thought. The Arkalon was quite clear on the matter. Mount Athan had been home to the gods on Verda's soil. Outside of God Fall it was the holiest place in existence. It was also unscalable, its smooth and unique exterior resilient to any and all climbing equipment. It truly was a place only for the gods.

Perhaps, Daijen pondered, that was why Aran'saur had been built at its base, where the emperor could rule in its shadow.

The city was a gem all of its own, the Vahlken's eyes taken there after following the sharp contours down the mountain. It sprawled across the land, daring to touch the very edge of the crystal. So vast was the capital that it could have swallowed The Saible whole and the city of Ehrendil with it. Like the mountain that towered over it, Aran'saur was a city with its own unique exterior.

Daijen had Valyra change her angle of approach so he could see it all in one sweeping vista. The city was a statement of victory, if not a testament to the power of the gods and their deeds and sacrifices for their people.

"I can't believe it's real," he uttered, his words too faint to reach Ilithranda.

A city without walls, Aran'saur was shaped like a crescent and built inside the gargantuan remains of a long-dead Leviathan. The monster's arching ribs cast shadows over the domes and spires while blocks of houses and markets nestled around what might have been considered hip bones. The creature's tail, some of which was partially buried beneath the earth, curled round, and buildings and giant warehouses hugged the standing plates and spikes of bone.

Daijen's sharp eyes narrowed on the behemoth's reptilian skull. While its lower jaw had been swallowed by land and time, its upper jaw remained above ground, sheltering a multitude of city blocks that could be accessed via roads situated between the teeth. Further up, gardens had been curated inside the four eye sockets, providing the dull bone with splashes of green.

At the highest point, sitting within a crown of bony horns and looming over the skull—and, indeed, the rest of the capital—was the imperial palace. It looked like a city unto itself, rising tier upon tier until it reached for the sky with a single spire of white stone.

The entire landscape, from ground to sky, was unlike anything Daijen had ever seen.

"Are you ready to enter the belly of the beast?" Ilithranda called out from astride Oaken.

Daijen tore his eyes from the view and caught sight of his companion. "Very funny!" he remarked.

Ilithranda pointed ahead. "You see the road up to the skull?"

There was but one road that led out from the palace, curving round the curled spine until it snaked down to the streets inside the skeleton.

"Aim for the base of that road!" she instructed. "There's a courtyard down there that can accommodate both of us!"

"Shouldn't we aim for the palace?"

Ilithranda shook her head. "We have the love and awe of the people! We should remind the emperor of that, if not the Skaramangians who surround him! Let us arrive at the palace gates with an entourage they cannot ignore!"

The people...

That sat with Daijen for the remainder of their flight. Since his transformation inside the pits of Handuin, he had only interacted with soldiers, whose trained sensibility afforded him some space and only a notch of apprehension. Now, however, he was about to set foot in the common streets of his kin, where ordinary folk went about their lives only ever hearing stories of the Vahlken and the war raging east of The Gap.

He had no idea what to expect.

The Aegres glided down and swept over the city several times, whipping up the capital's collective excitement. Daijen found it exhilarating, enjoying the speed with which Valyra weaved between the spires and cast the streets into shadow. He wondered if this was how the gods had felt so many eons past, when they had deigned to descend from Mount Athan and walk among the mortals.

Not that he was a god, Daijen reminded himself, tethering his pride before it ran away with itself. He was simply getting caught up in the spectacle of it all. In truth, the people watching them fly past would have been marvelling at the Aegres, something Daijen could have been accused of every day.

Following Ilithranda's approach, Daijen guided Valyra down to the courtyard at the base of the palace road. Crowds were already beginning to amass, swarming in from the four streets that spiralled into the courtyard. Had they descended even a minute later, the Aegres would have struggled to find space enough to land.

The roar of the people was intoxicating, but Daijen retained enough sense to steel himself, holding back any kind of smile. They were to be the warriors the tales spoke of, emanating that aura of discipline and control.

Valyra and Oaken bristled, unsettled by the mob pouring in around them. Valyra stamped her talons, clawing at the stone, while Oaken's wings twitched and his yellow eyes dashed from person to person.

"Easy," Daijen bade, patting his companion's neck.

It wasn't long before the city guard arrived, pushing their way through to come between the newcomers and the massing crowds. They did what they could to keep them from overwhelming the Vahlken while also trying to clear a path to the palace road. Daijen half expected Ilithranda to forge a path from atop Oaken, the Aegre's stride more than enough to force any person aside, but she was content to take it slowly. She wanted to be seen.

Keeping to his saddle, Daijen simply watched the crowd swell all the more until it was narrowed on the path. It took well over an hour to ascend the winding road. During that time, it was as if the city had suffered a great wound and its blood—the people—were gushing out.

If no one had alerted the palace to their arrival, the thunderous clamour of so many Andarens certainly would. The gates, however, were already open—albeit filled from gatepost to gatepost with a battalion of bronze-plated soldiers. Upon sighting the Vahlken, they rushed out in practised uniformity, encircling the Aegres while simultaneously walling off the mob with shields.

None dared challenge them.

Ilithranda brought Oaken a little closer to Valyra. "The people fear them," she remarked. "But they love us. He will hate that," she added with a creeping smirk that sharpened her features all the more.

It was no leap to assume she was referring to the emperor. Her father. Daijen thought of his last conversation with The Valtorak and wondered if the master of Ka'vairn had been worried about the wrong Vahlken.

Following her lead, Daijen guided Valyra over the threshold and into an enormous circular courtyard. Its centre was occupied by a colourful garden that had been landscaped into a spiral that surrounded a lush oak tree. The flowers were alien to Daijen, all a product of magic. Indeed, the tree seemed larger than an average oak tree, and his keen eyes were drawn to the veins of gold that ran *up* the trunk from some unseen source at its roots.

Enclosing the garden and the oak's massive canopy, the palace dominated Daijen's view. It had been built to impress, if not outright intimidate. So much of it appeared to be no more than slender arches of white stone and golden domes, the buildings partially concealed behind their extravagant façades. The central spire stood tall amongst it all, its walls corkscrewing into the sky.

Coming to a natural stop at the palace steps, the Vahlken dismounted as one and immediately gave their Aegres their full attention, meeting the creatures face to face. "Hunt," Daijen instructed. "Then rest. Keep one eye on the palace," he added, his gaze shifting to the side.

Valyra squawked her understanding and braced all four of her mighty legs. Her wings beat, blasting the soldiers that had escorted them with cold air. With Oaken close at her side, the Aegre launched into the sky once more. Standing alone now, surrounded by the palace guard, Daijen suddenly felt overly exposed—vulnerable, even.

He thought back to their descent into The Tomb on Nareene, where they had parted ways with the Aegres. Perhaps they shouldn't have been so quick to dismiss them this time. How much more leverage would they have had inside those walls if their mutated companions were standing by their side? If the palace's exterior was anything to go by, Valyra could definitely have fitted through its halls.

"What now?" Daijen asked, seeing that no one had come to greet them, or even direct them.

Ilithranda had lost some of her composure and now stood beside him a touch agitated. "They're going to make us *wait*," she deduced irritably.

The power dynamics were already beginning to grate on Daijen. "Is it going to be like this the whole time?"

"Yes," she stated. "Every emperor passes on their loathing for the Vahlken. He will have the instinctual need to impress his authority upon us at every turn." Ilithranda sighed, her fists balling at her sides. "Black Abyss," she cursed, taking to the steps.

"What are you doing?" Daijen asked quietly.

"Taking the power back," she grumbled, ascending the steps two at a time now.

With one stride, they passed between the pillars that stood between the steps and the palace doors. Curiously, the soldiers who had met them in the courtyard remained behind.

"They're not needed in here," Ilithranda informed him as he looked back over one shoulder.

Her comment led Daijen to better scrutinise their new surroundings. It took him longer than it should have to notice the archers looking down at them. Indeed, they were everywhere, hiding behind pillars, inside alcoves, and even inside the walls, their arrows aimed through narrow slits. Those he could see appeared to blend into their background, their skin matching the marble or thick drapes amid which they stood.

When one of them moved to better track the Vahlken, Daijen blinked. He could have sworn the archer's skin changed to constantly match their surroundings.

"Did you see that?" he asked as they passed through a set of arching doors.

"Changelings," Ilithranda nodded. "The work of the clerics. It doesn't last very long."

Daijen thought of his years in The Saible. "I've never seen anything like it before."

"Continued exposure to that kind of magic infects the blood," she replied. "They have to rotate the guard all the time. It's not practical outside of the palace."

Knowing there were unseen eyes on him, tracking his every step, Daijen felt unsettled.

Then there were the clerics themselves. Attired in white robes and bronze masks to hide their face and gender, they sat silently— one to every room and hallway. Hanging from a chain on their belts was a copy of the Arkalon, their only true companion through the centuries.

"It cannot be," came a bold and clear announcement.

Daijen came to a stop, noting that Ilithranda was standing rigid—unnervingly so. Unlike the archers, this Andaren was making no attempt to hide his whereabouts. His tunic was of a finery not found in the crowds that swarmed them outside the palace, a deep blue with accessories of gold. The tunic was brought together at his waist by a large belt that displayed an intricate pattern upon the brown leather. His hair was just as intricate, bound up at the back of his head with a knot of white silk.

He approached them from the side door, his golden eyes fixed solely on Ilithranda. "It cannot be," he said again, his tone mixed with wonder more than disbelief now. "Yet here you are, standing inside the palace once more. Even in death, the gods continue to move all the pieces."

"Barris Tanyth," Ilithranda named.

Daijen gave his companion a glance, detecting the acidity beneath her flat tone.

"Ilithranda..." Barris let her name hang in the air, as if he needed the time to believe what he was seeing. "You have returned... a *Vahlken*," he said at length, his voice full of surprise while he spared a curious glance down the adjacent hallway. "Even dead," he added with some amusement, "the gods maintain their sense of humour, it seems."

Even as he said it, Daijen detected the not-so-subtle tone of disdain in the man's voice, suggesting he gave the Vahlken as little credit as the emperor did.

Ilithranda said nothing, but Daijen could see all that she was holding back, the turmoil churning beneath the calm surface.

"And you are?" Daijen asked bluntly, drawing a look of derision from the smaller Andaren.

"Daijen of House Saeth," Ilithranda began, having found some of her reserves, "this is Barris of House Tanyth. Barris is the emperor's spymaster."

Barris made a sour expression. "Such a boorish title. All too human for my liking. I am merely a humble advisor to His Radiance."

"And what do you advise him on?" Daijen enquired, making a point to look down on the man.

Barris, however, did not shy away from the intimidating figure towering over him. "Anything and everything that threatens this institution," he answered simply, his gaze slowly shifting to land on Ilithranda again. "I have to say, I'm impressed. None have ever returned, let alone... a head taller," he said after gesturing at Ilithranda's height. "Tell me," he continued, and more seriously at that, "have you returned only for the Ankala... or has something *else* drawn you back?"

A crack split Ilithranda's calm exterior. "I have returned as a Vahlken," she declared. "There is naught but duty that could bring me back here."

A wicked smile cut through Barris's angular face. "What about your duty as a—"

The next word never filled the air, the spymaster having wisely chosen to shut his mouth when Ilithranda stepped into his personal space. His lips pursed, Barris slowly craned his neck to meet the Vahlken's violet eyes.

Daijen had no idea what the spymaster had been on the verge of asking nor why Ilithranda had reacted so threateningly, but it didn't stop him from having his sister's back. Hidden beneath his cloak, his left hand slowly rose up to grip the top of the scabbard on his hip. His peripheral vision caught movement in numerous locations, however, informing him that multiple guards had taken note.

"I am here as a Vahlken," she repeated, her voice low and uncompromising. "The very moment the Ankala is over, our business here will be concluded."

Barris narrowed his eyes. "You don't even want to know?"

To Daijen's dismay, Ilithranda—who always had a biting retort on the end of her tongue—gave no response.

No, it was worse, he realised. She wasn't even moving—not a single muscle. It was, Daijen knew, the quiet before the storm.

"Ilithranda."

He poured his warning into her name, hoping to break through the chain of rage uncoiling in her mind.

Not immediately, but soon thereafter, Ilithranda stepped back and gave Barris his personal space back. Her eyes were glassy, jaw tight. The spymaster had no idea how fortunate he was that Oaken had taken flight. Had the Aegre detected such a response in his companion, he would likely have torn the little man in half by now. As it was, he had Daijen to thank for his life.

Barris took a moment to smooth out his already immaculate tunic. "I was just on my way to meet you at the gates," he said after clearing his throat. "I expected you to land outside..."

"It's good for the people to see us," Daijen told him, seeing that Ilithranda was in no position to speak yet. "It reminds them that those who protect them are more than just a myth."

"I assure you," Barris countered, "they have only to look up at the palace to be reminded of those who protect them. Still," he continued pleasantly, as if they weren't at odds, "it is good that you are here. The Ankala begins at the pre-dawn hour." The spymaster glanced the way the two Vahlken had come. "Is The Valtorak close behind?"

"The Valtorak sent us in his stead," Daijen reported, offering naught else.

"I see. His Radiance will be... *disappointed.*"

"Perhaps, instead, he will be content to know that his kin guards the realm," Daijen interjected, garnering a disgruntled look from his companion and an unamused expression from the spymaster.

"This isn't The Saible," Barris pointed out. "Nor is it Ka'vairn. You will refer to His Radiance as such or by his title. Nothing else will be tolerated, not even from a Vahlken. As for the matter of lineage," he went on, directing his words at Ilithranda now, "your time to return and claim your bloodline ended upon being chosen for the path of Handuin. I fear your... *transformation* is a step too far. There has never been a Vahlken in the imperial family, though," he considered at length. "That might be a bridge worth building."

"I didn't come here to build bridges and I definitely didn't come back here to join the *brood*," Ilithranda stated, her voice knocked by a slight tremor while she regained control of her anger.

Barris visibly relaxed at that. "Then it would be best, I feel, to leave names out of it. As you said, you're here as Vahlken. Let it be that and that alone. No need to complicate matters."

"Agreed," Ilithranda was quick to reply.

A moment of silence followed, and it seemed Barris and Ilithranda were holding a soundless conversation. Daijen was becoming more bewildered by the second and might have voiced as much before approaching footsteps caused him to turn around.

It shouldn't have shocked him to see the two humans standing there, for he had often seen such fettered souls in and around The Saible, but they had all been bound in some way, be it manacles or iron collars. The two men—if, indeed, they were old enough to be considered as such—wore white robes that revealed much of their torso and arms, though it appeared their entire bodies had been painted white. Their bald heads were draped in fine chains of gold, the jewellery fixed via piercings in their scalp, nose, and ears.

Their attire aside, Daijen couldn't help but notice their physique. Unlike those who toiled in The Saible, whose living conditions bordered on torturous, the two men before him possessed accented muscles and good posture, suggesting they were fed well and given time to rest.

Barris Tanyth rounded the two Vahlken and ran the back of his hand up and down the arm of the nearest human. "Only the very best stock from every farm is chosen for life in the palace," he remarked. "They will be yours for the duration of your stay. Do with them what you will—I cannot speak to the needs of a Vahlken."

"I have no needs they can fulfil," Daijen was quick to respond, wholly uncomfortable with the situation.

Daijen could barely stand to look at them. They only existed in a life of uncompromising servitude because of the war orchestrated by the Skaramangians—they weren't the demonic fiends the clerics and the Arkalon made them out to be. They would be free, he knew, if only the war was at an end. He felt the weight of them then, the weight of them *all*. It was on the Vahlken to end the war—on *him*. Yet here he was, bartering words with a spymaster who could be a Skaramangian himself.

The urge to grab him by the throat and shake his secrets free was almost uncontrollable. Perhaps, when he was finished with Barris, he could tear through the palace and unearth every scrap of the Skaramangians. His blades would be slick with blood by the end. How many of their human pets would be thrown in his way to stop him?

"I don't need your eyes and ears following me around," Ilithranda said, cutting through Daijen's turmoil.

Barris gave a wry smile. "They are harmless, I assure you." The spymaster rounded the nearest human and turned him around by the shoulders. "Every human is branded with a tracking spell," he informed them, his hand running over an old scar in the centre of the man's back.

Daijen didn't recognise the glyph inside the circle, though, being the size of his hand, it must have been agonising to endure. "A tracking spell?" he said with disgust. "I have never heard of such a thing."

"The blessed warlocks are ever at work translating Ahnir's great bones. Even now, He who has seen The End is still gifting us magic. Better yet," Barris added with glee, "when activated, the spell inflicts enormous pain."He stroked the man's left ear as if he were no more than a pet. "They know they cannot hide from their masters," he purred. "Now, then, why don't they show you to your rooms?"

Daijen looked beyond the spymaster to the bright halls and chambers of the palace. "Are we not to meet the emperor?"

Barris held back a snigger and contorted his lips into a bemused smile. "Of course," he replied mockingly. "It's all His Radiance has thought about. Who wouldn't want to meet a pair of Vahlken fresh from the wilderness? I'm sure Emperor Qeledred would enjoy the reprieve from managing the expectations of the people. As you can imagine, there are a lot of moving parts when it comes to breaking with tradition. Still, His Radiance would rather suffer some criticism and bring a swift end to the war than have any more of his people die on the battlefield. Should I fetch him for you?" the spymaster asked, making a dramatic gesture down the nearest corridor.

There had been a time when Daijen would have taken the verbal assault, the mocking and ridicule. Not just because he had no idea how to respond but also because, in some way, he felt he actually deserved it.

But that Daijen was dead.

"Tell me, Barris Tanyth," he questioned, "if I break you, how quickly will *His Radiance* replace you?"

The spymaster did well to conceal his discomfort. He was an intellectual fighter, accustomed to sparring with words and tone of voice, his true intentions always hidden by the two. An outright threat was inelegant, even when delivered from the mouth of a killing machine.

"You will be summoned before the Ankala begins," he said, rather than address the obvious answer to Daijen's question. "Until then, I suggest you both take advantage of all the palace has to offer. Food, drink, entertainment—it can all be brought to your rooms. Should you wish to explore, an escort can be arranged." The spymaster made to leave, pausing only to face Ilithranda. "Regarding the *other* matter, if you change your mind, I will happily tell you where—"

"Thank you, Master Tanyth," Ilithranda interjected forcibly, moving aside to give him space.

The spymaster bowed his head and walked away.

Daijen glanced sideways at the waiting humans before turning his back on them. "What was that about?" he asked quietly.

"Nothing. He's just trying to put us off balance." Ilithranda sighed before her jaw tensed. "I didn't want to come here," she said through gritted teeth. "Why did you make me come back?"

Daijen could sense that there was so much more he wasn't being told, but he knew it wasn't the time to press the issue. He also knew better than to point out that Ilithranda had curbed his original plan herself, an intervention that had led them to that very moment.

He might have responded in some other way had Ilithranda not strode off, demanding to be shown to her room. Daijen waited until she had taken several steps before falling in behind his companion. He couldn't fathom what had really transpired between her and the emperor's spymaster, but he was certain there was more to her tale than she had shared.

Any thought of Ilithranda's past was banished upon the flash of red that caught his eye. Daijen came to a halt and his escort with him, though the man didn't dare challenge him. The Vahlken backtracked to the nearest archway and set his eyes on the procession of clerics walking two by two behind a revered figure.

Escorting them were cleric guards, a sect of warriors devoted to the religious order. They were easily spotted on the streets—just as they were now, in the palace—attired in a white cuirass, scarlet battle skirt, and silver helm and mask to conceal their entire head.

The clerics themselves, Daijen deduced, were more than just that. They wore dark red from the neck down, their heads concealed inside sloping bronze masks. They were *grand clerics*. For them to follow behind any other could mean only one thing.

Daijen Saeth was within twenty feet of the *master* cleric.

The Eldan.

The head of the Skaramangian snake.

Unlike those in his wake, the master cleric wore black robes with accents of red. His mask was more gold than bronze and flared at the sides in the style of eagle wings.

Seeing him sharpened Daijen's focus, reminding him why they were there. It seemed so clear to him now, yet it was an objective they hadn't even discussed in The Valtorak's office.

He was going to assassinate the most revered religious figure in all of Andara.

11

CHASING GHOSTS

Gallien might have laughed had The Green Leaf's words not been quite so absurd. "My father?" he echoed with complete disbelief.

Androma looked to be homing in on the wizard's voice. "Green Leaf, speak plainly," she bade.

If the old Rider could have seem him, she would have known that speaking plainly was becoming a fleeting possibility. The wizard's mental state was visibly deteriorating, his eyes relentlessly shifting to the spaces between them, as if he could see things that weren't there.

Yamnomora stepped in, a low and warning groan reverberating from deep in her chest. "I've seen this before. He's losin' it again."

"What are you talking about?" Gallien pressed, desperate to hear more of his father.

"Impossible," Androma rebuked. "Gallien has maybe four decades behind him. That's not nearly enough time. Besides, he would have succumbed to the weight of it all by now."

"What in the hells are you talking about?" the smuggler growled.

"It's not the weight of it," Aphrandhor announced, piercing

their cryptic conversation with some shred of strength in his tone. "I've spent two days trying to put it together, but it's all so... *broken*. Every memory is like a shattered piece of glass. Furthermore, it seems their edges are sharp, preventing me from delving beyond the surface."

Androma reached out and found the wizard's arm. "Green Leaf," she said softly. "You're not making any sense."

"Why did you mention my father?" Gallien demanded.

The wizard's attention snapped to the smuggler. "Your father?" he queried, as if it was occurring to him for the first time all over again. "Yes, your father. He is the key. He was *always* the key." Aphrandhor's face creased into agony. "What a fool I have been. I was a younger man..." he went on, explaining some unasked question.

Gallien could feel his frustration mounting, bordering on anger. "Androma, what in the hells is going on here? Why is he talking about my father?"

"I don't know," the old Rider replied, her tone clipped. "This only happens when he tries to read something with too much memory."

"What memories?" the wizard blurted, stumbling as he did. Cob caught him, abandoning his bow in the moment. "There are so few in there," he spat, gesturing at Gallien's head. "Only his name remains. I have never touched anything so... *damaged*."

Androma raised a hand to stop him in his tracks. "You said there is a weapon of power—one that hasn't been found yet. What were you talking about?"

"It *has* been found," Aphrandhor insisted, grabbing at Cob's arm. "It has been found and *hidden*."

"You've seen this in Gallien's mind?" Androma asked.

"Ye said there was nothin' there," Yamnomora reminded him. "Though that's not hard to imagine," she added under her breath.

The Green Leaf managed to part from the safety of the Kedradi, his free hand coming up as if to grasp something intangible. "His fractured mind is splintering my own," he hissed.

Retrieving a small glass vial from his belt, Cob was quick to pursue him. "Green Leaf," he said, offering him the yellow vial.

The wizard didn't hesitate. He took the vial and popped the small cork with his thumb before pressing it to his nose, allowing him to inhale the scent. The effect was immediate, widening his eyes and forcing the old man to gasp.

"What is that?" the smuggler asked.

"Glimmer salts mixed with safida spices," Cob answered. "It sharpens the mind. Good if you're bleeding out."

Gallien might have made a comment had the wizard not leaped into him, his staff left to fall so he could grasp the smuggler's shirt in both hands. "We need to prepare for their return!" he exclaimed. There was an urgency about the man now, as if he knew his time was limited. "The enemy has won this battle. They *will* bring about the Dark Ones. We need to start preparing and stop wasting our time trying to prevent the inevitable."

"Aphrandhor," the old Rider pleaded, "take a breath."

The wizard never took his eyes from Gallien's. "You were right. This was your father's," he said, glancing at the bracer on his arm. "He must have been the one, the one who stole it. What do you remember of him? Your father?"

"What do *you* remember of him?" the smuggler fired back. "You're the one wearing his bracer."

"We don't have time for this!" Aphrandhor barked in his face. "We must *prepare*! It's our only way forward." A wave of disorientation washed over The Green Leaf, sending him staggering away from Gallien, his boots piling the snow about his feet.

Cob was there, as always, to catch him and even guide him to a low boulder. "Sit," the Kedradi commanded flatly. "Breathe."

The wizard took a moment to collect himself. Rather than take too much time, however, he inhaled more of the salts and spices before the ranger could take the vial back.

"I wouldn't advise any more," Cob cautioned, returning the vial to his belt.

Aphrandhor's head turned to the morning sky, and he held the look of a man coming up for air.

"I... apologise," he whispered. "It's hard to explain," he continued, his attention having turned to the vambrace on his right arm. "Your mind, Gallien. It's chaos. And yet, I wish I had touched that chaos a little sooner."

"Why?" the smuggler grumbled, wondering if it was wise to pull on a thread that was so obviously fraying.

"Because that chaos is there to hide something," the wizard replied, a single finger in the air, "and it's only through seeing what *isn't* there that you glean the truth of what *should* be there."

Gallien was shaking his head. "What isn't there? What are you talking about?" he fumed. "I remember my life," he said with conviction, one finger pressed to his temple.

"But do you?" The Green Leaf countered. "You're a man always on the move. You never stop. You never look back. What do you really recall? Do you remember him? Your father? Can you picture his face? Can you hear his voice? What about his *name*?"

Gallien said nothing for a time, his mind working furiously as he looked back on his life. It was an uncomfortable sensation for the smuggler, who had ever been grounded in the present. He rarely looked ahead, and he did everything he could not to look back. But now, in this quiet moment, he found absences in his recollection—black spots where he felt there should have been something, *anything*.

His mother had died before he could come to know her, but that wasn't a memory so much as something he had always told himself since he had no recollection of her. His father had left him and Corben as teenagers. Their farewell to him was his only memory of their time together—he could picture the man walking away, the bracer fixed about his right forearm. It seemed a vivid memory, perhaps because of the pain it caused him.

With his brother by his side, they took up their father's crusade, searching the realm for relics and long-forgotten history. Then Corben had died, killed by magic while Harendun suffered one of its many sieges. Even the edges of that memory had begun to fade.

Gallien remembered his training after that, his prime years

given to the king's army. He had signed up in Caster Hold after leaving... He couldn't remember the passage from Harendun across the sea, but he knew that had to be it.

The smuggler glanced at Kitrana Voden, who had become a part of his life after walking away from the endless campaigns against the Andarens. He'd lived the life of a criminal thereafter, serving the worst of the worst in Thedaria. That led his memories to finding the skeleton beneath Harendun and his meeting with Androma.

Joran was all that followed.

"His name was Bragen Pendain," he finally announced, defeated by a degree of the truth. "He passed his name on to me and my brother, Corben. But," he caveated, hate in his eyes as he looked at The Green Leaf, "the last time I ever saw him, he told us to abandon the name. He said that if we continued to use it they would find us... and they would kill us."

"They?" Androma queried. "The Skaramangians?"

"*The Jainus*," the wizard said with certainty, taking the answer right out of Gallien's mouth.

"The Jainus were hunting your father?" Androma checked.

"That's what he said," Gallien confirmed. "They were after his work."

"They were after this," Aphrandhor corrected, holding up his arm to display the bracer. "You are right—it was your father's. At least, it was after he stole it."

"You *did* know him," Gallien cried accusingly, pointing a finger in the old man's face.

"No," Aphrandhor replied earnestly, though the effort brought on a coughing fit. "But I certainly knew *of* him," he eventually finished.

"Now who's lying?" the smuggler spat. "You're wearing his damned bracer!"

"I am telling the *truth*," the wizard asserted. "I never met any Bragen Pendain. But I heard the whispers like all others who trained in The Tower of Jain."

"What whispers?" Androma demanded.

"I was a young man at the time," The Green Leaf replied, his voice a croak, "and only recently appointed to work at the site in Akmar, in the very heart of The Silver Trees. I was told the bones would be there for study, but the relic that had been unearthed with them had been stolen."

"By my father?"

"By a *master thief.*"

"A thief?" Gallien questioned incredulously. "Sure—at times. But Bragen Pendain was no *master thief.* He couldn't have stolen anything from the Jainus."

"And yet he did. More so, he stole it using magic. *Powerful* magic."

"Maybe you need to sniff some more of those spices, wizard. My father tried his hand at everything, but *never* magic."

"Do you know that?" The Green Leaf challenged. "Or is it just a feeling?"

Gallien opened his mouth to state his knowledge on the matter but found himself tripping over his own memories—or lack thereof. It was a feeling, he knew, perhaps tarnished by his loathing for magic after it killed his brother.

Aphrandhor took advantage of his silence. "You don't enter The Silver Trees of Akmar undetected and successfully steal from the Jainus *without* magic. 'Tis impossible. Furthermore, it is his knowledge of magic that has fractured your mind."

Gallien was so stumped by the statement that his immediate anger was tempered by raw curiosity. "Speak plainly, wizard."

The Green Leaf shuffled on the boulder, appearing as fragile as an actual leaf that might get swept away in the breeze. "As I said, your mind is like a broken mirror. Every fragment reflects a moment from your life, but I cannot connect it to any other nor look beyond the surface. You talk of memories—of your father— but I saw none of it. I heard your true name as if it were an echo. Your love for Joran was the most real thing I felt. But there's more. So much more. I just couldn't... see it."

"What does that have to do with my father?"

"I would say *everything,*" Aphrandhor suggested, rubbing his arms to keep warm. "Taking the vambrace is proof enough that he knew his way around magic—*powerful* magic. Unless you have had a run-in with another wizard, your father is the only logical reason your memories are so splintered and out of place."

Gallien wouldn't hear it. "You don't know what you're talking about."

"I assure you, Mr *Pendain*, I know magic. Your mind has suffered under a spell—though I have never seen anything like it. Every memory I tried to follow spat me out somewhere else, sending me in circles. Even now, I am struggling to find the beginning and end to myself." His pale grey eyes landed on Gallien. "Only magic could do that. Though, I must say, I have never encountered magic capable of subverting the bracer. It compounds the fact that your father had access to spells unknown. Access to *knowledge*. Knowledge he used to locate more than just the vambrace."

"Another weapon of power," Androma concluded.

The smuggler made to respond, but his thoughts got in the way, giving him pause while he put the pieces together. "You think that's what's hidden in my mind?"

The wizard looked to be weighing up his choice of words. "Hidden? Erased? I cannot say for certain. I only know that your mind has been altered. Whatever you recall of your life, I cannot testify to its legitimacy."

"Stop," Gallien exacted. "Just *stop*." The smuggler took a much-needed breath. "This is getting us nowhere. My father is dead. You're just chasing ghosts," he told the wizard.

Aphrandhor maintained eye contact, though there seemed little spark behind them. "Ghosts? Who told you your father is dead?"

"I don't need telling. He was hunted by the Jainus and probably more besides. You can't outrun that forever."

It was pity with which the wizard looked at him now. "I was never part of the team assembled to retrieve the bracer," he began. "That task was left to the hunters—all from the worst the Jainus have to offer, more demon than man. It took them years, but... they *did* retrieve it." He raised the vambrace, a testament to the truth. "I was in charge of the site by the time they brought it back."

There it was, Gallien thought. That moment in time when he and his brother had been born—while his father had been on the run. He didn't want to believe that his father had stolen the relic, but he *knew* that vambrace. For whatever reason, he knew the bracer better than his father's image. And so there was but one conclusion: Bragen Pendain had stolen it. That alone was proof that he had no idea who his father really was.

"*When* they returned with it," the wizard elaborated, "they were quite clear. Your father isn't dead, Gallien. The hunters captured him in the end. He is *alive*."

"*That*," Androma interjected at speed, "is quite the leap, Aphrandhor. If he was taken alive, it was years ago. The likelihood of him *still* being alive is—"

"Higher than you think," the wizard cut in, leaving Gallien to stand alone, dazed and bewildered. "Prisoners of the Jainus are often subjected to time spells, slowing their lives down between interrogations. Depending on his value—which I would say is quite high, given what he did—Bragen Pendain could still be there."

Something snapped inside Gallien then, urging him forward until he barrelled into the frail wizard. He grabbed him by his robes and held him close, taking no notice of Cob and the scimitar of Draven bone suddenly in his hand. It was hard to get even a single syllable out, his question demanding a reprieve from his seething rage.

"Where?" he managed through gritted teeth.

Aphrandhor first raised a hand to calm the Kedradi, having him lower his blade, before that same hand came to rest over one of Gallien's. "Understand, the road I propose is not an easy one. You will need some of that fury to see you escape the hell I talk of—if we can even get inside."

"Speak," Gallien fumed, releasing The Green Leaf's robes to loom over him.

The wizard required a moment to right himself. "There is but one prison the Jainus have ever constructed. It is the same place where their beloved hunters are trained, for they themselves are the jailers."

"You can't be serious," Androma said, moving into Gallien's periphery. "We can't go there, Green Leaf."

"But we must," Aphrandhor replied, smoothing out his robes. "You don't turn your son's mind inside out to hide a mere trinket. Not only did he have knowledge of the bracer, he had knowledge enough to *take* it. Bragen Pendain was looking for these relics before either of us, Androma."

"Not *there*," the old Rider warned.

"He knows," the wizard insisted, his breath clouding the cold air. "And Gallien has seen it—the weapon of power! That is why his memories have been altered." Aphrandhor stood up dramatically. "We *must* prepare. The Dark Ones are *coming*," he hissed, sounding madder by the second.

"Will one of you speak plainly?" Gallien snapped.

Aphrandhor turned away from the old Rider, his focus landing on the smuggler once more. "We must go to Taraktor."

"What is that?" Cob asked, beating Gallien to it.

"The road to madness," The Green Leaf muttered, echoing himself.

"It's located north of Caster Hold," Androma explained, stepping in for the deteriorating wizard. "While I cannot speak of its prisoners, The Green Leaf is right—if your father is alive, that's where they would have taken him. And the Jainus are no strangers to time spells. It's... *feasible*."

Gallien couldn't believe what he was hearing. His father —*alive*. For decades, he had lived with the fact that he was dead. He had to be. Years had gone by with no contact, not even a whisper. The smuggler couldn't decide whether it was harder to believe Bragen Pendain might still be alive or that he had never really known the man, that he might be the son of a master wizard who had scrambled his son's mind to hide a weapon of power.

Gallien began to move away from the group, hardly aware of the violent exchange taking place in the mouth of the ravine.

"He wouldn't..." The smuggler swallowed and started again. "He wouldn't have done that to me. Or Corben. He wouldn't have messed with our heads. He always protected us. That's why he sent us away. To *protect* us."

"You're looking at it backwards," Aphrandhor told him, preventing Gallien from moving further away. "By erasing your memory, he *was* protecting you. Given his actions in Akmar, he must have known the Jainus were hunting for the same relics. He was likely trying to prevent you from crossing their path. To that end, he has hidden something deep inside you where your memories cannot align to make sense of it. As I pointed out, it's no mere trinket. He *must* have found another weapon of power."

"Fine," Gallien said, his tone clipped as he whirled on the wizard. "Unmagic me," he instructed, tapping his forehead.

"Excuse me?"

Gallien gestured at The Green Leaf's staff lying on the ground. "Use your magic and... you know, remove the spell."

"I'm afraid it doesn't work like that," Aphrandhor informed him. "I would have to know exactly what spell has been employed. Even then, there is no guarantee that there is a spell to counter it."

The smuggler let his head fall into his chest, dampening the frustrated sigh that escaped him.

"The answers do not lie with you," Aphrandhor declared. "You, as it turns out, Mr Pendain, are the *map*. And you lead directly to Taraktor."

Gallien's attention was swiftly diverted to the north, where he saw Kitrana striding away from the group.

"Kit!" he called after her. "Where are you going?" When the Nimean failed to answer, the smuggler glanced at Aphrandhor, a warning in his eyes that they were far from finished as he dashed away.

He called her name two more times before catching up with his old companion. It hadn't passed him by that she was crunching through the snow in bare feet or that her cloak was too small for her. It was a determined look that gnawed at him.

"What are you doing?" he demanded. "Where are you going?"

Kitrana looked at him as if he had lost his mind. "To Drakanan," she said simply before attempting to move on.

"Drakanan?" the smuggler repeated, though the truth of it soon dawned on him. "You're going for the sword."

"Of course I'm going for the sword. It's the only reason I'm on this dry hell. It's the only reason I've *ever* been here."

"You can't take the sword from Joran," he stated without thinking about it. "It's his only weapon."

"It was never his," Kit said firmly, turning on him. "It was never yours. I don't care if it belonged to a god or some mythical warrior. It was in the care of *my* people. As a battle maiden of the swordsworn, I am duty-bound to retrieve it."

Gallien frowned. "A what?"

"And as a Nimean," she continued without pausing, "I am bound by the blood of my people to claim that sword and set them free."

"What are you talking about?"

Kit closed the gap and grasped his shirt, holding him there while she quashed her anger. "You have no idea what I'm fighting for. This isn't the only world worth saving. At least up here, there's more than one of you. I'm the only one left. The only one who can make a difference. But I need that sword if I'm to do anything. So yes, I am going to Drakanan and reclaiming what is mine. You're welcome to come with me. I'm sure Joran would be happier with you there."

The Nimean left Gallien no time to consider his options, releasing his shirt and resuming her northerly heading without further delay.

Gallien watched her walk away, torn in two halves by the tug of his aching heart. He had just learned that his father might be alive—worse, he might be suffering under the magic of dark wizards. But he had longed to see Joran since the very second his mother's Aegre had taken him away. The smuggler took one step in pursuit of Kitrana before stopping to look back at his other companions.

The last time he had felt so torn was sixteen years ago, a baby in his arms. Then, he'd had left or right before him. One of those paths would have parted him from Joran forever. Of course, he had chosen Joran then. But he knew in his heart he wasn't choosing Joran this time, for the boy was exactly where he was supposed to be. If he pursued Kitrana. he would be doing so for his own selfish need to see his son again. The hard truth was that Joran didn't need him now. At least, he no longer needed him by his side.

"*We're still fighting for Joran,*" Andromated had said.

Now, that meant choosing the other path, a path that would likely see him parted from the boy forever. At least there was a chance to be reunited with his own father again. A possibility that had long laid beyond his wildest dreams. But Joran meant everything to him.

"Kitrana, wait!" he yelled, running after her.

"Gallien!" Andromated shouted, to which he offered no reply.

The Nimean only paused her departure when the smuggler was within a few feet. "You're coming?"

Gallien held onto his answer for a moment, unsure if it was, indeed, his answer. He was also captured by Kitrana's ocean-blue eyes and their unusual depth. "No," he finally said. "I'm no help to him there. And you're right. That sword was always yours. If you hadn't dropped it, my bones would be lying under Harendun as well."

Kit nodded her understanding and made to leave again, but then she paused and turned back to reach for his hand. She squeezed it tightly, much like the smile she offered him.

"Keep surviving," she told him. "I hope you win your war."

Gallien's smile was somewhat crooked. "I hope you win yours."

He watched the Nimean walk away for a while, his emotions churning like some great storm. With little thought, he reached into his satchel and retrieved the small red dragon scale. His thumb ran over the smooth surface while he thought back to the day he had lost Kitrana, as it seemed he was doing again. That was also the same day he had met Joran.

Before his feelings could consume him, Gallien gripped the dragon scale and turned about to march back to the others.

"If we're going to slow the Skaramangians down... If we're going to give Joran the time he needs," he began when he rejoined them, "then we need to be ready to fight beside him when the time comes."

"Careful, smuggler," Androma replied knowingly. "That's fighting talk."

Gallien gripped the hilt of his sword, applying some pressure to his belt. "I'm about ready for a good fight."

"Then we will need weapons," Aphrandhor replied, committing himself again to his argument. "Every piece of Andaren legend and even scripture details the gods' weapons as being pivotal in the battle against the Dark Ones."

"These would be the same gods that died, aye?" Gallien quipped.

"Yes," Aphrandhor admitted. "The gods died defeating them, but they *did* defeat them."

Gallien made a point to walk past Androma as he remarked, "I suppose it's left to *us* to make the sacrifices now."

Judging by her expression, the old Rider's own words weren't lost on her.

Finding the strength to rise, The Green Leaf scooped up his staff with a final statement on his cracked lips. "We make for Taraktor."

12

THE ANKALA

0 Years Ago...

4

It was to the sound of trumpets that the new dawn was ushered in. Added to that, the air was bombarded with drums, a cacophony that had awoken all of Aran'saur to a world of gloom. Amidst the soft glow of torchlight, Andarens lined the streets and peered out of windows and doorways to watch the procession of thousands.

Prisoners all.

Even from a distance, the Vahlken could hear the constant rattle of their manacles and chains. Murderers and thieves from every town and city in Andara, deserters who had fled from their posts in the east. They were all criminals seeking salvation for their lives, if not their family's honour.

Daijen observed their steady advance up the palace road from one of the many balconies that looked out on the capital. "We're going to be here for days.".

Beside him, Ilithranda bristled. "If not longer."

Daijen gave his companion a sideways glance. He hadn't seen such discomfort in her since they met the spiders in The Sin'duil—an encounter that would have challenged anyone's sense of courage. Having met Barris Tanyth, however, it seemed they had encountered a different species of spider. There was more to it, he knew. Ilithranda was hiding something from her past.

"Are you ready for this?" she asked him, the question taking the Vahlken by surprise.

"Are *you*?" Daijen countered, disliking the doubt he could hear in her voice. "You chose to come," he reminded her, "but you've been on edge since we arrived."

"I chose to come to stop you from using that damned bracer," Ilithranda snapped, if quietly. "And you have no idea what you're about to witness here," she added.

"I know they're all going to die," he said flatly, stating the common knowledge.

Ilithranda was shaking her head. "It's not that they die. It's *how* they die. And it will be *relentless*."

Daijen held onto his next question, noting the Andaren woman standing in the doorway, her physique hidden within the dark robes of the palace servants—a considerable step up from the branded humans. Her white hair was tied up high in a trio of knots, and her hands were pressed together at the waist. She waited patiently for the attention of both Vahlken before informing them that she was to be their escort to the throne room.

And so they passed through echoing halls of splendour and wall upon wall of portraits depicting various emperors and their lineage throughout the epochs. Of the numerous rooms and grand chambers they glimpsed, many were empty, their purpose unclear, if teeming with plant life, small trees, and a menagerie of colourful flowers. Indeed, many of the walls were layered in lush green vines and thick ivy. Here and there, the Vahlken even caught glimpses of birds flying overhead.

It was all to provide more cover, Daijen realised. His enhanced eyes missed little, including the Andaren guards standing statue-still amongst the plant life. Like those he had seen upon entering the palace, these Andarens had ingested the clerics' magic to change their skin colour, becoming almost perfect chameleons.

The further they journeyed into the labyrinth, the clearer it became that the palace's security had been improved overnight. They were everywhere, both obvious and camouflaged. Daijen had to assume that every local garrison had been emptied to furnish every corridor with so many soldiers.

The servant came to an abrupt stop at a seemingly random junction. She offered no explanation, keeping the Vahlken guessing until a set of ornate doors opened to their left. Behind an advance of soldiers, three imperators, and two castellans, there proceeded a short line of paragons and an even shorter succession of warmasters. The latter had come directly from The Saible, where they coordinated the war effort under the watch of the justiciar—who was notably absent from the procession.

Every one of them spared the Vahlken a look as they proceeded to the next set of doors. It was a mix of expressions Daijen had become accustomed to when around fellow soldiers. Some among them—typically lower in ranking—looked on the Vahlken with awe and surprise. As the line progressed and the rank increased, the expressions soured. It might not have been common knowledge that the Order of Handuin existed outside of imperial law, but it was well-known among those who felt the superior warriors should play a more active role in the war.

Daijen took it all in his stride and waited as patiently as he could. Their escort resumed the journey in the wake of the warmasters, who, apparently, were to be allowed entry into the throne room first. Being a head taller than them all, Daijen saw the golden doors before they could be opened. Twice his height and nearly as wide, they bore a raised image of the emperor, his arms outstretched as if he were welcoming the throng of people who looked up at him.

Their opening felt rather ceremonial. That is to say, *slow*. The throne room was revealed an inch at a time, forcing the line of generals to stop and wait. As the doors opened, Daijen felt his many years melting away, leaving him standing there a child, hungry with utter wonderment. It was agreed by all that the gods were dead, yet here he was, a messenger guard from a lowborn family on the verge of entering the imperial throne room upon invitation from His Radiance. How could the gods be dead and gone when his destiny had been so meticulously hand-crafted, for it must have been to have taken him from such obscurity.

When, at last, they were fully open, the imperial high command were led inside by their armed subordinates. Daijen was keen to get inside and see it all—to see the very heart of the empire he called home. Ilithranda looked to be feeling quite the opposite. Her head sank with every step, her eyes averted from the magnificence of the throne room. Somehow, she looked smaller, as if she had discovered a way to reduce her presence.

A stab of guilt tried to ruin the moment for Daijen. He shouldn't have pushed so hard to use the bracer. Together, they could have defied The Valtorak and planned their next step without accepting the invitation.

Such thoughts were banished the moment he stepped over the threshold and beheld the throne room in all its glory.

Six colossal pillars—each covered in relief from top to bottom —directed the Vahlken's eyes ever higher until he was looking at one enormous skeleton.

A dragon.

He had heard, of course, that a dead dragon could be found in the throne room, but actually seeing it with his own eyes was like stepping into the legend. More so, it brought much of his reading, his years spent consuming history books in Ka'vairn's library, to life.

"Dorgarath," he whispered to himself, though the name reached Ilithranda's pointed ears. Responding to her look of curiosity, he said, "The dragon. His name was Dorgarath. He was among the vanguard that attacked Tor Valan," he explained, his tale straight from the start of the war. "There are some texts that even suggest he was the first dragon to bring fire down on the city."

Ilithranda spared the suspended skeleton no more than a glance.

Daijen could hardly take his eyes away from it. The ceiling itself was mostly concealed by a canopy of luscious greenery, the leaves and stalks hanging so low as to filter between some of Dorgarath's bones.

Despite the distance that now lay between them, Daijen carried a piece of Androma with him, her perspective having bled into his own. What would she have thought to see a dragon so paraded? It was more than likely that she had known Dorgarath and his Rider and had done for centuries. What wrath Androma would have brought down on that chamber, where an immortal lay dead as a trophy.

The Skaramangians had a lot to answer for.

A hand lightly pressed the Vahlken's chest, an action that prevented him from walking into a stream. Quite perplexed, Daijen looked down, beyond Ilithranda's saving hand, and followed the channel of crystal clear water. It curved around, creating a ring of water inside the six pillars, forcing the group to ascend a short bridge and step onto a vast circle of white marble, an island at the very heart of the empire.

"Focus," Ilithranda mouthed at him.

Daijen accepted the instruction, aware that they were to watch each other's backs. He considered The Valtorak's warning that he was to let his old self go and the pride that came with it. So too, he knew, was he to let go of that child-like wonder that always hungered to see more of the world, to consume all it had to offer. Amidst the other-worldly splendour of Aran'saur, both would get him killed.

Continuing to follow in the wake of the warmasters, it was impossible not to walk over the golden sigil of House Lhoris, the broken circle and surrounding sunburst dominating the floor. Much like that broken circle, Daijen could now see that the perfect ring of water was broken by a small pool at the head of the chamber, where the empty Empyreal Throne loomed high atop a tower of steps.

The design of the room made little sense to the Vahlken. For all he knew, the pool and its ring of water was the emperor's personal bath. He could guess, however, that the three tall and elegant chairs lined up beside the base of the throne were intended for his three wives.

With as much grace and patience as possible, the palace servants ushered the various ranks of soldiers and generals into a line that allowed a clear path from the chamber doors to the throne. At the back of the line, furthest away from the throne, the Vahlken stood the tallest.

Then they waited.

It was an uncomfortable time, but time well spent by Daijen. He scrutinised the chamber beyond the great pillars, his trained mind naturally seeking out the places where enemies might ambush him. He found more doors than he had expected to, all built to blend into the walls. How many soldiers were stationed on the other side?

No, he thought. That was the wrong question. How many of them were Skaramangians? He had to assume the all were, including the warmasters standing to his right.

The mammoth chamber attempted to swallow the sound of the golden doors as they opened once more, but the intrusion on such quietude was enough to turn every head. All his years of training—years under Kastiek's tutelage—couldn't keep Daijen's heart rate from racing at the sight that greeted him.

In the place of his golden image, etched upon the doors, there now stood the flesh and blood of the imperial line.

A young male servant, standing rigid off to one side, cleared his throat. "Emperor Qeledred Isari Arad, the forty-first emperor of House Lhoris, who bears the sword and shield in the defence of the empire, keeper of the word, appointed one by blood and deed, bane of Erador, dragon-slayer, and servant of the light!"

It was with an air of unquestionable sovereignty that His Radiance strode towards the Empyreal Throne. His violet eyes were set on those steps and not once did they waver. It was as if the two were bound together by unseen forces.

Advancing over the small bridge, Emperor Qeledred approached their line, his plum attire shimmering with subtle accents of glistening minerals sewn into the fabric. His hands like-wise sparkled, each finger sporting a lavish ring of jewels. An opulent, if humble, circlet of silver crowned his head of thick white hair.

Then there was his scent. He glided past the Vahlken—likely unaware that their sense of smell was superior to the ordinary Andaren—and left his perfume in his wake. It was sweet, though grounded by an earthy aroma that reminded Daijen of the forest in summer.

Intoxicating was the essence that followed him, his three wives possessing an aura of different perfumes that each worked to seduce the Vahlken. Their fragrances were complimented by their exquisite beauty and model form, each walking perfectly in time with the others, their identical hair cascading down to within an inch of the floor.

Of the three, only one dared to glance at Daijen—a towering, if not intimidating, wall of muscle compared to them. The same could not be said of the two dozen children that followed them. More than half of them gawped at the Vahlken on their way past, and some even turned around so they might send whispers down the line.

Though the imperial family had entered the chamber like a shooting star against the black of the heavens, there were others among them worthy of attention.

The Praetorian Guard.

They formed a column on either side of the family, a protective barrier between them and the world. They moved with effortless grace, as if their white armour were simply a second skin. Of course, their actual skin was never to be seen, not even their faces, which were hidden behind masks each displaying a different expression. Of them all, Daijen found the grinning praetorian to be the most disturbing.

Daijen didn't know if he was to merely look straight ahead, as the others in his line were doing, but he found himself turning to seek out Ilithranda, if only to share the moment with her. The sentiment was not mutual. His Vahlken companion kept her eyes on the floor, revealing not a hint of violet. It couldn't have been to hide her heritage, for the imperial family were not the only ones in Andara to boast of such a beautiful eye colour—though it was rarer than the more common gold or even Daijen's icy blue.

Daijen decided that it was something else keeping her gaze from House Lhoris. He might have guessed it to be shame, though he couldn't fathom why. She had done well to get away from her life on the capital's streets and even better to ascend through the ranks of the army. And now, standing so tall as a Vahlken, she had attained the highest honour in the eyes of commoners and highborns alike.

Yet shame it was.

While the imperial family were ascending to their seats, Daijen and Ilithranda were ushered along with the others to find their place on the other side of the columned steps. Only when His Radiance had relaxed into the most august of thrones did the rest of his bloodline take to their own chairs.

Seemingly from nowhere, though Daijen deduced one of the hidden side doors had been used, a new procession entered the chamber. Rounding the edge of the water ring, until they could pass over the bridge were a dozen grand clerics. In the style of the emperor, they followed in the wake of the master cleric, who wore the same red robes as his lessers now. It was certainly the master of their order, though, still identifiable by the gold and bronze helm and its signature wings.

They crossed the circular island in total silence, their footsteps muffled by the light chains that hung from their belts and secured a copy of the Arkalon. All of them, including the master cleric, stopped before the pool and bowed to the emperor.

Upon rising, Daijen was sure the master cleric's gaze shifted within his mask and brought a pair of golden eyes to rest on the Vahlken, if only briefly. Though his face was concealed, it felt a knowing look to Daijen, as if the two had come eye to eye and knew that the other was truly seeing them.

"Your Radiance," the master cleric began. "Here marks the thirty-third Ankala."

"Let's be on with it then," Emperor Qeledred declared, his voice cutting through the chamber. "I would not have my sons and daughters continue this war in my stead."

The master cleric bowed again. "As you wish, Your Radiance."

Again, those golden eyes found Daijen before the mass of clerics dispersed. A pair of Andaren servants set up a small desk, chair, and roll of parchment beside the nearest pillar, the station soon assumed by one of the grand clerics. Others took up positions closer to the main doors or around the pool at the base of the throne.

"Bring in the first!" the master cleric called out.

It was left to the servants to open one of the majestic doors and permit entry to the first from the line of prisoners. Dressed in rags, the male Andaren stepped hesitantly into the throne room in manacles. He was immediately taken in by the splendour of the great chamber, but only until one of the clerics intercepted him and freed the man of his chains. He was then escorted across the bridge and brought swiftly before the imperial family.

Up close, it was clear that the prisoner was centuries old, perhaps nearing his five hundredth birthday. To a human, Daijen mused, he would have been better compared to someone in their late sixties, though he likely had another century of life ahead of him. At least he would have had he made different choices in his past life. He now stood on the precipice of death, as every Vahlken candidate did before the pools of Handuin.

A previously unseen servant entered Daijen's view with a cushion held in his hands. Unlike the others inside the throne room, whose hoods were drawn to conceal their faces, this servant wore naught but a loincloth to hide his modesty and a pair of plated gauntlets.

"The Helm of Ahnir," Daijen muttered under his breath.

So much of Andara's singular religion was grounded in that pierced helm. Not only had it been found beside the bones of Ahnir, but it had even granted visions of the future—a gift from the gods, the clerics had stated. Proof that they were real and that they favoured the Andarens above all other races.

Seeing it now, catching in the light that streamed through the tall glass windows, Daijen was almost humbled. Almost. The more he learned about the Skaramangians and the secret history of the world, the more his faith was challenged. Still, it was to be a moment he would never forget.

He missed the brief exchange between the master cleric and the prisoner, but it concluded with the old man entering the pool. He was closely followed by the bald servant who carried the Helm of Ahnir on a cushion. Once the prisoner had taken the helm from the cushion, the semi-naked servant excused himself and stood apart from the ceremony.

Ilithranda gripped Daijen's hand and squeezed it before letting go.

There was nothing to be discerned from her expression, the Vahlken's gaze fixed on the prisoner as he fitted the sleek helmet over his head. Daijen didn't know what to expect, but given Ilithranda's apprehension, his curiosity was quickly being replaced by a dark premonition.

"The days are shadowed by approaching night," the prisoner announced without warning, his expression blank. "The war to devour all wars has come again. He who lies entombed in the dark will rise and the fires with him. Death cannot hold him. He will stand amidst four pillars of his own creation, and with them he will harness the power of the world. Of *every* world. There is only—"

There was a wet *pop* and a gushing spray of red through the V-shaped slit in the helm.

Daijen jumped, though he did well to hide his reaction by partially turning to look at Ilithranda. She never took her eyes off the prisoner, whose body had already sunk into the water.

It did so without any head.

The Helm of Ahnir drifted free and dropped to the bottom of the pool. The near-naked servant went in after it, his own body momentarily disappearing beneath the darkening waters.

Off to the side, the grand cleric who had taken to the small desk was scribbling on the long piece of parchment. "He's recording the visions," Ilithranda whispered.

Still shocked at having just witnessed a man's head explode, Daijen missed the helm being returned to its cushion and the prisoner's body being dredged from the pool. The corpse was then unceremoniously dragged away by another servant, creating a snaking smear of blood that led to one of the side doors. Looking around, it appeared he was the only one shaken by the event. If anything, the emperor's children looked eager for more.

"We have heard this before," Emperor Qeledred said impassively, seated amongst his Praetorian Guard—who had taken up a seemingly scattered formation about the throne, each maintaining a different, if heroic, stance.

"Yes, Your Radiance," the master cleric agreed. "As well as variations of it."

"I was hoping for something more *specific*," the emperor continued. "Impending invasions. Battalion movements. The condition of Erador's fleet, even. Talk of some great war when we are already in the middle of one is of no use to me. Nor is this nonsense about pillars and the Black Abyss."

The master cleric bowed his head. "They are but conduits, Your Radiance. There are many paths ahead of us, just as there are many who will bear witness to those paths. The more who use the helm, the more we will see."

The emperor was already looking exasperated by the ceremony, and only one of thousands had died at his feet so far. Rather than offer a reply, he merely gestured at the distant doors.

"Another!" the master cleric demanded.

In no time at all, there was a young woman entering the pool, bewildered by her surroundings. She placed the helm over her head. She lasted longer than the old man, but what was a few extra seconds when every orifice was oozing blood—including her eyes? Again, Daijen was startled when her head exploded inside the helmet, adding so much gore to the pool. Though slightly different, her words had been essentially the same as her predecessor's.

"Fetch another!" the master cleric called.

An older woman came this time—perhaps older than the first to have succumbed to the helm's power. Like the others, she was struck by the magic of the helm.

"Six there were, and six there are," she reported. "Tempered by magic, they hold his voice in their hearts. Break the crystal, break the world. Break the crystal, break the world! Break the crystal, break the world!"

With every repetition, she became more shrill, her echoed warning only to be brought to an end by death.

Daijen winced as brain matter and shards of bone splattered against the white marble beside the pool. Once again, the bald servant had to enter the grim water to retrieve the helm. Bit by bit, his body was turning red from head to toe.

"The older ones don't last so long," Ilithranda said in his ear.

Daijen absorbed the information while bracing himself for the next prisoner. The spectacle was just as grotesque as the last—a young man parted head from body so he could deliver an indecipherable message regarding a possible future.

The Vahlken managed to stomach five more before he put his lips to Ilithranda's ear. "I can't take this," he whispered. "It's not right. Even criminals don't deserve this."

Ilithranda turned so he might see her violet eyes. "There's nothing we can do," she told him evenly.

"I can leave," he corrected. And he would have had Ilithranda's hand not gripped his wrist like a vice.

"We can't leave," she replied, her last word lost to the sound of another head bursting like an overfilled sack of wine. "This is considered sacred. Don't give them a reason to turn on us—it's what they want."

"Another!" the master cleric shouted across the vast chamber, his eyes on Daijen.

Inevitably, another prisoner soon occupied the dark pool. Daijen would have been surprised if the young man had seen twenty winters before arriving at his doom.

"The oldest demon from the oldest world slumbers beneath

stone and bone," he blurted, another slave to the helm. "The waters will boil, and the seas will rise. It cannot be tamed, it cannot be harnessed. It has no master but hunger. The Dawn-breaker will bring about everlasting night. Doom to the seas. Doom to the lands. Doom to the skies. The Black Abyss rises—"

Another wet *squelch* and a sudden *pop* interrupted the vision as well as his life.

"*That*," the master cleric emphasised, "was *new*. We shall record it and consult the Arkalon, Your Radiance."

The emperor was an example of perfect form upon his lofty throne. "I shall wait with bated breath, Master Cleric," he said dryly. "Perhaps another will enlighten us."

"As you say, Your Radiance."

Daijen closed his eyes as the next prisoner was summoned. "When will this end?" he asked Ilithranda.

"At sunset."

The Vahlken opened his eyes and scrutinised the ring of water that ran out from the pool. By sunset, it would be black with death.

He forced himself to watch the next prisoner.

Then he forced himself to watch a few thousand more.

13

BE CAREFUL WHAT YOU
WISH FOR

S at perched on the edge of the ravine, The Giant's Throat was laid bare beneath Grarfath. So too was the Andaren army, its many ranks squeezed between the ravine's high walls. Like a river with a slow current, they advanced on The Silver Trees of Akmar, steadily taking ground as they navigated the fallen Giants.

Growing tired of the sight, the son of Thronghir turned to the north, where he spotted the Kedradi ranger assisting the blind Dragon Rider towards the steep path they had found at the head of the ravine. It would take them down a near-vertical zig-zagging track to the forest floor, where they hoped to skirt around much of the invasion and make it beyond the region.

Close behind them was the smuggler, whose name had bewildered everyone.

It meant nothing to the smith. While he understood their simple language, he hadn't understood a word that had passed between the humans. They seemed to have been just as concerned with the smuggler's father as with the boy who had flown away on the Aegre. Grarfath couldn't see the connection between the two or how it mattered to the eclectic group.

But he had concerns of his own. Besides Kitrana Voden having walked away from them—and without even a farewell for the dwarf—he felt as if Yamnomora had stretched him over an anvil, and he was but to wait for the hammer to fall.

The hammer...

Yamnomora's fiery temperament naturally frayed any connection they might have, but losing The Anther had created a rift beyond bridging, it seemed. Having heard the wizard's speech, the smith knew that the hammer was, perhaps, even more important than he had given credit. But there was no changing what had happened.

He had thrown The Anther.

He had saved a life.

Grarfath huffed, wishing Yamnomora could see it that way. Instead, he was just the dolt who had undone months—years—of hard work to attain the weapon.

"I hear what ye're sayin', Green Leaf," came Yamnomora's blunt tone, "but how am I supposed to find it now? He doesn' know where he sent it! It could be anywhere!"

Despite his withered appearance, Grarfath still felt the weight of the wizard's gaze as it landed on him. Seated on the boulder once more, Aphrandhor had informed the others that he would be along shortly, though he would likely require assistance from the Kedradi, and that was before attempting to descend the cliff.

His long white beard flicked out to the side as the wind caught it. "Perhaps I might help you up, Master Grarfath?"

The dwarf eyed the liver-spotted hand extended before him, taking careful note of the vambrace encasing the wizard's forearm. Grarfath had heard the old man describe how the piece of armour worked—more magic, like The Anther.

More nonsense, the smith thought. He couldn't make heads or tails out of the stuff, lending him a natural distrust of magic.

"Ye're goin' to see into me mind?" he asked.

"Only if you are willing."

Grarfath licked his lips, feeling the bristles of his black beard.

Wielding the hammer had made him feel powerful, in control. The idea of someone using similar magic to peer into his mind made him feel quite the opposite.

"Wait," Yamnomora warned. "Ye're still reeling from *his* scrambled brains," she reminded him, gesturing at the distant smuggler. "Besides, Grarfath's got centuries behind 'im. Ye remember what happened last time..."

"I shan't pry," The Green Leaf assured her. "I need only look back as far as the ruins, when he last wielded The Anther. Two days of memory is no bother."

"Ye're sure ye can do that?" the dwarven warrior queried incredulously. "Remember what happened to ye. Remember what happened to *Daijen*," she added darkly, mentioning a name the smith hadn't heard before.

"He is not nearly so old," the wizard replied calmly. "And decades of practice have since followed. Now," he said, addressing Grarfath, his fingers flexing with invitation. "If you would."

With all the courage he could muster on that cold rock, the smith placed his hand in The Green Leaf's. Aphrandhor sucked in a breath, and his eyes closed for one precious heartbeat. It was the wizard who ended their interaction, retracting his hand. He clenched it numerous times while gathering his wits.

"Well?" Yamnomora pressed. "What'd ye see?"

"You hold a lot of memories. It is like a flood breaking through a dam," the wizard commented, rubbing his eyes. "Still, I was able to see what I needed to." Aphrandhor looked down at the smith. "Your emotions play a key part in controlling The Anther. I would say you must learn to wield *them* before picking up that hammer again. That said, you took to it as well as your mother did. Mordrith saved my life more than once."

"She had a strong arm," Grarfath muttered.

The Green Leaf looked to share in some of his grief. Like the others, he had only learned of Mordrith's death in the last two days. The wound was still fresh for the wizard.

"We will mourn her passing when we can," the wizard said.

"She deserved so much more. But she would have been proud to know that her son brought The Anther against the Skaramangians —especially against Slait."

Hearing the big Andaren's name brought back the memory for Grarfath, allowing him to see again the moment The Anther struck the brute, porting him from the ruins. "Do ye know where I sent it?"

"I believe so. You feared greatly for Yamnomora's life," the wizard observed, though his comment did little to soften her hard features. "At the same time, our clash with the Andarens reminded you of another battle." Aphrandhor looked away, as if he was drawing the memory out all the more. "You wanted Slait to be gone. Not dead—just gone, where he couldn't hurt anyone. It is my strong suspicion, Master Grarfath, that you sent The Anther home, to *The Morthil Mountains*."

Yamnomora swore in the dwarven tongue.

"Home?" Grarfath echoed.

"Not *home*, exactly," The Green Leaf specified. "Given your thoughts at the time, I would say you sent it to that battlefield. And The Dancing Sword of the Dawn with it."

The son of Thronghir recalled the battlefield in question. The Redbraids versus the Ironguards. It had been a bloody and violent affair, much like the battle atop The Ruins of Gelakor. It had also been the same day he met Yamnomora, when his whole life had been turned upside down.

"It's truly lost then," Yamnomora lamented, her feet set to rapid pacing.

The wizard gripped his staff in two hands as he twisted his hips to lay eyes on her. "Things are only truly lost if no one ever searches for them, my dear Yamnomora. And since the two of you will be returning to The Morthil Mountains in search of The Anther, I would say our odds are greatly improved."

"Ye can't be serious?" Yamnomora spat, immune to Aphrandhor's soothing voice. "If Slait an' The Anther ported into the middle o' Morthil, ye can bet both 'ave been swept up by Tharg an' his Skaramangian thugs."

Grarfath's attention was tugged by the mention of the dwarf, Tharg. He had been the one who ordered Mordrith's death, hounding her across the realm until finally accomplishing the dark task in The Swamps of Morthil. It gnawed at the smith that they had shared the same air, that he had even welcomed the wretch into his workshop.

"I think it is more likely," Aphrandhor countered, "that their sudden and dramatic appearance has drawn too much attention. The Skaramangians will be unable to act without revealing themselves, but you can be sure they will be scrambling to take control of the situation—all the more reason for the two of you to make haste."

Yamnomora was shaking her head. "We've jus' come from there!" she complained. "We risked life an' limb to bring ye the weapon. Hells, Mordrith gave her life protectin' The Anther from the Skaramangians."

Grarfath felt the bite of those words keenly. "I were tryin' to save ye," he muttered.

"Well, next time," Yamnomora expressed vehemently, "ye let me die, ye hear? What we're fightin' for is worth more than any *one* life. The enemy's winnin'!" she exclaimed, gesturing towards the Andaren army. "We need an arsenal."

Whether it was the cold, his empty stomach, or a combination of the two, Grarfath snapped and jumped to his feet. "What bloody good is an arsenal if ye've no one to wield it?"

"Bah!" Yamnomora growled, waving his remark away. "Ye talk like ye've any idea what we're really fightin' for!"

"I've heard enough to know the whole damned world is at stake!" Grarfath yelled back.

The Green Leaf cleared his throat, drawing the attention of both dwarves. "Perhaps this is a discussion best had on the *road*," he suggested, eyeing the path back to the north.

"I've no need o' 'im," Yamnomora fumed, making her way back to Bludgeon. "Ye can keep 'im," she called back.

"I think not," Aphrandhor croaked. "There's more to this smith than meets the eye," he went on, speaking of Grarfath as if he wasn't there. "His strength will be of use."

Yamnomora straddled the Warhog and patted one of the two enormous axes strapped to the saddle. "I've strength o' me own, Green Leaf."

"I am not referring to his *arm*," the wizard corrected. "If he is even half the dwarf Mordrith was, he will be a credit to our cause."

Yamnomora let loose something between a growl and a sigh. "So be it," she grumbled. "Pick up ye feet, smith. We've a thousand miles to retread," she said bitterly.

A flash of revelation crossed Aphrandhor's face. "Not necessarily," he countered, one finger rising into the air. "Not if you make haste."

Yamnomora looked at the wizard a moment longer before she too had that same look of revelation. "It's been two days already," she said cryptically, doubt creeping into her voice.

"Travelling without the burden of the rest of us will improve your speed," he pointed out. "You could still make it."

Yamnomora made a face to relay her scepticism. "That's a long time for any scar to stay open."

"True, but The Anther was used in the presence of the bracer, the axe, *and* the sword. Its power was tenfold. There is *hope*, Yamnomora," The Green Leaf added in the face of her doubt. "Do not let it dwindle," he pleaded.

The dwarven warrior slowly replaced her scepticism with true grit. "Then we will make haste," she said determinedly.

Grarfath threw his hands up. "What are ye talkin' abou'?"

The wizard managed a warm smile in spite of his obvious deterioration. "You will see soon enough, Master Smith." With a wince of pain, The Green Leaf rose to his full height. "Taraktor will take us north of Caster Hold," he called out, his own path taking him towards the southern head of the ravine. "As soon as you have The Anther, make your way there. I will be sure to leave word for you upon our return."

"Don' worry, Green Leaf," Yamnomora bade, guiding Bludgeon round in a tight circle. "If The Anther's for the takin', ye'll be seein' it again, an' us with it. Well," she countered ominously, "ye'll be seein' *me,* at least. The smith 'ere's gettin' his wish. Ye're goin' *home,* son o' Thronghir."

Grarfath had the sinking feeling it wouldn't be the home-coming he had hoped for.

14

THE FUTURE IS WRITTEN

0 Years Ago...

4

New light pushed through the lush canopy and filtered between Dorgarath's great bones, illuminating the imperial throne room in all its splendour. The pool and surrounding ring of water had been cleaned, the water replaced. The thick smear of blood that snaked from the pool to a side door had been wiped away, leaving polished white marble in its place. Even the pile of manacles had been removed away, all to be used again to bind of new prisoners.

Daijen Saeth occupied the same space as the previous day. That was true of his body, at least. The Vahlken's mind was struggling to stay grounded, haunted by the thousands of violent deaths he had witnessed. One after the next, he had watched his countrymen enter the pool to be dragged out moments later with a ragged necks.

Ilithranda had been right: it was relentless.

It spoke volumes about the imperial family and, again, proved

Ilithranda right. *"The imperial family doesn't live as we do,"* she had said atop The Ruins of Kharis Vhay years earlier. *"They simply watch from afar and enjoy the safety of their gilded cage."*

House Lhoris had detached themselves from the common Andarens—perhaps even the highborns. These weren't people being paraded and sacrificed before them. They were just cattle. Worse: they were bad cattle, tarnished by their crimes.

Daijen's attention was drawn to the golden doors as the first prisoner of the day was ushered inside. His perfect memory committed the woman's image as surely as the relief had been carved out of the pillars. He would soon remember her death just as well.

A sickly sweet smell assaulted the Vahlken's nose, a scent that preceded the master cleric. It seemed he had made a point of gliding past Daijen and Ilithranda on his way to the pool, if only so he could pause and utter words meant for their keen ears.

"I do hope you can stomach another day of revelation," he said provokingly, his winged helm revealing no more than his golden eyes.

There was no chance to respond before he continued to the pool and intercepted the prisoner. She was the lucky one, Daijen decided. Being the first, there was no pool of blood and brain matter nor a thick streak of red marring the pristine floor. She had no idea what death had in store for her—a blessing, if a pitiful one.

Into the water she descended, where she was soon presented with the Helm of Ahnir by the same meek half-naked servant. Daijen braced himself as the prisoner placed the helm over her head. All at once, her eyes glazed over and her voice was under the thrall of the helm's inherent magic.

"The skies will rain with blood," she began boldly. "Dragons will fall. Aegres will fall. The heavens will fall. He will wipe away the lines on the map, and the first empire will rise again—"

Daijen held his nerve this time, his flinch reduced to no more than a slow blink. As ever, the servant plunged in to retrieve the helm while others dragged the body away.

Emperor Qeledred—well rested by the look of the silver

freckles dotted about his nose and cheeks—stirred on his throne. "Have we had that before?"

The Skaramangian master cleric didn't need to consult the scribe recording the visions to answer. "No, Your Radiance. That was new."

The emperor settled back into the Empyreal Throne, his stony expression guarding his thoughts. "A good start then," he remarked optimistically.

Daijen intended to steel himself against the relentless deaths, if only to show the master cleric that he could, indeed, stomach it. But he didn't. He couldn't. Whether he embraced it as a strength or not, Daijen's humanity was a part of him, and no amount of time in the pits of Handuin could change that. He would feel every death. He would remember them all. Let the master cleric see that in him, he thought. Soon, it would be the last thing he ever saw.

One prisoner the another was led to the pool and, one after another, succumbed to its power. While some said nothing at all, their heads exploding without a word, there was a growing trend amongst the visions.

"*He*," Daijen whispered in Ilithranda's ear.

"What?"

"It keeps coming up. They keep saying *he*."

"That could mean anything," Ilithranda replied with a subtle shrug, her mind somewhat disengaged.

"This isn't the first time we've heard someone talk about a *he*," Daijen reminded her.

Ilithranda tilted her head just enough to lay eyes on him. "The curator," she mouthed, sharing some of his epiphany.

Daijen held a grave look about him. "I think we're missing something. Something *big*."

Ilithranda made no further comment, leaving them to stand shoulder to shoulder with the warmasters and watch the parade of death. Head after exploding head, the visions were given voice, and the cleric committed them to his ever-growing scroll of parchment. While it was painful to be a part of the ceremony, Daijen did his best to take in the visions, always aware that the helm offered branches of the future rather than *the* future.

By midday, after so many had died and the water was near-black with so much blood, the visions began to weave a new branch, departing from talk of a man shrouded in darkness and the rising empire around him. It was as if the visions were homing in, the futures being refined to a point that felt closer to the present. Closer to the war.

"The broken circle will live up to its blood and break the cycle of war," came the next proclamation on the matter. "One will stand between the two, *for* the two. Rider, Vahlken. Rider, Vahlken. Rider, Vahlken."

"She will ride scales and feathers..."

"He will master talon and claw..."

"Only he can end the war..."

"She stands between two worlds, a saviour and destroyer to both."

"Only he who stands in the shadow of kings can bridge the broken circle. Only he can usher in a new age of heroes. Only he can bring about... *a time of dragons.*"

After that nameless woman died a gruesome death, Emperor Qeledred sat forward on his throne, his violet eyes piercing the thick pool. "A time of dragons," he echoed.

The master cleric didn't respond immediately, his gaze as lost to the pool as his thoughts were.

"Master Cleric," the emperor pressed, his tone enough to convey any impatience. "A time of dragons would spell the end of Andara, would it not?"

"Forgive me, Your Radiance. I fell into prayer for a moment. I am compelled to remind the imperial court that the Great Ahnir shows us the future so we might intervene where He cannot. Nothing is set in stone. If there is, indeed, a future in which we see a resurgence in dragons and their wretched Riders, we must learn more so we might prevent it."

Daijen scrutinised the master cleric, sure there was more to it than that. Though he couldn't see his face through the bronze mask, the Vahlken was confident there was a hint of fear in those golden orbs.

"Bring forth the next!" the master cleric cried, sparing a moment to share a look with the grand cleric beside him.

A time of dragons...

It concerned them.

Besides a handful of futures that made little to no sense, the next few hundred were more refined when it came to visions of the figure that would straddle the line between Vahlken and Rider. More and more referred to a *him* rather than a *her*. The details concerning his appearance leaned more and more towards that of a Dragon Rider. But the Rider's dragon—and, sometimes, his Aegre —remained in obscurity, beyond the viewer's ability to comprehend.

Then came a word with weight behind it that rippled across the court, disgruntling the warmasters and their underlings while creating a wave of disgust throughout the imperial family.

"Abomination!" Emperor Qeledred raged, rising to his slippered feet.

"A half-blood," one of the warmasters muttered with derision.

Daijen tried to imagine it. A person with aspects of both cultures. What promise they held. What *hope*.

The court shared its outrage for a while longer, delaying the inevitable. Only after His Radiance had settled down did the others follow his example, allowing the clerics to continue with the grim ceremony.

And so on it went, as it would in the manner of blood and death. They saw the day out with thousands more committed to the Black Abyss, all in the name of progress.

As Ilithranda was, once again, in no mood to converse with him, Daijen was left to his own thoughts for the night. Sleep would elude him again, his mind tripping over the many visions he remembered so perfectly. He discarded the anomalous visions, focusing on the ones that had come up again and again, as if the helm was desperate to tell them something.

It seemed to the Vahlken's investigative mind that there were either two individuals or just one. In the latter case, the man in question would either end the war or make it worse. If the former proved to be true, then there was one figure who would bring about a new age of death and destruction and another who had the power to stop them.

There were too many variables for Daijen's liking.

Thankfully, none of the visions included a wrathful Vahlken hellbent on killing the master cleric.

As Daijen began to formulate a plan that might see him through to that end, a knock on his door informed him the sun was quickly approaching. He sighed heavily into his chest. Time had slipped through his fingers while he recalled the last words of so many doomed Andarens.

He was soon taken to hear the rest.

His heart sank at the sound of those golden doors opening. The numbness he felt upon witnessing the first head explode, however, was more concerning to him. Was it possible to watch so many men and women die in such gruesome fashion and feel nothing? He looked to the imperial family and found the disturbing answer.

To them, the visions were the more disturbing matter. The first dozen to enter the pool that day spoke of the same half-blood as being pivotal in the war, though it was never clear what kind of peace he was to usher in. The emperor himself pointed out that peace would only be attained when one side was annihilated.

Then came another nameless soul, an Andaren of middle age and gaunt physique. His eyes brightened as he beheld the throne room. Like all the others, he was parted from his manacles and led over the bridge, where the sigil of House Lhoris gleamed on the white marble.

Daijen narrowed his eyes on the prisoner's bare chest. He bore the brand of a deserter—a fellow soldier, then. His time in captivity had robbed him of his muscle and complexion. Still, he found the strength to fall prostrate at the sight of the emperor, his forehead pressed to the cool floor.

"Rise," one of the grand clerics instructed.

He was slower to reach the dark pool than his predecessors, but he outright hesitated at the sight. The smell alone must have gripped him with fear.

"No one can be forced," said the cleric at his back. "But your honour can only be reclaimed in there."

The deserter swallowed and entered the pool before being presented with the Helm of Ahnir. Like so many others, he appeared overwhelmed by the mere sight of it.

"Take it," the master cleric commanded.

"It is not too late to face the block," another cleric announced.

"Take it," the master cleric repeated forcefully.

The prisoner lifted the helm from its blood-soaked cushion, allowing the bald servant to retreat for a time.

"Put it on," came the order.

At the end of his road, the deserter placed the helm over his head. His eyes wandered over its red surface, slowly drifting out of focus until he was in the grip of the gods.

"In the shadow of kings," he began, words they had heard before, "with the blood of emperors. Son of darkness. Son of the first. He stands a Rider. He stands a Vahlken. He fights for life and delivers death. He is to be the light that holds back the dark. But the seed of darkness dwells within. It has but to hold out its hand and he will take it. The Black Abyss will be made manifest in their alliance. All will bow to the one who is *Pendain*."

The deserter spasmed in the pool and coughed up a dangerous amount of blood. Daijen glanced at Ilithranda, the two sharing the same questioning expression. Why wasn't he dead?

With blood streaming from his eyes, it seemed clear that he soon would be, but not before he sank beneath the surface. He was quickly dragged out and left to continue his spasms on the cold floor, the helm already reclaimed by the near-naked servant.

The master cleric turned to the throne. "At last, Your Radiance —*progress*. The abomination has a name."

"*Pendain*," Emperor Qeledred announced, his voice carving through the air.

"A human name, Your Radiance," the master cleric went on. "A pity. That will make finding him all the harder."

The sound of vomiting turned most eyes back to the deserter, who was now on his hands and knees as yet more blood poured from his mouth, eyes, and ears.

"He must be found," His Radiance declared, paying no attention to the bloody scene while one of his young daughters made her way up the steps to his throne. "This *Pendain* cannot be allowed to bring about such a vision. The destiny of Andara and its people cannot be steered by an abomination," he added, allowing the girl to climb onto his lap.

"Of course, Your Radiance," the master cleric agreed. "We will..." He trailed off, his gaze drawn down to the prisoner.

A head taller than the master cleric and with the eyes of an eagle, Daijen could see what the deserter was drawing on the floor, a symbol painted in his own blood. He knew that symbol well, as any Andaren would.

The master cleric kicked the prisoner in the ribs, sending him reeling while exposing the bloody sigil. "Your Radiance," he hissed. "The *Eikor*."

While word of an abomination had sent discord through the gathered party, mention of the Eikor—an ancient name—brought a palpable silence down upon the throne room. There was one among them, however, who found his voice before all others, if only a whisper.

"The Dark Ones," the servant muttered, fresh from the pool and coated in blood.

The master cleric's bronze mask snapped round to face the diminutive servant. From within one of his red sleeves, the Skaramangian freed a curved dagger. There came no hesitation as he swiped the steel across the servant's throat, swift and clean, adding his own blood to that which already clung to him. The cushion slipped from his gauntleted hands and the helm with it, creating a *clatter* at his feet.

It seemed a silent order had been given, for every cleric in the chamber immediately sought out one of the observing servants.

Like their master, they all produced a previously concealed dagger and turned on the helpless servants. One by one, they felt cold steel plunge into their hearts or stab at their throats until there wasn't a living servant remaining.

At the same time, the Praetorian Guard abandoned their various poses and assumed a protective battle formation about the throne.

Appalled by the sudden onslaught of innocents, Daijen stepped forward, his sabre already an inch from its scabbard. What calamity might have ensued had Ilithranda not held out her arm and barred his way. She gave him a subtle shake of the head, and there was a firmness behind her eyes that kept him back.

The explosive spate of violence came to an abrupt end, the master cleric stepping casually over his victim while cleaning his blade with a kerchief.

"Prudence, Your Radiance," he explained while pausing to pick up the fallen helm. "It would be best if the abomination's name and any mention of the Eikor remain with a trusted few."

"Agreed," the emperor replied, his response unnervingly even, though it proved enough to stand down the Praetorian Guard. "I would know more from the helm."

The master cleric glanced back at the golden doors. "We have exhausted thousands to learn this much, Your Radiance."

"Then imagine what we will learn after a few thousand more," he proposed, his fingers brushing absently through his daughter's long white hair.

The Skaramangian bowed his head. "Bring forth the next!"

"But father," the imperial daughter interjected, her voice sweet and innocent, "why hasn't his head gone *pop*?" she complained. "All the others did! That's my favourite part."

Daijen looked back at the prisoner who had spouted the problematic vision, the deserter forgotten in the carnage. Miraculously, he was still alive—if barely. He was looking up at the emperor with eyes as red as his skin. What agony there was in his expression, a pain none of them could comprehend.

Fortunately, his suffering came to an end in the same way as it had for the thousands before him, only without the helm, his head exploded across the floor, splashing up the master cleric's legs and robes. In the absence of servants, a group of the clerics' personal guard entered the scene and began dragging the numerous bodies away. They were careful to depart through the same side doors from which they had entered, thereby avoiding the awaiting prisoners who had no idea what they were walking into.

Best that the lambs don't see the axe coming, Daijen thought miserably.

While the bodies were being taken away, the master cleric returned to the spot on the floor where the deserter had drawn the symbol of the Dark Ones. He regarded it for a moment, as Daijen did from afar. It was a simple circle with four vertical lines—two running up from the bottom and two running down from the top. So simple a thing, yet so troubling.

Using his boot, the master cleric wiped the symbol away before meeting Daijen's gaze. There could have been no mistaking the Vahlken's fury, who felt his oath to protect the Andaren people had been compromised throughout the Ankala. However many would die in the name of tradition, Daijen Saeth vowed to add one more to the list.

———

Hours later, no sooner did he enter his private room than Daijen's gut spasmed and he threw his head over the side of his balcony, where he could vomit into the night. For three days he had held it together, but his mind's ability to recall every sight, sound, and smell now bound him to the deaths of several thousand Andarens. He had only to close his eyes and he was back in the throne room, watching one after another suffer agonising pain before losing their head.

It was barbaric.

He spat over the railing and let his head fall back to see an

ocean of stars looking down on Aran'saur, the city nestled comfortably between the bones of a long-dead monster. Daijen had rushed
from the throne room in the emperor's wake and retraced his way
to the room given him. There was so much swimming in his mind,
though it all felt as if it was swimming in a sea of dark blood.

The sound of triumphant music drew his attention to the city
below. The Ankala was at an end, and now the city would celebrate
under the belief that the Helm of Ahnir had shown them the path
to victory. There would be clerics on every street corner blasting
the false news to keep the masses in high spirits. To keep them
malleable.

In the distance, a streak of light shot high into the air and
exploded in a shower of golden dust, briefly banishing the night. It
seemed the clerics were adding their magic to their words, for the
firework was followed by more, each a different colour and size
designed to mesmerise the citizens of Aran'saur. Everything was a
tool in the hands of the Skaramangians.

The song of cracking stone broke Daijen's reverie. He looked
down to see that the railing he had been leaning into was beginning to break under the pressure he was exerting on it. He took a
calming breath and stepped back.

It didn't work. He was still furious. Furious with the imperial
family. Furious with his own people for having let them abuse
their power. Furious that the head of the Skaramangians was
permitted the freedom of the master cleric.

The Vahlken's fists began to clench into knots. It was time to
take action, he decided. He would land a blow their dark order
would not easily recover from.

Without deliberating with himself, Daijen leaped over the
balcony railing. Though he couldn't say when exactly, his mind
had already been working ahead of him, assessing the hallways
and patrol patterns and placements. It had also worked out a path
that would take him into the heart of the palace without the need
to use his door.

While he looked down at nothingness—a sure death—his
hand reached out and caught the base of the balcony, allowing him

to slow his descent while swinging back into the palace walls. All four limbs searched for purchase, bracing him in place. A quick survey revealed the route he would need to take in order to shimmy round to the east and then up, a path that would hide him from the exterior archers.

Scaling the palace was child's play when Daijen considered his decades trying to out-pace Kastiek on the cliffs about Ka'vairn. In no time at all, he was east and climbing, his ascent steering him clear of the patrols. Locating the throne room was easy enough, its large domed ceiling sitting at the base of the central tower.

A degree of Vahlken strength was then required to bend the lock on a hatch beside the glass dome. Once inside, and without having shattered any glass, he had the far more daunting task of getting down to the floor. There was nothing to hold onto and offer a way of descending with any kind of quiet control. It left him with one option.

Crouched on the lip surrounding the interior of the dome, Daijen let himself go and used his toes to push him out from the ledge. In little more than a second, he was crashing through the thick canopy, his limbs snapping vines and tearing leaves free.

It was the skilled work of the Weavers that prevented the air from being knocked out of him, an otherwise sure thing when slamming into the ultra-hard bones of a dragon. He clipped his head on the spine and flipped backwards before impacting the ribs. His momentum would have seen him roll off the side and plummet to the circular slab of marble below, but the Vahlken managed to find a handhold on the end of a single rib. And there he dangled, his weight pressing down on four fingers.

How easy it would have been to give in to the head injury—and judging by the blood tickling his left eyebrow, there was certainly an injury. Years of tutelage under Kastiek, however, had given his muscles a memory of their own. His free hand swung up and gripped the same rib bone, swiftly followed by his legs. Only then did he become aware that the great skeleton had been disturbed by his presence, its chains rattling lightly.

Perched inside the enormous ribcage, the Vahlken waited and

watched. The golden doors remained closed, the chamber eerily still. Daijen made his move and used Dorgarath's tail to put him within leaping distance of one of the six pillars. The severe relief that coated the pillar was more than enough for his fingers and feet to navigate and bring him to the throne room floor.

It was with satisfaction that he touched down, his infiltration successful.

The grand chamber, including the pool and surrounding ring of water, had already been vigorously cleaned. There wasn't a single trace of the thousands who had entered the chamber and died a horrifying death.

Jumping over the moat of clear water, Daijen made to cross the circular island in the heart of the room. His plan would see him leave the chamber and infiltrate the executive suites in the central pillar—there he would find his quarry.

Unless they found him first...

The Vahlken came to a swift stop, his ears detecting considerable movement beyond the golden doors. He made to move, but they swung open to a charging column of red and white. The clerics' personal militia crossed the bridge and took up positions around the edge of the circular island, boxing him in. The Vahlken naturally fell into a battle stance, his knees bent and one hand gripped about the hilt of his sabre.

His heart was racing inside his chest. How had they known to ambush him? He had avoided raising any alarm, his path to the throne room so unorthodox that none but a Vahlken could have succeeded.

Striding steps entered the chamber, and a cluster of Skaramangian warriors parted to allow another to enter the island. Attired in the same garb, his face concealed within a silver helm, the newcomer was a head taller than his peers, boasting a wider frame with broad shoulders beneath his white pauldrons.

His size mattered little to Daijen. The bigger his opponent was, the harder it was to miss them. He would cut him down first, the Vahlken decided. Perhaps reducing him to a pile of limbs would take some of the fight out of the others.

The larger one boldly stepped forwards, his left hand resting casually on the hilt of his sword. When he addressed Daijen his voice was a deep and heavy rasp, only worsened by the mask that covered his mouth. But it was his words that stumped the last son of House Saeth. Two there were. Just two.

"Hello, Runt."

15

IT'S IN THE BLOOD

In the shadow of Drakanan's entrance, Kassanda leaned against the frame, her arms crossed and her sandy cloak billowing in the icy wind. She watched Joran from afar while he interacted with Oaken, his young hands running up and down the Aegre's armoured beak. She had never seen one of the mutated creatures take a liking to any but their Vahlken companion, but there was certainly something between them.

It is most unusual, came the familiar rich baritone of Garganafan's voice, the dragon's words sparking from a place in the back of her mind. *I cannot decide if it is his familial heritage or his blood heritage.*

Kassanda's lips twisted in thought. **Is it because he's Ilithranda's son?** she mused. **Or is it because he has Vahlken magic in his blood?** The Rider sighed, the disappointment she had felt over the last two days now stirred with frustration—she had never enjoyed mysteries.

Whatever exists between them, Garganafan continued, *the boy can still be tested. If there is a Vahlken locked inside of him, unleashing it would prove instrumental in preparing his heart for the bond.*

Kassanda wasn't entirely convinced. **What if it's his blood? For** *all we know, it's the Vahlken magic in his veins that is preventing him from bonding.*

While that is a possibility, Garganafan agreed, his inherent wisdom shining through, *we both know that boy is not worthy of an egg yet. We can but train him and send him into the world once more. He must have a chance to prove himself.*

As ever, it was damned hard to argue with the dragon's logic.

We test him then.

Indeed.

Pushing off from the enormous door frame, the Rider donned her hood to provide her clean scalp with some protection from the elements. Before walking out onto the vast floor inside the towering horseshoe, Kassanda tapped into the bond that tethered her to Garganafan. She couldn't see the dragon from her position, but she knew where he was in the world, her eyes drawn up to the grey clouds that blanketed the sky.

Just knowing where he was always put confidence in her step, and so she walked out into the pale light of late morning and made her way to Joran and Oaken. She had given the boy two days to get his bearings and recover from their arduous journey to Drakanan and his near-death encounter with a wild adolescent dragon.

The time for resting was at an end.

"Tell him to fly away," she instructed when she was close enough that the wind wouldn't steal her voice from the air.

Joran turned around, noting her command before regarding the Aegre again. "He is wounded," the boy reported.

Kassanda tilted her head to scrutinise the torn sheets of chain-mail and red gashes that raked the creature's side. Garganafan's doing, the result of his claws dragging the Aegre from the lofty nest.

"He's lucky," she opined, echoing her companion's feelings on the matter. "There is none among his kind who could stand up to Garganafan. Now tell him to fly away—his presence will not be required today."

It was with some reluctance that Joran stepped back from Oaken and threw his arm out high. He ordered the creature to take off and received naught but a blank stare in return. He gave the command again, his neck craned to meet the Aegre's sharp yellow eyes. Nothing. Oaken retracted his head a notch when the order was given a third time, but he made no move to take off.

With a look somewhere between embarrassment and confusion, Joran turned to Kassanda with a shrug. "He won't go," he pointed out needlessly.

Kassanda didn't even need to ask, her feelings enough to prompt Garganafan's arrival. The dragon pierced the thick canopy, his considerable bulk pushing the clouds aside before his speed sucked them back up in his wake. Without the Rider in her saddle, he was able to plummet at a velocity that would have robbed her of consciousness. To that end, the bone-white dragon impacted the ground behind Oaken only seconds later, his landing enough to shake the earth.

It was with practised effort that Kassanda concealed her smile.

Garganafan's cool blue eyes had barely landed on the Aegre before he flapped his great wings and took off. Aggressive as their mutated kind were known to be, it seemed they possessed intelligence enough to know when they were outmatched—especially when wounded.

Joran watched Oaken fly as high as the surrounding cliffs before turning to face Kassanda. "He could be of use," he argued.

"Oaken's part in this war remains to be seen," the Rider told him. "As does yours." She began to circle the boy, her hand resting on the hilt of her silvyr blade. "Your training begins today," she explained, coming to a stop when she could see Drakanan behind him. "But first, I would know more of the clay I am to mould. You will meet me up there." Kassanda's dark eyes flitted up to the highest point of the horseshoe's southern curve.

Joran's mouth fell ajar as he took in the scale of the cliff. "How do I get up there?" he asked.

Kassanda waited until the boy was looking at her again. "You climb," she said simply.

Again, Joran took in the snow-covered cliff face and its jagged edges. "Climb," he repeated absently.

"I would be on with it," the Rider recommended. "It will snow before nightfall. When that happens, you will lose sight of your surroundings—you will be stuck, unable to climb up *or* down."

With more than a note of apprehension, Joran blurted. "Are there any ropes? Hooks?"

Kassanda began to stride towards Garganafan. "Your hands and feet are the only tools you can ever rely on. They will suffice." Without another word, she scaled her dragon's side, using one of the long straps that bound the saddle to his back.

Shall we? she spoke into their bond.

Garganafan crouched his powerful legs, his wings flexing out to his sides. Joran's hair and dusty cloak were blown out behind him when those magnificent wings fanned the air, taking the dragon clear from the ground. Kassanda gripped the handles that had been moulded out of the saddle, her belt already clipped to the hard leather in two places.

It was a short journey to the top of the cliff but exhilarating as always. In nearly seven hundred years, she had yet to experience any flight astride Garganafan that wasn't breathtaking. Unlike immortality, a gift of dragonkind that could only be appreciated over swathes of time, defying gravity and soaring through the heavens was a gift that always quickened the heart.

Using supplies and provisions from the many packs strapped to her saddle, Kassanda went about setting up a makeshift camp atop the cliff. The wind would have swept the flames of her fire away had Garganafan not curled his body around the site. It sheltered the Rider and gave her some time to sit and wait in peace.

She spent the subsequent hours reading one of the old tomes she had been carrying in her saddle bag for near on six months —*The Life of Vagandrad*, a Dragon Rider from before her time. Kassanda enjoyed the read with some cooked rabbit, her head resting against her dragon's pale scales. All the while, she noted an absence in the back of her mind. She knew the feeling well.

What are you not saying? she eventually asked him.

Garganafan stirred, his tail flicking up as his head tilted to lay one of his eyes on her. *You are deliberately distracting yourself.*

Kassanda looked out beyond the cliff edge, where only the sky could be seen. The light was dimming, and the clouds were beginning to sprinkle the realm in snow. It would be dark soon, and the snow would only get worse. Looking to the southern tip of the horseshoe, there was still no sign of Joran.

He will make it, she remarked. *Or he won't. His life is in his hands. It can be no other way.*

I am not talking about the boy, Garganafan replied, his gaze looming over her. *You are yet to acknowledge Androma's fate.*

Kassanda said nothing, her attention drawn conveniently to the flames.

Joran's description of the battle has but one conclusion, Garganafan reasoned. *Androma did well to survive all that she did after Maegar's passing. She deserves to be mourned, to be worthy of your grief.*

She deserves to be avenged, Kassanda corrected.

Perhaps, Garganafan accepted, *but that should not prevent you from coming to terms with her death.*

Again, Kassanda fell into silence, her emotions confined to a very small place in her mind, a place where even she would struggle to access them.

We have been here a long time, the dragon went on. *It is natural to feel lonely.*

A fraction of our life, Kassanda countered, *and even less than what's to come. Besides, I'm never alone,* she added, tapping the dragon with the back of her head.

Being alone *and being* lonely *are two very different things,* Garganafan responded. *You will always long for your own kind, just as I will always long for mine. Androma was our friend for many centuries. You must let yourself feel it, just as the boy feels for the father he has lost.*

Like you did when Aila was lost?

Kassanda regretted her barbed words the moment she gave them life. Fortunately, their bond was more than enough to convey that.

I am a dragon, Garganafan replied without shame. *When my rage burns bright, so too does the land I scorch. I will mourn Aila for many more centuries to come, just as you will for Rhaymion. Just as you must for Androma.*

Kassanda let her mind wander back, unwinding the decades that lay between now and when Baelon had defeated Rhaymion, the Dragonlord, in combat. Garganafan's hadn't been the only rage to burn the earth that fateful day. It was with a mix of emotions that she recalled the blood that had licked her sword—the blood of her fellow Riders. What a mess the world had become.

I have been grieving for Androma since Maegar died, she replied, keenly aware that her friend's immortality had perished with her dragon. *Now that she's gone, I would rather make something of her memory than simply dwell on it. Joran was her legacy. Androma gave her life to see him here. All I can do is honour that sacrifice.*

Hanun arain el mon arain, Kasandai.

Your heart is my heart, Kassanda.

Garganafan spoke the words in her native Dorneese, a reminder that they shared everything, including her memories of the tribe she had once belonged to in the depths of The Greenfold Forest—many lifetimes ago. Kassanda let her head rest against his side. *How do other people get through their lives without a dragon?* she wondered lovingly.

They climb instead of fly, Garganafan told her, his head turning to the southern point of the horseshoe.

Kassanda rose to her feet in time to see Joran's hands grip the edge of the rock. Clearly exhausted, the boy still succeeded in getting his legs over the lip and rolling away from the drop. The Rider approached and came to a stop at his side, her hood billowing about her face as the strong wind tried to take it from her head.

"On your feet," she instructed, her hand held out in invitation.

With a groan, Joran accepted the offer of aid and slowly rose from the ground. Kassanda took the opportunity to grab his arm, her fingers deliberately finding the tear in his shirt so she might feel the exposed skin.

He's warm to the touch, she said across their bond.

He carries the mutation then, Garganafan reasoned.

But to what extent? Ilithranda could have made that climb in half the time and gone on to slay a Mountain Troll.

He is still young and untested, the dragon pointed out as Kassanda and Joran made their way towards the fire. *As far as I know, there has never been a Vahlken child before. There's no telling how and when his mother's mutations will take effect.*

Kassanda thought of the instances in life where one's instincts were forced to reveal themselves. **Perhaps he needs pushing, then.**

"Drink this," she suggested, thrusting a waterskin into Joran's hands. There was still water in his mouth when she drew the extra sword she always had strapped to her saddle. "Take this." The Rider tossed the weapon at the boy, unimpressed by the way he dodged it rather than even trying to catch it. "Pick it up."

Looking quite bewildered, Joran swapped the waterskin for the sword and stepped away from the fire, mimicking Kassanda's steps. "Now?" he asked in disbelief.

"Your enemies will never give you time to rest," the Rider informed him.

"I can barely lift it," he complained.

"We shall see."

Her ominous reply was followed by a leaping attack. In the same fluid movement, she freed her silvyr sword of its scabbard and cleaved the air.

Joran naturally fell back in a bid to evade her, his poor footing more than enough to see him trip and twist to land on his shoulder. He cried out in pain, though it was not his shoulder but his leg that caused his suffering. Kassanda tilted her head and saw that the broken sword tucked into his belt had bitten into his thigh.

"Again," she commanded, returning to her starting position. "And you can get rid of that," she added, gesturing at the jagged sword with her own exquisite dwarven-forged blade.

On his feet again, Joran rubbed his injured leg before removing the broken sword from his belt. "I can't get rid of this," he protested.

"Don't be sentimental," she dictated. "It will only hold you back."

"I'm not being sentimental," the boy countered with irritation. "It's a weapon of power," he declared, holding it up so the firelight danced along the steel.

Garganafan's head lifted into the air, giving Joran a look of unease as he stood under those powerful jaws. *A weapon of power,* the dragon echoed, a note of awe behind his curiosity.

"It doesn't look like a weapon of power to me," Kassanda voiced for both of them. "They're said to be indestructible."

Joran tore his eyes from Garganafan to address the Rider. "I used it at the ruins," he explained. "It turned the Andarens to ash."

That sounds like power to me, the dragon remarked.

"To ash?" Kassanda queried, her doubt still audible.

"It looked a little different," Joran admitted. "The glyphs shone as if there was a fire inside the steel."

"And how did you come by it?" Kassanda enquired, a part of her undeniably hungry to possess so great a weapon.

"Gallien gave it to me."

"The smuggler? He *just gave* it to you?"

"He was already wielding the axe—another weapon of power," the boy added, as if it was common knowledge.

"An axe?" The Rider looked up at her companion, sensing his own excitement.

Weapons, Garganafan said eagerly. *Like The Anther.*

Kassanda acknowledged her dragon's comment, her desire to use the weapons against Baelon and his fellow traitors rising to the surface. "You're saying the smuggler possessed not one but *two* weapons of power?"

"The dwarf had one as well," Joran reported.

"Mordrith?" Kassanda had pulled the name from deep memory. "She was wielding the hammer?"

The boy shook his head. "She had a pair of axes—*huge* axes."

Again, Kassanda used her bond with Garganafan to pull another name from decades past. "Yamnomora, then," she corrected herself.

Joran's expression creased into confusion. "The other was a male dwarf. He was the one with the hammer. It had a blue glow about it."

Kassanda had again met Garganafan's eyes when something occurred to her—something she had failed to ask Joran in the excitement of his arrival.

"Androma would often travel with a companion," she explained. "An old man, a wizard. Was he—"

"The Green Leaf," Joran said, seizing Kassanda all the more.

"He was with you? Atop the ruins?"

"He was," Joran answered, albeit with a touch of grief.

The Rider turned away from the boy. *The Green Leaf possessed the vambrace,* she said into her bond with Garganafan. *That's three weapons of power in the same place.*

The dragon's head lowered a notch. *Kassanda,* he intoned, *if they perished in those ruins, then the weapons are in one of two places: among the dead or in the hands of the Andarens.*

Kassanda sheathed her sword and hurriedly gathered what supplies had been left about the fire. "Give me that," she ordered, taking back the extra blade from the boy.

"What's happening?" he asked with some concern.

Garganafan exhaled a sharp breath through his nostrils and extinguished the flames of the small fire.

"You should have mentioned the weapons of power two days ago," Kassanda chastised. "We make for The Ruins of Gelakor. With any luck, the Andarens have overlooked the weapons."

Joran's face dropped, as if he could already see the dead that awaited them. "We're leaving right now?"

"I would not delay any longer than we already have. The true power of those weapons is their ability to unbalance any war. I would bring them to bear against our enemy." Kassanda paused before ascending Garganafan, her eyes drawn to the broken blade. "I would take that for safekeeping."

Joran withdrew the weapon from her sight. "Gallien gave it to *me,*" he said quietly.

"And now you're giving it to me."

The boy retreated a step. "It's safe with me."

Do not push him, the dragon counselled. *For all we know, he is meant to wield the blade.*

He's meant **to wield the blade of a Dragon Rider,** Kassanda responded, her attention still on Joran. **He'll never reach that end if he's killed over a weapon of power.**

Garganafan tightened the cord of their bond, drawing out the unsaid truth. *That is not your reason for wanting the weapon. I see what you would do with it. What you would do with them all. The Skaramangians and their ill will are the enemy of us all. Baelon Vos can wait.*

Kassanda retracted her waiting hand. "Fine," she said to Joran and Garganafan alike. "But know the worth of what you possess, for there are others who will—others who would *take* it from you."

"I will protect it with my life," Joran vowed.

"No," Kassanda was quick to interject. "I do not warn you to protect the blade, but yourself. You are fated to bring about a time of dragons. Your destiny is worth more than any weapon of power. Should it ever come to it, choose your life over the sword."

Joran nodded hesitantly, his understanding of the matter evidently unclear. Kassanda chalked it up to naivety if not outright immaturity. Despite his harsh and dangerous upbringing, his youth was there to see. A babe in the midst of immortals.

How fragile the future was.

16

LEGION

0 Years Ago...

4

Daijen slowly rose from his battle stance, though his hand remained firmly gripped to the hilt of his sabre.

That voice. Those words. It had been fifteen years since he had heard them but his memory would never let them go.

The towering Skaramangian removed his helmet with one hand and tossed it away. There was a familiar grin waiting beneath, and so wicked it was.

"Slait."

The name escaped Daijen's lips like a blunt hammer fall.

Somehow, that terrible grin broadened across his pale face. "Don't send a messenger guard to do the work of a Vahlken," he declared, his hands now clasping the front of his belt.

Daijen spared himself a moment to scrutinise the once initiate of Ka'vairn—the psychopathic fool who had single-handedly diminished their order. The exile who had seen his brothers and sisters as his lessers. The betrayer who had slain Kastiek—the worst of his crimes.

He now stood before the Vahlken a sentinel of the Skaramangians, though he still wore the many scars of that fateful day in the eyries. His face was a patchwork, as if it had been cobbled together from numerous others. He still favoured a clean scalp, his pointed ears plain to see. So too was his rage, always simmering behind a cruel smile.

Hanging from his belt, as it did the clerics', was a small but thick copy of the Arkalon. It was the only book Daijen had ever seen Slait read during their many years together. How fitting that he should now be in the service of the clerics, a mask worn by the Skaramangians.

"Murderer," Daijen seethed, deciding that he would add more than one to the tally of dead.

Slait had the audacity to bark a laugh. "Is it murder to butcher animals?" he countered. "They were every one of them a heathen, a living blasphemy against the gods."

"They were your brothers and sisters!" Daijen yelled at him. "We were supposed to fight side by side, not against each other! I will see you answer for your crimes," he vowed.

"Crimes?" Slait fired back. "Says the one breaking into the throne room," he pointed out, gesturing at the grandeur about them. "You thought you were being so sneaky, hmm?" He laughed again and tapped his temple. "I know how you think, Runt. What was your plan? Infiltrate the tower and assassinate the emperor himself?"

"No." The word rang out, but not from Daijen's lips. "He was coming for *me*."

Slait moved aside to reveal the master cleric crossing the bridge, his usual entourage at his back—including the Helm of Ahnir on a plush blue cushion. Still attired in the same red robes as his fellow grand clerics, the one known as The Eldan entered the circle. How at ease he was, a testament to how safe he felt beside Slait. It angered Daijen all the more, stabbing at his pride.

"Well," The Eldan went on tauntingly, "here I am."

"The *apprentice*," Daijen intoned, translating the Skaramangian's title.

Golden eyes narrowed inside the ornate helm.

Quite sure of his abilities, Daijen knew he could free the dagger strapped to his right thigh and launch it at the wretch before he could even blink. That would bring an end to it. But he was also quite sure of Slait's abilities, for his body had been moulded by Handuin and his skills honed by Kastiek. The odds that he would intercept the blade before it could kill his new master were too high.

That left the Vahlken with little choice. He was going to have to slaughter every one of them and kill the Skaramangian snake up close.

"This isn't right," The Eldan announced, surprising Daijen with his conversational tone. "The Valtorak shouldn't have sent you to do what *he* cannot. And to send you as an assassin! It is beneath a Vahlken. You have been gifted a great power, and not by Handuin but by the gods themselves. Is it not the bones of Ahnir Himself that have elevated you? You are wasted at the beck and call of Ka'vairn."

Daijen offered The Eldan a wolfish grin of his own. "Your forked tongue won't bend my ear like it has his," he remarked, his blue eyes flitting to Slait and back. "I completed my training. I earned the *truth*."

The Eldan said nothing for a time, merely regarding the Vahlken. "The *truth*," he echoed. "Whatever *pieces* of the truth your order clings to, I can assure you, Daijen Saeth, you know little of our purpose in the world." He chuckled inside his mask. "You don't even know the meaning of *Pendain*. You think it's just a name?" He shook his head. "You're not just lost, you're misinformed. Join us and be a *part* of the truth."

"I know you would raise the Dark Ones," Daijen told him confidently. "Just as I know your true title is Eldan, not master cleric."

"I wondered what you might have learned from your trip to Nareene," The Eldan replied, his fingers clasped at his waist. "You did well to survive. I suppose I should thank you for that. New measures have been taken to ensure the site's continued security."

Daijen looked to Slait. "He doesn't deny it. The Skaramangians are not aligned with the gods. You're working to bring back the ones who destroyed them."

Slait responded with a pitying smile. "Our mission is reclamation," he stated. "We will bring back the gods and rebuild the heavens. But there is only one power in all the realm that will bring life back into their bones: the Eikor! When the Dark Ones walk again, the gods will return to repel them, only this time, we will fight beside them. The gods will not perish again," he vowed. "I see now how the Vahlken have meddled with those divine plans. How Handuin was corrupted by his grab for power."

Daijen could see it now. The Skaramangians had preyed upon his faith, upon his delusions and fantasies. Slait was a weapon to be wielded, and The Eldan knew exactly how to pull his strings. It also meant The Eldan would never divulge anything of the truth in front of the behemoth, lest the spell of manipulation be broken.

"You've leashed him well," Daijen concluded, his comment aimed at The Eldan—a fact that clearly outraged Slait. "I don't know what you really think there is to be gained from raising the Dark Ones, but I know I'm going to stop you. I'm not going to rest until your cult is dust."

The Eldan sighed inside his winged helm, his head shaking in disappointment. "I came here to bargain. You see, we each have something of the other's. I would have traded, but I see now that is to be impossible. The Valtorak has his talons in you."

Daijen frowned. "Trade?"

"Of course. You have a piece of Ahnir locked up inside that fortress of yours. Then there's the vambrace that has recently come into your possession," he added, revealing that the Skaramangians had also learned something from their trip to Nareene. "We require both," he continued. "I would have acquired them without blood, but..."

A chasm was slowly beginning to open inside Daijen. "You

would have me retrieve them," he deduced. "And traded them for what?" he asked, desperate to know what hung in the balance.

"For her life, of course," The Eldan replied, the answer obvious to him. "You see my man by the door? I have only to give the signal, and he will relay a message to those guarding Ilithranda's room. They tell me she sleeps like the dead. Even the legendary Vahlken are vulnerable while they slumber. But," he declared theatrically, "I can see you are not be bartered with. Too much bad blood, I suppose," he added, glancing at Slait. "We will kill you both and take what is rightfully ours."

His casual decree came with a flick of his wrist—the signal given to the man at the door. Simultaneously, Slait took one eager step towards Daijen, but his master held him back with a gesture.

"Take him to the brink of death," came the command. "I would like him to see the future before he dies."

Daijen followed The Eldan's gaze, which led him to the Helm of Ahnir, sitting idly on its cushion. The Skaramangian leader used the momentary distraction to slink away, retreating beyond the bridge with his entourage.

As one, the surrounding cleric guard assumed the same battle stance, their swords tipped towards the Vahlken.

"I trained them myself," Slait boasted, his own weapon yet to be retrieved from its scabbard. "Make him bleed!" he growled.

Daijen's mind should have been in that quiet place, the centre of the storm where the chaos of the world couldn't distract him. It was from that place that Kastiek had taught him to operate as a warrior, a keen device of Death itself.

But he was off balance. Besides his frustrating interaction with The Eldan and an unexpected reunion with his most hated enemy, Ilithranda's life was in jeopardy. He was envisioning a Skaramangian assassin slitting her throat while she slept instead of calculating the angles of defence and counter-attack that would see him live beyond the next sixty seconds.

The same muscle memory that saw him survive Dorgarath's hanging bones had him draw his sabre before the first attack.

A flourish of steel and a flick of his wrist batted not one but four incoming swords away. Distracted as he was, however, he failed to block a fifth blade that swiped across his cuirass. The silk of the Weavers kept the biting edge from splitting his skin, but the force of the blow remained a painful one that would bruise his chalky skin. It also staggered him, sending the Vahlken into a kick that reversed his direction.

Flung into a trio of Skaramangians, it was instinct that allowed Daijen to deflect two slashing blades and even deliver a sharp elbow to one of his opponents, but the kick that had shoved him into the fight also skewed his footing. The result was a stinging swipe of the third blade, the steel slicing through the edge of the leather armour protecting his right thigh. Daijen gave a stifled cry and dropped to one knee, positioning him perfectly for another kick.

The boot caught him square in the chest and flipped him onto his back. Most would have lain there, defeated and at the mercy of the many. But Daijen Saeth was not one to be counted amongst the majority. He was one of few to have been trained by Kastiek, to have fought and slain Dragon Riders, and to have delved into the dark depths of Skaramangian hell and survived.

He was a Vahlken.

It fell to him, and him alone, to remind them all of that cold, hard fact.

Flipping deftly back onto his feet, he did so now with his sabre and atori short-sword in hand. Crouched like a predator braced to spring, he took the measure of his foes. They had naught but their dulled wits to guide their swords, their mundane senses a barrier their skills could not surpass. The same could not be said of any Vahlken.

Like a pale demon, he rained hell upon his enemy. He would spin one way before pivoting the other, his two blades delivering a degree of fury no ordinary Andaren could handle. He batted aside their weapons and flicked his short-sword across throats and arteries, his every attack pre-calculated and executed with precision.

Within seconds of finding his feet, four of their number lay dead at his feet. Pressed by vengeance, if not their need to impress Slait, the rest of them tried to overwhelm him. Much like the first four, Daijen laid their plans to rest.

The first to strike was relieved of his blade before suffering the plunging attack of an atori blade to the heart. The Vahlken danced around his falling body, intercepted two incoming blows with his sabre, and kicked one of the guards so hard they folded in half and flew beyond the moat.

Hearing the distinct sound of steel cutting through the air, Daijen ducked under the unseen attack and spun on his knees to swipe his sabre across his enemy's midriff. Jumping to his feet, he blocked the sword of another and hammered the pommel of his atori blade into the Skaramangian's mask. The first blow knocked him back, but the second blow, fuelled by Vahlken strength, caved the plated mask into the guard's face. Blood shot forth from the eye and nose holes before Daijen created a brand new hole in his gut.

Seeing the last three beyond his dead and malleable foe, the Vahlken kept the corpse on his sabre and used him like a battering ram. Taken by surprise, one of the three was run through by the protruding blade, creating a skewer out of the elegant weapon.

The remaining two leaped at him, determined to be the ones to bring him down and win their leader's favour. Handuin's magic kept Daijen one step ahead, allowing him to parry both blades, one after the other, before executing a three strike manoeuvre that chopped through the leg of one, sliced the hip of another, and delivered a devastating backhand with the atori blade that sliced through iron and skull.

With blood spilling out of his ragged hip, the surviving member of Slait's students was already crawling away from the Vahlken. He whimpered and groaned as he came to terms with his impending doom. But it was not by Daijen's sword that he met that end. Before he could, Slait plunged his scimitar down through the guard's spine, delivering instant death.

"Pathetic," he muttered.

Streaked with the blood of his foes, Daijen strode towards the betrayer. "You're next."

A broad smile broke out across Slait's face. How familiar it was to Daijen, and always a prelude to an explosive attack. It was that kind of knowledge that prevented Slait's leaping thrust attack from spearing Daijen. Instead, the blade was rolled aside while the Vahlken pivoted around and threw up an elbow into the side of his enemy's head.

Slait took the impact and turned it into a forward roll between the strewn bodies. Daijen was of no mind to give him the space he sought and pressed his attack, coming at his foe with an onslaught of spinning blades. He forced Slait back step after step until he was by the edge of the island and on the verge of falling into the moat.

Proving his technique was just as balletic as Daijen's, Slait made the graceful leap to the other side and even parried the Vahlken's subsequent barrage as he followed him across the water. There they clashed, steel against steel, as they steadily rounded the moat and came upon the dais that supported the Empyreal Throne.

Fighting Slait was nothing like fighting the cleric guard. The betrayer's intimate knowledge of the Vahlken allowed him to anticipate Daijen's attacks and counterstrikes. Likewise, Daijen saw all his blows coming, recognising the way Slait would move fluidly through the plethora of combat techniques Kastiek had drilled into them. The only thing left to either of them was their environment, though how it could be used to their advantage came down to personal ingenuity.

Coming alongside the three chairs allocated to the imperial wives, Daijen sliced through the top of one and delivered a spinning back kick that launched the chunk of wood into Slait's head. He was able to dodge the unorthodox missile but not the jumping knee Daijen slammed into his chest. The betrayer hit the polished floor and slid several feet on his back before rolling his feet over his head to spring back into action.

He met Daijen at a sprint, his speed in such a short space unattainable by any ordinary Andaren. The Vahlken was still able to intercept the flurry of strikes and keep steel from touching flesh. Slait had pushed him back, though, giving him access to the steps that led up to the throne. He leaped and pushed off one of those steps and came back at Daijen with a pommel to the jaw. The force of it, if not the pain, was enough to turn the Vahlken around, where he suffered a battering shoulder barge to the back.

While his sabre was flung out from his grip, Daijen's atori blade was thrown forwards, beyond the circular pool in which he landed with an unceremonious *splash*. Before he could come up for air, there came a second *splash*. Slait heaved him up by his throat and slammed his head into Daijen's brow the moment he broke the surface. Before he could recover, the betrayer hammered his face with a knotted fist, sending him briefly underwater again.

Daijen wrapped his legs around Slait's waist, putting him off balance while dragging him down. There beneath the water, the titans of Handuin grappled for supremacy. But all it took was one misstep on the pool's smooth floor and Slait was suddenly behind Daijen, his arms coiled around the Vahlken's neck. It was a vice from which there was no escape, and so he was forced to breach the surface, where The Eldan stood waiting.

"You have fought well, Daijen Saeth. You have a tenacity worthy of Handuin himself. But, like your creator, you lack the strength to see our war to its end. Take heart, good Vahlken, for you will see that end before you join Handuin in the Black Abyss."

Daijen's attention was turned to the Helm of Ahnir, which The Eldan had personally carried across the throne room. He thought of the thousands who had donned the helm in that very pool. Was he to be one of them? Another line in the great tally? Deciding he wouldn't be, that his fight wouldn't be over until the war itself was dead, he writhed and struggled in Slait's grip, the water splashing about them.

"Hold him still," The Eldan commanded.

Slait's grip tightened all the more, reducing Daijen's ability to breathe, though he retained enough of his senses to observe the helm drawing nearer in The Eldan's hands while his entourage watched from afar.

Blood splattered across Daijen's face, forcing him to blink and miss the moment a Vahlken sabre shot through The Eldan's leg. The Skaramangian yelled in agony and dropped to the floor.

In his absence, Ilithranda could clearly be seen on the far side of the island, her bronze atori blade whipping left and right as she dispatched the grand clerics with brutal efficiency. Daijen could only imagine what she had left in her wake, though he had no doubt her room was currently occupied by dead Skaramangian assassins.

Her violent intervention had been enough to not only cripple The Eldan but also surprise Slait, evident from the slackening tension around Daijen's throat. Seeing that this was potentially his only opportunity to break free and complete his grim objective, the Vahlken threw his arm back and over his head, his hand gripping the side of Slait's face. A thumb to his enemy's eye made the betrayer squirm, turning him away from Daijen's clawing hand. It also put his right ear neatly inside the Vahlken's grasp. With one sharp tug, he ripped the ear free of Slait's head.

Slait roared with pain and released Daijen to clutch at his bleeding wound. As instructed, the Vahlken gave no quarter. Snapping about, Daijen grabbed Slait by the collar and pulled him in so he might feel the full force of his pummelling elbow. Three times he struck Kastiek's murderer, his strength increasing with each blow until Slait was no more than a floating body in a bloody pool.

The Eldan yelped, dragging Daijen's attention back around. The wretch was trying to crawl away, Ilithranda's sabre still lodged in his bleeding leg. The Vahlken tore through the water, his powerful legs ploughing through the resistance to take him up the steps and tower over The Eldan.

Retrieving his atori short-sword, a glance was enough to inform Daijen that Ilithranda was only seconds away from annihilating the last of the clerics. It was within that growing pile of death that he would see his deed to its end.

"What are you doing?" The Eldan cried, helpless to stop the Vahlken from dragging him by the heel.

"I'm going to extend you the same courtesy," Daijen replied, pausing to scoop up the Helm of Ahnir.

With a blast of strength, he tossed The Eldan into the heart of the island, the very middle of the broken circle of House Lhoris. The sounds of his agony pierced the chamber, drowning out the last breath of Ilithranda's final victim.

"Please," The Eldan pleaded, sensing his approaching doom.

Ilithranda ignored the snake and yanked her sabre free, eliciting another stark cry from the Skaramangian. The weapon removed, his wound began to bleed in earnest, a fact that his pressing hands could not stop.

"Was that Slait?" she questioned incredulously.

"This one dies first," Daijen vowed, placing his boot over the wound so his weight might add new dimensions of pain. "I've been watching you closely," he said when the man's screams died down. "You slaughtered the servants at the mere mention of the Eikor. That makes sense to me. You were protecting your secret. But the mention of a time of dragons rattled you. I saw it in your eyes."

"You saw nothing!" The Eldan spat.

Daijen's hand snapped out and ripped the helmet from The Eldan's head, revealing the Andaren beneath. There was nothing significant about him, his features those of all of his kin. If anything, he had the most forgettable face.

"We already know you fear the dragons. We know you manufactured the war—in part—to eliminate them. I imagine a *time* of dragons was not in the future you've been preparing for."

The Eldan gave his best expression of defiance. "You're so lost, little Vahlken."

Daijen let a bit more of his weight press down, drawing out a *hiss* of pain from the man. "Why do you fear dragons so? They weren't a threat until *you* started the war. Tell me *why!*" he yelled in his face.

It was, perhaps, the strength of his belief that formed The Eldan's next words. "There's nothing you can do. His return has been seen a thousand times over. The Pendain has been *seen.*"

There it was again, and from the mouth of The Eldan instead of an insane old woman or some obscure premonition. There was a *man* at the heart of the Skaramangian conspiracy. But who was he and what was his connection to the Dark Ones? That aside, The Eldan's mention of the one called Pendain confounded Daijen, drawing his brow into a furrowed knot.

"The Pendain," he echoed. "The one who will *stop* the war?"

The Vahlken failed to put the pieces together. Why would The Eldan speak of the one fated to bring about a time of dragons as if it was a good thing?

The Skaramangian began to laugh, and maniacally so. "Even when you hear the future, you still can't see it for what it is!"

Those barbed words stung Daijen's pride, tensing the muscles around his jaw. He had heard enough. "You're right," he agreed ominously. "Maybe I need to hear it one more time."

The Eldan's face dropped, and only a moment later, Daijen shoved the Helm of Ahnir onto his head. Frantically, he tried to remove it, his fingers desperately grasping at the rim, but Daijen prevented him, if only for a second. That was all that was needed to enthral him, snatching his mind from the present and hurling him into the future.

"Cast into the black, he drowns in shadow," came The Eldan's last words. "The Drakalis is without sight. He is without voice. He is to suffer for his betrayal, he who should have reigned beside the Pendain. But the darkness cannot hold him. His chains are destined to be broken by the power of Handuin. Break the crystal, break the world! Break the crystal, break the world! Break the crystal—"

Daijen didn't wince this time. He didn't even blink.

The helm clattered as it hit the floor and rolled to the Vahlken's feet, its interior slick with The Eldan's remains. What was left of his body lay motionless on the floor in an ever-growing pool of blood.

"What have you done?" Ilithranda uttered. "He could have told us more."

You didn't stop me, he thought, but he didn't voice it. "He was always going to take their secrets into death," he said instead.

The sound of splashing water turned both Vahlken to the ceremonial pool at the base of the throne. Slait was clambering out, a nasty and bloody gash oozing above his right eye. When he saw The Eldan, headless and disgraced at Daijen's feet, the roar that erupted from his lips was feral, a sound fuelled by blinding and righteous rage.

At the same time, the entrance to the throne room was filled with a swarming mass of palace guards. They froze upon sighting the many dead at the feet of the two Vahlken. Worse, they quickly realised the dead were grand clerics.

With blood running free from his torn ear, Slait tried to rise fully from the steps of the pool and staggered, his recent head injury yet to abate. "Heresy!" he bellowed, pointing at the Vahlken. "They have murdered the master cleric!"

There was a moment, it seemed, where the palace guard weighed up their numbers in the face of two Vahlken. While they hesitated, Ilithranda gave Daijen a clear instruction.

"Run!"

Following closely in her wake, Daijen was slowed only by his brief pause to retrieve the bloody Helm of Ahnir. He heard Slait roar in objection, a distant sound as the pair sprinted towards the tall, slender windows set above the hidden side doors. Ilithranda led the way, relying on her superior strength to make the leap up and through the nearest window. She fell into the night, unaware that Daijen had paused to find purchase on the lip of the frame rather than follow her down.

He looked back at the throne room, at the charging palace guard and the massacre beyond them. The Vahlken was about to let himself go when he noticed a figure in red rising amidst the dead clerics. It was another of their order, one who had been sly enough to play dead in the chaos of Ilithranda's attack. The cunning cleric crouched down and picked up the winged bronze helm that had sat on The Eldan's head. In one smooth move, he removed his own mask and donned the helm of the master cleric.

Daijen knew then that he had cut off the head only for it to be replaced by another before the body was even cold.

What could he do against such legion?

Added to that legion was Slait, an indiscriminate killing machine, a weapon in the hands of the Skaramangians. It felt a personal insult that the enemy would wield the power of Handuin. An insult he would see repaid tenfold. His time having run down, Daijen was forced to make the leap before the palace guard got close enough to hurl their swords at him. He fell back from the window, a chasm tearing through his insides.

Again, the enemy had suffered a blow yet somehow left Daijen feeling his victory was naught but hollow.

17
PLAYING THE ODDS

It was with quiet and measured steps that Gallien Pendain journeyed through The Silver Trees of Akmar. Strange and wonderful as it was, it felt alive, as if the forest was watching them, waiting for them to lower their guard.

The smuggler couldn't help himself. After hours of walking between the trees, he finally succumbed to his curiosity. Stepping over one of the shiny roots, he reached out for the silver bark. To his astonishment, it felt like any other tree. He had expected something more akin to steel, given its appearance.

The bark was not all that drew him in. Running like veins between the natural cracks in the bark was a silver liquid. It was running *up* the tree. With a single finger, he pressed between the cracks and withdrew a droplet. The liquid was thick, reminding him of sap as he rubbed it with his thumb. To his astonishment, the liquid began to gather on the end of his finger. The droplet reformed, and the silver liquid was sucked back into the tree by unseen forces.

Stepping back, Gallien tracked the unusual sap down the trunk and along the roots until he determined that the tree was drawing up the silver liquid from deep underground.

"'Tis the bones," The Green Leaf uttered, coming up on the smuggler's side. "The site lies at the heart of the forest. From there, the magic in the bones has interfered with nature."

Gallien surveyed the wizard beside him. It had been two days since they had descended the cliffs and entered The Silver Trees of Akmar. Two nights of rest had been good for the old man. His brief but overwhelming interaction with the smuggler appeared to be subsiding. Less and less were they finding him staring into nothingness, muttering unintelligibly under his breath. Gallien had refrained from asking him too many questions where his father was concerned, lest the memories shatter Aphrandhor's mind all the more.

Still, it had been all Gallien could think about. His father —*alive*. More than anything, he wished to quash the spark of hope in him. It was easier to live with the belief that he was long dead than it was to think he might see him again. And how might they find him? Taraktor was so foul a place that even Androma argued for another path. If he had been there for years—decades, even— and in the hands of wicked wizards no less, there was every chance the man they found would be a shell of Bragen Pendain.

Dead, alive, broken beyond repair. Gallien knew that he could not go on without knowing the truth anymore.

"Have you ever touched one?" he asked the wizard, looking from the bracer to the trees about them.

"No," Aphrandhor replied at length. "These trees are likely older than their ordinary kin. It is widely theorised amongst the Jainus that the bones have preserved the forest beyond its normal lifespan. Were I to touch one," he explained, "I might never wake from its memories."

"Why do you risk so much by wearing it?"

The Green Leaf regarded Gallien for a moment, his lips pouting and twisting in thought beneath his beard. "If I am not wearing it, others will," he answered wearily. "I have seen what it can do to the strongest of us. I would not have anyone else bear my burden."

The dark of night came to life as a fireball hurled overhead. The subsequent crash turned the company to the west, though they could not see the explosion or the damage it had undoubtedly wrought.

Gallien moved away from the wizard to stand by a different tree, his ear directed towards the heart of the forest. It was distant, but he could hear the sound of magic being discharged and the muffled cries of the dying.

Not distant enough, he thought.

"How long until we reach the southern border?" he demanded.

Standing beside Androma—who had taken their moment of rest as an opportunity to sit on one of the roots—was the striking form of a Kedradi ranger, his right boot propped high on a rock. It seemed so natural for the man to assume a pose taken right out of legend or myth, as if he embodied the heroes of old. Cob adjusted his grip on his bow and glanced at Aphrandhor, specifically his wounded leg.

"Another day and night. Maybe two."

"We are not yet halfway," The Green Leaf reported. "Until we get beyond the site, we risk an altercation with both sides of this fight."

Gallien sighed, his head tilting back to bring the silver canopy into view. Through the trees, he could see the tops of the mountains, their path having hugged The Spine to see them skirt around the bulk of the forest.

His attention returning to his companions, he considered what bad luck he had to be grouped with a blind woman and a wounded old man. If they kept to their path, taking the long route around the edges, confrontation seemed inevitable to the smuggler.

"We should cut across," he suggested. "The longer we're in here, the more likely it is we get into a fight we might not win."

Aphrandhor was shaking his head under his green hood. "I would not get any closer to the site than we already are. That is where the Jainus's defences will be strongest and the Andarens' attacks most concentrated."

"You're not thinking like a soldier," Gallien told him. "There were *thousands* of them. They didn't send so many just to attack the site from one side. Very soon, they're going to sweep round and surround the Jainus. When they do that, they will have soldiers spreading out in every direction to safeguard the assault. They *will* find us. We're better taking our chances now, before they get a stronger foothold."

"You're thinking like a smuggler," Cob interjected. "Playing the odds will get you killed."

"You don't win wars by being prudent," Gallien countered, his words an echo of Androma's. "It's time to be *reckless*."

"Gallien is right," the old Rider responded, beating Cob by a second. "The Andarens will seek dominance over the forest. They will do that by securing the perimeter. We *must* be gone from here before they do."

It was clear that the old Rider's words churned something in the wizard, her opinion evidently valued far more than the smuggler's. "Very well," he said reluctantly. "But know this: the Jainus guard these trees with more than magic and Giants. Keep your wits about you. We are trespassers here. We will be treated as such."

That seemed an obvious statement to Gallien, but there was something about Aphrandhor's ominous tone that suggested he was talking about something else. Something specific to the forest. It was enough to bring the axe into his hand, the cold steel filling his grip from nowhere.

———

While Gallien would have happily trekked through the night and made as much progress as possible, the group stopped to eat and sleep, allowing The Green Leaf more time to rest both his mind and his leg. It also gave the Andarens more time to claim ground, but the smuggler kept that observation to himself.

Instead, he followed from the rear while Cob led from the front, taking them on a direct south-westerly path. The heart of the forest would be on their right and dangerously close soon, but the natural gambler among them saw it as their only way through.

And so they advanced on that perilous path through the rising sun and into the afternoon. They paused at intervals, when

Aphrandhor began to fall behind. It was an agonisingly slow pace, however, whenever they got back to it.

Without her staff, Andromapa was forced to use her silvyr blade to explore the ground at her feet. The wizard, on the other hand, leaned on his staff so much the smuggler feared it might snap.

After little progress and a long day, the cold night returned to rob them of their fortitude. It was agreed, if reluctantly so, that they would refrain from starting a fire, lest it attract unwanted attention. Unable to shake the feeling that the trees were watching them, Gallien hated sitting in their embrace—and in the dark, no less. He pulled his leather cloak about him and kept his hood up, though it did little to keep out the cold and the feeling of being observed.

Then there were the distant rumblings, the tremors that ran through the earth. Giants were at work. Gallien imagined what chaos they were causing amongst the Andaren ranks. How many broken bodies littered The Silver Trees of Akmar now? How many Giants lay strewn dead, for that matter? The Andarens hadn't come to take prisoners.

"Your name," Cob questioned suddenly, his deep voice breaking the icy air. "Why Drakalis?"

The smuggler glanced at Andromapa and Aphrandhor, but the pair had slept through the Kedradi's question.

"I don't know," he replied with a shrug, his mind letting go of the distant warfare. "It was something Corben came up with."

"Your brother?"

"Aye. We were the Drakalis boys for some time," he elaborated, his memories bringing an old smile to his face. "I have no idea where he came up with it—a story he heard from Pa, most likely. It just stuck."

The ranger said nothing in response, content to return to silence with his bow propped up between his legs and against one shoulder.

"Can I ask *you* a question?" Gallien eventually said.

"Cob is not my real name," the Kedradi stated, anticipating the question.

The smuggler nodded along. "I was going to ask you why you're such an ass."

The ranger's eyes shifted to land on Gallien. Was there a hint of amusement behind that stony expression?

The smuggler decided to circumnavigate the matter altogether. "So what's your real name?"

Cob let his gaze wander over the forest before returning to their little huddle. "I'll tell you my real name if you tell me where you found that axe."

"I didn't find it," Gallien lied. "Corben did. Said he was somewhere outside of Harendun," he added, knowing a sprinkle of the truth always helped to sell a decent lie. "I took it when he died," he concluded, aware that the addition of a death would make it harder for follow-up questions.

"You weren't with him when he found it?" Cob pressed, proving that he existed outside the norm.

"No," Gallien told him flatly.

The ranger took a moment to absorb the short tale. "What of the sword?" he probed. "We didn't even know it existed, let alone that you were carrying it around in Andromas's satchel."

"Wait, wait, wait. You said you'd tell me your name."

"I said I would tell you my name if you told me where you found the axe," Cob reiterated.

"And I did," Gallien insisted.

"You lied."

The smuggler was taken off guard by the accusation, regardless of how accurate it was. He also didn't have the heart to compound his previous lie with another. "The sword belonged to Kitrana," he said instead. "I have no idea where she found it, but, if I had to guess, I'd say it came from the bottom of the ocean."

Cob looked away, his expression one of subtle revelation. "That explains her indifference to the cold—she's one of *them*."

Gallien lifted his head enough to see the ranger under the lip of his hood. "You know about them, the Nimeans?"

"Nimeans," Cob repeated, testing the name on his tongue. "My people have known about the Mer-folk for generations. I would never have guessed the legends to be true, that they can look like us."

The smuggler withheld his questions regarding the mysterious Kedradi and their legends, his concerns more present. "Why are you talking to me?" he asked bluntly. "You don't like me. You don't trust me. Or is this simply an interrogation?" he posed. "You'd do better buying me a beer."

"You're right," the ranger replied, his answer deliberately obtuse.

Gallien raised his waterskin. "Well, I'll always drink to that."

"I don't like you because you're just passing through," Cob explained. "It's the same reason I don't trust you. You would do and say anything to survive. Even now, you're not committed to this war. You're here to see if your father yet lives."

"I'm here to fight for Joran," Gallien hissed, so as not to wake the others.

"The only good thing you've ever done is take responsibility for that baby," Cob asserted. "But it doesn't change the fact that you chose *him*, not this *life*—not this *war*. Worse, fate has placed a weapon of power in your hands. I fear it will be wasted."

Gallien was about to give him a piece of his mind when the forest came alive around them. A wave of light seemed to wash over the trees, leaving them alight with thousands of twinkling stars. The smuggler was forced to shield his eyes while they adjusted to the brightness.

The spectacle of it drew him to his feet and finally disturbed the others, who were roused from their sleep. Gallien turned on his heel, taking it all in. Every tree, branch, and leaf was aglow with a soft white light, bringing their shadows into the night. Scrutinising the closest tree, he couldn't begin to count the starlight that shone across the surface.

"What is this?" he muttered in awe.

It was then that he noticed Androma's naked sword, the hilt gripped in her hand the moment she awoke. The blade itself was shining with the same starlight effect, a beauty even among the gleaming forest.

"Silvyr," croaked Aphrandhor, the slowest to rise.

"What's happening?" Androma demanded.

"The moon is out."

The old Rider physically relaxed. "You explain it," she sighed, ploughing the sword into the soil.

"The silver, you see," Aphrandhor relayed, a crooked finger gesturing at the trees, "is, in fact, sil*vyr*. For reasons unknown, the trees draw it from wells deep underground."

"Silvyr," Gallien echoed, his eyes now seeing coins where they had previously seen strange trees. "You could buy *Erador* with all this," he mumbled.

"Were it so easy to chop down," the wizard observed.

Gallien waved at the sparkling trees. "Why is it—"

"Silvyr is very reactive to the light of the moon," The Green Leaf went on, always happy to part with knowledge. "Much like the magic that governs this place, the reason for this reaction is unknown."

"It's beautiful," the smuggler whispered, his breath clouding the air.

Beside him, Cob was nocking an arrow. "We are not alone," he warned, bringing Androma to her feet.

"What is it?" she asked, her Dragon Rider blade returned to her grasp.

Gallien searched what little shadow there was between the trees but could not see as the ranger did. That didn't stop the axe from materialising in his hand.

"Wait here," Cob instructed.

"Where are you going?"

But Gallien's question went unanswered as the Kedradi walked off.

With great uncertainty, the trio could do naught but as instructed. They clumped together, back to back, with their weapons in hand, each searching with whatever senses they had for any sign of trouble. Gallien was reminded of the time Cob had peeled away when they were being hunted in The Morn Wood by Slait and his assassins.

"Are we bait?" he asked the other two, disgruntled by the idea.

"Don't underestimate him," Aphrandhor replied, his staff pointed at the trees. "Cob's instincts are rarely wrong."

"It's not his instincts that worry me," the smuggler told them firmly. "It's his methods."

"His methods will keep us alive," Andromo insisted, her sword held upright in both hands.

At a stride, the Kedradi returned to the small clearing, his eyes still scrutinising the forest about them. "I found only tracks, but I think we should move on."

The wizard's head twitched. "Tracks?" he questioned gravely. "What kind of tracks?"

"Horses," Cob reported.

"Andarens?" Aphrandhor was quick to follow up with.

"I wouldn't say so," the ranger answered as he collected some of their scattered sundries. "The tracks belong to horses with only four legs."

The Green Leaf became notably rigid. "Leave it," he snapped at the ranger, preventing him from collecting anything else. "We must leave at once." As fast as his leg would allow, the wizard resumed their south-westerly bearing.

Gallien's head whipped one way then the other as he looked from Aphrandhor to the others. "What's wrong?"

"I told you it was folly to get this close," the old man fired over his shoulder.

"Green Leaf?" Andromo pursued, both verbally and literally.

"Shh!" the wizard hissed. "We must be gone from here, before it's too late."

"What are we running from now?" Gallien probed, falling in behind them.

"You had better pray we're *not* being hunted," Aphrandhor said. "There is no outrunning *them*."

Gallien turned to briefly meet Cob's dark eyes, but there was no clarity to be found there. "Who's *them*?"

It was too late for a response, however, for the answer had already found them.

They attacked as one, their ambush coordinated and executed with precision. So fast was the trap closed on the companions that it took Gallien longer than it should have to realise what foe was upon them.

But there was no mistaking the horror unleashed by the forest. They thundered about the group, their hooves stomping at the ground as they brandished hooked swords, crude bows, and weighty hammers.

Gallien darted left and right to evade their charging entrance, and all the while, his mind could scream but one word.

Centaurs!

18

THE FORTY-FIRST

0 Years Ago...

4

Aran'saur was alight with celebration, its night sky a canvas of colour as the stars competed with the clerics' fireworks. The streets were filled with merriment in the wake of the Ankala, the people's spirits alive with hope that the war would soon be over. That Andara was that much closer to victory.

Little did they know that the real war had already found them and that it raged inside the imperial palace—in the very heart of their civilisation.

Running at full speed, Daijen Saeth was a terrifying sight to behold. Coupled with a display of his strength, which he used to reduce a set of double doors to splinters, he was a demon in the eyes of the palace guard. Six arrows—all fired from different places of concealment—whistled towards that door and found naught but an empty threshold.

The Vahlken was already halfway across the lofty hall by the time the hidden archers realised as much. Daijen paid them no heed, his own target the next set of double doors on the other side of the chamber. With a mighty *bang,* they relented to his shoulder barge, each panel of wood ripped from its hinges.

His dead sprint took him along one of the external bridges that connected one area of the palace to another. Despite the blood thundering in his ears, Daijen heard the smashing glass from somewhere above. A second later, the roof that covered the bridge nearly buckled under the impact. What followed was a pair of boots hammering the roof at an even greater speed than his own.

Up ahead, the door burst open to a group of cleric guards, easily identified by their penchant for red and white. There was no missing the Vahlken hurtling towards them, his bronze atori blade in hand. It was either credit to their courage or testament to the cruelty of their masters that saw the soldiers charge towards him.

It mattered little in the end. They were Skaramangians all. In Daijen's eyes, that rid them of any claim to be Andarens, therefore freeing the Vahlken from his oath to protect their lives. It seemed Ilithranda felt the same way.

Swinging in from above, she surprised the soldiers with an initial kick that launched one of their number through the railing and over the edge of the bridge. Unlike Daijen, Ilithranda still possessed her sabre, an elegantly curved length of steel that she immediately brought to bear against her enemies.

When Daijen finally slammed into the fray, he added his own blend of ferocity. Skidding through a gap in the chaos, the Vahlken popped up in the middle and flowed perfectly into Ilithranda's battle style. Together, they danced around the cluster of cleric guards, pivoting in synchronicity to deliver sweeping arcs of biting steel. It was within seconds, not minutes, that they found victory and stood towering over the dead.

Ilithranda, her face splattered with flecks of blood, glanced down at the helm Daijen had looped to his belt through one of the eye holes. "They will hunt us to the ends of the earth for that."

"Sheep don't hunt Aegres," Daijen replied flatly, making for the other side of the bridge.

"They have an Aegre of their own now," she reminded him, using his own terminology against him.

Daijen looked down at his right hand, his chalky-white skin darkened with Slait's blood. The Vahlken still felt stunned by his return—the Skaramangians, no less.

"Let him come," Daijen proclaimed boldly. "I'll take more than just his ear next time."

"You're doing exactly as The Valtorak warned," Ilithranda spat, halting him in his tracks.

Daijen looked over her shoulder, making certain there were none in pursuit. "What are you talking about?"

"You let your pride get in the way," she spat accusingly. "You shouldn't even have been out on your own!"

Daijen paused, hesitating over which point to argue first. "You haven't exactly been *present* since we arrived. I couldn't rely on you. And I don't need your permission either. I saw an enemy target, and I went after him. That's what we're supposed to do."

"Assassinating religious leaders in the middle of the throne room is *not* what we're supposed to do," Ilithranda retorted. "And we never said anything about stealing the damned helm!"

Daijen wouldn't hear it, shaking his head. "My pride had nothing to do with this," he argued, though his words rang hollow. "I just killed the leader of the Skaramangians *and* claimed a weapon of power. That's saving lives *and* crippling their arsenal at the same time. What were you doing? Sleeping?"

"You're lucky I wasn't," Ilithranda countered, stepping closer to him. "If it wasn't for me, The Eldan would have put that wretched thing on *your* head. Your insides would be decorating Slait's face by now."

Daijen opened his mouth to fire back, but any words he might have chosen would have been drowned out by the ringing of bells.

"We have to get out of here," Ilithranda asserted. She produced a Cuthar from her belt and blew into it as she stepped closer to the railing.

Daijen did the same, hoping the high-pitched whistle would find Valyra. "I think they're too far away."

"Then we're on our own," Ilithranda concluded. "The priority is to get out of the palace. Our only hope is to get lost in the city."

"We don't exactly blend in," he pointed out.

Ilithranda sighed, her frustration with him battling the logic he spoke. "Then we climb," she said, leaning over the railing and looking up. "The guard couldn't hope to follow us, and our chances of spotting Oaken and Valyra increase tenfold up there."

Daijen didn't need to look to know she was eyeing the central tower that stood sentinel over the grounds and Leviathan skull. "Those walls are too smooth—we would never reach the top."

"Agreed. Which is why we will have to go through the interior," Ilithranda said, already stepping over the last of the bodies to continue their escape.

"Wait," he called out, following behind. "Those are the imperial quarters. Do you have any idea how many guards will be posted inside that tower? They've already more than doubled them because of the Ankala."

"Afraid of a few *sheep*?" she jibed, her words aimed like an arrow at his pride.

"I won't kill innocent people," he told her, the pair pressing against the open threshold to spy the path ahead.

"No one is innocent inside these walls," she whispered.

"We took an oath to safeguard the lives of our people," he replied.

Ilithranda met his icy blue eyes before glancing at the massacre in their wake.

"They forfeited their lives in service to evil," he said succinctly. "The palace guard are just soldiers trying to protect their emperor. They don't deserve to die for that."

"And if the emperor bears their mark?" Ilithranda posed, thrusting her chin at the dead Skaramangians. "Are they not all in service to evil then?"

"I'm not killing them," he repeated.

"Do as you will—not that you haven't already," she added spitefully.

A step behind her, Daijen followed Ilithranda through the next series of corridors. They were forced to wait here and there, hiding behind pillars and statues or inside alcoves while patrols rushed through the palace. It seemed they had caused enough turmoil that the numerous guard posts were breaking formation to seek out the treacherous Vahlken. With patience and timing, the ruckus allowed the pair to move through a significant portion of the palace without causing another fight.

That was until Daijen pressed himself to a wall that wasn't actually a wall.

The changeling exploded into action the moment the Vahlken made contact. With surprise on her side, the camouflaged guard was able to strike Daijen across the jaw, pushing him back, before swiping a dagger across his arm and drawing blood. Staggered by the blows and taken aback by the illusion that confused his eyes, the Vahlken was attacked by another changeling on the other side of the room. The boot found him square in the back and pushed him towards the initial fiend.

By then, of course, his outrage at having been caught by surprise had banished the pain. He sidestepped the changeling and whipped out his powerful arm, his closed fist catching her in the chest. The air expelled from her lungs, the chameleon guard landed flat on her back and stayed there.

Hearing the cut of steel carve through the air behind him, Daijen kicked back without looking and sent the other changeling flying into the wall. The Vahlken paused, making certain the guard still drew breath as he lay prone on the floor.

"Someone will have heard that," Ilithranda warned. "We need to move."

Continuing with caution, Daijen was convinced that Slait was round every corner, waiting for them with a mob of cleric guards at his back.

"This way," Ilithranda bade, taking them through an open

archway and into a courtyard of florescent flowers and climbing vines.

Daijen noted the central tower was now looming in front of them, its spire impossible to see. Looking ahead, there stood a set of ornate doors, each bearing the sigil of House Lhoris.

Something didn't feel right to the Vahlken. Where were the guards? These doors would take anyone into the imperial quarters, where the emperor himself lay his head to rest.

Then Ilithranda froze, and Daijen with her.

The courtyard housed more than small trees, towering trellises, and enhanced flora. From the shadows, there emerged white wraiths.

The Praetorian Guard.

Daijen and Ilithranda naturally positioned themselves back to back in front of the ornate doors. Against any one of the praetorians, the Vahlken were undoubtedly the superior combatants, but against eight of them...

"You take the four on the left," Daijen suggested. "I'll take the four on the right."

The double doors at the base of the tower opened without warning, each handled by a praetorian. Daijen's gaze was instantly drawn to the figure standing on the other side, seen between yet more praetorians. He couldn't believe his eyes, the shock of it nearly disarming him.

"You have already made quite the mess of my throne room," Emperor Qeledred pronounced. "I would rather you didn't spill blood in my gardens too. I have been tending them for centuries."

Both Vahlken simply stared at him, failing to see what could only be a trap. But what trap would ever use His Radiance as bait?

"Come along," the emperor bade. "The entire palace is searching for you."

Daijen scrutinised the praetorians, who were blocking off any retreat. While they maintained their threatening demeanour, it was apparent that they weren't going to attack. If anything, their presence was more to usher the Vahlken inside the tower than start a fight.

Keeping their weapons in hand, Daijen and Ilithranda followed the emperor. So too did his masked guard, the last to enter before the doors were sealed in their wake. Beyond the antechamber, His Radiance led the pair into a domed, windowless room. Firelight from the fixed torches danced across the smooth walls, revealing a single point of interest at the heart of the chamber.

The hewn floor was a ring, its centre displaying a circle of exposed Leviathan skull that served as the palace's foundations. In the middle of that circle sat a dark spot, its edges jagged and bent downwards.

"You look upon the work of a god," Emperor Qeledred announced, his arms held out to his sides.

Were it not for his violet eyes shifting to the broken skull, Daijen would have believed His Radiance was referring to himself.

"Of all the Leviathans unleashed by the Dark Ones," he continued, "this is the only one to have received a name from our ancestors."

Quite aware of the praetorians at his back, Daijen remained on edge, unsure what was really happening here. Still, he maintained enough of his wits to know that there was no mention of a named Leviathan in the Arkalon.

"*Agannon*," the emperor declared, naming the ancient beast. He stepped off the marble and onto the skull itself, his attention taken by its jagged hole.

"There's no record of that in the Arkalon," Daijen felt compelled to point out.

The emperor's sharp gaze snapped up to meet the Vahlken's.

"Your Radiance," Daijen added, his words muttered more than anything.

"The Arkalon is but *one* source of history. Finding the omissions is a matter of knowing where to look." The emperor paused before continuing. "It was decided long ago that so foul a creature not be given the worth a name would lend it. After all, the glory should go to the gods, who died so we might live." Qeledred gestured at the broken section at his feet. "Aran'saur," he said, voicing the capital's name. "*Hammer stroke* in the old tongue. This is the blow that put Agannon down for good. Do you know your history?"

Perhaps more than you do, Daijen thought.

"Yes, Your Radiance," the Vahlken said. "The Arkalon states that the great Govhul descended from the heavens like a spear, that he struck the monster—*Agannon*—with his hammer."

Having seen some of what The Anther could do, Daijen had no doubt that it was the weapon in question. That would also suggest that the skeleton Mordrith had found beneath The Morthil Mountains was, indeed, Govhul.

"Straight through and out the other side," His Radiance remarked, his usually flat tone adopting a note of awe.

"You know the old tongue?" He was immediately unsure if he was even allowed to ask the emperor a question and braced himself for the potential rebuttal. "Your Radiance," he added.

"No," Qeledred replied with a scoff. "So crude and archaic a language has no place in our civilisation anymore. I learned of the meaning in my youth, on a visit to God Fall. I believe it is the only language the warlocks use to communicate with each other."

"Why are we here?" Ilithranda demanded, absent any formality.

It seemed with deliberate slowness that the emperor's eyes drifted to land on her. "She speaks," he said at length.

When he said nothing more, Ilithranda glanced at Daijen before setting Qeledred with a stern gaze. "Why are you telling us any of this? We're fugitives in your palace. We killed the master cleric and a dozen more beside him." She spared the Praetorian Guard a brief look. "We should be fighting, not talking."

"Would you prefer to fight?" Qeledred posed, without challenging her lack of decorum.

"I always prefer to fight," Ilithranda told him.

His Radiance nodded as he steadily rounded the chasm in the heart of the circle. "Well, I'm afraid there's no fighting in here. I come here to think." He stopped and turned, a bejewelled finger flexing to point out a cushioned alcove that interrupted the smooth, curving walls. "In the earliest days of my reign, I sat there and read this from cover to cover." He produced a small but thick leather-bound book from within his royal blue robes, reminding Daijen of the Arkalons carried by the clerics.

"What is that?" Ilithranda asked.

"An Arkalon," Daijen guessed.

"No," Qeledred stressed. "I am to be *seen* reading the Arkalon. I come here to read what I *shouldn't* be seen reading." He held up the book before tossing it over the chasm and into Ilithranda's hand. "It's a journal," he explained while she examined it. "From emperor to emperor, down through the epochs. The subject matter is quite specific."

Ilithranda spread the covers and displayed the pages to Daijen. The symbol of the Skaramangians looked back at him—a vertical line cut with two touching diamonds. Judging by how early on in the book it was, the symbol had been scrawled eons ago. Confirming that theory, the words around it and on the adjacent page were of the old tongue, Andara's ancient language.

"I know of the snakes that slither through my halls. We have always known. There are accounts in that journal that tell of them trying to adopt my predecessors to their dark cause. The House of Lhoris has *always* resisted."

"You might resist their cause," Ilithranda replied venomously, "but the House of Lhoris is no better than a puppet for the Skaramangians. They've been wielding your power since... well," she deduced, holding up the journal, "since they *gave* it to you. There would be no war with Erador if you didn't give the command."

"You know nothing of the power you speak," His Radiance countered. "It does not come from my will nor even my name. It comes from the *people*. They give me power, and *they* are very much in the grips of the clerics. Ours is one of religious law. If I am not in alignment with that, the people will rebel. I can assure you, that particular fire will be fuelled by the clerics."

Ilithranda beat her chest. "Then you should be using whatever power you *do* have and helping us—the ones fighting the real war."

"I am helping you," Qeledred informed her, gesturing at the

very chamber in which they communed. "You should be fighting for your lives right now."

"Giving us a history lesson isn't helping us," she rebuked. "And *telling* us you're not a Skaramangian and *proving* you're not are two very different things." Ilithranda looked at Daijen. "This could be a ploy to slow us down while they amass a larger force outside."

The emperor gave a short laugh. "You certainly sound like someone fighting the Skaramangians. But if it's proof you require..." He gave one of the white guards a subtle nod.

A moment later, two more praetorians appeared with the one who had left to fetch them, only they did not arrive empty-handed. Between them, they dragged Barris Tanyth by the arms, his face bloody and bruised.

"Show them," Qeledred commanded.

One of the praetorians used his thumb to pull down Barris's bottom lip, thereby revealing the small tattoo on the soft gum. The spymaster had been marked by the Skaramangians.

"I have been aware of Barris's true allegiance for some time," His Radiance explained. "Getting rid of him, of course, would raise too many alarms with his superiors. Your actions tonight, however, have presented me with an opportunity to replace him with one of *my* choosing." The emperor looked down at the broken spymaster. "Any last words, Barris?"

The spymaster opened his mouth, perhaps to plead for his life or maybe to use his forked tongue one last time, but his intentions would never be known. Before he could speak, one of the praetorians stepped in and ran a sleek dagger across his throat, the steel biting so deep as to severe his windpipe and vocal cords.

How numb Daijen had become at the sight of so much blood. It was a terrible volume that poured out of Barris's throat, darkening his robes and pooling about his knees. As the last vestiges of life ebbed away, the praetorians released the spymaster and let him fall face down on the floor.

"Another to be added to your tally," Qeledred commented. "What a pity," he added dryly.

Ilithranda stared at the warm corpse touching her boot.

"Killing one of them—even a wretch like Barris—won't dent their ranks. You *must* be able to do more."

"There are too many eyes and ears in my affairs," Qeledred informed her. "One of my wives is among their number. I am afraid the fight remains with you. To that end, I can aid your escape and see you live to fight another day."

The emperor moved away from the broken skull and made for the cushioned alcove. He reached for something hidden by the cushions and blankets—a concealed lever. Daijen heard the sound of a locking mechanism before the seating area was revealed to be a trap door.

"This tower is full of secret passages," Qeledred reported, one hand raising the seat out of place. "Go down and follow the path round. Keep going up. Do not be distracted by any of the doors."

"You know we're trying to get to the top," Daijen said, his tone indicating a subtle question had actually been asked.

"You require your Aegres to escape, yes? Why do you think I had the alarm raised? The Skaramangians would have dealt with you quietly. I only hope that your winged companions have heard the bells over the celebrations."

It was in that moment that Daijen assigned the emperor a degree of intellect he had held in reserve, having previously believed the man to be too pampered and ignorant to be intelligent.

"This is the first and, I suspect, last time we will ever meet," Qeledred went on, though his words were aimed solely at Ilithranda now. "I would speak with you a moment before we part ways for good."

Ilithranda met the eyes of her father, the violet of her own reflected in his. "We have nothing more to discuss." She tossed the imperial journal back to him.

His Radiance regarded the ancient tome before throwing it back to her. "The earliest entries are beyond my understanding," he admitted. "Any attempt I make to translate the work of my forebears would be monitored. At least in your hands, its secrets might be laid bare." Qeledred's imperial gaze fell on the helm hanging from Daijen's belt. "That, on the other hand, will have to be returned. I cannot let you leave with it."

Daijen made no attempt to give it back. "Besides being a barbaric form of execution," the Vahlken replied, "this lends the Skaramangians a sizeable advantage, Your Radiance. I am bound by oath to seal it in the depths of Ka'vairn."

The emperor maintained his uncompromising demeanour. "Slaying the master cleric in the throne room is a great insult to their order, if not the security of my palace, but it's an insult I can live with. The theft of that helm, however, is an insult that will bring my authority into question."

Daijen knew his mind on the matter, his feelings bound by his tenets. He made a point to look at Ilithranda, making certain he had her backing before the next round of violence ensued. Her nod was subtle, but it didn't escape her father, nor the Praetorian Guard.

As one, the white sentinels adopted a battle stance, their hooked swords raised high and low. Ilithranda, who had sheathed her sabre since entering the chamber, now drew the blade an inch, revealing a slither of the steel she would use to end them all.

"You value these warriors," Daijen stated. "You trust them with more than your life. You trust them with your *secrets*."

"My praetorians were born into their duty," Qeledred boasted.

Daijen made sure the emperor's attention was fixed on him when he posed his crucial question. "How many of them can you truly afford to lose?"

"For the Helm of Ahnir?" His Radiance took no more than a second to consider it. "All of them," he said simply.

Daijen's face dropped, so sure had he been that his words would bring peace, not bloodshed.

In the next few seconds, his mind ran through the inevitable fight. Using his extensive knowledge of Ilithranda, he predicted her attacks, defences, and counters first. From her position and proximity to the infamous guard, he knew where she would begin. That gave him his own starting point, a place from which their fighting styles would blend into one, forcing the praetorians to battle a four-armed opponent.

Qeledred, the so-called *bane of Erador,* raised his hand, a gesture that immediately put the praetorians at ease. His imperial violet eyes rested on the helm for a long moment before he looked at Ilithranda. It was impossible to say what the emperor was thinking, his steely expression likely having been trained into him from a young age.

"It is sacrilege to spill Lhoris blood," he remarked.

He knew who she was.

"While I would give their lives to retrieve the helm," Qeledred began, "I would not see my praetorians condemned to the lowest depths of the Black Abyss for their trespasses." The emperor sighed, a previously unseen look of defeat about him. "I can help you escape, but if you take that with you, I cannot stop what happens next."

Daijen predicted the ramifications well enough. "You would lay siege to Ka'vairn?" he asked in disbelief.

"I will have to order Ka'vairn's complete *destruction,*" the emperor specified. "Whatever your beliefs may be, Daijen of House Saeth, it is the belief of my people that the Helm of Ahnir is divine. It is in itself a declaration of power. That power must be situated here."

"So be it," Ilithranda declared, getting behind Daijen and reaffirming his bold decision. "Let's go," she bade, making for the secret passage.

Qeledred waited until Daijen was halfway inside the passage before calling out to her. "You left something behind the last time you were here."

Ilithranda stopped, her back to the emperor. Was that fear on her face, Daijen wondered? It was the rarest of expressions in her repertoire, but there it was to see.

"I don't want to know," she replied, ushering Daijen further down the hidden steps.

"But you must," came the emperor's imperative.

There was something in his tone, his choice of words, that

turned Ilithranda around. Father and daughter shared a tense moment of silence.

"Go," she instructed Daijen. "I'll be right behind you."

Daijen glanced at the emperor. "Are you sure?" he asked her.

"Go," his sister repeated.

With the Helm of Ahnir still very much in his possession, the Vahlken began the ascent. He moved ever upwards, following the often steep incline through the passage. There were doors on nearly every floor he passed, leading him to wonder which members of the imperial family were on the other side, oblivious to the intruder creeping through their home.

When, finally, there was naught but the hatch to the roof above him, Daijen removed the interior locks and opened the hatch. Walking out across the roof's flat surface, he was greeted by a view only attained from Valyra's saddle.

Aran'saur was awash with colour under a sky of fireworks. Every explosion exposed the Leviathan's bones—the bones of Agannon—and the buildings tucked in between.

More beautiful still was Mount Athan beside the capital. Its crystalline outer shell reflected the light in all its varying colours, revealing its many facets and edges. Not to be distracted, Daijen retrieved his Cuthar and blew into the night. He did so repeatedly until movement caught his eyes and turned him back to the hatch.

"Ilithranda," he called out, seeing the woman's shadow approaching him. "Are you hurt?" he had to ask.

She could only shake her head.

"What happened? What did he say to you?"

Ilithranda's absent gaze snapped to meet his own. How could any hold so many different emotions behind their eyes? She looked confused, as if she was calculating the unfathomable, while simultaneously appearing in complete despair. There was also horror behind her expression. Whatever revelation she had been exposed to, it had racked Ilithranda to her core.

Two piercing squawks cut through the night and distant celebrations, turning Daijen's attention to the starlit sky. Valyra and

Oaken were descending at speed, their massive wings flapping hard to land them safely atop the tower.

Seeing his winged companion was usually enough to bring a smile to Daijen's face, but not that night. He was haunted by Ilithranda's expression. He could but usher her to Oaken before he climbed astride Valyra. He shouldn't have needed to, but the Vahlken glanced over Ilithranda in her saddle, making certain that she had secured herself properly.

"You're a welcome sight, old friend," he said, patting his Aegre's muscled neck. "Take us home. We stop for nothing."

19
FOXES IN THE PEN

It was a glancing blow, a sword that Gallien deflected with his axe, but it was the swiftness with which the blow was delivered that took the smuggler from his feet. He hit the ground as hooves galloped past his head, kicking up the dirt as they went.

Years on battlefields had given him sense enough to know when Death was lingering, its outstretched hands waiting to pluck souls like a gardener might prune their flowers. It was this sixth sense that forced Gallien to roll aside, thereby avoiding another set of rushing hooves that sought to trample him. So too he did evade the scraping blade that had been swept across the ground in his wake.

Scrambling to his feet, he saw the green of Aphrandhor's robes between the legs of a Centaur. That same Centaur was struck by a spell, a brilliant and burning flash of magic that saw the creature rear up before crashing dead to the earth.

Clearly visible now, The Green Leaf staggered about, his staff unleashing destructive spells in every direction. When one of them, a blazing ball of fire, nearly slammed into Cob, the wizard called on his defensive spells and drew Yalaqin, his broadsword. A single wave of his staff and the steel was alight with flames, a weapon he brought to bear against the enclosing Centaurs.

Cob felled his own opponent after ducking under a swing and swiping his scimitar of Draven bone through the Centaur's legs. The almost human half of the creature cried out as it skidded across the forest floor. That cry was cut short when the ranger hammered the crab-like hook of his scimitar's tip into his enemy's skull.

Keeping his movements fluid, the Kedradi left his weapon lodged in the Centaur's head and pivoted to block an incoming hammer with his short-sword. Made from the jaw of some monster, it was all fangs, each the length of a man's hand. It allowed him to intercept the Centaur's sword and twist it from the creature's grip. A backhand to one of the horse legs followed by a mortal blow to its neck brought another Centaur into the arms of Death.

Gallien jumped and rolled, narrowly avoiding the spear that had been launched his way. He came up with a throw of his own. The axe flew quicker than the Centaur could move, and it was no small target. A yell of pain broke the din and the Centaur stumbled into a tree. It attempted to yank the weapon free of its horse ribs, but the axe was no longer there to grasp, leaving the wound to bleed all the more. Shocked and confused, the Centaur looked back at the one who had thrown it, only to find that same axe was being launched a second time.

When the axe, again, returned to Gallien's grip, it did so with another death added to its tally. There was no time to throw it at the next foe, who rushed the smuggler with a speed only a horse could match. While he managed to deflect the first jab of a spear, he could not defend himself against the hoof that caught him in the chest.

Both axe and precious air were parted from him as he was sent to the ground. Without delay, his chest informed him that it was on fire, despite there being no flames about him. While he tried to gulp much-needed air down, the Centaur pursued him, approaching with its spear angled towards him. It barked something unintelligible at the smuggler before adjusting its grip to hurl the spear.

How useless the axe was as it returned to his hand—it could not be thrown with any accuracy or force from the ground. And so there he would die, among the glowing trees of Akmar. At least he would die in a place of rare beauty, not something he thought he deserved. Nor was it to be his reality.

A staccato of lightning outshone the trees, assaulting the looming Centaur with nearly a dozen points of searing hot energy. It reared up, its jaw frozen ajar as its flesh burned and smoked. The ground trembled when it fell dead at Gallien's feet.

The smuggler would have thanked the wizard for his timely intervention, but his use of magic only attracted more Centaurs. Cob was already moving to aid The Green Leaf, his short-sword of fangs now replaced by his bow.

"On your feet!" the ranger yelled at him, his arm thrown out to direct the smuggler to Androma.

The old Dragon Rider faced two Centaurs. They advanced from right and left, though their approach seemed cautious considering their prey was blind. Gallien then noticed the pair of dead Centaurs lying behind Androma, who was also wielding one of their spears alongside her silvyr sword.

While his lungs still clawed for breath, the smuggler rose and readied the axe above his head. One good throw would send the weapon where it needed to go. A second throw would rid Androma of enemies altogether.

A strong and unrelenting grasp about his wrist brought his plan to a crashing end. The smuggler whipped around and looked up to see the Centaur who had surprised him. Its snarling expression was the last thing Gallien saw before a rock-like hammer collided with the side of his head.

———

Slowly, painfully, the world began to return to Gallien Pendain. What a strange world it was. The smuggler looked left and right to see the forest moving about him, as if the silver trees were sliding away. The rhythmic *thud* of hooves turned his attention away from the trees, where he discovered the truth of his situation.

His hands were bound and his ankles with them, only his ankles were also connected to a length of rope secured to a Centaur's midriff. He was being dragged along the forest floor—and, to his dismay, so were his companions.

Cob was beside him, similarly bound and unnervingly calm. On the Kedradi's other side, The Green Leaf was being dragged by his wrists instead of his ankles—a possible precaution given his penchant for magic. Gallien had to tilt his head back to see Androma; her predicament was just the same as theirs.

Before he made contact with any of them, the smuggler scrutinised their captors. The Centaurs numbered seven by his count, two of whom possessed all their gear and weapons, including Gallien's satchel and sword. Try as he might, being bound so tightly prevented the axe from coming to his aid.

The Centaurs themselves were among the meanest-looking things the smuggler had ever seen. Their horse bodies, all of varying colours and patterns, were painted with thick tribal tattoos that ran up their human torsos and across their elongated faces. Their hair was that of a wide mane, matted and home to feathers and small bones, that ran down their spine.

Where a rider would have placed their saddle, the Centaurs appeared laden with saddle bags, quivers, and a plethora of weapons and supplies. Despite their obvious arsenal, superior strength, and speed, they had taken the group captive rather than simply executed them. Gallien turned to Cob for answers.

"I thought you were dead," the ranger whispered, showing no sign of relief to learn the opposite.

Gallien experienced a flashing memory, reminding him of the hammer that struck a dangerous blow. "Why aren't *any* of us dead?" the smuggler replied.

The Kedradi glanced at Aphrandhor before answering. "They work for the Jainus, apparently. The Green Leaf thinks they're taking us to them."

Not for the first time, Gallien thought of the soldiers—deserters all—whom he had once witnessed be publicly executed by a Jainus wizard. The agony they had suffered while their skin burned from the ice that had slowly frozen them whole.

This wasn't going to end well.

The sun was beginning to rise when the Centaurs finally came to a halt. For the last hour, at least, the sound of war had breached the forest. The Andarens were closing in. Their catapults continued to rain fiery debris upon the forest, but it had become apparent to Gallien that the trees were immune to the flames, if not the missiles themselves. Such was the strength of the legendary silvyr.

Looking ahead, a group of men and women—all robed in Jainus garb—approached the stationary Centaurs. They exchanged words while the wizards spared the prisoners a glancing inspection. One of them, a woman of Androma's age—in appearance only—parted from the conversation and retrieved Aphrandhor's staff from the Centaurs. She examined it, taking careful note of the metallic mesh coiled about certain areas of the staff. The investigation led her eyes to The Green Leaf.

"Bring them," she commanded.

The remaining four Jainus moved to claim a prisoner each. A wave of the hand was enough to snap the rope that connected them to the Centaurs and free their ankles—not that they were permitted to walk. Gallien heard a number of his bones cracking and popping as his body was levitated from the ground. It was a deeply uncomfortable sensation that he was entirely powerless to fight.

Dragged through the air now, the companions were taken underground through a narrow tunnel that eventually opened up into a dome of hewn stone. At the dome's apex, the morning sun shone through a circular window of mottled glass, adding stark white light to the chamber's fiery gloom.

Despite all the activity about him, Gallien's attention was instantly taken by the enormous four-armed skeleton. In the heart of the chamber, it lay directly under the light and on the only patch of dirt that hadn't been paved over. Its limbs appeared strewn, suggesting it had found its rest without ceremony.

Struck down by a Dark One, Gallien assumed, before reminding himself it was all nonsense.

The wizard with Aphrandhor's staff in hand came to a stop, and the others with her. "Maester Harvish," she addressed, turning every Jainus head.

It was a bald man among them, however, who replied, his full black beard masking his moving lips. "What's this, Relia?" he enquired, all too calmly for a man surrounded by an army of Andarens.

"The Centaurs captured them south of here," Relia reported. "The green one was said to be using magic." She held up the staff for her superior to see. "He was using *this.*"

Maester Harvish narrowed his eyes at the object. "Demetrium," he muttered, spying the largest of the metallic meshes from across the chamber. His gaze then shifted to *the green one.* "My eyes deceive me," he said in wonderment, "for they cannot be looking upon Aphrandhor. No," he drawled, approaching the older wizard. "The Aphrandhor I knew would never be so foolish as to return."

The Jainus claimed the staff from Relia's hand on his way to stand before The Green Leaf, his eyes roaming over the details.

Then, using the staff to push back the wizard's hood, he declared, "It *is* you."

Floating beside The Green Leaf, Gallien noted the dried blood that streaked down from the wizard's hairline. He also sported a black eye and a graze across his crooked nose. The smuggler was impressed with the beating the old man had taken.

"Harvish," Aphrandhor said dryly. "You were hardly a man the last I saw you."

"*Maester* Harvish," the bald wizard corrected. "I have *you* to thank for that title. After all, in your absence, the site was passed on to Maester Bhor." Harvish chuckled under his beard. "Has there ever been a more incompetent wizard than Bhor? Besides you, of course," he added. "The Silver Trees of Akmar are under my domain now. The very future of magic," he elaborated, gesturing at the bones behind him, "is in *my* hands."

In the silence that followed, the chamber shook, raining dust from the domed ceiling. Gallien glanced at the circular window, wondering if they had just heard a Giant falling to its death or the impact of another catapult. Either way, it seemed the Andarens were almost upon the site.

"Maester Harvish," a younger wizard called from across the chamber. "Your orders?"

"Not now," Harvish replied dismissively, his attention still fixed on Aphrandhor. "Do you still have it?" he whispered, eyes wide.

Immobilised by the levitation spell, The Green Leaf was unable to prevent Harvish from pushing back the sleeves of his robe. The wizard's eyes grew wider still when he saw the vambrace on Aphrandhor's right arm.

The chamber shook again.

"Maester," Relia pressed, her view of the vambrace blocked by Harvish. "We must move the bones. We cannot hold them back much longer."

"Reports suggest they are sweeping east *and* west," another wizard informed.

"They will surround us soon," Relia insisted. "Our window to move south is closing."

"Silence," Harvish snapped, tossing the staff back to her. "The bones stay here."

"We cannot let them fall into the enemy's hands," Relia argued.

"Do not question me!" Harvish barked.

Turning back to Aphrandhor, he began to unclasp the plated vambrace—his prize. In the process, however, he touched The Green Leaf before freeing it from his forearm. As ever, it was brief, a moment in which the wizard slipped from the present and tumbled down the halls of someone else's memories. When he returned, it was with great alarm.

"Skaramangian!" Aphrandhor cried in accusation.

Harvish frowned, stepping back with the bracer in hand.

"He means to *give* them the bones," The Green Leaf explained.

The Maester's frown contorted into something between confusion and amusement. Then his expression fell altogether, revealing a cold and calculating man. "My masters will be most pleased," he said, holding up the vambrace.

Relia stepped in, "What's he talking about, Maester?"

His hand shot out, and with it came a light as bright as the sun, blinding all while burning Relia to a black husk. Her corpse flew across the chamber and caught the wizard responsible for keeping Cob aloft. All hell then broke loose as the darting Kedradi gave Harvish a moving target while the Skaramangian wizard became a target for his fellow Jainus.

Magic exploded across the chamber, and Gallien fell to his feet, his captor focused on bringing down the one who had turned on them. It soon became apparent that Harvish was not the only wizard to bow to a foreign master. On the other side of the massive skeleton, a young female wizard conjured an icicle from the moisture in the air and hurled it at the man who had bound Androma. The freezing spear took him in the chest and launched him into the wall.

Harvish was quick to forget about Cob, his magic turned on those who could kill him from afar. He erected shields left and right, blocking bursts of lightning and torrents of fire. Between them all, he retaliated with destructive spells, reducing much of the surrounding stonework to crumbling debris.

Gallien ducked and weaved through it all until he was able to dive into Androma, saving her from an incoming spell of blazing energy. "We need to get out of here," he growled, pulling her up by an arm.

The old Rider shoved him aside and intercepted one of the Jainus. The man yelped, his wrist bent such that the palm of his hand was touching his arm. His yelp turned into an agonised cry when the bone pierced the skin, the pain dropping him to his knees. Androma thrust the blade of her hand into his throat, silencing him for good.

"Where's Green Leaf?" she demanded, her words aimed in Gallien's general direction.

The smuggler was slow to respond, momentarily bewildered by the fact that Androma had somehow managed to free her hands. "He's over..." But Gallien's response trailed off when he failed to spot the green wizard.

A stray spell, rebounding off Harvish's shields, sizzled past the smuggler's ear, forcing him to the ground. There he spied Aphrandhor, the wizard crawling through the chaos to reach his staff, his hands still bound. He would have reached it too had Harvish not discovered him.

The Green Leaf had the air sucked out of him as the Jainus's spell swept him up in a storm, tossing him up to the ceiling. There he remained, pinned to the stone by unseen magic.

"I will add you to the prize!" Harvish yelled over the exchange of spells.

On the other side of the chamber, the female Skaramangian was holding back a pair of Jainus with a jet of flames. The rest lay dead about her, caught off guard by the sudden betrayal. The surviving pair were given a fighting chance when Cob leaped at the Skaramangian, his bound wrists wrapping around her throat. Her fire spell came to an abrupt end, her focus immediately shifting to her lack of air.

Being that much taller than the Jainus, the Kedradi arched his back and tried to raise his hands, applying maximum pressure to her airway. The wizard clawed his wrists and hands, desperate to free herself and gulp down much-needed air, but it was no use, leaving the wizard to rely on her true strength. Bringing both hands up towards Cob's face, her palms soon disappeared inside the light of new flames.

The Kedradi was forced to abandon his attack and push the Skaramangian Jainus away. Haggard from her brush with death, the Jainus was no match for the two wizards she had been fending off. Together, they applied fire and lightning. Within a few seconds, they overwhelmed her shields and wiped another Skaramangian off the map.

As a result, they gained the attention of Maester Harvish. While they made a mockery of nature, igniting the room with a multitude of colours, Gallien scrambled across the floor, finding his way to the nearest dead Jainus. From their belt he retrieved a knife before rushing back to Androma, who was clearly struggling to make sense of her environment amidst the raucous magic.

"Untie me!" he urged, putting the knife in her hand.

"Where's Green Leaf?" she asked again.

Gallien watched the sawing blade as it sliced steadily through the binding. "He's on the ceiling."

Androma paused. "On the ceiling?"

"Untie me!" he pressed.

The moment his hands found freedom, they were filled with cool steel again. At the same time, Harvish was murdering the last of his fellow Jainus. One failed to shield themselves against a slab of stone the maester hurled at his head. Besides caving in the man's skull, the subsequent spray of blood blinded the woman fighting at his side. It proved a fatal distraction as she missed the blinding spell that flashed across the chamber and burned a hole through her chest and out her back.

Gallien made his move—and furiously so.

The axe was let fly in a blur of silver, bronze, and gold. Harvish raised a hand and clenched his fist, an action that brought about an invisible shield. It flared as the axe struck and rebounded. Smug was the smile that stretched beneath the Skaramangian's beard— the smile of an arrogant wizard.

It completely fell away when the axe reappeared in Gallien's hand. He threw it again, flaring the Jainus's shield. Then again. And again. After the fifth throw, Harvish reached out with his magic and tugged the axe from the smuggler's grip. He held it, marvelling, for no more than a second before it vanished from reality and rematerialised in Gallien's hand.

"Now that *is* fascinating," he uttered. With a flick of his wrist, he unleashed branches of lightning across the floor, warding Cob away, the ranger having used his time to sneak up on the Skaramangian. "Good dog," he quipped before returning his attention to Gallien.

"That," he continued, eyeing the axe hungrily, "is quite the weapon you wield. A *weapon of power*. An *actual* weapon," the wizard specified. "We know of the helm. And the bracer, of course," he added, tapping the vambrace with his boot. "But we only knew of the hammer. Now, there is also an *axe*. Extraordinary."

The Skaramangian regarded Aphrandhor above him. "I have been somewhat isolated down here," he admitted, "but I still hear from on high. I know the trouble you've been causing out there. The blind Dragon Rider. The Kedradi ranger. The *wizard*. You're new," he told Gallien. "But you're most welcome," he said with wicked glee. "To think, I now possess *two* weapons of power *and* the unruly thorns in our side."

Gallien tried his luck, hoping that the wizard's ramblings had also lowered his guard. The axe cut through the air at speed, the blade destined to find the maester's head, until another flaring shield intercepted it.

Harvish laughed as the weapon vanished before hitting the floor and reappearing in Gallien's hand. "*Incredible*. Why does it obey you?"

The smuggler was poised to throw it again, his breath laboured, when Aphrandhor addressed the maester.

"Harvish," he rasped. "You're going to die down here."

The Jainus glanced up at him. "Was that a threat from the man pinned to the ceiling?"

"Not a threat," The Green Leaf informed him, his voice relaying the pressure his entire body was under. "You won't survive the Andarens."

"Are you afraid for my life, Aphrandhor?" Harvish replied mockingly. "You need not. I have friends among our pale cousins. I will be *rewarded*, in fact."

"They will reward you with a swift death," The Green Leaf told him confidently. "How many among their thousands bear your dark mark? They few will not be able to explain their allegiance with a human wizard, you fool. They will take what they want and be done with you."

The maester looked away in thought, clearly disturbed by the sense in Aphrandhor's warning. "This has all been arranged," he eventually replied, though Gallien knew the look of a man trying to convince himself.

"You making a shambles of the site's defences has been arranged," The Green Leaf countered. "You, *Maester Harvish*, are expendable."

A new quake rippled across the ceiling, raining more dust upon them. It was followed by the holler of Centaurs and the clash of steel. The Andarens had closed the net.

Gallien launched the axe again and again, forcing Harvish back with every throw while he constructed shield after shield. Cob skidded across the stone and scooped up Aphrandhor's staff before tossing it up to the wizard. The Green Leaf was able to move his arm just enough to catch it, reuniting him with the demetrium. He grunted with exertion, his spell distorting the air about him as it broke the maester's binding magic.

The Kedradi did what he could to soften the old man's fall, but Aphrandhor still cried out in pain. All the while, Gallien steadily advanced on Harvish, his arm powered by the need to survive as he threw the axe again and again.

His strength, however, was no longer required when The Green Leaf stepped in.

The wizard flicked out his staff and hurled spell after spell, each one creating a visible crack in the Jainus's shields. Harvish countered where he could but Aphrandhor deflected every spell, casting them aside before returning with a flash of deadly magic. Between them, they drastically altered the environment, littering it with patches of fire, slick ice, and shattered stone.

Their duel came to an end when Aphrandhor deliberately struck the stone between them, creating a spattering of sharp rocks, only to launch the debris at his opponent. While Harvish erected a shield to save him from the spray of pellets, The Green Leaf was already casting his next spell, a wave of concussed air that obliterated the weakened shield and slammed the Skaramangian into the far wall.

Doubled over and exhausted, The Green Leaf picked up the vambrace with a heaving chest. "We should leave while we still can," he managed.

"Is Harvish dead?" Androma enquired.

The wizard glanced at the prone Jainus on the other side of the chamber. "No. But his doom is assured."

"As is ours if we don't get out of here right now," Gallien insisted, making for the door. The smuggler paused when Cob presented him with his secured wrists, the binding easily seen to by the axe.

"What about the bones?" the ranger asked. "We can't just leave them."

Aphrandhor limped to his side and placed a hand on the Kedradi's shoulder. "This battle is theirs to win, remember. We must focus on winning the war."

"Let's go," Gallien cajoled, waving his arm at the door.

Cob reluctantly abandoned the chamber, and the group hurried through the narrow tunnel, following the slight incline that led them back to the surface.

What chaos awaited them.

The Centaurs were racing about, using their speed against the invading Andarens. They swung out and down, clipping them with hammers and putting their bronze armour to the test with swords.

But soldiers were not all that Andara had sent to conquer The Silver Trees of Akmar.

Clerics waded in, hurling vials and glass spheres of fluorescent liquid. The magic contained within brought a cruel death to any within range. Gallien glimpsed one Centaur as an orb of pink liquid shattered against its bare chest. Within seconds, areas of its skin began to stretch out of control, creating enormous growths before its bones did likewise and protruded into the outside world.

"Cob!" Gallien yelled, seeing the ranger veer off to the left. "Where are you going?"

The ranger leaped over a pair of dead Andarens and stopped in front of a Centaur, its corpse mangled by magic. One by one, Cob relieved the creature of weapons—*their* weapons. Androma's silvyr blade was placed directly in her hand, Yalaqin was tossed to Aphrandhor, while Gallien was reunited with his satchel and sword, the latter of which he decided to wield alongside the axe. The Kedradi had considerably more to take back, forcing the smuggler to dash out from their huddle and meet a charging Andaren.

He threw the axe before their swords could clash, but the Andaren proved agile and evaded the weapon with a sideways pivot. While he survived, his kin behind him did not, taking the weapon of power in the chest. Using his sword, Gallien blocked high and low, his arms immediately protesting the jarring sensation that ran up his bones. Deflecting the third blow with one hand, the smuggler came at his foe with the other—axe already in hand. Shock was to be his last emotion, his skull split with steel.

"Quickly," Cob urged, guiding Androma to the south, who had claimed an Andaren spear.

Gallien fell in behind The Green Leaf. Judging by the sound of explosive discharges, Aphrandhor wasn't the only wizard in the forest. Somewhere out there, the Jainus who had survived their maester's twisted machinations were fighting for their lives.

Southbound again, evading the erratic Centaurs and ever-intruding Andarens became easier. Both Cob and Aphrandhor used their long-range capabilities to beat back the encroaching Andarens, their arrows and spells reason enough to rid them of pursuers.

Still, it was the last throw of a cleric that nearly brought their company down to three. The vial shattered on the ground at Cob's feet, exposing the alchemical concoction to the air. The explosion lifted the Kedradi and flung him head over boots into one of the hardened trees. Aphrandhor saw to the cleric's end, unleashing one final spell to hasten their departure from the world.

Before rushing to the ranger's side, Gallien grabbed Androma by the hand and led her to the wizard. "Keep moving!" he yelled at them, his arm outstretched to the south.

The smuggler sheathed his sword and dropped the axe in the

dirt, freeing his hands to grab Cob under the arms and drag him away. Gallien glanced over the unconscious Kedradi, checking for any serious wounds, but he dared not take his eyes off the forest around them for too long.

He envisioned their escape, they few who had slipped through the narrowest of gaps as the Andarens closed their circle about the site.

Pausing up ahead, the wizard turned back to eye the two men. "They only want the bones," he remarked gravely, his staff still smoking from his most recent spell.

Feeling the weight of Cob in his hands, Gallien knew it would only take a single cleric to emerge and undo their plans to reach Taraktor.

"Just keep going!" he cried, urging both wizard and Rider to pursue the south.

Androma was shaking her head, spear in hand. "I hope you're right about this, Green Leaf."

The wizard looked directly at Gallien, his aged features creased with righteous determination. "I'm right."

PART TWO

20

HOME AGAIN

0 Years Ago...

4

Clearing the tops of The Hellion Mountains, Valyra tucked in her wings and dived into the valley. Ka'vairn was directly beneath them, protruding from the ancient rock like a beacon for all Vahlken. Oaken was close behind them, the black-feathered Aegre not one to be left behind.

Approaching the weathered stone and scaffolding at speed, both of them spread their wings and glided away from the fortress. Soaring on a bed of wind, the Aegres steadily turned around and made for Ka'vairn's courtyard.

Nestled in the corner, as he liked to do, was Aramis, The Valtorak's three-legged Aegre. He squawked once and turned his armoured beak towards the main doors, where its rider could be seen passing over the threshold.

The Valtorak was closely followed by Androma, the two dwarves, and...

Daijen's eagle-like eyes narrowed on the green figure at the back of the group.

Aphrandhor!

The wizard had arisen from his unnaturally deep slumber, his face now bathing in the afternoon sun. What promise his recovery held. That said, The Green Leaf looked a shadow of himself, his face gaunt and skin pale, his eyes ringed with dark halos. He also appeared to be using his staff as a walking aid now.

Valyra touched down in the courtyard, her talons sharp enough to leave an impression. Daijen rubbed her feathers and patted the creature affectionately. "You did well," he praised, impressed by her stamina. "Rest now."

Before we run out of time, he thought.

Both Vahlken descended their mounts and dismissed them with a gesture. It was impossible not to watch Valyra take off and conquer the sky, her wings buffeting the air and throwing Daijen's hair out. *Majestic* was the best word he could think of to describe his companion.

She could not distract him for long, the Vahlken soon confronted by the master of Ka'vairn. "I did not anticipate such a swift return," he remarked.

Daijen was already untying the knot on his belt. "There were unforeseen... *complications* that forced our hand," he replied.

He held out the silver helm for all but Androma to see. While there was some confusion from the wizard and the dwarves, The Valtorak gazed hard at the weapon of power.

"What have you done?" the master demanded.

"We need to talk," Daijen insisted.

"*I* need to sleep," Ilithranda informed them, not stopping on her way to the main doors.

The Valtorak raised an eyebrow at her unceremonious departure. "I suppose that was to be expected," he muttered, mostly to himself.

"What's going on?" Androma asked, shaking her head.

"Let's go inside," Daijen replied. "I will tell you all that I can."

————

Dusk was upon the valley by the time Daijen had told his tale in full. His impeccable memory allowed him to recount it all, though he spared them the many thousands of predictions he had been privy to, all of them heard before the same thousands lost their heads.

Following his conclusion, silenced reigned over Ka'vairn's extensive library but for the constant *crackle* of the fire. All but Androma stared at the Helm of Ahnir on the tabletop, its sleek shape reflecting the dancing flames.

"I can't believe you met the emperor," Aphrandhor said with a croaky voice, the first to speak. "At least we know he's not a Skara-mangian—that's something."

"That's nothin'," Yamnomora argued. "Didn' ye hear 'im? Ol' Qeledred is useless. He might 'ave his own mind, but he's still jus' a puppet. Worse, he's a damned *powerful* puppet."

"This Slait," Mordrith stated. "He's bad news, aye?"

Daijen nodded solemnly. "He might not have earned the title of Vahlken, but he survived the pits of Handuin all the same. He will be a dangerous weapon in our enemy's hands."

"We have a few dangerous weapons o' our own," Mordrith reminded them, her dark eyes glancing over The Anther beside her.

"Not like him," Daijen told her. "Beyond his abilities and skills, Slait is a purist. He believes every word of the Arkalon, a fact the Skaramangians have used to manipulate him. He truly believes he is fighting for the reclamation of the gods. In Slait's eyes, he might as well be a divine instrument put here to pave the way. He will never stop, and there are very few who can stop him."

"Wait until he meets the girls," Yamnomora declared brashly, referring to her axes as usual. "There's nothin' they can't stop."

Arguing with the fiery dwarf was a nonsensical exercise and, ultimately, a waste of time, leading Daijen's attention to The Valtorak, who had yet to voice his opinion on anything that had been said.

The master met his icy blue eyes only briefly before they

returned to the helm, before them. "You have doomed us all, Daijen Saeth."

The statement sucked all the air out of the room.

"It doesn't have to stay here," Daijen eventually replied. "I can hide it."

"That will make no difference now," The Valtorak deduced. "They know it's here, so here they will come."

"They were coming here anyway," Daijen pointed out. "With Slait on their side, they know we have the bone."

"They've always known we possess the bone," the master snapped. "The Skaramangians have never come for it because they lacked the resources required to take it by force. Publicly slaying the master cleric and stealing the Helm of Ahnir is all they needed to unleash the full power of The Saible on us. You've given them everything they could have hoped for. Now they get to declare us to be heretics, traitors to the Empyreal Throne. And for what?" he spat, picking up the helm. "We can't use this."

"But *they* could," Daijen fired back. "They would use that to murder our own people. The Skaramangians were using it to glean the future. How long have they enjoyed that advantage?"

The Valtorak tossed the helm back onto the table. "I warned you," he reminded him fiercely. "Your pride doesn't just linger—it swells!"

"My pride had nothing to do with this," Daijen seethed, outraged that the topic would be raised in front of others.

"Then you would lay your foolishness at the feet of your training? At the feet of Kastiek? Or myself?"

"I am a Vahlken," Daijen asserted. "I don't have to justify my actions to a glorified potions master." He regretted his choice of words the very second they left his lips. "I was there," he continued, reducing the venom in his tone. "You weren't. I acted only in the interest of the war. I have shown the enemy that they are not beyond our reach."

"You're right," The Valtorak responded. "Now they will be more cautious. They will be harder to find. Harder to hunt. Discerning friend from foe will become near impossible. All of which will be implemented by the new Eldan, who will already be putting his newfound power to use as the master cleric. Be it days or weeks, we will have to fight for this very stone."

With that, The Valtorak took his leave, his red robes billowing behind him.

Daijen sighed and let his chin sink to his cuirass. It had all made better sense in Aran'saur.

"What of the Ankala?" Andiroma asked, speaking for the first time.

Daijen took in the Dragon Rider, who had lingered on the periphery of the group. Despite the strip of dark cloth that covered her ravaged eyes, it was obvious the woman wasn't sleeping much. The Vahlken couldn't fathom how long it might take her to come to terms with the loss of Maegar, her companion of five hundred years. There was evidence of self-care, however—a good sign. Her blonde hair looked recently washed and her sandy cloak appeared to have been scrubbed. They were small steps, but steps nonetheless.

Intending to answer Andiroma's question, Daijen rose from his chair and miscalculated his footing. He stumbled but caught himself.

"Are you alright?" The Green Leaf asked him.

Daijen held out a hand to prevent any assistance. "I'm fine. I haven't slept for several days. It's starting to take its toll."

"Then rest," the wizard insisted. "We can talk more tomorrow."

The Vahlken nodded his appreciation and gripped Aphrandhor's arm in thanks. "I'm glad to see you on your feet again."

The Green Leaf offered him a warm smile. "As am I. Now rest."

Daijen paused in his departure and reclaimed the Helm of Ahnir. He had stolen it, after all. It should be his burden to bear.

It was a deathly sleep that awaited Daijen. So deep was his rest that even his memories eluded him, plunging his consciousness into a pitch so black it was an abyss, a welcome void.

———

Daijen awoke from sleep as if he had never slumbered at all, his senses and mind ever sharp. The angle of golden light piercing his room informed him that morning had returned to the valley. He had slept beyond the dawn.

His body felt new, as if the injuries he had sustained in the palace had never been inflicted. His fight with Slait flashed through his mind. Daijen had yet to fully process their duel or the fact that Slait had beaten him. Had it not been for Ilithranda's intervention, he—not The Eldan—would have worn the Helm of Ahnir.

Defeat was an old friend, he knew. The two had been brought together many a time thanks to Kastiek. Even Ilithranda had defeated him during numerous sparring sessions. Yet losing to Slait carried a sting like no other.

There had been a time when he was ahead in his training and the beatings he had thrown Daijen's way could be explained. But he had surpassed Slait, gone on to carry the title of Vahlken and wield a slaiken blade. Victory should have been *his*.

That sting struck his pride dead centre. Alone in his room, he felt small, his abilities all for naught. That sting tipped over into his guilt, reminding him that—again—Kastiek's murderer had foregone justice because he hadn't been up to the task.

Deciding he would put himself through a rigorous morning routine that would make him ache with pain, Daijen made for his door. He paused, his fingers hovering within inches of the handle.

The Helm of Ahnir was staring at him from across the room.

It looked such a simple thing. The only patterns it possessed were a couple of engraved lines that followed the contours back and down. There was the gash, of course, that left a jagged hole just above the right eye. The blow of a Dark One, it was said.

The Vahlken picked up the helm, his attention drawn to the only feature that even hinted at its divine nature. Sitting just above the eyes was a red gem no larger than a noht—a common coin. More intriguing was the black stone that rested *inside* the ruby.

It was with brutish curiosity that he tried to prise the red gem from its fixing. Alas, the helm would not relinquish its treasure, just as it would not its secrets.

Having tied it to his belt once more, the Vahlken left his room in search of others. His keen sense of hearing brought him to one of the balconies that overlooked the courtyard.

Tovun—the only initiate in all of Ka'vairn—was moving through his routines atop the ramparts. Elevated on the wall, he danced about the very edge of the fortress, risking death should he misjudge even a single manoeuvre.

The initiate's training was made all the harder by the sabre and short-sword he wielded. Each weapon possessed a different weight, a fact that would affect his balance on such a thin strip of stone. Still, he moved with grace and efficiency, his skills improving all the time in Daijen's absence.

The Vahlken thought to spar with the young initiate, to impart some of his own knowledge and offer Tovun more than The Valtorak's dogmatic point of view. But it would not be fair, he knew. To use the boy would not balm his wounded pride but make it worse. If anything, he should offer the young Andaren some advice. He had heard the initiate was bound for The Ruins of Kharis Vhay any day now, where he might find the Weavers. *Let the spiders be a shock for him too*, Daijen thought. After all, they had to be seen to be believed.

Abandoning the balcony, Daijen navigated Ka'vairn's labyrinthine corridors, always descending until he reached the Hall of Handuin, where, again, his ears detected life. The Vahlken's pace slowed when he laid eyes on the ringed table that sat in the heart of the lofty hall. Ilithranda sat upon the table's edge while Androma, Aphrandhor, and the dwarves were seated about her like an audience. Approaching them, Daijen also noticed The Valtorak, who stood apart from the company as a sentinel in red beside one of the pillars.

Androma turned to regard Daijen, her once beautiful eyes replaced by a piece of fabric. "A time of dragons," she uttered, and with considerable emotion.

Daijen looked at Ilithranda, who had obviously recounted

some of the Ankala. "That and so much more was proclaimed," he said. "It would seem there is a future in which it all hinges on one."

"This... *half-blood*," Aphrandhor confirmed, for lack of a better word.

Daijen nodded as he closed the gap and stood among them. "Whether they're a man or a woman remains to be seen. It seems a certainty, however, that they will be of both worlds. Human. Andaren."

"Vahlken or Dragon Rider," Ilithranda added, looking from Daijen to Androma.

"I fail to see how a Vahlken could bring about a time of dragons," Androma opined. "Surely this... *person* will be a Dragon Rider?"

"We won' know until we find 'em," Mordrith asserted.

"That will be quite impossible," The Valtorak announced.

"Ye could've said the same abou' *us* findin' each other," Mordrith countered, gesturing at the round table.

"It is impossible," the master continued, "because the future you speak of is just that: the *future*. It has not happened yet."

"How can you know that?" Daijen challenged.

The Valtorak looked at him for the first time, his violet eyes heavy with judgement. "Because the visions would have spoken of a male or female with certainty. As both have been seen, I would say the sex of the child has yet to be determined by nature. Ergo, they are yet to be born."

"Then this *time of dragons*," Androma lamented, "is years away."

"Decades," The Valtorak corrected. "Possibly even centuries. Or millennia. Or perhaps it will not occur at all," he concluded cynically. "The Helm of Ahnir is a fickle thing," he continued, his eyes having found the relic on Daijen's belt. "You're speaking of one in how many thousands of visions?"

"It was a recurring vision," Ilithranda stated. "That would suggest this child *will* be born."

"But what part will they play?" Daijen questioned, the weight of so many visions pressing on him. "There were other visions, ones that spoke of an individual who would be both a saviour and a destroyer."

"Again," The Valtorak pointed out, "that is the language of an uncertain future. Every individual lives a life of choice. By meddling, we threaten to tip the scales one way or the other. We should not know the future, just as we should not act on it."

"How can we not act upon it?" Androma argued. "A time of dragons is a time of *peace*. That's what we're all fighting for, isn't it? And there is no greater deterrent to war than dragons."

"The Skaramangians' fear of dragons might be the only truth we ever really uncovered," Daijen said, his words and tone just barbed enough to remind The Valtorak that their order hadn't accomplished nearly enough in the time it had stood. "Replenishing their ranks might be the only thing that changes this war."

"And stops 'em from resurrectin' the Dark Ones," Mordrith added.

Daijen and Ilithranda looked at each other at the same time, both drawn to the other by mention of the ancient foes. "The Eikor —the Dark Ones," Daijen translated, "were voiced in the same vision as this... *dragon saviour*."

"How so?" The Green Leaf enquired.

"Perhaps voiced is the wrong word," Daijen began before Ilithranda interjected.

"Their symbol was painted in blood on the floor," she declared bluntly. "The clerics then murdered every servant in the throne room so as to reduce the witnesses."

"They don' want folk knowin' abou' what they're really up to," Yamnomora grunted.

"Regardless," Daijen went on, "I would say the Dark Ones are connected to this unborn child."

"Saviour and destroyer," Aphrandhor echoed solemnly.

Daijen thought of the hundreds of visions, recalling them all with unnatural clarity, that had pertained to an individual—a *he*— who promised a great cataclysm. A *he* who would harness the power of the world, of every world and wipe away the lines on the map and see the first empire rise again—whatever that was. It made the Vahlken dwell again on the words of the curator, who had spoken of a man the Skaramangians appeared to be waiting on.

He was about to voice his concerns when Ka'vairn's master spoke up and, inevitably, evoked his ire.

"Pursuing any of this is folly," he expressed vehemently. "We cannot fight a war with unborn children and uncertain futures. You were to attend the Ankala to gather information—secrets— that the enemy held closely. You have returned with unnecessary blood on your hands and an artefact that will bring the wrath of the empire down on our heads."

"Killing The Eldan is no small thing," Ilithranda protested, rising from the edge of the table.

"You're right—it's worse. It's insignificant. Did he tell you anything of use before you blew his head off? The locations of any strongholds we might attack? Their plans for the war? Why they're keeping dead farmers in a tomb on Nareene?"

"*Cast into the black, he drowns in shadow,*" The Eldan had declared, his final words conjured by Daijen's sharp memories. "*The Drakalis is without sight. He is without voice. He is to suffer for his betrayal, he who should have reigned beside the Pendain. But the darkness cannot hold him. His chains are destined to be broken by the power of Handuin. Break the crystal, break the world!*"

Daijen thought to recount it for the group, but he feared it would only add to The Valtorak's argument that they had nothing to use against their enemy.

The Valtorak sighed with exasperation. "I see no course from here that requires your continued alliance. It is my strong sugges- tion that you disband and spread out. We might yet discover something crucial if we probe our enemy on numerous fronts."

Daijen squared himself against his master. "*The days are shad- owed by approaching night,*" he voiced, recalling a fraction of the visions he had borne witness to. "*The war to devour all wars has come again.* I heard that again and again and *again.* That warning came with a death. Every. Single. Time. I cannot ignore that. So instead of suggesting we weaken ourselves by disbanding, I suggest *you* go out there and do the only thing you're supposed to be doing: training more Vahlken."

The Valtorak remained as firm as the pillar beside him, unfazed by the harsh response. "Let them go while they still can, Daijen. Your recklessness is going to get them all killed."

The master didn't wait for a reply, his departure as swift and cutting as his words.

21

A HOLE IN THE WORLD

The Ruins of Gelakor were not as Kitrana Voden remembered them. Like then, of course, there were Andaren bodies strewn about the ancient site, cut down by steel or magic. But steel and magic were not all the Andarens had faced. She had learned later that the two Ydrits that had attacked the party had been tracking Gallien and his companions for days. Left in their wake was a bloody massacre of broken corpses and littered limbs.

The two monsters, great mounds of bloodied white fur, lay among the fallen, their hulking bodies the resting place of a dozen swords, spears, and arrows. What terrible hunger could so drive a beast?

The question transported Kit's mind to The Black Vault, where her people toiled under threat of death to free the Leviathan of legend. *There* was a beast of insatiable hunger, a creature said to be so vile it eclipsed nightmares. It sent a shiver down the Nimean's spine.

Navigating the dead, Kitrana made her way to the northern edge of the ruins, where Joran had taken flight astride an Aegre. From that lofty vantage, The Red Fields of Dunmar were a mighty canvas that dominated the horizon. In the twilight of the setting sun, the distant mountains were little more than a dark mist. Her destination lay just beyond that hazy line, where the mountains and cliffs shielded Drakanan from the world.

There she would reclaim the sword of Skara.

A litany of dangers crossed her mind at that thought. First, she would have to reach Drakanan on foot, taking her across a vast stretch of land without supplies. Then there were the Andarens. Though the army had advanced through The Giant's Throat, it was highly likely that they had left some forces behind in case of a flanking attack.

And if she managed to survive all that, there would still be the matter of Drakanan itself.

A single dragon would be enough to bring her quest to an end and Drakanan was home to their kind. Even if she were to face one of the fabled Riders instead, her fate would be the same. If, by some slim chance, she was permitted into their dwelling, how then was she to possess the broken sword again? If Joran said no, she would be in no position to take it from him.

The Nimean closed her eyes in despair. In that darkness, she saw her kin mining the rock either side of The Black Vault. How many had died from exhaustion and hunger before her very eyes? How many had been beaten to death or hunted for sport? Kit saw them all, including the cruel execution of Helaina, the Nimean princess. They were worth facing the odds—every last one of them.

"*The blade, broken for all,*" she muttered to herself, "*its power scattered to steal its sting. The blade, broken for all, its power to be guarded in the eye of the king.*"

It had been a while since she had recited those words, once found inside the temple of Atradon—the Water Maiden—where the sword of Skara had remained under guard for centuries. Lost to the Merdians, the temple and its history lived only in her now.

Her determination renewed, if not reforged into an iron knot, Kitrana turned from the view and searched for the zig-zagging path that would take her down to the valley floor. The *clatter* of hooves on stone, however, brought her to a sudden stop. Her large eyes scrutinised the ruins, the sound distorted by its own echo. The Nimean darted for the nearest piece of cover.

She regretted her choice almost immediately.

On the floor, her back pressed against the dead Ydrit, the monster's foul odour assaulted her nose, and she hated the feel of its fur between her fingers. The sound of approaching hooves breached more of the ruins, revealing the Andarens to be closer than she thought.

It was her training in the ways of the battle maiden that saw her seek out a weapon. With care, the Nimean began to remove one of the spears protruding from the Ydrit's side. The haft in hand, she paused and listened. It was only one horse, she deduced. A scout, perhaps? A deserter, even? Either way, they would join their kin in death when she let fly the spear. None would get in her way.

Adjusting the spear so it could be thrown from her right hand, Kit braced herself in a crouch, ready to spring up and deliver death. She waited, her senses honing in on the sound of hooves to give her a direction.

There!

Kitrana rose at speed, her stance that of a hero sculpted in stone. Her arm shot back, loaded with all her strength. At the last second, when her arm was committed to the launch, the Nimean saw the truth of the matter. While Kit was unable to stop herself from hurling the weapon, she succeeded in altering its trajectory just enough to see it sail wide of the mark. In so doing, she saved a pair of dwarves from certain death.

"What were that for?" Yamnomora yelled at her, the weapon wobbling in the stone beside her head.

Kitrana sighed with relief. "I thought you were Andarens," she explained, her voice hoarse from disuse.

Yamnomora made a point of looking back at Grarfath in the saddle. "Do we look like bloody Andarens?" she snapped, clearly rattled by her near-death experience.

Kit refrained from rolling her eyes and happily rounded the

Ydrit, putting its smell behind her. "What are you two doing here? I thought you were off to..." She trailed off trying to recall the prison Aphrandhor had spoken of. "To find Gallien's father," she said instead.

"We're to find The Anther," Grarfath replied, his answer eliciting a brief look of scorn from his dwarven companion.

Kit frowned and looked about. "It's here?" she asked doubtfully, a spark of hope ignited in her heart. With the hammer, she could avoid numerous obstacles between her and the sword.

"Not exactly," Yamnomora said cryptically. "It's not for yer business anyway. Ye've yer own fool's errand," she added, jutting her chin to the north. "Try not to get eaten by a dragon, eh?"

Kitrana offered the dwarf a venomous smile as Grarfath climbed down from the Warhog. While Yamnomora guided the beast away, Grarfath closed the gap to stand before the Nimean. Where before the smith had looked a fish out of water, he now looked a man simply burdened by more than he could carry. Kit had witnessed much of the derision Yamnomora had sent his way since losing The Anther—the source of his guilt, no doubt.

"I'm glad to be seein' ye again, Miss Voden," he said politely enough. "I thought we'd parted ways for good."

Kitrana's smile warmed for the dwarf. The Nimean glanced at Yamnomora—searching the ruins nearby—before returning her attention to the smith. "No one has said this to you," she told Grarfath, "but they should have." Kit laid a hand on one of his large shoulders. "You did a *good* thing."

Grarfath brightened, if only for a second. "Thank ye," he replied genuinely. "Not everyone sees it that way," he remarked.

Again, Kitrana laid her eyes on Yamnomora before she disappeared behind one of the broken pillars. "I suspect her ire lies not with you but with herself."

The smith's face creased into a confused knot. "Eh?"

"I have known warriors like Yamnomora," Kit elaborated, omitting that she was such a warrior. "They don't like to be saved. Worse, they don't like to be saved if it comes at a cost. Losing The

Anther is a price she can't swallow. She also can't blame herself because that would be admitting her own flaws."

"That's quite the insight ye've got there," Grarfath complimented. "I jus' thought she had a stone for a heart," he quipped.

Kitrana smiled with amusement. "Far from it, I'd say. Her heart burns with passion. Perhaps more than it can contain." When she finally looked down at the smith again, he was eyeing her with suspicion.

"Are we still talkin' abou' Yamnomora?"

The Nimean beamed at him, shielding any true expression. "No. We're talking about you," she said, diverting the conversation back to Grarfath. "Don't let her dissuade you. You are worthy of The Anther. You proved that by getting this far. You proved it by defeating that Andaren brute! None, not even Yamnomora, could best him. You wielded a weapon of power exactly as it was meant to be wielded: to vanquish evil."

Grarfath was unable to maintain eye contact, his attention altogether taken by his boots for a time. "Thank ye," he said at last.

"Over 'ere!" Yamnomora hollered from within the ruins.

Abandoning the Ydrits, Grarfath and Kit followed the sound of the warrior's voice until they arrived in a familiar place. The Nimean looked around, recalling their heated fight, shoulder to shoulder and back to back. It had been there, between the pillars and damaged walls, that Slait had descended on the group. The Andarens had piled in soon after and added chaos to the battle.

Grarfath looked to his right, where he had emerged with The Anther in hand. Following suit, Kitrana then tracked the hammer as if it had been thrown again. It led her gaze across the corpse-ridden clearing to the very spot where The Anther had struck Slait and the two had ported away.

The Nimean blinked.

She blinked again, sure that her eyes were playing tricks on her. "What *is* that?"

Resting five feet from the ground, there existed a tear in the fabric of the world. It was easily overlooked as, from many angles, it appeared to be no more than heat waves distorting the air. But, with patience, its supernatural state was revealed in the glimpses between those waves.

Kitrana was drawn in by the slivers of light that would come and go. "I've never seen anything like this."

"It's a..." Grarfath looked to Yamnomora. "What did ye call it again?"

"A port scar," the grizzled warrior announced, keeping Bludgeon's reins in a tight grip.

"The Anther did this?" Kit questioned.

"Aye. Not that it's got anythin' to do with ye."

The Nimean ignored the all-too-familiar response and moved closer to the phenomenon. "I didn't see this before. Does this happen everywhere you use it?"

Grarfath could only shrug.

Yamnomora planted a heavy hand on the smith's chest, moving him aside so she could better see the scar for herself. "Ye dolt," she jibed. "Still so much to learn. The scar wouldn' 'ave emerged right away. Takes a few hours. Some o' 'em only last a few hours. The fact that this one is still 'ere is testament to the power o' the weapons when they're all together. An' no," she stated, her attention shifting to Kitrana, "this doesn' happen every time The Anther is used. Only when the hammer itself is sent somewhere else. Understand?" she asked Grarfath. "Satisfied?" she asked the Nimean.

"Not even close," Kit commented under her breath. "What does it do?"

Yamnomora's mouth puckered and twisted while she deliberated. "It doesn' *do* anythin'," she eventually relayed. "How did Mordrith put it? It exists in two places at the same time. We can see it 'ere, but ye can also see it wherever the hammer ported to."

Grarfath looked like he had understood as much as Kitrana had of that explanation. "If it doesn' *do* anythin'," he posed, "why 'ave we come in search o' it?"

Yamnomora sighed and shook her head. "Exhaustin'," she muttered. "It doesn' do anythin'," she reiterated, "but if ye touch it, the scar'll pull ye in an' spit ye out—so *don'* touch it," she ordered sternly, one stubby finger pointed in Kit's direction. "Once ye move through the scar, it becomes unstable," she continued. "Collapses on itself—"

The world and Yamnomora's words were suddenly lost to Kitrana Voden.

There came no warning. No increase in discomfort. Just an agonising shot of searing hot pain, as if a molten rod had been rammed through the Nimean's back. She screamed and threw her head back, her spine arching severely. Her bones, boasting carti- lage more than anything, stretched beyond any human's norm. Her fingernails dug into her palms, drawing blood, while her knees buckled and she fell to the ground.

Through the haze of pain, she managed to see the dwarves, who moved frantically about her, bewildered by her sudden state of torment.

"What's happenin' to her?" Grarfath's voice could barely be heard over the blood pounding in her ears.

"Hold her down before she touches—"

Much like The Ruins of Gelakor, Yamnomora's command slipped from Kit's senses.

The Nimean could hardly make sense of her reality. She looked around, taking in a world that shouldn't have been there. The sky had been replaced by rock, its nooks and crannies illuminated by torchlight that revealed buildings crafted from the rough stone. From all around her came a buzz of noise, be it the hammering of iron, coarse shouting or even the merriment of bashful singing. The vast cavern was connected by a network of bridges and lifts, all of which were alive with the activity of... *dwarves*!

The Morthil Mountains. She was in Andara!

She was just as dumbfounded by the absence of pain, the torturous experience having gone as suddenly as it had begun. She was, however, left with a dull ache between her shoulders where...

Kit put one hand over the back of her neck, unable to reach the brand burned into her skin by the Merdians. What had they done to her? It was a question that would have to wait, for she soon found herself buried beneath Grarfath.

The dwarf materialised from nowhere and barrelled into the Nimean, taking her from her hands and knees. A second later and Yamnomora appeared with Bludgeon in tow. Only when the smith rolled aside did Kit see the port scar, though the phenomenon folded in on itself almost immediately and vanished from existence.

"Where is it?" Yamnomora was asking over and over again. She had released Bludgeon's reins so she might comb the area, but they had been spat out of the scar onto a flat plain of smooth stone— there was nowhere for The Anther to hide.

"It's not 'ere," Grarfath concluded miserably.

"It *must* be 'ere," Yamnomora protested, her hand thrown out to gesture at the empty space where the scar had sat.

But it wasn't there. Though that wasn't to say they were alone.

Their inexplicable arrival had alerted Morthil's inhabitants— specifically those in armour and brandishing steel. The horde descended the steps on both sides of the flat plain, pincering the intruders.

Death was almost upon them, Kitrana knew. Yet all she could fathom was the great distance that now sat between her and Joran.

Between her and the sword of Skara.

At the same time, she felt a cold dread seep into her bones, for beneath her feet, a Leviathan slumbered no more.

22
CLARITY BEFORE THE FALL

0 Years Ago...

4

It was a cold and bitter wind that met Daijen's bare chest. It might as well have been a warm breeze for all his skin could care. It didn't stop him from reducing the wooden dummies to kindling, his atori blade sweeping and slashing in carefully honed arcs. The Vahlken dashed, weaved, and darted between them all as if Kastiek's scrutinising gaze still lingered over him.

Amidst the debris, he was left standing tall, chest heaving after countless hours of exercise and rigorous drills. He had noticed Andromo some time ago, observing him from the edges of the training area, but only now acknowledged her presence.

"We have more," he said, gesturing at the broken dummies with the point of his short-sword. "I could set them up for you."

"I've never fought anything that stands still," she replied as a matter of fact. "I prefer something that can fight back."

Daijen knew a challenge when he heard one—decades in

Ka'vairn would do that. "I've been known to fight back," he quipped.

"Having seen the way you converse with The Valtorak, I'm inclined to agree."

The Vahlken glanced up at the northern tower that overlooked the courtyard. The Valtorak had retired to his office after their latest argument in the hall—that had been some days ago. Daijen wished to find some common ground again, but they repeatedly found themselves on the opposite ends of every opinion.

"Draw your sword then," Daijen bade, stepping over the splintered dummies to face his opponent.

Her long blonde hair caught in the passing wind, Andromeda did no such thing. "Ilithranda tells me you lost your sabre in Aran'saur," she said instead. "Am I to assume, then, that you're fighting with your atori blade?"

In naught but his trousers and boots, Daijen let his eyes wander over the bronze short-sword in his hand. "I am," he replied.

"You will find that even the precious silk of your Weavers is no match for the bite of my sword. I wouldn't want to break it."

Feeling like he had just lost some kind of competition, Daijen asked, "Then what would you suggest?"

Andromeda unbuckled her silvyr sword, the blade hidden inside its scabbard, and placed it on the stone at her feet. "We fight with steel." From within her satchel, the Rider removed two broadswords before tossing one in Daijen's direction. "Training swords," she said flatly, as if producing the swords hadn't caused the Vahlken to question his acute senses.

"How did you..." He tilted his head to see all of the satchel. "How did you do that?"

"Pocket dimension," Andromeda answered, one hand patting the bag. "A speciality of Aphrandhor's."

Her words were repeated soundlessly on Daijen's lips. "How does it work?" he asked, hungry for knowledge.

"If you can fit it," she said, stretching out the lip of the satchel, "you can store it."

"Fascinating," he replied absently, quite taken by the effect.

"*Practical*," Androma specified. "Especially if you wander the world rather than make a home in it." The Rider rolled her wrist several times, backwards and forwards, getting a feel for the weight and balance of the weapon. "If you hold back," she went on to warn him, "I will know."

"As you wish," he said with verve.

Without a sound, he pounced, leaving the ground altogether, his sword pointed down at his enemy. It should have been a clean win—a swift victory—yet he found naught but air into which to plunge his weapon.

Instead, he was immediately put on the defensive, swinging his sword up behind him to bat hers away from his spine. A quick pivot of his shoulders saw him evade the subsequent kick before he was forced to raise his weapon and deflect three more strikes from the Rider.

"What will you do about your sabre?" Androma asked, her question as sudden as her sword arm. "The one you left behind in the palace."

It made Daijen think about anything other than their duel, a fact that played right into the Rider's tactics. He managed half a word before Androma's sword was whipping round one way and then the next, high then low. He blocked up high and raised his right boot to avoid the low blow, only to find the training sword thrust towards his midriff, where the point pressed hard into his cuirass.

On her knees before him, arm outstretched to keep her sword aloft, Androma offered the Vahlken a wicked grin of satisfaction. "One to me," she said, scoring herself the victory.

Daijen's smile was tight and reserved as he batted her sword aside. "Again," he said hungrily.

"You never answered my question," Androma pointed out.

Assuming a new battle stance, his weapon held high so the steel rested across the back of his neck, the Vahlken assessed the Rider's body language, seeking out her potential attack. He saw none.

"I will forge a new one," he replied simply.

"A sword-smith too?" Androma asked, impressed perhaps. "They really do teach you everything here."

"I imagine you have servants at Drakanan," Daijen mocked with a hint of amusement. "I bet they shine your boots and butter your toast too."

Androma began to slowly walk around the Vahlken, as if taunting him. "We know basic smithing," she said without responding to his jibe. "Our silvyr weapons are obviously forged by the dwarves. Much like your slaiken blades."

Daijen used the Rider's last few words against her, hoping the sound of her own voice would drown out what little noise he made leaping through the air. Somehow, she knew. Androma dropped and rolled under his attack before springing back to her feet like a leaf skipping in the wind.

The second his feet touched down, the Vahlken reversed his course with a hand-standing backflip. He came down on his opponent with a hammering strike of his sword. Androma deflected it —as predicted—but missed his confusing jump, twist, and kick that found the side of her head. As his boot made contact, Daijen was sure to mould his foot around the back of her head and pull his strength just enough to take her down without breaking her neck.

Daijen walked in a tight circle to see the Rider picking herself up, one hand rubbing the side of her neck. "You held back," she stated with disappointment.

"You'd be dead if I hadn't."

"You hit hard," Androma admitted, cracking her neck. "I've been hit harder."

Daijen held back his witty response in favour of evading the Rider's lightning-fast swing. The tip of her sword scraped up his cuirass and missed his chin by a hair's breadth. There was no countering when Androma immediately advanced, using his leg and torso to elevate herself and land a kick to his face.

The courtyard welcomed him as it had so many times during his training. It still hurt, though not as much as his jaw. He stretched it, hearing the bones click as he rose back to his feet.

"Alright," he said wearily. "Don't hold back."

Androma gave him a disingenuous smile. "I warned you."

Daijen was on the cusp of making his move when the Rider fired off another unexpected question.

"Have you seen The Green Leaf today?"

The Vahlken's gaze wandered over the keep behind her. "No," he replied, keeping his answer deliberately short.

"You left the Helm of Ahnir with a wizard and haven't checked in on him?" she queried with genuine surprise.

"You said he was to be trusted, and I trust you. Besides, he proved himself at Nareene—"

Daijen cut his response short when forced to defend himself against another attack.

Their swords clashed again and again, always within inches of each other's skin. Deciding he wouldn't hold back this time, Daijen batted her blade aside and leaped sideways at his opponent. At the same time, his left leg whipped up, hammering his boot into Androma's chest.

His Vahlken strength launched her like an arrow from a bow, taking the Rider from her feet. She impacted one of the stable gates with enough force behind her to reduce the wood to pieces. Her journey, however, didn't come to an end until she skidded across the stone and struck the far wall.

Daijen was immediately weighed down by regret. He dropped the training sword and darted into the stable after her, but his third apology was drowned out by the violent rush of air that exploded from Androma's palm. It picked the Vahlken up like a leaf in a storm and threw him into the roof before tossing him back out into the courtyard.

With pain shooting through his back and chest, Daijen looked up from the ground and managed to see Androma through the wild strands of white hair that had fallen over his face. The Rider was walking out of the stables as one end of the structure completely collapsed in a plume of dust.

"That was good," she said without inflection. "But you can do better."

"You cheated," he accused her.

The Rider made a point of turning her head as if she were regarding the stables. "I use the gifts afforded to me, just as you use those afforded to you."

Daijen sighed, a feint more than anything, for his muscles were drawing on enough power to see him pounce from his prone position. At the same time, his right hand scooped up the training sword he had dropped, the steel scraping across the stone. For all his speed, the sound of the sword dragging over the courtyard floor was all Androma needed to hear to know he was coming.

The Rider sidestepped and deflected his swing before pivoting on her heel and retaliating with a swing of her own. They again fell into fierce swordplay, their dance taking them across the courtyard and up the staircase—a direction Daijen had purposely guided them towards. As predicted, Androma's reactions were slowed a fraction as she split her focus between his attacks and the steps themselves.

It was all the advantage the Vahlken needed to backhand his sword across his foe's torso and send her tumbling over the side of the staircase. Returned to the courtyard, Androma picked herself up and ran her fingers over the strike that had scarred the hardened plates of black leather. There was a single streak of blue amidst the black, a slither of scales.

Maegar's scales.

Sensing a natural pause in their sparring, Daijen approached the edge of the stairs, his weapon held low. He was about to offer Androma the opportunity to talk about the dragon when the Rider gripped the end of a step and pulled her weight up just enough to swing her leg into the Vahlken's knee.

Rolling shoulder over shoulder, Daijen used his tumbling fall to flip onto his feet. Androma came for him, using one hand on a step to lever her body round—specifically her boot. The Vahlken arched his back and narrowly evaded the blow before whipping his sword into her path. Steel collided in a rhythmic dance that only the best of warriors could have kept up with.

"You are defeated, Daijen Saeth," Androma declared.

Bemused by her words, Daijen raised an eyebrow as he paced the courtyard. "I don't feel defeated."

"I have centuries on you," she reminded him. "You are beaten."

The Rider's words were uttered as if a prophecy. Daijen, however, refused to accept it as such. He pounced, renewing their battle up the steps and across the ramparts. Their swords rang out, reverberating over The Dain'duil far below. It seemed hours they fought, the sun slowly passing through the sky until it began its descent into the west. Each came close to besting the other, to finding that moment of vulnerability or angle of attack that would secure their victory.

But there was no victory unless it was to be found in their impressive stamina, if not their tenacity. Daijen liked to think it was because they were so evenly matched, despite her centuries of experience, but he suspected Androma was becoming a shadow of her former self. While much of the bond between Riders and dragons was unknown, it was clear that their strength was a result of that bond. Without Maegar, she was becoming human again. The Vahlken couldn't help but wonder how many more sparring sessions it would take before he defeated Androma with ease.

But it was not that day. For all his attempts, the blind woman continued to intercept his strikes and slashing swipes.

"How is it," he finally asked with exasperation, "you are able to fight without your sight?"

Androma rose from her crouch and rested her blade atop one of her blue-scaled pauldrons. "Dragon Riders must be the light that holds back the darkness," she said, her words and tone suggesting she was reciting some kind of oath. "So we must learn to fight in the dark."

Daijen nodded along, taking her to mean that all Dragon Riders were trained to fight wearing blindfolds. "You deprive yourselves of your senses," he deduced, "so as not to rely on them."

"Precisely."

The Vahlken thought of his own training—his years learning to wield his enhanced senses—and managed a stifled laugh. "We are quite the opposite."

It was those enhanced senses that caught the subtlest of movements on the second floor of the keep. Daijen glimpsed Ilithranda at the window before she faded into shadow. Like The Valtorak, she had made herself scarce since the heated debate in the Hall of Handuin. More than once he had tried to find his companion of decades and enquire, if not demand to know, what had transpired between her and the emperor.

"I haven't seen her like this in a long time," he said without explanation. "Not since she first learned the truth about the war, about the Skaramangians."

Androma held the sword at ease and looped her arm inside his own before making for the steps leading back down to the courtyard. Daijen was more than happy to walk as such, the simple connection enough to ignite some long-forgotten emotions in him.

The Vahlken looked down at the woman beside him. She was so exotic in his eyes, her body a palette of colour. Her skin, while pinkish, varied in shades across her face and hands. So too did the freckles that dotted her cheeks beneath the blindfold. Her lips were dark by Andaren standards, a flush peach colour that Daijen found all too inviting. Then there was her hair, a golden mane of blonde that ran down her back.

"She hasn't spoken to me," Androma said, breaking the momentary spell she had seemingly cast over him. "I can try," the Rider offered, "but I sense only rejection awaits me at the end of that path."

"But she *does* speak to you," Daijen pointed out, a fact he had wanted to discuss for some time. "There is a most unusual bond between you."

"Unusual?" Androma contested as they stepped onto the courtyard floor.

"I meant no offence," Daijen was quick to reply. "Only that Ilithranda doesn't make friends easily. It took me *years*. And no small amount of blood," he added as a bleak afterthought. "And you don't come across as someone who... collects friends."

Androma tilted her head up at the Vahlken.

"Again," he said, "I meant no offence. Perhaps I'm just envious.

And *mystified*. I thought you both bound as nemeses after our meeting on the shore."

Androma said nothing for a moment, the training sword probing the ground in search of her silvyr blade. Reluctantly, Daijen broke away from her hold and retrieved the weapon for her.

"We are bound," the Rider finally replied, accepting the fine blade. "But not as enemies."

Daijen watched her strap the weapon to her belt and make for the keep. "Then as what?" he called after her.

The Dragon Rider paused and turned her mouth over one shoulder. "We are bound in *heartbreak*."

Her answer stumped the Vahlken, making him wonder if he really knew Ilithranda at all.

Androma stopped again when she reached the main doors. "We must begin preparations to secure the keep," she called. "You know this fortress better than I do. Speak to the dwarves and put them to work. Another day cooped up in here and they will destroy Ka'vairn before your army gets the chance."

Daijen heard every word, but his mind had got no further than that which bound Rider and Vahlken. By the time he had come to his senses again, Androma was gone, leaving him alone in the courtyard.

———

Within the hour, he had met with Mordrith and Yamnomora in the library, where he could present them with detailed drawings and maps of Ka'vairn. They had rejected his offer to take them through the fortress's strengths and weaknesses, informing the Vahlken that they would find them easily enough. Leaving them to pore over the ancient plans, Daijen went in search of The Green Leaf.

Even without enhanced senses, the wizard would have been easy to find. The discharge from his spells fouled the air and his constant muttering echoed down the cold hallways. Daijen honed in on him, bringing him to an area of the keep he seldom visited. It was draughty thanks to the many sections of broken stone that exposed Ka'vairn to the mountain winds. Much of the place was layered in silky sheets of ice, while numerous rooms were flooded from the rains.

Peering through an open doorway, the Vahlken spied the scaffolding that clung to the exterior. He imagined the catapult or ballista that had wrought such damage eons past when the emperor had gone to war with Handuin himself. History was soon to repeat itself—a dire thought that weighed on Daijen.

An ear-splitting *bang* grounded the Vahlken in the moment, returning his attention to the matter at hand. Daijen hurried through the last of the corridors until he came across a cloud of smoke coming from one of the chambers. Lying across the threshold was The Green Leaf.

"Aphrandhor," Daijen said as he aided the man back to his feet.

"I'm alright," the wizard assured him, dusting himself down.

"What happened?" Daijen asked, inspecting the room, his pale eyes piercing the fog to see the Helm of Ahnir sitting upon a pedestal, smoke rising from its slender curves.

"I will admit," The Green Leaf replied, "a touch of frustration has permeated my work. My experiments have yielded naught, and any attempt to remove the gem has failed miserably."

Daijen looked from the wizard to his staff on the floor. "So you hit it with magic?" he queried with some surprise.

"I had hoped to destroy the helm *around* the gem," Aphrandhor explained as he retrieved his staff. "As you can see, the helm benefits from the gem's protection."

The Vahlken crossed the room to better scrutinise the godly relic. "The *gem's* protection?"

"Oh yes, I'm certain the gem is the source of power. The gem *inside* the gem specifically."

Daijen narrowed his gaze, identifying the small black heart inside the ruby. "What makes you say that?"

"Deduction, I suppose." The wizard rounded the pedestal. "The helm allows the user to see potential futures, yes? That same power shouldn't also protect the helm from harm. That would be two *very* different spells laced into the same object. My theory is that the black gem provides the ability to see into the future, while the red gem protects it from being damaged."

Daijen rubbed a single thumb over the ruby, feeling its many facets. "Any theory on why it kills the user?" he asked, seeing the fatal flaw in the helm's design.

Aphrandhor's brow pinched, bringing together his feelings of curiosity and surprise. "I would have thought that obvious to *you*."

"To *me*?"

The wizard shrugged. "I assumed you carried the faith of your people, that the helm belonged to a *god*. That it wasn't meant for the minds of mere mortals."

The Vahlken made to speak but found his response lacking. "I have faith," he finally managed, his lips dry. "I have *hope*," he specified. "I must admit, my faith in the Arkalon has been shaken by all that I've learned. Did the gods truly walk among us? Was Mount Athan their home? Did we fight beside them against the Dark Ones? While I have seen the physical proof, something in my heart tells me..."

The Green Leaf tilted his head. "Tells you what?"

"That I'm missing something."

"I think we're missing more than just *something*," Aphrandhor agreed. "I have seen the skeleton in Akmar. Its skull is five times the size of ours. It couldn't have worn that helm if it wanted to. This was made for a *man*," he added, tapping the steel helm with his knuckles.

Daijen intended then to inform the wizard then of the individual so many visions had depicted, of a man who would bring about an ancient empire after raining destruction upon the realm. But it all felt too much to voice, the thousands upon thousands of visions that had all been tainted by bloody death. Still, he knew it all needed laying out so he might look upon it as he would a map.

"And I dare not touch it with the bracer," The Green Leaf went on, gesturing at the vambrace poking out of his satchel in the corner of the room. "The history of that helm is likely longer than that of any of the bones we discovered on Nareene. It would be liking falling down a well with no end. Imagine seeing every vision, every death, this wretched thing has caused. I would share in the fate of every poor soul forced to wear it."

Daijen folded his arms and sighed, aggrieved by the outcome. "So we can learn nothing from it," he lamented.

"You were still right to take it, Daijen," the wizard reassured him. "While it offers us no advantage, at least in our possession it does not offer our enemy the advantage."

"I fear the cost."

Aphrandhor looked to the destruction beyond the chamber. "Ka'vairn has withstood invasion before. It can do so again. Not to mention our little council of misfits. They will not be expecting the likes of us fighting by your side."

Though he did not doubt their abilities or their collective strength, Daijen knew the reality of pitting a few against the many. The Valtorak's words came rushing back to him. *"Let them go while they still can, Daijen. Your recklessness is going to get them all killed."* Each one was a weight that threatened to crush him.

"We need not be here," the Vahlken muttered, a spontaneous thought born of desperation and resentment.

"What's that?" the wizard questioned.

"We need not be here," Daijen repeated, boldly this time. "When they come for the helm," he elaborated. "The only thing of real value is the helm and what we have of Ahnir's skeleton—we could take both with us."

"And go where? We have exhausted our leads."

"No, we haven't," the Vahlken stated, a knowing look in his eyes.

The Green Leaf looked away in calculation before his gaze snapped back to Daijen. "You can't mean... You can't use the bracer on that bone," he told the Vahlken. "I thought you had been made to see sense."

"Think of the secrets locked away inside that bone," Daijen said provocatively. "It could be the key to unlocking *everything*. Presently, it would give us somewhere to start, somewhere not here. Let them tear Ka'vairn down brick by brick if they must. Our strength is not tied to any one place."

"While I agree with all of that," Aphrandhor countered, "I must protest your use of the vambrace. You have no experience with it. It's a very layered mechanism. You have to learn how to delve into the depths without plunging into the abyss. The more you press into the memory of something, the more you take on those memories and feelings as your own. If you touch that bone, you might lose yourself to it. You wouldn't know where you end and Ahnir begins."

"Staying here will be the end of us all," Daijen concluded, speaking more to himself than the wizard. "We need direction, something that will take us all away from here, including The Valtorak."

The Green Leaf sidestepped to block Daijen's view of the vambrace. "I cannot let you use it. You're too important to our cause."

What clarity Daijen experienced in that moment, his path laid before him, a path that would save them all and ensure the downfall of the Skaramangians at the same time.

The Vahlken displayed something of a pained smile, as if the compliment was too much to absorb. "As Androma said, you are a good man, Aphrandhor. What would *you* suggest?"

The Green Leaf sighed, his eyes wandering while he thought of a worthy reply. It was then, of course, in that instance of distraction, that Daijen's arm shot out. He caught the wizard in the throat with the inside blade of his hand, robbing the man of breath.

Quite shocked and lacking the required air, the wizard dropped his staff and wrapped his fingers around his wounded neck. Swift was the punch that Daijen landed in Aphrandhor's face, his strength withheld enough that he didn't break anything but powerful enough to throw the man's head into the back wall behind.

The scene had played out as clearly as the Vahlken had seen it in his mind, ending with The Green Leaf sliding down the wall in a crumpled heap. Stepping over his unconscious form, Daijen removed the bracer from the satchel.

His brief interaction with the satchel recalled Androma's words from earlier. *"A speciality of Aphrandhor's,"* she had said. The Vahlken peered inside the bag, finding naught but an eerie abyss therein. *Practical*, he thought.

He then picked up the wizard's staff and dropped it inside. It was a wonder to see the entire length of wood disappear into the void, though he marvelled at it for no longer than it took him to toss the satchel out of the broken window. There was no telling when The Green Leaf would rouse again, but at least he would be slowed without his magic.

With the bracer in hand, Daijen paused to claim the Helm of Ahnir. He would take both into the depths of Ka'vairn, where he would better the fate of them all.

23
HAUNTED BY HOPE

Despite the weight of the world that sat on Joran's shoulders, flying on dragonback made him smile from ear to ear. It was an entirely different experience to being astride Oaken, whose saddle had been designed with a more prone position for flight in mind. It had given Joran the feeling of being one with his mother's mount, as well as the feeling of safety, being so snug with the Aegre.

Atop Garganafan, the boy was upright as if he was astride a horse. The wind would have battered him were he not seated behind Kassanda, who, besides shielding him, had also rigged some of the saddle straps about his belt to keep him secure. Garganafan was significantly larger than Oaken too, his impressive wingspan taking them south at speeds he had never experienced during his solo flight on the Aegre.

It was exhilarating!

Something about being seated rather than lying made him feel like he was on a throne at the top of the world. The dragon beneath him added to that sense of power, lending to the belief that they could do anything and no one could stop them.

Garganafan glided low, bringing them under the clouds where

the last light of the setting sun could be seen in the west. It cast The Ruins of Gelakor in stark shadows and orange stone, making it appear far more beautiful than Joran felt it deserved.

Looking down on the ancient site, his stomach began to drop as a cool dread enthralled his spirit. Somewhere amongst the dead, he would soon be standing over Gallien and the others who had given their lives to see him fulfil his destiny. Joran tried to steel himself against what was to come, against the emotions that would overwhelm him. He was to be worthy of the dragon heart after all. He was expected to rise above such things, to command his emotions and not the other way around.

The feeling of alarm, however, did not settle but increased as Garganafan found purchase on the northern edge of the ruins. Only then was Joran able to see the carnage in all its gory detail.

"There are so many of them," he commented from the saddle.

Everywhere he looked, the ruins revealed more dead Andarens, their bronze armour gleaming in the dying light. The stone was marred by splatters and puddles of black where so much blood had dried.

"Tread carefully," Kassanda instructed as she began to dismount. "This place belongs to the dead now."

Joran swept his sandy cloak aside and followed the Rider down, mimicking her exact movements until he was upon the stone once more. To his right was the spot where he had said his final farewells to Gallien. It brought on a tightness in his chest that made him turn away from the area.

He turned in time to see Oaken gliding out of the sky. The Aegre circled high above them, reluctant, perhaps, to join them while Garganafan sat among the ruins. Instead, Oaken found a perch among the mountain stone that loomed over the site. From there, he merely watched them, a silent observer.

A silent *guardian*, Joran thought.

"He is a most unusual Aegre," Kassanda observed. "Absent their Vahlken riders, most return to The Hellion Mountains. Oaken treats you as if you are bonded."

"Androma said I have my mother's eyes," Joran recalled. "He seemed to recognise that."

"I would caution you against such a bond," the Dragon Rider warned. "When the time comes, you will be bonded to a dragon in more ways than one. I tell you now, no dragon will tolerate the lingering presence of an Aegre. The best thing you can do is order that the beast be gone." Kassanda left the matter at that. "Come," she bade.

Wondering how he could tell an Aegre to do anything, Joran returned his attention to The Ruins of Gelakor. "What are *they*?" he asked, his tone somewhere between horror and awe.

Kassanda followed his gaze and looked upon the two mounds of white fur surrounded by pieces of Andaren bodies. "Ydrits, I think," she replied. "I haven't seen one in some time."

Before Joran could reply, a blood-curdling shriek of what could only be pain resounded throughout the ruins. Only as it died away were they able to hone in on the scream. Kassanda was the first to respond, her racing movements swift and graceful. She navigated the corpses and broken stonework without disturbing anything before vanishing into shadow.

"Wait!" Joran called out, hurrying after her.

By the time he found the Dragon Rider, she was standing in a small clearing littered with bodies. She was alone. Joran looked around, noting the damaged pillars that encircled them and the tiers that rose beside them. It was from up there that Slait had fallen upon the companions.

Joran searched the dead and inevitably discovered the dark stains where he had cut down his foes, reducing them to sparks and ash. This place was also where Grarfath had thrown the hammer and rid them of Slait.

"There's no one here," he observed, baffled by the scream they had heard.

"Just ghosts," Kassanda said ominously. "Do you smell that?" she queried, crouching down to waft the air into her face.

"I smell a lot of things," Joran commented with disgust.

"I haven't come across that scent in years, but you never forget the odour of a *Warhog*."

Joran recalled the animal that had been in tow with the legendary stone bones. "The giant pig? The dwarves had one."

"The scent is fresh," Kassanda commented. "Most peculiar." The Dragon Rider stood up with resolve. "We need to search the entire site for any sign of Androma and the others. I will fashion us some torches."

That was not all Kassanda did. After handing Joran a flaming stick, she raised one hand into the air and opened her palm to the night sky. From her very skin, an orb of brilliant light was birthed into the world. It floated high and came to rest over the heart of the ruins. Where it failed to banish the shadows, their torches would see to the matter.

And so they parted, each searching a different area of the site while under the watchful gaze of Garganafan. It felt wrong to step over so many dead, even if they had been the attackers. In death, they looked truly at peace, their ashen faces frozen in the facade of slumber. That wasn't true of them all, however. It was all too clear which of the poor souls had met their doom in the face of the monstrous Ydrits. Beyond their ravaged bodies, they bore expressions of terror and agony.

Despite the butchery and gore that met him at every turn, hope was kindled in Joran's heart. Not only was Gallien absent from the slaughter, but so too were the rest of his companions. There was no sign of The Green Leaf or Androma. If Cob lay dead amongst the ruins he would surely have been surrounded by those he had felled, a monument to the Kedradi's prowess.

"I can't see them anywhere," he said upon reuniting with Kassanda.

"Nor can I," the Rider replied.

"Did they survive?" Joran blurted, well aware that his companion didn't have the answer.

"It would seem they did," she said, though there was still some doubt in her voice.

"What are you thinking?" he asked, his hope running away with itself.

Kassanda moved to see the dead heaps of fur that lay under the light of her orb. "I'm thinking the Ydrits provided enough chaos to allow them to slip through the Andarens. The only question is: did they retreat south or climb down and head north?"

At her question, Garganafan flexed his awesome wings and battered the ruins with a strong gust of wind. His flight was short, coming down atop the valley wall south of the ruins. He was entirely lost from Joran's vantage thereafter, leaving him to wonder what the dragon was even doing.

"Interesting," Kassanda muttered.

"Has he found something?" Joran's hope was up against his rising fear now.

"Fresh tracks—hoof prints and the scent of a Warhog."

"They went south then," Joran concluded, desperate to find his father.

"The tracks lead *into* the site."

"They doubled back?"

"If they did, they were all astride the Warhog. There are no prints besides those." Kassanda looked around the ruins. "I cannot say why the dwarves might have doubled back," she continued. "Then again, I cannot say why any other than Mordrith wields The Anther. We will fly further south, over The Giant's Throat. I would have answers, and I would know exactly what has become of so many weapons of power."

At once, the Rider began to make her way south, bringing her back to her dragon. Joran hesitated, caught between his need to know whether Gallien and the others had truly survived and the potential turmoil of discovering that they had perished elsewhere.

Clinging to the threads of hope, he followed in Kassanda's wake.

24
FALLING THROUGH TIME

0 Years Ago...

4

Believing he had been dissuaded from such a foolish path, there was none to stop Daijen descending into the darkest levels of Ka'vairn. The path ended where it always did—before the rounded slab of iron that barred all from the pits of Handuin.

With enviable strength, he pulled open the great door and entered the cavern. He thought to seal himself inside, using the iron bar to keep the door in place, but, considering the potential risks he faced, he decided to simply close it behind him. If something were to go awry, at least the others would be able to reach him.

Not that it would, he determined, spying the black bone resting in its alcove.

His Vahlken mind could handle whatever the bracer revealed to him—it was providence, after all. He was meant to be the one to uncover the truth, a task he had been given, with tools gifted to him by Handuin's alchemy. Through Ahnir, he would see all that had transpired before history could grasp it.

And, Daijen thought with a sliver of excitement, if Ahnir proved to be the god so revered in the pages of the Arkalon, he would surely see through the eyes of the divine. What wonders he might see! The beginning of creation, perhaps. Or the end of time and the dying of the light.

It was a hardship to stay grounded then, to remember why he was committed to the task at hand. He needed to strip back the Skaramangian order, to see their secrets so he might learn where to strike. Daijen dreamt of a single blow that would cripple the enemy and bring an end to the war.

Feeling the touch of cold steel in his hand, the Vahlken looked down at the Helm of Ahnir. It was a weapon of power, but only in the hands of those willing to slaughter thousands. Since it refused to part with its secrets and offer a bloodless advantage, Daijen perceived but one resolution.

None could possess it.

Giving it no more thought, he tossed it into the glowing white pit that churned with Handuin's magic. The helm sank without protest, its ruby and protected black gem plummeting into the depths with it.

He thought of his own experience inside the pit. Even if an initiate knew the helm was down there, they wouldn't have the faculty to search for it while enthralled by the potion mix. And there was no telling what would happen if a Vahlken returned to those waters. Given their potency, he concluded, it would be nothing good.

With the helm taken care of, he returned his attention to the black fossil. Standing before it, his eyes wandered over the many glyphs carved into the bone. They were as much a mystery to him as anything else. Handuin could not have said the same, for the warlock of old had translated those same glyphs to make the pits in that very chamber.

Not for long would they remain a mystery...

Daijen removed the vambrace given to him by the Weavers and

slipped his right hand inside the bracer of silver and bronze. He clipped it together, expecting to feel something, anything, but found it to be no different to wearing any piece of armour.

His arm outstretched, the Vahlken hesitated at the last second. It was doubt, he knew. Doubt in his own ability to see it through as he had claimed he could. But it was not his doubt. No. He had allowed the doubts of others to creep in and convince him he wasn't strong enough. They would have been easier to shrug off had they not come from his closest companions, including Ilithranda, who knew him best.

His eyes shut tight, Daijen hardened his resolve. He hadn't come this far by proving everyone's doubts in him to be true. Determined, his pale hand reached out and gripped the cold bone.

Nothing happened.

Daijen examined the bracer on his forearm and tried again. Nothing. What was he doing wrong? He hadn't seen Aphrandhor do anything differently. He touched it a third time before turning away in frustration, his fingers inspecting the clips.

Only then did he realise the cavern beneath Ka'vairn was gone.

The pits of Handuin and their white glow had disappeared, and the iron door with them. Daijen craned his neck as he now looked upon a towering hall of black stone. The Vahlken turned around, expecting to see the bone, and found himself confronted by a stranger—a *human*.

There was something about that man, something inherently dark, if not unnatural, that cooled Daijen's blood and set his heart to racing. Robed in black upon black, his head draped in a voluminous hood, the stranger stood eerily still, his cold eyes fixed on the Vahlken.

Daijen took a step back, his hand falling to the hilt on his belt.

"You have come to witness," the dark figure declared, his voice a deep rasp that set Daijen's hairs on end.

The Vahlken's lips parted in response, though he had no idea what he was to say—The Green Leaf had said nothing about interacting with the memories.

"I would not miss the fruit of your long labours, master."

The second voice turned Daijen on his heel, where he found another man awaiting him. Unlike the hooded figure, the new human was not intimidating. Robed in green and gold and cloaked in black, he emanated the aura of an ordinary person, his human features suggesting he was younger, with perhaps only a couple of decades behind him.

He came to a stop only a few feet in front of Daijen, his hands clasped by his waist and his head bowed in respect. "Has the hour arrived?" he asked, looking through Daijen.

A wicked smile cut the dark figure's square jaw. "As always, my apprentice, your timing is masterful. Come."

The Vahlken felt his body tugged in their wake, as if the memory was shrinking about him, before the hooded figure stopped mid-step and reached out for his apprentice's shoulder, as if he needed the support.

"Master?"

The dark figure reached under his hood and covered his eyes in discomfort. "He's trying to find me," he whispered.

"*The Drakalis,*" the apprentice named, fear casting his eyes upwards.

Daijen had heard that name before, spoken by The Eldan—a future voiced for him and Ilithranda alone.

The master staggered. "He would pluck the secrets from my mind," he hissed.

Daijen looked around, wondering who he was talking about, for there were none in that hall but they two.

The hooded man moved away from his apprentice, his anger flaring as he snarled at the air.

"Your treachery knows no bounds!" he yelled into the vast hall. "I know it was your black heart that sparked this rebellion! If you would glean anything from my mind, then witness your fate, *betrayer*! I will doom you to shadows and dust for all time," he vowed, his voice laden with venom.

His dark promise delivered, he waved his hand through the air, his fingers dancing to create extraordinary patterns. The distortion about him was barely visible, perhaps only to Daijen's eyes. The illusion faded the moment he lowered his arm, and he exhaled a long sigh.

"He is banished... for now. Gelakor and the others will have him probe again in time. This rebellion must be quashed." The dark figure rolled his shoulders and shrugged, as if he was unburdening himself of the problem. "To the matter at hand."

Daijen's attention was drawn to the middle of the grand hall, where the master waved a bony hand over the floor. The stone there had been arranged to display a circle that contained an array of interlocking patterns and was lined with mysterious runes. Reacting to his movement, segments inside the circle began to retreat into the floor, revealing a pitted level beneath the hall.

The smell struck Daijen as a blow, bringing a hand up to his nose. He was instantly reminded of his time in the throne room during the Ankala when all he could smell was that noxious vat of blood.

This was so much worse.

The pool of blood at the base of the Empyreal Throne could have filled the pit twenty times over it was so vast. Curiously, the blood was boiling, releasing bubbles of steaming air into the hall.

The apprentice took a step back from the edge. "Is that... blood, master?"

"I have been preparing it for months," the dark figure replied.

"What animal could provide so much?" the young apprentice asked.

"The *human* animal," the master informed him with glee. "Every village along the western coast was required."

The apprentice dampened his look of horror before turning to regard his master. "Villages?"

"Thanks to the sacrifice of the men, women, and children of those lands, my dominance and the security of the entire realm have been assured."

It looked too much for the apprentice to swallow, and he tore his eyes from the hooded figure and returned his attention to the pit. So too did Daijen, disturbed by the hulking shapes that moved and disturbed the boiling surface.

"I have uncovered a great depth of magic in blood," the master went on, sounding so pleased with himself. "A depth even my master failed to touch. With the right blood, volume, and careful preparation, it can be used to push all the boundaries of the magic world."

The insidious wizard cackled, his laughter echoing about them. "Can you imagine it? No limitations. I won't need to crush this rising rebellion. They will tremble in my shadow and flee to the wilds, preferring to live like animals than challenge me. Verda will be mine, and I shall keep it so."

The boiling blood was disrupted by a greater force that began to churn the sickly liquid, causing it to splash up the walls and onto the floor at the apprentice's feet.

"Yes," the master rasped, and eagerly so. "Rise."

Without warning, the blood began to spill over the edge and spread across the hall floor. It rushed around Daijen's boots and splashed up the pillars and scattered furniture.

The pit was rising...

The nameless fiend was beaming inside the shadows of his hood. It was a marked contradiction to his apprentice, who looked as if he would have retreated were he not standing beside his master.

Daijen could make no sense of what he witnessed, for it seemed such a wicked place could not stand the divine presence of Ahnir. If this was *after* the war with the Dark Ones, his bones would have had to be present for the bracer to have brought him to that point in time, yet the Vahlken could not spy them anywhere.

All he could do was wait and watch.

Before the blood could reach the hall's interior walls, those that had disturbed the pit from within began to take shape. What Daijen beheld almost brought him to his knees, but instead, he staggered back into a pillar. Four of them there were, crouched on one knee and dripping with blood.

"Arise, my children."

And so they did, bringing them to a height twice that of any man so that they towered over master and apprentice. By their sides rested four slender arms of toned muscle, each limb ending in a three-fingered clump of large knuckles. Faceless and hairless, their smooth and sizeable heads sloped up and back into a rounded stubby point. Entirely sexless, they stood naked in their grey flesh upon two muscled struts shaped in the manner of a horse's hind legs.

Daijen knew exactly what he was looking at, though the truth of it hollowed him out, leaving all his hope and faith to drain away.

Standing before him, at the feet of their human creator, were those that had been worshipped by all of Andara since the time of the first epoch.

The gods!

25
QUAKES IN THE DEEP

There had been no fighting back. Even Yamnomora had surrendered, though her dismay looked to have been a distraction as The Anther was, again, lost to them Kitrana Voden—a fish out of water amongst the hardy dwarves of Morthil—had simply raised her hands and waited to be wrestled and bound by the armoured soldiers. Grarfath had endured the same rough handling, his wrists bound in iron and chained to a thick leather belt around his waist.

Of them all, Bludgeon had proved the hardest to arrest. The Warhog put two of the soldiers on their backs and nearly gored a third with his tusks. It was the combined effort of three charging dwarves that toppled the pig and allowed them to bind it. Their handling of the animal greatly angered Yamnomora. She hurled abuse at them, threatening to break free of her manacles and insert her boot into particular cavities.

It was, of course, an impossibility. The site had been guarded by a little over two dozen soldiers, all plated from head to toe and bristling with swords, axes, and spears. Added to their troubles, the four had ported into a deep rectangular pit, preventing them from any kind of escape.

Having been marched up the steps, Grarfath looked down at the site. While it was empty now, the last time he had been there, the pit had been a battlefield. The fighting had been vicious, a bloody affair between the Redbraids and the Ironguards as they settled their differences in the old ways.

The Green Leaf had intuited correctly, it seemed, the smith having recalled the memory while fighting amongst the surface ruins. If only he had been thinking of his home, Grarfath chastised himself. The dwarf couldn't help but wonder then if he even had a home anymore. Swept away with Yamnomora, he had missed the deadline to pay both the Guild Lord of the Underborns and The Banking Federation.

The facts of his existence were unavoidable. He was un-guilded, a son of the Underborns no more, and his family home had been absorbed by the lords of all profit, The Banking Federation.

How wrong he had been to believe that things couldn't get any worse. For a time, rock bottom had been living on the verge of losing his home and workshop, the labours of his father passed down to him. Then, an unexpected adventure had cast him from the place of his birth and put him in danger, his very life threatened by those who had murdered his mother.

A sliver of success—that concept held aloft by every dwarf—had been within his grasp as he literally held The Anther, a weapon of power from myth and legend.

That too he had lost, his failures culminating in that very moment in which he found himself in irons. Added to that, he was now under the gaze of his kin, who had ceased their many activities to observe the newcomers—the prisoners.

Of the expressions Grarfath could see between the surrounding guards, most were curious rather than judgemental. The smith had to assume their inexplicable appearance was the cause since the trio had done nothing illegal to warrant their public arrest.

"Why were so many guardin' an empty pit?" he whispered to Yamnomora beside him.

The dwarven warrior scowled at him. "Why do ye think?" she

retorted. "We ain' the first to jus' pop out o' thin air down there. That whole site's a security risk now. Ye can bet yer last kronum that entire pit'll be filled with stone before long."

Grarfath looked back, spying the pit through a slight gap in their armoured escort. He imagined Slait porting in, the behemoth killing machine a shock to all. The smith couldn't help but wonder how many had died putting the mutated Andaren in irons.

Looking back, Grarfath laid eyes on Kitrana, who marched behind them, head and shoulders above every dwarf. The Nimean appeared haggard, though it had nothing to do with her short, tattered cloak or bare feet. Her skin was paler than ever except under her bloodshot eyes, where the pigment had darkened. It could have been lack of sleep, or even water, given her origins, but the smith suspected the recent bout of severe pain was the cause of her dishevelled look.

"Eyes front!" one of the soldiers barked in the dwarven tongue, clubbing Grarfath about the shoulder with the base of his axe.

Unable to rub the site, the smith simply rolled his sore shoulder and obeyed his captor. As he did, the sturdy ground beneath his feet shuddered. The quake travelled up, freeing dust from every crevice and knocking over sundries. A distant scream echoed from somewhere inside the mountain city but none gave it any mind.

"That were a big one," someone from the mob remarked, and gravely so.

"What were that?" Grarfath asked aloud, if quietly.

"Who knows?" Yamnomora grumbled.

"In all me years, I've never known so much as a tremor run through Morthil," he insisted.

Yamnomora's response was as unintelligible as it was noncommittal. Deciding not to press her, Grarfath simply continued to move as instructed. Within the column of soldiers they passed through hall after hall, journeying ever deeper into the heart of Morthil. It was there that the smith heard a familiar ruckus.

The protesters made their presence known everywhere, chanting and crying out for the attention of their fellow dwarves.

Grarfath looked over the various mobs, reading their signs that spoke out against a hollow culture of profit and naught else. They desperately longed for the old ways, when the stone bones paid homage to the gods, when their faith unified them, instead of being where at odds over coin as they were now.

How many times had Grarfath seen his mother among them? Hers had been an ardent voice among the throng. It had been the beginning of the end for their workshop.

"Where do ye think they're takin' us?" he eventually asked his red-headed companion, keen to think of something else.

Yamnomora glanced at him before jutting her stubbled chin ahead of them. "Up there, I'd say."

Grarfath looked at the path before them, over the helmed heads of his fellow dwarves, and spotted the grandest set of steps in all of Morthil, each riser between them plated with gold, lending to the appearance that they approached nothing less than a golden wall. It was, of course, where those wide steps ended that shot the smith's heart with a shard of ice.

His gaze climbing ever higher, Grarfath's eyes wandered over the inverted mountain that hung from the ancient rock. The stairs touched the lowest point of that mountain and were the only way in or out of the royal domain, for inside that stoney hive dwelled the High King and his blood kin.

"We're goin' up there?" he uttered absently.

"Looks that way," Yamnomora mumbled.

Grarfath swallowed, his apprehension growing with every step they ascended. The matter was made even worse when he noticed the ballistas sitting on rocky outcroppings from the royal fortress, each angled to fire their bolt at those on the golden staircase. Directly above the top of the stairs was a balcony that housed three enormous cauldrons, their contents steaming. The dwarves who stood guard beside them had only to upend the vats and their boiling cargo would be poured upon those below.

Then there were the fabled pendulums fastened to the cavern walls. Grarfath spied them in the distance; great knots of iron bristling with spikes. It was said that each of the six had been individually measured on their thick chains to ensure that they swung inches above the steps and not through them. Such contraptions would maximise the loss of life while preserving the well-crafted, and expensive, floating staircase.

The smith in Grarfath marvelled at the ingenuity and even wished to see the deadly pendulums at work, though without any loss of life.

Another quake gripped the halls of Morthil, bringing with it a light rain of dust. It also rattled the pendulums' heavy chains. Just the threat of them breaking loose was enough to produce beads of sweat across the smith's brow.

"That ain't right, I'm tellin' ye," he muttered in Yamnomora's ear.

Warm light bathed them all, stealing Grarfath's attention. At the top of the steps, the great seals had been removed, and the mammoth doors opened from within. Upon reaching the highest point of their lengthy ascent, they had arrived at the lowest point of the royal fortress, where the trio was handed over to a new set of soldiers.

Like those who had escorted them through the lofty halls of Morthil, these soldiers bore the sigil of Clan Greyhelm—a crown shaped like The Morthil Mountains themselves. An exchange began between the two groups, though their words were masked by the flames of the blazing hearth in the heart of the entrance hall.

Placed beside Kit, Grarfath took the opportunity to ask her if she was alright. "That was some pain ye were in," he added.

"I think my pain is the least of our worries," she replied.

"Silence!"

The dwarven word was barked from a soldier clad in copper-coated steel and a thin grey cloak. He rounded the hearth with a savage-looking mace in one hand, the weight of it straining the veins in his thick arm.

"I am Korgan, son o' Kol," he proclaimed in his booming voice. "Everythin' inside these walls falls under my protection. Ye dogs are guests. Act as such, an' I'll treat ye as such. Mess with yer new jewellery there," he warned, gesturing at their manacles, "an' I'll treat ye... *differently.*"

The way he rested the mace over one shoulder was more than enough to translate that final word.

In his wake, they were led up one of the twin curving staircases that brought them to the next floor. A short foyer lay before them, ending with a set of silver doors that could have accepted ten dwarves abreast. Grarfath's experienced eyes scrutinised them all the more and saw the unbelievable truth of them. He couldn't fathom the cost of so much silvyr!

Added to the cost of the raw material and general shaping were the intricate carvings depicted on their surface. Across both doors was the mighty dwarf known as Duun, son of Darl, his boot resting upon one of the dead Talakin—the shadowed beasts of legend. And there it was. The Anther. If only it was the real thing and not an image forged from silvyr.

Korgan, son of Kol, pointed to a spot in front of the closed doors. "Wait 'ere," he commanded before leaving them to order the guard into new positions.

Kitrana, who couldn't have understood a word the dwarf had barked, fell in beside Grarfath. "Where *are* we?" she asked quietly.

The smith glanced over one shoulder to make certain Korgan couldn't hear them. "In our tongue, it's called Khardunar," he informed her grimly.

"What does it mean?" she asked.

Grarfath thought about it. "It's the sound made when a hammer strikes steel on an anvil."

"That seems oddly specific," the Nimean said in hushed tones.

"It's all about temperin' the steel," the smith explained, wondering how to explain that the Greyhelms saw themselves as the ones who had tempered the wild steel that was the dwarven race in times long past.

"It is home to one of your guilds?"

Grarfath gave a mirthless chuckle. "Wouldn' that be simpler. No Guild Lords 'ere, Miss Voden. Khardunar is home to the Greyhelms an' the throne o' the High King 'imself."

Kit looked down at him. "I didn't know your people had a king."

"Oh aye. High King Glaive, son o' Thold. A good king by all accounts. He were crowned in his youth. No more than a pup, they say. His father died o' somethin', I can't remember. Glaive were the one who decreed new laws that brought peace to the guilds. This were centuries ago, mind ye."

"Would ye two stop witterin' on?" Yamnomora interjected. "We ain' meetin' the High King so he can pat us on the back. There's goin' to be questions followed by three short but swift executions."

The smith's alarm could be seen in the whites of his eyes. "Executions?" he repeated a little too loudly.

Korgan abandoned the guard and snatched Grarfath by his leather tunic. "Ye will wait in silence," he said threateningly, "or ye'll be crawlin' into the throne room with two broken legs."

Grarfath looked into Korgan's pale green eyes and saw every bully The Banking Federation had sent to intimidate his father before being harassed himself. It set the smith's heart to a hammering beat. Korgan was a big dwarf by any standard, and he wouldn't be carrying such a heavy mace around if he didn't know how to wield it, but they were fleeting facts in the face of Grarfath's mounting rage.

Korgan's eyes, however, were not all that Grarfath saw.

There, upon his thumb, was a ring like so many others the brute displayed across both hands. Except this ring housed a dull red gem with a single white pattern. Grarfath had seen that pattern before—the mark tattooed on the arm of a dwarf who had attacked and, potentially, slain his mother.

His threat delivered, Korgan moved away again, leaving the smith to face his companions and mouth a single word. "Skaramangian."

Yamnomora sighed. "Perhaps the executions won' be so swift after all."

Before Grarfath could balk at her response, the extravagant and impenetrable doors of silvyr began to part. They did not move on hinges but were slid aside into cavities hidden within the walls.

A greater extravagance awaited the trio inside, where the throne room glistened with enough jewels to give the starlight envy. So too did it shine with gold, be it in the polished floor or the straight-edged pillars.

As they were ushered over the threshold, Grarfath noted the thick veins of silvyr that ran through the golden floor. Only the most skilled of dwarves could have worked the silvyr as the design demanded.

Once inside, it became clear that the throne room was a vast hall capable of housing hundreds, if not thousands of guests. It was tiered both high and low, with stairwells leading to a pitted level that displayed ancient relics, weapons, and treasures on pedestals or secured within glass cases. To the sides were spiralling steps of yet more gold that ascended to a floor that wrapped around the entire chamber, providing a viewing balcony from which to marvel at the splendour.

Besides the mass of wealth on display, there was one item that had likely been placed inside to steal the attention of every guest. To call it an item was an understatement, Grarfath knew, for it dominated the back of the chamber and engulfed all three thrones with ease.

"What manner of beast is that?" Kitrana muttered.

The smith approached the gargantuan skull and upper jaw, his gaze dancing across its many fangs and teeth that sat row behind row. He had seen its depiction before, like so many dwarven children who enjoyed the old stories, but it had always been painted or a mere sketch. To see it with his own eyes was as awe-inspiring as it was terrifying.

"A Stonemaw," he eventually answered, feeling the heat of the flames as they passed between two hearths.

Korgan brought them to a halt well before reaching the dais and the thrones thereon. Of the three, only two were occupied, leaving the central chair notably empty. To the left sat she who could only be queen, Urlusa, daughter of Aenir. On the far right,

Grarfath knew he must be looking upon her only son, Throden, a prince renowned for his prowess with a double-sided axe— hearsay to be sure, the smith reasoned, given the size of his puny arms.

Both sat under the shelter of the Stonemaw's upper jaw, their thrones, much like the empty one between them, crowded and piled with jewels and trinkets as if they meant nothing, though even a handful could change the lives of several dwarves.

"Kneel!" Korgan snapped.

Slowed by the language barrier, Kitrana suffered a kick to the back of the knee, bringing her down beside Yamnomora.

"It is to be expected, Korgan," came a deep and rich voice from the upper level. "There are few who can keep their wits in the face o' a Stonemaw—even a dead one."

Like the others, Grarfath looked back over one shoulder to locate the source of the voice. He was easy to find, descending one of the spiral staircases in robes of emerald and bronze. The High King of Morthil was one of two figures to have occupied the highest tier; the other remained at the top of the steps, content to watch.

Tharg.

As it had with Korgan, Grarfath's heart began to beat like thunder in his chest. There stood the dwarven Skaramangian who had hunted his mother and, ultimately, given the order to kill her. It made the smith sick to his stomach to know he was in council with the High King. Was he there spreading the disease of his secret order? Or were the Greyhelms simply another branch of those who worshipped the Talakin? Either way, Grarfath felt like rending his chains and using them to choke Tharg to death.

Reaching their floor, High King Glaive approached them in all his majesty. His fingers gleamed with ornate rings while his thumbs were hooked into a belt of fine leather and a clasp of bejewelled gold. About his neck hung a chain of pure silvyr inlaid with sapphires, draped low to cover his barrel of a chest.

Like his wife and son, the High King boasted skin a shade darker than Grarfath's. He sported no hair upon his domed scalp but glorious was the thick beard that threatened to abandon all colour. Upon that dark brow sat his crown of silvyr, the stubborn metal shaped to match his sigil and the jagged points of The Morthil Mountains.

Rounding the trio, Glaive stepped onto the dais and craned his neck to stare in wonder at the giant skull. "Do ye know the story o' their kind?" he asked.

Sensing the rhetorical nature of the question, Grarfath kept any answer to himself.

"Morthil was their domain," the High King went on. "Many o' the halls we use today were adapted from their burrows. They were, o' course, an unruly breed o' creature. Not to be tamed or herded. Yet there was one among our ancestors who dared to challenge that notion. One who not only guided 'em to further our great kingdom but also put an end to the threat o' 'em when the work was done. Do ye know his name?"

Grarfath, again, withheld his response, assuming the High King wished to speak the name. It was with expectancy, however, that Glaive stared at them.

The smith swallowed and wet his lips. "*Duun, son o' Darl,*" he said.

The High King narrowed his eyes, though they flitted between Grarfath and Kitrana. "Ye speak man's tongue so she would understand," he concluded, his tone having lost its wonderment and adopted a rigid edge. "I would not sully me tongue with their uncivilised words. Humans are only good for one thing: profits."

Glaive pivoted swiftly, his emerald robes flapping dramatically as he took to his throne. While only a coincidence, the fresh quake that rippled through the stone of Morthil added a note of theatrics to his seating. Either side of him, the piled jewels were disturbed, creating a miniature avalanche of shining wealth. The High King glanced here and there, a notch of concern about him.

"Duun, son o' Darl," he eventually continued, as if there had been no interruption. "A legend amongst our people. A true hero o' the ages. So tell me, Grarfath, son o' Thronghir, how did it feel to wield the weapon that made 'im so?"

The smith's face went blank. His name had just come from the lips of the High King. It should have been an impossibility since they hadn't been questioned at all since porting into Morthil. By way of answer, his gaze was drawn up and to the side, where Tharg still observed silently from the surrounding balcony. Tharg had known the identity of both himself and his mother, who had uncovered The Anther years earlier.

"Ye look surprised," Glaive remarked. "Should a king not know his people?"

"Ye don' know 'im!" Yamnomora snarled. "Just like ye don' know me! Ye only know what that *snake* whispers in yer ear!" She turned her head towards Tharg and spat on the floor.

Heavy and deliberate were Korgan's footfalls. Coming up behind Yamnomora, he raised his mace, the weapon made ready to crush her skull.

"Not 'ere," the High King commanded, his words able to stop Korgan from following through. "The splendour o' me throne room won' be marred by the blood o' such an insignificant creature as this." Glaive held his hands out to the chamber. "This is a place o' words."

"Ye Greyhelms 'ave been wieldin' yer *words* like hammers for millennia," Yamnomora retorted defiantly. "Ye've probably killed more with yer voice than I 'ave with steel."

The High King paused, his dark eyes locked with hers. "I do not doubt it," he replied menacingly.

Hopeless was the laugh that broke free of Yamnomora's chest. "So that's it, is it? The Skaramangians sucked ye in with... what? The promise o' more?" The dwarf made a point of looking around at the extravagance that surrounded them. "Aye, because ye're in need o' that."

Glaive remained calm, in control, as he bartered words with the warrior. "Every Skaramangian joins the cause for their own reason. For some, it is greed. Others seek power, to dominate. We 'ave our grunts—like yer mother, Grarfath—who feed off the lies that offer hope o' a better world, a world o' heroes an' gods instead o' profits an' success. The latter is not for the likes o' Lord Tharg up there. Oh no, he knows what world he's livin' in an' how it works. An', as ye can see, the Greyhelms are in no need o' treasure, an' we already wield the power to dominate."

Yamnomora spread her weight out across her knees and straightened her back. "So ye're a true believer then," she reasoned miserably.

A smile cut a line of white across Glaive's face. "As was me father before me. An' his father before 'im. Ours is a proud line that goes back to the beginnin'. Back to the very days o' Duun 'imself." The High King shuffled forwards on his throne. "Who do ye think it was that finally put 'im in his place? Ol' Duun drew his line in the sand an' declared that every dwarf were on *his* side. But that were not his right. He didn' speak for all o' us. There were those o' us who didn't jus' see sense in livin' in the shadow o' the Talakin but *thrived* under his rule. Still, he were a hero in the eyes o' many by then. There was no bein' rid o' 'im," he complained, gesturing at the silvyr doors that had now been shut.

Yamnomora frowned, knotting the muscles around her eyes. "*His* rule?" she questioned, her eyes darting about in thought. "What are ye abou'?"

The High King chuckled to himself. "A loss in translation as far as ye're concerned."

"Yer Grace." Tharg's warning voice cut across the grand chamber.

Glaive waved his adviser away. "They're chained an' on their knees in the heart o' Khardunar, my Lord Tharg. They'll never see anythin' beyond these walls again," he added with glee.

"Their fate is no mystery, Yer Grace," Tharg replied. "I'm thinkin' o' others best kept in the dark..."

Grarfath followed Tharg's shifting gaze to a sealed door that sat on the opposite side of the throne room.

The High King's mood soured immediately. "The Eldan made a mistake with that one," he grumbled, an opinion that put Tharg visibly on edge. Glaive waved his hand again, dismissing the topic. "Ye'll be tellin' me how ye got back into Morthil now," he commanded. "I know ye don' possess The Anther, so how did ye do it?"

"The only thing we'll be tellin' ye," Yamnomora countered, "is where ye can *put* The Anther."

"There is more we would know," Tharg interjected again before the High King could respond. "The company they keep has long been a thorn in the order's side. Perhaps we should begin the interrogations in earnest, Yer Grace? Were The Eldan here, he would—"

"But The Eldan is not 'ere, Lord Tharg!" Glaive interrupted, still reeling from Yamnomora's insolence. He paused while he clenched his jaw furiously under his greying beard. "Under the mountain, *I* am king," he declared self-righteously. "These are *my* prisoners, not *his*."

"O' course, Yer Grace," Tharg replied with a bow of the head. "I only meant to press the sensitive nature o' the matter."

"It has not escaped me," the High King shot back, his eyes finding Lord Tharg above them.

Still, Glaive took a breath while he counselled himself. Mention of The Eldan had caught him off guard, it seemed. Grarfath knew nothing of the man who held the title, but he couldn't imagine how terrible he was that the High King of Morthil would consider his judgement.

"Send word to Aran'saur," Glaive eventually announced, his tone more measured now. "Inform The Eldan we 'ave allies o' the Vahlken in our custody. I would 'ave them exhausted o' all they know before his response though."

"Very wise, Yer Grace. Perhaps the matter should be handed over to our *guest*," Lord Tharg suggested. "It would keep all o' 'em out o' sight at least."

"This pleases me," the High King said. "Would ye like to meet yer inquisitor?" he asked of the prisoners.

Lord Tharg rounded the balcony and knocked on the side door.

Glaive rose from his throne and came to stand before the trio. "It would be typical to receive the offer o' yer life in exchange for information abou' now. But we'll not be doin' that. Ye will, all three o' ye, die inside these walls. How much ye suffer before that end is up to ye."

The side door opened from the other side, though the guards who were doing so found themselves shoved through when a considerably taller figure strode into the throne room. Despite his size, his footsteps were far lighter than Tharg's beside him. They walked together no longer than it took the newcomer to leap deftly over the balcony rail and land beside the dais.

What shred of hope that might have lingered in Grarfath was extinguished then, for he kneeled in the shadow of Slait, The Dancing Sword of the Dawn.

26

ENEMY INCARNATE

0 Years Ago...

4

Though he had never seen one with his own eyes, Daijen knew from the descriptions of both Mordrith and Aphrandhor that he was looking upon the gods.

Even bound in their dull flesh, dripping with blood, they possessed a distinct skeletal structure that matched perfectly with all that he had heard of the gods. And there they stood, soaked in the blood of innocents, awaiting their master's word.

What hell had he been brought to?

Images of the Black Abyss were conjured all the more when dark smoke was steadily expelled from their pores. The smoke surrounded each of them, coalescing and deepening in shadow until all four of them were clothed and hooded in long draping robes in the style of their master.

"Let me hear your sweet voices," the sinister wizard requested.

As one, the four enormous beings raised their heads. Daijen

recoiled at both sight and sound, their featureless faces peeling apart from a single vertical seam to unleash a noise, a resounding barrage, that assaulted his ears. As the sound tailed off, only the wizard's laughter could be heard.

The apprentice looked on with confusion. "I don't understand, master. You said you were amassing your work, your knowledge of magic. I thought you were creating a book."

"My grimoire," the master uttered. "Yes. And so I have," he proclaimed, arms outstretched to the four. "Come now. You have ever been the brightest among my disciples—there has never been one more worthy of being my apprentice. Can you not guess what I have done?"

Edging closer, the apprentice kept shoulder to shoulder with his master. "I have never seen such creatures," he confessed.

The master let loose a barking laugh. "Are they not a marvel? Each of their bones I have sourced from worlds more terrible than this, from monsters great and small. Whole now, they are beyond the skill of any man, a foe to life and Death alike."

"I don't understand, master." It seemed to pain the young man to admit as much.

"You still have much to learn, apprentice. But that is no bad thing," he added soothingly, one bony hand coming to rest on his pupil's shoulder. "It is the gaps in our knowledge that make us strive, that let us never tire from the greatest of works." The hooded wizard gestured at his new creations. "You cannot see my spells upon them, for they are etched into their very bones."

A flash of concern ran across the apprentice's face before being replaced by realisation. "A living grimoire," he muttered.

"Yes," the master drawled. "A spellbook spread between four pillars of unending loyalty, encased in flesh and muscle where no other might glean my work." The dark figure gestured at one of the workstations scattered about the hall, where a large desk sat between shelves, cauldrons, and stacks of parchments. "Books can be stolen, their secrets spilled forever with the turn of a page and prying eyes. I should know. It was *my* prying eyes that stole magic from Barad-Agin."

The apprentice spat on the floor at the sound of the name. "Had you not, master, we would have all been devoured by his Leviathans."

A crooked smile breached that shadowed hood. "Always quick to my defence. You are a good apprentice. You are a good *Skaramangian*," he specified with pride.

Mention of that name sharpened Daijen's attention.

"I would safeguard my magic," he went on, gesturing at the man-made gods. "I would not have it fall so easily into the hands of others. I have entombed them," he beamed, "and they shall accompany me everywhere, serving as a source of knowledge *and* protection."

"Such a thing has never been," the apprentice observed, a hint of awe in his voice now. "What are they to be called, master?"

"I call them *Golems*," the wizard announced. "Though I would not leave them as such. Made of magic, they are to both contain magic and *unleash* it. They are deserving of true names." The hooded figure paused, regarding his apprentice for a moment. "I have heard the name given to me by the people of Verda," he said, his voice low and deeply unsettling.

"Master..." the apprentice began, almost apologetically.

"The Eikor," the wizard declared. "So say the men of the west. To the dwarves, I am The Talakin. You speak the eastern tongue as I do, apprentice. Tell me: what is the translation?"

The younger man swallowed his fear. "The Dark One."

Daijen felt a wave of nausea overcome him. How wrong they had been! The Eikor, the Talakin—the Dark Ones. The Arkalon was wrong, perhaps even deliberately so. There was no *them*. Just *him*.

The Dark *One*.

So terrible was his legacy that every race under the sun knew of him by some name or other.

"I have taken no offence," the wizard interjected. "Insects weren't meant to fathom the work of gods. They are fickle creatures. For generations they called me saviour. Hero. *The Pendain*! Following the Battle of Carstane, I was The Dancing Sword of the

Dawn for generations. Their limited minds interpret my new work as an act to destroy."

Daijen couldn't help but step closer to the wizard. "Pendain," the Vahlken muttered. That name had spread like a wildfire through the visions of the Ankala. With ease he conjured the memory of the deserter who had spouted the first vision.

"In the shadow of kings," he had pronounced, *"with the blood of emperors. Son of darkness. Son of the first. He stands a Rider. He stands a Vahlken. He fights for life and delivers death. He is to be the light that holds back the dark. But the seed of darkness dwells within. It has but to hold out its hand and he will take it. The Black Abyss will be made manifest in their alliance. All will bow to the one who is Pendain."*

It confused Daijen all the more, for the one called Pendain was spoken of as both hero and villain.

"They have not the sight to see the truth," the apprentice added, cutting through Daijen's thoughts.

"My predecessor would have destroyed it all," The Dark One stated. "He unleashed something he could not control. The Leviathans should have been left to slumber in the nameless deeps of the world. As I did then, I will save the world again," he said earnestly, his attention turning up to his Golems. "I will end the in-fighting and the corruption. I will quash the little tyrants that rise up and spread pain and suffering. I will bring peace unlike any the world has ever known."

The Dark One ceased his dreaming and turned to his apprentice, his tone lowered to the reality of their situation.

"I am content for the name Skara to fade from history. But I would not suffer the same for my *sons*. Of human flesh, they were too weak to survive the torments of this world. They each succumbed to the wrath of Barad-Agin. The same will never be said of my *new* children, whom I gift those same names. Behold, apprentice, you are the first to look upon Meliax, Govhul, Yohem, and Ahnir," he proclaimed lovingly.

Daijen slid down the pillar, the strength in his legs sapped by the names he had worshipped since childhood. Yet here they were, given to these Golems, creations all of The Dark One. The stark truth added to the layers of ruination that had been Daijen's foundations. It was all a lie, a fabrication. A *manipulation*. The Skaramangians had to be behind it—they who wore the cloth of religion so they might steer civilisation.

No.

So they might still serve their master's plan. *The Dark One's plan.*

To what end, he still could not say, for the truth remained beyond his understanding. He had been led to believe that they existed to uncover the Dark Ones, those beaten back by the gods, who had died in the act. But then what, he had to ask, had beaten them back—beaten *him* back?

Investigative was his thinking, his mind shaped and moulded by the ways of the Vahlken. The answer was formed by the pieces he held. A single word took shape on his lips, and he knew it to be true.

"Dragons..."

The war between Erador and Andara had been started to achieve a single end: eliminate the threat of dragons. At the same time, they would acquire the Golem skeleton resting among The Silver Trees of Akmar. With all the skeletons in their possession, the Skaramangians would have access to The Dark One's *living* grimoire.

But there was more, he knew. There had to be. Amassing the dark wizard's knowledge of magic couldn't be their only reason for millennia of manipulation and war.

He thought of The Tomb on Nareene.

"This is where he will remember who he is," the old crone had said. They were awaiting his return.

His return.

Daijen looked at The Dark One again, perplexed at how this man of flesh and blood, who had walked the earth thousands of years past, could ever return to that wretched place beneath Nareene.

The Vahlken was drawn to the circular slab beneath the Golems, where the pit of blood had previously sat in the floor.

There, he had seen skeletons brought to flesh and life from naught but idle bone. Did the Skaramangians possess the knowledge to recreate the pit?

It was likely they did not, for the answer lay scattered across all four of the Golems. There was revelation in that, for now he knew why the Skaramangians truly desired the ancient skeletons. Even then, lost within memory, he could still hear The Valtorak instructing him to question his deductions. Without proof, he could but cling to theory.

It was enough to make some of his deductions unravel. Even if the Skaramangians had the knowledge of the grimoire in its entirety and they reproduced such a vile pit of necromancy, they would still need The Dark One's skeleton. Not only had Nareene housed hundreds of skeletons, but they knew for certain that at least one of them was naught but a humble farmer.

Aggravated by his lack of clarity, Daijen looked down at the vambrace on his arm. He shut his eyes and willed his desire to be gone from that dreadful place. He had to return to warn the others, if not mount an assault on God Fall, where the rest of Ahnir's bones were being studied.

Yet he remained.

Upon opening his eyes, that bleak hall and its sinister occupants still surrounded him.

Rising to his feet, absent the blood that could not cling to his ethereal presence, Daijen tried to put some distance between himself and the Golems. He sought a window, a chance to see something else that might settle his thoughts, but there were none. The hall was just as enclosed as the magic inside those wretched creations was.

Looking down at the blood that pooled around him, Daijen saw himself reflected in the gruesome liquid. But there was more than just himself in that reflection. Above him were clouds asunder with lightning, though the flashes they produced had no effect on the black hall. His gaze drawn up to the phenomenon, the Vahlken was forced to blink as cold rain fell upon his face.

Wiping the water from his eyes, Daijen feared his mind had

broken, shattered like glass. Gone was the dark hall and its gothic design, the open world now laid out before the Vahlken. A storm churned overhead, spitting lightning and blasting the air with terrible thunder. The rain fell in relentless sheets, soaking the muddy land under his boots.

Through it all, a roar rippled across the vista and found Daijen's ears. Turning to his left, he was faced by a kingdom of stone, a city encircling a mighty fortress that clung to the cliffs at its back. Again, that roar *boomed* across the land, a chant, it seemed, from those who dwelled beyond the high walls.

Under those stormy skies, the city unleashed a salvo of fiery arrows that tried to defy the rain. For a moment, they lit up the darkness, and it was as if the stars had descended beneath the black clouds. Predicting the fall of the arrows, Daijen couldn't help but retreat several steps. It was all so real. The wind picked up his hair, and he felt the rain on his skin. Surely he would feel the sting of those arrows too.

He was never to know.

The arrows graced the sky but not the earth, each of them burning up into a shower of sparks so bright Daijen was forced to look away. Wondering what they had been intended for, the Vahlken turned around, where the land stretched out across plains only seen in the staccato flashes of lightning.

Amassed there was a small force of cloaked figures, their identity concealed by their hoods as much as the storm. Skaramangians, Daijen knew, for three banners stood in their midst, each displaying that most dreaded sigil.

The Dark One, who seemed to suck in the shadows about him, stood at the tip of their arrow. Daijen also recognised the apprentice beside him, though the younger man now sported a goatee and looked to have aged by a handful of years.

The apprentice and all those about him were insignificant compared to the four black pillars standing sentinel beyond the hooded disciples.

The Golems.

They loomed ominously over them all, shrouded in their robes of floating shadows.

A distant *twang* returned the Vahlken's attention to the city. His sharp eyes soon discovered the enormous slabs of stone sailing through the night sky. Again, he felt that trepidation under the shadow of impending death, doubtful that he would survive the memory.

As with the flaming arrows, The Dark One unleashed his magic to thwart his foes. One clawing hand swiped through the air, and with it the work of the catapults was undone, as every boulder was torn from its flight and brought into a vertical drop.

The Dark One let loose his wicked laugh, an unnaturally loud and rasping cackle. "They throw sticks and stones at us," he announced with amusement.

The ground shook, but the falling slabs were not the cause. The Golems were on the move, their great strides enough to part the disciples.

"Ahnir!" The Dark One called forth.

Of the four, one advanced beyond the others, heeding its master's beckoning voice. Its insidious aura was expelled in an almost physical wave that made Daijen's hairs stand on end. What tapestry of lies had been woven to turn such a fiend into a god?

The Dark One glanced up at his creation. "Something with fangs and claws, I think." He looked up again as a second thought occurred to him. "And something *hungry*," he specified.

The grey flesh of its featureless face peeled left from right, revealing row upon row of small fangs. The noise it produced was tenfold what Daijen had heard in the black hall. It beat back the thunder as a mighty trumpet and hurtled across the realm in waves that the Vahlken felt against his chest.

The moment Ahnir stopped, when its faced sealed up, the wisps of its shadowed cloak flew out, towards the city. Daijen could hardly fathom what happened next, his mind racing to catch up with his eyes.

From within the darkness of Ahnir's cloak, there came a torrent of monsters. They rushed from the Golem's shadows, frighteningly swift on their legs of sharp bone. As one, they tore across the land between The Dark One and the city of stone, their hundreds turning into thousands.

Like Androma's bottomless satchel, it broke everything Daijen knew of the physical world, of the matter that could occupy space. His inability to comprehend the situation didn't stop the creatures from advancing on the city, their column spreading out across the field. Somewhere between spiders and scorpions, the beasts let loose an ear-splitting shriek, a cacophonous warning to the people behind the walls.

"No dragons here." The Dark One's voice wormed through the air, finding life in the shadows of the Vahlken's cloak. "No Riders to stand for you. Open your gates, *King* Hellion, and kneel. You have until my pets reach your home. Or remain in your gilded hall, if you must, and I will let them scale your walls and *feast*. Either way, I will have what is rightfully mine before the dawn."

His voice retreated back into the shadows whence they came. Daijen was struck by terrifying awe—how could a man use the shadows and dark places of the world to project his voice across such a distance?

Yet he had, for the message had been heard loud and clear. Such was obvious when the tall gates began to open and a single man parted from the crowd to kneel on the threshold. They had submitted. Though not favourable, Daijen knew it to be the wise decision given the likelihood that the city was brimming with families who couldn't hope to defend themselves against an enemy so vast and abhorrent.

It was to the confusion of all that those monstrosities did not stop. Daijen turned to regard The Dark One, as did the apprentice beside the wretch. The twisted wizard made no attempt to leash the beasts still racing from the shadows of Ahnir's cloak.

"Master?"

The Dark One silenced his apprentice with a finger to his own lips. "Listen. You might just hear the first screams."

Indeed they did. The screams of innocents found life despite the storm, echoing across the plains. Inumerable monsters ploughed through the open gates and scattered amongst the streets, while others scurried up the outer walls and poured in from above.

"Did he not kneel, master?"

"Of course he did," The Dark One replied. "But taking his throne was as inevitable as it was easy. The real work we do here must be everlasting."

"The real work?"

"To sow fear in the hearts of men," The Dark One said eagerly.

Daijen Saeth looked out at his enemy, seeing now that they were not legion but *one*. Of all the horrors he had witnessed and the visions he had heard during the Ankala, the memory in which he stood brought one forth.

"He who lies entombed in the dark will rise and the fires with him. Death cannot hold him. He will stand amidst four pillars of his own creation and with them, he will harness the power of the world. Of every world."

What had been the mere words of a potential future were now incarnate before Daijen's eyes.

27
THEDARIA

Gallien was sure to keep his hood close about him, lest the light of day touch his face and betray him. Thedaria was a city of eyes and ears, and every one led back to the same place.

The Padoshi.

For a little over sixteen years, the smuggler had succeeded in staying a step ahead of the crime boss, and where the gap had closed, Gallien had bloodied his hands. If there was any truth to the Mighty Kaliban, the god was certainly laughing at him now.

On the outside, Thedaria was a city of beauty and promise, but Gallien knew it to be rotten, a place where the helpless were enslaved to those who held power.

Without meaning to, he conjured memories of his time in the Padoshi's employ. Even when he hadn't been breaking the law, the smuggler had been present and witnessed atrocities born of a twisted mind. He could still smell the blood and hear the tearing of flesh. The screams haunted him too, echoing in his mind.

If only he had made those memories before his father ravaged his mind, he thought. At least then he would be able to sleep for more than a few hours at a time.

There, on the edge of The Misted Road, the smuggler's thoughts returned to his father—or at least they tried to. Reluctantly, Gallien had begun to see that Bragen Pendain was more of an idea than anything else. He maintained emotions surrounding the man, feelings that informed him of distant memories where those emotions had first been nurtured. He just couldn't grasp them.

While Gallien felt violated by the intrusion on his mind, he couldn't help but foster hope of finding his father alive. It was that hope—a fool's hope, perhaps—that gave him the courage to follow the road to Thedaria's main gates.

The Green Leaf led the way, the group restricted in pace, as the wizard was, by his wounded leg. That same restriction had lengthened their trek from The Silver Trees of Akmar, now far to the north, adding days to their journey.

Thedaria, however, was not the welcome sight it should have been. Gallien had voiced his desire to acquire supplies and be on their way within hours of entering the city, thereby forgoing the luxury of a real bed and a hot meal prepared by someone else.

Again, Aphrandhor's injury had made itself known. Outvoted by the others, he was to spend at least one night in Thedaria so that the wizard's leg could be properly seen to and medicines procured.

"It's been nearly twenty years since you were there," Androma had pointed out during the debate. "The Padoshi's memory might be long, but the same cannot be said of the thugs he employs. Your face will be just one of thousands inside those walls."

Approaching the open gates, Gallien didn't feel one of thousands. He felt eyes on him. The smuggler tried to keep his head down, but the call of sailors turned his attention towards the river in the south. As always, The Treeling was littered with ships, great and small, as they brought trade to Thedaria. The sailors called out to the villagers who lined the river, cheerful, perhaps, to have anyone but their fellow crew to converse with after untold weeks at sea.

A painful knock against Gallien's shoulder dragged him from the view and grounded him as he crossed the threshold.

"Watch where you're going!" a man growled at him, rubbing his own shoulder as he departed the city.

His heart pounding, the smuggler's pain was drowned out by a surge in adrenaline. It left him on the verge of running or fighting —it was hard to say. Either way, the axe had returned to his grip, emerging from nowhere to fill his hand.

Cob was quick to react and moved to conceal the phenomenon before anyone noticed the orange glyphs. He lightly grasped the smuggler's wrist, encouraging him to keep the weapon of power hidden within the folds of his cloak.

"Breathe," he urged softly, leaving Aphrandhor and Androma to continue on. "Focus. You cannot walk around carrying an axe. Especially one so fine as that."

As the distance between the wizard's vambrace and the smuggler's axe became too much, the glyphs faded to that of dull steel again.

Gallien had a barbed retort for the ranger, but he knew the Kedradi was only trying to keep him alive. The man had become somewhat tolerable since their escape from Akmar, a fact the smuggler attributed to his actions. Had he not dragged the unconscious ranger through the trees and then carried him for many miles, the Andarens would have seen to his end.

While Cob had acknowledged the feat, he had yet to actually thank Gallien.

Still, he had curbed some of his blunt attitude towards the smuggler in recent days. While Gallien couldn't say he liked the ranger, he no longer felt like punching him in the face every time he looked at him.

"I shouldn't be here," he muttered.

"And yet you are. You can only walk the path you are on. Take heart that you do not walk alone."

Gallien absorbed the ranger's words and took the instructed breath while they stood amidst an ever-moving mob. He felt the weight disappear from his hand, the axe taken away by the calm winds that blew through his mind.

Cob nodded approvingly. "Good. You must practice this. The sharpest weapons are only achieved by honing them."

Gallien frowned. "Am I the weapon?" he asked, being wilfully ignorant. "Or are you saying I need to sharpen the axe?"

The ranger could clearly see Gallien's intention had been to mock, though he did little more than take a breath himself. "Perhaps we shouldn't linger," he suggested, turning to join the flow of people.

With his hand resting on the hilt of his sword instead, Gallien followed Cob, and the two caught up with the older pair. Androma's new staff—adapted from an Andaren spear—glided left and right at her feet and granted her a wider berth than most. Her progress was still slow, her knowledge of the streets obviously limited, while her companion was walking with a limp.

"Take my arm," Cob said, guiding the old Rider.

Gallien came up on The Green Leaf's side. He noted the dark stain on the robes about his left leg. Added to that, the wizard looked pale and haggard, much like he had after touching the smuggler's mind. How far could they really get before he collapsed and made a scene in the streets?

"How good are you lot at picking pockets?" the smuggler asked of his companions.

"There's no need," Cob informed him, patting the pouch hanging from his belt.

Gallien scrutinised the size of the pouch. "Thedaria's not cheap, Ranger."

"Coin is not our problem," Aphrandhor commented. "Finding somewhere to spend it without alerting the Padoshi, on the other hand..."

Sixteen years, Gallien knew, was a long time for things to change inside a city like Thedaria, but if it was anything close to what it was, there was only one place that offered them the best chance at moving unseen.

"This way," he bade, having the group change direction.

Cob glanced at the street sign. "The Stilts?" He shook his head of dreadlocks. "We need shelter," he pointed out.

"That's why we need to go this way," Gallien countered.

"Those slums offer no safe harbour," the Kedradi argued. "The desperate souls who dwell there are certainly in the Padoshi's pocket. They would sell out their mothers if it pressed coin into their hand."

"It's the only place we'll blend in," Gallien said, gesturing at their collective grubbiness, which now included Cob, whose fine shoulder cloak and battle skirt of blue and gold had been tarnished and ripped. "If we cross the river, we'll stand out like a sore thumb," he went on, nodding at the bridge that connected the first two rings of the city. "And if you can afford to go any deeper than that, you had better be able to prove you're related to the Skolls." The smuggler jutted his chin up at one of the green flags that blew in the breeze, depicting the Blood Lord's sigil of a fish shot with an arrow.

Androma planted her staff on the ground beside her. "How are we to avoid so many eyes and ears eager to report four new and wealthy strangers in The Stilts?"

"I'm not saying we will," Gallien replied honestly. "In fact, we probably won't. Nothing happens here without the Padoshi finding out. But this is the path we're on," he said pointedly, his eyes falling on Cob. "If we *must* stay here, The Stilts at least offer a warren of streets to get lost in. That might be our only chance of getting out of here."

The Green Leaf glanced at his companions. "To The Stilts, then," he declared.

———

Following the city's outer ring towards the river in the south, the group were able to observe the steady decline of Thedaria. The streets became filthier, littered with debris and wayward souls who slept under the stars. Moving ever deeper, the eyes that landed on them were suspicious, cast from shadowed doorways and cluttered alleys. Deeper still, the very ground ran out, as if it dared not support those who inhabited The Stilts.

"I see the name is well earned," the wizard remarked.

Gallien looked out on the shacks and crude cabins built atop each other, extending over The Treeling itself. On a forest of wooden stilts, the shanty town creeped ever closer to the inner ring, with visible construction across numerous sites. Only the Blood Lord would keep them at bay, if not the Padoshi himself, for The Stilts—if left unchecked—would soon bridge the gap and prevent ships and boats from entering the city proper.

The sprawling mess of it was but one aspect. The smell was another. The frigid air of winter could not still the odours that drifted out of the area. It seemed the last place to take anyone to treat a wound.

"There's no need to be picky here," the smuggler told them. "Anywhere with enough beds will do. And don't be tempted to overpay," he added. "They'll assume we have something to hide and our time here will quickly run down."

The group accepted his expertise on the matter without argument. And so they departed Thedaria's hard ground and stepped onto the boards over the river. Every street and bridge was busier than life in the city, though most of The Stilts's malnourished population could be found lazing about in a stupor or getting into brawls over scraps.

It was a place of abandonment.

Be by it their loved ones or civilisation itself, the people of The Stilts had been left to their own devices without resource or aid. Even The Gilded were notably absent, saving their sermons for the people who were considered to actually matter. Gallien pitied them, they whose very souls had been disregarded.

But they were not to be underestimated, Gallien reminded himself. Each of them was a nerve ending that connected in some way to the Padoshi. With that in mind, he kept his gaze lowered and refrained from making eye contact with anyone.

"This'll do," he said reluctantly.

Cob read the sign above the door. "The Seadog," he murmured, quite unimpressed.

"I'm sure there is a cosy charm inside," Aphrandhor commented optimistically.

"That's what The Stilts is known for," Gallien quipped. "Its *cosy charm.*"

The door creaked as they entered, drawing the eyes of every occupant—all three of them, one of whom was the maid behind the bar, a woman of many decades with skin closer than anything else. She chewed her gums, assessing the newcomers, while the two men seated at a table by the only window peered over the top of their tankard.

Gallien took the lead, reaching the old maid first. "Four rooms," he said gruffly, aware that manners were not to be expected of this inn's typical clientele.

The maid barked a harsh laugh. "*Four* rooms? Does this look like The Baskelon?" she shot back, gesturing to the Blood Lord's palace on the other side of the river.

"Four beds then," Gallien countered.

"I've a room with *three* beds," the maid stated flatly. "Four and a half marks per bed. Take it or leave it."

The smuggler shook his head. "That's robbery. We'll give you *three* marks per bed and an extra half mark since there's four of us. Take it or leave it."

The maid licked her cracked lips. "Leave it," she replied, as if she wasn't in dire need of the business.

Gallien was about to continue negotiations when The Green Leaf inserted himself. "We shall happily pay you four marks each, madame, if we might only have those beds immediately."

"Happily?" the smuggler mouthed, scowling at the wizard. Only then did he notice that the older man was struggling to stand, and the dark stain on his green robes appeared to be damp again.

"Done," the maid replied. "Coin first."

Cob removed the required marks from the pouch on his belt. Despite having no ill intentions, Gallien's opportunistic nature gave him cause to make note of the Kedradi's wealth, if not the fact that monster hunting was a lucrative business. Not that he had any interest in the latter. Short-lived were the rangers of the world. Just behind smugglers who betrayed the Padoshis of the world...

The room they were shown to was just that—four walls, a door, a window that looked out on the river, and three grubby beds. What was left of the day was given over to gathering supplies, chiefly those that could be used to aid the wizard's wound. Cob sourced it all, having returned to better parts of the city where clean bandages could be found and herbalists sold medicinal goods.

The ranger tended to The Green Leaf's wound, exposing the leg to reveal the bite of the Andaren arrow. Cob created a paste from the supplies he had acquired and filled the wound after cleaning it. Aphrandhor gritted his teeth throughout and almost lost consciousness when the paste was applied. Gallien had to hand it to him—he was one tough old piece of leather.

As the wizard began to fade into slumber, the smuggler bit into an apple while his attention slid across the room. Androma was in the process of removing her rags and cloak, all of which was in need of washing. Sure that he was about to see her naked form, Gallien was about to avert his eyes when he glimpsed the most brilliant blue.

He stared at her from his perch beside the window, for she stood amongst them a vision of dragon scales. The undersuit clung to her like a second skin, disappearing into her boots. Scale upon blue scale, the natural armour coated her as if she herself was a dragon.

Gallien might have commented had he not caught Cob's eyes. The ranger shook his head, a warning against any topic that brought up her dragon, Maegar. The smuggler was content to leave it be—and, indeed, all talk. He finished his apple and joined the wizard in sleep after it was agreed that Cob would stay up and take the first watch.

For two days they remained in that room, their supplies only replenished when the ranger went out for them. The Stilts was a

place of sporadic noise, be it day or night, with fights and merriment breaking out at all hours. Gallien could only watch it all from
the grimy window while they waited for The Green Leaf's strength
to return.

It was still agreed, however, that it would be quicker to find
passage and sail down The Treeling to enter The Drifting Sea. From
there, they could be taken up the coast to Caster Hold, where trade
was essential for the battalions stationed there. It would cut out
days from their journey and allow them to retain some strength
upon reaching Taraktor.

With that in mind, Cob and Androma set out on the second day
in search of a viable ship and a captain in need of some extra
marks. Gallien's concern for them only began to grow after the sun
had set.

"I thought they'd be back by now," he remarked, unable to
count the number of ships in harbour.

The Green Leaf sipped his hot tea, unperturbed by their
absence. "There are few, if any, out there who could challenge such
a pair. Do not be burdened, Mr Pendain, they will return. You'll
see."

The use of his real name reminded Gallien of the heated argument between them, atop The Ruins of Gelakor. A tinge of guilt
stabbed at the smuggler now, aware that he had wrongly accused
the wizard when, in fact, Aphrandhor could be the reason he might
be reunited with his father. After seeing the way he had been
treated by the Jainus in Akmar, his barbed comments about being
one of them seemed out of place.

Such thoughts ruminated for another hour before Gallien felt
the need to voice them.

"I'm sorry," he began, voice breaking from disuse.

"What was that?" The Green Leaf asked, his fingers working
the wrappings of a fresh bandage.

Gallien abandoned his perch and moved to help the old man.
"I'm sorry," he said again, discarding the old bandage. "I have a
history with wizards and magic... As well you know," he added,
tapping the side of his head. "I've only ever witnessed it be used to

punish or conquer. It killed my brother. When I saw the bracer on your arm, it was easy to assume you had played a part, that *magic* played a part."

The smuggler swallowed, hating every second of his bloated apology.

"I was without a part to play," Aphrandhor replied soberly. "I called myself Jainus when your father stole the vambrace, just as I did when he was caught by the hunters. I didn't find the strength to act until it was too late for him. What has been done to you—and your family—is a wrong I cannot undo, but perhaps I can help to make it better. If your father is to be found in Taraktor, I *will* see him freed."

Gallien finished wrapping the new bandage. "Thank you," he said, caught off guard by the wizard's genuine response. It was foreign to the smuggler that anyone would accept responsibility for their actions, especially those from decades past. The Green Leaf had gone up in his estimations—a rarity in Gallien's life.

"Magic is misused in this world every day by humans and Andarens alike," Aphrandhor went on. "In truth, I hope that more than peace will come out of Joran's destiny, that he will spark a new beginning for us all. Perhaps then, magic will save our loved ones instead of robbing us of them."

Gallien nodded in agreement, though his thoughts were already circling around Joran. He missed him more than anything and hated thinking of the trials he would have to endure without him.

"You've been fighting this war for along time," he said, distracting himself from Joran. "That's a long time to dream about what *could be*."

"Is there anything better to fight for?" the wizard queried with a warm smile. "Joran will see us to victory," he continued with conviction. "We have only to buy him the time he needs."

The quick fall of numerous footsteps clawed at Gallien's attention, drawing his gaze to the window and the creaking planks beyond. The smuggler moved away from the wizard's bed and pressed himself against the wall. Peering outside, he counted twelve men striding along the boardwalk.

"I think it's *us* who have run out of time," he muttered with dread.

"What is it?"

Gallien needed no more than a glance to know that the twelve were not natives of The Stilts. Their clothes, while hardly lavish, were too clean and intact, each item costing more than the average citizen of The Stilts could scramble together in a month. It didn't escape the smuggler that they were all armed with a sword at their hip, a weapon beyond the clutches of the locals.

Narrowing his eyes through the rain, Gallien paid close attention to the man who led the group. Fileus Fod, a rather ridiculous name for a man better known as Mr Grim. The smuggler didn't realise until that moment what a pleasure it had been to go so many years without seeing the Padoshi's most favoured executioner.

The axe now in hand, Gallien dashed across the room to gather his things and attach his sword. "We need to get out. *Now*."

"The Padoshi?" Aphrandhor questioned, wincing as he put weight on his injured leg.

"They found us." Gallien's words came out as one.

Leaving all else behind, the pair departed their room and descended the stairs as quickly as the wizard's leg would permit. They had seconds, Gallien knew, until Mr Grim and his thugs rounded the building and found The Seadog's entrance.

"Oi!" the old maid called out. "Hang about!" she insisted, as if she feared them leaving.

Gallien ignored the obvious conclusion, as well as the inn's treacherous owner, and hurried for the door. Under the pouring rain, the smuggler looked to his left as Mr Grim and the Padoshi's goons rounded the corner. Both parties came to a sudden stop. Gallien locked eyes with Mr Grim's only eye, his square-like head hidden within his hood.

It was wicked glee behind the executioner's toothy grin.

"Fileus!" Gallien called out jovially, well aware that the man despised his given name. "A lovely evening for a walk, eh? Or, perhaps, a *swim?*" he added suggestively, half turning to regard the wizard beside him.

The Green Leaf stepped forwards, raising his staff into the air in both hands. That wicked grin was wiped from Mr Grim's face as swiftly as his feet were taken from the wooden planks beneath him. Along with his thugs, Fileus was hurled back by the localised storm that ripped through the street and flung them into dark waters. Much of the boardwalk and stilts below were destroyed in the process, threatening the foundations of the surrounding buildings.

"Run!" Gallien gasped.

As fast as he could, Aphrandhor fled in the smuggler's wake, the pair narrowly avoiding the demise of The Seadog, its front half snapping away in a shower of splinters to slide into the bleak waters. The maid remained standing behind the bar in utter shock, her mouth ajar.

Wizard and smuggler were soon gone from the area, throwing themselves down every next street to get some distance. Only when Gallien noticed he had rounded two corners without Aphrandhor did he stop and double back. The Green Leaf was leaning against a wall, chest heaving, while he pressed one hand to his wounded leg.

"We can't stop," Gallien told him. "The water will slow them down, but they'll be on us soon."

"You knew that man," Aphrandhor said between breaths.

"They call him Mr *Grim*. He's the Padoshi's favourite hound. He won't return to his master without me."

"Go, then," the wizard urged. "I will do what I can."

Gallien was about to nod his appreciation and run, his self-preservation always first to kick in, when something stopped him. Rooted to the spot, he looked from The Green Leaf to the end of the street, half expecting to see Mr Grim.

Why had he not fled already? The wizard had proved himself more than capable of holding his own. He even thought of the terrors that awaited him in the Padoshi's grip, yet he still did not run.

He knew the truth, of course.

Joran wouldn't have run away. Joran wouldn't abandon his companions to certain death. Joran would fight for what was right —the purest chord in the boy's heart was righteousness, after all.

"Come on," he insisted, hooking his arm inside the wizard's. "There's maze enough for us both to get lost."

Moving slowly through The Stilts, the pair navigated the gloomy streets. Always the smuggler tried to keep the river on his left, taking them further south, towards the villages that lined The Treeling. Here and there, it became an impossible task, the unsteady rise of shacks or the tower of crooked cabins blocking their path.

Then came the barking commands of the Padoshi's men. Gallien looked back over one shoulder and spied them bursting through a crowd that had been playing some kind of betting game in the middle of the street.

"There!" one of the thugs cried, dripping wet.

Aphrandhor pivoted on his good leg, staff rounding with him. Gallien's ears popped at the blast let loose, though the spell was far more contained this time and caught a single man in the chest. Still, it was enough to fold in his limbs and launch him back into three others.

A jostling noise turned the smuggler to an alleyway beside them—two more. He let the axe fly with all his strength behind it. Shoulder to shoulder in the tight space, the Padoshi's men couldn't hope to avoid it. The one on the right couldn't, at least. He went down with the weapon protruding from his chest, the steel having cleaved through his sternum with ease.

The survivor continued his charge and came at Gallien swinging. The smuggler drew his sword and blocked the incoming blade, holding it aloft, while he willed the axe to return to him. The thug's surprise was short-lived, for by the time he noted the axe in Gallien's hand it was ploughing into the side of his head.

"Sorry, chaps." Aphrandhor's apology preceded his staff, which he stamped into the planks of the boardwalk.

His magic rippled down the street, upending every plank of wood and splitting the stilts beneath. Those holding cards and placing their bets plummeted into the cold water before another of the Padoshi's thugs followed them down.

A group that included Mr Grim came to a skidding stop at the edge of the street, where the spell had faded. "Drakalis!" Fileus Fod roared, his hood drawn back to reveal the trench-like scars that ran over his shaved head.

Gallien sheathed his sword and shot the man his cockiest grin before gripping the wizard by the arm. "Let's go!"

Deeper still they weaved through the narrow streets of The Stilts, drawing suspicion from all they passed. Almost every tap of The Green Leaf's staff made Gallien wince, the *crack* of it striking the planks getting louder the more he leaned into it. The smuggler's instincts told him to part ways with the old man, that the noise he made would alert their foes or that his slow speed would doom them both.

Nevertheless, he gripped the axe a little tighter and remained at the wizard's side. There was every chance they could make it back to the river and find a rowboat that would take them to the inner ring. From there, they could—

Aphrandhor went down, thrown onto his back.

Gallien only registered the club that had swung around the corner when Mr Grim appeared holding it. The Green Leaf didn't stir, a trickle of blood running down from a gash in his left eyebrow. There was no time to check on him and see if he had survived the blow, for Mr Grim and his remaining thugs were filling the street.

Fileus pointed his club at the smuggler. "What a bad boy you've been, Gallien."

The air was cleaved by the ringing of steel as Gallien drew his sword again. They wouldn't take him alive, he decided.

If only he had known about the man creeping up behind him.

28

ONCE THERE WERE HEROES

0 Years Ago...

4

Hurled through time again and again, Daijen fell to his hands and knees as he slipped from one place to another. Since witnessing the Golem, Ahnir, unleash an army of monsters upon King Hellion and his city, the Vahlken had been forced to stand amidst battle after battle, condemned to observe the slaughter. With every new location and time, it seemed the Skaramangians swelled in numbers, the men of east and west taken in by the power of The Dark One.

Throughout it all, a question had begun to arise. It had niggled and gnawed at Daijen, but he was certain that some of the places he had been dragged through time to were well within the lands of Andara. He even wondered if The Hellion Mountains had been named for the king he had glimpsed. And so the question had gained weight.

Where were his people?

Where were the Andarens?

The battles that had raged about him were fought by humans and dwarves. Why had his kin not risen to challenge The Dark One and his forces? It troubled the Vahlken, though he hardly had the time to fathom it, his mind squashed and stretched as he fell deeper and deeper into the past.

On all fours, he had landed on the very edge of a ravine, his head protruding over the long drop. Accustomed to heights, it did not dizzy him, though he looked up in the hope of orientating himself. Before him was a cavernous valley, a great scar on the land that cut from north to south. Above the vista reigned the stars in the heavens, their majesty on display in the absence of any clouds.

Rising to his feet, the sound of heavy, yet familiar, footsteps turned him on the spot. Two of the Golems were walking along the flat top of the ravine, their four arms swaying gently at their sides. As the memories had gone on, Daijen had noted that the four Golems were rarely seen as a collective, their power and authority required elsewhere in order to keep The Dark One's empire stitched together.

He couldn't explain how he knew, only that he knew for sure that the Golem on the left was Ahnir, the one to whom he was tethered.

The wizard himself was present atop the ravine, guarded on either side by his towering sentinels. At his back, there followed a procession of Skaramangians that reached back as far as the eye could see, all donned in black armour and dark cloaks.

The Dark One had adopted a different attire since Daijen had seen him last. While he still sported his obsidian cloak and hood about his head, his robes had been replaced by elements of gold armour, lending him the look of a warrior.

Looking to the north, where The Dark One was leading his forces, the Vahlken was met by a temple of some kind, its architecture new to his eyes. It jutted out from the mountain and touched the edge of the ravine, its hewn stone shaped into domes and vast archways. Clinging to the domes and spires were mighty statues, gothic in design, as they reflected the image of dragons. Beyond it, the ravine dropped away into a flat canvas all the way to the horizon.

"You will come no further!" a stout voice boomed from the temple.

The Dark One came to a stop and his forces behind him. He paused there, under the stars, his thoughts his own. Then he pulled back his hood with both hands, revealing his features in the pale moonlight. A square jaw beneath a set of strong cheekbones was the foundation of a sharp face. Equally sharp was his mohawk, a strip of white hair that ran over his scalp into a long braid that collected in his hood.

Daijen would have placed the man in his forties, perhaps early fifties, though his exposure to humans was limited enough to cast doubt on that. It was all the harder to determine given the number of small scars that chipped away at his features. More unusual were the scaly patterns about those scars, as if the skin around the old wounds mimicked that of a lizard.

"Come now, Gelakor!" The Dark One shouted back. "Is that any way to welcome an old friend?"

A set of tall but narrow doors flung open in the temple's southern wall. Torchlight spilled out, casting a long shadow from the man standing on the threshold. Unseen by them all, Daijen moved closer, putting himself between the opposing men.

The one named Gelakor strode out from the temple, unafraid of the forces that had amassed at his door. Behind him, his cream cloak flapped in the cool night breeze. Upon his chest, he wore a cuirass of silver dragon scale, the design reminiscent of Androma's undersuit. Caught in the moonlight, Daijen's eyes were drawn to the axe in his hand.

The resemblance to Mordrith's hammer, the fabled Anther, was immediate. The silver haft was coiled in a graceful twine of copper that engulfed the elegant curves of the weapon's blade.

The man himself was close to The Dark One in age, if perhaps few years younger. His muddy blond hair fell to his shoulders, framing a face of stubble and a singular scar that ran down his brow and over his left eye.

Soon after he departed the temple, three others cast their own shadows and followed Gelakor outside. Daijen moved again to better see them all, the group collectively dressed in the same armour and cloak as Gelakor, though each boasted a different colour.

The Vahlken marvelled at them as they stood before The Dark One, they the few who dared to challenge the many and the powerful. He wondered if he looked upon the earliest, if not the first, Dragon Riders of Verda. Daijen had to look twice at one among them, astonished to see a *dwarf*.

He stood head and shoulders beneath his peers, though his width looked to be making up for it. Raven black was his hair, tied back to expose every crag and crevice of his pale face. Even then, everything below his nose was equally black, concealed by his considerable beard. The scales that decorated his armour were a dark and muddy red.

As if seeing a dwarven Dragon Rider wasn't surprise enough, this one was holding The Anther. It was exactly as it was in Daijen's time, only it was wielded by a different dwarf.

Beside the dwarf was a tall and slender man who wore a very familiar vambrace. The Vahlken glanced at his own, despite his surety that they were identical.

Standing on the other side of Gelakor was a woman who bore more scars than all of them combined. The war had ravaged her such that she even wore an eyepatch, the strap easily seen in her cropped hair. Like all the others, she wielded a weapon worthy of attention.

Daijen stared in wonder at the sword in her hand, its accents of gold and copper binding it to that of the axe, hammer, and bracer. What power it must hold, the Vahlken thought, though its unique properties remained a mystery.

The Dark One greeted them with a warm smile. "It is good to see you all again."

"Ye see us often," the dwarf replied. "Ye're always jus' too far from the battlefield to barter words," he added venomously.

"Duun, son of Darl," The Dark One said happily enough. "How does my hammer feel in your grip?"

Duun hefted the weapon. "The Anther belonged to Qif," he retorted gruffly.

The Dark One's smile faltered. "Qif," he said wistfully. "I miss her still."

Only Gelakor's barring arm stopped Duun from advancing on the wizard. "She'd still be 'ere if ye hadn' slain her in cold blood!" he spat. "Brigabhor too if yer heart hadn' been so black!"

"I warned you not to get in my way," The Dark One responded.

"Was it not you, Skara, who trained us to *get in the way?*" Gelakor posed. "We were to stand for the people," he said righteously.

"To what end?" The Dark One blurted, his anger flaring. "With the very weapons you wield, I, not you, defeated Barad-Agin. I lost everything fighting for that peace—for *their* peace!" he roared, pointing at the world unseen. "How many years did we spend instilling kings and queens? How many years did we waste sowing their alliances and keeping the monsters at bay? All we did was make it *worse.*"

Gelakor raised his chin a notch. "You have lost your way, Skara."

"No," The Dark One drawled. "I *was* lost. Lost to a vision of what could be. Lost to a world that could only be dreamed of. Even now, under the guardianship of the *Dragon Riders,*" he added mockingly, "how many suffer and die needlessly in your realm of peace? I have seen it with my own eyes. The murderers, rapists, thieves—they still *thrive!* The urge, the *desire,* to dominate, to spread torment, and *take* all that they can is a living thing that *beats* in the heart of every man! Your lands are infested with these vermin, these would-be conquers —barbarians who would rob parents *just like me* of their children!"

The Dark One took a breath and lowered his voice. "They are allowed to do so because of the freedom we granted them. Because of the fools we put on their thrones. You're all too arrogant to see the truth. That *we* are the reason for so much suffering. It is our responsibility to take the power we wield and *use* it. We, the *immortals*. We, who will *never* forget the past."

Gelakor was shaking his head. "You can't hear it, can you? You sound just like *him*. You were his apprentice once. Now I wonder if you ever stopped calling Barad-Agin your master."

"That darkness you see in me is what beats in *their* hearts!" the wizard spat. "I would undo it. I would replace that insidious desire with *fear. Paralysing* fear. That is the true power we harness."

"You had the chance to rule!" Gelakor fumed in his face. "Those wasted years you speak of. How many times did the people ask you, *beg* you, to lead them on the throne?"

"I dwell on those years every day," The Dark One confessed. "It is with shame that I consider the hundreds, the thousands, that died because of my fear. I was too narrow-minded to see that Barad-Agin's words weren't a poison in my ear but a warning. He was right, Gelakor. His vision lacked execution, but *he was right*. Freedom leads to chaos. Chaos leads to suffering. And that suffering," he declared, arms wide, "has led to *me*."

Duun shrugged in the face of the speech. "All I hear is madness."

"It is madness, son of Darl, that the blockheaded mind of a dwarf might ever bond with a dragon. Yet here you stand, an anomaly as well as a mockery to the order *I* started."

Daijen stared at The Dark One and was held there by revelation. Skara had started the order of Dragon Riders...That could only mean *he* was a Rider.

That explained the voice that had plagued Skara's mind on the night the Golems were born—he had been hearing his dragon, the one he had called The Drakalis. Furthering the revelation, it seemed they were on opposing sides, a most unusual scenario given the intimacy of their bond.

"Why did you request this meeting, Skara?" Gelakor demanded before Duun could reply with equal venom.

"I hoped words might triumph," The Dark One told him.

"You are deluded, prince of monsters," the woman berated.

"We told you before—we will never join you. You have pressed us to violence, and violence you will have."

"Nathara," the wizard addressed her. "Any more violence and there will be nothing left of you," he jibed, eyes wandering over the tapestry of scars on her face. "But I did not come all this way to ask for your allegiance. Were you all to kneel this very moment I would still part your heads from your shoulders for your betrayal."

"Get to the point," Gelakor ordered.

"I came to ask only for what is rightfully mine," The Dark One explained, his gaze drifting from left to right as he looked upon the weapons of power.

A new wave of tension rippled across the Dragon Riders. "You came all this way," Gelakor concluded, "to ask your *enemies* for their weapons? Nathara was right, you are deluded, but I would never have thought you such a fool."

Daijen couldn't say he knew The Dark One, but he knew the expression on his face. He had predicted their response.

"You've met Meliax and Ahnir," the wizard began, half turning to regard the faceless Golems. "So too have you met Govhul and Yohem, though you might have noticed their absence. Right now, they stand ready to unleash The Shadow Realm upon the fair people of Ungala."

The Riders' tension morphed into unease.

"Ah yes," The Dark One went on. "You thought the city was safe nestled so deep in your territory. Perhaps you shouldn't have accepted my request to meet and thinned your defences."

"Impossible," the tallest of the Riders determined. "You have come from Nareene in the west. Ungala is too far away for your *creatures* to have reached it yet."

"You think them slow because they keep pace with little old me, Qirann. I assure you, my children are just as swift on land as any dragon in the sky. Give me what is mine, or I will have them shroud Ungala in monsters and darkness."

The Dragon Riders said nothing for a time, determining, perhaps, the validity of The Dark One's threat.

"You doubt me?" the wizard enquired. "Ahnir has only to open his mouth and his voice will carry unheard to all but his brothers in Ungala. By the time you got there, the white city would be red with blood."

"You really believe we would just hand over weapons that will increase your power?" Gelakor questioned. "We are still sworn by the oaths you had us take when we bonded with our dragons. We will bring fire and light to any and all who toil in the name of evil."

"You are blind to evil," The Dark One scoffed. "Just as you are deaf to the truth I speak." The wizard sighed with impatience. "If it makes it easier for you all, you may keep the weapons. I only desire that which lies *within*."

Daijen looked again at the weapons of power. "Within?" he echoed, his words for him alone.

"We each earned these weapons," Gelakor voiced proudly. "And we each wield them to uphold our oath. You cannot have them, nor that which they house."

"I don't recall you earning that axe, Gelakor. I *do* recall *gifting* it to you."

"I recall saving your life time and time again," the Rider countered. "That is to be *my* shame." Gelakor hefted the axe. "Can the mighty *Eikor* not summon it to his grip?"

The Dark One glanced at the weapon. "Whatever spell you have enacted upon my work, it will fade upon your death."

Gelakor stood firm in the face of the threat. "And *that* is the only way you're getting it."

"But how many more will die first?" the wizard posed, his head tilting up towards Ahnir.

"Unleash The Shadow Realm if you must," Gelakor replied. "But know that we did not accept your request to meet lightly, nor were we the *only* ones to accept it," he added knowingly.

The wizard looked back at the man with curiosity, though it soon melted from his face, leaving an ever-darkening expression of concern. His gaze fell away from the Riders, and he scanned the night sky. Just as Daijen had seen before the birth of the Golems, The Dark One's features creased in pain, staggering him on the spot.

"Can ye hear 'im, laddy?" Duun asked, a smug grin beneath his bushy beard.

The haft of Gelakor's axe slowly slid down his grip. "He's coming for you, Skara."

It was with ferocity that The Dark One turned on the Dragon Riders. White fury burned in his eyes, as if his gaze alone might raze the world. His reaction was mimicked by Ahnir and Meliax, their shadowed robes drifting wide as they opened their depths to The Shadow Realm. From within each, a set of enormous spider-like legs began to probe the world of Verda.

Daijen knew he could not be harmed by the memory, yet his feet retreated from the nightmare unfolding in front of him. He retreated further still when the temple moved. What he had believed to be statues clinging to the shadowed stone were far from such.

As one, four dragons flapped their wings, gaining height so they might descend upon the Golems and gathered Skaramangians. Terrible and fierce were they, their unbridled wrath so plain to see.

Yet Daijen Saeth saw no more, just as none saw the Vahlken fall from the edge of the ravine. Like a stone, he fell from the ledge and from the Golem's memory until a great abyss swallowed him whole.

29
LEVERAGE

Crouched upon the southern edge of the valley, Kassanda looked down the sheer cliff at the head of The Giant's Throat. It was there the tracks ended, suggesting Androma and company had taken the dangerous path to the forest floor below

"What madness drives them so?" she muttered under her breath.

"They're alive," Joran kept saying to himself, his hope having expanded into elation after discovering the tracks of three men and a woman.

Kassanda looked back at the boy over one shoulder. "Why would they travel south, through the forest, while the Andarens occupy the region?"

Joran shook his head. "Getting me to Drakanan was all they talked about. Our journey was ever north."

The Dragon Rider sighed, dissatisfied with the mystery as well as the fact that they had missed them. Rising from her crouch, she followed the edge towards the valley itself, where she could look down on the mouth of The Giant's Throat, a watcher unseen by the thousands of Andarens who camped inside and on the fringes of the silver trees.

"They have taken the forest," Joran remarked.

"They did not come for the forest," the Dragon Rider replied darkly. "Their prize lies within, and they guard it well."

"What prize?" the boy enquired. "The bones?"

"Androma told you of them?"

"The Green Leaf," Joran answered. "He told me they were the source of magic in these lands. That the Andarens have one of their own in the west."

"They are a font of knowledge where magic is concerned," Kassanda corrected. "They are not the *source*."

"Either way," Joran argued, "we cannot let them leave with the bones. We both know the Skaramangians are behind this."

The dragon heart that beat in Kassanda's chest demanded that she fall upon that forest with all the wrath and ruin she was capable of. Without Garganafan, however, who could not pass through a forest of unyielding silvyr, it would be left to her to pierce the Andaren hide and fight her way to the bones. Again, the dragon heart within her beat with a boldness that would have her believe she could do such a thing.

But her responsibility towards Joran and his training allowed a sliver of reason to enter her mind, a shadow of inevitability she could not ignore. Even a Dragon Rider could not stand against an entire army and live. Who then would see to Joran? Baelon Vos? His training would suffice but his ideology would taint the boy.

No... she said into her heart. Now was not the time to intervene. Stay the course. Play her part. Bring about a time of dragons.

"Come," she bade, rising to her feet.

"We're going down there?" Joran asked.

While there was trepidation in his voice, Kassanda detected the eagerness too. "You are keen to prove yourself, but earning the dragon heart is worthless if you die under the shadow of a thousand arrows."

"But—"

The Rider stopped and turned on him, her words cutting

through his own. "Confronting an army without one at your back isn't the definition of courage. 'Tis death. A *fool's* death at that."

Frustration flushed the boy's cheeks. "How am I supposed to bond with an egg if I avoid danger?"

"I can hear it in your voice," she revealed. "Your apprehension. You still fear death. You would mask it with courage, but courage cannot be something you pick up or put down. It is not to be worn like armour or wielded like a sword. True courage must come from within. It must come out in you with every beat of your heart."

Looking somewhat hopeless, Joran shrugged. "How do I achieve that?"

"When you fear the death of others more than your own," Kassanda voiced.

"I already fear that," Joran stated. "I'm here, aren't I? Trying to become some kind of warrior. If you think it hasn't crossed my mind that I will likely *die* fulfilling my destiny, then—"

"You only *think* you fear the death of others more," the Rider corrected him harshly. "It is the instinct of every living creature to fear their own death. When the moment arrives, self-preservation will force you to make a choice. Even then, should your courage hold, it still might not be enough to bond with an egg. Flashes of bravery aren't enough. You must know who you are. You must know who and what you stand for."

"That's maddening! What does that even mean?"

"It means you are above all things that might trap the hearts of men. Fear, doubt, arrogance... even love."

Joran looked at her like the bottom of his world had just fallen out. "I'm supposed to be without love?"

"That's not what I said," Kassanda replied impatiently. "You are to *rise above* it, not be *ruled* by it. You must be able to kill what you love if your duty demands it, Joran. The darkness that would take this world is not easily conquered. It will demand *everything* of you. To have the dragon heart is to have unwavering valour. Unyielding honour. Unending sacrifice."

Clearly deflated, Joran moved away to regard the glistening forest below. His need to do good was inherent—that much was clear. While that had been enough to see him begin his training, it wasn't necessarily enough to see him finish it. The world didn't need a good warrior. It needed a *great* Dragon Rider.

Kassanda's thoughts were dulled when she felt a presence pressing against the periphery of her mind. She looked south, over The Silver Trees of Akmar, in search of her eternal companion. Garganafan was a distant speck, but she could feel him closing in.

"What are we to do, then?" Joran asked with a softer tone. "If they only came for the bones, they will eventually retreat north." The boy gestured at the valley behind them. "There's nothing to stop them. Their path back to Andara is clear."

"Messenger birds will have been sent from White Tower when they invaded," Kassanda informed him. "Even now, the army will be approaching from the south—and the Jainus with them, given what is at stake. They will never reach The Red Fields of Dunmar."

"What if the Andarens outrun them? They have only to stay ahead until they reach Andara."

Kassanda opened her mouth to respond when Garganafan flew within range of communication.

The south lands are empty! No one is coming!

The Rider turned away from Joran to see the dragon approaching. **Perhaps they have been delayed out of Caster Hold,** she suggested. **The Jainus will take The Misted Road through The Spine—you wouldn't have seen them.**

Even if both are true, Garganafan countered, *they will not get here in time. Those bones already belong to the Skaramangians.*

Kassanda turned her head so Joran couldn't see the muscles tensing in her jaw. **Were there any signs of Androma and the others?**

None, but they have days on us.

Or they're still inside the forest, Kassanda replied, her inner tone one of grave concern.

"What's going on?" Joran enquired, having learned to spot when the companions were in conversation.

"There's no sign of Androma or your father. Or the army," she added quietly, her hands resting on her hips.

"No one is coming?" the boy questioned, and rightfully so.

"We cannot know the tactics of the king," she said, feeling obliged to defend His Grace.

"What tactics? This is letting them win!"

Kassanda heard his words but more so his tone, the latter a jibe at her personal inactivity. "You still believe we should go down there and intercede?"

"Isn't that what you're supposed to do? You have a dragon!"

"Have you heard nothing I've said?" the Rider lambasted, frustrated by his learning curve. "What good would it do to kill a few hundred, even a few thousand? They would still overwhelm us. Garganafan too," she added, ignoring the dragon's wordless protest in the back of her mind. "We would die. You would die—and your destiny with you. The enemy would still leave with its prize. That isn't just the logical outcome; it is the *only* outcome. You *will* heed my wisdom on this."

Joran stormed off, chuntering miserably to himself. He only made it as far as the clifftop, however, before he was forced to stop, lest he fall over the lip. While it certainly hindered his dramatic departure from their argument, it didn't stop him from calling back to her.

"Kassanda? What's that?"

The Dragon Rider followed the boy's upward gaze, to where the cliffs in the west rose ever higher over The Throat, their heights topped with snow, and the cloud cover was low, brushing the lofty stone. She sighted the trickle of loose rocks and pebbles cascading down the cliffs, their origins lost to the clouds. Further to the left of the tumbling stone, wisps of cloud were disturbed by something moving at speed along the clifftop.

I'm coming, Garganafan said before she could call him.

Kassanda spared the dragon a glance, noting the considerable distance he still had to cover. She was on the verge of encouraging his speed when a distinct and familiar shape took form on the edge of the cloud cover. Two bat-like wings flexed wide, and a long tail curled out of the mist to lick the clear air. Reared up on its hind legs, the dragon came down into a vertical dive, its wings tucked in now.

Relief flooded Kassanda, and she lightened the grip on her hilt. "It's Obrin," she said aloud, communing with both Joran and Garganafan.

"He is a friend?" the boy enquired.

"Of many years," Kassanda confirmed. "As is his dragon, Melanda."

Violet scaled, Melanda was a dragon who shone brilliantly in the midday sun. Though smaller than Garganafan, as all other dragons were, Melanda was still considered large amongst her kin.

Strange, Garganafan voiced in Kassanda's mind. *Melanda did not reach out to me.*

It is to be expected, the Rider replied. **They've been patrolling the same hundred miles of coastline for forty years—alone. Even amongst immortals, that's no small amount of isolation.**

Though Garganafan did not respond with words, Kassanda could feel his unease. She couldn't help but adopt it, her companion's wisdom far beyond her own. It was that unease that had her give Joran a once-over, regretting now that the sword she had given him was strapped to Garganafan's saddle. There on his belt, however, was a weapon of power, albeit broken.

"Conceal it," she directed, having the boy hide it better within his sandy cloak. "And stay behind me."

"I thought they were friends?"

Kassanda said nothing, content to wait the remaining seconds in silence until Melanda glided over the valley and came down at their side. The ground shuddered under the impact and the air buffeted them as her wings flapped once and hard.

Under the gaze of Melanda's red eyes, Kassanda bowed her head. "Your splendour has been long missed by these old eyes."

The dragon bowed her head in return. While typical, Kassanda was surprised at Melanda's silence. Through her bond with Garganafan, with whom Melanda could commune telepathically, Kassanda should have had a clear line of communication.

She's not letting me in, Garganafan informed her, his concern growing steadily from afar.

"Kassanda," Obrin called, descending from his saddle in a single bound.

The two Riders collided in a tight embrace. "Obrin. It has been too long, old friend."

Obrin stepped back, his long dark hair and beard a tangled mess. Indeed, he looked a man who had kept to himself for many years. Even his eyes had a wildness to them. His attire, of course, was identical to Kassanda's, his sandy cloak caught in the high wind, exposing the plated black leather that coated his undersuit of violet scales.

"Who is this?" he asked, forgoing any kind of familiar greeting.

Kassanda didn't need to turn to see that Joran was the one in Obrin's sights. "He is... This is Joran. He is my ward."

Obrin's green eyes twitched. "Ward?" he echoed, looking about—looking for the boy's *dragon*. "He has bonded?" the Rider asked with great surprise, keenly aware of their dwindling numbers.

"Not yet," Kassanda was forced to admit.

Obrin tilted his head, scrutinising Joran's appearance. "My eyes must deceive me. An Andaren stands before me, yet so too does a man. A child of enemies?"

"His mother was Andaren," Kassanda announced evenly, as if it was hardly a matter of consequence. "Why are you here, Obrin?" she queried, changing the subject.

Obrin looked like he wished to continue their previous deliberations, and so his answer was short. "The Andarens—perhaps you missed the ten thousand soldiers down there," he added with amusement. "I thought you and Garganafan were safeguarding the eggs," he said, steering the conversation away from his presence in the valley.

"How did you get wind of the invasion?" Kassanda persisted, finding it unusual that he had learned of the inland hostilities from his coastal patrol.

"I was north of The Deep," he explained, naming the expanse

of sea that sat mostly within Erador's domain. "The smoke from White Tower can be seen for miles."

While that might ring true, Garganafan said, *I still cannot look into Melanda's mind to see the truth of it. Something doesn't feel right.*

"Garganafan has swept the south lands," she informed Obrin. "There is no sign of our soldiers. Perhaps together we can keep the Andarens from entering the valley," she suggested, an attempt to tease out their reason for being there. "Dragon fire should make them think twice," Kassanda went on. "It would give our forces time to amass."

Obrin was nodding along, seemingly in agreement. "You left Drakanan in pursuit of the Andarens," he reasoned absently, his gaze turning north before wandering back to Joran. "Should you not return with your... ward? Baelon would have those eggs, Kassanda. Garganafan's presence is all that has kept him at bay."

Kassanda held onto her response while she glanced up at Melanda and then out at the approaching Garganafan.

Do not provoke him, her companion warned. *Keep him talking.*

Kassanda knew that to be the best course of action given the distance that still sat between them, but the mention of Baelon— the great traitor—was like a fire beneath her simmering anger. It bubbled over, driving her to ask a question that should have waited until she had a dragon at her back.

"You are familiar with Baelon's wants?"

Her words changed everything.

Melanda's head slowly began to rise, her claws digging steadily deeper into the stone. Her Rider, confident beside his dragon, didn't stiffen but raised his chin, a defiant man prepared to defend his choices.

"Tell me, Obrin, what was your price?" she demanded, provoking him all the more. "What could Baelon Vos offer you that would cleave you from your oaths?"

Obrin had an air of relief about him, as if he was thankful the charade could end. "Patrolling empty shores and dissuading Andaren warships every few years gives one time to think, to dwell on what was... and what can be."

It took a great measure of Kassanda's strength to keep her blade sheathed. "I thought you were stronger than that—both of you," she jibed, looking up at Melanda. "To have sought out Rhaymion's murderer. Aila's butcher," the Rider added, making sure to strike at the dragon with her words.

"We did no such thing," Obrin told her. "Baelon came to *us*. For weeks he stayed by our side. We would talk late into the night and dream together high above the clouds. He shared his vision for the Dragon Riders. For the *world*. Kassanda, there is a place for you in that world. Just meet with him. Listen. I didn't have the sense to understand it back then. The chaos. The bloodshed. It all happened so fast."

"I know of his vision," Kassanda said boldly. "Dragon Riders aren't meant to rule. Immortals have no place dictating the lives of those doomed to die. We safeguard their world so those flashes of life might mean something. So no, Obrin, I will not listen to his *madness*. I will hold to my oaths."

"Damn your oaths and the line of kings that have held you to them! Our order has nearly faded into shadow because of the Etragon bloodline! Even now, at our very feet, the war spills out of control," he fumed, gesturing at the forest below.

"Like the king and his council, you lack Baelon's foresight, his *strategy*," Obrin continued. "The Andarens believe they are retrieving one of their gods down there. Whether that's true or not, their *belief* can be used against them. We have only to take it from them, and the entire war can be bargained for. That's *real* leverage. Leverage the king could have used were he not so fearful of the Jainus. Baelon does not share that fear. He will reshape this war, quash it with a single stroke. Generation after generation will thank us, Kassanda. On both sides."

"That's why you're really here then—to steal from the thieves." Kassanda gave a dour laugh. "How low must Baelon stoop? I suppose he doesn't have to," she realised. "Not when he has robbers like you to do his bidding."

Stop antagonising them! Garganafan urged.

Melanda let loose a rumbling growl from deep in her chest, her fangs parting just enough for Kassanda to see the blood that stained them and the gore of her previous meal clinging to dark gums.

"There is to be a new age of Dragon Riders, Kassanda," Obrin declared. "Should you cling to the past, I must warn you: Baelon's orders are very clear when it comes to renegade Riders."

Shield yourself! Garganafan roared in her mind.

The dragon's intuition was right. Melanda inhaled one sharp breath and exhaled, allowing her to utilise the glands on either side of her tongue. The two streams of liquid jetted from her maw and mixed into a fire unlike any conjured by man.

As those flames came to life, so too did Kassanda's shield, the magic brought into being as she raised a single knotted fist. The shield flared every colour, its spherical shape revealed by the engulfing fire. The Rider was taxed on two fronts, for the intensity and heat of Melanda's breath were magnitudes beyond any physical blow, and she was also forced to expand the shield to encompass Joran behind her.

Outside the protective bubble, the stone was scorched black, smaller rocks were reduced to ash, and the snow for fifty feet in every direction was melted away. Though Kassanda could no longer see Obrin—or anything—through the flames, she knew he too must be shielding himself, his proximity enough to burn skin down to the bone.

I'm coming! Garganafan yelled again and again into their bond.

Just tell me when she stops, Kassanda replied, her next bout of magic itching to be unleashed.

It seemed a lifetime before Garganafan reported as much, at which point her brow was dripping with sweat from the exertion. While flames still licked the edges of her shield and ground around them, masking Melanda and Obrin, Kassanda threw both arms out wide, freeing the spell that had been steadily building inside her. It shattered her shield and expanded in every direction at great speed, banishing the remaining flames and scattering the shattered stone.

Melanda's head was thrown aside by the force of it while Obrin was cast back, his feet scraping across the ground until he teetered on the lip of the clifftop.

"Get back!" Kassanda shouted over one shoulder. Her command was accompanied by a spell, a shockwave that plucked Joran from his feet and tossed him away.

Garganafan's sharp eyes pierced the distance and saved her life again. *Dive!* he commanded.

Kassanda didn't hesitate, her body springing and twisting through the air, carrying her from certain death as Melanda's jaws clamped shut just where she had been standing. The Rider rolled across the stone and came up with her silvyr blade sliding out of its sheath. She flicked the sword from right to left, deflecting Obrin's leaping attack.

The two Riders collided again and again in concentric circles, the ring of their silvyr echoing over The Giant's Throat. Obrin was rusty, his form lacking discipline. Years of inaction, Kassanda deduced. Whereas she had full use of Drakanan's training arenas and equipment, he had enjoyed decades where Melanda's presence alone was a deterrent.

Joran's distant shout, however, spoke of his danger and tore at Kassanda's focus. The boy had hurled himself from a boulder, narrowly avoiding Melanda's scraping claws. She gnashed her maw at him, missing Joran by inches due to his trip and subsequent fall. He crawled as fast as he could and had the good sense to roll aside before one of Melanda's huge feet hammered the stone.

I'm coming! Garganafan promised again.

Not soon enough, Kassanda knew, and she herself was tangled in a duel that would prevent her from intervening. She thought to kill Obrin swiftly, but the rage it would ignite in Melanda would be disastrous for them all. What was it Obrin had boasted of on Baelon's behalf?

Leverage...

Kassanda feigned her next counterattack and pivoted on the spot. Her padded elbow snapped up and round, slamming into Obrin's nose, shattering the structure therein and splattering his cheeks and lips with blood. Twisting her hips, the Rider brought her silvyr blade across in a two-handed grip, its edge slicing through the black leathers about his midriff and putting Melanda's violet scales to the test.

They endured, as she knew they would, but the pressure behind her blow was still enough to shift their alignment and find a sliver of flesh beneath, evidenced by the line of red that now decorated the sword.

Obrin was thrown back by both attacks, his attention split between the blood pouring out of his nose and the blood staining his armour. Kassanda burst forwards and planted a boot on his chest, launching him onto his back. She had only to step forwards and cut the air with silvyr, bringing the blade to his throat. The weapon was pressed just enough to draw blood. It was also enough to get Melanda's complete attention.

"Leave him be!" Kassanda barked at the dragon. "Fly beyond Garganafan, and I will release Obrin!"

Melanda's front right leg shot out and pinned Joran to the ground. Slowly, she dragged him beneath her looming jaws, the stone etched by her claws.

An external pressure surrounded Kassanda's mind, a feeling that manifested as a cold touch at the base of her skull. Garganafan accepted the presence, and his mind formed a bridge between them all, allowing the violet dragon to speak.

Remove your blade from his neck, Melanda issued, her voice silky smooth, *or I will crush the boy.*

Obrin's arm whipped out, his hand reaching for the hilt of his fallen sword. As the silvyr clattered and scraped across the stone, Kassanda hammered her heel into his wrist and applied a notch of extra pressure to his throat.

"Be still, Obrin," she commanded. "Grown-ups are talking."

Joran cried out, his voice naturally strained.

I will grind his bones into the stone, the dragon threatened.

"You will fly away," Kassanda corrected her. "Or you will answer to Garganafan."

I could kill both of you and begone from here before he arrives.

"And you would do so without your Rider," Kassanda reminded her, altering the angle of her sword to cut afresh into flesh.

Obrin squirmed and Melanda exhaled a sharp breath through her nostrils. One of her claws lifted from the ground to hover over Joran like a guillotine.

She will not yield! Garganafan warned her, his words for Kassanda alone. *She cannot!*

The Rider knew as much—what dragon would bow to the threats of a human?

She will kill the boy! Garganafan asserted gravely.

I don't need her to yield, Kassanda replied knowingly. **I just need her eyes on me.**

Garganafan had been so fixed on their location that he had missed what was occurring on his periphery. So too had Melanda, who was taken by painful surprise when Oaken crashed into her at terrifying speed.

Aegre and dragon came together in a tumbling collision of limbs and wings, their combined bulk slamming into the base of the next cliff. Joran was sent rolling a few feet in the same direction but was soon on his feet and sprinting away from the battle of claws and talons.

Oaken's armoured beak clamped around the back of Melanda's neck. The force of the Aegre's bite, combined with the silvyr-tipped armour plating, was enough to pierce scale and hide, drawing a mighty roar from the dragon.

Melanda unleashed her fiery breath upon the rising cliff, sending the flames up and across where they threatened the Oaken's feathers. The Aegre had no choice but to release the dragon's neck and dart aside. All aggression, Oaken did so with a swiping strike across Melanda's face, his talons dragging red gashes down to her jaw. It was enough to stop the jet of fire but not enough to stop the dragon from swinging her tail.

The Aegre was hurled aside, a portion of the blow absorbed by the sheets of chainmail and armour he wore. Still, Oaken was slow to rise, his right wing twitching and bleeding across his dark feathers. Melanda pursued him without thought, her roar splitting the air as she stomped across the stone.

It was with the confidence of an apex predator that the dragon came to tower over the Aegre. One good bite across the neck would break his bones and bring an end to Oaken. It was the kind of close, personal kill a dragon enjoyed when their rage was at its peak, to feel their foe die in their jaws. It was most satisfying, Kassanda knew.

But the Aegre, it seemed, was just as crafty and agile as his rider had once been.

His feint revealed, Oaken leaped up, propelled by his back legs. His front talons dug deep into Melanda's open maw, pressing into gums while keeping the jaws open at the same time. The dragon's pain was immediate but tempered compared to the agony that followed when Oaken ripped out half of her tongue.

The Aegre retracted his talons and fell onto all fours with a meaty and ragged chunk of tongue hanging from his beak. His feathery face free of emotion, Oaken blinked once and dropped his prize. Having witnessed his kin in battle many times, Kassanda knew that aggression was all the instinct they had, and Oaken did not disappoint. His wings flapped once, taking him high enough to pounce on Melanda's back.

While the beasts' fight was renewed in earnest, Obrin took advantage of the distraction. Kassanda was too late to shield herself from his magic, the force of it throwing her back. As with his fighting prowess, his spellcasting was left wanting, the source ill-defined due to underuse. As a result, Kassanda was quick to recover, her sword still in hand.

Ill-defined or not, it was all the time Obrin needed to rise with his blade in hand. Worse, he turned to intercept Joran, who skidded to a stop before he entered the rogue Rider's swing. The boy might have succumbed to Obrin's superior skills there and then had a white dragon not come into view.

Garganafan was almost upon them.

"Melanda!" Obrin yelled, abandoning any potential fight with Joran. "Melanda!"

The dragon was in a fight for her life. Besides the talons that continued to pierce and rake her sides, she looked to be suffering terribly from the wound in her mouth. There seemed no end to the blood spilling over the edges of her gums, always oozing between her fangs. Only when her Rider's warning sank in did she move to free herself from the battle.

Raising her left wing, she batted Oaken aside and lashed at him with her tail, taking his legs out from under him. One vigorous swing of her horned head clubbed the Aegre under his beak and threw him into the face of the higher cliff.

Without a threat or so much as a last word, Rider and dragon came together and plummeted into the valley. Kassanda ran to the edge, making certain they were fleeing. Indeed they were, flying north through The Giant's Throat—away from Garganafan.

The white dragon thundered down onto the clifftop. He was bristling, a fact that was likely obvious even to those who weren't bonded to him. Kassanda could feel the vein of guilt mixed with the fear he had harboured.

All is well, old friend, she said into their bond. *I am not be undone by traitors—cowards all.*

I should hunt them down, the dragon seethed.

"Oaken!" Joran yelled, running over to the Aegre.

Kassanda flicked some of Obrin's blood from her blade before sheathing it. *There has been enough bloodshed for one day.*

Garganafan reluctantly agreed, though he hungered for the thrill of the hunt. His hunts always ended the same way.

Crossing the gap between them, Kassanda caught up with Joran, who was running his hand over Oaken's neck. The Aegre's feathers were all the darker for the blood that coated them. Still, the creature stood proud on all four of his legs.

"You are proving hard to be rid of," Kassanda remarked, meeting Oaken's yellow eyes. She regarded Joran for a moment, the boy only alive because of the Aegre's interference. "Perhaps it wouldn't hurt to have something of Ilithranda by our side," the Rider mused, earning a warm smile from Joran.

We must return to Drakanan, Garganafan insisted.

Kassanda was on the verge of agreeing with her dragon when her recent words came back to her. "No," she said aloud, garnering a curious look from Joran. "We must hold to our oaths."

Garganafan looked down at her. *But the eggs...*

"Their fate has ever been their own," she told him softly. "They will bond to whomever they are destined to."

Joran looked from dragon to Rider. "What are you talking about?"

Kassanda looked south, over the silver trees. "That skeleton must not leave Erador. It cannot be allowed to reach the Skaramangians. I don't know what plans have been set in motion to meet this invasion, but there will be an assumption the Andarens intend to push further south."

"Might they?" Joran queried.

"Unlikely. The Skaramangians will want to ensure the skeleton reaches Andara. What better protection than an entire army?"

Then what path are we to take? the dragon asked.

"The armies of Erador will not arrive in time—not on *foot*," Kassanda specified. "If they were to set sail from Caster Hold, they could shore up in the north, between White Tower and Argunsuun. The Andarens would find their homeland blocked by ten thousand spears."

Joran looked inspired. "That might actually work," he said. "But how do we get an army to set sail from Caster Hold?"

Kassanda turned to the boy. "*We* can't. But I know someone who can."

30

THE POWER OF WORLDS

4

0 Years Ago...

Daijen opened his eyes from what had felt like a deep, dark slumber. Quick were his senses to take in the environment and fill his mind with information. He knew well the scent of a forest. So too did he recognise the feel of leaves against his skin and the touch of soil beneath his fingers.

Lying on his back, partially buried in foliage, he looked up and spied the sky between the canopy. It was the burned orange of twilight, of the setting sun and the passing of another day.

The silence was notable. Palpable, even. There was no bird song nor any audible sign that the forest about him harboured life. The Vahlken might have considered the forest dead had his ears not detected the distinct *snap* of twigs and the rhythmic crushing of foliage.

Daijen sat up, all too familiar with that particular rhythm— that particular gait. From behind a tree strode a Golem on its horse-like legs, the cause of such quietude. Its shadowy robes floated about it as if caught in a breeze all of its own.

It could only be Ahnir, Daijen knew. What fresh hell was he to witness now? He recalled then his fall from the cliff, a mistake that had cast him from one memory into another. It was the first time he had done anything, deliberately or otherwise, that had affected his place within the Golem's memories. Even now, he could not will the bracer to set him free and return his consciousness to his body within Ka'vairn.

The Vahlken froze.

His musings had split his attention, causing him to miss what was taking place right in front of him. Ahnir had stopped in his tracks. The towering Golem stood eerily still. Daijen looked around, seeking the source of whatever had transfixed The Dark One's hideous child.

Slowly, deliberately, the Golem's hooded head began to turn towards the Vahlken. Its smooth face of featureless grey skin looked down at Daijen. He held his breath, as if he were the prey caught in the gaze of a predator. It was impossible, he told himself. However the Golem perceived the world, it could not perceive *him*. In memory, he was a watcher, an ethereal observer, and no more.

And yet...

There it stood, head bowed, as if it were looking at him. Daijen didn't know what to do. Could he fight the thing? What difference would that make? The Golem was only a memory, an echo of what was. Since the Vahlken hadn't been present in that moment in time, they couldn't interact at all.

"This isn't real," he told himself.

The cold air felt real, drifting out of the black shadows of Ahnir's ethereal cloak. From within those dark folds, it could unleash monsters never seen on the face of Verda before. Daijen tore his eyes from those depths and looked up at the Golem. The creature tilted its head like a curious dog.

Then it left.

Ahnir resumed his full height and continued its stride through the woods. Daijen took a breath, one white-knuckled hand gripped to the vambrace on his forearm. It ignored his every command to leave and, instead, dragged him deeper and deeper into memory. He could handle it, the Vahlken told himself, thinking of Aphrand-hor's debilitation.

He held onto that belief as he trailed the Golem. It walked for another mile before the trees fell away and they entered a vast clearing. The distance was concealed by the mountains that towered over the forest, though the Vahlken's icy blue eyes were fixed on that which lay before him.

The Tomb.

"I'm on Nareene," he uttered to himself.

His gaze lifted, taking in the black pyramid. In his time, the pyramid was mostly buried beneath the island, its glassy capstone all that protruded. It sat upon Nareene in all its glory now, a behemoth of obsidian stone, a promise of dark things.

Daijen could feel the memory contracting about him, ushering him into a jog to catch up with Ahnir. He was too late, however, and the memory imploded about him, shrinking to a single point before expanding into a new one.

Bathed in torchlight and the flames of surrounding hearths, the staggeringly tall chamber was familiar to Daijen, only there had been a colossal pillar at its heart when he had seen it last. That same pillar had crashed into a hollow beneath it, taking with it the many skeletons it housed. Now, in the ancient past, the chamber looked to be one enormous workshop.

A wizard's laboratory, he knew.

Candles were scattered about, like stars brought down from the heavens to bring light to scrawls, bubbling cauldrons, and a plethora of hideous experiments. Here and there, the Vahlken heard the lame moan of some poor soul chained up or bound to a table, there to await the horrors of The Dark One. Further still, the Vahlken could hear distant screams of torment, their pain carried through the labyrinth of the pyramid.

Without a sound, Ahnir positioned itself by one of the surrounding hearths and stood motionless. Daijen then noticed the Golem's brothers, each stationed as Ahnir was, like black pillars on the laboratory's periphery.

Overwhelming though the environment was, Daijen's attention was honed to a single point in that terrible place. With a nervous glance at Ahnir, the Vahlken began his journey into the centre of the chamber. He navigated the workbenches and puddles of blood, drawn to the flurry of sparks.

In the light of those sparks, he discovered Skara, The Dark One. Absent his robes and armour, he was down to naught but trousers and boots, his bare chest a slab of glistening muscles and scars. Beside a giant forge, he looked more akin to a blacksmith than a wizard, his belt laden with tools as he worked over an anvil.

Daijen paid The Dark One little attention, his sense of awe and wonder entirely stolen by the source of the sparks. Flickers of lightning flashed between the sparks, all dancing on the edge of a *portal*.

The Vahlken had never seen anything like it. Through the tear in space, he could see what looked like the roots of a tree, only they were far too big to belong to any tree. The bark was as white as snow, and the ground between them shone as if the heavens had been trapped beneath a foot of clear water.

He knew The Dark One had boasted of monsters from other worlds—from The Shadow Realm—but he had thought the Golems his only access to such dark and twisted places. What he gazed upon now was more heaven than hell, a world of light and mystery.

What magic was this?

The answer could be found beneath the portal. As it had been with the Golems, a section of the floor had been pitted and filled with blood. Using the dark magic of Barad-Agin, who had unleashed the Leviathans in Verda's earliest age, Skara had discovered new and twisted ways to use blood magic.

From the pool, thousands of droplets were drawn up, lost to the edges of the portal. They were feeding it. With the blood of innocents, The Dark One had opened doors to other worlds.

"Here they come."

The voice drew Daijen to a man previously hidden behind Skara. The Vahlken had to look twice at the old man, for he recognised his eyes between the grey hair and beard that hid much of his face. It was the apprentice, he realised. That young man who had been present for the birth of the Golems now stood with a stooped posture, his robes clinging to a fragile frame.

"Good," The Dark One replied, scrutinising his work upon the anvil. "I need *more.*"

Between the tools laid down on the anvil, Daijen spied fragments of red crystal. While his curiosity was piqued, movement from the portal demanded his attention. Shifting from one world to the next, a man stepped over the threshold and entered the chamber.

The Vahlken had seen enough death to know when its shadow lingered over the living. The man, haggard and sporting numerous wounds, could barely stay on his feet. Indeed, he soon succumbed to his pain and dropped to his knees beside the anvil, though The Dark One took no notice of the man, so consumed was he by his work with the red crystals.

"Where are the others?" the apprentice enquired.

The man looked pained to raise his head, revealing burns across his skin. "Dead," he croaked.

"Do you have it?" the old man demanded callously.

The dying man lifted one closed hand to his master, but before he could reveal the contents, his entire body suffered magic Daijen had never witnessed before. From feet to head, his skin was transformed before them, converting the man of flesh and blood into the bark of a white tree. His last breath was one long exhale that ended with the sound of strained wood.

"He makes fifty, my lord."

"A necessary sacrifice," Skara told him, striking the largest of the red crystals with a hammer.

The apprentice pulled a lever built into the floor. A mechanism sounded beneath the stone, drawing Daijen's eyes down to that sickly pool of blood. Litre by litre it drained away, revealing the runes carved into the pool's sides. As the viscous liquid disappeared through channels and grates, the portal shrank until it finally closed in on itself, leaving the vast chamber in the light of torches and candles alone.

From within his robes, the apprentice retrieved a serrated blade. Gripping the servant's wooden hand, he began to saw it free from the body. Despite the years that had weathered him, the old man managed to prise open the stiff fingers. The wooden digits splintered and snapped, exposing the severed palm.

The Vahlken moved around the anvil to better see what had been brought back from the other world—what had cost the lives of fifty men. Pinched between finger and thumb, the apprentice held up a leaf of startling red—the same hue as the fragments of crystal upon the anvil. It caught the light in such a way that Daijen had to assume it too was made from crystal.

The apprentice discarded the wooden hand so he could turn the leaf and inspect its every facet. "Small," he said, clearly disappointed. "But intact."

Sweating from the rigorous hammering, The Dark One paused long enough to say, "Ready another group."

"Should we better prepare the next batch, my lord? If only so they might be more successful."

"It would do no good!" The Dark One fumed. "The tree takes umbrage with its leaves being plucked and its power being harnessed. If the price is life, then life we shall gladly pay. Ready another group," he instructed again.

The apprentice bowed his head, an act that threatened to cause him to topple over. "My lord," he said obediently before nodding at another servant waiting in the shadows. The younger man hurried off, his words bringing death to expendable Skaramangians.

Having already returned to his work, The Dark One carefully brushed the pieces of red crystal off his anvil and into an iron pot with a lid. Without touching the pot, the wizard placed it inside the forge, his open hand guiding it to the shelf with magic.

Using the same spell, he removed an identical pot that had been sitting in the forge and subjected to the intense heat. A flick of his finger flipped the lid off and he levitated the contents out and onto the anvil.

Several pieces of red crystal now lay beside the intact leaf the apprentice had laid down. The Dark One scrutinised those pieces.

"Hold out your hand," he ordered.

The apprentice hesitated, though only for a heartbeat. Skara's fingers danced in the air, lifting the pieces to settle on his apprentice's palm. The old man's arm naturally twitched, expecting the inevitable pain. It was with disappointment, not surprise, that he then held them unharmed.

"Quite cool, my lord."

The Dark One seethed before his rage bubbled over. He balled his fist and struck the whole leaf atop the anvil. Whatever magic powered his hammering blow, it was enough to undo the bonds of iron and snap the anvil in half with an almighty *crack*. The leaf, however, lay on the floor, between the pieces of iron, still very much intact.

"If it's not malleable," he raged, "I cannot construct the shell! Without a shell, I cannot contain the heart within! Do you know what happens then?" he roared in his apprentice's face.

"I have seen Mount Athan with my own eyes, my lord."

Shoulders hunched, Skara turned on the forge, the flames reflected in his dark eyes. "You have seen nothing," he uttered. "Pray that you never do," he added ominously.

Daijen thought of the mountain, a titan overlooking Aran'saur, its surface slick with crystal from top to bottom. Given all that he had learned he knew, again, that the Arkalon was wrong. Mount Athan was home to no gods and never had been. What The Dark One was referring to, however, sent a chill down his spine.

"I need more *heat*," Skara growled.

"I will have construction started on a larger forge immediately, my lord."

The Dark One lashed out with his magic, creating a brilliant flash of purple light that destroyed the forge, sending pieces of twisted iron and broken stone across the chamber in a torrent of wild flames. It seemed the fires would have spread, licking all that they could in a bid to consume and engulf, were it not for two of the Golems. They stepped forwards from the shadows and inhaled the flames, sucking them into the darkness of their cloaks.

"There is no forge of man's design that can provide the heat required," The Dark One snapped. "I created the first gems using *dragon fire*," he explained, gesturing at a workbench.

Daijen moved around the apprentice, most curious as to what Skara was referring to. Upon the workbench he discovered nothing of note, except, perhaps, for a pair of empty stone moulds. The Vahlken might have ignored them entirely had he not recognised the shape of one.

His fingers traced over the smooth stone, feeling the impression of what would shape a helm—*the Helm of Ahnir*.

Daijen thought of the helm he had recently cast into the pits of Handuin. Had it not housed a black gem within a ruby? He looked back at the shattered anvil, where the crystalline leaf had landed. He was witnessing the creation of the helm.

And one other...

Looking back at the workbench, he examined the second stone mould. Unlike all the other weapons of power he knew of, this was not to be wielded in battle or worn to protect. It was a *necklace*. At least, it would be. For now, it was naught but an impression.

But what did the crystal leaves have to do with it? The Dark One spoke as if they were imperative to forge the helm, but he had seen no such gems fixed to any of the weapons nor the very bracer he currently wore.

Daijen desperately wished to grab The Dark One and force the answers from him, for even witnessing history unfold with his own eyes was not enough. He needed to understand so much more.

"How then, my lord, are we to acquire the necessary heat?" the apprentice asked. "Perhaps we might capture a dragon and force the fire from its maw?"

Skara was shaking his head. "Your edge dulls with age, apprentice. Dragons can communicate with each other over miles—many miles when in distress. It would bring *him* to my door."

"My lord, you need not fear—"

"Do not say his name!" The Dark One bellowed. "And do not speak of my fear as if you might grasp it. The only fear I harbour is for a world of chaos. A world of unbound freedom and the suffering it brings."

"I only meant to instil your power, my lord," the apprentice replied meekly. "There are none who can challenge you now."

Skara turned to regard the stone moulds, though it looked as if he was staring at Daijen. "Barad-Agin believed the same of himself. Only in the light of Dawnbreaker did he finally see the truth." He closed the gap, coming to stand beside the Vahlken and the empty moulds. "I am not so foolish as to believe my immortality will last. This can only end with *his* death," he specified with determination. "But there are other ways to live forever," he purred, one finger following the edge of the necklace mould.

"Then the stones must be crafted, my lord," the apprentice said encouragingly. With slow and careful steps he made his way to his master's side. "Instruct me. I would see to the fires you require."

It seemed Skara's mood was that of a pendulum as he now looked down at his most trusted servant with something akin to love. "Your loyalty is a source of strength to me," he said, planting a hand on the apprentice's shoulder. The Dark One's eyes glanced over the shorter man and were quickly drawn back to something on the other side of the chamber. His hand withdrew, and he moved away without explanation.

Daijen was close behind, spying the large canvas on the wall and Skara's destination. The Dark One stood before the map of Verda with a look of revelation about him.

"My Lord?" the apprentice croaked.

"In the absence of Mount Athan, there is but one place in all of Verda that possesses the heat I require." The Dark One smiled. "It's as if nature itself is calling to me, willing me to bring order to its world." He pressed one finger into a solitary island beneath Erador. "Kanofell," he announced.

Daijen narrowed his eyes, noting the volcano depicted in the heart of the island. He knew nothing of the place, a piece of land that had played no part in the war between east and west. As far as the Vahlken knew, it wasn't even populated with Eradorans in the present day.

The apprentice didn't appear to share his master's enthusiasm. "What of the Kedradi, my lord? They would never grant an outsider access to the forges therein. It is with good reason that their island is surrounded by sunken ships—"

"*Erador's* ships," The Dark One was quick to interject. "All too often are they attacked by the kings of the east. How many times have they been subjected to sieges and invasions?"

"Not one has succeeded, my lord. The Kedradi defend their home well."

"They are inventors, warriors, philosophers of art and war alike. They can be reasoned with."

"But," the apprentice countered, "it would cost too many lives just to reach their shores, my lord."

"They would not turn away a *friend*, I think," The Dark One replied cunningly.

The apprentice frowned under his hood. "Friend, my lord? The Kedradi have no friends beyond their borders."

"I will not present myself as The Eikor, or The Talakin, or even The Dark One," he replied, voicing the many titles the people of Verda had given him. "To the Kedradi, I am simply the enemy of their enemy. Furthermore, I shall come before the House of Thayne as a friend bearing a gift." Skara turned back to regard the stone moulds. "What nation would refuse the gift of foresight? To know your enemy is coming before they even know themselves."

The crevices etched into the apprentice's weathered face creased all the more. "You would give them the helm, my lord?"

The Dark One looked down at his apprentice, his initial amusement at such a question turning to pity. "No, old friend. I would use their greed to access their forges and the fires of their black mountain, if only so I might forge that which I can use against them." Skara sighed and placed his hand upon the old man's shoulder again. "You have ever been the finest of my Skara-mangians."

The apprentice managed to look up at him. "My lord?"

"Hush now," The Dark One whispered. "Since you were a boy, you have served faithfully by my side. I am only saddened that you will not live to see the world I promised you. I only hope you meet the abyss knowing you have done *good* work."

The apprentice saw the truth of his situation, his eyes widening in desperate plea. "My lord, please, I have many more years of—"

Snap!

Unnatural was The Dark One's speed, though perhaps mercifully so. His neck broken, the apprentice crumpled to the floor at his master's feet, never to see the world he had given his life for.

"Have my ship prepared!" Skara called out, his words sending unseen feet rushing through the halls. "I travel alone. Ahnir, see him added to the pits. His blood will still serve my ends."

As commanded, the looming Golem crossed the chamber, its black cloak washing over everything without disturbing anything. Daijen waited to one side, ready to observe the unceremonious removal of the dead apprentice.

The Vahlken wasn't ready for what happened instead.

Ahnir turned away from the corpse and gripped Daijen with its upper arms, lifting him several feet from the floor. It was a crushing grasp from which there could be no escape, his arms pinned to his sides.

The Dark One turned around, irritation on his face. "Ahnir? What are you doing?"

Daijen felt the air forced from his lungs as the Golem launched him across the chamber with the strength of twenty men. Slamming into the stone, the Vahlken was engulfed by a numbing darkness.

31
A TOKEN

I t was with pain that the world came back to Gallien Pendain. His senses tried to inform him of his environment, but his memory made a mess of things, working furiously to understand what had happened. His hand naturally moved to the source of pain and discovered the crusted blood on the back of his head.

It came to him then. He had heard the creaking of wood behind him before... nothingness. He had been struck unawares it seemed, the ambush sprung perfectly.

He opened his eyes and groaned at the sight that awaited him. The dungeons were all too familiar, set beneath the Padoshi's complex in Thedaria's eastern district. He had been ensnared by the city's largest spider, and, like every spider, the Padoshi did not keep prisoners for long.

"Gallien," came a croaking voice.

The smuggler was hit by a wave of fresh pain as he tried to rise from the damp floor. He was made aware of other injuries then, across his ribs and down his legs. Mr Grim had thrown him a beating, apparently.

"Easy," the same voice bade. "You were not handled well."

Gallien managed to sit up against the wall of his cell and spy

The Green Leaf through the bars. One side of his face was streaked with dry blood, and his left eye was horribly bruised. He was notably absent his staff.

"Are you alright?" Gallien asked, his hope sapping with every passing second.

"I fear my age has become more of a hindrance than I liked to believe," he replied wearily.

"They were less than half your age and you still sent them flying," the smuggler pointed out. "I'd say you've still got some fight in you."

"But not enough, it seems," the wizard lamented. "What can we expect from our captors?"

Gallien looked around, noting the empty cells about them. "Nothing good," he muttered.

The sound of heavy locks and chains turned the attention of both prisoners to the door on the far side of the dungeon. "Wakey, wakey, rise and shine!" boomed Mr Grim's voice. "The night is still young!"

Still groggy, Gallien couldn't find the strength to fight back when a pair of unarmed thugs hauled him up and dragged him through the lavish complex.

It was just as he remembered it. Lush flowers and reaching vines between gold pillars and trellised windows that overlooked Thedaria. Rugs lined every hallway and even hung from the walls, great tapestries costing a small fortune. Statues and busts sat in corners and littered the gardens dotted throughout, each depicting a hero from the stories of old. The Padoshi loved such tales, he recalled. The rooms of his private quarters had been stacked with tomes and bards' tales that brought such colour to the gallant warriors of legends.

With Aphrandhor being dragged in tow, they were brought to the grandest chamber in the complex, if not all of Thedaria, for not even the Blood Lord could boast such wealth. The grand doors were opened ahead of them, presenting Gallien with a nightmare he had failed to outrun.

The Padoshi of Thedaria.

The most powerful man west of The Spine lounged on his throne, his impressive girth so swollen as to conceal much of the striking chair. Absent a shirt, his bare chest was a canvas of foods he had devoured that morning, all atop a menagerie of tattoos. His every finger sparkled with jewels, the rings only able to be removed if cut from the bloated digits.

His neck remained forever hidden, squashed between his glistening bald head and round shoulders. It was known, though never openly discussed, that the Padoshi hated the touch of any and all hair, forcing him to have his body shaved every day, eyebrows and all. The same could be said of his concubines, of which there were six lounging about his throne.

So imposing was his previous employer that Gallien hardly noted the chamber's host of occupants. They were sycophants all, people of standing or general wealth who wished to stay in the Padoshi's graces. Always they would surround him, enjoying his food and drink while basking in his presence. No matter their reputation, each one was a criminal. Under his rule, they twisted and broke every one of the king's laws to see his ends met.

Along with the band, their raucous energy came to suddenly quieted at his arrival. Perhaps the Padoshi had created some buzz about his capture, for the smuggler had not been well known during his employment. His betrayal, however, had sent ripples across the Padoshi's empire.

Both he and Aphrandhor were dropped unceremoniously at the foot of the throne, their backs guarded by Mr Grim and his lackeys. Off to the side, one of the guests made to leave with a woman on his arm.

"Blood Lord Skoll!" the Padoshi called out, halting the man to whom the king had entrusted all of Thedaria. "Leaving so soon?"

Skoll stood a little straighter, his rake of a form standing rigid in the eyes of all. "It seems we each have matters to attend to," he said curtly.

"Stay," the Padoshi insisted, his tone dropping into that of a command. "You are, as always, my guest of honour, Blood Lord. I would not have you miss such a *reunion*." With his final word, the

Padoshi's gaze landed on Gallien. Black and ever hungry, they were those of a shark.

Skoll returned to the sidelines while everyone else waited for the Padoshi's next word. Though sweating profusely, the crime lord sat comfortably in that tense silence, the only sound coming from his mouth as he scoffed a handful of nuts from the bowl beside his throne.

"Obedience," the Padoshi announced with satisfaction, gesturing loosely in the Blood Lord's direction. "A small price to pay for peace in one's life. Infinitesimal when that peace comes with such great rewards. Am I not fair?" he asked the smuggler. "Am I not understanding? Mistakes are made every day on both sides of The Spine. Mistakes can be corrected. Improvements can be made. Weeding out the problems is how I *strengthen* my kingdom. But," he intoned, doing his best to lean over his gut, "wilful disobedience is a *disease*, a scourge that has the power to undo all my labours."

Gallien gave a muffled laugh, deciding his last few minutes on Verda's green earth would be amusing if naught else. "Your labours?" he questioned. "Picking up nuts is all the labour you get done these days."

Sudden movement from behind was halted when the Padoshi raised his fingers from the flat of his armrest. In his peripheral, Gallien saw Mr Grim lower his fist and assume his position once more.

"There's that wit I remember so well. You would have been twice the smuggler if you hadn't always felt the need to run your mouth off."

"Running your mouth off is half the job," Gallien quipped.

The Padoshi laughed, putting his guests ill at ease. "Your tongue shall be the last to go," he finally declared, and ominously so. "Tell me then, while you still can, why would you be so foolish as to let my products run free like that? Time and coin was well spent procuring them all."

"Products? They were *children*, you piece of—"

The Padoshi slammed the back of his hand into the bowl,

sending nuts flying everywhere as he jumped to his feet. He was unnaturally fast for a man of his size. "Yours is not to question!" he growled, spit spraying the smuggler. "I didn't pay you for your morals! I paid you because you didn't have any!"

He waved one thick, bulbous finger across the many guests. "Look at them, Gallien. Wretches all!" he spat. With one hand, he imitated a mouth eating rapidly while his lips smacked together. "Bottom feeders in silk and gold. They only eat the scraps I throw away, but damned if they don't come crawling back for more. How dare you think you are better than any of them. How dare you think you are better than *me*!"

"I wouldn't say that," Gallien replied from his knees, chin raised defiantly. "I mean, look at you. You're *twice* the man I am." Amusement split his lips into a broad grin.

The Padoshi's right eye twitched. Here was a man unaccustomed to *defiance*. He reached out and placed his hand against the smuggler's cheek, his touch disturbingly tender. "You shouldn't have run, Gallien. Had you taken your punishment like a man, we could have avoided all this ugliness. Alas, this moment was inevitable, I suppose."

The crime lord turned his attention on the gathered crowd. "Let it be known across all of Erador, the Padoshi of Thedaria does not suffer the disease of betrayal. It shall be excised, piece... by piece."

It couldn't be helped. Under the scrutiny of a madman who wielded power like a child might a toy, Gallien felt threatened enough to conjure the axe. Aphrandhor's vambrace was only feet away, causing the glyphs etched into the axe's curved steel to emit a purple glow, adding to the spectacle. There came an audible gasp from the crowd and Mr Grim rushed to lock Gallien's arm and wrist in a vice-like grip. The Padoshi stepped back, his brow furrowed in confusion and great surprise.

Gallien tried to resist Mr Grim's intervention, but his arm was being bent beyond its abilities. He released the axe but the second it hit the piled rugs, it ported into his other hand. Two more of the

Padoshi's thugs shoved The Green Leaf aside and tackled the smuggler, pinning him face down.

"Give it here!" Mr Grim snapped, prising the weapon from his fingers. Of course, he held it for no more than a precious moment before it vanished and reemerged in Gallien's hand. Confounded, the favoured executioner leaped to grapple the smuggler's other arm. "Hold him down!" he barked.

"Fascinating," the Padoshi drawled, his voice enough to silence all.

Gallien groaned in pain as Mr Grim bent his wrist, forcing him to drop the axe. The Padoshi picked it up, clearly taken by the exquisite weapon. As ever, it abandoned his grip and returned to the smuggler, eliciting a giggle from the crime lord.

"I *like* that," he crooned. "Make it do that again."

Pain was applied to Gallien's wrist, and the scene replayed for all to see.

The Padoshi clapped his hands with excitement. "Incredible! Magic is such a rarity," he purred. "The Jainus are swift to find those who dabble with it. Swifter still are they to *keep* their secrets." The crime lord pinned the weapon beneath his bare foot, where his baggy trousers tickled his ankles. "Such a *fine* thing," he complimented. "Too fine for a lowly smuggler, I think. Tell me, what spells enthralled it so? Tell me and your suffering shall be greatly reduced, traitor."

Struggling to breathe under the combined weight of three men, Gallien adjusted the angle of his head so he might reply. "You have to stand it up," he began, "and then *sit* on it. That's the truth," he said, doubling down on the obvious mockery.

Sharp agony pierced his shoulder as Mr Grim applied pressure to areas that were only meant to bend one way. Impatient, the Padoshi picked up the fallen axe again, his knuckles paling under his intense grip. Yet still the weapon of power absconded in search of its master.

Judging by the expression tearing across the Padoshi's face, he was beginning to feel somewhat humiliated. His small eyes darted from person to person, as if he was daring them to comment.

"I would have it," he seethed, his attention returned to Gallien. "And I would have it *now*. Release it to me, Mr Drakalis, or I shall leave you in the care of Mr Grim."

Gallien recalled Mr Grim's speciality—a flayed body wasn't idly forgotten.

"I have no idea how it works," he answered with frustration, the truth finally parting from his lips. "I was the first to touch it in god knows how long. It won't leave me alone."

The Padoshi straightened up, assuming his tall stature. "Perhaps if you were dead, it would seek a new master," he mused threateningly. "But death is so *boring*. I have such magnificent plans for you. I can't tell you how important it is to me that you suffer before you die." The Padoshi's face lit up with epiphany, his joy quickly reflected by the oblivious onlookers. "The answer is simple! Mr Grim... cut off his hand."

"With pleasure."

Gallien's mind went numb, sure that he had misheard the tyrant. Only when he felt Mr Grim being replaced by another did alarm spread rapidly through his mind. He writhed and fought back with all he had but it wasn't enough, for his body was pinned and his arm outstretched with the axe in his grip.

"No!" Aphrandhor cried, but the wizard was silenced by a backhand from his captors.

From his belt, Mr Grim retrieved a cleaver, the steel crusted with old blood. "Hold him still! And someone get me a hot poker," he ordered. "We don't want him to bleed out and die on us."

Gallien fought all the harder and felt another thug wrestle his thrashing legs. His head forced to one side, he could only look up at the Padoshi, who stood there, grinning with anticipation.

"Your agony was to be gift enough," the crime lord announced over the scuffle. "So kind of you to bring me more, Gallien."

The smuggler roared with effort and received a pummelling for his defiance. He could hear the approaching *sizzle* of a scalding-hot poker. It opened a pit in his stomach, which threatened to eject its contents.

"Turn his head," Mr Grim commanded as another tied their belt around the smuggler's arm. "I want him to see."

Rough hands grappled the smuggler's head and turned it to face his pinned arm and the axe in his grasp. Beyond Mr Grim, who was eagerly awaiting the hot poker, he saw Blood Lord Skoll merely observing, a goblet of wine in hand. How could he be so calm knowing what he was about to witness?

"*Breathe*," Cob had urged him, the ranger's words coming back to him. "*Focus.*"

At once, Gallien ceased his protesting and exhaled. It was damned hard to find any level of calm, and his focus was immediately snatched when the poker arrived, its end burning bright orange. He shut his eyes and concentrated on his breathing, telling himself over and over again that he was alright.

"Let's be on with it then," Mr Grim said, his smile evident in his voice.

Gallien squeezed his eyes even tighter, willing the axe to disappear.

Yet it remained.

He heard Mr Grim get down on his knees, and a new hand gripped his forearm, above the wrist. A touch of cold steel pressed against his skin as the cut was lined up.

Gallien held his breath, his teeth clenched.

A single sound from the chamber's entrance pierced the stillness—a man clearing his throat.

When the chop never came, Gallien dared to open his eyes.

Mr Grim's arm remained aloft, paused before the gruesome stroke with the cleaver in hand. All heads had turned to the main doors and the newcomer who had halted the evening's entertainment.

"Sorry for the interruption, big fella," the stranger began, though his slow and lazy tone suggested he was far from apologetic. "I saw the door was open, so I let myself in. You don't mind do you?" He walked casually towards them, nodding politely and waving at the high-born scum with a wiggle of his fingers. He helped himself to a goblet of wine held aloft on a servant's tray. "That's good stuff that is," he decided after a swig.

Gallien was utterly perplexed. The man before him was somewhat raggedy in appearance, a low-born who could hardly afford decent clothes and likely hadn't washed in some time. A mop of grey hair, unkempt and greasy, fell to his shoulders, touching a drab cloak coated in muck and patchwork repairs. His face couldn't decide whether it sported a beard or simply days of growth.

The Padoshi squared his rounded shoulders and puffed out his chest. "Galahart," he said with derision.

Gallien and Aphrandhor looked at the newcomer with fresh eyes, for there was only one Galahart of note. The smuggler had met two other men who went by that name, and both had claimed to be the king's spymaster. This Galahart was a third iteration and distinctly different to his counterparts, one of whom had been skewered by Slait, his body pinned to the ceiling of a tavern.

"You bring the *king's* business to my home," the Padoshi said assumingly. "I am honoured."

At the same time, Blood Lord Skoll quietly sank into the crowd about him.

Galahart was about to respond when he noticed the buffet table and its many platters of food, delicacies from across Erador. Diverted to the table, he began stuffing his pockets with whatever he could fit inside, a chicken leg gripped between his teeth.

"You put on a good spread, I'll give you that," he remarked, tearing a piece of chicken from the bone. "Are those prawns from The Dawning Isles?" He scooped up three and pocketed them.

"Help yourself," the Padoshi said, clearly unamused.

Turning away from the food, Galahart wandered towards the throne, picking chicken from his teeth as he did. "I'm here because..." He trailed off, having spied someone in the crowd. "Is that *you*, Skoll?" The spymaster bowed his head. "Good evening, Blood Lord. Good of you to represent the king amongst such... *esteemed* folk."

Skoll's discomfort reached new heights, his attention divided between the Padoshi and the spymaster. He eventually bowed his head in return and averted his eyes, quickly finding something of great interest on the floor.

"What can I help you with, Galahart?" the Padoshi asked, donning a long silk robe of pearl white, handed to him by one of his many servants. "Surely you are here to extend an invitation to the king's table in Valgala? I have some wonderful *opportunities* I would love to discuss with His Grace."

Galahart made a show of patting down his clothes. "Alas, I must have left that invitation in my other pockets. I'll be sure to bring it next time."

A disingenuous smile twitched across the Padoshi's face. "Then how may I be of service to the King of Erador? As you can see, I'm in the middle of finalising my employee's resignation."

"I can see that," Galahart replied, taking another bite of chicken and washing it down with a mouthful of wine. "Unfortunately," he went on, his food still visible as he chewed, "this man," he indicated Gallien with the chicken leg, "and this one," he added as an afterthought, pointing at the wizard, "are to come with me."

The Padoshi remained still, a living wall of flesh, while his hairless eyebrows fought valiantly to raise the thick slab of skin that was his forehead. "Is that right?"

"Afraid so."

The Padoshi looked down at the smuggler. "Most curious. Is he for hanging? Because if he's bound for death, I would happily take that off the king's plate."

"That would be the king's business. I'm just a facilitator."

"Don't sell yourself short, Galahart. We both know there's far too much blood on your hands for such a simple title."

The spymaster ignored the comment and finished his goblet of wine before tossing the empty vessel into the hands of a bewildered high-born. "I'll just be taking them then," he stated, wiping the excess wine from his stubble.

The Padoshi did not move, nor did any of his men. "I'm confused, Galahart. What could a pitiful smuggler such as Gallien have done to earn the attention of the king's spymaster?"

Galahart shrugged. "From the king's lips to your ears, his words are absolute. These men are to be handed into my custody."

"You have received word from the king?" the Padoshi questioned incredulously. "Yet they have been my guests for no more than *hours*. That's not nearly time enough to get word to *and* from the king. It would seem your little birdies informed you of their capture in The Stilts and you came with all haste." Again, he looked down at Gallien. "What an intriguing tale you weave, Mr Drakalis."

"I could have word sent to the king," Galahart countered. "Of course, the missive would have to detail your lack of... *clarity* on the matter."

A mischievous grin spread across the Padoshi's cheeks. "You do that. In the meantime, I think I shall hold on to my new guests."

Gallien foresaw the future that lay ahead of him. It would be filled with long days of torture and interrogation while the Padoshi emptied him of secrets, secrets he believed pertained directly to His Grace. There was nothing the crime lord wouldn't do to have the king neatly inside his silk pocket.

Galahart finished the last of the chicken leg and threw the bone on the floor. "That might complicate our relationship."

The Padoshi's face screwed up in mock concern. "Well, we certainly don't want that, do we?" The crime lord looked away, thinking hard on the matter before he was struck by an idea. "Perhaps a token, then," he said cheerily, glancing at his favourite executioner.

Mr Grim brought the cleaver down with all his strength, severing Gallien's hand at the wrist.

The axe vanished from the dismembered limb as shock and pain elicited an ear-splitting roar from the smuggler, who could only watch as the Padoshi picked up his hand and tossed it at the spymaster.

"Tell our good king he will have his men one piece at a time."

Without warning, the glowing poker was pressed into the bleeding stump, magnifying Gallien's pain tenfold until blissful oblivion swallowed him whole.

32

WHERE THE LIGHT MEETS
THE DARK

0 Years Ago...

4

A spray of cold water brought Daijen Saeth back into existence. His eyes snapped open in time to see the next ocean wave crash into the shore, the water reaching high before soaking him through. Disorientated, he rose to his feet, taking in the stone port that stood defiantly against the relentless sea. Its waves were being driven hard under the lash of a great storm that ignited the distant night sky with lightning.

Broken ships littered the shallows between the larger vessels that had docked along the port. Those that were still intact and sailable sported sigils of blue and white, each depicting the image of a spear running down the spine of an open book.

It took Daijen a moment to recall the sigil, his impeccable memory sifting through pages he had perused as an initiate. It belonged to the Kedradi, Erador's most southern and reclusive tribe.

Turning inland, the Vahlken was met by a view of destruction. He stood on the very edge of a fort, perhaps, though it looked to have branched out with numerous buildings beyond its walls. All stood in ruins now, with smoke rising from every hole and crevice. Small fires could be seen through windows and broken doorways. Entire sections of the outer wall had been pulverised, creating a landslide of rubble that led down to the port.

Like dark wraiths, the four Golems stood as eerie sentinels amidst the battlements, unmoving and ever watchful. Though they could not boast eyes, they each faced the raging sea, their attention adrift from the wreckage about them. Curious, Daijen turned around again, casting his sharp eyes over the stormy waters.

All but a Vahlken would have missed it.

There, in a single flash of lightning, was the silhouette of a dragon in flight. Soaring on bat-like wings it crossed the sea and circled once over the smoking ruins. Its landing only added to the destruction, the hewn stone no match for the bulk and swaying tail of a fully grown dragon.

The Golems had no reaction to the dragon's presence, nor the Rider who climbed down from its silver scales. The same could not be said of the Rider, who stopped and took note of every hooded Golem. From nowhere, a fine axe materialised in his hand, filling his grip with steel, with a weapon of power.

"Show yourself!" Gelakor bellowed, his pale cloak billowing.

Daijen caught movement in his peripheral vision, turning him to the shadowed archway that led into the fort. From that darkness came one who had adopted that very essence into his name. He did not, however, appear from that tunnel in his customary blacks but as a regal king.

His purple cloak blown out behind him, Skara crossed the port in golden armour, his white mohawk and long braid exposed without his usual hood.

"*To the Kedradi, I am simply the enemy of their enemy,*" he had said to his apprentice.

Daijen was beginning to get to grips with his new place in

time. It seemed The Dark One had indeed shed the trappings associated with his title and gone before the noble Kedradi as something else entirely. He now stood victorious upon Erador's soil with a powerful new ally at his back.

"Do you like what I've done with the place?" Skara asked mischievously, arms held out.

"Broadcastle has stood for centuries," Gelakor replied, placing them on Erador's southwest coast. "It was from here we planned our final assault against Barad-Agin. You, me, Qif. Last I was here, there were many families who called this place home." The Dragon Rider looked to be barely containing his rage. "You would raze it in a single day," he seethed.

"A single *morning* actually," The Dark One corrected, and casually so. "The Kedradi are most efficient. And they do so loathe the mainlanders and their warmongering."

"What poison could you have whispered in the shadows that would rally them to your wretched cause? *You* have been the source of war for decades. You are the very embodiment of warmongering."

"I didn't offer them war," Skara told him. "I offered them freedom. *They* chose war. Like most, they believe it is the only path to freedom. Even you hold such beliefs."

"I hold to the belief that killing you will save millions," Gelakor retaliated.

"Your belief lacks conviction, old friend. How many of these little chats have we had since parting ways? Do the others know, I wonder?"

Some of Gelakor's fury seemed to ebb away, replaced by sorrow. "They do not hope as I do."

"Hope?" Skara echoed, the word and its meaning perhaps foreign to him.

"Hope that you will see sense," the Dragon Rider answered. "Hope that you will lay this madness to rest. Hope that you will reunite with—"

"Do not speak his name!" The Dark One spat. "You cling to a fool's hope if you think such a thing could come to pass. I know it was him who turned you all against me. The sting of his betrayal will *never* fade!"

"Betrayal?" Gelakor repeated incredulously. "He is the very definition of goodness. He saw that in you too. That's why he *chose* you. That's why he convinced his kin to give us their eggs. We would all be ash beneath Barad-Agin's heels if it weren't for him."

A *crack* of thunder shook the skies above, a herald to the rain that began to fall upon Broadcastle in relentless sheets. The storm had found Erador's shore, as if nature's most turbulent mistress would witness the clash of immortals for herself. Yet it could not touch the two men. As the rain met the previously unseen shield of each warrior, it simply bounced off, leaving them and the stone about them perfectly dry.

"Cling to him as you do your hope, Gelakor, and see where it gets you," Skara provoked.

"Without him, you are bound for dust," the Dragon Rider reminded Skara. "The same cannot be said of him."

"You think I cannot kill him?" The Dark One questioned, a challenge in his voice. "You think I *will* not? Have I not proved myself a dragon-slayer?" he jibed, eliciting a rumbling growl from the silver dragon behind Gelakor.

"I don't doubt your wickedness. But we both know you will never settle for a mortal life. Who would continue your *great vision*? One of your Skaramangians? Orvax will torch them all," Gelakor added, nodding his head back at the dragon.

"I thought I taught you to never underestimate your enemy," Skara replied.

"You taught me *everything*," the Rider admitted. "That's why you know you're already beaten."

The Dark One let loose a rattling laugh. "The only victories you've ever boasted were standing at my back. Even now you talk of beating me when we stand in the ruins of *your* defeat. Wasn't Broadcastle under the protection of the Riders?"

"This is you *scrambling* to keep the Kedradi onside," Gelakor argued. "You think I don't know the real reason you sought them out? You don't need allies when you can conjure nightmares from other realms," he added, gesturing at one of the Golems. "I was there, remember? I was there when you forged the first stone in dragon fire. And you're making more. How many years have you toiled in the furnaces and forges of their mountain now?"

The Dark One moved closer to the edge of the port, where the sea splashed up and over the stone. "That's why you're here then," he guessed, a sharp smile on his chiseled face. "You've come to see if there's any truth to the whispers that have reached you."

"You don't deny it," Gelakor observed. "You're forging new stones."

Skara pursed his lips, a touch of amusement about him. "I'm forging the *future*. You only have yourself to blame. Had you given me what is rightfully mine, I wouldn't have been forced down this path. But I should thank you. Your defiance sparked an idea, an idea that I might forge something *better*. After all, a smith should only ever improve on their work."

"The Kedradi will see through your deception," Gelakor promised. "Try as you might, appearing as you once did will not be enough to conceal your true self. When they see the snake they've let into their home, they will cast you into the same fiery doom you would use to further your madness."

"Madness? No, old friend. When my work is done on Kanofell, I will have achieved clarity. The future will be clear to me. Not just that, but it will be mine for all eternity. So you can tell *The Drakalis* his days are numbered, for I will unshackle myself from his black heart and steal his last breath."

There was real concern etched across Gelakor's face, as if he knew enough of the man before him to fear the depths of his dark designs. "You know we won't let you. All you've done is risk the lives of the Kedradi."

Skara laughed again. "You would never assault that island— not even to kill me. The cost would be too great for your fragile conscience. All you can do is wait and see what I do. Hasn't that been the way we've played this game? I act, you react."

Gelakor adjusted his grip on the axe. "If it's a reaction you're looking for..."

"Try it," The Dark One antagonised. "I will prise that weapon from your cold fingers and take its heart for my own."

As one, the four Golems began to make their way down from the ruins, each harbouring the promise of death. The cracking of stone could be heard beneath Orvax's claws. A sharp jet of steam shot from his nostrils as he bared his fangs and raised his horned head.

"This won't be like last time," Skara warned. "You shouldn't have come alone."

Gelakor hefted his axe and fell into a battle stance. "Who said we came alone?"

The sky flashed above, and a deafening boom of thunder ripped across the night, a trumpet calling forth an army to war. Daijen was taken aback by the sight, his feet ushered into a retreat from the sea.

"You're not the only one with allies," Gelakor announced smugly.

The Dark One turned to the crashing waves, whipping his purple cloak out behind him. Standing beside Daijen, he looked out on an army conjured by the sea herself. They were launched from the water like arrows, their number steadily filling the stone port until they blocked any view of the stormy horizon. Though in appearance they were akin to humans, the Vahlken noted enough differences to know they were most definitely not.

Mer-folk.

Barefooted, their pale skin could be seen under their extraordinary attire, a mix of unknown materials that clung tightly to their flesh. Most sported bold tattoos, thick patterns of varying colours that weaved all across their bodies. Dull was the steel of their weapons, their arsenal of spears, tridents, and swords.

The sound of *clinking* armour and chainmail turned Daijen around. From the ruins of Broadcastle came the fighting Kedradi of Kanofell. Donned in their blue, cream, and gold, they appeared a regal force of war. Preparing to meet the Mer-folk, they wielded the finest of weapons, instruments of steel and death likely forged in the great furnaces Gelakor spoke of.

Daijen felt his mind protest at the sight, as if he knew something wasn't right. Something to do with their weapons. With the *steel*. He had read all that had ever been amassed of the Kedradi in his time, and yet...

His memory failed him.

The Vahlken was left only with the feeling that past and present weren't in alignment. While he could reconcile differences in culture over the course of eons, he could not accept that his impeccable memory was faltering. He had no choice but to let it go, for both sides charged into battle, plunging him into chaos.

So too did Skara and Gelakor. The Dark One and Dragon Rider collided in a flash of magic and steel. Their fight soon spilled over, taking the lives of Kedradi and Mer-folk alike. And they were not the only immortals to wade in.

Orvax snapped his jaws and ensnared one of the Golems— Meliax, Daijen knew, though he could not say how. The dragon flicked his head and hurled The Dark One's creation into the choppy seas, where it was ensnared again by something monstrous, a nightmarish fiend of the ocean depths brought into battle by the Mer-folk.

An unimaginable heat washed over the violence as Orvax unleashed his fiery breath. The flames would have engulfed Yohem had its almost vaporous cloak not inhaled the inferno, sucking the blaze into an icy void between worlds.

Ahnir and Govhul retaliated. Towering over both forces, they sprinted through the battle, adding to the carnage as they knocked down and trampled any and all to death. At the edge of the bloodshed, they leaped with the strength of twenty men and grappled the silver dragon about his head and neck. Orvax swung his mighty head, hammering Govhul through a thick wall and out of sight.

All four of Ahnir's hands pulled and clawed at Orvax's face, threatening his blue eyes and scraping his gums. It irritated the dragon, who had no way of dragging the Golem from between his horns. He thrashed and writhed, his tail demolishing one of the

Kedradi's ships and launching debris across the port. Holding onto the dragon, however, was only part of Ahnir's assault.

From within the shadows of his black cloak, there came a swarm of... *things*. Daijen had never seen anything like them before, a breed of monster between a spider and a crab. No larger than a human hand, they scurried out of the depths of the Golem's cloak and spread across Orvax's face and even into his jaws.

Ahnir jumped down, leaving the little fiends to work their way around the dragon's body and wings. It was difficult to discern what they were doing, but Orvax had abandoned his fight with the Golem and was throwing himself into the rubble of Broadcastle in a desperate bid to crush them it seemed.

Daijen caught himself smiling.

He banished the expression and quashed the satisfaction rising in him. It was a touch of elation, he knew. How could he feel anything even close to that at such a sight?

The Vahlken looked up and to his right and met the featureless face of Ahnir towering over him. It was dread that gripped him then, a frigid pit that sucked all the heat out of him. He had been stuck down in the depths of Ahnir's memory for too long. It was the only logical explanation for the momentary glee he had experienced.

Panic began to rise in him, seizing his chest. He was losing himself to the Golem, a creature born of loyalty to The Dark One. Without thought, he began trying to remove the vambrace from his arm, and yet it wouldn't budge. It was as if it had bonded to his very skin.

Daijen stumbled and staggered in his fruitless efforts, oblivious to the battle raging around him. Only when The Dark One himself cut across his path did the Vahlken cease his attempts to be free of it.

Skara was a terror to behold. He waded through the Mer-folk with magic that pulled them apart, turned them inside out, and even fused some together. Between it all, he unleashed staccatos of lightning, spears of ice, and flames that charred any and all.

Gelakor pursued him, his axe hacking through the Kedradi

forces. The weapon of power flew from his hand to take life after life, always reappearing in his grip out of thin air. As the Rider impacted The Dark One, Ahnir flung aside the knot of warriors beside Daijen.

The Golem was striding towards the Vahlken.

Step by step, Daijen retreated from the monster. It would do him no good, of course—he was bound to the creature. Inevitably, it caught up with him, only this time, the Golem did not reach for the Vahlken. Instead, it walked through him, the shadows of its cloak enveloping Daijen until his world was an absence of life and light.

33
WRATH BEFORE RUIN

I t was some survival instinct that demanded Grarfath avert his
eyes, lest he provoke the predator standing over him. Slait,
however, possessed an inexplicable quality that didn't just fix
the dwarf's eyes on him, it also prevented him from blinking. As
such, he took in every detail of the one his brief human companions had named *The Dancing Sword of the Dawn*.

While all of the surface folk were tall to a dwarf, Slait was
damned tall, intimidatingly so. It seemed unnatural to a dwarf that
any being could stand at such a height and maintain their balance.
Of course, Grarfath had also learned that the Andaren was no ordinary surface dweller—he was a Vahlken.

His face and bald head bore scars of old, some as fine as a
strand of hair, while others marred his features with thick and
raised gashes of grey flesh against his ghostly pale skin. His ears
were pointed in the manner of every Andaren—at least, his left ear
was. Where his right ear should have been was a ragged stump, as
if it had been roughly torn from his head.

As he had while fighting in The Ruins of Gelakor, The Dawn
Sword still wore his white armoured cuirass and long battle skirt,
both mixed with patterns of deep red. His appearance, in a word,

was grubby. His great travels and penchant for violence had blemished his attire with dirt and splatters of blood.

The smith recalled how easily Slait had bested Yamnomora amidst the ruins. His strength and speed had been unmatched, a killing machine even amongst Kedradi, wizards, and old Dragon Riders. He would have likely slaughtered them all had The Anther not slammed into his back.

The Anther...

There it was, gripped in his chalky-white hands. The gold, bronze, and copper caught in the firelight of the hearths, amplifying its exquisite craftsmanship. Grarfath didn't realise until that very moment how much he had missed the feel of it in his grasp. However much he had longed for his life to return to the way it was, the power he had wielded in that hammer had been intoxicating. In battle, a foreign place for the smith, he had drunk in that power and enjoyed the simple pleasure of fighting to survive.

While he had known there was so much more to be done with The Anther in one's possession, he still feared the responsibility that came with it.

Not that *he* possessed it anymore.

"You," Slait said accusingly, and in the dwarven tongue. "You're the one who sent me here with a hammer in my back."

Grarfath didn't know what to say.

Yamnomora never had that problem. "That weak spine o' yers could o' done us all a favour an' *snapped*."

Slait's golden eyes shifted to the red-head. "I will enjoy breaking you, she-dwarf. Long have you troubled the Skaramangians."

Yamnomora chuckled to herself. "Ye're goin' to break yer bones tryin' to break me, laddy."

The Dawn Sword sneered as the throne room vibrated around them—another quake that disturbed the heaps of gems and coins stacked around the three dwarven thrones.

Slait whipped his head up towards Lord Tharg on the surrounding balcony. "Have them bound and put in a cart. I will transport them to Aran'saur myself."

Lord Tharg cleared his throat and glanced at the throne, leading Slait's gaze to the High King—who no longer looked amused.

"Ye don' give commands 'ere, Andaren," King Glaive stated.

"I speak for The Eldan—"

"SILENCE!" the High King bellowed. "Ye are a guest not jus' in the halls o' Morthil but within the very walls o' me ancestors, boy. Ye're not to speak but *listen*! Lord Tharg," he continued, now ignoring Slait altogether, "why does he wield *my* hammer?"

How small Tharg appeared under the gaze of both The Dawn Sword and the High King. "Like the bones, Yer Grace, any weapon o' power is to be sent to God Fall. I imparted it to Slait so he might see to its safe arrival."

"Do those damned warlocks not 'ave enough? We sent 'em the bones, bones *we* unearthed at great expense! That's two they possess—an' the helm to boot. If Emperor Qeledred can keep his fancy helmet, I say The Anther should stay with the Greyhelms."

By the expressions shared by both Slait and Tharg, it seemed to Grarfath that the High King was walking a fine line between loyalty and heresy. Such was the greed of a king, he supposed.

"The Eldan was quite clear, Yer Grace," Lord Tharg tried to continue, but Glaive's raised hand was enough to halt his words.

"Who is king of these mountains, Lord Tharg?"

The aged dwarf cleared his throat again. "Ye, Yer Grace."

"Then stop givin' me the commands o' others. These are *my* prisoners an' that is *my* Anther. The people want a hero," he muttered. "I shall give 'em one."

Slait stepped towards the throne. "Blasphemy!" he spat. "The Eldan's every action is to further the work of the gods—to see them returned. Who are you, king of hollows, to stand in the way of that?"

Glaive jumped from his throne, outraged, and his son with him. "I will not be spoken to like that by some zealous half-wit! Ye are to relinquish that hammer right now," he fumed. "Outside o' that, ye'll eat, sleep, an' breathe when I tell ye to."

"I do not bow to kings," The Dawn Sword replied defiantly.

"Ye *will* bow to me!" the High King growled, hammering his fist into his chest. "Or ye shall be broken, lad. Broken an' sent back to yer master in a box."

Slait managed to stand a little taller, his grip adjusting the position of The Anther in his hand. "You overreach, good king. You cannot see beyond the crown on your head. I shall put it in a way a dwarf might understand: you are naught but a *cog*, son of Thold. While every cog is important, they can all be *replaced*."

The High King's right eye visibly twitched, his wrath reaching its apex. "'Tis good that ye know a thing or two abou' cogs, lad, because the machines I'm goin' to put ye to will blind ye with agony. Korgan!" he commanded, naming the muscled dwarf at Grarfath's back. "Arrest this fool, an' bring me that hammer!"

"Yer Grace!" Lord Tharg cried out.

His words were akin to raindrops on the mountain stone. The High King had been offended in his own home, his very station diminished by a foreigner within earshot of his wife and son. He would have retribution. And so Korgan moved as his king demanded, the dwarf's spiked mace brought down upon Slait in both hands.

Grarfath was already turning his head away, hoping to save his eyes from the explosion of blood after that mace caved in Slait's skull. What had seemed inevitable, however, never came to pass. Korgan's blow missed The Dawn Sword by an inch, though it was by no mistake of the hardy dwarf. The Vahlken-trained Andaren had simply evaded the strike with a single, if impossibly swift, sidestep.

Using only the power of one arm, Slait backhanded The Anther across Korgan's face, dropping the dwarf dead at Grarfath's knees, his face staved in and neck broken.

The High King's jaw fell open.

"Lord Tharg," Slait called out. "Perhaps you could remind the king that this weapon and these prisoners are the property of the Skaramangians and, therefore, subject to The Eldan's authority. An authority," he said deliberately to Glaive, "that the Greyhelms have long bowed to... and been rewarded for doing so."

Tharg looked a dwarf whose arms were being physically torn apart. In the end, he said nothing, his head bowed in submission to the High King—the one who commanded every spear under the mountain.

"GUARDS!" Glaive roared.

From every door, seen and unseen, there came line upon line of armoured dwarves. They soon filled the throne room with shields, spears, and axes, their bearded faces concealed behind masks of iron.

Slait turned slowly on the spot to take them all in. He didn't look impressed.

"Ye're goin' nowhere good, lad," Glaive told him wickedly.

"My oath is to the gods," The Dawn Sword reminded him. "And they have seen fit to place their weapon in my hands."

Stepping closer to the three prisoners, the Andaren raised The Anther. He had only to bring it down and they four would be gone from Khardunar—and a portion of the High King's extravagant floor with them. For all his speed, though, The Dancing Sword of the Dawn could not evade the bolts from two crossbows, each fired only feet from where he stood. The first penetrated the armoured tasset that protected his thigh, dropping him to one knee. The second slammed into his shoulder, making short work of his cuirass to embed in the muscle beneath.

Still, the brute only grunted at what would have reduced others to a wailing mess. It was enough, however, to falter his swing of The Anther and give a trio of dwarves time to rush him. They grappled him in full plate, a painful collision that grounded The Dawn Sword on his back. The hammer was prised from his grip, the theft eliciting a roar of anguish from the Andaren.

A fourth soldier parted from the wall of bristling iron, a hammer of his own in both hands. He stepped over Slait and thundered the weapon's haft into his forehead. The Dancing Sword of the Dawn went deathly still.

Grarfath watched it all from only feet away. He further observed The Anther being offered to High King Glaive, the weapon raised horizontally in two hands as the solider dipped to one knee. With relish, the son of Thold accepted the hammer, as if he was Duun himself reunited with his oldest companion.

That was all Grarfath, son of Thronghir, was to witness, his view blocked by the same hammer-wielding soldier who had sent Slait into slumbering oblivion. The smith could only see the guard's eyes, but they betrayed a broad grin beneath his iron mask. That was the last thing Grarfath saw before the hammer was raised and he shared in the Andaren's oblivion.

It was not to last, however, for the skull of a dwarf is thick and stubbornly.

The smith came to as he was tossed into a damp cell. His hands managed to break his fall, saving his head from further injury. The sound of *clattering* iron bars and *rattling* keys turned him around from his place on the floor. The cell had been sealed, his jailor already departing.

Looking through the bars he discovered Kitrana Voden on the other side of the passage, the Nimean still unconscious. In the cell beside her was Yamnomora, who rose unsteadily to her hands and knees with a trickle of blood running down from her brow.

It was, again, some deeper instinct that drove Grarfath to survive that turned him to face the cell connected to his own.

Two golden eyes looked back at him, each set within a face that looked chiselled from white stone. Slait sported a dark bruise above his right eye, a small gash running through the patch of dark skin. Nevertheless, the Andaren appeared fully alert, his recovery significantly swifter than the dwarf's.

"Vast is our world," The Dawn Sword rasped, "yet you had to send me *here*."

"Next time, I'll be *holdin'* the hammer that strikes ye down. Ye won' be goin' anywhere after that."

The Andaren's face lit up, and he edged forwards within his cell. "So you do speak! And with steel in your voice. A pity it takes iron bars for you to find your courage."

"I had courage enough to strike ye," Grarfath argued.

"From afar," Slait countered. "And in the *back*."

The dwarf groaned. "Ye're jus' sore because ye got taken out o' the fight by a lowly smith. I heard 'em talk o' ye afterwards. Ye must think ye're really somethin' to be usin' a name like *Sword Dancer*."

"The Dancing Sword of the Dawn was a warrior unlike any you stone bones could fathom," Slait hissed. "Like your great Duun, he came from an era of heroes."

"Is that what ye are?" Grarfath replied incredulously. "A hero?"

"I am the herald of reclamation," The Dawn Sword declared.

"Ye're a *prisoner*," the smith informed him bluntly.

"He's bound for death is what he is," Yamnomora chipped in, leaning against her bars. "How sweet that ye should meet yer end at the hands o' yer own."

"These are not my people, she-dwarf. They have forsaken their oaths. The Eldan will see to their demise, if not that of all your kin."

"The Eldan?" Yamnomora echoed with venom in her voice. "His neck'll snap jus' as easily as any other wretch who bears yer mark." The dwarf laughed to herself. "Especially if all he's got is *ye* to protect 'im! Ye must've been only feet away when Daijen blew the head off the last one."

Their conversation—if it could be described so politely—went over Grarfath's head. Indeed, his attention had slipped altogether. At first, he had attributed the vibrations beneath his feet to another quake, but then the distant sound of chains reached his ears. Added to that, he heard the distinct sound of cogs and gears working in tandem. He bade the arguing pair be quiet, but they continued to hurl barbed threats at each other.

"Will ye both shut it!" he finally barked, his eyes rising to the ceiling as he tracked the mechanisms coming to life behind their cells.

"What is it?" Yamnomora demanded, clearly keen to return to insulting The Dawn Sword.

Her question was answered by the dungeons themselves. All four cells began to rise from the ground, leaving the stone path below. Within seconds, they were free of the chamber entirely and rising above the block, each cell fixed to an array of cranes and pulleys. The cranes pivoted away from the dungeons and moved the cells so they now hung over a sheer drop of at least a mile.

Grarfath held onto his bars, fearful of the swaying that rocked his small world. "What in the hells is this then?" he complained.

Through the bars, he could see that the dungeons had been located in a protrusion of stone that jutted out from the higher tiers of Khardunar. From his new position, the smith was able to spy the floating staircase that connected the Greyhelms' fortress to the rest of Morthil and even the colossal pendulums fastened to the cavern walls.

"This is goin' to make things a little harder," Yamnomora muttered miserably.

"*What's going on?*"

The human words came from Kitrana, who had been roused, it seemed, by the sudden movement. She rose slowly into a sitting position in her cell, her demeanour notably groggy until she took in her dire surroundings. Wide were her blue Nimean eyes as they drank in the gut-wrenching chasm beneath them.

"*We're prisoners o' the High King,*" Grarfath told her, adopting man's tongue. "*Is yer head alrigh'?*"

The battle maiden edged her way towards the bars and dared to peer over the edge. "*How did we—*"

The Nimean's question was cut off by her own blood-curdling scream.

The smith pressed himself against the bars, though he was never to reach her. "Kitrana!" he yelled.

It was no use. The pain that split through her was blinding, just as it had been in The Ruins of Gelakor. She clawed at her back, the source of her agony, but her constant writhing and thrashing prevented her from doing anything but enduring the torment. Throughout it all, there was but one other sound to accompany her misery: laughter.

Slait's amusement boiled Grarfath's blood. "Shut yer gob!" he shouted at the Andaren.

The Dawn Sword's vile laughter only faded after Kitrana's

anguish came to an end. The Nimean remained where she lay, panting for breath, her knees curled up into her chest.

"*Are ye alrigh', lass?*" Grarfath called out.

"*I don't know... what's happening to me...*"

Kit's voice was weak, her words barely heard over the distance between them.

"*You should never have run away, girl!*" Slait remarked, the Andaren sitting comfortably now with his back against the bars.

Grarfath frowned. "*Run away? What are ye jabberin' abou'?*"

"*Your companion is the property of another. Where did you find her?*" he asked offhandedly. "*Most of the farms are west of Morthil—too far for any wandering dwarves to come across. I cannot believe so slight a thing slipped past The Saible.*"

To Slait's eyes, the smith realised, Kitrana Voden was a human. *His* mistake. "*She ain' no slave o' yer kin,*" he said, eager to put the brute down.

"*Tell that to the one who branded her,*" Slait retorted, a smirk cutting into one of his cheeks.

"*Branded?*" Kit repeated weakly, her arms finding just enough strength to turn her and face The Dawn Sword. There was a look of revelation about the Nimean, her right hand probing the skin over her shoulder.

"*You are bound to your master by magic, foolish girl. So long as you bear the brand, they will find you anywhere in the world. Running away has only ensured you will suffer before you die.*"

Kitrana managed to sit up and lean against the bars. "*They're coming for me,*" she uttered in despair.

High above the halls of Morthil, they heard the next quake before they felt it, their cells shaking as the tremors moved through the stone and into the cranes. Unlike the others they had experienced, it was followed by a distant outcry, a chorus of terror that echoed through the caverns.

"*Now what?*" the smith wondered aloud.

His attention was diverted to the rocky wall on his right, his gaze drawn by the sound of splitting stone. To his dismay, small fissures began to run wild through the rock, raining dust into the chasm below.

The cranes *creaked* and the chains *rattled* under the strain, dropping the cells half a foot. The iron fastenings that kept the heavy mechanisms pressed to the walls began to warp, their bolts losing their place in the stone.

On his knees, Grarfath slid across his cell to better see the halls of Morthil. Far below, where the city's many districts sat shoulder to shoulder beneath the hanging Khardunar, bridges that had stood for centuries fell away and buildings could be seen to wobble, with some of the taller ones actually toppling into the streets, causing more screams to filter up to the prisoners.

Yet all this was background noise to something else. Something terrible. Something powerful. It reminded the smith of rushing wind, the herald of a storm so wrathful it threatened to tear away the roots of Verda's ancient earth.

Then he saw it.

Rising from the depths and spilling through every passage.

The ocean herself had come to swallow The Mountains of Morthil.

34
THE SACKING OF KANOFELL

0 Years Ago...

4

The cold and numbing embrace of Ahnir's ethereal cloak was almost a comfort to Daijen. For the first time in his life, there was no war, no conspiracy—he had found a place beyond death where he could simply *be*, a place where he wanted for nothing. It had swept him from the shores of Broadcastle, snatching away the clash of Kedradi and Mer-folk. Gone was Orvax and his wrath, a perilous rage he shared with his Rider, Gelakor.

It seemed an injustice, then, that he should be cast back into memory.

Daijen Saeth staggered out of the darkness, freed from the folds of Ahnir's inexplicable magic. Taller than everyone around him, the Vahlken looked out over the heads of hundreds, perhaps thousands. Men they were, humans all, bound by one of two sigils.

Those who fought in armour of silver and flowing red cloaks bore the familiar dragon's head, the very same Daijen had seen imprinted on Androma's dark leathers. Their foes battled in the blue and cream of the Kedradi, their pointed spear and open book displayed on their cerulean cloaks.

That same sigil could be seen on the banners hanging from the rooftops, though it shared the fabric with another sigil. The Skara-mangian symbol reigned alongside the spear and book, a symbol Daijen now knew to be the banner of The Dark One.

Their war filled the streets of some unknown city, a ruckus of ringing steel and defiant cries. Everywhere Daijen looked, men from both sides were succumbing to death, run through by swords or picked off by Kedradi archers positioned high on the rooftops.

A deafening roar breached the din of battle, moving the Vahlken's attention above the white walls about him. Orvax's silver scales flashed overhead, the dragon's appearance heralding destruction. His tail swung low, dragging through the rooftops of two buildings. Slabs of white stone and deadly chunks of debris rained down on the street, though there was nothing left of the Kedradi archers, each of whom had suffered a crushing death.

The ground quaked under the impacts and the cries of men fell short, yet Daijen's gaze was kept ever high. In Orvax's wake, the Vahlken's eyes were fixed on the mountain that loomed over the city, the white stone clinging to its great roots in the earth.

It was no mountain, the Andaren realised, but a volcano! Black smoke rose steadily from its angled top, illuminated from below by the fiery glow therein. Mount Nuvata. The name came to Daijen as if it had been spoken into his mind, into the deepest depths of memory. So too did he know now that he stood upon the island of Kanofell, the ancient home of the Kedradi.

How could he know such things?

A towering shadow walked past him, pushing through the battle with stride alone. The indomitable Ahnir knocked any and all aside as it advanced towards Mount Nuvata. The brave few who fought under the banner of the Dragon Riders burst forth from the fighting and attempted to bring the Golem down.

The first of them managed little more than raise his sword before half a dozen monstrous hands sprouted from the inky depths of Ahnir's intangible robes and dragged him into the darkness. Another received a backhand from the Golem, hurling the man across the street and back into the fray, where he met a Kedradi spear. The third red cloak was plucked from the ground by his head. He screamed as his helm was wrought and crushed into his skull. Ahnir discarded the body without a care, not to be slowed.

The galloping of hooves turned the Vahlken to his left as they crossed a large junction. Two riders in silver and red thundered down the street on horseback, their swords arcing high and low to the detriment of every Kedradi around them. Upon sighting Ahnir they spurred their mounts on, determined to be the ones to end the infamous Golem. It was not to be.

All four of Ahnir's arms shot out and grappled one of the horses, lifting it bodily from the ground. In the same motion, the Golem slammed it into the adjacent horse, shattering bones and bursting bodies in one fell swoop. The creature made not a sound as it departed the carnage, its grey hooves trailing large prints of blood through the streets of Kanofell.

Relief and satisfaction settled over the Vahlken, his nerves sedated by the sight of the dead soldiers. Unlike before, a degree of effort was required to rid himself of the feeling. He should have been dismayed at their deaths, that they had failed to destroy the wretched Golem.

The sound of batting wings drowned out the battle, and a rush of wind surged between the buildings. Daijen turned in time to see a dragon land in the street, its bulk bringing an end to numerous fights. With one breath, a jet of fire tore through the corner of a building and exploded out the other side, torching a dozen Kedradi soldiers advancing on the crossroads.

The dragon caught sight of Ahnir, its orange eyes a tone lighter than its burned orange scales. It let loose a roar so terrible it broke even the courage of the Kedradi, who fled the immediate area. The Golem didn't so much as flinch. Again, Daijen adopted the creature's confidence, puffing out his chest in defiance of the dragon. So too did he experience Ahnir's desire, though it was not a desire to destroy the dragon but something else...

It was a yearning to return to their master.

Its master—Daijen forced the correction upon himself.

As his fingers, again, tried to prise the bracer from his arm, the Golem clenched its four hands and flexed its arms wide. The physical world bowed to the magic imbued upon Ahnir, allowing something considerably larger than the Golem to burst forth from the hidden realms nestled in the shadows of its cloak. The Vahlken fell back, his body thrown to the ground by his own instincts.

The monster exploded from Ahnir, its bat-like wings extending to launch it into the starlit sky. For the time it flew over the buildings and circled back, Daijen was convinced Ahnir had birthed another dragon, for the creature possessed so many of the same features. Its face was framed by horns that spread out across its back and down its spine, ending in a dragon-like tail of bony protrusions.

The ground shook as it impacted the street, there to challenge the orange dragon. Only then did Daijen see the differences. As well as being smaller than the dragon, it only boasted two legs, so the beast moved along the ground in the manner of a bat, using its thumb-like claws in the bend of its wings. It did not roar in the face of its bigger opponent but hissed, revealing a jaw brimming with small fangs.

A *Wyvern.*

The knowledge belonged to Ahnir. Now, it belonged to Daijen. The Vahlken shook his head, feeling more than just the creature's name coming to him. He whipped his head back to the fight, all too aware of what was about to happen.

The dragon ignored the Golem for the moment and unleashed its furious voice. It was immediately followed by an inferno, the flames spat from the two glands inside the dragon's mouth. The Wyvern ducked its head and stood its ground, allowing the fire to engulf it.

In the wake of the dying flames, the monster raised its head, its scales smoking from brow to tail. It hissed again and revealed glands of its own. Daijen knew there would be no need to shield his eyes, for Wyverns could not produce fire from the concoction of fluids.

The jet of steaming liquid crossed the gap between foes and bathed the dragon's head, splashing into its eyes and mouth. The dragon recoiled and managed half a roar before its voice became distorted and gargled. It staggered to the left and fell through the wall of a building, demolishing its ground floor. An avalanche of hewn stone then fell upon the dragon, burying its burned orange scales in a plume of dust and rubble.

The Wyvern ascended the debris and dead dragon beneath before rearing its head back to let loose a shrill hiss. As it pushed off into the sky to battle more of its cousins, Ahnir turned back to Mount Nuvata and renewed its stride.

Daijen was pulled along, a witness to the bloodshed. While it seemed the Kedradi were the superior force, their fighting techniques and fine blades outmatching the Eradorans at every turn, the islanders were completely undone by the dragons. The Vahlken turned on the spot while trailing the Golem, observing the dragons as they plunged out of the night, each a bolt of fiery retribution.

They torched entire streets in a single pass, blackening the walls and bodies alike. With claws and tails they smashed and collapsed whole districts, punishing the Kedradi for siding with The Dark One.

Then there were the Riders themselves.

Daijen caught sight of one as they neared the winding steps that led up to Mount Nuvata's lustrous entrance. He recognised the Rider as Nathara, who had stood beside Gelakor and the dwarf, Duun, when The Dark One had first demanded his weapons be returned to him. Just as she had appeared then, the Rider bore the heavy scars of war upon her shaved head, including an eyepatch.

She stood a lone warrior in a large courtyard, where she was to face a knot of Kedradi without aid. They quickly swarmed her, attacking from all sides. Their weapons were exquisite, their steelwork rivalled only by the dwarves, though none compared to that which Nathara wielded.

Dawnbreaker!

Ahnir had spied the blade using whatever supernatural senses it had at its disposal. Daijen had never heard the name before, but he could feel the pull of it, the Golem's eagerness to snatch it from the Rider for the glory of its master.

Nathara pivoted, twisted, and flipped between her attackers. Her every counter was deadly, arcing the weapon through back-hands and slashing the steel across flesh. That same steel burned through the Kedradi, disintegrating their skin in dark gashes, the edges aglow with burning orange. So too did it melt through their swords, leaving them defenceless to her blows. It was a bloodless battle, their wounds being no more than ash.

Her prowess, however, only attracted more Kedradi. They rushed her from every street and alley, each determined to be the one to claim the unimaginable victory. They might have claimed such had a thunderclap not brought Duun, son of Darl, into the fray.

With The Anther in hand, the dwarf had ported from some-where else, bringing with him the debris he had left behind. Side by side now, both Dawnbreaker and The Anther came to life. While the glyphs and fine shards lining the sword sizzled bright orange, The Anther adopted a blue hue.

Duun grinned at the mob surrounding them. "Now ye're goin' to get it," he promised them.

The Kedradi were a fighting force who embodied all that it was to be brave—they did not flee. But before they could mob the Riders, Nathara raised Dawnbreaker and proved the weapon's name was well-earned.

Daijen shielded his eyes from the light that poured out of the steel, its power banishing the shadows. The Kedradi surrounding them were instantly blinded, some having dropped to their knees with blood oozing from their eyes. Nathara dashed in, taking no prisoners, for Dawnbreaker's magic was now amplified by the presence of The Anther. Rather than tearing through the men like butter, it reduced them wholly to sparks and ash.

Doling out damage of his own, Duun waded in with The Anther. The Kedradi were awash in the blue glow, if only for a moment before the dwarven Rider slammed his hammer into them. Their cuirasses were staved in and their bones shattered, both incapable of standing up to the power of his swing. There was more to his attacks, however, than just the strength of his arm—Daijen almost stopped walking beside Ahnir to stand and stare at the nightmarish scene.

Every one of the Kedradi struck by Duun was ported inside another of their kin. The product was a hideous amalgamation of two men, their bodies fused together. In some instances, the dwarf combined more than two of them, porting three or four into one abominable being that possessed too many limbs and heads. It was death to them all.

Ahnir paused before the courtyard was gone from sight. Daijen could feel the Golem's temptation again, a prize of not one but two weapons of power on display. Part of the Vahlken willed Ahnir to enter the battle and reclaim the sword and hammer—damned if he couldn't close off that whisper in his mind. The Golem abandoned the idea of its own volition, subject to a much stronger feeling.

Urgency.

Daijen's attention was pulled up to the gargantuan archway of gold and silver that sat atop the winding steps. The Dark One was in need.

Ahnir set off at great speed, a pace even a Vahlken could never hope to match. As such, Daijen experienced a strange sensation, as if he was being ported from place to place, always ascending the mountain, until he was on the threshold beneath the burnished entrance. He now looked out on the capital city of Kanofell. Nithrael, he knew it to be, the name sparking in his mind.

Nithrael was burning.

A handful of dragons rained fire upon the white city. Still

further off, their sails illuminated in the moonlight, a scattered fleet of ships fled the island under the Kedradi banners. Families, Daijen guessed, with women, children, and the aged who couldn't hope to fight the Dragon Riders and their forces. They escaped the mayhem without harassment from the dragons or, indeed, the invading fleet of ships that had amassed on the beaches. This wasn't genocide, then, but a punishment. The Riders were sending a clear message to the realm: side with The Dark One and suffer their wrath.

The Vahlken was dragged away from the sight when Ahnir reached the arch and dashed inside. They were soon confronted by a handful of soldiers in red cloaks, their fear palpable in the shadow of the Golem. Proving their fear to be warranted, the dark depths of that unnatural cloak unshackled a monster. It was not one monster, however, but hundreds.

No larger than a finger, the red creatures burst into the world on small wings, their numbers lending them the appearance of leaves caught in a strong breeze. A Humming Swarm. Daijen knew of them, native as they were to The Fangs in Andara's southern lands. Every Andaren knew to steer clear of them. The human warriors standing between Ahnir and its master had no choice but to face them.

Swinging their swords and even raising their shields was useless against the Humming Swarm. The little monsters moved through their cluster like the wind might blow through the branches of a tree. Within seconds, the soldiers became hard to see through the red mist. After only a few seconds more, their garbled screaming stopped. The Humming Swarm deserted their meal as quickly as it had engulfed them, making for the city. In its wake lay a group of slick skeletons encased in armour.

Ahnir continued its advance into the mountain, unhindered by its towering height thanks to the Kedradi's grand architecture. The air became distorted by heat as they penetrated Nuvata's thick walls and entered the legendary forges of Kanofell. Daijen would have liked to explore it all, spying only glimpses of the workshops that branched off from the main corridor, but Ahnir was quite intent on its destination, taking the Vahlken into the very heart of the volcano.

Hellish was the heat that rose from the great vat of magma below. The platform that Daijen stepped onto could only have been constructed by magic and those capable of shielding themselves from the extreme conditions. That rationalisation led the Vahlken to the one who had likely built it all.

Skara was slowly rising from the floor, his purple cloak tattered and singed with trails of smoke lifting from the damaged fabric. At his back was the forge itself, set at the base of a stone circle that stood upright on the far edge of the platform, its interior alight with flames.

Limping towards him was the Rider, Gelakor. He flexed his fingers, and the axe materialised in his grip. "Your reign is at an end, Skara!" he yelled over the roar of the volcano. "So too are your dark works," he added, tossing something metallic on the floor at his feet.

The helm!

It was just as Daijen had last seen it before he threw it into the pits of Handuin. Set high between the eyes was its red gem—the red leaves taken from another realm. This was where The Dark One had finished his toil, rending and reshaping the extraordinary leaves to his will. A shell, Skara had called it, to encase something of great power, something that had caused Mount Athan to sit within a crystal shell of its own. Whatever that was, it rested inside the red gem, a stone of obsidian.

"If that thing takes another step," Gelakor warned, his gaze turned back over one shoulder, "I'll cast your precious helm into the fires." He nudged it with the tip of his boot.

The Dark One looked pained to straighten his back. "You should have let me finish it, old friend. I could have shown you the world I'm trying to create. You would have kneeled at my feet to see that world made manifest."

"My dreams are haunted by visions of what you would make of it!" Gelakor spat. "How many more centuries must I endure them?"

The Rider shook his head, his exhaustion more than merely physical. "I will burn this world if it means purging you from it."

"Don't you see?" Skara demanded. "It's that same belief—that same *absolution*—that burns in me! Unlike me, you're *wasting* your strength, Gelakor. You should have taken that passion and applied it to something everlasting. Your efforts would have Verda set alight for eons, its people and history torched by your misplaced wrath. For too long you have been plagued by the whispers of a dragon in your mind. They are *animals*!" he raged. "They debase our thoughts! They even have the power to subdue our very will!"

Gelakor pointed his axe at The Dark One. "Your words are a poison, wizard!"

"You cannot trust them!" Skara argued.

"You would say anything to stay your execution," the Rider fumed. "I'm going to drag you from this place if I have to. You will stand before the people of Verda so you might look them in the eyes during your final moments. For their satisfaction, I will part your head from your shoulders."

"I thought I was to be devoured," The Dark One commented, adjusting the gold chain about his neck, the pendant hidden beneath his cuirass. "That was the last thing he said to me, you know. That he would swallow me whole and alive so I might suffer at the very end."

"No dragon should have to kill their own Rider, even one so wretched as you," Gelakor replied grimly. "I shall spare him the pain."

"How virtuous of you," Skara remarked.

"You broke his heart," Gelakor said, his tone saddened. "You were The Pendain, Skara! He was The Drakalis! That was supposed to mean something! You ripped all that away from him. He will never be the same. I can only hope that he takes another Rider so his spirit might be reforged."

The Dark One began to laugh, a maniacal cackle that bested the volcano's roaring. "There are no Riders where I'm sending him!" His wicked laugh increased all the more. "There are worlds beyond this one. Worlds where even dragons are just *prey*. I will cast him into that shadowed realm. Perhaps I will abandon Orvax to such a fate," he taunted. "They can keep each other company in the abyss."

Gelakor leaped at Skara, his boot knocking the helm towards the jagged edge of the platform. As the two collided in battle, Ahnir threw itself across the stone, one bony arm outstretched. As the helm teetered on the lip, the Golem grasped it in a single massive hand, saving it from a fiery doom.

Every blow of Gelakor's axe was met by a spell that prevented the steel from cleaving through The Dark One. Whenever Gelakor used magic of his own, Skara would deflect it, if not absorb the spell, and fire it back, twice as powerful. They danced across the platform, disturbing the tools and upturning the benches with their fury.

They finally locked together, Skara having intercepted the axe by the haft while Gelakor's free hand gripped The Dark One by the throat. Skara responded in kind and grabbed the Rider by the throat, keeping the two joined in a battle of wills. Their conflict might have gone on had it not been for dramatic intervention.

The Anther impacted Skara across his golden cuirass, launching him back towards the upright circle of fiery stone. He skidded across the hewn floor and slammed into the base of the forge, striking it a moment before The Anther scraped over the stone and stopped beside him.

Daijen turned as Ahnir did, preparing to challenge Duun, son of Darl. But the dwarf was not alone. Beside him, Nathara raised Dawnbreaker, its intense light spilling out, bathing the Golem such that the shadows of its cloak retreated, revealing the creature's body within. Ahnir recoiled from the power of the sword, taking refuge on the edge of the platform, the helm dropped from within the grasp of its many hands.

"The city o' Nithrael stands upon the edge o' its doom!" the dwarven Rider declared boldly. "Kanofell has fallen! Ye're at the end o' yer rope, Dark One!"

Skara rose to one knee, wiping away a trickle of blood that ran from a gash above his left eye. "You have robbed me of an ally, dwarf, no more. My forces on the mainland have continued to amass during my years on this island. You have done no more than win the battle. At great expense, I imagine," he added with a smirk.

"Your years have been wasted here," Nathara told him, careful to keep Ahnir in her limited peripheral vision as she scooped up the helm. "We will destroy your work, just as we will destroy all that you have ever built."

"Save your breath, Nathara," Skara warned. "You have so few left."

Nathara snarled at The Dark One, a threat brimming behind her teeth.

"It's hard to imagine your own end, isn't it?" Skara continued, getting ahead of her. "But I've *seen* it," he intoned, glancing at the helm in her hand.

"More lies," Gelakor hissed. "Command that *thing* to jump into the fires," he barked, pointing his axe at Ahnir. "Do it, Skara, or I will—"

The Dragon Rider stopped when he noted the hungry grin spreading across The Dark One's face. Following his cold eyes, Gelakor turned around to see Nathara placing the helm over her head.

"No!" Gelakor cried.

"I would see for myself—"

Nathara's words ended there, taken as her gaze was by the visions.

Gelakor lashed out, striking the helm with his axe. It tore through the steel, scarring the helm before flinging it away. Duun caught Nathara's collapsing form and crouched to hold her in his arms.

She was already seizing. Blood oozed from her eyes and ears and trickled out from her nose. Her breathing had become audibly difficult, as if the Rider was choking on her own spit.

The Dark One picked up The Anther. "Tell The Drakalis I have what he's been searching for."

Gelakor spared Nathara an extra moment, witnessing her grow

still in the clutches of death, before facing his enemy again. What rage there was behind his eyes.

The Dark One offered a presumptuous smirk. "Until next time, old friend."

Ahnir leaped, arriving at Skara's side in a single bound. When the Golem landed beside him, The Dark One brought the hammer down, striking the stone with all his might, and Daijen was sucked in from afar as all three were ported from the fiery heart of Mount Nuvata.

35

THE ONE AND ONLY

I t was with the eyes of a ranger that the Kedradi scanned the streets of Thedaria. Through the last hours of the night and into the late morning, Cob had scoured The Stilts—or what was left of them. Aphrandhor's particular flavour of destruction was easy to see. There wasn't much else in the world, let alone the slums, that could wrought such damage.

Having abandoned The Stilts with a single scrap of information, the ranger had walked the streets of the city proper in search of the Padoshi's premises.

"Carried 'em out, they did," a young boy had told him in exchange for a few marks. *"An old man and some fella."*

When probed as to who the men doing the carrying had been, the boy wouldn't accept any amount of coin, his lips sealed on the matter. That alone informed Cob that the Padoshi was behind it all. There were none who would speak against him. As a result, he had failed to locate the crime lord's home, for any mention of the man silenced all.

Infuriated and concerned for the wellbeing of his companions, the Kedradi eventually returned to The Broken Sabre. It was a cosy little tavern situated on a busy crossroads, its framework painted a calming green. Inside, he found Androma in the same booth he had left her in. The old Dragon Rider had insisted on accompanying him, if not going her own way to cover more ground. The idea had been quashed when Cob pointed out her lack of knowledge regarding Thedaria's layout. Most reluctantly, she had agreed.

Sliding into the booth to face her, he offered a sigh by way of greeting.

"I thought you were a hunter first and foremost," Androma commented, likely having identified him by his scent as much as his sigh.

Cob looked out the murky window beside the booth, hardly noticing the passersby while he considered what he *really* was first and foremost. Like so much else where his culture was concerned, it was not to be shared with outsiders, even ones he trusted.

"It's hard to hunt a monster that leaves no tracks," he replied gruffly.

"Have you tried the Leaf District?" Androma queried. "I hear it's where all the highborns live. I imagine the Padoshi has quite the complex."

"I tried," Cob said. "Too many eyes. The Leaf District is under the watch of the homeguard," he explained, having noted the soldiers on patrol in that area.

"I wouldn't have thought that would be a problem for a Kedra-di," came a nasal voice, carried on notes of a commoner's tone.

Cob turned to scrutinise the man standing beside their booth. His odour struck the ranger immediately, making him wonder how he had failed to detect the stranger the moment he entered the tavern.

Draped in a tattered grey cloak and attired in common, if stained, clothing, he stood with a confidence Cob rarely saw in any man, fearless almost. He hooked a few strands of scraggly grey hair behind one ear and gestured at the seat beside Androma.

"Do you mind?" he asked, taking to the seat regardless.

The old Rider looked outright insulted as she was forced to shuffle along, though it might have been his stench that truly irked her. "And you are?" she demanded, one hand shielding her nose.

"Normally," he began quite casually, "I'm something of a messenger. Today, however, I'm in the business of *delivery*."

With that, the stranger placed a severed hand on the tabletop.

Cob was able to conceal his displeasure as much as his surprise, but he recognised the hand—at least, he recognised the tattoos that ringed the thumb and middle finger. It broke his mask of stoicism, revealing something of the rage that bolted through him. In that same instant, he drew the slender dagger of curled Wither bone from his belt, its pommel decorated with three vibrant feathers of red, purple, and blue. He drove the tip into the table, right between two of the stranger's fingers.

Taking his lead, Androma's hand whipped out with a knife already in her grasp, the steel now pressed against the man's throat. "What is it?" she asked the ranger.

Cob's reply was blunt, if brimming with anger. "He just put Gallien's hand on the table."

Androma's response was delayed by shock, but when her reaction had its moment, the old Rider applied enough pressure to draw a thin line of blood from the stranger's neck.

"Easy, Androma," the man bade, his hands rising in surrender.

"How do you know my name?"

"Well, it's not like we three haven't met before," he replied, chin raised.

"Who are you?" Cob questioned, his expression a promise of violence.

The stranger licked his cracked lips. "I suppose I look a little different to the last time we met."

Androma's head twitched, and she withdrew her blade half an inch. "Galahart?"

"The one and only!" he beamed.

The Kedradi slowly sat back, retaking his Wither blade as he did. Casting an eye across the tavern, the ranger did his best to unravel the patrons, searching for those in the spymaster's employ. Every one of them appeared as ordinary as the next, without a single tell-tale sign that they were more than they presented to be.

Yet Cob was certain that some, if not all, were spies in their own right, just waiting for Galahart's command.

"I've met *three* of you now," Androma stated sourly.

"And thrice you have been blessed," Galahart replied sarcastically.

Cob pressed his finger onto the table beside Gallien's severed appendage. "Speak plainly, spymaster, or I will add *both* of your hands to his."

"Did you skip breakfast, Mr Cob?"

Androma returned her blade to his throat. "Speak," she hissed.

Galahart carefully placed two fingers against the flat of the dagger and pushed it away. "Your boy's got himself tangled in a web of his own making, I'm afraid. The old fella's got caught up in it too."

"Is Gallien alive?" Androma asked.

"He was when I left. Kaliban only knows what's been chopped off since then."

"And The Green Leaf?" Cob pressed.

"He's been roughed up a bit. *Big* egg on his head." Galahart imitated a lump on his own forehead. "To be expected, though," he added, picking through the scraps of food on Androma's plate. "He did give Mr Grim the runaround. Killed some of his boys too."

"Mr Grim?" the ranger echoed.

"Fileus Fod," Galahart named. "He's as thick as they come—nothing but a bag of hammers between his big, stupid ears. But he's one *mean* sod. He's the one who parted the smuggler from his hand there."

"He's the Padoshi's man," Androma assumed.

"His right hand," Galahart specified before covering his mouth and glancing at Gallien's body part. "Poor choice of words."

"Why have you brought this to us?" the ranger asked, keen to move on.

Galahart munched on a boiled potato while pouring all the salt onto the table. "Because," he began, his finger drawing a symbol into the pile of salt, "we're fighting the same enemy."

There upon the tabletop, was a vertical line with two diamonds at its heart.

The Skaramangians.

"I employ all manner of beasts," Galahart went on. "Men who will do anything for coin. Men who will do anything in service of their king. Men who will do anything as long as they get to kill someone. Unfortunately, none of them can challenge the Skaramangians like you lot have. Hence my predicament and the gruesome nature of my delivery," he explained, gesturing at Gallien's hand. "I tried to treaty with the Padoshi, but he was having none of it. He *really* wants to make that smuggler suffer, and he'll kill the wizard too—just for fun."

"You wield the power and authority of the king," Andromia reminded him. "Surely there is no Padoshi in all the realm that would so boldly stand up to that."

"This particular Padoshi is a problem unto himself, I'm afraid. I have a few daggers in the shadows, but he owns the armour in this town. Even the Blood Lord bows to him. Save marching an army on Thedaria, there's nothing I can do."

"Then march the damned army and free our companions," Andromia insisted.

Galahart gorged on another potato while laughing to himself. "Since you're here at all," he managed amusedly through his mouthful, "and not in Drakanan as you intended, I'm assuming you were forced south by our pale cousins from the west. I can't exactly divert several thousand soldiers just so we can topple some crime lord." The spymaster paused while he washed his food down with Andromia's drink. "On the matter of Drakanan," he said lightly, "I'm assuming the boy got to where he was supposed to go."

The old Rider took what looked like a calming breath. "Joran is in Drakanan," she answered.

"Well there's that at least," Galahart commented, wiping his stubbled jaw. "I need to get you lot back in the *real* fight," he continued. "The Andarens haven't been spotted anywhere in the north, which tells me they've gone south, straight to Akmar."

"They have," Cob confirmed.

"Then they'll have taken ownership of the skeleton by now," Galahart concluded. "That puts two in their hands and none in ours."

"Where are the king's men?" Androma demanded.

"Wherever the king's told them to be, I suppose," the spymaster responded bluntly. "The real question is: where are *you* going? Even without the boy, you're still in the fight. So where were you going before the Padoshi stuck his nose in?"

Cob wished he and Androma could confer with their eyes, the ranger unsure how much to divulge to the mysterious spymaster.

"There is another weapon of power," Androma revealed, her confidence omitting the murky waters of Gallien's troubled mind or the extraordinary way in which Aphrandhor retrieved the information.

Galahart's casual, bordering on lazy, demeanour sharpened a notch. "You're not pulling my leg?"

"It's believed to be more powerful than any of the others," the old Rider reported as a matter of fact.

The spymaster chuckled. "What? More powerful than a helmet that shows you the future?" When no response came, his demeanour sharpened all the more. "What is it?"

"We don't know yet," Androma confessed. "The answer lies in Taraktor."

Galahart blinked and swivelled his head on Cob, his eyes questioning the Kedradi as to whether Androma had lost her mind. "Is she joking?"

"She never jokes," the ranger replied.

"Taraktor?" the spymaster repeated with utter disbelief. "You won't find any answers there. I've lost plenty of men trying to get eyes and ears behind those black walls. Only the damned can enter. I mean, think about it. A *Jainus* prison. The worst of the worst get condemned to that place. Mad wizards driven insane by their own magic. And you definitely won't find any weapons of power there. I'd know if the Jainus had one."

"That is our destination," Androma said evenly, not to be put off by the spymaster's description.

Galahart drummed his fingers on the table while his lips pouted and twisted in thought. "Who told you to look there?"

Cob leaned forward. "You have *your* sources, spymaster, and we have *ours*."

"Like you said," Androma spoke up, "the enemy will soon be in possession of two skeletons and all the magic they contain. It's a critical step for the Skaramangians, one that might be enough to bring about the return of The Dark Ones."

Galahart made a face to suggest he didn't put much stock in the legend.

"We must be ready for that day," the old Rider continued. "Adding another weapon of power to our arsenal will only improve our odds of victory. To that end, we *need* Aphrandhor and Gallien."

"Given your heading," the spymaster quipped, "it might be a mercy to leave them in the Padoshi's hands."

"Will you help us or not?" Cob interjected, a hint of aggression in his tone.

"Easy, big fella," Galahart bade, his hands coming up again. "You make it sound like I haven't helped you already. If it wasn't for me, you'd still be running around Valgala with The Dawn Sword on your tail."

"These daggers you have," Androma probed. "The ones you keep in the shadows. Might they be of any assistance?"

Galahart sighed. "They're a useless bunch, to be honest. Best to let people like the Padoshi think otherwise though."

"Then why are you here?" Cob growled.

The spymaster shrugged. "Maybe I felt sorry for you, eh? Walking the streets for hours on end like some lost puppy. Your feet must be knackered."

"You can judge the state of my feet after I shove them up your—"

"Alright, alright," Galahart cut in, looking somewhat bored now. "Like I said, I need to get you lot back in the fight—this war's proving a distraction there's no getting around. I can tell you exactly where to find your friends and how to get there unseen. What's more, I can get you on a ship—a *good* one, not those poxy little things you've been looking at. Passage to Caster Hold will put you within spitting distance of Taraktor."

"And in return?" Androma asked.

"The same thing I've always wanted from your little band of rogues: *results*. If there is another weapon of power out there—find it, and do us all the favour of using it."

Cob raised his hand, feeling that they were getting ahead of themselves. "Passage to Caster Hold is one thing, but we'll never even reach the ship if we can't free our companions. What we really need are swords. Call on your men."

Galahart winced. "Honestly, they'd just get in your way, mate. These fellas aren't trained. They've just adopted a life of violence and, in some cases, a really bad gambling habit."

The ranger gritted his teeth in an effort to contain the flash of anger that ran through him like a hot iron. "Today is not the day to test me, spymaster."

"I disagree," Galahart countered. "I think today's the perfect day to put you to the test. Your people are renowned warriors all. But you, Mr Cob, are something *extra* special, aren't you? The last son of House Thayne."

Cob stiffened at the sound of his family name.

Galahart glanced at the feathers attached to the Wither blade. "Those are Thayne colours, aye?"

The Kedradi swallowed, composing himself. "How could you know that?"

The spymaster made a hopeless attempt to straighten his severely crumpled shirt. "The same way I know you were trained by the best swordsmen in all of Qalanqath. The same way I know about that chip on your shoulder. Your family carries quite the history. I wonder, do your friends know your ancestors' part in all this?"

Cob remained perfectly still, a cobra poised before the strike.

Galahart leaned back. "You've got a murderous look in your

eyes, Mr Cob. Don't look so shocked. It's my job to know things. Besides, everyone wants to be *my* friend—even in your sister."

"The Padoshi of Thedaria would appear to be an exception," Androma observed dryly.

"He prefers *assets* to friends," Galahart reported. "And, save for our good king, I am *nobody's* asset. That said, you are not permitted to kill the Padoshi."

Cob required an extra moment to ground himself in the conversation, his mind still reeling from the mention of his family name and even his sister. That and more had been uttered by an *outsider*. It seemed an impossibility to the Kedradi, an insult even, for it spoke of betrayal. Why would his sister—the embodiment of their most sacred laws—break with their most ancient traditions. And to one who reported directly to the King of Erador, no less?

The ranger forced it all aside for the time being and addressed the injunction that had just been thrust upon him. "You don't have authority over me," he reminded the spymaster.

Androma flexed a single finger, pausing any further argument. "Why?" she asked the king's man.

"The Padoshi is part of a larger network that, while corrupt from the ground up, does provide services the crown finds... *convenient* from time to time. That's not to say you can't get a little creative. Any damage or loss of... *assets* you might cause extracting your friends is acceptable. Just leave the big man alone."

Cob's iron cuirass knocked against the table as he leaned forward. "I'm to leave that wretch of a man alive because your king benefits from his illegal deeds?"

"From time to time," Galahart underlined, as if that made it acceptable. "Listen, if it was up to me, I'd shower you with coins to part him head from shoulders—if you could find his neck, that is. But it's *not* up to me. And whether you like it or not, you're on the king's soil. His Grace doesn't want the Padoshi taken out of the picture yet."

The Kedradi sat back, making his dissatisfaction abundantly clear to the spymaster.

"I can see this offends your noble Kedradi sensibilities," Gala-

hart noted, his jaw working as if it was trying to undo a knot in the
muscle. He looked away, a single finger now tapping incessantly
on the tabletop. "There's a gallery on Konyven Street," he began.
"Paintings and sculptures mostly. The highborns love all that sort
of stuff. It's owned by Blood Lord Skoll. Of course, it's the Padoshi's
really. There are vaults behind most of the big paintings—filled to
bursting, they are."

The spymaster paused, rising from the table. "My boys are no
good in the kind of fight you're in for, Mr Cob, but they are good at
making a bloody mess of things. I'll have them do what they do
best at the gallery. That should divert a considerable number of the
Padoshi's guard."

"And the ship?" Androma questioned, not one to let the details
slip.

"The Raven. The captain owes me a favour."

It was subtle, but Cob noticed the curious twitch of Androma's
head. "The captain?" she enquired lightly.

"Captain Addison," Galahart informed her. "I'll have him
waiting for you, but he won't want to be in harbour come the
dawn, so you'd best be on with it." The spymaster made to leave,
pausing only to turn back and gesture at Gallien's hand. "Everything you need to know about the Padoshi's place is on the hand,"
he said with disturbing indifference. "Be seeing you."

———

Standing by the shore of Thedaria's outer ring, Cob looked beyond
the river and set his eyes on the enormous mansions and
complexes that lined the city's inner ring. Some of the view was
blocked by the ships and boats that bobbed on the water, but there
was nothing large enough to conceal the Padoshi's home.

Having waited for nightfall, the crime lord's fortress was now
alight with torches and candles now. The flames upon the walls
were routinely interrupted by patrolling guards and distant
shadows that passed by the windows.

Cob took one last look at the instructions crudely scribed on

Gallien's palm before tossing it into the cold water. Galahart had been quite clear that crossing the river at high moon would be the best time to infiltrate the fortress. He had also used the word *swim*, ruling out any possibility of using the bridges.

The Kedradi regarded the old Dragon Rider beside him. She hadn't said much since the spymaster had brought them the smuggler's hand. Androma carried her concern like a tight knot in her chest, the unease restricting her voice. She had considerably more respect for Gallien than he did, and she certainly liked him more than he did. That said, the ranger felt a cold grip about his heart when he thought of the Padoshi robbing the man of further body parts.

"He's survived worse," Cob commented into the night. "The Green Leaf too. They only have to survive a few more hours."

"You have a plan?" she asked, keeping her emotions on the matter firmly quashed.

"Of course," he replied confidently.

When he said nothing more, the old Rider tilted her head questioningly. Following his continued silence, she asked, "And do I have a part to play in this plan?"

"I was hoping you would knock on the front door for me."

"I think I can manage that."

"You know the captain," the Kedradi stated, having come to the conclusion some hours ago. "Or the ship, at least," he added, hedging his bets.

"Captain Bail Addison," the old Rider announced. "He's an old acquaintance of Gallien's, from his pirate days."

"Of course he was a pirate," Cob replied, with no lack of judgement in his voice. "How do *you* know him then?"

"Joran had just been born," she explained, her voice still absent the warmth of emotion. "He was days old, and we were stuck in Harendun. It was Captain Addison who transported us to Caster Hold—for a *price*," she added, her tone adopting the first inkling of emotion, be it regret.

"Can we trust him?" the ranger asked.

"No," she answered bluntly. "Whether it be loyalty or fear that binds Captain Addison to Galahart, he remains a pirate, a man of *opportunity*. As always, we must guard ourselves against any and all. That shouldn't be a problem for someone trained by the *best swordsmen in all of Qalanqath*," she remarked, her words barbed.

"He called you the last son of House Thayne," the old Rider stated, her voice inquisitive. "They are your kin?"

"I can reveal no more than you already know," Cob told her, the creed of his people weighing heavily upon him.

The Kedradi looked down at her, a woman—a warrior—he respected above all others, and wished he could tell her everything. She deserved that much. Even more so given the life she had sacrificed in pursuit of their enemy.

"*Tradition*," his mother had always said, "*is the life blood of any culture. Without it, we will lose our history, our sense of self, and our ability to protect what is ours.*"

"*It is a punishment*," his father had opined in one of the rare moments his madness had abated. "*Chains put upon our people by their own decree.*"

Those same chains, Cob knew, had been crafted by the deeds of House Thayne.

That was his legacy.

Cob might have said more, cryptic though it would have had to be, had he not noticed something in the distance.

"What is it?" Androma asked, likely hearing the *creak* of his twisting leathers as he removed and discarded his heavy cuirass.

"Smoke."

Its source was, perhaps, a mile north of the Padoshi's complex, and the smoke—a deep black—rose ever higher into the night. The glow of flames could be seen between the surrounding buildings and was accompanied by the distant ringing of a bell. Cob looked up, spying the moon at its apex.

"Galahart's men have risen to the challenge, then," Androma surmised.

The Kedradi removed the arrows from his quiver and held them in a tight bundle. "Now we swim."

36

THE DRAKALIS

4 0 Years Ago...

The cacophonous roar of battle woke Daijen Saeth from a death-like slumber. The Vahlken was standing in a large alcove built into the sloping wall of a black pyramid, looking out on a field of death —he was on Nareene again, in The Dark One's palace.

Azad-guul...

As on Kanofell, Ahnir's knowledge passed seamlessly over to Daijen, revealing the palace's true name. He might have pondered on its meaning, aware, somehow, that the translation was at his fingertips, but the battle below drew him in.

Plated in black armour and draped in flowing green cloaks, the Skaramangians fought in the defence of Azad-guul and their dark master. Amassed against them were the knights of Verda, an army of silver and red.

They clashed in bloody violence, their armour bashing together and their swords ringing out across the battlefield. Their cries of war and death mixed together, interrupted only by the thunderous bellows of the Trolls who lumbered through the chaos with mighty hammers in hand. Like the green cloaks, the Trolls wore armour imprinted with Skara's dreaded sigil, the mark of the Skaramangians.

Untethered, the towering monsters swung their mallets and hammers, sweeping through the ranks of red cloaks with unbridled rage. The free men of Verda were thrown wildly into the air, their bodies crushed and left broken amongst their kin.

They were not without rage of their own. Clusters of soldiers rushed the Trolls where they could, thrusting and jabbing their spears, the steel tips finding the gaps in their armour. Daijen witnessed the death of one, its fall taking it back into the ranks of Skaramangians—at least four were flattened beneath its bulk.

To the Vahlken's surprise, the red cloaks were reinforced by a contingent on horseback. They pierced the battle from the east, riding into the masses in colours of blue, cream, and gold.

The Kedradi!

In the wake of The Dark One's deception, it seemed the people of Kanofell had seen the truth of things. Daijen had to wonder how many weeks, months, or even years had passed since their city of Nithrael had been sacked.

Perhaps in their attempt to make amends, they had added their skill and steel to the free men of Verda. The Skaramangians were chopped down on the eastern flank, no match for the mounted riders from Erador's south.

And so the melting pot was brought to the boil, the blood spilling across every inch of the land, soaking the dirt beneath boot and hoof.

"What a lovely day."

The outrageous remark turned Daijen to his left, where The Dark One was observing the cloudy sky, The Anther in his grip. Time had certainly passed since Kanofell. Skara's wounds had faded altogether, replaced by small reptilian scales. His style of attire had also changed, for he now stood a sentinel of gold, from his cuirass and battle skirt to his cloak and bracers.

He stood a fitting emperor, worthy to rule over all of Verda.

Memory pressed upon the Vahlken then, taking him back to that same pyramid in his own time. Daijen recalled the ancient mural painted on the wall in the depths of Azad-guul. A golden figure there had been, standing before the black pyramid as seven dragons approached from...

Daijen turned his gaze to the north and spotted them immediately. Seven there were, just as he had seen on the wall. The dragons had plummeted through the cloud cover and now soared through the sky, soon to bring their wrath upon Azad-guul.

Skara's demeanour changed in that moment, the would-be emperor adopting an aura of seething hatred. His fists clenched, and his jaw stretched tight across his face. Reacting to their master, all four of his Golems stepped forward, rising to the challenge.

"No," Skara commanded, halting any action they might take. "He must be close if this is to work. We must meet with words, not battle. I need to draw him in," he added wickedly.

The Dark One held out his hand, beckoning one of his human servants. Daijen moved, unseen by Skara, to observe the servant approaching her master. In her hands was an ornate chest laced with gold foil and a clasp shaped into the Skaramangian sigil.

"Come then, *Drakalis*," Skara bade, his tone mocking the ancient title. "Come and claim what is yours."

Dragonlord...

Daijen found the translation deep in his mind, as if it had always been there.

He stepped back and craned his neck to see the object removed from the chest and lifted high in The Dark One's hand.

The Vahlken's jaw dropped.

Held high above the battlefield, in clear sight of sharp reptilian eyes, was a *dragon egg*. Daijen knew that egg, its dark purple outer scales all too familiar, for he had held it himself. Held it—and *lost* it.

For just a second, he relived that moment, when the hulking pillar of stone had retreated into the pyramid's deepest depths and destroyed the chamber in which he had discovered the egg. It had been cool in his hands, if only for a brief time before it was cast from his grip. He had been lucky to survive the collapse, and Androma beside him.

But what significance did it hold now? Or *then*, he corrected himself, losing his orientation in the timeline. Daijen had a sinking feeling, sure that deeds dark and insidious plans were about to unfold.

"Remember, children," Skara said, addressing his four Golems. "You work together this day. Only combined will you overcome our great foe."

The creatures gave no response, physically or verbally, their master's command always enough.

A roar that preceded the dragons, a single, bone-chilling sound that hollowed Daijen out. It was as if his every instinct had frozen in fear, rooting him to the spot and surely also the grim fate that awaited him.

So too did it impact the forces locked in combat. While they stayed their swords and gazed at the sky, the Trolls—creatures ruled entirely by their instincts—turned and fled, crushing allies and foes alike in their panicked retreat.

Threading the line between unrivalled beauty and a nightmare given flight and fire, the largest and fastest of the dragons landed first—he who had torn the world asunder with his roar. Shaking the earth on the northern edge of the battle so as to avoid crushing the ranks of red cloaks who bore the sigil of the Riders, the colossal dragon began its deliberate approach.

Seconds later, six others touched down behind him. Daijen instantly recognised Gelakor astride the silver Orvax and Duun, son of Darl, mounted on his dragon of muddy red scales. While they had seemed titans before, they were now dwarfed in the shadow of The Drakalis. *The Dragonlord.*

The opposing armies moved aside, the forces peeling apart like a torn thread. As the lone dragon approached, The Dark One descended the steps, his Golems at his back. As they had for the dragon, red and green cloaks alike fell away, granting Skara a clear path across the field.

Daijen accompanied them every step of the way, his attention never wandering from the gargantuan dragon and its unyielding gaze, its piercing eyes.

Eyes of *violet*.

Set against a black face, the dragon boasted scales of the purest obsidian, a natural armour that only accentuated his eyes all the more. There was a storm also behind those eyes. A ferocity that bordered on madness. A fury that would never know an end.

Skara came to a stop, The Anther still in hand and the egg nestled in the crook of his other arm. He stood a moment, waiting for the black dragon to halt and tower before him. The Dark One took a breath—to steady himself perhaps. Of all who had opposed him, he hated this one the most. The betrayer.

Raising his chin, Skara uttered the name he had forbidden all others from voicing.

"Malliath..."

The dragon exhaled a sharp blast of air from his nostrils, blowing out The Dark One's golden cloak.

Skara hefted the egg. "He could have been a prince if you had stood by me."

Malliath's head twitched, his violet eyes landing on the egg.

"Yes," the Dark One said. "I gleaned the truth from Icerys's womb in her final moments—before I slaughtered her like a pig and ripped out her egg. Your *son*."

The ground relented beneath Malliath's claws, the dirt churning as he unleashed a resounding rumble from deep in his chest. The soldiers crowded around the scene took several steps back.

"I told you I would take everything from you," Skara reminded him. "Your kind are so much easier to kill after you've peeled every scale from flesh. Icerys was stubborn, though. She didn't die easy... or *well*. A good mate for you, I suppose."

Malliath raised his head to the sky and cracked the air with his deafening voice. A lamentation, perhaps. Or a pained cry for the love he had lost. Either way, it poured cold dread into the bones of every man on Nareene.

"You have a choice to make," Skara told him, the only man who had managed to stand his ground in the face of Malliath's roar. "Bow your head and swear your allegiance to me, now, before the men and dragons who so blindly follow you into rebellion. Or," The Dark One posed, "watch me toss your only offspring, the only thing you have left of Icerys into The Shadow Realm."

To underline his point, Skara held the egg out, where he could so easily throw it into the abyss that dwelled within the folds of Ahnir's cloak.

"What will it be, Malliath?" The Dark One yelled. "Are we to have *war* or *peace*? How many more shall die because you think you know what it is to be *good*? How many more shall suffer the freedom you've bought them? The very same thing that crushes them! Choose!"

Malliath remained eerily still, an extraordinary sight for a creature so large. Yet still he was, his violet eyes fixed on the egg alone. It seemed an impossible choice to make, albeit a choice Daijen couldn't empathise with. While he felt the weight of many lives on his shoulders, he had no children against whom to leverage that responsibility.

Thousands held their breath, waiting for the dragon's response.

At last, when Malliath's face creased into a grimace and he bared the hundreds of fangs that lined his jaw, the world had its answer.

"So be it," Skara muttered.

Keeping the egg to himself, rather than tossing it into the abyss as he had threatened, The Dark One stepped back. At the same time, the Golems stepped forward, shielding their master behind a black wall of supernatural cloaks. As Malliath opened his maw, revealing a thick, slimy tongue between his deadly glands, Ahnir and his brothers enacted Skara's intended plan.

Daijen had never seen the Golems work together, combining their magic into one powerful force, but it was swift and terrible.

Their dark and ethereal robes became as one, creating a single portal between them. Muculent tentacles, each as broad as a tree, shot forth from the darkness and ensnared the black dragon, wrapping around his throat before he had the chance to scorch them from the earth. While he thrashed, more tentacles emerged from The Shadow Realm and tied themselves around his front legs.

Beyond Malliath, the six dragons who had accompanied him broke into a mad dash across the field. They were not to make it in time. Whatever fiend lay on the other side of the veil, it had the strength to drag Malliath inexorably towards The Shadow Realm. His claws protested and his wings batted the air, but to no avail.

"If it's the last thing I ever do," Skara shouted over the strong winds being sucked into the portal, "I will force your son from his egg and make him *bleed* for your betrayal!"

There was a fire behind Malliath's eyes, The Dark One's promise landing just as he had intended.

Then the dragon was gone, his physical form squeezed and stretched beyond natural law. He was pulled into a realm of monsters and pain.

It was just as Daijen had seen in the mural, in the lowest chamber of Azad-guul—the black dragon swallowed by darkness.

The moment his tail vanished, the four Golems separated, ending the vast portal that had existed between them.

Orvax was upon them.

The silver dragon leaped, his claws a promise of vengeance. The battle that ensued was not for Daijen's eyes, however, the Vahlken swept from memory when Ahnir grabbed him by the shoulder and yanked him back.

Instead of skidding over the blood-soaked ground, Daijen slid on his back over a polished floor.

Everything had changed. It was night time, evident by the black skies that hung over the jagged hole in the ceiling. Rain poured in, cast out of rolling clouds that cast lightning across the heavens.

Daijen turned on one shoulder and was immediately face to face with Ahnir. The Golem was sprawled on the stone floor, two of its four arms severed above the elbows. One of its legs appeared to have been crushed while the other remained pinned under heavy debris from the ceiling. From its many wounds, including a gash across its featureless face, white, sickly blood oozed and spread across the floor.

There was still life in the creature. Though sluggish, it moved this way and that in an attempt to break free. Unable to deny his connection to the thing, Daijen felt pressed to aid it. His strength was no use, of course. He couldn't change what had already happened.

The loud *ring* of steel turned the Vahlken around. His eyes wide, Daijen took in the heated battle playing out before him. The Dark One, wounded and his breath laboured, stood encircled by three Dragon Riders. Gelakor lashed out with his axe while Duun came at Skara wielding Dawnbreaker. The third Daijen recognised as Qirann, who wore the bracer and had confronted The Dark One atop the valley.

Daijen glimpsed Qirann amongst the living for no more than another second. With The Anther in hand, Skara required but one blow. The hammer clobbered Qirann across his chest, a two-handed strike that would have caved in the ribs of any man. While his scale mail might have stood up to the attack, there was naught he could do to subvert the magic of the weapon. In a flash of light, he was ported from his place in the battle to the inside of a broken pillar.

Death was instantaneous. Fused with the stone, only two of his limbs and his head were visible, protruding from the pillar at painful angles.

Duun, son of Darl, roared with anger and threw himself into The Dark One. They wrestled across the floor, their weapons *clattering* on the hard stone. They traded fists and sharp elbows, their armour *clinking* under the barrage of rain.

Their grappling tussle came to an end with both combatants holding firmly to the haft of The Anther. The dwarven Rider was quick to plant his boot in Skara's chest and push off. They were parted forcefully, the hammer still in Duun's grasp as he rolled over his own head.

The Dark One bared bloody teeth as he flipped onto his feet, Dawnbreaker in hand. He rolled his wrist, getting a feel for the weapon. "It's been too long," he uttered.

Only then did Daijen realise Skara was not as he had been moments ago, outside the pyramid. Gone was his golden attire and flowing cloak, replaced with a cuirass of bronze that displayed his bare arms and robes of black, as he was accustomed to wearing. Gone was his well-trimmed mohawk and long braided ponytail, his hair having grown out into a mane of white that fell past his shoulders.

Again, the Vahlken had been swept up in the winds of time and hurled into a memory years on from Malliath's doom. Considering the massive hole in the ceiling and the chamber in which they fighting, Daijen had to wonder if they were even in Azad-guul anymore.

Fearless, Gelakor leaped at The Dark One. Axe and sword met between the two, the steel of one scraping and sliding along the edge of the other in a hue of purple and orange. Despite the injuries both had sustained up to that point, they both fought with a style and grace no mortal could hope to achieve. The many lifetimes they had spent honing their skills and even developing new techniques were on display, their fight taking them across the chamber and back again.

Duun added his own brand of violence. He began by repeatedly slamming The Anther into the floor, porting himself sporadically from place to place. Besides being disorientating, his actions were a clear threat, a countdown to his ultimate attack.

And attack he did.

The dwarf ported in beside Skara and swung low, using the hammer to take out his legs. No sooner was The Dark One on his back than The Anther was coming down on him. Yet a flash of green and a staccato of lightning took Duun from his feet preventing the hammer from ever landing. Before he hit the floor, Skara was already turning that same magic on Gelakor.

The human Rider had his defences ready, his raised arm and clenched fist the source of a shield that absorbed the relentless lightning. It was but a distraction, however, a blinding diversion that allowed Skara to find his feet and charge Gelakor.

The two men collided in furious battle again. Daijen's decades of rigorous training saw him note the change in Gelakor's technique as the Rider adopted a more evasive and erratic style. He was evading Dawnbreaker at all costs, the blade capable of reducing him to ash with a single cut. In order to use his axe to its full potential, he needed to get some distance, allowing him to throw it repeatedly—and it seemed Skara knew as much. The Dark One hounded him across the chamber, skidding across the wet stone on one knee if it meant keeping up with the Dragon Rider.

A single-handed strike from Skara melted through one of the pillars without resistance, allowing him to twist the blade and threaten Gelakor's midline in the same motion. The Rider ducked and weaved, countering where he could, his axe the only thing capable of blocking Dawnbreaker and defying its power.

"I suppose this was inevitable," The Dark One rasped, shoving Gelakor back with his shoulder. "It was always to come to this— you and I to the death." Skara began to pace, falling into a circular pattern with the Rider. "I had hoped Malliath's demise would see an end to your rebellion. Yet here we are, all these years later, and your heart still burns with the fire he sparked in you."

"Malliath saw what you were becoming," Gelakor replied, his chest heaving. "And that spark isn't just in me. It's an everlasting flame that now lives in every Dragon Rider. Long after you're dust, it will still burn bright. Malliath's legacy will spell the doom of any who seek to replace you."

A distant chorus of roars found their way through the broken ceiling and into the chamber, defying the constant *clatter* of rain. Skara half regarded the sky above. "You've done well to grow the ranks," he said, his voice lacking genuine sincerity. "If only we had been able to bring this many dragons to our fight with Barad-Agin. It would have been a short battle."

"They are a force for good—*your* words," Gelakor reminded

him, pointing his axe at his foe. "The moment Malliath turned against you, your corruption should have been *blindingly* obvious to you!"

"You've brought, what, fifty dragons to my door? How can you not know them as I do? They are just as corruptible as we are, Gelakor! They can be troubled by *greed*. They can harbour a desire for *power*. You just have to find the right dragon," he added, his smile a promise of more evil to come.

Gelakor saved his words and let his axe fly. The precision and force should have been enough to kill any man, but Skara proved himself so much more. Dawnbreaker slashed through the air, a flat line of steel before The Dark One's face, and deflected the weapon of power. As it was wont to do, the axe returned to the Rider's hand, and he let it fly.

Skara was on the move now, advancing at speed. Gelakor was relentless, throwing the axe high and low, only to have it batted aside every time. The gap closed, and the pair were forced back into hand-to-hand combat. Soaked through, their wounds spilling blood into the rain that coursed over them, they gave everything they had.

Movement from the shadows caught Daijen's eye. A servant of The Dark One—an apprentice, perhaps. He hid behind a pillar, watching fearfully as his master fought for his life. His attention momentarily diverted, the Vahlken missed the dwarf recovering on the other side of the chamber.

Duun made himself known to all when he brought The Anther down, hammering the tip of Dawnbreaker into the stone. His face burned and still smoking, he bared his teeth at Skara, his dwarven tenacity enough to keep the sword pinned at an angle.

Gelakor didn't hesitate.

With strength only a Dragon Rider might command, he swung the axe from over his head and cleaved through Dawnbreaker, snapping the length of steel in two.

The expulsion of raw magic was enough to fling all three of them in different directions. Duun slammed into a wall while Skara and Gelakor skidded and tumbled over the floor.

By the time Daijen had lowered the hand shielding his eyes, The Dark One was on his feet. Though he limped, Skara was still able to tower over Gelakor before he could recover.

A glint of gold drew the Vahlken's sharp eyes to The Dark One's chest. His necklace had been freed from its place beneath his bone cuirass. It sat just above his heart, a golden frame occupied by a red ruby and a heart of viridian.

Daijen recalled the empty moulds from the depths of Azad-guul. One, he knew, had become the helm, confiscated by the Riders before it could be completed. But what of the second mould? That which had been shaped as a necklace?

Fresh waves of rage creased Skara's features as he regarded the broken sword in the middle of the chamber. "You have no right to undo my works," he glowered. "No right!" The Dark One reached down and snatched Gelakor from the floor with both hands.

Holding the axe by the single handle that sat behind the bladed head, the Rider had only to punch out as Skara dragged him near. The weapon cut through his cuirass and sunk deep into flesh. Daijen knew enough about anatomy to know The Dark One had just suffered a mortal blow, the artery feeding his heart likely severed.

Skara gasped, his hold on Gelakor already weakening. He staggered back, step after step until he was in the middle of the chamber, under the rain again. The axe vanished from his chest, recalled by the Rider, and The Dark One fell to his knees. With one hand to his cuirass, he peeled his palm back to stare at the blood spilling from the wound.

"It is done," Gelakor announced.

Losing his grip on the world, Skara collapsed onto his side as his apprentice darted from the shadows.

"My lord!" he cried, turning him onto his back.

Duun was already striding over, teeth clenched and hammer gripped within white knuckles. Gelakor stepped in and halted the dwarf from slaying the young man.

"There has been enough bloodshed," he declared. "Let the

news spread," he added, nodding his head at the distraught Skara-mangian.

What life remained in The Dark One saw him raise tentative fingers and touch his apprentice's cheek. The apprentice, in turn, gripped the ruby pendant in both hands, as if he was doing his best to conceal it. Still, he could not blot out the red glow in its entirety, the light finding its way through the narrow gaps between his fingers.

It *was* a weapon of power.

Worse, Skara's apprentice was using it...

"Oi!" Duun yelled. "What's that abou'?"

By the time the dwarf had ripped the man away from The Dark One, the pendant's red hue had dissipated. Duun might have noticed the bewildered look on the young man's face or, perhaps, the terror as he looked at his master, but the son of Darl was already stolen from the moment, realising that he now stood over a dead Skara.

"That's it then," he said. "It's finally over."

A turbulent mix of emotions ran across the apprentice's face, but it was not enough to stop him from jumping to his feet and running away. He did so with the ruby pendant, Daijen spied, the chain having snapped when Duun tore the boy off his master.

"What were all that abou' then?"

Gelakor, looking about ready to drop to his knees with exhaustion, could only shrug. "An attempt to heal him, perhaps. Let him go," he said wearily. "Our work here is not finished."

"Oh?"

Gelakor didn't say anything for a time, resting, perhaps, in that moment of long-awaited victory. It seemed to Daijen that it was not everything the Rider had dreamed of. When he finally rose, he moved towards Qirann's dead body, still protruding from one of the pillars. He whispered some kind of prayer over the man before closing his eyes and removing the vambrace from his arm.

"Ye can't be serious?" Duun asked, catching on.

"I told you we would, and so we shall. These weapons are too powerful for any one person to wield, even a Dragon Rider. We will scatter them across the realm—hide them from all." Gelakor picked up the broken sword by the hilt. "Give this to Atradon," he instructed the dwarf. "Her people can take it into the depths of the sea. *We* will conceal the blade and disperse the others."

Duun was distracted, his attention fixed on The Anther in his hands.

"It's time, old friend," Gelakor said encouragingly. "We must rid ourselves of *all* his work."

"Are *we* not o' his work?" Duun posed. "Was it not Skara's own hands that brought Orvax's egg from the other side?"

Gelakor placed a hand on the dwarf's pauldron. "Some things cannot be undone, brother. It's up to us to make sure the order stays in the light, as Skara once intended."

The dwarven Rider nodded solemnly until he caught sight of Ahnir. "An' what o' their wretched kind?" he sneered.

"His grimoire is even more dangerous than his weapons," Gelakor remarked. "They too will be scattered to the winds. Let them fall into myth and legend. They shall be wiped from the annals. Our own history can make no record of them. It will be as if this never happened."

"What abou' the others?" Duun asked tentatively. "The *pale* ones?"

That particular description tugged strongly at Daijen's attention.

"I'm not for likin' whatever the wretch intended for 'em," the dwarf continued.

"Their numbers have already grown beyond our control," Gelakor reported, shaking his head.

Movement caused them all to turn, but it was Daijen whom Ahnir was reaching for. The Vahlken only briefly glimpsed the creature between long and bony fingers before its entire hand pressed into his face.

Smothered in darkness, Daijen Saeth was cast from all memory.

PART THREE

37
VALGALA

Having soared beside the very pinnacle of Mount Kaliban and left The Spine of Erador behind, Garganafan took the party of three ever southward, his wings gliding steadily east until The River Kyber glistened below under a midday sun.

It was a party of *four* now, Joran realised.

Flying beside the white dragon was an Aegre of black feathers and weathered armour. Oaken had become a welcome member of their group since his intervention atop The Giant's Throat. There had been no further talk of exiling the creature from Kassanda, a fact that pleased Joran greatly.

He had come to enjoy not only the creature's presence but also his name. How wonderful it was to speak a name his mother had held dearly. It was something they shared, even though Ilithranda was no longer able to voice it.

Seated behind Kassanda, Joran let his gaze drift from Oaken to Garganafan. While he had marvelled at the incredible view since departing The Giant's Throat, he had taken little time to admire the dragon himself. Garganafan was a sight to behold, a spectacle of nature that spoke of an artistry only Verda herself could create.

As they glided over the realm, Joran noted the small white scales that formed the outer layer of Kassanda's pauldrons and vambraces. They weren't *all* white. Here and there, he spotted the most exquisite gold scales nestled amongst the white. Looking out over the dragon, he soon began to spy the same haphazard pattern across his body. Massive as he was, those golden scales—though still few—were the same size as a person's head.

Kassanda was looking at him over one shoulder, a question in her eyes.

"The gold," he said, close to her ear. "It's beautiful."

The Rider glanced over her companion, her features softening as she did so. "Garganafan's scales carry a rare trait amongst his kin," she began. "Though slow by any measure of time, his scales have been changing colour since he hatched. One day, centuries from now, he will be entirely *gold*."

"Incredible!" Joran exclaimed, imagining such a magnificent sight. "Is gold a rare colour amongst dragons?"

"Not particularly," Kassanda informed him. "But changing from one colour to another is rare, though not so rare as his breath."

"His breath? You mean the fire?"

Kassanda shook her bald head. "Garganafan doesn't breathe fire," she replied, surprising Joran all the more.

"Then what *does* he breathe?"

"I'm sure you'll see soon enough," the Rider answered ominously.

Joran drank in the dragon lore, desperate to become a part of it himself. It was also pleasing to hear Kassanda's voice. The Rider had been more stoical than usual in the wake of their fight with Obrin and Melanda. Despite knowing what it was like to face a dragon, his nerves still more than a little frayed, he couldn't fathom the betrayal she felt. To have called someone friend—brother—for hundreds of years and then have them turn on you was unimaginable to him.

"We're here," she called as Garganafan banked slightly to his left.

Beyond the dragon's horned head, Joran gazed at the gleaming white jewel that sat in the middle of endless green fields. The River Kyber snaked across the plains and disappeared inside the white walls of Erador's ancient capital—Valgala. From their lofty height, the city's interior lake could be seen glistening like a mirror under the midday sun.

It was a wonder to see the capital from the heavens as well as in the light. When last Joran had been within Valgala's walls, it had been a night full of violence and blood. He had only to shut his eyes to see Slait pinning Galahart to the ceiling of The Whistling Pig, a sabre rammed through his gut. What a mess The Dawn Sword had made of the others under the spymaster's employ. Joran and his companions had been forced to abandon Valgala that very same night, aided by... another Galahart.

He tried to shrug off the trauma of it all. His was to be a life of violence, a destiny fulfilled by the point of a blade. He had to adopt the way of the warrior—and quickly at that. As Kassanda had said, *"To have the dragon heart is to have unwavering valour. Unyielding honour. Unending sacrifice."*

While Joran knew there would be opportunities to grow in those areas under Kassanda's mentorship, he couldn't help wondering how their trip to Valgala might test him. The second of the two Galaharts he had met that fateful night had told him the king desired an audience, though, given the importance of his training, it would have to wait.

As they drew closer to the capital, Joran felt that meeting was inevitable, for the one whom Kassanda sought—the only one who could move Erador's armies—was none other than the king himself. A sinking feeling began to grow within him, and not because Garganafan was descending. So far in his life, there had been very few people who desired to meet him and not also seek to either control him or kill him. He couldn't see how a king, a notoriously greedy and selfish breed of creature, would be any different.

A piercing squawk from Oaken pulled Joran's attention away from the city and his spiralling thoughts. The Aegre called out again before reducing his speed and falling behind. Joran looked back to see his mother's companion veering away from their intended destination.

"Where's he going?" Joran asked, raising his voice over the wind.

Kassanda glanced back. "He has the good sense to stay away from Valgala. The walls are bristling with enough ballistas to bring him down. Let him go. He's followed you across the country once. He can do so again. Now hold on," she instructed.

Joran gripped her around the waist as Garganafan plummeted towards the green plains below. It was a rush, both exhilarating and terrifying all at once. However he felt, it was clear to Joran that he couldn't live the rest of his life without the feel of a dragon beneath him—there was nothing more inspiring, if not outright intoxicating.

Garganafan spread his pale wings and glided around the city at great speed, allowing the people of Valgala to see him. Ringed about the lake, the rooftops were steadily filled with men, women, and children clamouring to glimpse the white dragon. Garganafan flew from north to south before turning to fly over the capital itself, his shadow running over the streets until he raced over the lake.

Kassanda patted Joran's clinging hands. "Brace yourself."

Joran looked ahead to see the spires and central tower of the king's palace, the white stone touching the northern shore of the lake. It was quite apparent that there was nowhere large enough within the city's walls for a dragon of Garganafan's size to land—a fact that made their heading all the more worrying.

"Where are we going?" he asked with concern.

Garganafan answered the question with action, his claws skimming the surface of the water before his legs and torso followed suit. Plunging into the lake, the dragon created a mighty splash and rippling waves that crashed against the shore, rocking small boats and big ships alike.

His powerful tail swaying like a rudder in the water, Garganafan swam until his claws were able to sink into the lake's depths. The dragon walked the remainder of the distance, lowering himself further until Kassanda and Joran could climb down and jump across to the stone port.

The walkway ran straight through the harbour and ended at the base of the palace, where a considerable contingent of red cloaks—Valgala's homeguard—were emerging from. With spears in hand, they approached the newcomers in two lines, their armour creating a raucous *clatter*.

Upon stopping, one of the soldiers peeled away to meet them directly, his cuirass emblazoned with the sigil of the king—a plunging sword, the blade coated with dragon scales.

"Valgala welcomes you, Dragon Rider," he greeted with a bow of his helmed head. "I am Captain Hawkins of the palace homeguard."

The captain's gaze shifted repeatedly towards Joran, always wandering over the pointed ears that protruded from his snow-white hair and violet eyes. His discomfort abated somewhat when he realised Joran wasn't a full-blooded Andaren, his pink skin telling a different story. There remained some apprehension in his demeanour, though, if not outright derision. While he had clearly decided Joran wasn't a threat, he was still disturbed by the sight of a half-blood.

"Captain Hawkins," Kassanda replied, focusing the man, "I seek urgent words with the king."

"It would be my honour to escort you."

Following in the captain's wake, Joran attempted to raise the hood of his cloak and conceal what he could of his Andaren attributes.

"No," Kassanda ordered, one hand catching his arm. "A dragon does not hide what they are."

Reluctantly, Joran let go of his hood and left his white hair and pointed ears on display. Stepping between the watchful home-guard, he entered the palace shoulder to shoulder with Kassanda. Therein awaited an opulence the young man had never seen before. How anywhere could be so clean was beyond his under-standing, though the army of servants who scurried about like ants gave him some idea. Posted throughout were more of the homeguard, though some blended in with the suits of armour on display or the life-size paintings and tapestries of knights that hung from the walls.

Braziers and hearths brought light to every corner of the marbled palace, but its architecture had clearly been designed with the sun in mind. Almost every passage and chamber they moved through allowed something of the natural light to filter through, lending a soft glow to the king's towering halls.

They were taken ever upwards, ascending grand staircases and passing under gold-trimmed archways. Joran glimpsed a two-storey library through an open door, the books situated on shelves of dark oak, the highest volumes reachable only by climbing one of several brass ladders. Alas, they were not taken inside but ushered towards a set of black doors displaying the king's sigil.

Standing between them and the doors, however, was a single figure, a tall man of perhaps sixty years. His copper hair was losing its colour, though what remained was short and brushed back— well maintained, Joran thought. There was not a crease in sight on his jacket of black and gold, and his tall, dark boots were just as clean as everything else in the palace. He was an odd sight to Joran's eyes, who had traversed much of the realm in recent weeks.

If his attire didn't scream highborn, his expression would have been enough. A lithe man, his cheekbones stood proud over a trimmed beard of fading copper and tight lips. Piercing blue eyes watched them intently as they approached. It was perhaps his stern gaze, though, that stopped Captain Hawkins and his men from accompanying them any further.

"Kassanda Grey," the Rider declared, voicing her family name in front of Joran for the first time. "You may announce us," she added, nodding at the black doors.

Those tight lips managed something of an amused smile. "I know who you are," he replied, his voice as rich as his fine clothes. "It is a relief that the mighty Garganafan and his Rider, Kassanda Grey, still hold true to their oaths."

"Who *are* you?" she asked unapologetically.

"A humble servant of the court," he informed her. "Not a *court servant*, I should point out. The difference is rather startling."

Kassanda said nothing but let some of her impatience show.

The stranger remained where he stood, not to be perturbed by the testy Rider. "Why is *he* here?" he demanded, his blue eyes falling on Joran.

Kassanda's obvious irritation was replaced by confusion as she looked from one man to the other. "You know each other?" she asked.

Joran shared in her confusion. "I've never seen him before," he insisted.

"He's supposed to be in Drakanan," the man continued, speaking only to Kassanda, "bonding with a dragon egg. I lost good men keeping The Dawn Sword occupied to ensure as much."

Joran was sure then that he knew the stranger's identity, though he couldn't quite believe it. "Who *are* you?" he asked.

Looking somewhat impatient himself now, the man answered curtly, "I am Galahart, Chief Advisor to His Grace's security council."

While Joran's eyes widened at the familiar name, Kassanda's eyes twitched, narrowing for no more than a second. "You're the infamous spymaster I've heard so *little* about."

Galahart flashed his teeth. "Even a *little* is more than I'd like, though there is much to be gained in reputation, I suppose."

Kassanda cut through the nonsense. "The ways of our order are not your business, spymaster. Joran is with me. That's all you need to know."

"Be that is it may," Galahart accepted reluctantly, "you might find his being here a... *complication*."

Joran's curiosity bested his trepidation, forcing a single word to blurt from his mouth. "Why?"

"Joran has been adopted by my order," Kassanda put it bluntly, speaking over him. "Are we not welcome in the House of Etragon?"

Galahart raised his chin. Then he smiled, as if he were starting again. "Dragon Riders have long been welcome in the house of the king. I can only assume you have come with news of the northern invasion."

"I have. Urgent news. So, if you please..."

The man didn't budge. "The palace is not as it once was," he said, his voice lowered. "This old stone is home to more than just *my* eyes and ears. The Jainus have made themselves known in recent years. Through their connections in The Gilded, they have applied religious pressure to House Etragon. Furthermore, they have applied their magic to the bloodlines. All the great houses have accepted their meddling, allowing the Jainus to use their spells on highborn mothers."

"Why?" Joran asked, not entirely sure he wanted to hear the answer.

"Their magic ensures the children are born with desirable attributes, aesthetically speaking, though some under our supervision have exhibited an unnatural level of intelligence or physicality for their age. The wizards' involvement also comes with the promise of a healthy baby and a speedy recovery for the mother.

"This kind of interference grants them powerful allies, all of whom require balancing where the king is concerned. To that end, they stand in court," Galahart reported, glancing over his shoulder. "As I'm sure you can understand, there is a delicate balance between the throne and the wizards. Information is the highest form of currency."

"The flow and obstruction of information is *your* business, spymaster," Kassanda countered. "I am here to say what I must."

"You are a warrior, yes?" Galahart replied, his question rhetorical. "You understand the subtleties of manoeuvring one's foe, lest the blow merely wound. When *I* strike, I like to know my enemy will not get back up."

"I didn't realise The Jainus were our enemy. Or The Gilded, for that matter."

"My predecessor imparted much to me before his death, but there was one piece of sage advice that has always stayed with me. *Everyone is your friend until they're not.* Do you know who taught him that?" Galahart tilted his head, as if he were a teacher trying to tease the answer from her.

Kassanda's jaw hardened. "Baelon Vos."

"Baelon Vos," Galahart echoed, drawing out the Rider's name. "For nine hundred years, the throne and every king who sat upon it called him friend. Then, some forty years ago, Baelon and his merry band of renegades changed the board—no warning. Every circle about the throne had to be drawn in. What loyalists remain within your order are few and far between—the Riders can no longer be relied upon.

"The Jainus know this," he continued. "They have always been one step away from real power, but thanks to your order, they never crossed the line. Now, they lean into The Gilded like never before, wielding religion like a weapon. Their influence over The Gildessa is absolute. She has her priestlings spreading propaganda on every street, ever tightening the chord between The Jainus's magic and the will of Kaliban. In short, they have begun plans to squeeze House Etragon out of the picture, leaving the throne for them."

The spymaster sighed, glancing over Kassanda to the soldiers who had escorted them. "If only The Jainus, The Gilded, *and* Baelon Vos were the sole source of our problems," he lamented. "Say what you must, Rider, but do not speak of the Skaramangians. The king knows they exist, but I have yet to unravel the wizard who stands for The Jainus. I would keep them at arm's length wherever possible."

"You are neither king nor Dragonlord," Kassanda reminded him. "My allegiance is to them and them *alone*." The Rider stepped closer to the spymaster. "Presume to control my voice again, and you will spend the rest of your days struggling to speak at all."

There it was, the dragon that lived within all Riders. Joran saw that most ferocious and noble of creatures flash across Kassanda's face and breathe life into her words.

Galahart's expression, on the other hand, suggested he wasn't taking the threat seriously. Still, the spymaster bowed his head and knocked once on the doors at his back.

They were immediately opened from the other side, flooding the foyer with light. "Tread carefully," he whispered as they passed over the threshold.

Kassanda's responding gaze was sharp, if brief, for her attention soon turned to the throne room beyond. Joran did his best to mimic her confidence, taking a quick step to remain by her side. He slowed, however, and his focus on the Rider waned as his eyes were taken upwards.

The throne room of House Etragon was unlike anything Joran had ever seen, a stupefying and imposing splendour he could never have imagined after a life on the road with Gallien.

Entering between two rows of statues, each a regal figure of twenty feet in height, the short corridor opened up to a circular floor surrounded by tiers of white stone benches. Behind them stood four colossal statues that reached for the domed ceiling, the hands of each capable of holding the smaller statues that formed the entrance. Joran's violet eyes noted the crowns upon all of them, even the smaller ones, and deduced them to be ancient kings of Erador.

Between the four enormous statues, the domed ceiling was supported by a ring of tall pillars, allowing the elements to access the chamber. Situated within the central tower of the palace, above most of the city, the wind that blew through the pillars picked up Joran's sandy cloak and white hair, dragging them to the west, where the afternoon sun cast the chamber in strips of golden light.

Passing beyond the column of smaller statues, Joran and Kassanda stepped onto the circular floor of black stone, a stark contrast to the white of all else. Directly ahead, the ring of tiered benches came to an end, allowing space for the throne of Erador.

While it did not sit above all the tiers, it sat well above Joran's head, a block of white stone shaped into a dragon's head, horns and all. The throne sloped back and up in the manner of a scaled dragon's neck, ending in line with the highest tier of the surrounding benches.

It was also empty.

As the black doors shut behind them, another was opened to

the side, where pitted steps led to a chamber unseen. Voices found their way up into the throne room, followed by a group of men. It was, of course, the man leading the group who captured Joran's attention.

Though his clothes were likely of the highest quality, they were simple by comparison to Galahart's. His white shirt and trousers were mostly concealed by a long but delicately fine coat of charcoal grey that touched his ankles. He boasted no crown nor even a plethora of jewellery, displaying only a single, if large, ring on his right index finger.

Kassanda dropped to one knee, her fist pressed to her left breast. "Your Grace," she uttered.

Joran was a second behind her and soon found himself looking at a pair of dark boots slowly approaching him.

"Leave us," the king commanded.

Joran tilted his head to see five men—highborns all—depart the chamber, the grand doors opened by servants who had remained silent in the corners of the short corridor. They too were given the command to leave by Galahart, though the spymaster was sure to stay *inside* the throne room when he closed the doors.

"Rise," the king bade, his voice a touch softer now.

Joran stood up and found himself eye to eye with the most powerful man in all of Erador. He was, perhaps, in his early fifties, though the man had managed to retain much of his hair colour, boasting a good volume of short but curly auburn with only spirals of grey here and there. His beard had not fared so well, greying almost completely with tufts of white about his chin.

It seemed fitting, given the well-chiselled statues of kings long past, that the sitting king would have a square jaw and a hand-some face. It stood out to Joran then when he noticed that the man before him also sported a handful of scars. A considerable one cut through his jaw and beard on the right side, ending just below his eye. Another, deeper still, marred his forehead, interrupting his left eyebrow. The rest were shallow: a slice across his nose, a line through his bottom lip, and what might have been a burn on his right temple.

IN THE SHADOW OF KINGS

None detracted from his looks, and his physical stature spoke of a man who maintained a good level of training. It was his eyes, dark wells of oak, that spoke of a richness to the king, of a life that had seen more than the comforts of a palace. They softened the hard edges of his face, making his scars all the more a curiosity.

They lingered on Joran for a while, drifting only to look past him at Galahart. The spymaster's response remained a mystery to Joran, who dared not turn his back on the king. When that royal gaze returned, the king scrutinised him even more, though he paid more attention to his violet eyes than his hair and ears.

An awkward silence hung in the vast chamber, prompting Kassanda to speak again. "Your Grace?"

Cajoled from his reverie, the king blinked and regarded the Rider. "Forgive me," he began, turning and taking only a few steps up to his throne before casually sitting on the steps themselves. "We have been on a war footing since before I was born, but recent activity in the north demands my advisors meet every five minutes to deliberate and conject," he explained wearily. "I do hope you've come with news."

"This is Kassanda Grey, Your Grace," Galahart said by way of introduction so as not to risk his king's embarrassment. "She rides upon Garganafan."

"That would be the huge dragon in my lake, I suppose," the king quipped, amusement pulling at his lips. "I should like to meet him."

"Garganafan would be honoured, Your Grace," Kassanda replied with a curt bow of the head.

"The honour is mine. I have never met one of your order. The secret schism that exists between the Riders began before my reign. Your absence on the battlefield is keenly felt, though your efforts along the coast are much appreciated. I'm told many an invasion has been turned back by those still loyal to my house."

"A time of dragons is coming, Your Grace," Kassanda vowed, a subtle glance thrown at Joran. "Those still loyal have long memories. The old ways will not be forgotten."

The king offered her a warm smile. "I long for those days. Like the kings before me," he added, gesturing up at the statues that looked down on them, "I fear my time will pass before this war finds its end."

"Perhaps," Galahart interjected, "the Rider has brought news from west of The Spine."

"That is my hope," the king declared. "The Andarens made quite the mess invading our fair lands. Then... *nothing*. They just vanished. Conjecture and rumour would have me split my army to all four corners of the world. "

"The Andarens are no longer in the north, Your Grace," Kassanda reported. "After storming White Tower, they turned immediately south, through The Red Fields of Dunmar. By the time we caught up with them, they had taken ground beyond The Giant's Throat. The Andarens now occupy the region of Akmar, though their activity is centred around The Silver Trees."

Joran didn't miss the subtle glance the king gave to his spymaster. "The Silver Trees," he echoed.

"Thedaria would be the obvious target," Galahart concluded. "From there, the Andarens could flank Caster Hold before going on to invade the south. It would certainly give them the resources required to push north and bring the war to Valgala."

Kassanda was shaking her head. "It is my strong belief, Your Grace, that the invading force will go no further south."

The king raised his eyebrows. "You think they will cut through the mountains," he inferred. "The Misted Road would bring them directly to this city. Though it is a treacherous path."

"No, Your Grace," Kassanda countered, a politeness in her tone that Joran was unaccustomed to. "The Andarens have no need to invade further because they have what they came for. They will retreat to Andara with their prize, ensuring its safe delivery to the warlocks."

Again, the king glanced at Galahart. "Their prize?"

"Yes," came a voice from above, raising Joran's gaze to one of the thick pillars. "I too would like to know of this... *prize*."

There was no mistaking the woman—a Jainus. She descended the steps that cut through the stone rows and moved to the corner of the throne, where she could look down on all of them, including the king. Her robes of deep red hid her feet, though a tight belt, laden with pouches and the sundries of wizards, pulled it all in about a narrow waist. Like any highborn, her black hair was immaculate, trimmed meticulously at the shoulders.

"This is Marinen," the king said, his demeanour sinking somewhat. "Marinen stands for the Jainus in my court. She is a valued advisor in these trying times."

"This is the first I have heared of an assault on The Silver Trees of Akmar," the Jainus announced. "As you know, Rider, that region has long been under the care of my order."

"Then I am sorry for your loss, Mistress Marinen," Kassanda replied evenly, "for you have lost many brothers and sisters tending to that great forest." The Rider returned her attention to the king. "The Andarens are camped within the trees, Your Grace. It is theirs. As is the skeleton at its heart."

"Skeleton?" Marinen was quick to question.

Joran turned to regard Galahart, whose disappointment was no more than a fleeting expression. When the boy looked back at the king, the ruler of Erador was already looking at him, and intently so.

"The Andarens believe it to be one of their gods," Kassanda explained. "Whatever it is, those bones offer the enemy a new source of magic. We cannot let it fall into the hands of—"

"What are you talking about, Rider?" the Jainus interrupted, moving across the front of the throne. "Those trees are a phenomenon my people have been researching for centuries. There are no *bones.*"

Kassanda straightened up. "We cannot let those bones fall into the hands of the Skaramangians," she said, forging on.

"The hands of *who*?" the Jainus demanded.

The king sighed, a bemused smile pulling at his beard. "If you have any cards to play in this game, Marinen, now is the time to lay them out. If you do not, I will have to ask you to leave in the care of Galahart."

There was an obvious battle taking place inside the Jainus, her allegiances tripping over one another. With contorted lips and a sour expression, Marinen made her way down the steps, past the king, and onto the chamber floor.

"Are all Dragon Riders so blunt as this one?" she asked aloud. "That name is not to be bandied around. The eyes and ears drawn to it travel as far back as Aran'saur."

Galahart rubbed his eyes and pinched the bridge of his nose. "A lot of manpower could have been saved if you had just come forward with this knowledge, Marinen."

"Does this mean your spies will stop searching my chambers while I'm not there?" she countered.

The king raised his hand, silencing further argument. "Do the Jainus have anything to offer on the matter?"

Marinen hesitated. "Word has likely reached The Tower of Jain by now," she reasoned. "But it has not found its way to Valgala yet. If plans are in motion to reclaim the bones, they are not known to me."

The king looked her in the eyes. "Omissions tear away at the truth just as much as lies do, Marinen. I am aware that your bond with The Gilded is stronger than it is with the throne, but we three institutions are one cord, a single tether between the people and Kaliban. How are we to work together if one of those cords is frayed by the others?"

The Jainus made to respond, but, again, the king held up his hand.

"Reach out to your superiors. Learn what you can. Report anything less than the whole truth to me, and my palace will shrink dramatically in your eyes. How long do you think the great Magus will keep you in office after that?"

Marinen opened her mouth only to have the king speak over her again. "Go," he commanded. "Bring me something useful."

The Jainus looked offended, on the edge, perhaps, of rebelling against the king. It would be a step too far, Joran considered. Outright defiance was too overt given the wizards' subtle efforts thus far. Besides, it was clear that mention of Marinen's superior, the Magus, was enough to remind the Jainus that she was under the command of others.

"Your Grace," she said with a bow.

"Apologies, Your Grace," Kassanda offered once the black doors had closed behind Marinen.

"Not necessary," the king replied, sweeping his curls back. "We have long suspected the Jainus's knowledge of Skaramangian affairs. We know they are not allies, otherwise they would have handed that damned skeleton over years ago. You've saved us a lot of time, Kassanda. Besides, it's the politics of it all that slows us down. Now is the time for action."

"She could still be lying," Joran blurted, drawing all eyes to himself. He licked his lips and swallowed his anxiety. "Marinen may well report this meeting to the Skaramangians, not the Jainus," he explained.

The king smiled. "Quite right," he stated. "An astute observation. Fear not. Galahart's people will be following her every move from this chamber. We will soon learn the truth of her allegiance."

Joran looked from the king to Galahart. "You wanted this?"

"No," the spymaster said bluntly. "I would not have warned you otherwise. That said, an opportunity is not to be squandered."

"I should like to speak with your war council if I may, Your Grace," Kassanda voiced. "I have a strategy in mind that might see us turn the tide."

"Very good," the king replied. "Galahart, have the council gather as soon as possible in the war room. See that my guests here are given quarters in the meantime."

The spymaster bowed. "As you command, Your Grace."

Just as it seemed the trio had been dismissed, the king spoke again, halting their departure.

"I would ask that you stay behind, Joran. I missed you during your last visit to Valgala. There is a matter I should like to discuss with you."

Kassanda frowned. "What matter?"

The spymaster stepped forwards, his words stern. "Yours is not to question the king, Kassanda Grey."

"Joran is my ward," she reminded him.

"You know my name," Joran observed, absent the required etiquette. "You know... You know who I am?"

The king of House Etragon raised his hand, a calming gesture. "It's alright, Galahart. Yes, Joran, I know who you are. For all my spymaster's secrets, he has made me aware of the half-blood hunted by the Skaramangians. The one believed to bring about this *time of dragons* your master spoke of. It's not every day you meet someone with a *real* destiny."

"Your Grace," Galahart interceded delicately. "Perhaps this can wait until after the war council? Time is of the essence if we are to prevent the skeleton from crossing into Andara."

It appeared that the king begrudgingly agreed. "After, then."

The very moment the black doors sealed shut behind the trio, Kassanda and Galahart turned to face each other.

"You will mind your words in front of the king."

"Why does the king seek a private audience with my ward?" Kassanda demanded at the same time.

"That would be the *king's* business."

"Joran's fate is in the hands of the Dragon Riders," Kassanda told him. "It is not his place to meddle or manipulate."

"I warned you," the spymaster retorted, speaking as if Joran wasn't standing right next to him. "Bringing him here is a complication..."

38
THE LAST DAYS OF MORTHIL

As if it were a monster rising from the depths of the world, the sea invaded Morthil with a deafening roar. It found every street, alley, and crevice, sweeping dwarves from their feet. Entire buildings were washed away, pushed over the edges and into the chasms.

Grarfath gripped the bars of his hanging cell and pressed his face into one of the gaps. "What's happenin'?" he cried.

None could reply, their troubles only just beginning.

The cranes that kept them aloft began to groan and lose their couplings to the cavern wall. Chains and bolts were being stressed beyond their limits. The prisoners were powerless to do anything. Anything but fall.

One after another, the cells and the cranes that held them fell away. Grarfath hit the ceiling, where he remained plastered until they stopped mid-fall. He struck the floor, the wind momentarily knocked from his chest. It seemed something of the crane mechanism had maintained its hold on the ancient stone, leaving all of them hanging at awkward angles.

They swayed from side to side, their momentum sure to wear

down the stubborn bolts and fastenings. The smith yelled in surprise when his cell collided with Slait's. The mutated Andaren bashed his head against one of the bars, splitting his left eyebrow. It wasn't enough to keep him down, however, and he soon rose to assess their perilous situation.

His words were stolen when they began falling again. Grarfath could hear Kitrana and Yamnomora shouting wildly over the sound of rattling chains and groaning metal. When those chains pulled taut, though, everyone's direction changed again. Acting like a hammer, the combined cells of Grarfath and Slait swung sideways and slammed into the others.

To the sound of exploding stone, Kit and Yamnomora's cells were forced through the side of Khardunar, punching through the outer wall to one of its chambers. Their cells were mangled such that Kitrana was able to squeeze through a gap, while Yamnomora had only to bend an already crooked bar until she could slip through as well.

Though dazed and likely wounded, they rushed to the jagged hole in the side of the king's palace, looking on in despair as Grarfath continued to swing back and forth towards them. The impact had caused the smith more injury, but he had strength enough to rise and steady himself with the bars. With wonder, he observed the opening in his cell, an entire wall of bars cleaved free when it had hammered the others' cells.

"Jump!" Yamnomora yelled.

"*Jump!*" Kitrana added in man's tongue.

"You'll never make it," Slait said behind him, their cells seemingly fused together after the initial collision.

"Oh, I'll make it," the smith vowed under his breath.

He waited—timing was everything.

The cell swung back and forth, the chains threatening to drop them at any moment. Yet even when he drew near the palace wall, Kitrana and Yamnomora still seemed impossibly far away.

Grarfath bent his knees, ready to propel himself. "Ye can do it," he said over and over again.

"Jump!" Yamnomora barked, her gaze above the cells, where the calamity continued to unfold.

A feeling of doom came over the smith. He knew then that if he delayed one more time, he would perish. And so he leaped, throwing his hands out as he did. Had he been a human or an Andaren, the dwarf would have made it, his fingers just grasping the edge of the interior floor. As it was, he missed the edge by half a foot.

In the grasp of nothingness itself, he felt himself about to fall to that doom he had felt overshadow him. But strong are the fingers of a dwarf, and stronger still are the muscles in their arms. Luckily for Grarfath, it was Yamnomora's arms that had caught him.

"I've got ye!" she hissed, her voice strained.

Looking up, the smith could see that Kitrana was slowly but surely heaving Yamnomora back inside, though the dwarf herself was instrumental in bringing Grarfath up the ledge. Even when he had his hands on the floor, she continued to grasp at his belt and yank him up.

Suitably exhausted, the trio lay on the floor, panting for breath.

The sound of rending metal was enough to turn them back towards the hanging cells. Since jumping free, Grarfath's cell had parted ways with Slait's and fallen into the chasm below. The Dawn Sword now stood clinging to his bars while his cell swayed from side to side. Atop his cell, the rings of metal that kept it attached to the chains were slowly warping and snapping.

"Dance yer way out o' this one, Dawn Sword!" Yamnomora yelled at him.

Slait paid them no attention, his golden eyes wandering over the edges of his cell where it had been entwined with Grarfath's. The damage was clear to see, the sheets of metal having been over-lapped and then pulled apart with repeated collisions.

Though he risked hastening his demise, Slait began pushing the corner of broken bars away from the rest of the cell. His muscles bulged and his teeth ground together with sheer exertion until it began to relent, allowing him space to climb up and find purchase on the flat roof.

The metal rings had done all they could, finally snapping. The cell plummeted towards the watery darkness below, leaving Slait hanging by one hand, his fingers clenched about the only chain that remained.

"He's a crafty kud, I'll give 'im that," Yamnomora muttered. "Come on," she urged, tapping the smith's arm. "Leave 'im to dangle. We need to get The Anther an' get out o' 'ere before the water rises."

Leaving The Dawn Sword to his fate, the trio navigated the two heavily damaged cells and the scattered rubble, departing the chamber with what strength they could muster. The halls of Khardunar were lavish and large, larger than any dwarf required. It was also a labyrinth of stairwells, mezzanines, and dead ends. Fortunately, the chaos outside the palace was causing chaos *inside* the palace.

Thundering boots could be heard almost everywhere, the king's guards charging about on royal orders. They looked to be securing items here and relocating items there—safeguarding their king's treasures while the people drowned.

Grarfath slowed down and turned back when he realised Kitrana was no longer running by his side. The Nimean had paused by an open window that looked out on the dwarven realm below. Until the water could fill the chasm beneath Khardunar, the sea would continue to rush through the streets, claiming lives every second.

"*It's my fault,*" Kit whispered. "*This is my fault.*"

"*What are ye talkin' abou', lass?*"

"*I woke it up,*" she uttered.

Grarfath stumbled over his response. "*Ye woke what up?*"

The Nimean looked down at him, grave concern marring her fair features. "*The Leviathan.*"

The smith frowned, shaking his head. "*The what? Ye're not making any sense.*"

"Come on!" Yamnomora growled, turning her companions back to the palace interior.

She ploughed into a Greyhelm guard, ending any conversation about monsters in the deep. She was sure to grip his hammer in both hands and twist the weapon up and round. The dwarf was sent reeling into the wall, a boot shoved into the base of his back for good measure.

Yamnomora came away from the brief encounter with the hammer already swinging to catch a second guard charging from round the corner. His pauldron took the brunt of the impact but her strength was still enough to take him from his feet.

Grarfath dashed in, jumping on the guard before they could recover. With the powerful arms of a smith, he pummelled the loyal Greyhelm while Yamnomora saw to the first guard, his own hammer used against him.

His breath ragged, Grarfath stood over his beaten foe, knuckles bloody. *"How do we get out o' 'ere?"*

"There's only one way in an' out o' Khardunar," Yamnomora replied, relieving the nearest guard of his dagger.

Kitrana stepped away from the window. *"We're just walking out the front door?"*

Yamnomora slipped the knife into her belt and tossed the hammer to Grarfath. *"O' course not. We're goin' to use The Anther."*

The smith shared an uneasy look with Kitrana before replying. *"An' how are we to get that back? Ye can bet it's not left the High King's side."*

Yamnomora offered a wicked smile. *"We'll ask 'im for it."*

With that, she was off, taking to the next corridor before descending one set of stairs in order to ascend another. They worked their way around a vast mezzanine, hiding in alcoves and behind statues when required.

"Do you know where you're going?" Kit asked, her voice hushed.

"No," Yamnomora answered bluntly. *"I'm jus' followin' the activity,"* she explained, gesturing at the dwarves moving through the hallways.

"This is going to get us killed," the Nimean opined.

"The Anther is our only ticket out o' 'ere," Yamnomora retorted.

"It's also the only reason we're 'ere," the dwarf added, pressing her back to the wall.

"The Green Leaf said we need an arsenal," Grarfath reminded Kitrana, though he recalled that the Nimean had chosen a path of her own. *"Ye've seen what that hammer can do. We can make a real difference with it."*

The smith turned back to Yamnomora, who was looking at him intently.

"What?" he whispered.

Yamnomora stared at him a moment longer. *"Nothin',"* she said, though it seemed she was looking at him for the first time. *"Let's go."*

When a big enough gap presented itself, the trio crossed the corridor and cautiously entered a chamber that boasted naught but statues of past Greyhelms. Moving swiftly, they passed through the door on the other side—only to enter the throne room itself. They were on the top floor of the mezzanine structure, able to look down on the massive skull of the Stonemaw and the treasures that lined the lowest level.

There seemed to be more activity in the throne room than the rest of Khardunar combined. Dwarves, both soldiers and servants, darted from relic to relic and filled chests with jewels and coins. With the queen and prince huddled to one side, the High King stood in the middle of it all, directing the work with The Anther in hand.

"Don't miss a single gem!" he cried. "Be quick abou' it!" he bellowed. "Handle that with care!" he commanded.

Striding through the main doors, Lord Tharg made directly for his king. "Yer Grace!"

The High King pointed at a set of antique armour. "Make yerself useful, Tharg! Carry whatever ye can!"

The Skaramangian dwarf waved his hands in warning. "We cannot abandon Khardunar, Yer Grace!"

Glaive shook his head. "Have ye looked outside? This entire region is to be swallowed by the damned sea! No. Me family an' all that's ours is to be taken to the Bozun District—it's the highest cavern in all o' Morthil. Once there, we can see to the pumps an' activate the drainage system," he said confidently. "If it still works," he added with significantly less confidence.

"No, Yer Grace," Lord Tharg protested. "We're already cut off from the other caverns. Everyone is tryin' to get up 'ere!"

The High King's brow creased into a knot of muscle. "Everyone?"

"The entire region! The water has driven' 'em up. The guards are keepin' 'em at bay for now, but they're amassin' down there!"

"Well they can't come into the palace!" the High King protested. "We've not the supplies for 'em all."

"Agreed," Lord Tharg replied. "I suggest redirectin' the guard to the base of the steps, Yer Grace. They need reinforcements down there."

"*What are they talking about?*" Kitrana asked.

"*Letting everyone drown,*" Grarfath seethed.

Glaive clapped his hands, garnering the attention of his guard. "Put everything back where ye found it! Get to the steps! None can enter Khardunar!"

"Very good, Yer Grace," Lord Tharg complimented, as if it had been the High King's idea all along.

"Do we know yet the cause?"

"There were a lot o' talk comin' out o' the undercity, Yer Grace. I heard rumours o' water comin' through Torlin's Doors."

The High King raised an eyebrow. "Torlin's Doors?"

"Aye, Yer Grace. That whole area is known as The Well—it's as far down as we've ever gone."

"Where the bones were discovered?"

"Aye, yer Grace, along with The Anther."

"Well now we know what lurks beneath that stone," Glaive remarked dryly. "Damn the sea!"

Grarfath considered what Kitrana had said to him, of the Leviathan she had supposedly woken in the deep. The High King had no idea what really lurked beneath his city.

The rest of their conversation was lost, their words drowned out by the clamour of armour and marching boots as the soldiers departed the throne room.

"Khardunar rests a little above sea level," the High King went on once the din had subsided, straightening an ancient helm returned to its display. "We 'ave only wait it out."

"An' those in the other caverns, Yer Grace?"

"They 'ave their own evacuation tunnels," Glaive replied offhandedly, waving a dismissive hand through the air. "The Erabus Cavern is likely lost by now," he reported, as if all those lives didn't matter. "An' if the water truly came from beyond Torlin's Doors, the undercity's already been wiped away."

Grarfath's heart broke as the truth of that settled over him. All those people. The families. The children. All kin of the Underborn guild, as he was and Yamnomora beside him. How many of them could have survived? Even a few would be a miracle. And there were no miracles in the halls of Morthil. Only profits and losses.

Before Yamnomora could make her move, and her obvious outrage suggested she had been on the cusp of action, Grarfath descended a handful of steps on the nearest spiral staircase and leaped over the railing.

Lord Tharg crumpled beneath his bulk, his face flattened to the polished floor. From both his mouth and nose, blood sprayed across the veins of silvyr that ran through the golden surface.

Rising up, the smith kept his knee pressed into the back of Tharg's neck and maintained enough pressure to ensure he didn't move.

"Ye!" the High King roared, pointing the hammer. "How did ye escape me dungeon?" His attention was diverted when Yamnomora and Kitrana descended from the top floor, both jumping over the rail to land beside the smith. "Guards!" he cried.

"Give me The Anther," Grarfath demanded, his hand open and ready to receive. "Give it to me, or I'll break his neck."

Glaive barked a laugh. "Ye think his life means enough to me that I would part with a weapon o' power? Ye should o' stayed in yer forge, smith. Ye're in over ye head."

"Give it to me!" Grarfath raged, desperate for his anger to

outweigh his conscience—only then could he see his threat through to its end.

"Go ahead," Glaive suggested, The Anther resting over one of his large shoulders. "Kill 'im. After that, ye'll 'ave to face me," he said with devilish conviction. "I can assure ye, son o' Thronghir, I've not been sat in that throne all me days. The best warriors in all o' Morthil 'ave seen to me instruction. Hell, at least I'll 'ave some entertainment up 'ere!" he laughed.

"Yer people are dyin' out there, an' ye would seek entertainment?" the smith growled. "Ye're not fit to be High King! An' ye're definitely not fit to wield that hammer," he added defiantly.

Glaive snorted and hefted The Anther. "Fancy yerself the title o' Hammerhold, do ye? Think ye can take on the mantle o' Duun 'imself? *Ye*, a lowly talentless smith who couldn' live up to his father's skill. Yer mother's lucky I had Tharg 'ere put her out o' her misery," he jibed. "The shame she'd feel to see what an embarrassment ye've become."

Grarfath snapped. His wrath had finally reached its crescendo and demanded a physical outlet.

It demanded *vengeance*.

In the act of jumping to his feet, he pushed his knee down with all his weight atop it. *Crack.* Lord Tharg died right there on the throne room floor, a pathetic death after so many centuries of conniving under Skaramangian rule and thriving on the wealth of a dwarven lord. Grarfath might have relished in it were he not flying at the High King in a fit of rage.

For all the lies that had spilled out of his royal mouth during his long reign, Glaive had spoken the truth where his instruction was concerned. The smith punched naught but air, receiving, instead, a blow to the chest from The Anther's pommel. Bent over in pain, the High King's knee rammed up into his face, sending him to the floor with a bloody nose.

At Glaive's feet, his breath momentarily stolen from his lungs, Grarfath spied a handful of armoured guards rushing in through the main doors. Yamnomora paused on her way to challenge the High King, her warrior's mind calculating where her violent talents were needed most. Drawing the dagger she had claimed as her own, Yamnomora stepped over Tharg's corpse—spitting on it as she did—and rooted herself between the oncoming guards and their sovereign.

"Another step, lads, an' I'll throw ye a beatin'," she warned.

Without plate or a significant weapon, they failed to see her as a threat, their charge never faltering. Grarfath couldn't see Yamnomora's face, but he didn't need to in order to know the dwarf was grinning. She dipped low, tackling the first of the guards about his waist. One deft flip launched him over her shoulders and onto his back, where Kitrana Voden was already waiting to deliver a solid heel to the face.

The stubborn dwarf grabbed another by the leg and twisted his knee out of place, bringing him down where she could cut across his face with an elbow. "Get The Anther!" she yelled back at the smith.

Kitrana slipped her toes under the edge of a fallen sword and flicked it up into her waiting hand. Suitably armed, the battle maiden added a secondary line of defence, intercepting those who got past Yamnomora. They were doing their job so Grarfath could do his.

Rising to his feet, he stood face to face with High King Glaive, his wife and son now taking shelter behind one of the thrones. The older dwarf unclasped his cloak and shrugged it from his ornate pauldrons, grinning as he did.

"The Greyhelms 'ave survived every catastrophe to befall our people. Every civil war. Every natural disaster. Who are *ye* to bring us down, smith?"

The High King's question struck Grarfath in a way he hadn't anticipated. Who was he, truly, to stand there and challenge the descendant of kings? How, even, had he come to stand in the heart of Khardunar, Morthil's most ancient source of power?

However reluctant he was to hear the answer, it came to him from a recent memory, the words carried by Yamnomora's voice.

"*Ye're not gettin' it, are ye?*" she had said, huddled around the fire in the cold ruins of Tor Valan. "*Ye're the Hammerhold now.*"

Upon the death of his mother, that weighty title had been passed to him. It wasn't a question of whether he liked it or not, he now realised. It was a question of what he was he going to do about it.

Grarfath wiped the blood from his moustache. "I'm the Hammerhold," he declared boldly. "An' *that* belongs to me."

Glaive glanced at The Anther. "Come an' get it then."

The smith bolted forwards. Any disbelief that he was actually fighting the High King of Morthil was numbed by a simple instinct: he would have to kill if he wanted to survive.

Glaive wasn't to make it easy. He sidestepped with the grace of a lighter, younger dwarf and rolled The Anther up into Grarfath's gut, lifting him to his tip-toes. A swift kick to the hip reunited the smith with the lavish floor, sending him tumbling over his limbs.

Not to be deterred by his lack of fighting skill, Grarfath picked himself up and roared in defiance as he attacked again. At the last second, he leaped and came down on the High King with a knotted fist that boasted boulders for knuckles. Glaive took the blow squarely on his jaw and reeled, spitting blood as he pivoted to regain his footing.

Grarfath's powerful arms were just getting started.

Before his foe could swing the hammer, he thrust a fist into Glaive's kidney once, twice, and a third time up into his nose. The High King grunted in pain before he landed on his back and groaned, his entire weight having come down on his spine.

With a jolt of confidence, Grarfath advanced on his enemy, believing—as any brawler would—that a prone opponent was as good as beaten. But when he got close enough, Glaive twisted his legs about one of the smith's and scissored him at the knee, bringing him down and into a jab from The Anther. Grarfath's head snapped back, and he crumpled at the base of the dais that housed the thrones.

"Ye've a good arm," Glaive complimented him on his way back to his feet. "A pity ye've no idea what to do with it."

Grarfath didn't see the kick, but he felt the impact slam into his ribs and shove him onto the dais itself. He rolled in pain, grunting and moaning, watched all the while by Glaive.

"It's fittin', I suppose," the High King mused, booting Grarfath a second time. "The first dwarf to call 'imself the Hammerhold was slain in this very chamber, an' by me own blood no less. Maybe that's the *real* legacy o' the Hammerhold. To die at the hands o' a Greyhelm."

The smith reached out, his fingers finding the pile of gems and coins amassed about Glaive's throne. As The Anther came up—a promise of doom—Grarfath rolled over and threw the handful of treasures, striking the High King in his round face. He cried out, eyes shut tight, and missed the smith by an inch, the hammer cracking the floor instead.

Grasping the haft, Grarfath launched a boot up into Glaive's gut and parted him from the weapon of power. As the High King staggered back and, ultimately, fell over, the smith used the throne to pick himself up. The prince started forward to challenge him, but his mother, the queen, held him back with both hands. Bloody and bruised, Grarfath ignored the young fool and closed the gap, The Anther scraping across the floor behind him.

"All me life I've lived in the shadow o' someone else's legacy. Me father. Me mother," he added, a recent addition given all her work to eliminate the Skaramangians. "I'm not to be livin' in Duun's an all," he declared with some fatigue. "I think I'll forge me own path. Startin' with the end o' yer wretched reign."

Quicker than it seemed possible for a dwarf of his size, Glaive sprang to his feet and charged, grabbing the haft of the hammer before it could strike. His grip was stubbornly firm, preventing Grarfath from snatching it back.

"Did ye really think a bit o' grit an' a few words would give ye the strength to actually beat me?" the High King rasped in his face. He yanked The Anther towards him, pulling Grarfath into ranger to land a devastating headbutt.

The smith lost his vision just long enough to miss his own fall. He now lay on his back, looking up at Glaive.

"Ye've spent all yer life hammerin' steel." The High King kicked him in the face, rolling him over. "It's a little different when the steel hammers back, eh? Did ye think all 'em guards standin' abou' were 'ere to protect me?" He barked a laugh. "They're 'ere to protect what I represent: the power o' Morthil!" Another boot found Grarfath's ribs, shooting pain through his chest. "I've been fightin' since I could walk, son o' Thronghir. I don' need no protection."

"I'll be the judge of that."

Slait was less than a second behind his own words, each of his powerful arms coiling around the neck of the queen and prince. They thrashed to no avail, their struggle at an end when The Dawn Sword twisted his arms and snapped their necks simultaneously.

Glaive cried out, his roar somewhere between rage and heartbreak. Abandoning Grarfath, he ran across the dais and swung for his pale foe. With one hand, Slait grabbed The Anther, preventing the weapon from completing its swing, and with the other, he gripped the High King by the throat. The smith could hardly fathom the strength required to lift a dwarf bodily from the floor, let alone with the power of a single arm.

Glaive's eyes bulged in his thick head, his gaze beyond the hulking Andaren, looking at where his wife and son lay dead on the floor.

"You have betrayed your oaths to the order," Slait condemned, bringing Glaive's attention back to him. "You have forsaken the path of the Skaramangian. You have abandoned your fealty to The Eldan."

The High King squirmed and writhed, his feet kicking out uselessly. He relinquished his grip on The Anther and tried futilely to peel The Dawn Sword's fingers from his neck.

"In so doing," Slait continued, and without a hint of strain in his voice, "you have placed yourself in opposition to the gods. I was put on this earth to slay any and all who do so."

Glaive managed to prise just enough of Slait's grip away to utter broken words. "The... Eldan... has... lied to you."

"You think you deserve last words?"

"There... are... no... gods."

Slait's anger flared—a terrifying sight. He dropped The Anther and wrapped both hands around Glaive's skull. For the rest of his life, Grarfath knew he would never forget the sound of the High King's death. His garbled wail of agony. The *crunch* and *crack* of his imploding skull. The wet *splatter* of blood. Then the quietude of death itself, Glaive's body having made its final sound.

Surviving on instincts, something told Grarfath to claim The Anther. He scrambled behind Slait and rolled aside the moment he felt the cold steel in his hand. The Dawn Sword was already upon him and would have ensnared him had he not rolled away so swiftly. His reach, however, was not to be underestimated. A long, powerful leg shot out, launching the smith from the dais and across the polished floor.

As the dwarf landed, so too did the hammer several feet away, shattering an ornate vase before coming to a stop. Light of foot was The Dancing Sword of the Dawn, his advance seen, not heard. Grarfath spied the behemoth through the strands of his scattered dreadlocks. That grit he had previously found seemed so far away now, his conviction dwindling.

"I'm the Hammerhold," he muttered under his breath, his right fist steadily clenching into a knot.

"It is a blasphemy that you would wield The Anther," Slait was saying as he came to stand over the smith.

Grarfath responded with action, coming up by the lead of his fist. His first two slugs caught The Dawn Sword in the gut, and he ended his combo with a solid punch across the jaw. Slait took it all, his tongue exploring the cut on his lip.

The backhand was so swift that the smith wasn't entirely convinced his enemy had moved. Still, he flew into a pedestal and found himself partially buried beneath a suit of armour, a great pain lancing through his cheekbone.

"I'm going to enjoy killing you, dwarf—"

Slait broke off, turning towards the sound of steel scraping across the floor.

Doing his best to find his feet, Grarfath watched as Kitrana

Voden picked up the fabled hammer. Curiously, she paid The Dawn Sword no heed, her attention fixed solely on the smith.

Sudden and deep was the pit that opened up inside of Grarfath. It was her eyes. Everything he needed to know could be found there.

"*I'm so sorry,*" the Nimean uttered.

"No!" both Grarfath and Slait cried in unison.

But there was no stopping The Anther as it thundered into the floor at her feet.

39
THE DRUMS

Through shadow and slivers of cool moonlight, a soaking-wet ranger scaled the Padoshi's fortified home. Any handholds were few and far between, and all of them shallow, but the Kedradi had spent much of his youth climbing the sheer cliffs of The Gold Rise in Erador's south, where his people had made their home in the desert lands of Qalanqath. With experienced fingers and toes, he made short work of the hewn stone.

His ascent was made all the easier thanks to Galahart's distraction in the north, where the Padoshi's treasures were at risk. There were none to greet him on the rampart nor any to spy him on the other side, where his hands and feet braced into the corner of the compound to control his quiet descent. Cob landed in a well-maintained garden of low hedges and thick rows of flowers.

Had his mission not required some urgency and no lack of stealth, he might have paused to admire the arrangement and their combined scent. Such natural beauty did not readily occur in the baked lands of Qalanqath—a beauty he had come to silently appreciate since venturing into Erador's north, where nature had more opportunity to blossom.

The sound of barking orders sharpened his attention, directing him beyond the garden. He pressed his back to a wall, where the corner sheltered him from those stationed inside the compound's entrance. Under shelter, in the gloom of a few torches, the Padoshi's thugs were being ordered to different stations about the compound. They were all of them unaware of the wolf that had already entered the pen.

"Quit your moaning and get moving!" the one in charge yelled. "I don't want any blind spots!"

"Come on, Dagnar," a lazy thug complained. "There's no one crazy enough to attack this place."

"Well there's someone crazy enough to attack the gallery," Dagnar countered. "You all heard Mr Grim. We're to lock this place down."

Cob reached for the dagger of Wither bone on his belt. The curved blade was slender, like the talon of a bird, only its edge had been worked to produce a line of sharp bone. His hand was drawn to the three feathers hanging from the weapon's pommel. As he would, he made to rub one of them between his finger and thumb —a ritualistic habit.

The ranger stopped before gripping the feathers.

His fingers were trembling.

Looking down at his hand, Cob observed the constant vibration that ran through the digits. Seconds later, he began to feel the tremor working up his knuckles and into his hand.

How long had it been since he had spilled blood?

The number of days didn't matter. The answer was *too long*. Within minutes, he knew, his other hand would experience the same thing. Then both of his arms would succumb to the tremors, and his entire body would follow soon after. How many times had he seen his father go through the same thing before the seizure took him?

It only got worse after that, when the madness sank in.

Flashes of memory pressed upon him, taking him back to the halls of his youth. He, again, watched from a hiding spot while his father raged and spread destruction about their home. He would shout at people only he could see and hear, blaming them for his plight. To this day, Cob had never seen anything more terrifying than his father's anger, a white flame that burned only to destroy.

The Kedradi's mind was returned to the present by a familiar sound. He knew without question that he alone could hear it.

The drums.

They beat like the call to war in his chest. Always they followed in the wake of the first tremor—a countdown to madness. The rhythm would only increase, drowning out the sounds of the world like blood pumping in his ears. What began as a single drum soon grew to a chorus, demanding he take action.

There was only one way to beat back the curse placed upon his ancestors. Only one way to satiate it. Drawing the dagger, he clenched the hilt until his dark knuckles paled.

A rapid beat found his ears, a pitch too high to be the drums that *boomed* in his mind. It was the sound of a wooden staff knocking on the compound's large doors—specifically, the normal-sized door situated inside one of the larger doors.

The chatter and hubbub in the entrance came to a sudden stop. "Who in the hells is that?" one of them asked.

Cob heard a sword being drawn.

"Out of the way," Dagnar commanded. "No one's getting in here tonight."

Again, the entrance resounded with the sharp knocking of a wooden staff.

"Whoever you are," Dagnar called out, his hand moving the narrow slider at eye level, "you can piss off—"

The distinct sound of steel plunging through skin and bone was the only signal Cob needed. If the beat of the drums in his mind was anything to go by, it wasn't a moment too soon.

He rounded the corner and broke into a dead run. The surprise barely had time to register on the face of his first victim, who suffered a deep slash across his throat. As he fell to his knees, eyes bulging and hands gripped to his bleeding throat, so too did Dagnar fall back like a plank of wood, a dark pitted wound where his left eye had been.

Having well and truly invaded the entrance interior now, Cob grabbed one thug's shoulder and used him to leap up and run around the corner wall, bringing his boot arcing round into another's face. In time with the drums, he felt the impact against his foot and then again when his body hit the ground. The thug whose own body had supported the ranger never had the chance to retaliate, his torso slashed twice in rapid succession before the Wither bone was driven into his heart.

Two more came for the Kedradi, lunging with swords. The angle and timing of both attacks was a matter of calculation—one Cob was quite proficient in. The ranger had only to pivot once, his shoulders and hips twisted deliberately to see him evade both blades at the same time while also bringing him into striking distance with his shorter dagger.

Up went the Wither bone, pushing through the soft pallet beneath the jaw before going on to deliver a mortal blow to the thug's brain. Even as he fell to the ground, the Kedradi was already ramming the last of them into the wall, stabbing the man relentlessly in the face as he did. By the time he impacted the wall he was dead, unable to do anything but slide down the stone in a puddle of his own blood.

The drums continued to beat into every crevice of his mind, the *boom... boom... boom...* gripping his very bones. The curse demanded more before it would let him enjoy some semblance of sanity.

"Are you quite done?" Androma asked from the other side of the doors.

"Not even close," he muttered to himself.

He opened the door for her, and the old Rider passed over the threshold with a blood-soaked knife. "Very good," Androma praised evenly. "All without the ring of steel," she added, a hint of admiration in her voice. "I'd say our arrival went unheard."

"Getting in was the easy part," he reminded her.

With one hand clinging to his arm, Androma followed the ranger's lead as they navigated the gardens and made their way towards the main building inside the Padoshi's walls. They stopped once in the shadows beside a large statue, where they waited for one of the sparse patrols to pass them by on the ramparts above. The Kedradi hated waiting, the curse insisting that he scale the wall and eliminate the two men.

"There's a lot of activity inside," Androma said, focusing him.

Cob's gaze wandered over the numerous windows, all illuminated by candlelight, and saw what the old Rider could hear. "The bulk of the guards left behind are securing the main house," he reported. "There looks to be a lot of servants too. That's a lot of eyes to avoid."

"I don't care!" boomed a deep voice from inside one of the chambers. "I want everyone down there! Find who did this and bring them to me!"

Cob placed an arm across Androma and pulled her back in line with him, concealing them further in shadow as the doors to the main house were flung open. A group of thugs strode out into the night.

"Make it very clear when you see Mr Grim," that deep voice called after them, halting the group on the path, "I want whoever did this *alive!*"

"As you command," one of the men replied before the doors to the house slammed shut again.

"This has got Galahart's stench all over it," one of the thugs concluded. "Spread the word. I want him found."

Androma tightened her grip on Cob's arm. "They will discover the bodies," she whispered.

Cob glimpsed the group between the planted trees, counting six in total. Killing six armed men without attracting attention was a near-impossible task.

"*Cloak yourself in chaos,*" his first tutor had instructed him all those years ago, "*but do not get pulled into it. You are to be the eye of the storm—not the storm itself.*"

It had taken him a long time to grasp the meaning behind his mentor's words, a master amongst sword masters. Now, with nearly forty years behind him, the ranger knew exactly how to orchestrate a storm from its quiet heart.

Without warning, he abandoned the shadows, entering the thugs' midst with no more than a calm step. He dropped the first after running his dagger across his throat—a silent death that would not alert the two in the lead. As great alarm spread amongst the other three, he launched the Wither bone with a casual backhand, sending it directly into the heart of the nearest one.

As both men fell, the ranger was already pivoting, his scimitar of Draven bone coming up in one hand. His feet executed the twist and his hips followed round. As did the swinging scimitar. The two who had witnessed his brutal attack went down one after the other, their faces torn asunder by the blade's curved edge.

As Death claimed them for its own, the two thugs in the lead were just turning around, terror deforming their expressions as they reached for the swords on their belts.

It was no use. Their reaction time was poor at best and the fear that had already gripped their hearts prevented them from taking evasive action. A swift jab to the throat prevented one from crying out, while a hammer blow from the scimitar cracked the skull of the other, silencing him forever. A final, two-handed strike removed most of the survivor's head, adding his body to the rest.

For a time, there was only the sound of Cob's breathing. To the Kedradi, it competed with the ever-present drums that were only just beginning to fade. He had spilled more than enough blood already, but the curse was always slower to dissipate than it was to come on.

Confident that the brief fight had gone unnoticed, missed by those who had wandered much further along the ramparts, the ranger moved the bodies from the path, retrieved his dagger, and returned to the shadowed gardens in search of Androma. To his irritation, the old Rider was no longer there. He hissed her name, his search taking him back to the path and dangerously close to the main house.

A light tap of her staff directed him to the collection of buildings south of the main house. There he found her beside a wall, her hand pressed flat to the stone, head tilted to one side.

"We need to find a way inside," he said, careful not to chastise the legendary warrior for wandering off.

"Our friends are not in there," she replied, nodding her head at the main house. She made a point of sniffing the air. "Perfume, food, sweat. I am following a fouler scent," she explained, turning her sightless eyes towards one of the buildings to the south.

"Of course he has his own dungeon," Cob remarked.

Being made of bars, the door did nothing to contain the putrid odour leaking out of the dungeon. Cob knew the smell, detecting the decay of flesh and notes of human waste. Under it all was the heady scent of blood.

"Who in the hells are you?"

It seemed to Cob that the guard had been on the verge of a nap when they entered unannounced. The ranger nodded at the only other door inside the entrance, quick to adopt the part of a Padoshi thug.

"The boss wants to see the prisoners," he answered gruffly, a response made only to bide time while the guard rose from his chair to block their path.

The man scowled up at the Kedradi. "I don't know you. And who in the hells is she?"

Cob's hand snapped up, striking the guard in the throat. As the man's head dipped forwards, his ability to breathe taken from him in an instant, the ranger reached out with both hands and yanked sharply to the right. *Crack.* His neck broken, the guard fell dead at Cob's feet, where the ranger was able to easily retrieve the keys from his belt.

Eleven men had died since he had entered the Padoshi's grounds, and still he heard the drums resounding in the back of his mind. Since Androma couldn't see, he raised his left hand, monitoring for any tremor. It was still there, but at least it appeared to be contained.

Beyond the other door lay a spiralling set of steps that led down into the compound's foundations. A place where the sun could never bring the hope of a new day.

The smell only got worse as they descended. The walls were damp, and the ceiling dripped with cold water. It wasn't a particularly large dungeon, able to house no more than a dozen prisoners at a squeeze.

In the gloom, Cob searched the cells between the bars. There was certainly evidence of previous prisoners, the floors and walls smeared with blood and excrement. It was so damn cold that the Kedradi would have been surprised to learn any prisoners survived long enough to be tormented by the cruel Padoshi.

"It's alright," came a light voice from the corner. "You're going to be alright. You'll see. Everything will be just fine."

"Green Leaf?" Androma called out.

Movement directed Cob to the cell in the northwest corner, where the shadows were thickest. There they found them, their companions huddled together in the far corner. They were both freezing, their limbs trembling. Both were pale, haggard from their rough incarceration, though Gallien fared the worst. He was so pale he might have been a living corpse, his clothes and blond beard splattered with blood.

The ranger's gaze was drawn to the smuggler's right hand—or rather, where it should have been. The bloody stump was layered in green cloth, the strips evidently torn from Aphrandhor's robes.

"Androma?" the wizard cried. "Cob!"

Using the keys he had taken, the Kedradi opened the cell gate and rushed inside to aid them. While he still possessed something of a limp, The Green Leaf was able to rise on his own and assist Cob in picking up Gallien.

"He wanted the axe," the smuggler rasped, finding the ranger's dark eyes. "I did what you said," he continued, lips trembling. "I couldn't make it go away."

Cob glanced at Gallien's wrist. How much harder his life would now be. He looked at the smuggler again, his previous prejudices melting away as he was forced to reassess the man and what he had lost in their fight against the enemy.

"You did well," he told him earnestly. "You did well."

"Are you hurt?" Androma asked, her free hand exploring the wizard's face.

"I have suffered no more than rough hands," The Green Leaf said. "And they could not see the bracer for what it is," he added, holding up his arm. "How did you find us?"

"A mutual friend," the old Rider explained cryptically.

"Galahart?" Aphrandhor queried incredulously.

"He has his uses," Androma admitted by way of confirmation.

"We have to get out of here," the smuggler urged, his gaze distant and unfocused.

"Galahart has secured us a ship," Cob informed him, one arm wrapped around Gallien's waist to guide him. "It will take us to Caster Hold."

Despite how cold he was, Gallien's face was dripping with sweat by the time they had ascended the stairwell. Cob sat him down on the only available chair while he helped Aphrandhor search the racks, chests, and cabinets on the far side of the chamber. There they found the smuggler's sword and leather cloak, along with the wizard's belongings, including his staff and blade, Yalaqin.

"My bag," Gallien rasped, glancing at the satchel hanging by its strap.

Androma found it with her probing hand and slung it over the smuggler's head and shoulder.

"Can you help him?" Cob enquired in hushed tones, his eyes darting from The Green Leaf's staff to Gallien.

"I was never much of a healer," Aphrandhor confessed. "Furthermore, there is still much unknown in that field of magic. I have witnessed disastrous side effects to both parties."

The Kedradi nodded his understanding and ushered the smuggler to his feet. "Our ship leaves at dawn, with or without us," he warned.

When Gallien failed to lift his sword, the weight of it too much for him, Androma stepped in and sheathed it on the smuggler's belt. "I will help him," she said, as if she could see the apprehension in the ranger's expression.

"Stay behind me," Cob instructed them all, his hands removing both his bow and an arrow from over one shoulder.

Outside, they stepped under a twilight sky as the sun pushed back the veil of night. How peaceful the sunrise was, unaware yet of the blood that had been spilled in its absence. To Cob's relief, it rose in silence, the cursed drums pounding inside his skull now mercifully gone.

"This way," he bade, his arrow nocked.

Gallien stopped, halting them all. With true hate, he looked upon the Padoshi's main house, his gaze wandering from window to window.

"We have to leave," Androma insisted.

"He's in there," the smuggler whispered, murder in his eyes.

Cob placed a hand against Gallien's chest, drawing his attention. "That fight is for another day."

Given what they were up against, it seemed an agonising age before the smuggler reluctantly nodded his head.

Their departure was significantly slower than their infiltration. Aphrandhor limped, his staff making even more noise than Androma's, which tapped incessantly across the stone path. Added to what sounded like a cacophony in Cob's ears, Gallien coughed every few steps, his wounded arm cradled close to his chest. And damned if the main gates didn't seem so far away.

They managed to pass the six corpses the ranger had hidden before the alarm was raised. It came from the ramparts, though it appeared the guard had spied the bodies left in the main entrance. Still, his cry had reached the Padoshi's dwelling, where it sparked new activity. As the man came running along the rampart, he inevitably spotted the four companions and even pointed at them, his lips parting to shout as much. The arrow that found him sank deep into his chest, robbing him of his voice before it claimed his life.

Looking back, the doors to the main house were, again, flung open to reveal a fresh group of killers on the Padoshi's payroll. Nocking another arrow, Cob took aim, finding the narrow gap between Aphrandhor and Gallien. With a satisfying *twang,* and the group of killers was reduced by one.

"Keep going!" the ranger insisted, letting his companions pass him.

"We leave together," Androma asserted.

"Go!" Cob snapped, setting another arrow to his bowstring.

As the trio continued their slow escape, the Kedradi added another death to his tally. The arrow caught its target in the face, springing him back in a dramatic flip. By the time he had nocked another arrow, the remaining thugs had seen sense and scattered, abandoning the path altogether. Cob replaced the bow over his head and unclipped the Draven scimitar from his belt.

From within the maze of tall hedges they came at him, each a harbinger of their master's vengeance. Yet Cob danced around them, pivoting and weaving without a single counterattack. Besides dizzying them, he was ensuring greater chaos by allowing them to amass about him. None of them had received any kind of formal training, let alone training on how to work together as an effective unit. They bashed into each other, their swords and axes colliding in their failed attempts to kill the ranger. Some even tripped up, meeting the path before another accidentally kicked them in the face.

When he was ready, when he had taken the measure of each fighter, the last son of House Thayne unleashed his many years of strict tutelage. His scimitar, carved from the rib bone of an adult Draven, stood up to the strength of their steel with ease. He batted and deflected their blades aside, his shoulder cloak and battle skirt spinning with him as he dashed from foe to foe.

"You must flow through battle as the river flows through the rock," his oldest instructor had told him. *"Always moving, the water cannot be stopped."*

Cob hardly registered the men dying around him. He would strike with his scimitar and move on, always deflecting and attacking a new opponent. Eventually, he was stepping over bodies and faced with fewer and fewer men. As the last of them hit the ground, his cry ended with the fall of his scimitar, the ranger heard the discharge of magic from further down the path.

Beyond the hedges, Cob watched as another of the Padoshi's thugs flew as high as the ramparts. A *crack* of lightning illuminated the entrance before smoke could be seen rising into the early morning air. The Kedradi broke into a run, a fact that saved his life from the incoming arrows. Two of them—from the ramparts to the north. The archers hounded him down the path, firing haphazardly as they did.

While the arrows still searched for him, Cob exploded into the compound's main entrance. Only two of those who had opposed the trio remained on their feet, a number that was cut in half when the ranger leaped and came down with a solid fist, clubbing the thug in the centre of his face.

As he struck the wall and fell into unconsciousness, Androma pinned the last of them to the large door with her staff. A quick horizontal shove from the Andaren spear collapsed the man's windpipe before she whipped the end of it across his face.

Gallien had stood slumped against the interior wall for the duration, his head resting against the stone. There was no fight left in the smuggler, his strength sapped by blood loss.

"The door," Cob instructed, looking at The Green Leaf.

One blast from his staff blew the small door from its hinges, leaving the large gates with a significant hole in their defensive capabilities.

"I just meant open it," the ranger commented, guiding Gallien back into Androma's care.

Aphrandhor shrugged in a half-hearted apology. "The Padoshi is lucky this is *all* the damage I've wrought."

On the streets of Thedaria again, Cob turned back to the compound, his bow having already replaced his scimitar. The two archers who had harassed him from the ramparts were now atop the gates and taking aim.

With many more years of practice under his belt than they had, the Kedradi required less than half the time the Padoshi's thugs needed. His arrow sailed high, plunging into the head of one before either had fired. The death of his comrade was enough to see the surviving man take cover and stay there.

"Go!" Cob hissed, pointing down the river.

There was a search party on their tail almost immediately. Slow as they were, and not wishing to leave a trail of bodies in their wake, the companions were forced to duck into alleys and hide behind crates and carts. For a short time, they tried to lose their pursuers in the streets about the great mansions and towers. Time, however, was against them. Doubling back on themselves, they made for the river once more.

There were too many ships and boats to count along The Treeling's shores, but only one had its crew flying about the deck. Along its port side, *The Raven* was painted in bold white.

"This is it," Cob said, waiting at the base of the ramp, ensuring that the other three made it on board.

A broad figure barred the way, his hands resting on his hips. "Gallien Drakalis," the man voiced with a drawl.

For the first time since being rescued, the smuggler's expression something other than blank exhaustion. "Addison," he croaked miserably, a scowl pulling at his brow.

"Get him on board and be quick about it," Addison commanded, stepping aside while his gaze surveyed the streets beyond. "The last thing I need is one of the Padoshi's fellas seeing you in *my* company. We make good coin here."

The companions shuffled onto the ship's deck, where Androma managed to keep Gallien upright, biting into his energy reserves.

The Raven's captain noted his severed hand, eliciting a chuckle from the big man. "Still pissing people off, are we? Mr Gibson!" he called before Androma could return stern words. "Bring me the sea!"

"Aye, Captain!"

As the sun peeked over The Spine of Erador, Cob watched the city of Thedaria pull away to the fading echo of drums. How long before the countdown began again? Madness was always coming for him. Given that Taraktor was to be their destination, he mused, perhaps madness was coming for them all.

40
A NEW PATH

Upon entering Valgala's war room, Joran had craned his neck to take it all in. While only a fraction of the size of the throne room, it still possessed a grand space, including a second floor. Like the ground floor, it was occupied solely by books and scrolls and the occasional table on which to peruse them. The late afternoon bathed the whole chamber in light, the waning sun flooding in through the tall arching window in the far wall.

How quickly the war room had crowded, and all about the largest table that dominated the heart of the ground floor. Dozens of eyes scrutinised that table and the three-dimensional map carved out of the original wood. Like the king's many advisers, Joran examined the map of Erador and Andara, looking specifically at the forces of red and white placed upon it.

A collection of white statues stood in The Silver Trees of Akmar —the Andarens. The red statues were split, the king's men stationed predominantly outside the city of Freygard, far north of the capital. It had been explained early on in the meeting that those battalions had been ordered forth from Valgala itself to meet the invasion beyond The Spine, believing that the Andarens intended to follow the road south, attacking as they pushed on. What remained of Erador's forces were positioned in Caster Hold, along with the fleet.

Joran's attention was drawn across The Drifting Sea, just north of Caster Hold. There he saw the city of Harendun, where he had been born in the middle of a siege. Standing upon the city was a small collection of grey statues. He recalled an earlier conversation with Galahart, though not the one currently standing beside the king. Conversing with Androma, the other spymaster had revealed that Harendun now sat as a fiefdom all of its own under the rule of Vander, a Dragon Rider who answered only to Baelon.

A man the king had referred to as General Dorrick, pointed at the Andaren forces in Akmar with one liver-spotted hand. "Their only move is south, Your Grace. Their army will require resources and supplies after such a journey, not to mention their conflict with the Jainus. If we send word to our men in the north," he suggested, gesturing at the red statues outside of Freygard, "we can have them double back and..." The general sighed. "I'm loathe to order such a force through the mountain pass, but The Misted Road would allow us to amass at Thedaria. I would advise moving the men from Caster Hold at the same time," he added, directing everyone's attention to the hook of land in the west. "Both forces could pincer the enemy as they advance south, beyond Akmar."

The king was nodding along, clearly in agreement. He might even have said as much if Kassanda hadn't interjected. Standing directly opposite General Dorrick, the Dragon Rider reached out and moved the white forces, positioning them north of The Giant's Throat.

"What if the enemy moves north instead?" she posed, glancing at the spymaster. Galahart's expression was unreadable, but he was subtly shaking his head—she was not to speak of the Skaramangians.

"North?" the general blurted, a touch of amusement about him. "That would prove a massive waste of energy and supplies.

They're on Thedaria's doorstep," he pointed out. "If we don't move our forces now, we *will* lose the city."

"The Andarens have not come to invade," Kassanda reported to the gathered council. "If that had truly been their intention, they would have followed the northern road and attacked Drayshon before going on to Freygard."

"Forgive me, Rider," General Dorrick cut in, "but you don't send an entire army if your intention is *not* to invade."

"They sent an army to ensure their success. And they sent an army to see that it was not short-lived."

The old general scowled at her before looking at the others crowded around the table. "Do all Riders speak in riddles?"

"General Dorrick," the king intoned. "Kassanda Grey is a Dragon Rider. Afford her the respect of such a title."

The highborn general looked to have a problem with his jaw, though he managed a bow of the head. "Apologies, Your Grace" he said. "I only wish to understand your *guest*."

Kassanda didn't respond right away, her dark eyes locked with those of the king, a silent question posed in the Rider's expression. The king looked to consider the request before responding with a curt nod. At this, the spymaster closed his eyes, a look of exasperation about him.

"The Andarens were quite deliberate in taking their southern route," she explained. "Their target was never more than The Silver Trees of Akmar. Therein lies a source of magic they intend to return to their warlocks in Andara."

"A source of magic?" the general was quick to question.

Joran looked at his mentor, wondering just how much she would divulge. It was eminently possible the Skaramangians had eyes and ears inside that very room.

"There is a reason the Jainus have long held sway over that region, General Dorrick. You will have to take up the specifics with them. But know that source of power now lies in the hands of the enemy. They will depart our lands with it and increase their arsenal of magic."

"Kassanda speaks the truth," the king said before a series of questions could leave the general's lips. "Mistress Marinen is yet to return, but she has gone in search of answers from the Magus. Given their regard for The Silver Trees, I would imagine a cadre of wizards has already been issued from The Tower of Jain. I can't imagine they will send enough, however, to defeat an army so vast."

"They might not even catch them if they're moving north," Galahart added.

The king looked to Kassanda. "You said you have a strategy in mind?"

"Yes, Your Grace," she answered. "Their path north remains clear—we can do nothing to catch them." The Rider began moving the statues, placing the Andarens on the strip of land between White Tower and The Watchtower of Argunsuun. "Our only hope is to delay them, preventing them from crossing back into Andara." She repositioned the red statues in Caster Hold, pushing them north through the waters of The Deep until they stood beside the Andarens.

"At the same time," she continued, using a stick to move the forces collected outside Freygard, "we flank the enemy. By sea and by land, we can box them in and reclaim the source of magic before they cross into Andara."

The general didn't argue immediately, his eyes narrowed in thought while his gloved hand cupped his well-trimmed goatee. "Our numbers in Caster Hold are not so great," he admitted. "We would be pitting a considerably smaller force against the might of the Andaren army. There's every chance they would be crushed before we flank them."

Kassanda glanced at Joran before addressing the problem. "They will not hold the line alone. Garganafan and I will accompany them."

This seemed to surprise the general, even please him. "It has been some time since a dragon has flown into battle. It will be like the old days."

And so the discussions and possible variations on their

strategy continued, each of the king's advisors contributing something from their unique perspective. They all did so between stares at Joran. It was clear his mother's heritage was a distraction, lumping the young man with a sense of unease. He wished to draw his hood and conceal his pointed ears and white hair, to disappear from sight altogether. It was only Kassanda's words that kept him at the table.

"A dragon does not hide what they are."

Still, Joran used the mingling at the end of the meeting to slip away, keen to be unseen for a time. He glanced back at Kassanda, making certain her conversation with two of the advisors was distraction enough. Departing the war room, it was only a short corridor and a single stairwell back to the throne room. He entered via the same door the king had used when first they met, bringing him out onto the circular floor.

As before, his eyes were drawn up to the colossal statues that stood inside the ring of tall pillars. The kings of old looked down on him, their long shadows cast across the floor and the tiered rows at their feet. The wind infiltrated the chamber, blowing through the gaps between the pillars and picking up Joran's sandy cloak as he approached the throne of Erador.

How, Joran wondered, had he come to be in this place? It seemed only yesterday he had been working in the kitchen of The Brass Giant, Gallien beside him. Now, with a Rider's cloak on his back and their boots on his feet, he looked upon the throne.

As unbelievable as it was, his thoughts drifted back to Gallien. Where was he now? What was he doing? Was he still in Androma's company? Was he still fighting for the cause, or had he finally got his life back?

While Joran desired the answers, he was just glad in his heart that Gallien had survived The Ruins of Gelakor, that somewhere out there in the world, he lived. He had given up so much to keep Joran safe all those years. Didn't he deserve a path of his own choosing?

In truth, Joran hoped selfishly that he had remained opposed to the Skaramangians, if only because such a path would likely reunite them someday.

His thoughts were banished when the door opened again, admitting the king this time. Alone, he paused upon sighting Joran. It seemed, if only for an instant, that he was relieved of all the burden he carried.

"Joran," he said, stepping into a strip of golden sunlight—the last of the day.

Suddenly conscious of his presence in the throne room, Joran bowed his head. "Apologies, Your Grace. I was..."

The king held up a hand. "There's no need to apologise. It's not easy having so many eyes on you, is it?"

"Most of them looked at me like I'm a spy," Joran remarked.

"Their great, great grandfathers were younger than you when the war started," the king replied. "I fear Andarens will always be their enemy, even when this is all said and done, Kaliban willing."

"You would make peace with Andara?" Joran enquired unthinkingly. It was so easy to forget he was talking to the king.

"It is my duty to always strive for peace," he said, wandering towards the steps that led up to his throne. "The alternative would see one or even both our peoples destroyed." He shook his head in despair. "You saw all those books, the ones lining the war room? I didn't grow up in the palace, so I haven't had nearly enough time to read them all. Those that I *have* read all say the same thing: the path to peace is forged through war." A pall of hopelessness came over him. "I have fought in this war. I can tell you, Joran, there is no peace to be found in it. Bloodshed begets bloodshed. It is my reasoning that peace—*real* peace—must be forged another way."

"The Skaramangians will never stand for peace," Joran stated. "Do you know of The Dark Ones, Your Grace?"

"I know the Skaramangians believe them to be more than legends. That they will fuel the war as long as it conceals their work to resurrect them. They are fanatics, Joran. I hold no stock in their beliefs. I only know that weeding them out is like trying to catch smoke. Then again, there's no prophecy about *me*. You're the one said to change it all."

Joran felt the atmosphere shift, as if they were finally getting to the reason the king had desired an audience with him. He didn't like it, recalling his mentor's words to Galahart.

"Joran's fate is in the hands of the Dragon Riders. It is not his place to meddle or manipulate."

"You're on a path foreseen to bring about a time of dragons," the king went on. "I understand the value in that. The Skaramangians fear them, and rightly so." The head of House Etragon paused, his attention wandering briefly over his ancestors before landing on Joran once more. "Is that what you want?"

Joran would have blurted the affirmative had he not been so surprised by the question. Of all people, he would have thought the King of Erador wouldn't want him to have a choice, lest he choose a path that allowed the war to continue.

"It is," he finally answered. "I will do what I must if it brings peace to *both* realms."

The king looked confused. "Peace? What does your destiny say of peace?" Seeing that Joran had been stumped, he added, "There seems to be an assumption—put on you by others, I assume—that a time of dragons will bring about peace."

Joran's focus was sharpened all the more in that moment. He had never taken that perspective before. And why would have? It had been Androma who had imparted it all to him, her own point of view skewed by her past.

"Do you know what was said that day?" the king enquired, sitting on the steps at the base of his throne. "Do you know what those poor souls voiced into the world before the Helm of Ahnir took their lives?"

Joran recalled Androma's words, realising then that they had been her accounts of the visions rather than what was actually declared.

The king, it seemed, was better informed, for he spoke the exact words into that, the grandest of chambers. "Only he who stands in the shadow of kings can bridge the broken circle. Only he can usher in a new age of heroes. Only he can bring about *a time of dragons.*"

In the wake of his rich voice, there was silence for a time as the words were absorbed by the white stone as much as by Joran.

"It speaks of peace," the boy insisted. "I don't know what all of it means, but... a new age of heroes. A time of dragons. Those are good things."

"You don't need heroes in a time of peace, Joran. Heroes are called upon in battle. Dragons are good peacekeepers," the king conceded. "They're also good at killing people by the thousands." He shook his head, ruffling his curls. "At what price will that peace be won? We know the helm shows many possible futures. Isn't there one where you don't have to raise up heroes? Where you don't have to lead armies into battle? Isn't there a future where just your very existence is enough to... *to bridge that broken circle?*"

Joran wasn't just confused, he was conflicted. Whether he was supposed to or not, he turned away from the king, his thoughts racing. He had never considered any other option. He had been excited at the idea of a destiny, of becoming a Dragon Rider, of being plucked from his lacklustre life on the road beside Gallien. Taking a breath to calm his thoughts, a single point came to mind —a question.

Slowly pivoting to face the king again, he asked, "How do you know what was said? You know it word for word." Putting the dots together, there seemed only one conclusion. "Did Androma tell you? No," he quickly answered for himself. "Androma said she had never met you."

"Androma," the king echoed, savouring her name like a fine wine. "Alas, I never had the pleasure. I have heard a lot about her though."

That was just as surprising as the king knowing one of the prophecies word for word. "From who?" Joran had to ask.

"The same person who told me about the Helm of Ahnir." The King of Erador said nothing for a moment, a warm smile spreading beneath his beard. "You have her eyes," he said softly.

Joran's thoughts and feelings immediately went numb. "You... You knew my mother?" It was all he could think to say.

"For a time," the king admitted. "Not nearly long enough," he added sadly.

There was a glaring conclusion staring Joran in the face, yet his mind was entirely unable to grasp the impossibility of it.

"Are you..." He didn't know how to voice it.

The king rose from the steps and descended to stand face to face with him. "Yes," he said, his voice little more than a breath. "I'm your father, Joran."

41
RIDDLES IN THE DARK

Kitrana Voden did what she could to fend off the dwarves of Morthil, the guards who fought under the banner of the Greyhelms. But damned if the stone bones weren't strong, their skin a tough leather and their armour bulky and all-encompassing. The Nimean found it to be a better tactic to present herself as an obstacle, slowing them down long enough for Yamnomora to do what she did best.

The sound of something heavy and metallic striking the floor turned her attention over one shoulder.

The High King, Glaive Greyhelm, lay dead before his throne. Such a small and pitiful thing he seemed in death. All the more so in the looming shadow of The Dawn Sword, his killer.

He would soon boast the same of Grarfath Underborn, who lay sprawled beneath a suit of antique armour. The dwarf was bruised and battered, though the smith had proven himself more than just that, for he was still alive where many warriors would have already perished.

But the son of Thronghir could not hold Kit's attention. On the other side of the polished floor, lying amongst pieces of a broken vase, was the source of what she had heard.

The Anther. A weapon of power. It was unattended.

In a word, the hammer was *freedom*.

It could take her far from that place, a place she had never intended to return to. Her journey to finding the sword of Skara had already gone sideways—perhaps even backwards, given her imprisonment at The Black Vault.

Kitrana thought then of that wretched hell. Of the Nimeans who toiled endlessly to dig through the rock so they might unleash the Leviathan for the Dread Queen. How many had died since her escape? How many more would die until she returned with the sword of Skara and eradicated the Merdian threat?

Her time on dry land had been so turbulent, and there had been times during her search for the broken blade that her life beneath the waves seemed a distant dream. But her years of captivity and torment were a recent memory that burned brightly in her mind. That was where she was needed. That was where *her* battlefield was. For too long she had been embroiled in the affairs of surface-dwellers. Their troubles were their own.

As a battle maiden, Kitrana Voden's duty had been to safeguard the sword of Skara for the sake of her culture. She would, again, wield that relic, the Nimean vowed. The broken sword would be found and reclaimed from Joran. Reforged, that which she had protected would help her to protect that which mattered most.

Her people.

Kit didn't even recall walking to the hammer, nor picking it up, yet suddenly there it was, in her hands. Slait and Grarfath looked at her, but it seemed the dwarf knew what she intended. So much of her argument melted away in the smith's gaze, and the Nimean was reminded of the lives at stake beyond her watery world. It wasn't selfish, she told herself. It was sacrifice.

"I'm so sorry," Kitrana uttered, wishing she could take the smith and even Yamnomora with her. But who among them could truly defeat The Dawn Sword? If she didn't go, at that very moment, he would slaughter them all.

Grarfath and Slait yelled as one in protest.

As The Anther swung up, the Nimean thought of Drakanan,

where the Aegre had taken Joran to fulfil his destiny. Only once had she walked upon The Dragon Path out of Drayshon. It had been many years ago, during her earliest exploits with Gallien. They had been investigating an ancient site south of the road, where she had hoped, as ever, to discover the broken blade of Skara. The great statues that lined the path every few hundred yards had captivated her imagination, embedding themselves in her memory for a time such as this.

The hammer slammed into the High King's floor and let loose a shockwave that revealed a glimmer of that distant and snowy path. But it was not enough to port the Nimean, and the effect faded, leaving her standing in the throne room, locked in the cold stare of Slait.

The Dancing Sword of the Dawn forgot all about Grarfath and strode towards her with murder in his eyes. The seconds that followed were precious and filled with more protests from the smith. Kitrana ignored them—ignored them all. There was no one but her in that chamber. And her *will*.

The Anther struck the ground once more, with all her strength and focus poured into it. Slait's purposeful stride turned into a dash, his long, powerful legs making short work of the distance between them.

Thoom!

A brilliant flash erased the throne room and Slait with it.

Kitrana stumbled forwards, The Anther slipping from her grip before she fell to her knees. Having ported several times now, the Nimean was able to recover and gather her wits enough to see the dragon standing in front of her.

Falling back, Kit scrambled across the broken ground, which was now a mix of polished marble, a vein of dwarven silvyr, and the hard rock of Erador's northern lands. All the while, she looked wide-eyed upon the looming dragon, its head and body coated in the snow that whipped across her face from the east.

Relief flooded through the Nimean when she saw the truth of it. A statue. One of many that lined the path to Drakanan.

Behind her, on the other side of the road, was another dragon statue, its body rising at least twenty feet from the ground so its neck and head could arch ominously over the path.

She had done it, then. The Anther had brought her back to her mission.

But at what cost? The question arose from nowhere and filled her mind with images of dwarves drowning in their homes. Of Grarfath and Yamnomora dying at the hands of Slait.

With some effort, the Nimean quashed the question and the thoughts that accompanied it. There was only the sword. First, she would follow The Dragon Path to Drakanan and reclaim the hilt from Joran. Without considering how hard that might actually be, Kit then thought about step two. Finding the broken blade.

Grarfath having the life choked out of him.

Yamnomora having her neck snapped.

Those images flashed before her eyes, a promise of the haunting regret that would follow her to the end of her days. She flung her head back and let loose a roar, her shame and duty colliding with such force that her emotions demanded an outlet.

Picking herself up, her bare feet crunching through the pebbles and snow, she collected The Anther and began her journey further north. Immune to the cold weather that plagued the region, the Nimean was able to put some thought into the elusive broken blade. Thankfully, those thoughts took her back to her earliest days as a battle maiden, a welcome distraction from what she had just left behind.

She could see the hilt so clearly in her mind, as it had been in the Temple of Atradon—the Water Maiden. What remained of its broken blade was partially buried in the stone of its personal podium, as if the hilt was always welcoming a hand to grip it. It never did, of course. The battle maidens, warriors from every culture under the waves, were to ensure the sword of Skara was never wielded again.

Kitrana could see the interior of that chamber as if she were currently floating in it. The domed ceiling had been carved from the rock shelf in which the temple was situated, its curved walls depicting the story of the fabled weapon. She knew well the tale of

Skara, the great warrior who had bested the Leviathans and brought peace to the water world. It was the last panel of relief that had interested her in the days that followed the Merdians' unprovoked attack.

The imagery depicted her own people, the Nimeans, meeting with a surface dweller on the shores of some unknown land. They were handing the broken blade to the stranger, the weapon presented ceremoniously in two hands. There was an inscription etched into the stone—the words exchanged on that fateful day.

"*The blade, broken for all, its power scattered to steal its sting,*" read the first line, supposedly voiced by one of the Nimeans.

"*The blade, broken for all, its power to be guarded in the eye of the king,*" the surface dweller had been recorded to reply.

Many philosophers from every culture under the sea had theorised on that response. Some debated the king in question, as there had been several beneath the waves at that time, while others believed he was referring to the King of Erador, if Erador had even been established at that time.

By now, it had become unpopular to theorise about it at all since the weapon had been broken and scattered for an important reason. To locate the blade was to put the entire world in danger.

It was only the Merdians' world Kitrana intended to put in danger. She vowed on The Dragon Path, there and then, that she would break the sword again when her people were free and their enemy defeated. The Nimean thought of the consequences should she do otherwise. The Dread Queen would use the sword of Skara to unleash the Leviathan, securing her rule and the dominion of all Merdians.

For hours she walked the path with that nightmare hanging over her—and what a thin path she had chosen to tread.

"One step at a time," she murmured to herself, her ears bombarded by the wind. She didn't even have the hilt yet, and the riddle concerning the blade's location remained a mystery.

In the eye of the king...

That single line had followed her all the years she had walked the surface. There had even been times during her imprisonment at The Black Vault wheen her mind had wandered while she picked at the stubborn rock. There was one place she had never searched for the broken blade, a place where only a handful of people were free to roam. The palace in Valgala. Perhaps the blade was hidden where only the King of Erador could see it? In his chambers or in view of his throne?

As she began to consider the insurmountable task of breaking into the palace, the landscape before her began to take shape through the falling snow. The cliffs rose high around her, presenting the Nimean with an enormous alcove set into the mountains, a horseshoe lined with vast caves from top to bottom.

Drakanan!

Kitrana instinctively moved to take shelter behind one of the great statues along the path. Blindly, it seemed, she had walked into a land of dragons—real ones. Her big eyes roamed over the curved cliff face, searching for any sign of the flying creatures or their Riders. It was eerily quiet, save for the incessant wind. Every cave entrance was pitch black.

The Nimean felt a presence settle over her, like a little fish caught in the sights of a predator. It was an instinct born of her ancestry, she knew, a trait of the Mer-folk—and not one to be taken lightly. Looking around, high and low, there was nothing to suggest that anyone—or *anything*—was observing her. Yet the feeling persisted.

Moving on, Kit dashed from statue to statue, always pausing to reassess her surroundings. She heard something in the wind. The sky offered naught but thick rolling clouds and more snow. What had she heard? It came again, like the billowing of a cloak caught in a strong breeze.

Closer to the head of the horseshoe now, Kitrana could make out a set of black doors built into the base of the cliff face. Sealed shut, they revealed the sigil of the Dragon Riders. It wasn't far. A run that could be measured in seconds.

Kitrana swallowed and looked back, her eyes scanning the land and sky. Nothing. Perhaps she had imagined the noise.

Run! her instincts screamed.

Breaking cover, the Nimean made for the doors at a dead run. It felt agonisingly slow compared to the speed she could travel underwater. It was so much worse when pitted against a creature with flight.

That billowing sound was now accompanied by a hideous roar. Looking back, Kit's entire vision was eclipsed by a dragon of mottled yellow and black scales. It glided down towards her, maw extended to reveal rows of pointed teeth. It had no Rider nor a saddle—only hunger.

Running for her life, Kitrana threw herself into the doors, her hands fumbling with the large iron ring. She groaned, mimicking the door, as she heaved one of them open. It was slow, the slab of metal and wood resisting her strength.

A terrifying shadow overcame the entrance, and the dragon's wings stretched wide to slow itself down. It also angled the beast to bring its front claws to bear. As they flexed to reach out and snatch the Nimean from the ground, Kit wedged herself through the available gap, the edges of the doors scraping against her cheek and the back of her head.

The second she fell beyond the doors, the dragon thundered into them, its claws slamming it shut again. On the floor, Kitrana lay on her side, her chest heaving as she clung to The Anther. The dragon bellowed outside, shaking the stone beneath her. Its wings buffeted the air again, then grew distant in its departure.

For a time, Kit remained on the cold floor. She did her best to think of anything but those open jaws and the cruel fate she had just escaped—and by a hair's breadth. This was not how she imagined her arrival would go. There had been thoughts of sneaking in, perhaps even surveying Joran from a distance for a while to see if the hilt could be stolen without notice.

That was an impossibility now. Her arrival must have been heard throughout every hall in Drakanan. Yet none came to investigate. Minutes went by and she had heard nothing but her own ragged breathing.

Able to see perfectly in the absence of any light, it almost passed her by that she was lying in complete darkness. Where were the Dragon Riders? Where was anybody? It stood to reason the home of dragons would never require any guards, but there had been no one to stop her from entering what should have been a secure fortress.

Kitrana thought of the dragon who had greeted her. Had the weather been fair, there was a good chance she would never have made it within three hundred yards of the doors. Still, it all seemed a little odd to the Nimean.

Rising to her feet, she was immediately startled, and almost blinded, by the torches that sprang to life along the walls. On and on they went, bringing light to the lengthy corridor. Doorways and branching tunnels were soon illuminated, though she had no idea where to start.

With tentative steps, she began to explore beyond Drakanan's entrance, The Anther held high where it could rest on one shoulder. With no indication of where to go, she decided to follow the draughts.

Every new turn activated the dormant torches, illuminating the next passage. She checked doors here and there, with most being locked. Those that were open revealed rooms that varied in size and design, some being made for a single occupant to sleep in while others simply housed supplies.

The largest chamber she came across—and, indeed, had to cross to explore further—was some kind of dining hall. Long tables and benches ran from wall to wall beside an extensive kitchen area. Like everywhere else, however, it was entirely unoccupied.

Moving on, the blazing torches revealed more tunnels and passages that burrowed through the ancient rock. Everywhere she went, there was more evidence that Drakanan had been designed to house a great many Riders.

So where were they all?

Opening a set of double doors, a chamber even larger than the dining hall lay before the Nimean. Workstations were scattered throughout, with forges and anvils in between. Racks lined the walls, displaying a variety of weaponry and armour types. There were even a handful of training dummies and sacks of sand hanging from the ceiling.

Weaving between it all, Kitrana spotted an alcove filled with boots and a line of sandy-coloured cloaks beside it. She might have overlooked them and moved on had she not considered her appearance. Of all the races that walked the surface world, none could withstand the weather like she could. And, she had to admit, the ground was most uncomfortable under her feet. With a glance back at the doors, the Nimean searched for a pair of suitable boots —pausing only to remove the plated toe-caps and guard.

With a new cloak that actually fitted her height, she discarded the tattered one Yamnomora had given her and returned to the passage.

Water!

She could smell it. Taste it even. Like a human chasing precious air, she followed the smell and then the sound. And what a glorious sound it was! The door was partially open, leading her into a chamber so massive it could have swallowed the dining hall and workshop combined. To her delight, it was entirely filled with water.

On the far side of the bathhouse, water poured out of the natural rock and fed the rectangular pool, its surface dancing with the reflections of the surrounding torches. Somewhere inside the pool, she guessed, was an outlet, where the water could continue its journey through an underground river. She didn't really care, flinging her new cloak and boots aside.

The Nimean dived in, her body relishing in the transformation. Her lungs expelled the last of her air and closed off, no longer required. In their place, Kitrana's skin, along with a lining inside her mouth, began to take the necessary oxygen out of the water. At the same time, her fingers and toes secreted a natural oil that quickly coagulated to form a webbing.

It was bliss!

For a creature of her speed, there was very little space to swim, but she enjoyed every moment of it. Length after length she swam, pausing only to break the surface and briefly dive out and back in.

Exploring the depth, she discovered it was no more than ten feet, yet she still placed herself at the very bottom and rested in peace.

For a time, she could think straight. It also helped to remind her that the water was her world. It was where she belonged. It was where her loyalties belonged. Urged to return to the oceans, Kitrana reluctantly departed the pool, her body reversing its breathing apparatus. The webbing between her fingers and toes soon dried up and crumbled away.

Her cloak and boots donned once again, she gave the pool a long look before closing the door and moving on. For untold time she searched in vain, lost to the labyrinth of Drakanan. So long did she search that, eventually, the Nimean even resorted to calling out for Gallien's boy by name.

Nothing.

Feeling the cold hooks of hopelessness deep in her gut, Kitrana finally stopped to rest. She cared little for where she was, her back finding support against the nearest wall. Sliding down to the floor, her shadow flickering in the torchlight, the battle maiden shut her eyes and let her head hang over her chest.

She alone occupied that most ancient of places. Joran had gone, if he had ever even arrived. For all she knew, the boy had fallen to his death from the Aegre. Given what she had heard of the mutated beasts, it was also possible that the Aegre had landed somewhere else and eaten him.

Either way, the hilt was lost to her.

Again.

Finding the broken blade had felt like a near-impossible task, but at least she had been halfway to completing the weapon. Finding both halves, with no idea where to begin searching, was utter folly. Every Nimean beneath the sea would be dead and the Leviathan dug free from its prison before she found even one.

Whatever remained of her life now would be a twilight existence. In death, she would find no reprieve, her fate, like all else, in the hands of The Hag. She would be judged and cast into the Dry Lands, never to swim in the Eternal Waters.

As all of her emotions collided in a perfect storm, she threw her head up, intending to scream at the top of her lungs. But no sound escaped her lips, her thoughts and feelings muted immediately by the blue glow illuminating the passage.

It was coming from The Anther, its glyphs and fine shards alive with the inner light. Hope rocketed up her throat, driving the Nimean to her feet. She had seen the effect before—twice, in fact. The first had been in the old city beneath Harendun when first she had discovered the axe with Gallien. The second had been in the ruins atop The Giant's Throat when so many weapons of power were brought together.

Her eyes wide and mouth ajar, she stared in wonder at the hammer. From the moment she had witnessed Grarfath wield its power in the lowest depths of Morthil, she had known it was important to her own cause, that it would, in some way, aid her mission. And she had been right.

The Anther could sense its kin.

There was another weapon of power nearby.

Kitrana moved away from the wall and held The Anther out before her, using it for navigation. Moving right, the blue hue began to fade, turning her back. Moving along the passage, the light returned before fading again. Following its prompts, the Nimean was returned to the spot where she had rested against the wall.

It wasn't just a wall, however.

She craned her neck to take in the relief carved across the stone. Men and women, cloaked and stamped with the sigil of the Dragon Riders, genuflected before another figure—a man. A *crowned* man. They were kneeling before a king. The King of Erador.

"Of course," she whispered, seeing now that her people had given the blade to the Dragon Riders—who else could have ensured it would remain safe?

Kit hefted the hammer and presented it before the wall. The light intensified, increasing all the more until it was touching the relief.

"It's in the wall," she muttered.

Naturally, her free hand began pushing against the stone, searching frantically for some kind of mechanism or seam. It wouldn't budge. She growled in frustration while also feeling a spring of joy and excitement in her chest. Still, there was no moving the wall.

Feeling the weight of The Anther in her hand, the Nimean considered the rather blunt option. It was a weapon of power, after all. It would make short work of the stone. Equally, it was a *weapon of power*. She had limited knowledge regarding the magic that dwelled within it. What if she struck the wall and ended up back in Morthil?

Too dangerous.

Kitrana placed the hammer on the floor, removing it as an option. There had to be another way. Stepping back, she looked at the image as a whole. There was a sun in the corner, its light depicted as straight lines running diagonally across the carving. Standing in that light, the king stood over the Riders, a closed fist upon his chest as he accepted their allegiance. It was full of small details, drawing the eye to the swords resting on the Riders' hips and even the creases in the billowing cloaks.

The king himself stood regally, his robes flowing out around his feet, a line of tall cliffs at his back. He wore rings and a large necklace as well as his crown, his trappings befitting a man of his title. It seemed a shame, really, that such an exquisite piece of art was destined to dwell in the dark of Drakanan for all time.

Something about the king stood out to Kitrana. Perhaps it was that he stood while all others bowed before him. No, it wasn't that. There was a detail she knew she could see but couldn't put her finger on. Her eyes narrowed and twitched as her gaze slowly rose and, finally, came to rest on his head.

That was it.

While the Dragon Riders knelt before him, the king wasn't actually looking at them. He wasn't even looking straight ahead. The artist had purposefully turned the king's head so the viewer could only see one of his eyes. Furthermore, it seemed the king was looking far to his right, where the sea could be seen to meet the shore beyond the Riders. Why would he be looking at the sea instead of those bowing at his feet?

"The blade, broken for all," she recited, "its power scattered to steal its sting. The blade, broken for all, its power to be guarded in the eye of the king." Kit stepped closer to the relief. "In the eye of the king... In the eye of the king!" she exclaimed.

Alas, the one and only royal eye was too high for her to reach. Running to the nearest door, she kicked it in and looked for something, anything, that could lend her height and support. In a room of supplies, she found a crate, its contents light enough for her to push it down the hall and up the base of the wall. Without delay, she climbed onto the box, her hand reaching slightly above her head.

She hesitated. Was this the moment she had been working towards for so long? It had to be, her journey laid out by Atradon Herself, for no other could have weaved such circumstances that brought her to that place—and with The Anther no less. This was to be a moment of divinity, a blessing from the Water Maiden.

Her fingers pressed into the eye of the king. It moved. By half an inch, it sank into the wall. There was a distant *click* somewhere inside the stone, followed by a series of mechanisms and *rattling* chains. Only when the wall itself began to move did the Nimean jump down and drag the crate away.

Slowly, the detailed relief began to disappear, and the slab of stone lifted into a space in the ceiling. Dust rained down, filling the passage with a smoky haze. Kitrana waved the air in front of her face, desperate to see what was on the other side.

With a resounding *boom*, the wall finally came to rest in the rock above. Stepping through the cloud of dust, Kitrana Voden entered the hidden chamber, her presence igniting a single torch therein.

As her eyes came to rest on the chamber's sole inhabitant, a distant sound echoed through the halls of Drakanan.

She was not alone.

42

IN THE SHADOW OF KINGS

The foundations of life itself shuddered inside the deeps of Joran's mind. All that he knew—that he *thought* he knew—came crashing down upon itself. Initially, he chose to believe that the king was lying, then that he was just wrong. But he could see it in the man before him—his own reflection. Joran knew he had his mother's eyes, ears, and hair, but the structure of the king's face was all too familiar.

"That cannot be," he whispered.

"And yet it is," the king told him, his dark eyes having adopted a glassy sheen. "You *are* my son."

He reached out, as if to touch the boy's cheek, but Joran retreated a step, his shock gripping him body and soul.

The king took no offence at his expression, advancing no further. "And you are so much more than that," he continued earnestly. "Tell me, Joran, what do you know of your mother? Has Andromo spoken of her?"

Joran seemed to be having trouble regulating his breathing, but he managed to nod his head. "She was a Vahlken," he muttered.

The king nodded along. "Did Andromo tell you her name?"

"Ilithranda."

It looked to bring some comfort to the king, to hear another say her name. "I suppose that's all she said," he reasoned. "That would keep things simple. It would keep you on the path to becoming a Dragon Rider."

Some small part of Joran's world, one that still made sense, took umbrage with the insinuation. "What are you getting at?"

"Your heritage is more complex than Androma would like it to be. But none of us can outrun the blood in our veins. You should know this already, Joran, and I'm sorry you're hearing it now, from me, after learning that I'm your... Well." The king took a steadying breath. "Your mother was Ilithranda of House Lhoris, a daughter of Emperor Qeledred and a princess of Andara."

So nonsensical were his words that Joran let out a short, sharp laugh of disbelief. "No," he said flatly, a word none should ever say to a king. "My mother was a Vahlken."

"And a damned good one," the king agreed heartily. "But your mother was illegitimate. Were it not for her father's blood, she would have been killed inside her mother's womb. Andaren scripture protected her, prohibiting the spilling of Lhoris blood. That didn't mean she couldn't be cast out, however. Ilithranda fought hard for her place amongst the Vahlken. Still, she was a Lhoris. You have that same claim."

Joran didn't know what to say. The king had no reason to lie to him. It just didn't make any sense.

"Do you understand now? There's another path. You are a child of Etragon blood *and* Lhoris blood. You're not just the product of any union between our two peoples. You're a union of the *thrones*." Stepping back, he swept his hands up and across the enormous statues that looked down on them. "You, *Joran Etragon*, stand in the shadow of kings who have come before you. You also stand as a son of the broken circle, of House Lhoris. What will you do?" he challenged. "One of them *will* be destroyed if you stay on your path."

It was all too much for him to hear at once, let alone answer a question of such magnitude. "My name is Joran Pendain," he uttered, unable to meet the eyes of his apparent father.

Something about the king softened then, as if he realised he had pushed too hard, too fast. "Pendain? Was that *his* name? The smuggler who cared for you."

"Gallien," Joran said, wishing more than anything that he was standing beside him.

"Should we ever meet," the king vowed, "I will grant him the title of Blood Lord and afford him any land that is mine to give. He did what I could not. I would see that debt paid handsomely."

Again, Joran didn't know what to do with that information. Gallien being a Lord of the Blood was almost as absurd as Joran being the Prince of Erador. And a prince of Andara... Looking up at the domed ceiling, he took a much-needed breath, hoping it would quash the rising urge to vomit.

"This can't be true," he said absently, and with no idea where to begin.

"My wife and I have no child," the king stated, pivoting the conversation just enough to focus Joran. "There is no heir," he specified. "That throne is legitimately yours to inherit. If we could convince the Jainus and The Gilded to support that claim, the people would come to accept it. Think what good that could do. It could be the beginning of *real* peace talks. It could be the beginning of a new world, one where both realms learn to live together. They just need to see that it can be done," he finished, gesturing at Joran.

Joran hadn't even been aware that his feet had taken him to the base of the throne, where he seated himself on the steps. *I'm Joran Pendain*, he said in his mind, repeating it over and over again in the hope that it would ground him.

"I'm sorry, Joran," the king said again, coming to join him on the steps. "This isn't how I imagined this conversation would go— and I've imagined it for years. You're owed so much more. You *deserve* so much more. I'm sorry I wasn't there to see to that."

"How could... She was a Vahlken," Joran tried again, lost in the maze of it all. "How could..." He shrugged, at a complete loss.

"Our pairing does seem an unlikely one," the king admitted. "My journey to the throne was not... *traditional*. Like I said, I didn't grow up in the palace. I didn't even have the name Etragon until I accepted the crown."

Joran turned to the man, a question behind his confused expression.

"I grew up a lordling—a son of a Blood Lord," the king explained. "In my youth, I was Edris Vanhaven of the Blood Valayan. By the grace of Blood Etragon, our line has ever ruled over Elderhall in the east."

"Edris," Joran repeated, voicing the name that had remained a mystery all his life. Of course, he had heard the name, it being that of the king, but never could he have imagined it would mean so much more to him.

"Upon my coronation, I took the name Edris *Andalan* of Blood *Etragon*." Seeing Joran's brow furrow further into a questioning expression, the king elaborated. "Given that we were in a time of war during my ascent to the throne, it was heavily advised—for the sake of the people's morale—that the name Etragon continue through to victory. It's not uncommon for kings to take new names when they're crowned," he added with a shrug, as if changing one's name was a small detail.

Feeling that he might drown in all that he had learned, Joran grabbed hold of what tether he could and focused on one matter at a time, hoping all the while that his mind would make sense of it all while he questioned the king.

Questioned his *father*.

"If you were of Blood Valayan," he began, "how did you get put on the throne?"

"Tragedy," King Edris said simply. "The Valayans are cousins to the Etragons. Our blood has always bonded us to the throne, if from a distance. Still, that distance remains closer than any claim to be made from the other Blood Lords. When King Talasar died, and his family with him, *I* was next in line."

"They *all* died?" Joran questioned incredulously.

The king nodded solemnly. "It would have been the year you were born. Valgala was rife with disease—The Red Pox. It killed so many, including the king, queen, and their two sons. The king's sister was an infant when she died, and his brother died years earlier in a hunting accident before he could sire children. There were no Etragons left after The Red Pox. It took them all in a *week*."

As sobering as that was, Joran still had questions. "You were *next in line?*"

The king paused, reassessing his response. "My father, your grandfather, was next in line." He licked his lips, his demeanour sinking somewhat. "Had he not been in Valgala, visiting the king of all people, it would be him upon that throne today. As it was, he caught The Red Pox and died in the west wing a few days after the royal family."

"I'm sorry," Joran offered, unsure what else to say.

"He was a good man, your grandfather. You would have liked him. He was very... open-minded. He saw the world for what it could be, not what it is."

"You were his only son?"

"No," the king replied, his answer bringing a smile to his face. "The Valayan line is survived by my brother and sister. They both have families of their own. As the oldest, the throne was mine to assume. My burden."

Joran accepted all the information, his mind able to follow the path that led to his biological father becoming king and taking on the Etragon name. What he couldn't understand, however, was his mother's part in it all. King Edris had said nothing that explained their *unlikely pairing*.

"How did my mother—a Vahlken—come to meet the King of Erador?"

Edris looked out across the throne room, his gaze distant, beyond that chamber. "I wasn't a king when we met. Just a lordling with a chip on his shoulder." He sighed, looking weighed down by the memories. "The war had raged for centuries, a fact that was taking a toll on the entire country. Erador's army was finally beginning to dwindle, with many finding ways to avoid being conscripted.

"King Talasar had the idea to inspire the people. He commanded the first-born sons of every great bloodline to join the army. I had no choice but to submit for training, though I had been trained to fight in Elderhall since I could walk. I eventually found myself in Caster Hold, placed in charge of a battalion, and given a single order: conquer our enemies."

"You were a soldier," Joran replied, recalling what Kassanda had said of his true father.

The king nodded. "I led many campaigns on Andaren soil. I enjoyed victories. I was lucky enough to survive and learn from defeats. I gained something of a reputation for strategy, and the numbers under my command increased. Inevitably, I caught the attention of the Andarens. They started baiting us, setting traps and ambushes. We had to begin questioning every scrap of intelligence.

"We thwarted them all, but, in the end, it didn't matter. We were ordered to invade Harendun. *Again.* The Undying City does not yield easily. For weeks we laid siege, and for weeks they kept us at bay. I was impatient for victory. I thought a small team could penetrate an area of their defences and open the way for more to follow. But they knew Edris Vanhaven of Blood Valayan was amongst the invaders. They were always looking for me."

"What happened?" Joran asked, absorbed now.

"They killed my men and captured me. They went on to repel our invasion, but I was long gone by then, shipped south to the island of Agandavael."

"What's on Agandavael?"

"The Triden," the king answered, his tone lending some gravity to that place. "It's much like our Caster Hold, home to the Andaren fleet. It houses the largest contingent of Andaren soldiers after The Saible. It's also where I met Ilithranda."

Edris paused there for a moment, perhaps recalling that time perhaps. "By then, she had been fighting the Skaramangians for years. But when I met her, she was fleeing a tragedy of her own. She sought comfort in the numbness of war. When she wasn't keeping us off their shores, she was training Andaren soldiers to be better fighters."

Joran wished he could imagine her, see her face. "You were her prisoner?"

"Eventually. She watched the way I was treated for days... or maybe it was weeks," he pondered. "Unlike everyone else, Ilithranda knew Erador wasn't the real enemy. That everything had been manufactured by the Skaramangians. She took pity on me. Though it would have been better if she had taken pity on me *before* they broke most of my ribs," he added with a touch of humour.

Joran repositioned himself on the steps to better face the king. "They didn't execute you?"

"I was to be taken to the mainland, where they could transport me to Aran'saur. I think I was to be paraded before they took my head. Obviously it never came to that."

"She protected you," Joran concluded.

"None dared challenge her, not even the paladins running The Triden." The king gave a half-hearted laugh. "I remember a missive once came from the capital, from Aran'saur. It bore the sigil of the archjusticiar himself—bar the emperor, he controls the entire Andaren army. A very important man. A very *powerful* man. It was a thinly veiled order to release me to the paladins so I might be transported to Aran'saur."

"What did she do?"

King Edris smiled wistfully. "She threw the missive in a fire, right in front of a paladin." He laughed again. "You should have seen his face. He couldn't do a damned thing. Only once did I think it would come to violence—this was months into my captivity." The king grew serious again, his tone dropping several octaves. "I hadn't realised, not until that moment, that she would actually kill for me. Not that it came to that. Oaken landed at her back, and every one of them lost their courage."

"Oaken!" Joran blurted.

Surprise washed over the king's face. "You know of him?"

"I have *flown* on him!" Joran exclaimed. "He's here!"

Edris straightened up. "You've flown on an *Aegre*? Wait. Oaken is *here*?"

Joran stumbled over his response. "He's close by." His words all seemed to come out at once, but he managed to inform the king of Oaken's involvement at the ruins and his subsequent proximity. "He separated from us when we approached the city."

The king looked to the dim sky between the pillars. "Oaken... I should love to see him again." There was a note of sadness to him, as if meeting the Aegre again might break his heart all the more.

"My mother loved you," Joran murmured, wondering how it would feel to actually experience such a thing.

Edris tilted his head, his response reserved while he thought about it. "In her own way. And in time, yes. Your mother was... complicated. Ilithranda was born before the war broke out. She was centuries old. Add to that her start in life, her connection to the imperial family, and several of our lifetimes on the battlefield... And that's all before she became a Vahlken and started fighting the *real* war. She was broken in more ways than one. I like to think that, while we were together, she was a little less broken. If still entirely lost."

"How long were you together for?" Joran asked.

"Three years," the king was quick to reply, as if that number had been with him for the last sixteen years. "Oaken flew us south after we fled The Triden. For three unbelievable years, we lived in The Fangs. The beaches there are more beautiful than any in The Dawning Isles."

"I have seen neither," Joran admitted.

"In the future I spoke of," Edris said coyly, "you would rule over one and be welcome at the other."

Joran couldn't entertain that particular path, his mind swimming with revelation. "Why only three years?" he asked, changing the subject.

"I haven't known you nearly long enough, Joran, but I can see that you're a person who knows what it is to have a sense of duty. Yours, if I'm not mistaken, is a duty to others, even those you have never met. That duty drives you to do what is *right*, seek out the truth and, ultimately, help those who cannot help themselves. It is commendable, given your life on the road, where you are always a target for others.

"I too have a sense of duty. Mine was instilled in me by my father, as it is in all lordlings. First is our duty to Kaliban, the one true god. Then our king and all those of Blood Etragon. Thereafter, we have a duty to serve the people of Elderhall and the honour of our bloodline. Those of Blood Valayan do not take their duty lightly, and it called to me all the while I was away.

"I tried to ignore it, and for three years I succeeded. But, eventually, it demanded attention. I needed to know how the war was going. Where had my men been sent? Had the Andarens retaliated and invaded Caster Hold?" The king sighed, his head dropping to his chest. "Those questions and more haunted me night and day."

Rising from the steps, Edris wandered into the open space before the throne, that most royal of seats stealing his attention for a moment.

"If I could go back..." he began before coming to an abrupt stop. "We went to Harendun. It was still in the hands of the Andarens. It didn't take Ilithranda long to get the answers I sought. Being a Vahlken opens every door. And if it doesn't," he quipped, "they just kick the door in."

Seeing that Joran wasn't amused by the comment, King Edris continued. "That was when we learned of The Red Pox in Valgala. As you can imagine, news of the entire royal family's death spread like a wildfire. There were celebrations in the streets of Harendun for days. Their clerics told everyone it was a sign that reclamation day would soon be upon them."

For a short time, Edris paced the polished floor, struggling with the past.

"I couldn't believe they had all perished," he eventually continued. "I thought for sure one of the princes must have survived. I needed to know for certain because... because I knew my father was next in line. I agonised over it, Joran, but I knew I had to go back to Erador and see for myself. I have often wondered what life I would be living right now if we had just stayed in The Fangs, out of the war and the politics."

Joran couldn't even begin to imagine the life he might have lived with both of his parents in lands untouched by the Skaramangians and their machinations. "How did you get back to Erador?" he asked, wishing to keep his mind away from dreams of what never was.

"Oaken," the king said simply. "Ilithranda knew of a narrow gap where the Dragon Riders were unable to extend their patrols. She warned me they couldn't wait for too long. I... I promised her I would return in time. That we would return to our life after I knew the truth of it."

King Edris turned away from Joran, concealing his face and, perhaps, the emotions he couldn't hide in any expression. When he turned back, he looked pained by the memory of it all.

"I never returned," he confessed.

Joran thought of his mother and Oaken, waiting idly for days, maybe even weeks. What had she gone through in that time? Had she worried about him? Had she hated him? He would never know, but he was saddened to imagine her on the day she chose to fly back to Andara, alone.

"Why not?" Joran asked, his throat dry.

The king gestured at the lofty chamber they occupied. "My timely return was seen as something of a sign from Kaliban," he explained. "I learned that my father had been in the palace, that he had come to request more resources be applied to finding me in Andara." Edris's fist clenched at his side. "He died trying to find some way to save me, and I didn't even need saving."

"They made you king," Joran stated, voicing the reason that his parents never saw each other again.

The king stared at him, likely sensing the judgement in his voice. "I had everyone's eyes on me," he said by way of a defence. "If I had returned to Ilithranda, they would have followed me. That would have put both of you in danger."

Joran's head twitched. "You knew?" he blurted. "You knew she was pregnant?"

Edris closed his eyes for a time, perhaps to keep any tears at bay. "Yes," he replied. "She wasn't showing, but we knew she was with child."

He abandoned us.

The thought flashed through Joran's mind like lightning.

"My duty was tenfold," the king tried to expound. "You can't imagine the weight of it, Joran. Like you, all I had ever wanted to do was help my people. And just like that," he said, snapping his fingers, "my people were no longer those of Elderhall. It was every soul in Erador. Added to that, Ilithranda had told me everything about the Skaramangians. I had to do something."

Joran stood up, his emotional range diminished almost to utter numbness now. "The only thing you had to do was be there for her. She died giving birth to me in the middle of Harendun while your men burned it down."

"Joran," the king said pleadingly.

"Do you know who *didn't* have to do something?" Joran replied. "Gallien. He didn't have to do a damned thing. But he did. He *chose* me. I'm not Joran of Blood Etragon. I'm not Joran of House Lhoris. I'm *Joran Pendaïn.*"

It was against every protocol, but the king did nothing to stop Joran from turning his back on him and storming out of the throne room.

43

A SHORT REPRIEVE

Gallien Pendain was awoken by pain, his closest companion of late. It burned in his wrist and shot up his arm, throwing him from the hammock in which he had been sleeping. With an unceremonious *thud* he struck the floor and groaned as new waves of pain washed across various body parts. If only they could have taken away the agony in his wrist.

Blinded and disorientated by the pain, he tried to pick himself up just as he had a thousand times before. A costly mistake. The stump that now formed the end of his right arm pressed into the floorboards and, together with his left hand, bore all his weight. The torment that followed was like a thunder clap, and it felt as if Mr Grim had brought that searing hot iron to bear once more.

Gallien cried out and fell again, his right shoulder taking the brunt of it this time. The smuggler lay there for a time, cradling his wounded arm close to his chest, his face creased while he battled the pain. When, at last, he could open his eyes, he dared to look at the stump.

It was bleeding, the fresh bandages already staining crimson. He couldn't recall the old ones being changed. Indeed, he struggled to recall the events that had led him to...

Where was he?

He didn't need to look around to be given the necessary clues. He could feel the floor swaying gently beneath him. The smell of salty air found its way through the dense musk that permeated the room of hammocks. Beyond his environment, he could hear distant shouts and calls from sailor to sailor.

It came all back to him then. Their escape from the Padoshi's compound. Reaching the docks at Thedaria's edge. The Raven.

Then his memory conjured the broad image of Captain Bail Addison. A pirate. A mercenary. An old mentor.

A killer.

The smuggler saw glimpses of the last few days, though they were little more than shards in his memory. How many days and nights had they been aboard The Raven?

Without the answers, his attention was naturally drawn back to the bloody stump where his right hand should have been. Gallien could still feel the pressure exerted on him at the Padoshi's feet, the weight of the men who kept him pinned, helpless, unable to defend himself. He had tried so hard to make the axe disappear.

His desire for retribution, combined with the sense of violation and injustice he had suffered, was enough to make him mad with rage. Fuelled all the more by his pain, Gallien hammered the back of his head into the floorboards and roared with all his might, his face flushed red.

His thoughts turned to dark and twisted desires, conjuring images of what he would do to the Padoshi to slake his hunger for vengeance. They were interrupted, however, when the cabin door opened, flooding the gloom with stark light. Shielding his eyes, Gallien was soon able to lay eyes on Androma.

"Gallien?" she called, her hands extended and searching his empty hammock.

"I'm here," he croaked, using what he could to pick himself up.

"You're hurt?"

Everything hurt. There didn't seem to be a single part of him, be it mind or body, that wasn't suffering.

"I'm fine," he lied.

"You sound awake, at least," the old Rider remarked. "Come. The air will do you some good."

It seemed odd to grip the blind woman's arm for guidance, yet she knew the way, and he still felt hollowed out. How long had it been since he had eaten and drunk properly?

At the top of the steps, The Raven's deck opened up, revealing its crew busy at work. Beyond them, the rolling waves of The Drifting Sea dominated every horizon under the midday sun.

The wind cut across the deck, blowing through the rigging to find Gallien. It skimmed the razored hair above his ears and threatened to undo the knot that kept his blond hair collected on his crown. His brown leather cloak billowed to the east, brushing against Androma's tattered rags.

It was glorious, and yet the smuggler dashed to the port side railing and wretched into the sea, his brow dripping with sweat. Androma's hand found his back as she appeared at his side. If she was concerned, her stern expression—her only expression—did not show it. Looking at her, Gallien saw her blindfold was splattered with speckles of blood—the blood of those who had kept him captive.

The old Rider breathed in the sea air. "Here we are again, you and I. Same waters. Same ship."

"No Joran," Gallien added, a sadness about him.

"His training will have begun by now. His dragon might even have hatched already."

That was little comfort to the smuggler, who just wanted to have his son by his side. That wasn't entirely true, he realised. He didn't want Joran to see him as he was, so wounded and broken. He didn't even want the boy to know that his mind had apparently been hollowed out by his father and that he, Gallien Pendain, was no more than a shell of a man, his family name all that had been left to him.

"He still has it, you know," Androma commented, pulling the smuggler from his reverie.

"Who has what?" he queried, wincing as the pain in his wrist lanced up his arm again.

"Captain Addison," the old Rider specified, and quietly. "He has the atori blade I gave him as payment all those years ago."

Gallien frowned, recalling the tense conversation and Androma's abrupt bartering. "He still has it?" The smuggler scanned the deck in search of the pirate. "I told him where to sell it."

"Well, he didn't," Androma concluded. "Cob saw it on his belt."

Gallien considered what he knew now that he didn't back then. "It was hers, wasn't it? The blade belonged to Joran's mother."

"Ilithranda," the old Rider confirmed. "It should be with Joran. It is his birthright."

The smuggler turned his head and scrutinised his companion. Her expression remained the same, yet he could see something else beneath the surface. Resolve.

"Don't even think about it," Gallien advised.

"About what?" she replied coyly.

"You know *what*. We're on his damned ship, Androma. You can't just steal it back and expect us to ever reach Caster Hold. Addison'll dump the lot of us into the drink and be done with it."

"You believe my methods to be so obtuse?"

Gallien shook his head. "I've only just got away from the grips of one tyrant. I'd rather not piss off another in the middle of the sea. Leave it alone, Androma."

"We sail under the protection of Galahart," she reminded him.

"The spymaster?" Gallien asked, his hazy memory recalling something of the man's name during their escape from the Padoshi's compound.

"He was in Thedaria," Androma confirmed. "At least, a *version* of Galahart was in Thedaria. He secured The Raven for us."

The smuggler sighed. "He's not to be trusted."

"Which one?"

"Both," Gallien replied without thought, aware that Captain Addison's loyalties could always be bought out by a higher bidder.

"Galahart knows our destination is Taraktor," Androma went on. "He knows a weapon of power hangs in the balance."

"You see the folly in trusting a man whose title is spymaster?"

"Of course, just as Captain Addison sees the folly in betraying such a man."

Gallien might have barked a laugh were he not in constant pain. "Don't rely on that. And don't dwell on the blade. Better to forget it even exists."

Androma said nothing, which really said it all. Gallien could accept that he didn't know the depths of what the atori blade meant to the old Rider. He could only hope she accepted their mission to Taraktor as more important.

"Thank you," he said, wiping his mouth and changing the subject. "It would have been a slow death."

"I did very little," Androma admitted. "What more is needed when you're standing behind a Kedradi ranger?"

Gallien looked over his shoulder and spied Cob on the other side of The Raven. He was hanging over the side, his feet braced against the railing while one hand gripped the sheets. The sea sprayed him with every dip in the waves, and the breeze blew out his shoulder cloak and battle skirt. Even his long dreadlocks were picked up in his wake.

The smuggler caught a glimpse of green in the corner of his eye. Aphrandhor was nestled in the bow of The Raven, his hood knocked back by the wind. He held his staff close to him, the one thing that would have made the biggest difference to them. Even without it, the wizard had been his only comfort, a steady presence in the aftermath.

"I would speak with The Green Leaf," he said, peeling away from the railing. The smuggler paused, placing a hand on the old Rider's shoulder. "And *thank you*," he said again, with earnest.

Slowly, he made his way to the bow, ignoring the many looks his wrist received. Aphrandhor stood a sentinel, slightly starboard of the ship's figurehead. Gallien tried to remember the first time he had seen the raven head carved out of the prow, but the memory escaped him—like so many others.

"Green Leaf?"

The wizard was startled, apparently in a world of his own until the interruption. "Gallien!" he exclaimed, greeting him with a genuine smile. "Look at you on your feet! Very good."

The smuggler couldn't help but mimic the smile, though his was much quicker to fade.

"Are you well?" he asked, his gaze lingering on the dark bruise and nasty gash marring Aphrandhor's forehead.

"I've a headache that won't shift but apart from that…" The Green Leaf's eyes drifted down to Gallien's wrist. "You suffered far worse."

"Imagine how I would have looked a week from now. I'm not sure I have enough parts to lose and still live," Gallien jested half-heartedly, his attempt at levity falling flat.

"You were very brave," the wizard stated, and sincerely. "I don't intend to patronise," he added. "I only mean to say…" The Green Leaf licked his lips and started again. "There aren't many who could have stood up to a man like that. Most would have succumbed to fear. You didn't even beg. I'd say there's more to you than meets the eye, Mr Pendain. A lot more. I look forward to the day your memories are restored and I might meet the whole you."

Gallien could only bow his head in thanks, his lips pressed into a tight and reluctant smile. He didn't deserve such kind words from the man he had accused of murdering his father. He had said that and so much more to the old man's face that he now regretted.

"I judged you harshly," Gallien said, his words just carrying above the waves crashing into the bow. "Unfairly," he added. "I know it's only a chance that I might see my father again, that I might even save him, but I wouldn't have that without you. And you got me through the worst night of my life, so thank you on both accounts."

The wizard absorbed the considerate words before replying. "There aren't many of us fighting for the light. The Skaramangians have so few enemies. And, while I know there are some who doubt your place in all this," he said, sparing a glance for Cob, "I for one am glad you fight with us, Gallien. It can be quite the blow to always be underestimated, but in your case, I feel it is you who always deals the *last* blow."

The smuggler indicated his stump. "I'm not sure how much use I'm going to be in our next fight."

"Yes," The Green Leaf sighed. "there is always a *next* fight, isn't there? Luckily for you, you travel with a Dragon Rider *and* a Kedradi warrior. If there was ever anyone to instruct you in the ways of single-handed combat, it would be them."

"Drakalis!" the captain's voice boomed across the deck.

Hearing his pseudonym, Gallien steeled himself for the exchange to come and slowly turned around. "Captain," he replied amicably.

Round and tall, The Raven's captain blocked out the ship behind him. "I've scraped things off me boot that look better than you, lad!"

Gallien didn't reply right away, his eyes falling temporarily on the bronze short-sword tucked into Addison's belt. "I won't lie," he said. "I haven't felt this bad since... well, since I was one of your crew."

The captain chuckled from a place deep in his chest. "Still got your wit, I see. Glad the Padoshi didn't chop that off and all!"

It was a biting remark, but Gallien wasn't one to feel the sting of words. "You're still carrying the atori blade?" he stated, his tone questioning.

Addison admired the weapon on his belt, his chunky fingers coiling about the hilt. "Oh aye! I took it to your man in Caster Hold. Told me he could sell it, just like you said."

Gallien's brow pinched in confusion. "You didn't want the coin?"

"He didn't have *enough*," the captain reported. "I wanted double his offer, but he wouldn't budge. So I held onto it, thinking all the while that I would track you down and gut you with it. But the attention it got me!" he boasted. "Every tavern from Caster Hold to Thedaria gave me free drink and food to tell them the tale of how I killed a Vahlken for it." The big man laughed to himself. "I tell them something different every time! I've even killed a couple of folk with it too. Damned sharp, and stronger than any blade I've met in a fight."

Gallien offered him his signature smile, though it never quite reached his eyes. "Well, I'm glad you didn't gut me with it."

"There's still time, Drakalis. There's still time..." Addison said before walking away to shout orders at his crew.

"A charming man," Aphrandhor commented.

Gallien leaned against the port side railing, his wrist cradled close to his chest. "The quicker we get off this boat, the better," he muttered.

The wizard regarded him for a time, his thoughts his own until he voiced the question brewing in his mind. "That name: *Drakalis*. 'Tis an unusual one. How did you come to adopt it?"

Being the second in their group to ask as much in as many days, Gallien repeated the same off-hand answer he had given to Cob.

"Corben came up with it," he answered, recalling his brother's idea. "I think it was from one of Pa's old tales—something he read in a tomb knowing my father." Not that he did know his father, the smuggler thought, unable to remember any of those tales himself.

"You might be right," The Green Leaf agreed. "If I'm not mistaken, it's from one of the old tongues we know so little about. *Drak*," he pronounced clearly, "means *dragon*. It is common knowledge—among scholars and the like—that Drakanan translates to *dragon lands*. In your case, we have Drak-alis. But, I confess, I do not know the translation for *alis*."

Something deep inside Gallien's mind told him, quite firmly, that he knew the exact translation. Yet the smuggler couldn't think what it was, as if there was a wall between him and the knowledge he possessed. He felt it was more proof that his father had used magic on him to hide something.

A weapon of power.

The Green Leaf gave him a measuring pat on the shoulder. "We will make sense of all this soon enough," he promised.

Gallien nodded and patted the old man's arm before walking away, following the starboard rail back towards the cabins. Just beyond the main mast, Cob hopped off the railing, blocking the smuggler's path.

The Kedradi looked him up and down, his head tilted to one side. "You look terrible."

Gallien nodded along. "I keep hearing that."

"Have you heard about your smell?" Cob quipped, a rare grin breaking out across the ranger's face.

It managed to crack a portion of the smuggler's stoicism, and the two men shared a quiet laugh.

"In Qalanqath, my people have a saying: *What doesn't kill you will only try harder next time.* I promise you, Gallien Pendain, when next the Padoshi of Thedaria tries to kill you, I will be at your side, and we will face him together."

Gallien didn't know what to do with the kind words, so he fell back on his humour. "Are you starting to *like* me, Kedradi?" Cob's demeanour changed in the blink of an eye, and as he folded his arms, he cast his dark eyes out to sea. "If I'd known all it took was chopping off a hand I would have done it back in Hemon."

The ranger met him eye to eye again, ignoring his humourous remark. "You have shown true commitment to our cause. That makes you tolerable at best."

Gallien narrowed his gaze. "You *like* me," he jibed.

"I am glad you have survived this long. Take from that what you will."

The smuggler laughed silently to himself before allowing a notch of seriousness into his tone. "Thank you. Whether you were doing it to save me or The Green Leaf, you got me out of hell. I'm indebted to you."

"We went into that wretched place for both of you, and I would do it again," Cob confirmed. "You can serve some of your debt by letting me clean your wound and change the bandages." Gallien made to protest, but the ranger cut him off. "If it gets infected, you will become a different kind of burden."

The smuggler looked at his wrist and regretted it. He had managed to avoid examining it in the light of day—even covered in bandages, it was hard to bear. "I can still feel it," he said, sure that he was wiggling his fingers right there and then. "It actually hurts."

"Phantom pains," Cob informed him.

Gallien nodded in agreement—he had heard the term before. "I saw it a lot when I fought for the king. After the battles. Men—boys really—crying out about pain in limbs they didn't even have."

"Time will bring healing," the ranger said. "So too will clean bandages. Come."

With great reluctance, the smuggler followed the Kedradi and accepted what he knew would bring more pain and followed the Kedradi.

44

DRAGONLORD

There were sounds, distant and loud, echoing through the stone halls of Drakanan, but Kitrana Voden hardly noticed them. Her world had shrunk to that single chamber, an alcove hidden for millennia inside the walls—kept safe in the eye of the king.

With The Anther in hand, Drakanan's secrets were laid bare, the weapon reacting to its kin. The Nimean put the hammer to one side and moved through the dusty haze that fogged the alcove. The blue light from The Anther mixed with the orange glow that tinted the floating dust. There it was, resting horizontally on a stand that supported it at both ends.

The blade of Skara!

There was no mistaking it for what it was. Glowing orange, the runes etched down the fuller were the same as those that decorated the hilt as well as The Anther and Gallien's inexplicable axe. The bottom end of the blade was broken, the steel jagged. Kit had looked upon the hilt enough times to know that the broken ends matched perfectly.

She had found it!

Tentatively, Kitrana picked it up in both hands, parting it for the first time in thousands of years from the stand. It was a dream, she was sure. Decades of anticipation only lent to her disbelief. Yet there it was, cool and most definitely real in her hands. Even the edge was still sharp, the steel immune to rust. Were she human, tears might have streaked down her cheeks.

Holding the blade close to her chest, the Nimean did her best to come to terms with the profound moment. The hilt had been with her for so long that it seemed an injustice that she should finally hold the blade alone. To that end, it felt an injustice that she not only needed to track down the other other half but also reforge them, and with so few resources to call upon.

Kit's thoughts naturally returned to Grarfath, a capable smith by all accounts—*his* accounts. What hell was he going through? Had the water consumed them all? It seemed unlikely, given the depth of the chasm beneath Khardunar, but they remained trapped with The Dancing Sword of the Dawn. That would be peril enough.

The sound of grinding stone found its way to the alcove, and, Kitrana acknowledged the disturbance. Moving back to the hall, the blade still gripped in one hand, the Nimean cocked her head and waited, listening.

Voices. They were muffled, the sound bouncing off too many walls.

A spring of hope swelled in her heart. Joran! The Water Maiden had truly blessed her. Picking up The Anther, she dashed down the corridor, pausing regularly to hone in on the voices. Drakanan was something of a labyrinth, but she soon came across a hall already illuminated by torches. It was instinct, perhaps, that cautioned her against rounding the corner.

There was more than one voice, meaning Joran was accompanied by another. It could only be a Dragon Rider, who would likely take umbrage with a stranger wandering their passages—and with two weapons of power no less. Her approach would have to be delicate, for she needed that hilt, and the Nimean doubted she had the skill to take it while the boy was in the company of a Rider.

She took a breath and composed herself before peeking round

the corner. The chamber was tall but relatively narrow and occupied by six pillars and no more. Like much else in Drakanan, the walls were layered in relief and ancient paintings, but it was the far wall that caught her eye, for the stone appeared to have been lifted into the ceiling as it had in the secret alcove.

The chamber beyond looked vast, the rock having retained its natural jagged appearance. It looked to be tiered, as if row upon row had been carved out of the sloping floor. Two figures came into view, forcing Kit back into hiding.

"Six," a woman said, her tone full of disappointment. "We're hardly going to build a new age with six eggs."

"What good are the eggs if we don't have the Riders?" came her companion's voice.

A cold dread seeped into Kit's flexible bones. That was not Joran's voice.

"Patience," a third voice bade, halting the other two in their tracks. "We have time on our side. Trust in the Dragonlord."

Kitrana dared to peek again, spying three of them this time. It seemed the third had been hidden behind one of the pillars, waiting for the others to emerge. The two who had departed the vast chamber carried a chest each, the boxes deep and ornately crafted. All three of them wore the garb of the Dragon Riders, each displaying the colours of their dragon in the scales that layered their vambraces and pauldrons.

Legendary as they were, the Nimean's instincts told her to pull her neck in and remain as still as possible. She thought about using The Anther then, the weapon capable of porting her to safety. But she considered the last time she had wielded it, recalling the need for more than one blow to make it work. If that happened again, the Riders would be upon her before she could swing a second time.

"Something to say, Raya?" that third, older voice enquired.

"I trust in the Dragonlord, of course," she began, her tone suggesting otherwise, "but we all know why we're here *now*."

"Raya..." the second voice cautioned.

"We're all thinking it," Raya pointed out.

"*What* are we all thinking?" the third voice pressed.

"These eggs have sat here for years. The only reason we're collecting them now is because Garganafan isn't here."

"Your point?" The third voice had adopted an ominous tone.

"It speaks of fear," Raya said plainly.

"The Dragonlord fears nothing," the third voice insisted.

"Then why now?" she countered.

"Raya!" the second voice hissed.

"Be careful," the third voice counselled. "Heretical is your tone, Raya. I recall Ithira, *your* dragon, being among those who brought down Aila that fateful day?"

"I know my part in what happened, Haldar," Raya said defiantly, naming the Rider. "Rhaymion was challenged because he showed weakness. Fear. Is it not our place to hold the Dragonlord to that same accountability?"

Haldar chuckled to himself. "Do you intend to challenge the Dragonlord for his title? What about Ithira? Does she fancy her chances against Kalaghan?"

"Neither of us intend to challenge," Raya stated, the strength of her voice depleted somewhat. "I speak only of observation."

"I would advise keeping your *observations* to yourself," Haldar intoned. "The Dragonlord does not fear Garganafan. Of all the dragons in the realm, it would weigh heavily on him to slay one so powerful. What a better *ally* Garganafan would make. What a better empire we might make with him at our side. Kassanda too."

"Of course," Raya responded, "I see the—"

"You see nothing," Haldar cut in. "That is why Baelon Vos is the Dragonlord and you are not. *He* sees our future and would rather achieve it without losing anymore dragons. A noble goal. That said," Haldar added slyly, "I would enjoy seeing you challenge him, if only to see you learn a valuable lesson."

"I meant no disrespect," Raya said, her voice suggesting she had bowed her head.

"I will not speak of this," Haldar promised, "but you would do well to guard your thoughts on the matter. There's no telling what Kalaghan might discern the next time he opens his mind to Ithira."

The tension growing in Kitrana built to such an extent that her grip around Skara's blade broke the flesh. She grunted, stung by the pain, and let the steel slide until the point hit the floor. For such a small thing, it might as well have made a sound to rival the roar of the ocean. She didn't need to look to know the three Riders had been alerted to her presence.

The Nimean bolted.

For precious seconds, she heard naught but her own breath and boots striking the floor, but the thundering of boots soon followed in her wake. There was hardly time to calculate her direction, and the torches struggled to keep up with her speed, often leaving her in the dim light of the blade and hammer. Worst of all, wherever she went, the torches revealed her location, allowing her pursuers to maintain the hunt.

Fearing she would be caught in those cold halls, it was with relief that she caught sight of the natural light pouring in through Drakanan's main doors, left ajar by the Riders. With as much power as she could muster, the Nimean sprinted the length of that final corridor, slamming into the door before pushing on through the gap. Without thought, Kit raced down the path between the hulking statues. She had no plan, her feet spurred on by fear alone.

It was that same fear that clouded her mind, preventing her from seeing the obvious: if the Riders were present, so too were their mounts...

Numerous shadows swept over the ground, and the wind was whisked into a frenzy about Kitrana. She skidded in the snow, coming to a stop as a monstrous dragon dropped out of the blue sky. All four of its clawed feet cracked the ground, its wings flaring like a bat's at its sides. The beast's long neck unfurled, raising its head into the air where it unleashed a deafening roar.

Four more descended into the horseshoe, each with their own tone of roar or hiss, their wings flapping and tails whipping. Predatory eyes tracked her every micro-movement.

Kitrana's attention was, of course, brought back to the dragon that had blocked her path. Its scales were of deep honey speckled with silver and bronze, a contrast to its bright green eyes, both of which looked upon the Nimean as if she were an ample snack. Between and above those exquisite eyes was a singular horn almost twice that of a man.

It was a killing machine with wings.

Behind her, the three Riders she had overheard came to a stop on the path. Kit expected them to seize her, to take The Anther and the broken blade from her. Instead, all three of them dropped to one knee and bowed their heads, the two chests placed on the ground in front of them.

"Dragonlord," Haldar voiced reverently.

Turning back to the dragon, the creature had brought its wings in and lowered itself into a crouch, revealing the man astride its saddle. The Dragonlord beheld her for a time, regal upon his leather throne. It seemed a bone-breaking drop, but he suffered no such injury when he dismounted and began to approach.

He cut a striking figure, even beside the mammoth dragon. Older than she would have expected of a Rider, he sported a well-trimmed beard and short hair of white and grey, reminding her of a military general. His pauldrons lent him a broad and intimidating silhouette, each a reflection of his dragon's scales. Unlike the others, who wore layered armour of dark leather beneath their sandy cloaks, the Dragonlord wore a cuirass of bronze, his cloak and battle skirt jet black.

Coming to a halt in front of her, he tilted his head while his eyes roamed across her body. Kit noted the scar that ran up from his collar and across his jaw, interfering with his beard, but it was his cold and calculating eyes that held her attention. It was like looking into the eyes of a shark.

"Obrin!" the Dragonlord called out.

To Kit's right, a violet dragon crouched as the other had, allowing its Rider to more easily find his way to the ground. "My Lord," he replied, crossing the gap, his mane of wild hair thrown back in the wind.

"You said the half-blood was a boy," the Dragonlord remarked, his eyes fixed on Kitrana's pointed ears, both of which had been revealed by the breeze.

"He is, my Lord. This is not him."

The Dragonlord narrowed his eyes. "Who are you?" he asked, glancing at the weapons of power in her hands. "*What* are you?" he asked more pointedly. When she failed to answer, the one-horned dragon exhaled a sharp breath through its nostrils. "Easy, Kalaghan. Why don't we start with names? I am Baelon Vos, Dragonlord. And you are..."

The Nimean wondered if she was experiencing her final moments in this life. "Kitrana," she managed. "Kitrana Voden."

"Well met, Miss Voden. Perhaps you could enlighten us. Why are you trespassing on ground most cannot find the courage to even look upon?"

Kit tried to answer but failed to find the moisture to part her lips, let alone the right words.

"Perhaps it has something to do with those," the Dragonlord mused, looking at the weapons. "Is that a sword?" There was wonder in his voice.

Kitrana moved her bleeding hand so the blade was concealed behind her leg. "I'm sorry for trespassing," she croaked before clearing her throat. "I assure you, I haven't taken anything that wasn't mine to claim. I'll just be on my way."

The Dragonlord sidestepped, blocking her way with a bemused smile. "While I could overlook the cloak and boots, Miss Voden, I cannot let you pass with weapons of power in your possession. Now, you strike me as an intelligent woman. As I'm sure you can imagine, there are two ways we can proceed."

Kit glanced at Kalaghan, well aware of her options. "I... I can't give it to you," she whispered, despair creeping in. Her hope couldn't help but quaver under the gaze of so many predators, including the Dragonlord.

Curiosity flashed across Baelon's face. "You can't?" he echoed incredulously. The Dragonlord looked at those of his order and the winged beasts beyond, astonished, it seemed, that he faced such defiance. "I was mistaken," he admitted. "You clearly lack the intelligence to know when you should submit."

"I wasn't trained to submit," the battle maiden revealed, finding a thread of courage and holding onto it with both hands. "I see no reason to start now," she declared, falling into a battle stance.

At the same time, the three Dragon Riders at her back rose to their feet and freed their swords in unison. Besides the Dragonlord, Obrin moved to do the same before his master held out a calming hand.

"Let us have words before blood," he insisted. "You speak of training. Did someone send you?"

Kit could feel her fear mounting, determined to bury her. When backed into a corner, however, there was only one place her fear could go. *Anger.*

"I'm here to take back what rightfully belongs to my people," she fumed, doing her damnedest to maintain her grit.

"Your people?" Again, Baelon scrutinised her pointed ears. "Anything you took from in there belongs to *my* people."

"It came from the sea," Kit declared with conviction, "and it shall be returned to the sea!"

Baelon looked at her with revelation in his eyes. "Oh... You're one of *them.* I haven't met one of your kind in centuries."

"You don't need it," she protested, hefting the broken sword. "You probably didn't even know you had it."

"Fascinating," the Dragonlord commented, ignoring her completely, examining the Nimean in a whole new light. "We came for the eggs," he went on, addressing his fellow Riders, "but it seems we're leaving with so much more."

"You don't need them," Kitrana argued, glancing from hammer to blade. "You have dragons! Magic! Silvyr swords! Please!" she pleaded, her time clearly running down. "You don't know what I've gone through to get this far."

"I look forward to hearing your tale, Miss Voden. Yours are a curious people."

Baelon held out his hand, his fingers flexed expectantly.

Kitrana didn't yield, her mind racing. She had seconds, if that, to think of a solution. The crushing truth pressed upon her, making it all the harder to see a future in which she lost possession of both weapons and her freedom was, once again, taken by another. The idea of fighting back flashed through her mind, folly as it was.

That scenario boiled down to one question: who would kill her first? Running away posed a similar conundrum. Surrendering was the only choice that left her with the future possibility of escape, with or without the blade.

That didn't mean she had to give them everything.

Could she find a notch of redemption while spiting the Dragon Riders? Only if it worked, she knew. It all came down to willpower, something the Nimean had spent a lifetime building. Like a tsunami, the waters of her mind washed away all distraction, leaving her with a single image to focus on, to make real in her eyes, as if she was in that very chamber.

As the Dragonlord lowered his hand and sighed, perhaps resigning himself to the violence he would have to resort to, Kitrana tossed the broken blade at him. The steel flipped high, causing Baelon and the others to look up as he reached out to catch it.

It was in that moment of distraction that the battle maiden made her only possible move.

The Anther flew from her grip, its head of gold and bronze hurtling towards the nearest statue lining the path. The moment it left her hand, the Nimean knew she had thrown true, the power of the weapon drawing energy from her.

In a flash of light, explosion of stone, and *clap* of air, the hammer punched through the fabric of reality and vanished from Drakanan.

Drained of what energy she had left, Kitrana stumbled and staggered. The light of the world began to fade in her periphery, and her conscious mind slipped further and further into numbing darkness. She barely registered the strong hands grabbing her as she fell.

As the blue sky above began to dim, swallowed by shadow, Baelon Vos looked down on her in his arms. Behind his mask of disappointment, there was a quiet fury burning in his eyes.

His image stayed with her in the dark to come, her energy ebbed to its last.

45
CALAMITY

As Yamnomora slew the last of the Greyhelm guards, his armoured body slamming into the floor, the atmosphere inside the throne room was sucked into a tense void. Slait stood over the spot where Kitrana Voden had just hammered The Anther, porting her, and her alone, to safety. Where there had once been polished marble and veins of silvyr, there were now patches of rocky earth and snow, the latter having never previously graced Morthil's interior.

She was gone.

Grarfath could hardly believe it, his heart stung by betrayal. It was quickly drowned out by despair, the hammer their only hope of escaping the rising waters. Seeing the fury burning behind The Dawn Sword's eyes made the smith wonder if he would live long enough to drown.

The Andaren's fists balled into knots at his side before he lashed out and kicked a pedestal over, knocking the antique gauntlet from its perch with a *clatter*. His bald and scarred head whipped around, turning his golden eyes on the dwarves. He looked from one to the other, likely calculating how he would murder them.

"Is there another way out of this wretched place?" he demanded.

Surprised to still be drawing breath, Grarfath looked to Yamnomora, who seemed to share some of his confusion. "Ye're not goin' to fight?" she asked, wielding one of the fallen guards' swords.

"That depends on whether you know another way out of here," Slait replied. "This is Khardunar. They must have built escape tunnels in case of invasion."

"Tunnels to where?" Yamnomora countered. "We're hangin' from the cavern roof!"

"Up there then!" Slait growled, pointing to the ceiling.

"I don' bloody know!" Yamnomora growled back, shaking the sword in her hand. "I don' live 'ere, an' I didn' build it!"

Slait took a threatening step towards the dwarven warrior, prompting the smith to speak up.

"Glaive said the other regions will 'ave taken to their evacuation tunnels. This region has been cut off. He said we'd 'ave to wait it out up 'ere."

"Wait it out?" Slait barked. "By the gods that dwarf was a fool! Even if the water fails to swallow Khardunar, we're so high we'd drown before we reached the bottom of the steps, never mind the tunnels."

The Dawn Sword roared and kicked one of the dead dwarves, flinging the corpse up and into the wall.

"The steps," Grarfath muttered, his thoughts going to those being held back by the Greyhelms. How long did they have before the water swept them over the ledge and into the chasm beneath Khardunar?

"Where are *ye* goin'?" Yamnomora questioned, seeing the smith stride towards the open doors.

"The guards down there are keepin' everyone back—they're goin' to get everyone in this region killed. They don' even know the one who ordered 'em to hold the line is dead," he added, gesturing to the High King's body.

"What are *ye* goin' to do abou'it?" Yamnomora asked, though she never took her eyes from Slait.

Grarfath crossed the threshold, shrugging as he did. "I haven' thought that far ahead."

"You're wasting your time!" Slait called after him. "We're all doomed down here. At least their end will be swift," he added miserably.

Yamnomora hefted the sword in her hand. "If it's a swift end ye're lookin' for..."

Slait turned away from the dwarf, his pace set to a listless wander. It was the last Grarfath saw of him before the throne room was behind him and the grand steps were before him.

The city below was steadily being claimed by the water as towers and buildings that had stood for millennia were brought down. The masses dominated the plateau at the bottom of the steps, where thousands tried to push past the armoured contingent of Greyhelm guards. It was by the point of spears that they were kept at bay.

Grarfath descended a single golden step before the sound of cracking rock and creaking steel fell upon him. Looking up, his gaze was drawn to the colossal pendulums fixed to the cavern walls and the semi-circular blades at their ends. The dwarf thanked the old gods that they remained where they were before pressing on.

The smith hollered and yelled as he drew nearer to the guards, but his voice could not carry over the crying of children, protests of parents, and the roar of the approaching sea. He barely slowed when he crashed into the back of one guard, shoving him forwards and disturbing their entire formation.

"Stop!" he cried. "Ye've got to stop!"

The guard to his right gripped him roughly by the shoulder and yanked him back, his spear soon to follow. Grarfath rolled aside, narrowly missing the point of the weapon as it bore into the ground.

Grabbing the shaft, the smith ensured the spear remained where it was while he jumped to his feet. The Greyhelm, however, was trained to never give an inch when defending Khardunar, and so he thrust an armoured fist into Grarfath's face, knocking him back onto the steps.

"Wait!" the smith shouted, one hand waving while the other cupped his cheek. "Ye don' understand! He's dead!" Whether he heard him or not over the din, the lone Greyhelm continued to advance, driving Grarfath further up the steps. "The High King is dead! THE HIGH KING IS DEAD!"

The guard faltered, failing to ascend the next step. Two more at the back of the Greyhelm formation turned around, having heard the smith's declaration. One of the two patted the guard in front of him, turning his attention to the steps.

The guard who had punched him pointed his spear. "Ye lie!"

"Would I be standin' 'ere if he were still breathin'?" Grarfath countered. "He's dead! Tharg too! Do ye hear me!" The smith projected his voice over the guards. "High King Glaive is dead! Lord Tharg is dead! There are no Greyhelms 'ere! Ye're doomin' yer own people for nothin'!"

Another of the guards broke away from their row to face the smith. He gripped his spear in two hands, a threatening gaze piercing the slits in his visor. It became all the more threatening when he took to the steps.

"This ain' the time for vengeance!" Grarfath told him, taking another step up. "We need to get everyone up there!" He looked over at the falling buildings and encroaching waves. "We're runnin' out o' time," he fumed, teeth grinding.

I'm the Hammerhold, he thought, trying to bolster his resolve.

Absent any hammer in his hand, the thought rang hollow, deflating his courage. How could he take on the mantle of the Hammerhold without The Anther? He was just a smith.

A sharp yell turned the dwarf's attention to the edge of the Greyhelms, where one of the guards had pushed back a small child with the pommel of his spear. The mother reacted violently, bashing the Greyhelm about the visor. She received a backhand from the same guard, who went on to pull a dagger from his belt and hold it threateningly at the father's throat.

Something snapped inside the smith. His resolve be damned. He didn't need it when his blood was boiling so.

The Greyhelm rising to meet him couldn't have predicted an unarmed and untrained dwarf would throw himself down the steps, but that was exactly what Grarfath did. His weight impacted the guard and took them both down to the plateau, where they crashed into several legs. The ripple effect was devastating to their formation, each dwarf taken out by the one behind them.

Grarfath gripped the Greyhelm beneath him by his helmet and hammered his head repeatedly into the stone. He didn't stop there, rising faster than those encumbered by so much armour. Kicking one aside before he could get up, the smith claimed a fallen spear, swinging it and jabbing it to clear something close to a path.

"GO!" he roared at the masses.

The distinct sound of steel cutting through armour and biting into flesh turned the smith back to the steps. Yamnomora was clearing the way in the only manner she knew. With bodies at her feet, she paused to nod approvingly at Grarfath before returning to what she did best.

One of the Greyhelms reached out from the ground, snatching at ankles. Grarfath plunged the spear down, driven on by righteous rage.

"Run!" he urged, shoving and kicking the guards.

There came distant cries as some of the Greyhelms were pushed over the lip and into the chasm. There was nothing they could do now, the swell of people too much to quell. Any who managed to find their feet and fight back were dragged back down by many hands, where they succumbed to the stampede.

Feeling the water wash around his feet, Grarfath turned to spy the rising sea between the masses. It was minutes away from creating a powerful waterfall that would begin to fill the chasm beneath Khardunar.

"Go!" he yelled. "Up! Up!"

Grarfath heard the screams before his eyes discovered the cause. Along with great slabs of rock, the fixings that had secured the pendulums for centuries fell into the chasm. Like the arm of a god, one of the pendulums arced slowly across the cavern. Swinging across the steps, the huge blade sliced through three dwarves without an ounce of resistance. But it was the subsequent shock and fear that inflicted more damage. Their sudden stop sent a wave down through the ascending mob, casting a dozen into the chasm.

"Keep goin'!" Yamnomora cried from the base.

It took precious seconds for those in the lead to find their courage. Even then, there were only a few seconds more before the pendulum swung back towards them. Pushed forwards by the swell, those who tried to stop in time were thrust into the thick blade, their violent deaths sending another shockwave down through the masses.

More rock and steel fell from the cavern roof, plummeting past the stairs at frightening speed. "No," Grarfath uttered, helpless but to watch as another pendulum broke free of its fixings.

Passing only inches above a particular step, the second blade swept mercilessly through the fleeing dwarves. More lives were taken in a spray of blood, and more lives were lost to the darkness below.

"Grarfath!" Yamnomora called, pushing her way through to him. "We need to get up there an' direct 'em!"

Together, they muscled their way into the throng where it narrowed to meet the bottom of the steps. Yamnomora remained on one side of the lower pendulum while the smith continued up, positioning himself just above the higher one. Taking control of the flow, they were able to instruct their kin when to stop and when to go.

It was just too slow.

The water was coming for them.

Those still on the plateau were wading through it to reach the steps, their home crumbling behind them. As much as Grarfath wanted to urge his people on, he had to keep stopping them for the blade to pass.

It seemed the survivors of Morthil were truly doomed when the third and final pendulum lost its place. Unlike the others, however, the rock securing the end of the pendulum was shattered by cracks.

Grarfath's jaw fell open as he watched the entire pillar of steel drop away from the cavern ceiling. "Hold on!" he warned, but there was nothing to be done for those in line with its fall.

The golden stairs shuddered as the pendulum plunged through them and down into the roots of the mountain. In its wake, several steps were entirely gone, along with any who were unfortunate enough to have been climbing them. Adding to the death toll, half a dozen more fell over the edge of the stairs, their footing compromised by the quake.

"Keep going!" Grarfath insisted, desperate to know if Yamnomora had been killed or cut off from the rest of the steps. "Go!" He ushered the last on his side beyond the swinging pendulum and up to Khardunar.

Descending enough steps to put himself on the other side of the pendulum, he was relieved to spot Yamnomora standing at the top of the severed steps. Relief quickly turned to dismay when the smith saw the impassable gap that now separated the two halves. Rushing down to the bottom step on his side, Grarfath foolishly looked over the lip and down into the abyss. Damned if his hands and feet didn't tingle and begin to sweat.

"Are ye a'right?" he called down to his companion.

"I can't make that jump," Yamnomora replied grimly. "They're ain' none that can."

Grarfath caught sight of the small faces poking out between legs and cloaks. "What abou' the children? Can ye toss 'em up?" he asked desperately, unable to contemplate Yamnomora's fate in the moment.

The red-headed dwarf glanced back at the little ones among them, her heart visibly breaking. "No," she answered with agony.

Distant screams echoed up from those still at the base of the steps. The water was flowing so strongly now that parents had to pick up their children while the elders among them were dragged down into the chasm. They were running out of time.

Shaking his head, desperately trying to come up with a solution, the lowest pendulum swung from left to right, its path taking the huge blade right through the gap in the steps. The speed of it swept the smith's dreadlocks out and picked up his beard. Grarfath swore under his breath, realising the possibility of constructing any kind of bridge from materials in the palace would fail. Their only options were to jump or...

The dwarf looked at Yamnomora before looking back over one shoulder, where Khardunar hung from the cavern stone. "Wait there!" he commanded needlessly.

"Where are ye goin'?" Yamnomora shouted, seeing the smith take to the steps.

Grarfath saved his breath and charged up to the palace. The crowds made it all the harder to reach the throne room, but there was none among them capable of stopping the powerful smith from getting through. Shoving past the last of them, most of whom were staring at the wonders inside the great chamber or at the dead king himself, Grarfath laid eyes on their only solution.

Slait was slouched in the High King's throne, one leg hanging over the armrest. He looked a man resigned to his fate, oblivious even to the masses that had flooded the throne room.

"Ye!" Grarfath called, hurrying towards the Andaren. "I've need o' ye!"

"I've already searched the upper levels," The Dawn Sword replied miserably, his golden eyes never straying from his lofty boot. "It seems old Glaive over there thought he was safe from everything in his golden palace."

"Ye're a Vahlken, aye?" Grarfath began, ignoring his comment.

Slait turned to look at him. "Come to insult me before I drown, have you? Take a care, smith. My mood sours."

"I mean ye're strong, aye? Fast too. I'm in need o' both," he added urgently.

"Leave me be, dwarf."

"The steps are broken," Grarfath reported, stepping dangerously close to the killer. "There's still hundreds down there, stuck on the other side. They can't make the jump an' they don' 'ave the strength to throw anyone up. But *ye* could do it," the smith told him, his tone almost pleading. "We 'ave to go, *now!*"

Slait's attention returned to his boot, his expression unfazed by the calamity. "Die down there, die up here. What does it matter?"

"They don' 'ave to die at all!" Grarfath growled, stepping so close to him now that The Dawn Sword could throttle him. "Help us! Please! Ye claim ye're 'ere to do the gods' work. Surely even *yer* gods can't abide needless death."

"We're all going to die down here, smith. I can only be glad the gods slumber in death, lest they see my failure with their own eyes."

Grarfath changed tack. "Ye don' 'ave to fail. This doesn' 'ave to be the end. Dwarves are the best engineers in all o' Verda! We're natural problem solvers. Ye can bet someone 'ere can figure out a way to save us. Ye can also bet we're goin' to need every able body to see it done. Help us an' we'll help ye reach the surface again. I give ye me word."

Somewhere in the middle of his speech, Slait's head had twitched, as if the Andaren had been hooked by an idea. "There's no way out of here," he finally replied, seeing the ruse.

"They said the same thing once abou' gettin' *into* the mountains," Grarfath countered. "But we did it. There's nothin' we stone bones can't get around. Or *through*. If we're to maximise our chances o' doin' that, we're goin' to need every dwarven mind we can get." The smith straightened up. "What say ye?"

The Dawn Sword's expression gave nothing away, but the next time Yamnomora looked up the steps, the dwarven warrior beheld the most unexpected saviour.

As the pendulum swung between them, Slait leaped the gap with a single graceful bound. Uneasy was the stare between him and Yamnomora, but it only lasted until he picked her up and launched her towards Grarfath's waiting hands. She just made it, one foot finding purchase against the bottom step while the smith caught her wrists.

Grarfath was flooded with relief to have her by his side again, and the two of them worked together to grab every dwarf Slait threw up to them. It was slow but steady, the priority given to the children and their mothers. Slait was a testament to the power of the Vahlken, his muscles pumping relentlessly as if he were some dwarven machine. Still, the line seemed never ending and the waters continued to rise all the while, claiming more lives.

As the waters rose, the situation found a way to get worse. The lower section of the steps began to wobble, the stone at its base cracking and slipping away from the cliff. Screams and cries for help worked their way up to Grarfath, but it was Slait who saw the inevitable coming. Abandoning the dwarf he had been about to throw up, The Dancing Sword of the Dawn bent his knees and jumped, taking him cleanly to the safety of the upper steps.

"What are ye doin'?" Grarfath yelled.

"It's coming down!" Slait retorted. "Let's hope we have the dwarves we need," he added knowingly.

Grarfath was powerless to stop him from striding up the steps, back to Khardunar.

"Coward!" Yamnomora shouted after him.

The smith turned back to those stuck on the lower steps. They were already rushing down, back to the plateau and surging water. The broken steps fell away before the last few could make it, and so they plummeted with the broken steps towards the watery darkness below. That still left hundreds on the plateau, huddled and terrified. How long did they really have before the sea carried them into the abyss?

"Wait!" Grarfath called after The Dawn Sword. "There has to be another way!"

With Yamnomora, they chased after Slait, avoiding the highest pendulum and entering the palace once more. No shoving was required this time, the mob parting to allow The Dawn Sword to pass through.

"We can't jus' leave 'em down there!" the smith persisted, his words aimed at Slait's broad back.

"Unless you can fly, smith, that's exactly what we're doing." The Dawn Sword continued towards the throne, leaving Grarfath to stand beside Tharg's corpse. "I suggest you start *problem-solving*," he asserted, taking to the throne like some king.

The smith wiped the sweat from his brow, wondering how he was supposed to think clearly when all he could see was his fellow dwarves trapped on the plateau. Yamnomora was saying something to him, or perhaps she was saying it to Slait, but Grarfath didn't take it in. His thoughts felt like they were moving at great speed and standing still all at the same time.

How could he save them all?

How could he save any of them?

The answer came to him in a flash of light and a clap of air, causing his ears to pop. Like everyone else in the throne room, Slait included, Grarfath Underborn could but stare in utter disbelief.

46

OATHS OF BLOOD

O f all the places Kassanda Grey had been trained and trained others, the central spire that overlooked all of Valgala was possibly the most distracting. The city was a beauty to behold, its white walls speaking of virtue, while the enormous lake at its heart seemed a reflection of its purity. It was a monument to what the human mind and hands could bring into the world.

But it was not the source of Joran's distraction.

Not once did the young man look beyond the vast balcony, taken in by the magnificent view. He moved through the drills she had been teaching him, and clumsily so. He missed crucial steps, mishandled the hilt of his training sword, and failed to observe his proximity to the balcony rail.

Still, he had persevered since dawn, his loose shirt now stained with sweat—though not nearly as much as it should have been, given the hours he had been at it. It seemed his body conserved energy at a better rate than the ordinary man or Andaren, just as he regulated his temperature better when exposed to the blistering cold.

There is a Vahlken in him, Garganafan remarked confidently.

Kassanda glanced beyond the rail, catching sight of her companion's white scales breaking the lake's surface. *He does not exhibit their speed or their strength,* she commented.

Not yet, the dragon replied knowingly.

The Rider scrutinised the boy's movements. *I have seen him display a degree of Vahlken balance and precision. He already has excellent core control, always sure of his footing and environment.*

But not today, Garganafan said, finishing her thought.

No... Not today.

"Stop," she commanded.

Normally able to come to a perfect stop, as if beheld by some spell, Joran continued halfway through his manoeuvre before coming to a halt.

"Your mind wanders," the Rider announced.

"I'm fine."

"I didn't ask about your feelings," Kassanda pointed out. "I stated a fact. I would say you've lost your edge somewhere along the way, but you never had it to begin with. You have met the new day, yet your mind remains in the past. How might we remedy that?"

Joran rubbed his left eye and wiped some of the sweat from his brow before pushing his white hair back. "Apologies, master," he said curtly. "I'm just... frustrated. It's been two days since the war council. Why are we still here? I thought we were to accompany the fleet out of Caster Hold."

"And we shall," Kassanda told him evenly, searching his eyes so she might discern truth from lies. "It takes time to get word across the country, not to mention the preparations required to ready an entire fleet. Caster Hold will be in chaos right now. Your training is still a priority and the palace offers us a safe place to conduct it."

That answer clearly didn't satisfy the boy, his wrist rolling to swing the sword round and round.

Kassanda drew her sword, the silvyr blade singing as it tasted the air. She moved to stand directly in front of him, an obvious challenge.

"What are you doing?" Joran asked.

"What does it look like I'm doing?"

The boy licked his lips and swallowed once, his purple eyes glancing at the sword in her hand. "It looks like we're to spar, except you're still wielding your silvyr blade."

"Top marks," the Rider quipped. "But what we're actually doing is sharpening your focus. I don't know what really troubles you, but I can bet it will fade under threat of pain."

"How am I supposed to—"

Kassanda leaped, literally cutting through his words. Joran had the sense to dart backwards, his keen sense of balance keeping him light on his feet. Was that Vahlken speed? If not of the body then certainly of the mind.

Displaying a boldness he had yet to earn, the boy struck back, his steel blade batting her sword aside before coming down with a chopping blow. The question of his speed was answered then, for the Rider easily brought her weapon to block the attack above her head. A solid fist to his chest ended their clash and sent the boy skidding across the smooth floor.

Rubbing his chest, Joran picked himself up with a scowl. "You cheated."

"You cannot cheat in a fight for your life. The sword is but one weapon. You must learn to use all at your disposal."

Joran feigned his agreeing smile and dashed towards her, his boot coming up to find her gut. Kassanda's superior speed saw her retreat just enough that the kick found naught but air, while her free hand whipped up to cup his heel. Joran should have been put off balance, vulnerable to a swift kick to his inside leg, but the son of Ilithranda used her hand to flip his entire body up and over. That second boot would have clipped her jaw had she not had the speed of a Rider.

Nonetheless, Joran had not had the training to execute a follow up attack, smooth as his recovery had been. Kassanda barrelled in, rolling his sword away to expose his torso. Her free hand shot out, her rigid fingers stabbing into the nerve cluster in his shoulder, before slamming her pommel into his chest. Having pulled her punches, he remained on his feet, allowing the Rider to jump and twist.

The wind was forced from his lungs by the boot planted in his sternum. Once again, Joran slid across the floor, his sword falling from his grasp. He slapped the floor with his palm, his face flushing with anger.

"Again," he demanded.

Kassanda flicked his resting sword with the tip of her own, sending it into his waiting hand. As he came on, weapon rising high, the Rider flipped the hilt in her hand so the silvyr ran up her arm. With little effort—much to Joran's increasing irritation—she then evaded his every attack by no more than an inch with a pivot here and a twist of her shoulders there.

As she had predicted, his rage won out and he ceased flowing through the moves she had taught him. He brought the sword down in two hands, aiming for her head.

It was then that Kassanda returned her blade to the duel, raising it to meet the hammering strike. Feeling the jar run down through her arms, the Rider questioned whether she had just experienced a portion of mutated strength. Either way, it was not enough to beat her defence, and his emotions prevented him from spotting the biting dent in his sword.

When he came at her again, Kassanda sidestepped as she blocked, aware of what was about to transpire. As damaged steel collided with unyielding silvyr, Joran's training sword shattered into pieces. Concluding their match, the Rider whipped his back with the flat of her blade, the edge just cutting into flesh.

Joran cried out in pain, one hand reaching over his shoulder. "I was never going to win while you fight with a silvyr—"

The boy clamped his mouth shut when the Rider's blade was tossed in his direction. Taking it firmly in his grip, he tested the weight of it, hefting it this way and that while examining both sides of its length.

"Do you think that will make a difference?" she asked him.

"Yes," he answered obstinately.

Kassanda refrained from shaking her head or rolling her eyes.

"What good is the weapon in your hand when you fail to see who you bring it against? You let your emotions cloud what should be obvious to you."

His jaw firm, Joran managed to control his tone at least. "And what's that?"

"You faced an opponent you cannot beat," the Rider said plainly.

Joran frowned. "If I am to think like that then surely I will never earn the dragon's heart."

"I'm not talking about bravery. I'm talking about strategy. Using *this* before *this*," she explained, tapping her head and then her breast. "You should have accepted that this was an opportunity to learn, not gain a victory. You will fight more than common soldiers out there. It is inevitable that you will face a warrior of skill equal to a Rider, if not a Rider themselves. You should be observing how I move, how I counter. You should be pushing me to see what I'm capable of. Know your enemy, Joran. Only then will you understand what it takes to beat them."

The boy's head sank into his chest, the sword held low at his side. If her words had been heard, he was reluctant to acknowledge them. *Youth*, she mused miserably.

"Put this on."

Joran accepted the strip of cloth produced from her belt. "Over my eyes?"

"Well I don't want you to wear it as a neckerchief," she replied dryly, making for the potted plant just inside the balcony door.

While Joran concealed his eyes, the Rider snapped off a branch, its length not far off a sword's. Kassanda slashed the air with it, satisfied with its durability.

"Now what?" the boy asked.

"Now we shall really test your focus," she said menacingly.

"My focus is fine," he insisted.

"That is not what *I* have observed. Something gnaws at you, competing for your attention. What could be more pressing than your training?"

As Joran opened his mouth, his lips already shaping into a

negative response, Kassanda struck the back of his legs with the branch. The boy yelped and brought the silvyr sword up in both hands.

"Use your senses," she encouraged. "Listen for the creak of my leathers, the pad of my boots, the sound of my voice." Her words trailed off as she ducked and whipped the branch out again, catching him across the shins.

"Ow!" he yelled, waving the sword out in front of him.

"Catch my scent in the breeze," she continued, her voice turning the boy on the spot.

Her cloak blew out in the wind, ruffling to Joran's right. He backhanded the area, swiping at no more than air. Kassanda flicked the end of the stick and scratched the side of his cheek. The boy growled and lashed out at empty space.

"You left the war council with haste," Kassanda commented, preying now on his mind.

"What of it?" he asked, turning to face her voice.

"To my eyes it looked as if the king followed you." She paused then, assessing his expression for any hint that she was on the right track. "Did you speak with him?"

"No," he replied all too quickly.

Kassanda struck again, whacking his sword arm this time. Joran nearly dropped the weapon before twisting the hilt and striking at her. The Rider intercepted his wrist with one hand and whipped him across the back again, deliberately hitting him where the silvyr had drawn blood.

Rather than give into the pain this time, Joran thrust the blade behind him, forcing Kassanda into retreat. Pivoting, he then pursued her, dragging the blade diagonally left and right as they moved across the balcony. Twice he reduced the size of her stick, chopping through the slender wood like it wasn't even there. Eventually, the Rider had to duck and roll away, making noise as she did. Joran rounded on her, the silvyr in his hand slicing through the air.

He stopped, unaware that she was standing atop the railing

beside him. His head tilted, listening for her over the incessant wind.

"Over here," she whispered, drawing the sword over the railing. She was gone immediately, of course, somersaulting over him and onto the balcony once more.

A clip around the back of his head informed him that he needed to narrow his focus.

"What is it about this place that troubles you so?" she queried. "You were all wonder and awe," the Rider remarked, always moving. "Now you brood. What am I not aware of?"

"Nothing," he grumbled, honing in on her.

They danced again, and the boy received another strike for his efforts. "There can be no secrets between master and apprentice. It is my duty to strip you of all that would hinder you in keeping to your oaths. If something stands between you and what must be done, let's have it and be done with it."

Joran tore the blindfold from his eyes. "This is pointless," he fumed, tossing it away.

"Dragon Riders must be the light that holds back the darkness," Kassanda informed him. "So we must learn to fight in the dark."

"That's very poetic," Joran admitted, "but if I can't see, I can't fight."

"Would you say the same of Andromalda?" Kassanda countered. "You must have seen her fight amongst the ruins. Was she unable to fight without her eyes to see?"

"I can bet it would have helped."

"Did it help you earlier? You never took your eyes off me and yet you still bled for it." Kassanda discarded the stick and took her sword back. "There's always more going on than what you can see. Every Rider must come to learn this lesson. Never accept, always question. Never rely on one weapon or one sense. Use everything at your disposal. You will never inspire by the mere swing of a sword. You must be *more*."

There came a sharp knock against the archway that led into the domed chamber. The Rider might have dismissed whoever sought to interrupt her lesson were it not the King of Erador himself. Kassanda bowed, as was expected of her. It was with embarrassment and the promise of punishment that she turned her gaze on Joran beside her, who did not bow.

King Edris entered the chamber, making his way towards the balcony. "I come with news, good *and* bad, I'm afraid. I thought I would deliver it myself."

"Your Grace," Kassanda began. "You could have sent word, and we would have gladly descended to the throne room."

The king waved the notion away. "Any excuse to see this view," he said wistfully, admiring his city below. His eyes did linger on Joran, however, while the boy notably looked anywhere else. "I quite like having a dragon in the lake, though I hear the local fishing has all but died," he added with some amusement.

"Garganafan has been known to have that effect on the wildlife," the Rider commented with a tight smile.

"You said you have news, Your Grace," Joran reminded him, much to his master's ire.

"I did," King Edris confirmed, his gaze returning to find those young and violet eyes. "The fleet is almost ready to set sail for the towers. Were you to leave today, I'm sure they would be ready to depart upon your arrival."

Kassanda bowed again. "That is good news, Your Grace. With a swift northerly breeze, we should be ashore before the Andarens reach their home soil."

"Yes, though not the good news I come bearing," the king specified, looking to Joran. "I have had word from Thedaria. Your companions yet live. They have crossed paths with my agents there."

At last, a genuine smile lit up Joran's face. "They have seen Gallien?"

The king nodded. "And the others. A wizard, a blind Rider, and a Kedradi ranger by all accounts. Your friend, Gallien, keeps quite the company."

"My *father*," Joran corrected, a notch of defiance in him.

The king's jaw twisted out of shape, his eyes narrowed, as if he couldn't bring himself to agree or disagree. "My agents are not all they crossed paths with," he eventually said. "Apparently, Gallien has something of a chequered past—history with the Padoshi there. It's caused some friction and no small degree of violence. Still, my people have seen them safely from Thedaria, though I would advise they steer clear of the city upon their return."

"Return?" Joran questioned. "Where are they going?"

"Therein lies the *bad* news. They are bound for *Taraktor*."

Kassanda was sure she had misheard the king, but she felt the same confusion across their bond, and Garganafan heard *everything*.

Madness, the dragon opined.

"Taraktor?" the Rider echoed incredulously, noting the blank expression on Joran's face. "Why would they go there?"

"What's Taraktor?" the boy asked.

"I am yet to receive a more detailed report, but it would seem they are on the hunt for a weapon of power, one yet to be claimed by either side."

That still made no sense as far as their destination was concerned. "That hunt would take them to *Taraktor*?" Her tone continued to be laden with disbelief.

"What is it?" Joran had raised his voice above theirs now. "What's Taraktor?"

Kassanda looked her ward in the eyes. "It's where the Jainus keep all their nightmares."

"It's a prison, of sorts," the king detailed. "My predecessors and I have long left it to the wizards, as we have The Silver Trees of Akmar. It is said to be a dark place, a wretched stain on the land. Those who venture too close never return."

"Where is it?" Joran persisted. "I've never seen it on a map."

"I confess I have never known," the king informed him. "I leave such things to Galahart."

"You won't find it on any map," Kassanda explained. "It's not somewhere the Jainus want people poking their noses in."

"You know where it is," Joran reasoned.

"I do," the Rider said.

The boy looked at her expectantly. "Where is it?"

"You do not make demands of me," Kassanda told him. "And what would you even do with such knowledge? Besides the obviously foolish."

"I would go to their aid," Joran declared.

The Rider folded her arms. "As I said..."

"If they are going somewhere none ever return from, I would—"

"What?" Kassanda interjected. "What would you do? Join them in never returning? That's death, Joran. Or worse: imprisonment under the Jainus. You're meant for something more than that."

"They're searching for a weapon of power," he pointed out. "That's worth the risk."

"Worthy of death? Listen to yourself. They've already been through hell to get you this far. They have bled so you can train. So *train*."

Kassanda was suddenly conscious of their audience. Of all in the realm, the king should not have to witness such a dispute. Added to his own eyes and ears, their abrasive tones had also brought a handful of palace guards to the open archway.

"Forgive me, Your Grace. And my ward. His young blood yearns for action and rejects wisdom."

Joran looked at the king, his gaze somehow silencing the most powerful man in Erador. "My blood," the boy muttered, an expression of reluctant revelation about him.

"Joran," King Edris intoned, his voice full of warning. "You cannot call upon your blood without consequence. Trust me."

What's happening here? Garganafan mused.

Kassanda looked from the king to Joran without an answer for her companion.

"Is this the path you want?" King Edris asked the boy.

"My path is still my own," Joran replied defiantly before turning to face Kassanda. "I'm just using everything at my disposal."

While Kassanda sensed her own words were about to be used

against her, she couldn't fathom how, nor could she ask before Joran continued.

"You swore your oaths to Blood Etragon and the throne of Erador," he stated, his gaze like iron.

"I did," the Rider confirmed, still unsure where this was going.

"Then by my blood and the throne rightfully mine, your allegiance is sworn to *me*. As the son of King Edris Andalan Etragon and Prince of Erador, I would have you tell me where to find Taraktor."

Garganafan's shock was in harmony with her own, the two companions unable to voice their surprise. Kassanda could only looked at the king, the only one who could shed light on the truth of it. His silence was deafening.

"Imposible," she uttered.

"Says the Dragon Rider," the king countered. "We live in an improbable world, not an impossible one. Joran *is* my son. Your oaths are to him as much as they are to me."

Kassanda could only stare at Joran for a time. But the truth was the truth, a crushing weight her duty could not deny. "North of Caster Hold," she revealed, obeying the... *prince*. "It clings to the eastern cliffs between Erador and Nareene."

Joran nodded in satisfaction. "Then I too am bound for Taraktor," he said, making to leave.

The Rider frowned at his back. "You are forsaking your training," she called after him, but he did not respond as the baffled guards parted for him. "You would let him go?" she demanded of the king, any thought of protocol forgotten. "He is your only heir. You know where he's going."

"You heard him. His path is his own. I will not make a king of the boy by trapping him in this gilded cage. If he is truly destined for the throne, he must find his own way there, as I did."

Feeling that everything was unravelling about her, Kassanda bowed to the king. "If you would excuse me, Your Grace."

"You're leaving for Caster Hold?" he asked, pausing her departure.

"Instruct them to set sail as soon as they are ready. With or without me."

————

After failing to catch up with Joran inside the palace and having no joy tracking him down on the streets of Valgala, Kassanda did the only thing she could and took to the air.

Circling the city, they could see many coming and going, but of the six roads that fed into the capital, two of them were without activity since one led to The Tower of Jain and the other to the narrow gap through The Spine of Erador. That made spotting the only person in that area all the easier.

Garganafan banked to the west, gliding down towards The Misted Road and its sole occupant. Joran's sandy cloak billowed northwards, the wind determined to take it. He had no supplies and no weapon save the broken blade tucked into his belt, yet there he was, trekking into the depths of the mountains in the middle of winter.

Damned fool, she cursed.

He means well, Garganafan reasoned. *Sometimes that can make us do foolish things.*

He's the son of the king and grandson of the Andaren emperor with a future that has the potential to see our numbers swell. He doesn't have the luxury of being foolish.

Just saying all that reminded Kassanda of the weight upon his shoulders.

Landing behind him so as not to seem threatening, Garganafan shook the earth, cracking the road. His wings flared once before closing about his sides, buffeting the boy. Kassanda was on the ground in seconds, disheartened to see that Joran was still walking towards the mountains.

"You can't just walk away from this," she called after him.

"I'm not walking away from anything," he replied, finally turning to face her. "To have the heart of a dragon, you must stand up to your foes. Be *defiant* in the face of death. Your words! Those are your words, and that's exactly what I'm doing."

"You *will* stand up to them," she promised. "But not now. And not like this."

"Then how? With a dragon at my side? With a silvyr blade in my hand? You're training me for something that hasn't even happened. That might never happen! You said it yourself: by knowing the future, we've changed it. We're just wasting time. I should be with them, helping however I can. So should you. Because of me, you're not guarding the eggs from Baelon. We've both got somewhere better to be than training for something that might never come to pass."

With that, he turned back to the west.

"I can't just let you abandon this path," Kassanda asserted. "What's been seen… It's too important. If the Skaramangians fear a time of dragons, then shouldn't we—"

A sharp squawk drowned her out, a strong gust of wind running through her cloak. Descending from above, Oaken flapped his wings until he was on the road in front of Joran, his armoured beak flashing in the sun. His scarred face and chipped horns framed his cold yellow gaze. The Aegre did not cower in the face of Garganafan as he should have.

Joran hesitated until Oaken stooped his front half, allowing the boy to ascend his mother's saddle. Though he looked only a shadow of a true Vahlken, Joran appeared comfortable astride the Aegre.

"Fight this war however you will, Kassanda Grey! And I will do the same!"

Dragon and Rider watched as Oaken launched himself back into the air, taking Joran into the west.

To Taraktor.

47
THE FALL OF KHARDUNAR

The Anther stood proud in the heart of Khardunar, its head partially buried in the floor and surrounded by stony debris. The shock of its arrival sent a gasp throughout the survivors, a prelude to the silence that followed and occupied the throne room with an iron grip.

Grarfath looked from the hammer to Slait, who was poised to spring from the High King's throne. All the mutations in the world weren't going to help him reach The Anther before Grarfath, the weapon directly in front of him. As The Dancing Sword of the Dawn propelled himself across the dais, the smith claimed the hammer, knowing exactly where he wanted to go.

Timing was everything, something a good smith knew all about, and so he thundered The Anther into the floor just as Slait was upon him.

A relentlessly cold wind swept over the pair, who now occupied the surface world, where the elements blew in from the east to meet the mountains. Slait flew over the dwarf, completing his leap as they were ported miles from Khardunar.

"Ye 'ave me thanks for savin' those that ye did," the smith

called out, moving away from the impact site. "It's the only reason I ain' stavin' yer head in right now."

On all fours, Slait tried to orientate himself in the world. "Where are we?" he rasped.

Grarfath looked to the west, where The Morthil Mountains rose to dominate the land. "The Bronze Doors o' Orgunthain," he announced, pointing The Anther at the distant slab of iron carved into the rock. "Don' worry, ye won' be alone for long."

With that, the smith hammered the ground at his feet and returned to the depths of the earth, where he was almost knocked from his feet by the rushing water gushing over the plateau's edge. So loud was it that he barely heard the shock of those around him, their eyes wide at witnessing the miracle of his arrival.

"Who are *ye*?" they asked, clinging to their loved ones, waiting to die.

There was no time to answer them, for the surge of water was now bringing large chunks of debris onto the plateau. Wading towards the nearest group, Grarfath swung from high to low, searching for the ground beneath the water. It wasn't much, but it was apparently enough to stagger the magic therein. The effect was weak, distorting no more than the air around the dwarves, revealing slivers of the surface world.

There came many questions as to what he was doing and what phenomenon they had just witnessed, but the smith had to focus, to block them out, and think only of that dry earth beyond The Bronze Doors of Orgunthain. When the hammer failed to port them a second time, the dwarf twisted the weapon so the head was pointing down, as if he might plunge it like a dagger.

Holding it high, Grarfath, son of Thronghir, dropped to one knee and drove The Anther's head straight down. The magic engulfed six more dwarves who stood around him, porting them all to the surface with a splash of water. As with all who experienced the power of The Anther for the first time, those who had been saved fell about, disorientated and confused, desperately trying to hold onto the contents of their stomachs.

Through the staggering dwarves, Grarfath glimpsed Slait in the distance, on his feet now. Having deliberately ported a hundred yards from where he had left The Dawn Sword, there was no risk from the behemoth while he ported again.

The rising waters parted as he returned to that desolate plateau, if only for a second before swelling about his legs. His muscles twinged, a sting almost about his lungs. He knew then the real risk, and it had nothing to do with the mutated Andaren. The Anther would inflict its cost with every use.

"Me son!" a father shouted, rushing towards Grarfath. "What did ye do?"

"He's safe!" the smith reported. "Gather round! Quickly!"

Having no choice but to trust him, the father closed the gap but left Grarfath enough room to wield The Anther. So too did others, taking their chances with the inexplicable dwarf. They were all petrified, holding their children close and above the rising water.

Grarfath repeated his actions, plunging the hammer straight down at his feet. Again, a handful of dwarves were ported up and out, bringing them into the light of the surface world. Careful to have chosen a slightly different location this time, he was, again, beyond the reach of Slait, who was wandering close to the previous group.

Feeling some of the drain reaching up through the muscles in his neck, Grarfath gripped The Anther in both hands and ported away. After repeating the process three more times, his fatigue ever increasing, the smith realised he needed to port more people at a time before the water became so powerful it pushed them all over the lip.

As the sea closed in about his legs again, the dwarf's knees nearly buckled. By now, he had gained the trust of those around him, however, and they hurried to surround the smith, pushing the children through the gaps. He pictured his environment in his mind, finding those he intended to port. It was more than twice the number he had been saving. He didn't doubt The Anther could do it; by every legendary account, the weapon had been used by Duun himself to move The Nheremyn River.

He doubted his strength.

"Please," one of the mothers pleaded beside him, her daughter gripped to her chest.

One scream turned into many, dragging Grarfath's attention to the ruins of their city. The water had swelled and was now rising ever higher to wash over the plateau. It was not coming alone. Carried by the wave, one of the fallen towers was about to roll over the survivors before being tossed into the chasm.

Seeing that they were all to be crushed, any notion of doubt or strength was banished from the Underborn's mind. He could only act, and so he did.

The *clap* of air was muted by the water, but it did nothing to quash the power of The Anther, or the one who wielded it. As they ported once more, chaos was unleashed upon the surface world. A considerably larger body of water was dumped on the land this time and, with it, over two hundred dwarves. Soaking wet, they fell over each other, blinded by the bright sky and sick to their stomachs from the portation magic.

As always, Grarfath felt the bite in his muscles as if he himself was the source of power from which the hammer drew. Yet he did not collapse as he desired to, his body retaining enough strength to keep him upright on one knee.

He looked at The Anther in his hand. If anything, it had consumed less of his energy. That seemed impossible given the increased number of people he had ported, but he couldn't deny the difference he felt.

With no more than slumped shoulders, he tilted his head to see all who had accompanied him from the doomed plateau. The smith couldn't believe it. He had saved them. *All* of them. His relief, mixed with a notch of pride, helped to combat the terrible drain he was experiencing.

As the eyes of his people began to find him, to look upon him in wonder and thanks, Grarfath remembered the others still trapped down there, inside the walls of Khardunar. Yamnomora was among them. The cantankerous dwarf had been something of a pain, even spiteful at times, but she was the first person to mean something, anything, to him in a long time. She was the first person to have believed in him, declaring him the Hammerhold when she was more than capable of wielding The Anther herself.

That bond formed a new chord of strength in the smith, a chord that granted him access to new wells of reserves. As Slait bounded over, crossing the gap to reach him, Grarfath inhaled one big breath and raised The Anther. When it landed, he was standing on the broken floor of the throne room.

His gaze was weak, roaming lazily over the mob that filled every tier of the grand chamber. One amongst them burst through the wall of onlookers and ran to his side. Yamnomora skidded on her knees—just in time to catch him. She was saying his name in his ear, but her voice sounded so distant.

Grarfath found her green eyes and raised a hand to place his palm to her stubbled cheek. She saw something in him—that much was evident in the way she beheld him. It was, in itself, a source of vitality, fortifying him. Still, he didn't stop her from helping him stand up.

"I did it," he whispered, his voice incapable of anything more. "I got 'em out."

"I know," Yamnomora replied, a genuine smile breaking the hard lines of her jaw. He had never noticed how nice—how warm —that smile was. Or maybe he was imagining the smile. It was hard to say.

The floor beneath them shuddered, and all of Khardunar groaned.

"That keeps happenin'," Yamnomora reported gravely.

Grarfath added a groan of his own as he slowly rose to his feet. He looked about, noting the dust raining down and the cracks beginning to appear on the walls. "It's goin' to fall," he uttered, drawing Yamnomora's hard gaze. "It's headin' for the chasm," the smith said with all confidence.

He took in the faces about him. They were all just as doomed as those up to their knees in water had been.

The Hammerhold would save them all, he told himself, thinking of the mighty Duun. If he was to make a legacy of his own, it could not be less than that of his predecessor. Yet the thought of it was as a great shadow darkening his world. He knew the energy required to port so many—energy he did not have.

A fresh quake ran through Khardunar, threatening its place in the cavern roof.

Something strong gripped his shoulder, turning the smith's attention back to Yamnomora beside him. She was looking earnestly into his brown eyes, searching, perhaps, for something of the dwarf his mother had spoken of. The dwarf who would be worthy of wielding The Anther.

"It's time to raise that hammer if ye can," she said.

He would prove himself such.

"Bring everyone as close as ye can," he rasped.

Having used the hammer to help him stand, he now adjusted the haft in his hand, preparing to swing it. As Yamnomora began to usher everyone closer to him, Grarfath regarded the weapon, specifically the way he was holding it. When porting a larger surface area, he had held The Anther so the head was pointing down.

With what little mental clarity he had left, the dwarf considered the hammer with the mind of a smith. Any good tool had many facets; even a hammer had more than one side. What if...

Those two words spawned many questions, making him wonder about how, exactly, The Anther was meant to be used. Could it be that the top of the head, when plunged straight down, was intended to port the wielder and those around them? That would make sense if the front of the hammer—the side traditionally used—was intended to port enemies or objects, things he could strike. Or *parts* of enemies, he mused, thinking back to the Three-Headed Dread Serpent he had decapitated in The Swamps of Morthil.

Then there was the difference he had felt using it that way. He had certainly retained energy, otherwise he wouldn't have made it into Khardunar.

The palace shook again, as if his thoughts had weight. How long did they have? Minutes? Seconds? The pressure was tenfold in the eyes of so many. There was at least three times the number he had saved on the plateau.

And Yamnomora was among them.

What had it come to that such a dwarf as her was his only friend? Still, after years of solitude in the wake of his father's passing, and the years before that when he had failed to connect with anything that couldn't be placed on an anvil, he was grateful for that friend. Cantankerous as she was.

"It's now or never," she remarked, her green eyes scanning the ceiling.

Crowded around him, dwarves of every guild looked at him expectantly. In that moment, there was nothing to separate them, nothing to tell them apart. The Boldbanes watched him with the same despair in their eyes as the Frostbeards. The Ironguards held their children fiercely close, as did the Redbraids between them. They were one people, huddled around their hope.

As he had on the plateau, Grarfath Underborn dropped to one knee and rammed the head of The Anther into the floor beside his boot. Its power was undeniable, expanding through the vast chamber in a wave that could only be glimpsed as light. In the same second as the hammer hollowed out the heart of the Greyhelms' ancient home, Morthil itself released the palace from its embrace, plummeting it into the dark void and cold waters below.

The light of day was blinding and oh so welcome.

Hundreds of dwarves stumbled and staggered about the flat plains outside The Bronze Doors of Orgunthain. Some cried out in relief, others in disbelief. In the middle of them, Grarfath collapsed onto all fours, his fingers just about holding onto the haft of the hammer. It felt so much heavier than before. Just opening his eyes was a hardship as his every muscle cried out in need of rest. In his chest and in his ears, he could feel his heart beating rapidly.

With numb hands, he pushed himself up, defying his exhaustion. He was helped by other hands, Yamnomora being the only one not affected by The Anther's magic.

"By the old gods," she breathed, "how did ye do that?"

Grarfath thought to explain his findings where the hammer

was concerned but found his voice just as weak as everything else. Instead, he allowed her to take some of his weight as he dipped his head onto her shoulder, The Anther still upright at his feet.

Yamnomora patted the back of his head, where his dreadlocks were gathered into a tight knot. "Even yer mother couldn' 'ave done that," she said, her words just audible over the hubbub.

When her body tensed, the smith forced himself to raise his head and follow her gaze.

Slait was coming.

His long legs saw him stride easily through the masses, his golden eyes locked on Grarfath. A pit of despair opened inside of him. How was he to fight such a fiend now? He gripped The Anther but failed to lift it more than a few inches from the ground.

"Easy," Yamnomora bade, moving to place herself between them. "I'll take care o' this."

Grarfath wished to protest. Was it not his place to protect them? Had the Hammerhold of old not been the greatest warrior of his time? Were he Duun, son of Darl, The Dancing Sword of the Dawn would be a smear on the end of The Anther. Instead, the smith was sure he would vomit before he swung the weapon.

As Yamnomora puffed out her chest and squared her shoulders, Slait began to slow down. While it might have been believable that the red-headed warrior was the source of his hesitation, the truth was something else entirely.

Not far from the heart of their mass, where Grarfath stood, the Andaren found himself entirely surrounded by a growing number of dwarves. Though weaponless, they still possessed their legendary strength and outnumbered the Skaramangian assassin six hundred to one. They deliberately moved to form wall after wall of hardened dwarf, fixing Slait with a cold stare that promised an abundance of violence if he misstepped.

"Out of my way," he demanded.

His next step was mimicked by the dwarves who directly surrounded him. None of them were warriors, and they all hailed from different guilds, but they were each strong, with arms thicker than Slait's.

"Which one of you wants his skull crushed first?" The Dawn Sword asked.

"Ye might kill a few of us, aye," Yamnomora called out, "but ye can't kill all o' us, big man. We'll bring ye down, be sure o' it."

Slait snarled, his top lip curling to reveal a fang. "The hell you will," he growled.

The Andaren stomped forwards, backhanding the first dwarf to reach for him before gripping the next by the throat and using him as a battering ram. A testament to his mutations, The Dawn Sword managed to push through three rows of dwarves before those behind piled on and brought him down under their sheer weight.

As Slait succumbed to his beating, so too did Grarfath succumb to his exhaustion. He managed to slap the back of Yamnomora's cuirass as he fell forward and found her waiting arm was enough to stagger his collapse. But it was not enough to keep his eyes open, nor his mind conscious.

And so the son of Thronghir slipped into the deepest slumber of his life, and well earned it was.

48

STEPPING OFF THE ROAD

It was a crisp dawn in the east, the light of a new day bringing Caster Hold to life. From the deck of The Raven, Gallien's view drifted over the naval town. It had become something of a city over the last two hundred years, if a misshapen one due to the needs of the king's men.

Where they would usually be found on the outskirts of any populace, there were barracks upon barracks in the heart of Caster Hold, all surrounding the main fort—an ugly collection of blocks and ramparts that allowed the Etragon sigil to be seen from anywhere.

Gallien gave the plunging sword of dragon scales no more than a glance, his attention quickly taken by the activity around the docks. Each ship was being loaded with hundreds, if not, thousands, of crates and barrels, the great cranes operating from the safety of the shore. Of course, the smuggler could barely see any of that through the dense mass of soldiers.

Caster Hold was bleeding, its every street and alley gushing with red cloaks, their steel plates shining bright in the dawn. Gallien had seen this before, up close. He remembered well walking among them, plated and cloaked in the king's colours as they prepared to invade enemy lands. History was repeating itself.

"What's going on out there?" Androma asked, though how she had known he was standing there was a mystery.

Gallien cradled his bandaged wrist a little closer to his chest, briefly regarding the blind Rider before returning his gaze to the shore. "If I had to guess, I'd say they're going to invade Harendun, but the last I heard it was under the occupation of a *Dragon Rider*."

"Vander," Androma confirmed.

It seemed a fine coincidence that she would voice his name while the smuggler was rubbing the red dragon scale that belonged to Vander's beastly companion. He looked down at it, gripped between finger and thumb. It had been a while since he had retrieved it from the bottomless satchel. He had forgotten how sharp its edges were.

"We were lucky to get out of Harendun when we did," Androma commented. "Vander retained every one of those soldiers. The ships too. Now he has an army all of his own."

"Good for him," Gallien replied absently, his thoughts cast back to the last time he was in that part of the world. Joran had been only a babe then, and he had yet to love the boy. He missed him terribly.

"What is that?" Androma asked, her sightless eyes angled down at the railing, where the smuggler toyed with the single scale.

Deciding her ears and nose were better than all of his senses combined, Gallien just accepted her seemingly supernatural perception of the world. "It's a dragon scale," he said simply.

"You carry a dragon scale?" she asked, her interest piqued.

The smuggler shrugged. "I picked it up in Harendun."

Androma's head twitched. "You have one of Herragax's scales," she concluded.

"The red dragon? Aye. I found it in the street, right after I watched Vander murder one of our own. Hells, he would have killed me too if he had seen me."

The thought of it still sent a shiver down his spine.

"Vander murdered a human soldier? Why?"

"Stole his kill," Gallien put it simply. "Vander was fighting a Vahlken. The soldier stabbed him in the back and killed him. I guess Vander wanted the glory."

Androma's expression fell, along with her shoulders. "I always wondered how he died," she said quietly.

The smuggler looked at her, brow furrowed. "The Vahlken? You knew him?"

"His name was Tovun. He was an initiate at Ka'vairn when I met him. A good man. I helped to conclude his training with..." The old Rider trailed off and turned her head to the sky. "It seems like a lifetime ago. Everything used to feel so fresh in my mind. I could recall everything, even from centuries ago. Now I struggle to recall last week."

"I'd rather forget last week," Gallien quipped, though he paused to wonder just how much he had been made to *forget* already.

"Why do you carry the scale?" Androma enquired.

The smuggler shrugged again, uncomfortable with the vulnerability between them. "I've been out of my depth for sixteen years. Probably longer," he admitted. He licked his lips, finding it easier, somehow, to talk knowing she couldn't see him. "I don't know. I suppose it reminds me that I didn't die. That maybe I'll survive the next thing."

The old Rider chuckled to herself. "I live every day thinking the opposite. Maybe the next thing *will* kill me."

Gallien let his eyes wander over her weathered face. How much had she seen? How much had she done? Androma was a piece of history, her knowledge guarded by skills she had acquired over her many years of life. Now that he thought about it, Androma might be the noblest person he had ever met.

"I hope it doesn't," he replied, getting no more than a tight smile in response.

Androma's hand wandered down to Gallien's side, her fingers

brushing against the rough leather of the satchel slung over his shoulder. "You've taken good care of my bag, at least."

Gallien tugged on the strap, feeling somewhat protective over it. "I'm not one for magic and the like, but damned if this isn't brilliant. Everyone should have one of these. There were many times when Joran and I had to leave somewhere in a hurry. If we'd had to lug even half of the supplies I keep in here, we'd both be long dead by now."

"I keep meaning to ask The Green Leaf to make me a new one," the old Rider replied. "That satchel saw me through many hard times. I'm glad it was a boon to you and Joran. I like to think I was still with him in some small way."

Gallien was missing Joran too much to dwell on his time with him and, perhaps, the time he would never have again. "How does it work anyhow?" he asked, his tone a bright note in an otherwise souring conversation.

Androma whipped her head around. "You mean to say you never figured it out? After all these years?"

Gallien blew out his cheeks. "I put stuff in and I pull stuff out. As long as it fits through the sides..."

The Rider was silently laughing to herself. "You have to know what you've put in to pull it back out."

The smuggler nodded along, despite disagreeing with the statement. "But I've felt other... *things* in there." He thought of the objects his hand often slipped between to remove the desired item.

"That's because there's so many things in there," Androma said knowingly. "Between the both of us, it's likely been filled almost to capacity. Even pocket dimensions have their limits."

Gallien raised an eyebrow. "How am I supposed to clear it out if I don't know what's in there?"

"You break the spell." Androma pinched the front of the satchel and held it up to the light, illuminating the faintest of runes etched into the leather, creating a ring around the whole bag. "Or you keep filling it and let all your sundries fall out."

Gallien patted the near-flat satchel. "Good to know."

Soon after, The Raven dropped anchor and settled neatly into the docks, finding the only space available, and dropped anchor. An official from the fort was already waiting with papers for Captain Addison. They intended to fill his coffers in exchange for the use of his hold—a familiar job to The Raven's crew. Still, Bail Addison did not answer the call, even as the ramp was extended and the official ascended to the deck.

"We should go," Androma urged, gripping Cob under the arm. "Now."

The Green Leaf was close behind. "Did Galahart make mention of any help on this end?"

"Now, Aphrandhor," the old Rider insisted.

Gallien narrowed his eyes in suspicion, watching his companions descend to the dock. He gave The Raven's deck a lasting look as he followed behind, curious as to where the loud and abrasive captain was. He had never missed an anchor drop.

"Androma," he called after her, his leather cloak flowing out behind him.

The old Rider continued to usher the trio onwards, towards solid ground. Gallien called her name again only to hear her voice beckon him on.

Then came the distinct sound of outrage. The doors to the captain's cabin swung open, Addison's voice carrying across the docks. Looking back, Gallien glimpsed Bail shoving the official aside as he ran to the starboard railing, his eyes scanning the docks.

"There!" he cried, the word *booming* out of his broad chest. "Get 'em!"

Not to question their captain, a dozen of The Raven's crew charged down the ramp and took to the docks, swords and daggers in hand.

"Not again," Gallien complained, breaking into a run. "Why do I always end up getting chased on these docks with you?"

"I believe you were to blame last time!" Androma retorted, running beside Cob and Aphrandhor.

Though she couldn't see him, Gallien looked directly at the old Rider. "What did you do?" he demanded. She said nothing, content to be roughly guided along the docks at speed. "Androma! What did you do?"

A group of red cloaks broke away from the stone shore and descended the wooden steps to block their escape. The companions had no choice but to stop, caught between the two. Gallien reached out with his only hand, snatching at Androma's tattered robes.

"What did you..." The smuggler was drawn to the hilt poking out of the shadows of her cloak. He would have recognised it anywhere. "You stole the atori blade," he hissed.

"It doesn't belong in the hands of a pirate," she spat.

"It was a trade," Gallien pointed out, glancing over her shoulder to see the mob of pirates approaching them.

"Not a fair one," Androma argued. "This should be enough to buy an entire army."

Gallien's stress was plastered across his face. "You don't steal from a pirate," he fumed. The closer both parties got the more he saw their chances of reaching Taraktor slipping away, and with them, any hope of rescuing his father.

"It's a concept he should be used to," Androma said dryly, if unhelpfully.

The red cloaks halted, hands grasping hilts on their belts. Their presence was enough to stop the pirates from going any further, though Captain Addison couldn't be stopped from barrelling through to the front of his men. His lips twisted while his small eyes assessed the predicament.

"Gentlemen," he said, looking at the red cloaks. "You can go ahead and arrest this lot—thieves all!"

"I will not have a pirate call me a thief," Cob declared boldly.

"That one," Addison identified, pointing at Androma. "That one drugged me, she did!"

"Underestimating your weight is what I did," Androma corrected.

"You see! A confession that is! Arrest her!"

Gallien looked back at the red cloaks, wondering why, exactly, they weren't doing anything but keeping them there.

"What are you just standing there for?" Addison barked. "Check her! She's got what's mine! I want that sword back, witch!"

At last, the red cloaks parted, making way for an aged commander, his rank there to see in the golden fin that lined his helm. "You all fit the description," he said gruffly, eyeing the companions up and down. "That The Raven?" he asked, nodding at the ship.

"Aye!" the captain growled, a hungry grin on his face. "The blind one stole from me!"

The old commander didn't look amused. "You expect me to believe this blind woman stole from *you*? Is that what you want everyone in Caster Hold to believe?" he added, his words tugging at the threads of Bail's reputation. What else did a pirate really have? "Return to your ship, Captain. The king has need of your sails."

There was fire in Addison's eyes, his blazing gaze cast over the four companions. If the shore hadn't been lined with red cloaks, Gallien knew the man would have taken his chances and had the soldiers and their commander slaughtered right there on the dock. What he'd do to the four of them would be far worse... and slower. As it was, the odds were against him, his life and his vessel both at risk.

"Galahart and his ilk are a fickle lot," Addison informed them, his tone dripping with venom. "The very moment you lose his favour, I'll be there, waiting. You'll see."

Then the pirate walked away with his crew in step.

"Must we make enemies everywhere we go?" The Green Leaf remarked, following the ranger between the red cloaks.

"You must be the Kedradi," the commander said assumingly, though Cob's dark skin and arsenal of bone weaponry removed much need to guess. "Galahart sent word of your arrival. We've horses and supplies ready, though we were given no destination, so you've food and water for three days."

"That will do," Cob replied, speaking for them all.

"Quarters have been made available to you in the keep," the commander went on, his voice like gravel.

"We won't be staying the night," the ranger announced, his words causing The Green Leaf some dismay. "Where are the horses?"

Escorted by those same red cloaks, the companions were led through the streets of Caster Hold. Addressing the wizard's upset, Cob explained that they didn't need to be looking over their shoulder for murderous pirates. Aphrandhor understood, of course, and agreed wholeheartedly, but it was clear his wounded leg was eating into his resolve.

Still, they paused in their departure to clean and redress Gallien's wrist. The commander made the fort's physician available to them, and the smuggler thanked Kaliban he did. Without essence of the poppy, he would surely have blacked out from the pain. As it was, the pain was only enough to make him sweat through his clothes.

Clambering onto a fresh horse, his bandages neat and spotless again, Gallien watched Cob assist Androma into her saddle while one of the soldiers aided Aphrandhor, his injured leg requiring him to use a step.

"I've met one or two of Galahart's agents in the past," the grizzled commander commented, his neck craned up at them. "Never seen the likes of you lot though."

"Needs must," The Green Leaf replied cheerily.

The commander could only nod at that. "And don't worry about Addison and his boys. We'll see they don't trouble you."

"Appreciated, commander," Androma replied, her hands clinging to Cob's waist.

Looking up at the late morning sky, the ranger turned their horse around. "Let's gain some ground before nightfall."

The commander's face creased in confusion. "The road's that way," he directed, pointing east.

"Our heading is north," the wizard reported, guiding his horse just so.

"North?" The commander gave a mirthless laugh, glancing at his men. "There's nothing north of here but rocks and sea."

"Then rocks and sea be our destination," Aphrandhor replied with a curt bow of the head.

Gallien bowed his head at the commander and almost brought his fist to his chest, as he once did as a soldier. Instead, he directed his horse to the north, following his companions between the trees and into the wilds.

49
EXODUS

For two days, Grarfath Underborn slipped between reality and a world of dreams. His very mind felt heavy, allowing him no more than seconds at a time to glimpse the world about him. The sky was always dazzlingly bright, if pale. There were always faces looking down on him, hands and damp cloths brushing his face.

Then it was back into the deep wells of his dreams, where he was frequently swallowed whole by great chasms or chased through a labyrinth by a giant Andaren. Sometimes he found himself drowning in endless waters, sinking into a cold abyss. There he saw Kitrana Voden, emerging from the black like an angel to rescue him.

Whenever he broke the surface, however, it was Yamnomora who greeted him, pulling him ashore. Hers was a constant presence through the halls of his dreams, just as she was always there when he eventually opened his eyes.

Under a starlit sky, he finally opened his eyes without the almost immediate need to close them again. The smith was able to turn his head and survey his surroundings, crowded as they were.

Sitting up, the furs that had protected him from the bitter cold fell loose. Hundreds—no, thousands—of dwarves were packed together, huddled or sleeping around fires. Beyond them, he recognised the flat lands that stretched on into the night, The Ice Plains of Isendorn. At his back, The Morthil Mountains rose up, shadowed and hidden in the heavens.

Looking to his left sent a stabbing pain through his right shoulder. Grarfath winced and began to rub it, aware that he always wielded the hammer with his right arm.

The Anther!

Alarm ran through him, his pain forgotten, as he searched in vain for the weapon of power. He was flooded with relief to discover it nestled between Yamnomora's arms and legs; the dwarven warrior had fallen asleep with it. Those frantic few seconds, however, were enough to rouse her. Like coiled springs, her eyes snapped open, the chips of green drowned out by the flames reflected there.

"Grarfath," she breathed, scrambling to his side.

The smith tried to move to greet her properly, but his muscles refused to fully support him. Yamnomora caught him and kept him firmly on the hard ground, The Anther still gripped in her other hand.

The disturbance alerted others, turning eyes on Grarfath. A single whisper acted as a spark, igniting a wave of whispers and hushed words that rippled through the survivors.

"Easy," Yamnomora bade, her eyes flitting to his forehead. "Ye knocked yer conk pretty bad when ye fell over."

Grarfath touched his brow and winced again, pain lancing through his skull. "I feel like I've been used as an anvil," he said wearily. The smith tilted his head to see past Yamnomora, sure that his eyes deceived him. "Is that Bludgeon?"

Yamnomora glanced over her shoulder and returned with a grin. "Oh aye, that's 'im a'right. A survivor, that one."

"How?"

"He's a prime stud," Yamnomora replied, as if it was obvious. "When they took us prisoner, they must 'ave sent 'im to the farms in the southern caverns." The dwarf nodded to the north. "He came out o' the emergency tunnels with everyone in the Braccus District."

"They got out?" Grarfath was reinvigorated at the news.

"We've been trekkin' south along the mountains for two days," Yamnomora informed him. "They've been pourin' out o' the tunnels," she reported, nodding at the uncountable dwarves around them. "Even a few Underborns made it," the warrior added, a thread of hope in an otherwise devastating knot of death and destruction.

"Truly?" Grarfath uttered, searching their number as if he could find them by their stone bracelet alone. Without thought, he ran his fingers over his own bracelet, feeling the small stones his father had made from the ground upon which he had been born. It was a unique trait of the Underborns and now all the rarer.

"An' that's not all," Yamnomora went on, lowering her voice. "News o' what ye did has travelled fast. Everyone ye saved in the Royal Quarter has told *someone* who weren' there."

Grarfath paid closer attention to his kin, who continued to stare at him, passing words between themselves. "What are they sayin'?"

He felt The Anther as Yamnomora placed the cool steel under one of his hands.

"They're sayin' ye're the Hammerhold reborn."

The smith didn't know what to say at that, though he decided it was a little premature. Surely the real Hammerhold would have saved Morthil?

"Ye doubt it," Yamnomora stated, observing his reaction.

"I want to be," he replied, his voice lacking conviction. "But I'm jus' a smith. Ye saw me down there. I'm no fighter. I can swing a hammer, sure, but that ain' enough to be the damned Hammerhold. An' the only reason I've got this far is because o' ye. If ye hadn've dragged me along I'd 'ave gone back to me workshop by now. I'm no hero, Mora."

The dwarven warrior opened her mouth but looked to have been caught out by her own name. Grarfath expected her to rebuke him, clarifying her full name, yet she took a breath and looked over at their fellow dwarves.

"I don' think Duun ever called 'imself a hero," she began, accepting her nickname without comment. "It were everyone else who called 'im that. Ye ask any one o' 'em that should 'ave died on that plateau or in Khardunar. *They'll* tell ye what ye are. So don' go listenin' to this." Yamnomora pressed a finger to his temple. "Listen to *this*," she instructed, putting that same finger to his chest. "No one told ye to go back again an' again. Ye did it because ye knew it were right, an' ye knew ye had the power to do it. That's all ye ever need."

Grarfath didn't know what to say as he absorbed her words. He soon found himself unable to really think about it, his mind beginning to dull. His exertion must have been obvious to Yamnomora, for she soon urged him to lie down and finish his night of sleep.

———

Dawn had come and gone when Grarfath next opened his eyes, the sun having glided its way to late morning. Their makeshift camp was alive with activity, every fire being used to cook food or boil water. The chatter of his people was a constant buzz interrupted only by the snorts and squeals of roaming Warhogs.

What a joy it was, though, to see dozens of children running and playing throughout the encampment. Whether he had saved them or not, he was just happy to know so many of their younger people had survived the greatest cataclysm of the age.

Rising from the pebbled ground, his furs abandoned, Grarfath became the epicentre from which silence spread across the vast camp.

"The Hammerhold!" one of the children exclaimed.

Their cry broke the dam, and Grarfath found himself being rushed by a mob. He would have retreated had he not been standing at the roots of the mountain, where the stone rose at his back. The smith held out his hands to slow them, but it was no use

—he was cornered. There was no speaking to any one of them, their words of thanks and praise overlapping into a single noise.

Humble though he was, the lack of food in his belly and the desert in his mouth made him impatient to move past his new-found celebrity. Thankfully, Yamnomora had the strength to peel them apart and place herself between the smith and his crushing admirers.

"A'right, a'right!" she bellowed in their faces. "Let's give 'im some space, eh? He's not eaten for days, an' he's barely had a drop o' water pass his lips! Unless ye want 'im to drop dead right 'ere, I suggest ye all go back to yer business o' packin' up! We'll be movin' on before long!"

Many hands reached out to touch his arms and cloak before he was alone with Yamnomora again. Now that he had heard it, he couldn't help being aware of the severe growl in his stomach or the hollow feeling in his legs. He was sure he could eat an entire cow were it presented to him.

Yamnomora thrust The Anther in his hands. "Here. Try not to forget this, eh? Probably best ye're seen with it."

Grarfath nodded along, his concentration slipping. "Do ye 'ave any food an' water?"

"Ye'll not want for much amongst this lot," she replied with a knowing smile. "Let's find ye somethin'."

Yamnomora wasn't wrong, and the two of them enjoyed the generosity around them. They consumed supplies from a variety of camps so as not to impact any one group of survivors. While Grarfath remembered what it felt like to be whole again, the larger camp continued to pack away all that they had managed to bring with them through the tunnels.

Through the chaos of it all, the smith caught sight of a pale and bald head. Moving to better see it, he found himself looking upon The Dancing Sword of the Dawn amidst his kin.

Looking miserable, the huge Andaren sat upright on the freezing stone, his wrists, arms, ankles, and legs all bound by a number of different things, from chains and ropes to scraps of material and leather. A strip of cloth cut between his lips, preventing him from speaking, while those around him were sure to keep a weapon of some kind always in hand.

"Where are ye goin'?" Yamnomora asked, though it was soon apparent.

The dwarves parted without needing to be asked, making way for the Hammerhold as he came to stand before Slait. His golden eyes looked up at the smith, piercing and cruel. There was a vow behind those eyes that he would murder Grarfath the moment he was free.

"Ye didn' kill 'im," Grarfath said, pointing out the obvious as Yamnomora caught up with him.

"Not yet," she replied menacingly. "I always thought to lop off his head with one o' me girls, but both are lost to the waters now." She crouched down so they were eye to eye. "I jus' can't decide how I'm to end ye."

Executing The Dawn Sword jarred with the smith. "We shouldn' kill 'im," he said bluntly, knotting Yamnomora's brow all the more.

"What's that?"

"He's a... *Skaramangian,* aye?" Grarfath had been sure to lower his voice before naming him as such. "We should hand 'im over to the others—the wizard an' the likes. Let 'em question 'im. He might help 'em find this weapon o' power they're searchin' for."

Slait's gaze narrowed on the smith at that, his curiosity clearly piqued.

"He's not for knowin' a damned thing," Yamnomora countered. "His *betters* 'ave been feedin' 'im swill since he joined their ranks. Gobbled 'em up, didn' ye! Ye stupid kud. He still thinks his lot are fightin' for the gods an' not the promise o' the dark."

"He's got to know somethin'."

Yamnomora shook her head. "He's a *zealot.*" The dwarf turned on the Andaren, her anger getting the better of her. "Ye don' know up from down, do ye?" she asked Slait directly, pulling his head back by his scarred scalp. "It's because they've used yer faith against ye. Ye're jus' a tool to 'em. A weapon they can aim an' fire," she growled.

As Grarfath was about to call for calmer heads, a disturbance turned him around, towards the sounds of folk complaining and small stones being trampled under heavy boots. Approaching the smith was a group of dwarves—highborns all—and a cadre of Morthil guards at their back.

"What's this, then?" he asked, his question turning Yamnomora from the Andaren brute.

The warrior groaned. "This lot," she said with loathing. "A couple o' 'em are officials, ministers from the Greyhelms' court an' the Banking Federation. The three in the lead are the real problem."

Grarfath scrutinised them in particular, noting the guilds they belonged to. The dwarf leading the way bore thick tattoos that formed an intricate pattern across his face and bald head and could even be seen covering his hands. A Boldbane, then. No... Not *just* a Boldbane. *The* Boldbane. The dwarf striding towards him was the guild leader, his long coat, silvyr necklace, and fine clothes elevating him beyond the simple status of a rich guild member.

Beside him, to his left, was a dwarf who clearly belonged to the Redbraids. While his mohawk was grey with age, he had deliberately retained a patch of hair to the right of his scalp where his red braid could forever hang. Like the Boldbane, he wore clothing and furs far too expensive for any ordinary dwarf, and his silvyr necklace was near-identical to that of the Boldbane.

On the right strode the leader of the Frostbeards, a guild whose members always kept their beards in a tight braid, not a single hair out of place. He was just as aged as the other two and attired in finery and jewels.

"Where's the Ironguard?" Grarfath asked before they were in earshot. He had seen them scattered amongst their number, but their guild lord was notably absent from the group before him.

"Lost to the waters they say," Yamnomora answered. "Ye can expect these three to fight over the survivors. Ye watch. Ye won' 'ave to pay any fee to join their guild no more. Jus' pledge yer undyin' loyalty to 'em. They need numbers now."

"Why are they comin' for me?"

"They've been sniffin' around ye for the last two days. Like I said: everyone's talkin' abou' ye."

"This is the one?" The Boldbane demanded incredulously, jabbing one stubby finger at him. "This is the *Hammerhold*?"

"Aye, guild lord," one of the soldiers answered.

The Boldbane looked him up and down, unimpressed. "Ye're the *smith* I keep hearin' abou'?" he asked rhetorically.

"Grarfath, son o' Thronghir," he replied, raising his chin. "I'm o' the guild Underborn—"

"No ye're not," the Boldbane told him plainly. "The Underborns are gone. Ironguards too."

"Is that it?" the Frostbeard interjected, his greedy eyes on the hammer in Grarfath's hand.

"He wields The Anther," Yamnomora announced, and loudly so.

A spatter of mutterings ran through the surrounding crowd, including a brief, if quiet, exchange between some of the guards.

"I see a fancy hammer," the Boldbane voiced. "Crafted by a smith as skilled as yer father, I'd wager," he added accusingly.

"It's true!" came a cry from the crowd.

"He saved us all!" another yelled.

"Let's see, then," the Boldbane challenged.

Even with sleep and food in his belly, Grarfath knew he didn't have the energy to feed The Anther.

"He's the Hammerhold," Yamnomora reminded the guild lords, "not a performin' Warhog. The proof o' it stands around ye, breathin' the same air. Every soul from the Royal Quarter should rightly be dead, buried under the mountain. Grarfath nearly died gettin' us out o' there. Unlike the High King!" she shouted, pivoting to project her voice. "The Greyhelms commanded we be kept at bay, for the waters to sweep us into oblivion while he stayed safe in Khardunar!"

"Enough!" one of the nameless ministers barked.

"Treason!" another snapped.

"If that truly is The Anther," the Frostbeard cut in, "then it should be in the hands o' a leader, someone worthy o' Duun. By the power o' me guild, I demand ye hand it over, son o' Thronghir."

The Boldbane turned on his fellow guild lord. "Why should *yer* guild wield The Anther? It's the Boldbanes that will lead dwarves back to Morthil."

The Redbraid stepped forward, speaking for the first time. "Grarfath, son o' Thronghir, I am Guild Lord Yannis, son o' Yannagar. I formally invite ye to join the Redbraids."

"Hang abou'!" the other two protested.

"I would make ye special advisor to meself," Yannis went on. "The Anther would remain yers, but ye're to swear allegiance to me an' me guild right 'ere, right now."

"I offer the same," the Frostbeard blurted. "An' a home for every Underborn survivor," he added, sweetening the offer.

"Bah!" the Boldbane spat, waving at the air. He closed the gap between them so Grarfath could only see the tattooed guild lord. "I'll make ye chief warsmith," he uttered softly—a seductive proposal, given the power that came with such a title. "Ye can be at me side when I unite our people under one guild."

"What's he sayin'?" the Redbraid grumbled.

"Let it be our names carved into the stone o' Morthil, eh?" the Boldbane continued, his words for the smith alone.

Grarfath was overwhelmed and under the scrutiny of his entire people. He also felt threatened with the Boldbane planted firmly in his personal space, a feeling that only added to his disorientation.

"What say ye?" the Boldbane questioned impatiently.

The smith eventually stepped back, gaining some perspective, both literally and otherwise. Beyond the eyes that bored into him, The Morthil Mountains loomed tall, hiding the west from view. Their jagged teeth kissed the clouds that drifted ever southward. It appeared so calm, the surface untouched by the mayhem and calamity that wrought destruction in its depths.

Whether it was an epiphany or the whisper of the old gods, Grarfath looked upon their ancient home, now in ruin, and felt a sense of peace. It was all gone, their history and the trappings of their culture, wiped away by a cleansing flood. But so too was the stain of the Skaramangians and the religion of profit that had been installed to remove heroes and idols. Even the gods.

They had a chance to start again, just what his mother had hoped for. What she had fought and died for.

If they were to achieve something new, something better, it could not be in the skeleton of the old world. Not that they could, the smith reasoned. The Boldbane spoke of returning to the halls of Morthil, but there would be no liberating it from the water, not in their lifetime.

Grarfath looked to Yamnomora beside him, his eyes pleading for a notch of the confidence that made her so bold. The warrior gave him a simple nod, her support absolute.

The son of Thronghir looked about and stormed over to ascend the nearest cart. Now above everyone, he hesitated, unaccustomed to so much attention. He had never seen so many dwarves in one place. Again, Yamnomora clenched her jaw and gave him a reassuring nod.

Grarfath turned his gaze deliberately on the guild lords. "No!" he proclaimed, gathering as much authority into his voice as possible. "I don' know what the future looks like for our people!" he continued, his voice booming to all now. "But I know in me heart that future cannot be in Morthil!" There looked to be some friction among the onlookers at that. "How many generations will be forced to scratch a livin' off these barren lands while we drain the halls an' caverns? If we even can! The works o' our forefathers lie beneath the water now! Beyond our reach!"

"We are o' stone an' bone!" the Frostbeard roared, his outrage flushing his cheeks. "We aren' afraid o' a little hardship, smith!" His response was met with both argument and agreement from the masses.

"By all the profit," the Boldbane added, "we will never give up Morthil!"

"There's nothin' left o' it to claim!" Yamnomora yelled.

Grarfath raised one foot to rest on the rail of the cart. "For too long 'ave we settled on this soil! Soil so named for those who claim it! The Andarens hold fast to their lands, an' they would remind us we dwell in their realm by the grace o' their pale emperor! For too long 'ave we lived in the middle o' their war with Erador! Profits be damned, I say!"

They were heretical words, he knew, but that didn't mean they weren't meant to be voiced.

"The old gods didn' breathe life into our ancestors so we might serve the east an' west!" Grarfath went on, shouting over the hubbub that had erupted. "We were to be a proud people! We were to work the rock an' stone an' by the sweat o' our brow make an honest livin' off the roots o' the earth!" He had them again, their attention fixed on him. "The only profits we should seek are those found in the richness o' our deeds! Live an' die on these icy plains if ye must, but there's nothin' in those halls that will grant ye that chance."

"What about our homes?" one dwarf called out.

"Our businesses!" another yelled.

"We can' jus' leave our dead to watery graves!"

"Our time 'ere is ended! Our place in the world is out there!" Grarfath used The Anther, and deliberately so, to point away from the mountains. "A new age o' the dwarf is beyond that horizon! An age where we might reshape the earth as the old gods intended for us! There we will make new homes an' build new industry! An' I say we let the dead slumber still! It does not serve the livin' to die savin' the bones o' the dead!"

"What should we do?"

"Where should we go?"

Those questions and many more were hurled from the great mass, the more heated of them stirred by the guild lords.

Grarfath held The Anther straight up and waited for calm to return. "I'm not up 'ere because I 'ave all the answers! An' I'm defiantly not up 'ere because I'm lookin' to lead ye all! I'm tellin' ye what ye need to hear! What ye do with it is up to ye! *Ye!*" he emphasised. "Not yer guild lords! Not the Bankin' Federation! I'm puttin' Morthil behind me this very day! Accompany me if ye wish —I vow to only swing The Anther to serve our people!"

The Boldbane pointed directly up at the smith. "The only company ye'll find is irons! Arrest this heretic!"

Grarfath jumped down from the cart, coming face to face with the guild lord. It was enough to pause the advance of the guards, who had heard all the rumours of the one who wielded The Anther.

Angered by their hesitation, the Boldbane made to snatch the hammer for himself. He succeeded in gripping the haft under the golden head but failed to anticipate Grarfath's strength. And that was not all. Instead of pulling back on the hammer, away from the raging dwarf, the smith pushed forwards, thrusting the top of the head into the Boldbane's chest.

The air *clapped* and a blinding flash exploded from the point of impact as the Boldbane was ported five steps back and sent reeling into the other guild lords and ministers.

Grarfath marvelled at the hammer, his awe reignited as the weapon had displayed yet another ability. Never had he ported anything, let alone a person, without also losing The Anther in the process.

He was not the only one to marvel, the dwarves about him having shared a collective gasp. It was a show of *real* power.

His wonderment only lasted a few seconds, however, as his energy was reduced again by the magic. Yamnomora was already there to support him, her arm and hand under his elbow.

Embarrassed and disrespected, the guild lords picked themselves up, shrugging off the aid of the guards. They each had daggers in their eyes and a promise of retribution, but it would not be in that moment. Not when so many swarmed the Hammerhold, offering their agreement and pledging to follow him anywhere.

———

It was some time—hours it, seemed—before Grarfath and Yamnomora were able to make their way though the dwarven population and emerge to their south, where The Dorth Road lay before them. In that time, the smith had been praised by some and nearly assaulted by others, his message not received gladly by all. Still, when he looked back, the road was overflowing with sheer numbers, his following secured.

His people's *future* secured.

With naught but onwards ahead of them, Grarfath kept to the path, his fingers playing with the stone bracelet around his wrist. For all his words and even his feelings on the matter, a part of him was saddened to be abandoning his homestead. It had been his parents' home and their parents' before them. He gripped one of the smooth stones between finger and thumb. At least he would always have a piece of Morthil with him.

That would do.

50
TARAKTOR

Cob's dark hands grasped tightly about the reins, his knuckles paling. His heart was in the grip of dread—not at that which lay before him but at the sound in his ears.

Drums in the deep of his soul, returning to plague him, to usher him down the path of violence so it might be satiated with blood. Those drums would chase him across the known world and into the wilds beyond.

As the injustice of it burned bright in his mind, the truth of the rhythmic drumming trotted up the rise. The beating was that of hooves and they belonged to the smuggler's horse, the last to reach them. It was a relief to the Kedradi, who let go of his reins and scrutinised the steadiness of his left hand. The curse remained at bay, it seemed, content with those he had butchered in the Padoshi's home.

For now...

Joining him at his side, Gallien set his gaze to the beast of black iron that clung to the white cliffs. "What in the holy mother of Kaliban..."

His fear of the drums abated, the ranger was able to assess the landscape with clarity. None but a few monsters had ever struck fear in the Kedradi's heart, but there was something malevolent and wicked about Taraktor that did just that. Its every tower, wall, and rampart was sharp, like the jagged teeth of a hungry behemoth.

Like the hook of land on which it had been built, Taraktor's central spire rose up and curled over the sea, as if it were the claw of a gargantuan black dragon. Some of its buildings were sprawled across the flat land, where its main gates were located, but the fortress boasted a collection of towers, balconies, and protruding blocks down the cliff face on which it perched.

Between the sharp fangs of iron, enormous figures, hooded and robed, had been positioned like gargoyles, their ghoulish faces marred by pain. It was a place for the damned, a hell on earth.

It seemed an odd thing to see something so baneful in the light of a pale grey sky when surely so sinister a place should only exist in the darkest of nights. Yet there it was, not to be found on any maps but nonetheless standing tall on Erador's hook—and in the east, no less, where each day it would be greeted by a golden dawn that could only wish to hide its light from the iron claw.

To the ranger, who had seen all manner of beast in the world, be it created by nature's hand or man's, Taraktor was an offence to the land. He hated to imagine what it was like on the inside.

Looking at Gallien again, Cob had to wonder how the smuggler's father might have survived such a place, time spell or not. His instincts told him there was naught but death inside its razored walls, but he could not bring himself to say as much and dash Gallien's hope, nor their collective hope that Bragen Pendain would reveal the location of a hidden weapon of power.

His attention lingered on Gallien for a time. He was sickly pale, his eyes dark. Two days of hard riding and little rest had been taxing for the smuggler, who was still desperately recovering from the loss of his hand and no small volume of blood.

While he knew it would be prudent to rest there for a while, the Kedradi didn't like the idea of closing his eyes in the shadow of Taraktor for any amount of time. Added to that, their enemy's plans were always moving forwards. How long would it be before the Skaramangians brought all three skeletons together? How long after that before they brought their new magic to bear and returned the stain of the Dark Ones to the earth?

Their choices weren't just limited, they had dwindled to one: find Bragen Pendain and build an arsenal of divine weapons. Then the real war would begin...

"How do we get inside?" Androma asked, ever practical in her thinking.

It undoubtedly helped that she couldn't see the nightmare born of the wizards' world.

The Green Leaf guided his brown mare to stand between them and their destination. "Its walls cannot be climbed," he reported. "We would find the cliffs equally treacherous."

The ranger considered that, of their party, one had an injured leg, while another possessed a single hand. Then there was Androma, who, without her sight, would inevitably fall to her death.

"I could make the climb," he proposed. "Infiltrate it as I did the Padoshi's compound."

The wizard shook his head. "It's not our wounds that would keep us from the walls but the spells placed upon them. The cliffs too. Remember, Taraktor was designed to be a prison. Everything about that wretched place was made to keep its occupants from getting out. Those same spells will stop us from getting in."

Cob glanced at the staff in Aphrandhor's hand. "What about *your* magic?" he posed, thinking of the time they had broken into the port office in Allisander during their hunt for Gallien and Joran. "You could levitate me over the wall. I could open the door from the inside."

The Green Leaf looked from the Kedradi to Taraktor, his old face creased with doubt. "Those walls are taller than they look from here. It would be a long way to guide you up."

"You could do it," Cob replied encouragingly.

"But could I do it before we are discovered?" Aphrandhor countered. "I could not defend myself *and* see you to the top. We would both perish."

"We didn't come all this way just to look at it," Gallien said with frustration. "You must have some idea of how we get inside."

The wizard looked at the smuggler, his eyes narrowed as he saw the same deterioration that Cob had noted. "I do," he admitted, if reluctantly. "Though, now I am here, in sight of madness made iron, I am... unsure."

Androma adjusted herself in the saddle behind Cob. "You have led us this far, Green Leaf. We trust you."

The wizard regarded Taraktor, his face concealed by his green hood, until he turned back to gaze upon them all. "Deception," he declared.

———

The late morning had drifted into early afternoon by the time the four companions were on the final approach to Taraktor. Of the three horses the commander had gifted them, two had been released and sent galloping back down the path they had come, sure to find their way back to Caster Hold.

So too had they stripped themselves of obvious weapons and strapped them to their only remaining horse, ridden by The Green Leaf alone. Trailing the wizard, Cob, Androma, and Gallien were forced to walk one behind the other, each bound to the other and, ultimately, the horse via a length of rope stored in their supplies.

The ranger was sure to keep his wrists close together, simulating the tight knot that was supposed to be binding his hands. Behind him, Androma did the same while Gallien was pulled along by a simple knot about his good wrist.

They were prisoners now, though their deception was still weak in the Kedradi's opinion. While it might have been believable that they three were criminals of the magic world, The Green Leaf did not look the part of a Jainus wizard anymore. In place of their dark robes, he had opted for green many years ago. It would surely raise questions.

Aphrandhor had reassured them that the mark of the Jainus would be enough, the sigil tattooed on the inside of his left forearm and, apparently, put there by magic and not the artistry of human hands and ink. Such things could be tested, the wizard had said.

Cob maintained his doubts.

With the roaring sea on their right, its crashing waves just audible from atop the cliff, the companions closed the gap. Soon, Taraktor dominated their view, towering over them just as it towered over the water. Closer now, the ranger began to observe damage to the fortress, his eyes darting from one area to the next.

Outside the walls, where the grass had yellowed around the black keep, there sat huge chunks of twisted iron and all manner of debris, most of which had sunk into the earth on impact. Looking up, he could see the towers from which they had come, though that could only mean the source of the damage had come from *inside* Taraktor.

The lower ramparts were just as broken, with whole areas bent out of shape, exposing the prison inside. One of the lookout towers that dotted the ramparts was entirely missing from its place on the high wall. The Kedradi discovered it further out in the west, where the husk had been left to rust in the tarnished grass.

Here and there, jagged lines tore through the walls, revealing portions of the interior and the halls within. As with the debris littered about the outside, the iron of those walls looked to have been peeled away from the inside, the metal curled outwards.

When, at last, they arrived at the main gates, there was no doubt in Cob's mind that something nefarious had taken place. As with all else, the gates had been twisted and wrought out of shape from the inside.

The Green Leaf brought his horse to a stop and looked back at him, the same concern on his face. The ranger slipped his hands from the rope and instructed the others to do likewise as he reclaimed his weapons.

"What's going on?" Andromap asked.

"Something isn't right," Gallien muttered first, the smuggler having seen all that the Kedradi had.

"I'm going to need a little more than that," the old Rider replied with a notch of irritation.

"There's no one here," Aphrandhor explained, dismounting. "There should be hunters atop the walls. They should be *everywhere*."

"Something has happened here," Cob detailed for the Rider's sake. "There's evidence of an attack almost everywhere. Even the gates are open."

"Open?" Androma echoed.

"*Broken* would be a better word," the smuggler opined.

"This is impossible," the wizard uttered, his right hand running over the twisted metal of the nearest door.

"This is *old*," Cob specified, having moved closer to investigate the doors for himself. "Look at the edges. Rusted." He looked out across the broken tower tops scattered about the land. "They're *all* rusted. This isn't new. Whatever happened here, it was some time ago, *years* perhaps."

"That cannot be," The Green Leaf insisted. "The Jainus would not abandon Taraktor. *If* it suffered some attack," he stressed, "they would rebuild, make it stronger."

"I see no deception here," Cob remarked. "Though I see fresh tracks," he added, crouching to inspect the grooves in the dirt. "A horse and cart have been through here." He stood up, looking back the way they'd come. "More than one I'd say. These tracks have been made over time. Some are older than others."

Gallien used his teeth to untie the knot about his wrist. "I'm going in there," he announced, his determination pushing through his obvious fatigue.

Cob met The Green Leaf's eyes, both agreeing that forward was the only option while also agreeing that neither knew what to expect. His quiver returned to his back, the Kedradi gripped his bow and loosely nocked an arrow, keeping the two together in one hand. Androma retrieved the Andaren spear she had been using as a guide stick and the atori blade. She was followed by Aphrandhor, who led the horse on foot.

The wizard halted the mare before removing its saddle and

reins. "I think this is as far as you go, my new friend. I will not keep you here." He ushered her south and watched the horse trot away. "No need to doom another, eh?"

The Green Leaf was, perhaps, the bravest man Cob had ever met, having faced things in the fight against the Skaramangians that would have crippled a man with fear. But as his grey eyes rose high to look upon its arching spire, Taraktor was enough to mar his expression with trepidation.

The ranger did what he could to hold fast to his self-belief. He was yet to find that foe who could bring an end to his days. There was no reason he would cross them inside those black walls.

Passing between the twisted gates, the companions entered an uncomfortably small courtyard, its space predominantly occupied by an ugly statue. It depicted a tall and hooded figure resting his foot upon the back of a naked man, his face carved forever in agony. The hooded man—a hunter, no doubt—was missing an arm and several fragments of his robe, the stone shattered like so much else of Taraktor.

Without delay, they passed the statue and headed up the short steps to the narrow set of doors tall enough to permit entry to a man three times the Kedradi's height. Still, those two doors were only wide enough for one of them to pass through at a time.

Consumed by the towering beast, they entered a world of dust and decay and, indeed, close quarters, the ceiling soon sloping down until it was only a few inches above their heads. It was frustratingly cramped, the tight spaces doing well to maintain the heavy musk that dwelled throughout.

Even when the hallway opened up, it only did so to a junction that offered the most unusual options for progression. There was a set of stairs to the left, each step protruding from the wall, that led up to a space in the ceiling just wide enough for a set of shoulders. There was another staircase on the other side of the junction, though they descended five steps before rising again to a different square opening in the ceiling.

Directly in front of them sat a round door of wood and iron, its surface displaying the sigil of the Jainus. Or at least it had, the symbol having felt the touch of fire at some point, charring much of the wood to black.

If those three options weren't enough, there was also a square door set into the floor with a ringed handle in its centre.

"This is not what I expected," Gallien said, as the group crowded into the junction.

"Don't touch me," the wizard instructed, raising his right hand and the vambrace that encased his forearm.

"That's going to be hard in here," the smuggler told him, careful to avoid that all-seeing hand.

A distant *boom* sounded from parts unknown and found the huddled companions. Cob couldn't say whether he had heard just the one sound echoing through the fortress or several *booms*.

"What was that?" the smuggler asked.

"I am as new to this place as you are," the wizard replied miserably. He peered over their shoulders, his eyes narrowing to see through the gloom now that the light of the world had dimmed beyond the doors. "As I said, Taraktor was designed to keep its prisoners inside. We have entered a maze only the hunters can navigate."

"Did they have to make the maze so damned small?" Gallien complained.

"It's uncomfortable, isn't it?" the wizard replied. "Another design feature I'm afraid. It's to instil the feeling of being swallowed whole, as if you're being slowly digested by a monster. A monster that eats your *hope*."

"Where to?" Androma queried, always ready to move on.

The Green Leaf considered all four of their options. "Let's shed some light on the issue," he said, stamping his staff once on the floor.

A torrent of fire exploded from the branched end and quickly found it had nowhere to go. Cob grabbed Androma's arm and dragged her down as the fire spread across the ceiling in every direction, the flames licking at the walls around them. Gallien too dropped into a crouch, his only hand coming up to shield his eyes.

Aphrandhor brought an end to the ordeal when he tossed the

staff away, though the heat remained, distorting the air. The wizard fanned the smoke with his hands and looked at the burned stone before regarding his staff in confusion.

"What happened?" Androma demanded.

"That was supposed to be an orbling," the old man informed them. "An orb of light," he clarified, seeing Gallien's puzzlement.

Cob placed a hand on the wizard's shoulder, questioning the man's health with no more than a look.

"I fare well," The Green Leaf assured him. "I know the difference between the two spells," he added, his tone suggesting his comment was obvious. "I had no intention of conjuring a living flame."

The ranger picked up the staff and gave it back to him. "Try again."

"Is that a good idea?" Gallien questioned, his gaze roaming over the recent damage.

Aphrandhor licked his lips and held out his hand, his expression gripped in concentration. A globe of liquid light began to rise from his upturned hand, taking shape as it lifted away from his skin. With only an inch between the spell and his hand, however, the orb froze over and fell back into his palm. The wizard turned the block of ice in his fingers, examining its smooth surface with increased confusion.

"Madness," he muttered.

Androma reached out and found the orb of ice in his hand. "What's happening here, Green Leaf?"

"The truth of this place is worse than I feared," he said, looking at his staff again. "It's as if the demetrium has been neutralised. I have no control over my magic."

"Why would that be a design feature?" the old Rider pressed. "Prisoners would have been stripped of any and all demetrium long before they were thrown into this hell."

The wizard lifted his hooded head, his gaze so distant he might have been looking through time itself. "I don't think it is. I think something else caused this."

"The same thing that caused all the damage," Cob reasoned.

Without a word, Gallien removed the only torch from its fixing on the wall and set it alight using the flames that still licked at the wooden door. "I'm going that way," he announced, his impatience audible as he placed the torch in Androma's grip.

"Why that way?" Cob questioned, a single eyebrow raised.

Gallien shrugged. "Call it smuggler's intuition."

With only one hand, he required an overt level of exertion to open the door. Cob thought to aid him, seeing how exhausted Gallien looked after their simple walk up to the fortress, but he sensed in his companion a need to prove himself, if only *to* himself. Instead, the ranger took aim, his bow pulled taut and the arrow pointed at the opening.

Aphrandhor was the first to advance beyond it, his green robes dull in the dismal light until Gallien reclaimed the torch from Androma. Cob wished to get in front of The Green Leaf as soon as possible, for the wizard was all too vulnerable without his magic.

It seemed the old man shared that thought, though rather than let the Kedradi pass him, he drew Yalaqin from his belt. The steel blade was the first to find daylight again, a soft beam of dusty sunlight that penetrated Taraktor through one of the damaged walls.

"What happened here?" Cob questioned, his fingers running over the melted edges where the wall was broken.

"Nothing good," The Green Leaf replied, having come to a stop a little further on.

The companions moved to examine whatever the wizard had discovered, though Androma required a description. The Kedradi wasn't entirely sure how to begin. He had never seen a skeleton fused upright into a wall before, its jaw hyperextended and bones blackened.

"He died in pain," Gallien observed, as if he was recognising an old friend.

The wizard reached out and tentatively handled the only item that still clung to the skeleton's neck, fused there by magic.

"A medallion?" Cob queried.

"The mark of the hunters," Aphrandhor confirmed, the round pendant sitting on the end of his fingers.

The ranger could just about make out the Jainus sigil on the tarnished metal, though the four-pointed star also bore a weaving snake—an addition made solely for the hunters.

"Let's keep going," the smuggler urged, his eyes already on the corridor ahead.

"This could still be a trap," the Kedradi reminded him, well aware of what hastened the man.

Gallien frowned and looked back at the skeleton. "Does this look like a trap? One of the jailers is in the wall."

"This is a place of magic. We cannot trust everything we see."

"It's what I can *hear* that troubles me," Andromam interjected, her comment silencing them both.

Cob cocked his head, one ear pointed down the narrow hallway. The sound was muffled to begin with, but now and then there came a clear, crisp word, spoken with a man's voice. As quietly as they could, the companions moved towards the noise, the ranger's hands positioned deliberately about his bow.

Rounding the next corner, it was clear that the hunter they had discovered in the wall had been luckier than his comrades and managed to flee long enough to enjoy a few more seconds of life, though they had likely been seconds filled with dread.

Cob didn't even bother trying to count the number of skeletons fused into each side of the corridor. Most of them were fused together, their outstretched arms narrowing the hallway all the more.

Like their lone friend, they all looked to have suffered in their final moments of life. The fact that they were all facing the same direction and all so close together confirmed for the ranger that they had been running away from something. Or someone.

One behind the other, they slowly navigated their way through the bony limbs, contorting their bodies to fit through the awkward gaps. It was much worse for Andromam, who had to physically feel her way through to the other side.

As one, they paused upon hearing that distant *boom* again. This time, however, Cob felt the resounding vibrations through the floor.

Torch in hand, the smuggler was first to get through the corridor of death, his eagerness subduing any caution.

"The light," Cob hissed.

Gallien held the torch at arm's length while he peered around the next corner. Seeing the light bouncing off the walls around his blond companion, the ranger held up an arm. The smuggler looked back at them and nodded his head in the new direction, clearly having discovered the source of the voices.

The damage to the new area was tenfold what they had seen so far. To the Kedradi's eyes, it looked as if something truly powerful had exploded and obliterated everything in a fifty-foot radius, including the floors below and above. The result was a large mezzanine-type structure, its sides comprised of jagged stone and melted iron at every interrupted floor. From their vantage, they could see into chambers high and low that had all suffered the loss of a single wall.

"Make sure you have enough supplies," came a voice from below. "There's a good chance you'll get trapped in the east wing."

"For how long?" a much younger voice replied.

Cob tilted his body ever so slightly, so his eyes were able to look down at the inhabitants. The lowest floor had the surface area of numerous rooms, as if the walls had been knocked through after the loss of the ceiling. Its corners were piled high with tomes, scrolls, and loose parchments, all precariously close to flaming candles and torches. Dotted between were cots and blankets, surrounded by enough sundries to suggest the occupants had been there for some time. There were even a couple of desks and chairs on one side where they might work outside their sleeping quarters.

He counted three men and a woman. The younger voice he'd heard must have belonged to the boy, who was not even twenty years old. They all wore the dark robes of the Jainus, the fabric glistening with copper where the woven demetrium caught the light.

"It could be hours," the oldest of the wizards told the boy, his white hair cropped so fine his scalp was visible. "Or it could be days. The walls do as they will."

"Can't we stop them?"

"The magic that governs this place was instilled in the iron long before we were born. It would take some effort to undo, and since we dare not use a spell to light so much as a candle, our efforts are best utilised elsewhere. Brodrick will accompany you," he went on, gesturing to the other man. "Do as he does and listen well, young novice. Taraktor might be dead, but its jaws will still snap at you."

"As you say, Inquisitor Vorn."

With considerable backpacks and all manner of supplies and tools hanging from their belts, the two wizards departed the makeshift living area via a door in the corner.

"We ask for fresh supplies," the woman complained in their absence, "and they send half of what we requested and a boy who doesn't know his arse from his elbow."

The older wizard hardly paid her any attention. "Where is Rogun? He should be back from the cells by now."

The woman shrugged, navigating her way across the littered chamber. "He's an odd one. Let him be, I say."

"I would run a tighter ship than that, Gilly," the old wizard remarked, and firmly so. "We have a schedule for a reason. Trust me. I've spent more years than all of you put together in this wretched place. I've seen wizards deviate from the plan before. Taraktor will not tolerate it."

"He was investigating *twelve* again," Gilly replied, her tone suggesting she was unbothered by her superior's stern response.

The older wizard sighed. "We've learned all we can from that cell," he said, pointing at a particularly large stack of bound scrolls. "Rogun knows that."

"He's too new to know that," Gilly replied, taking to her cot. "He just needs to get twelve out of his system. I was the same."

"Weren't we all."

Aphrandhor stepped back from the broken edge, his staff and blade held close to his person. "Inquisitors," he breathed. "I was among their ranks before being reassigned to The Silver Trees. They must be here to investigate, but..." The wizard trailed off, thinking.

"They've been here for a long time," Cob concluded, thinking along the same lines.

"It certainly looks that way," The Green Leaf agreed. "Years," he mumbled in disbelief.

Cob looked to Gallien. He was deflated, making his sickly condition appear all the worse. The hope he had harboured for his father was quickly dwindling. So too were the ranger's hopes that they were on the right track to possessing another weapon of power.

"It would seem the Jainus know little more than we do," Aphrandhor continued quietly. "I've never heard of an investigation taking so long."

"Let's go and ask them then," Gallien suggested, a notch of aggression about him.

"That would not be wise," The Green Leaf cautioned.

"Why? They can't use magic either. We have the advantage," the smuggler pointed out, nodding at the ranger.

"That doesn't mean they won't *try* to use magic to defend themselves," the wizard theorised. "We should not push them. They could kill us all, themselves included."

"I for one would like to know more about *cell twelve*," Androma murmured, her words little more than a gentle breeze on the air.

"As would I," Gallien declared with dangerous determination, his feet seeing him retreat back into the passage.

Every instinct Cob had told him not to follow the smuggler, that to do so would lead him into the belly of a beast from which there would be no return.

Yet bound he was to walk where shadows rule, for there he would find his enemy, and there he would end the curse that had plagued his line for so long.

PART FOUR

51
CONSEQUENCES

0 Years Ago...

4

For the first time in his many decades, Daijen did not awake with the clarity of a Vahlken. His icy blue eyes were slow to open, the world a blur beyond his nose. His mind was groggy, his thoughts slipping away from him, not a tether to be grasped.

He could hear Gelakor's voice in the distance, the Rider's words naught but a drone. It began to change, however, morphing into a female voice. Didn't he know that voice? How strange it was for his perfect memory to have something, anything, just out of reach.

The voice boomed in his sensitive ears. "Incoming!" it called, the word funnelled through the narrow window in his room.

The whole chamber shook, and dust rained down from the ceiling. Daijen pushed himself up from the bed, his instincts flaring with great alarm. The edges of it all were just too dull for him to fully grasp his situation.

"Ahnir," he called out, his voice little more than a hoarse whisper.

Where was the Golem?

His strength was too slow to return, and the Vahlken staggered from wall to wall until he fell through the door. Daijen knew immediately that that couldn't be right. There was no interaction between him and the world of memory. Yet there he was, lying amidst a pile of splintered wood.

The stone beneath him shuddered again.

The Vahlken wiped his face and picked himself up, using the wall to help support himself along the corridor.

He could *feel* the cold stone.

There was something familiar about his environment, like the woman's voice that he'd heard in bed. Still he could not place any of it.

Instead, he followed the noise that drifted in from the end of the hall. The light piercing the slitted windows was an outright assault against his eyes, a sensation he hadn't experienced since before his transformation in the pits of... in the pits of...

Daijen groaned, the name eluding him.

Shielding his face, the Vahlken shoved the doors open at the end of the hall and stumbled into the outside world. He was on a large stone balcony overlooking a vista of mountains. His eyes constricted and dilated repeatedly, bringing those mountains into focus again and again. It was dizzying, and he lurched towards the balcony railing without any balance.

Stopped by the railing, he collapsed to his knees, his gaze forced to retract to his surroundings. His vision returned just in time to see a fiery ball impact the eastern ramparts, blasting fragments of stone in every direction. The rogue flames fell upon the stable roof, dancing across the wood at speed in a bid to engulf it.

He could *feel* the heat.

"Ahnir?" Daijen muttered, seeking some kind of stability.

Figures dashed across the courtyard below, scooping up buckets of water as they did. One after another they threw the water over the fire, quashing it to naught but black smoke.

He could *smell* it.

While the other figures ran back to their posts, one of them stopped with Daijen caught in their gaze. They could see him.

She could see him.

"Ilithranda," he croaked, the name pushing through the fog.

"Green Leaf!" she cried over one shoulder.

His weight supported almost entirely by the railing, Daijen's eyes followed the direction of the call and located a young man in green robes and a mishmash of armour.

The *wizard*, he knew. As the truth came back to him, Daijen's mind was slammed by memory. For just a moment, The Green Leaf was replaced by another wizard—*the* wizard.

Cloaked and hooded in black, Skara stood on the steps of the ramparts, looking back at the Vahlken.

Daijen blinked—hard. The Green Leaf returned to his vision, along with the man's name.

"Aphrandhor," he rasped as Ilithranda scaled the wall and hopped over the railing with feline grace.

"Daijen," she uttered, catching him before he fell onto the stone. "You're awake," she said in disbelief.

"Awake," he repeated, struggling to rend reality from memory.

"Ilithranda!" a woman called up. "Bring him inside!"

Daijen turned his head and spied her through the stone balustrade of the railing. Her blonde hair was radiant under the sun, though her features were partially concealed by the strip of fabric that crossed her eyes. In one hand, she wielded a fine sword of silvyr, the pommel a golden dragon's head, and in the other, she held a staff, the wooden tip pressed against the courtyard stone.

"Androma," he whispered.

"Come on," Ilithranda insisted, picking him up under one arm.

Daijen shut his eyes. "This... Is this real?" He shook his head. "It's not real," he told himself—he was simply dreaming within Ahnir's memories, his consciousness lost to time.

A deep and guttural squawk ripped through the chaos around the Vahlken. It was a sound that spoke to his very soul, slicing like talons through the haze that blinded him. Daijen opened his eyes at once to see an indomitable Aegre land in the courtyard.

"Valyra!" he exclaimed, finding, at last, some strength in his voice.

The Aegre's back legs supported her bulk, armour and all, while her front legs perched atop the balcony railing, her large talons curling round to touch the floor. Mighty and majestic was the eagle head that towered over both Vahlken, her beak plated in steel and tipped with silvyr.

Daijen looked up into Valyra's yellow eyes and found himself. He pulled away from Ilithranda until he could reach out and place one hand on her beak and the other on her feathers, just below her left eye.

"Valyra," he said again, her name and touch grounding him in the moment, in reality.

"Incoming!" a gruff voice warned from the distant ramparts.

The fortress shook again, and the sound of cascading rock resounded from the east. Daijen moved to look past Valyra and discovered a pair of dwarves atop the ramparts. The Anther pulled entirely at his focus, gripped as it was in the black hand of a female dwarf. Her name was on the tip of his tongue, but it seemed inconsequential compared to that which she wielded.

He *needed* it.

The Anther didn't belong to her.

It was to be returned to the *master.*

Daijen started forwards until his right leg gave out and he stumbled back into Ilithranda's arms. It was enough to put him back in control of his own mind. At the same time, he looked back at the ramparts and knew the dwarves to be Mordrith and Yamnomora. Allies both.

Friends both, he corrected, the thought requiring some effort.

"Let's get you inside," Ilithranda said, guiding him back into the fortress.

Ka'vairn!

The name came to him as they descended the interior stairwell and arrived in the main hall. The Hall of Handuin! He was home, at last.

Ilithranda lowered him into an armchair that had been placed by the circular table in the centre of the hall. From where he sat, the Vahlken could see the empty throne at the head of the chamber, where Handuin himself had once held council over the earliest Vahlken.

He could also see the main doors to the keep, which had been flung open to flood the gloom with daylight. Four silhouettes cast long shadows over the floor, approaching with haste.

Aphrandhor was the first to stand over him. He was dishevelled, as if he had donned the mismatching armour as fast as possible. His short blond hair was unkempt, and his goatee had begun to spread in the manner of a beard. Most obvious was his black eye. Daijen's memory questioned the cause of the bruising before recalling that he had been the one who had delivered the punch himself.

The wizard held his staff to one side. "It is a marvel you survived," he remarked. "Given the lack of food and what little water we've managed to get past your lips, you should be dead."

"He is a Vahlken," Androma announced, her own staff ceasing its rhythmic tapping against the floor. The Dragon Rider looked in his general direction. "You are a fool, Daijen Saeth," she chastised before her tight lips curled into a warm smile. "But you are a fool I would keep around. I am glad you have returned to us."

"He looks half dead," Yamnomora stated, her large axes held low by her sides.

Mordrith was the last to arrive, coming to stand shoulder to shoulder with her red-headed kin. "Half dead or not," she said, "we could use whatever strength ye can muster, Daijen."

"Give him a moment," Ilithranda replied firmly.

"Have ye seen what's beyond yer gates?" Mordrith retorted. "There's no moment to be had." The dwarf's eyes fell on Daijen. "The fight is upon us. They've come for the helm, lad."

"The helm," Daijen echoed, his gaze drifting down to The Anther in Mordrith's grip.

Again, he was overcome with the urge to snatch the hammer from her grasp. The Vahlken had the sense to shut his eyes, even clamping one hand over them.

"Daijen." It was The Green Leaf who had addressed him, taking one step closer to the armchair. "Where *is* The Helm of Ahnir?"

Gone, Daijen thought with clarity, a second before his memory caught up and reminded him that he had tossed the helm into the glowing pits of Handuin. It was a fleeting thought, however, a flash that was drowned out by a weight in his mind, the pressure applied by the mention of the Golem. Furthermore, the Vahlken was enraged to hear the wizard ask of the helm, as if it was his to claim! As if he had any right to it!

Righteous fury saw Daijen leap from his chair and throttle The Green Leaf, picking him up in a single hand. Numerous voices cried out before hands grappled him from all angles. It was Ilithranda alone who had the strength to part him from the wizard.

Yamnomora was quick to use the haft of an axe and beat Daijen back into the armchair, where she could press the curved blade to his neck. "What were that abou'?" she growled.

Mordrith and Androma helped Aphrandhor rise from his knees. The wizard held one hand to his throat, coughing all the while.

Grounded in reality once more, Daijen stuttered with his apology.

"What just happened?" Ilithranda demanded of him.

"We haven' got time for this," Yamnomora pointed out.

"It's alright," The Green Leaf rasped, standing by his own strength. "It's the bracer. His mind is struggling to peel one reality from another."

"What does that mean?" Mordrith asked, waving The Anther in her hand.

Daijen had to look away, feeling the tug of a foreign consciousness as it sought to control his actions.

"It means he touched something he shouldn't have," Ilithranda scolded. "What were you thinking? That damned bone is thousands of years old!"

Daijen wished to respond with all that he had learned, to justify the great risk he had taken, but there was so much inside his mind. Just thinking about it was like pouring molten steel into his head, his memories and sense of self obliterated by the weight of Ahnir.

"How long?" he queried, his head supported by the wing of the armchair.

"We found you five days ago," Ilithranda told him. "I thought you were going to waste away in that room," she added quietly, a note of sorrow in her voice.

Ka'vairn shook again, its ancient stone clinging stubbornly to the mountains.

"What's happening out there?" Daijen was sure the answer was within his grasp, but he could only think of the assault on Kanofell and the Kedradi's subsequent exodus.

"The very thing I warned you would happen," came the sternest voice of them all.

The group parted, allowing Daijen to see the oldest living Vahlken. He had no name, his title a cleansing mantle that wiped away such personal affectations. He was The Valtorak, of course, the title rising from the murky depths of Daijen's ragged memory.

Like Ilithranda, the master of Ka'vairn wore his vambraces and tanned cuirass, the leather and padding concealing the silk of the Weavers beneath. His cloak of victory, a pelt from a brown bear that had roamed The Dain'duil centuries earlier, was draped over his sloping pauldrons and touched his ankles. Upon his belt was the atori short-sword, its copper blade a display of the Weavers' craftsmanship, and his sabre, gifted to him before Daijen had even been born.

In his hand, as always, was his slightly curved staff of wood. Its purpose had long baffled Daijen, for The Valtorak had no physical ailment to warrant it. A sign of his position, perhaps, though he had never read of such a thing in Ka'vairn's extensive library.

Calling on his memories proved to be a mistake. The real pain that accompanied it drove his head into his hands. It was as if his own mind was rejecting itself in favour of Ahnir's.

"You will look at me when I'm talking to you," The Valtorak commanded, waiting until Daijen's bloodshot eyes peered over his hands. "Your actions in Aran'saur have compromised this fortress, its secrets, *and* its potential to keep fighting our true enemy."

"My actions," Daijen whispered, desperately trying to recall them.

He tried to backtrack from tossing the helm into the pits and punching Aphrandhor. For one glorious moment, he remembered with clarity the flight home astride Valyra. Beyond that, he saw flashes of the Leviathan—Agannon—whose great bones were lost amidst the towers and spires of the capital city.

The palace...

He had been inside the emperor's palace.

The Ankala!

Thousands of deaths flashed before his eyes, adding up to a volume of blood that ripped him from the Hall of Handuin and landed him in another time and place.

Gone were his friends and allies. Gone was the grey stone of Ka'vairn. The Vahlken now stood in a circular pit, buried up to his knees in dark red blood. He recognised it at once: the birthplace of all four Golems.

"Arise, my children."

Skara spoke just as he had the first time Daijen had witnessed the memory. How different it was to be looking *up* at The Dark One, standing beside his young apprentice. On either side of the Vahlken, a naked Meliax, Yohem, and Govhul rose to join him. There was no Ahnir in that grim pit, for Daijen himself stood in the Golem's place.

In the blink of an eye, it was all gone. He was standing directly in front of The Valtorak, back in the Hall of Handuin. The master of Ka'vairn raised a thick white eyebrow, likely wondering, as Daijen was, why the weary Vahlken was on his feet at all. His strength and balance waned, forcing Daijen to grip The Valtorak's cuirass. With one strong arm, the master kept him on his feet.

"He is useless to us like this," he said to the others.

"I can fight," Daijen replied, battling fatigue and dizziness to stand on his own.

"And you *will*," The Valtorak told him firmly. "It is *you* who has brought this fight to our door. You will see them turned away. Or you will die trying." The master looked past him. "Ilithranda, go to my lab in the east wing. You know the vials he requires."

"You said we were to save those," she reminded him.

"Until we were at our last," The Valtorak said, nodding in agreement. "I would rather increase the number of fighters who trained under Kastiek than enhance our strength in the final hour. Go."

"What vials?" Daijen asked, omitting the fact that he could see all four of Skara's Golems in the hall, lurking in its corners

"Potions," The Valtorak reported. "They will speed up your recovery. But you must still eat, drink, and sleep. You have withered for too long. Even magic has its limits."

Meliax and Yohem came to stand over the group, their featureless faces angled down at Daijen. He couldn't help but look up at them before turning on the spot to gaze up at Ahnir and Govhul.

"What's he lookin' at?" Yamnomora asked.

"He has the memories of a god," Aphrandhor informed them. "I can only imagine what he's seeing."

Ahnir reached down with one of his lower arms, his fingers splayed to grasp Daijen about his face. Knowing all too well that such a thing would tear him from the moment, the Vahlken pushed past Androma and Mordrith, falling to his hands and knees. He scrambled across the floor, desperate to get away from the Golem.

Pressed against one of the pillars, he could only wait and watch as Ahnir crossed the hall to reach him.

The Valtorak was shaking his head. "Foolish boy. Confine him to his chamber. See that he eats and drinks. He will be needed before the end."

That was the last thing Daijen heard before that massive grey hand engulfed his senses.

52

CELL TWELVE

I t was with inexplicable confidence that Gallien navigated the narrow passages and winding steps of Taraktor. A smuggler's sense of direction, he decided. He was sure, if asked, that he could point to north and south, the prison's interior maze unable to deprive him of his bearings.

He led them this way and that, the torch in his hand. There was little for the flames to reveal, the walls and doors identical at every turn, as if they were all slick with the same oil. They had gone up, taking various stairwells and even a couple of ladders through tight gaps and small archways.

"Not that way," the smuggler had said at one junction.

His companions had agreed when they realised that the shadows could not be banished by the flames of the torch, as if the darkness was feeding on the light.

Feeling a breeze tickle his beard, Gallien pushed open the door to his left. The dim light of early evening exposed the room, entering through a large, jagged hole in the eastern wall. Gallien looked out on the waters of The Deep. Further out, he could just make out the hazy outline of Nareene on the horizon, the largest of the islands inside Erador's hook.

His attention returned to the chamber. It was clearly a kitchen, though he hated to think of the labour required to get food and supplies to that particular part of the prison. He couldn't help but think of Joran then, the two having worked in many a tavern kitchen over the years. It was a strange thing to both wish the boy was with him and be glad that he be spared such an awful place.

A cold pang of dread churned his gut, as so many had since he first set eyes on Taraktor. It was, indeed, an awful place, an awful place his father had been imprisoned in for untold years. It was sickening to think of the torment he must have endured, trapped behind those black walls.

Soon, he thought. *If you're in here, old man, I will find you.*

Entering the exposed room, it easily boasted the most space of any chamber they had come across, with a ceiling twice that of the halls. It was there, of course, that the smuggler's gaze was drawn. His eyes watered, and his mouth fell ajar. Looking back at him was a dead man, and recently dead at that, his body pinned to the stone by every knife and sharp object in the kitchen.

Gallien blinked, and as if by some spell, the man of flesh and dripping blood was gone, replaced by a skeleton in rags.

"Gallien?" Aphrandhor was beside him, scrutinising the horror on his face. The wizard regarded the old corpse above. "I fear there are more dead than living in these halls." He squeezed the smuggler's shoulder—an apology, perhaps, for what seemed an inevitable conclusion.

Still bewildered, Gallien gave the skeleton one last look before following his companions through the door on the other side of the kitchen. Doing his best to rid the image of the dead man from behind his eyes, the smuggler shuffled past Androma and Cob to join Aphrandhor at the front, where he could use his torch to light the way.

"You've done well thus far," the wizard commented, somewhat bemused. "Which way do your instincts say now?"

Gallien examined the branching corridor, his choices down to three doors. While he was not informed by any *instincts,* he noticed the numerous pot marks that had long ago shredded the wood around the lock on the right-hand door.

"This way."

The Green Leaf stayed close behind, leaving Cob to direct Androma, though the old Rider assured him she only needed a direction and not a hand. Only a few feet beyond the door, and they stopped again to listen to the distant *boom*, the sound and vibration passing through all of Taraktor.

But this time, it was not so distant.

Gallien turned around to look at his companions—just in time to see a new wall slide out of nowhere and slam across the hall, separating them from Cob and Androma. Aphrandhor hammered the pommel of his sword into the new wall, shouting their names through the iron. Their responses were muffled and soon drowned out entirely by the continued shifting of walls in the immediate vicinity.

"Move!" Gallien barked, darting down the passage.

One after the other, smuggler and wizard dived into the next chamber before another wall sealed off the corridor behind them. No sooner were they inside than a third wall burst from conceal- ment and shot towards the pair, threatening to split them up while chopping the chamber in half.

Gallien instinctively reached out to grab Aphrandhor and pull him towards his side of the wall, his fingers flexing to reach those green robes. But there were no fingers. There wasn't even a hand, no matter what his senses told him.

It was only good fortune that The Green Leaf had the good sense to roll towards him—and not a second before the wall slotted into its new position.

Taraktor settled after that, its latest seizure having changed the interior layout. The two men slowly rose, their eyes roaming over the new semi-circular chamber and the two doors that hadn't been there previously. There was no looking back, the way they had come now unrecognisable in the new configuration.

"Left or right?" the wizard croaked, his sword dragging across the stone as he scooped it up.

"Does it matter? This place will spit us out wherever it wants."

Retrieving the torch at his feet, the smuggler tucked his wounded wrist close to his chest and gestured for his companion to open the left door. The corridor beyond was just as cramped and dark as every other. It took them to stairs that went down before going back up—a seemingly useless design—as well as up stairs that clung to the walls of windowless towers and overlooked bottomless pits.

It was hard to say whether the walls shifted within minutes or hours, but Gallien began to suspect that it was entirely random, having once survived a sliding wall that moved only seconds after everything had apparently settled.

They came across no more inquisitors, nor did they hear any in those dark passages. Nor did they detect a trace of their companions, though the wizard assured him that Cob and Androma were more than capable of taking care of themselves, even going so far as to remind the smuggler that *they* had rescued *them* from the Padoshi's grip.

But this was not Thedaria...

The frequency of skeletons increased, including one that floated endlessly across the ceiling, defying all laws of man and beast. They found another pressed to a wall, its top half a crumpled mess of bones while everything below the waist was encased inside a block of ice, where the legs remained perfectly preserved, the ice equally untouched by time or temperature.

"What kind of magic is this?" Gallien felt compelled to ask upon finding yet another cluster of poor souls fused to the walls and ceiling.

"If I had to guess," The Green Leaf replied with a whisper, "I would say we're looking at *raw* magic."

"What does that mean?"

"You saw my spell go awry after we arrived," the wizard stated. "That's what happens without demetrium to focus a wizard's magic. It's raw, unchecked, *dangerous*. Your thoughts and emotions cloud your desire, and the intended spell suffers for it. A simple flame can turn into a volcanic eruption. Telekinesis or levitation can turn into a storm capable of uprooting mountains. More often than not, the user wounds or kills themselves in the process."

Gallien nodded along, absorbing what he could through the fatigue and constant pain that harassed him. "Raw magic," he echoed. "The sort of thing a prisoner would have to resort to if they wanted to escape."

Aphrandhor passed by the latest clump of fused skeletons, his sword now sheathed on his hip so he might investigate the dead. "This does look like a prison break," he admitted. "But like so many others, these men were all running away... together."

"What of it?"

The wizard handled a scrap of cloth that had survived whatever magic had killed them all, the strip hanging from an arm. "Not all of these men were hunters. This one was a *prisoner*."

Gallien scrutinised the fabric and saw that it was of the lowest quality and not to be afforded to the Jainus's prized hunters. "They were all fleeing the same person," he determined.

"So it would seem," Aphrandhor agreed, moving on.

The smuggler hesitated to follow in the wizard's wake, his gaze lingering on the skeleton that had been a prisoner. He looked at the skull—or what remained of it. Could that be his father?

"Gallien," Aphrandhor called softly. "I need the light. And best we stay close, lest the walls have their way."

It could have been hours that passed before the walls shifted again, their progress having taken them deeper into the black heart of Taraktor. Shoulder to shoulder, the pair were presented with a new direction that opened up to a chamber of naught but black iron. They turned left and right, searching for the next door, stairwell, or ladder, but discovered only dead end after dead end.

"We're trapped," Gallien stated gravely.

The Green Leaf's old eyes narrowed at a spot in the middle of the floor. "I think not."

The smuggler lowered the torch to better see the markings carved into the stone. It was a perfect circle, its interior edge lined with runes and glyphs. "What is it?" he asked.

"I'll show you." The wizard stepped into the middle of the ring and indicated that Gallien should accompany him.

There came a brief scraping of stone as the slab inside the circle began to rise. Gallien braced his legs to steady himself, unsure of the magic being used. Holding the torch with his only hand, he felt all the more vulnerable.

"This is a common way to get about in The Tower of Jain," Aphrandhor reported on their way up.

Effortlessly, silently, they rose towards the ceiling, where an identical slab of stone was already ascending, allowing them to reach the floor above. There they stopped, and The Green Leaf stepped off the platform. Gallien mimicked him before watching both pieces of stone descend, returning to their original places without any mechanical support.

"Wizards," he muttered under his breath.

"Gallien," his companion cautioned.

Quite astonished, the smuggler craned his neck to take in the size of the tower they had entered. It must have been the great hook that loomed high over the prison and the cliff upon which it sat, for the top could not be seen as it curved to the east.

He turned on the spot, observing the square shape and zig-zagging steps on all four sides. They rose up and up, cutting between floor upon floor—countless they were. So too were the cells that lined every floor, their numbers crudely painted on the flat of their iron doors.

A cold wind howled through the tower, whipping up the smuggler's leather cloak and the wizard's green robes. It wasn't hard to find the source: the gash in the left-hand wall was so massive a horse and cart could have passed through without trouble.

The tower's jagged wound offered a view of the outside world, where the moon had come to reign over the night sky, the water below only to be seen by its pale light reflected in the waves.

Gallien moved closer to the opening, seeing now that it also sloped down, the magic having torn through several floors below as well. He couldn't fathom the power required to rip through so much iron and stone.

"Look for number twelve," Aphrandhor said.

Gallien nodded his chin at the second floor up. "Don't need to look far," he replied dryly. That particular cell was missing its door, the walls around it blackened and crumbling. Looking to the other side of the tower, the smuggler found the door, the iron partially buried in the wall, put there by something with a lot of power behind it.

Like everything else in Taraktor, the steps up to the cells were unusually narrow and not at all even. Yet Gallien still bounded up them with what energy he could muster, desperate for answers. He passed three cells on his way, all empty, their doors ajar after the locks looked to have been wrought out of shape.

Cell twelve.

Gallien Pendain stood upon its threshold, his feet refusing to go any further. It was dread, he knew. That cold, unyielding grip that squeezed all the courage and virtue from the hearts of men.

He had felt it before, when The Dancing Sword of the Dawn had appeared in The Edda Highlands, there to kill Joran while he was just a babe. He had felt it again watching Joran fly away from The Ruins of Gelakor astride his mother's Aegre. And, more recently, he had experienced that same dread when Mr Grim had raised his axe, preparing to take his hand.

It was not for himself that he endured that icy grip about his heart. It was for his father, who he knew, without a doubt, had been locked inside cell twelve. It was all there in the blood, scrawled across every wall and in a language that belonged to the Pendains alone.

"Wait!" The Green Leaf hissed, struggling to catch up.

The wizard peered inside the cell, careful not to step inside. His eyes drifted high, leading Gallien to a complex pattern of runes carved into the stone. Perfectly straight, the pattern ran along every wall, ringing the cell.

"What is that?"

"A time spell," Aphrandhor reported. "Any living thing trapped inside would perceive the world at a fraction of its pace, slowing their ageing to a crawl. It's a useful warding spell if your prisoner is

something of a mystery. The Jainus can keep them almost indefi-
nitely, waiting for more information to come to light before inter-
rogating the prisoner again." The wizard pointed to a patch on the
wall to their left. "You see the break in the pattern, where the runes
are interrupted? That will have broken the spell."

Gallien stepped inside, looking at his companion as he did.
Aphrandhor had spoken the truth, for the smuggler was
untouched by any such spell.

There was so much more inside that cell than the writing, of
which there were hundreds of lines, but Gallien was drawn to the
smoke slowly drifting up from a set of candles in the corner. Scattered about them, he noted several pieces of parchment, ink and
quill, and a pack resting against the wall, its flap peeled back to
reveal food supplies inside.

The smuggler returned to the doorway, his eyes darting from
floor to floor, cell to cell, searching for the Jainus.

"What's wrong?" Aphrandhor demanded.

"The inquisitor is here," the smuggler whispered. "Rogun," he
added, recalling the name from hours earlier.

The Green Leaf joined him in the search, though neither discovered anything to suggest they weren't alone. "We must remain
vigilant," Aphrandhor warned, ushering Gallien inside the cell.

The old wizard, who must have seen everything during his
long life, stopped a foot inside cell twelve and looked on in horror,
mouth agape. As Gallien's had, his grey eyes wandered from wall
to wall, struggling to take in any one detail as there were so many.

"This was his cell," the smuggler uttered, his voice low, though
not out of fear of the inquisitor but out of pity for his father.

"How can you be sure?"

Gallien didn't really want to go any further into the room, but
he crossed it to highlight one of the larger lines of writing at
shoulder height. "Corben, my brother, would write everything like
this. Father taught him, and Corben taught me. At least, he *tried* to
teach me. He was always the smart one."

The fine muscles around Aphrandhor's eyes twitched as he

looked from the writing to Gallien and back. "Your father taught you this language?"

The smuggler gave something of a shrug. "He made it up. Corben said it was a way of documenting his research without fear of competitors and the like. Bragen Pendain wasn't the only one out there looking for valuable relics. I should know. I ran into a few myself."

"Your father invented this language?" the wizard questioned incredulously.

"Aye. I suppose he was a little paranoid, but so was Corben, come to think of it."

The Green Leaf moved across the cell, careful not to stand on the inquisitor's belongings. "Gallien, this is a *real* language."

The smuggler frowned, and not because of the shooting pain he felt running up from his injured wrist. "Real? No, no, no," he uttered in quick succession. "Only the three of us could use this. That was the whole point."

The wizard looked at him like he was suddenly faced by another man. "Gallien, you've seen this writing before and *recently*. These glyphs," he continued, gesturing at every wall, "were carved into the stone at The Ruins of Gelakor. They were *everywhere*."

Gallien was already shaking his head. "That's impossible. My father made this up when we were children."

"You were *there*," Aphrandhor told him, pointing as if the ruins could be seen at the end of his finger.

"I didn't stop to read the walls," Gallien argued. "We almost *died* on that rock."

His line of reasoning thwarted, the wizard took a breath, clearly thinking of a fresh avenue. "You really didn't see the glyphs?" he asked again, frustrated.

"You told me they were unreadable," the smuggler reminded him. "That no one had ever managed to translate them. Why would I waste my time looking at words I can't read?"

"Trust me, Gallien. As someone who has spent considerable

time looking at different languages, I know what I'm talking about. These glyphs are *identical.*"

Gallien looked hard at the wizard. He did trust him. "You're saying my father knows how to read and write in a language that's been dead for what, millennia? And no one else does. Not even the best scholars in the realm."

It still didn't sound like the man he remembered, though he had come to accept that all of his memories of the man were potentially fabricated at this point.

He also noted the tense with which he had referred to his father—his hope that Bragen Pendain yet lived had turned to unshakable belief.

Aphrandhor held out his hand to the grim walls. "The proof is written in *blood.*"

The writing wasn't all that decorated those dank walls in blood. Between the scrawled lines of ancient glyphs, Bragen Pendain had drawn images, places, faces... *monsters.* Each of the four walls served as the canvas for one larger image that his father could only have achieved by standing on his rickety cot. Gallien pivoted on the spot, looking from one to the next.

"What are they?" he asked without really meaning to.

Depicted in blood, each image was that of a tall, lithe figure, robed and hooded with four arms.

Four arms...

The smuggler was taken back a number of years to Harendun, when he and Kitrana had discovered the Andaren god buried beneath the city. That enormous skeleton had also possessed four arms, but why would his father be drawing images of the Andaren gods?

"You tell me," Aphrandhor replied knowingly. The wizard pointed at the glyphs beside each figure, inscribed at an angle by bloody fingers. "You said your brother taught you."

Gallien licked his lips. It had been some time since he had used their secret language—not since Corben had been killed before any of this madness had begun. Moving to the nearest wall, he tilted his head to see the words that appeared to be connected to that figure. It was on the tip of his tongue, the curls, flicks, and dashes slowly emerging from the depths of his mind.

Handing the torch to The Green Leaf, the smuggler used one finger to trace the first glyph. He hesitated, his fingertip half an inch from the dried blood. He clenched his fist just the once, reminding himself that he was no stranger to blood.

Pressing his finger into the glyph, he began to trace the word, as if he were the one writing it. "Meliax," he muttered, the name ringing in the halls of his memory.

"One of the Andaren gods," Aphrandhor confirmed. "And the others?"

Gallien remained where he stood for a time, his mind drifting across an endless sea. He stared at the bloody figure, seeing it take shape as if it were only now being drawn on the cold wall. Looking down, his right hand had returned, his palm and fingers coated in so much blood he couldn't see his own skin.

"Gallien?"

His name ended the dream, leaving the smuggler to behold the stump at the end of his arm. He swallowed and turned to face another wall, his brow dripping with sweat despite the chill. The next one came to him a little easier.

"Ahnir," he said, who the wizard confirmed was another of the four gods. "Govhul," he announced, reading the third wall.

"Let me guess," Aphrandhor interjected as Gallien turned to the final wall. "Yohem?"

Gallien nodded, translating the words swiftly now. "Why would my father draw the Andaren gods?"

"I would ask *you*," The Green Leaf replied, "but I get the feeling he has erased those answers from your mind. Do you know what *this* is?" he asked, indicating one of the drawings wedged between the lines of glyphs.

The smuggler moved to the back wall, opposite the door, to examine the image. "It's a pyramid," he said, familiar with the shape and little else.

"Your memories of your father are shattered, but you still recall your time with your brother, Corben, yes? Did he ever speak of a pyramid?"

Thinking of his brother only conjured the one memory—his death. Deciding he didn't want to probe his memories any further, Gallien simply shook his head. "Does it mean something to you?"

"There are very few pyramids in this world," Aphrandhor told him. "Even fewer still intact. But there is only one with ties to the Skaramangians." The wizard looked away, his gaze penetrating Taraktor's iron. "They call it The Tomb. I was there some decades ago."

"Where is it?"

The wizard's expression suggested he couldn't believe the truth of it. "On Nareene."

Gallien looked to his left, through the doorway, at the great gash that marred the side of the tower. He had seen Nareene that very day, the island a hazy line on the horizon. "What did you find there?"

"Questions. And *monsters...*"

The smuggler returned his attention to the pyramid, his eyes caught by the glyphs written along one of its diagonal edges. "Azad-guul," he read. It was little more than a flash, but the pyramid took shape in his mind as he did so, its black walls glistening under a bright sun.

The wizard's eyebrows furrowed. "What was that?"

Gallien ran his finger along the name. "Azad-guul," he repeated, seeing nothing this time.

The wizard grimaced as he consulted his own weathered memory. "This is beyond me," he whispered, before his eyes brightened. "Now *that* I know," he said confidently.

Gallien turned to study one of the other walls, perhaps the messiest of the four. Packed tightly between the streams of ancient words, Bragen Pendain had drawn numerous weapons of power. Aphrandhor had spotted the vambrace first, the image depicting the teardrop relief that sat atop the forearm.

A few inches over, Gallien recognised the axe he hadn't seen since his hand had been chopped off. A part of him hated it now, the weapon having become a source of desire for the Padoshi of Thedaria, a desire that had led to so much pain.

Beneath the axe, they looked upon The Anther. They could only hope that Grarfath and Yamnomora had found a way to retrieve the weapon, though they were likely still on the road back to The Morthil Mountains.

Off to one side, near the corner of all the glyphs, was the Helm of Ahnir. Gallien had never seen it before and was surprised to discover the helm of a god would look so ordinary. There was every chance, of course, that his father had never seen it and the bloody image was merely his interpretation. It was also firmly in the hands of the Andarens and beyond their reach.

The smuggler's eyes returned to the mass of words and images, soon to land upon the sword. He wondered then what might have happened to Kitrana Voden. She must have reached Drakanan by now, but what had she found there? Had she seen Joran again, training to be a Rider? Had she been turned away by a dragon? Or worse?

Gallien hated not knowing her fate. The first time they had been separated, beneath Harendun, he had assumed death—a plausible outcome, given that she had been dragged away by a monster. But now? Joran might have given her the broken blade. The Nimean could already have returned to the seas with her long-awaited prize, though she was still without the rest of the blade.

The Green Leaf stretched out an arm, his fingers hovering over an image that had been painted on the wall centrally, just beneath the depiction of Ahnir. "What are *you*?" he mumbled.

Gallien tilted his head to see past the flames of the torch in his face. There, scrawled amongst the other weapons of power, was a necklace.

"That doesn't look like much of a weapon," the smuggler commented.

"You could say the same about this," the wizard replied, his eyes glancing over the vambrace on his arm.

"*This* is the weapon you think my father knows about?" Gallien asked, his disappointment audible.

"Why else would he have drawn it alongside the others?" It was clear to see that Aphrandhor was excited by the discovery. "This proves my theory is correct. Look at it," he instructed. "Do you remember anything? Anything at all?"

Despite his doubts, Gallien did as the wizard asked and looked at the bloody image again. Nothing about the necklace conjured a memory or even a feeling, but he continued to stare at it, aware that it could be the reason they had travelled so far and risked so much.

He turned to report his lack of ideas—only to find The Green Leaf was gone. The smuggler alone occupied the cell, its door whole and sealed shut from the outside. Again, his hand had returned, only now his feet were bare and his belly was aching with hunger.

The madness was creeping, like a spider crawling up his spine, working its way to his mind. Then it came all at once, and he flitted about the room, slamming his palms onto the walls and door. He flipped the cot and threw the meagre blanket away, feeling the weight of years pressing down on him.

On his knees, he came face to face with the bloody weapons of power smeared onto the wall. He focused on the necklace and felt the weight of it about his neck. For just one fleeting moment, it was a comfort to him.

"Gallien."

Aphrandhor's tone was firm, as if he had been calling his name for some time.

The smuggler blinked, a droplet of sweat streaking down his temple. He was on his feet, boots on, standing beside the wizard. He looked at his stump, the sight of it grounding him.

"You know this," the wizard concluded, his staff pressing into the necklace.

"I don't know... I don't know *what* I know." Gallien wiped the sweat from his brow and pinched the bridge of his nose. "What did he do to me?"

"Alas, he tried to keep you from all of this," The Green Leaf reasoned. "I'm sorry you have been dragged back into it. But you must know where it is. Bragen Pendain must have hidden it before the hunters captured him."

Just thinking about that scenario inflicted a degree of pain on Gallien, forcing him to shut his eyes and push past the bolt of pain that ran through his head.

"Do you know what it says?" Aphrandhor pressed.

The smuggler took a breath before looking at the image again. There were many words written around the necklace, just as there were around all of the weapons, but there was one on the inside of the chain, just above the pendant. The whole word was curved to match the shape of the necklace, its letters written more delicately than elsewhere.

"What does it say?" the wizard pressed.

"Immortality."

A noise from the doorway turned both men around. Standing there, his dark robes cascading over his ankles, was a man—a Jainus. He was a few years younger than Gallien by the look of him, his blond hair greying about the temples. Wide-eyed, he stared at Gallien, oblivious to the wizard beside the smuggler.

"You must be Rogun," Aphrandhor began, his knuckles whitening around his staff.

"You can read it," the Jainus said absently, taking no heed of The Green Leaf's words. "You can read it," he said again, his mind working furiously behind his eyes.

"Neither of us can use magic here, Rogun," Aphrandhor pointed out. "So perhaps we should just talk. We might learn more from each other. You're here investigating, just as we are. Why don't we—"

Rogun bolted, vanishing from the doorway in a dark blur. Gallien took off after him, his shoulder crashing into the door-frame before he pushed away and ran along the cells. The Jainus, however, was not suffering from any of the ailments that plagued the smuggler, and so he was already bounding down the narrow steps.

Gallien called after him, but there was no stopping Rogun as he sprinted across the base of the tower. Having expected him to stop on the circular platform and descend into the bowels of Taraktor, it surprised the smuggler to see the Jainus leave it behind. He was, instead, running for the great gash that opened up one side of the tower.

By the time Gallien was running past the circular platform, Rogun was already out of sight . The outside world fought to penetrate the tower, blowing out his cloak as he began to carefully climb down the uneven slope. Here and there he had to leap to cross a drop that fell into a chamber below, but he was soon three floors down and stepping onto a long and narrow balcony that clung to the prison walls.

They were just below the top of the cliffs now, the light of the moon offering a view of the sea alone. The sea—and a fleeing Jainus. The wizard ran along the balcony, his hand gliding over the railing. He looked desperate, wild even. Gallien called out for him to stop several times, but Rogun kept going, his gaze cast repeatedly out to the east.

"Let's just talk!" the smuggler shouted over the frenzied wind.

Rogun stopped in the middle of the vast balcony and looked back at him like an animal trapped in a corner.

"You can't use magic, and I'm in no mood for a fight," Gallien rasped, out of breath. "Let's just go back inside."

The Jainus's expression slowly morphed from desperation to realisation and, eventually, reluctant acceptance. Then he jumped.

Gallien pressed himself against the railing, helpless to do anything but watch as the wizard plummeted to the rocks below. Before he met his end, however, Rogun thrust out a hand and banished the night, forcing the smuggler to shield his eyes.

Like a shooting star, his spell rocketed high and curled over the sea. At its apex, the spell exploded, creating an even bigger ball of light before fading away.

Gallien looked down, the Jainus not to be seen amidst the rocks and crashing waves. Finally, the sound of footsteps caused the smuggler to turn—Aphrandhor was approaching as fast as his wounded leg would allow.

"What was that?" Gallien asked.

The wizard had no answer, but his expression said two words.

Nothing good.

53

THE SIEGE OF KA'VAIRN

0 Years Ago...

4

Flitting in and out of sleep, Daijen struggled to comprehend the days and nights, his body sweating all the while. It was new to the Vahlken, having only experienced as much after great exertion— enough to exhaust the average Andaren to death.

With what clarity he could muster, Daijen ate and drank the food and water that was routinely left in his room. He rarely saw the person who put it there, though when he did, he couldn't be sure if they were real.

Ilithranda was the only one who left a lasting mark. In his delirium, Daijen fought The Valtorak's potions, their taste so vile as to convince him he was being poisoned. His sister's strength, however, was enough to overpower him and see the potions past his lips.

"Come back to me, Daijen."

Her words echoed through his mind, repeating time and time

again. More than once, the sound of Ilithranda's voice was enough to prevent him from slipping into ancient memory.

There were also times, in the darkest of night, when he was convinced Skara was sitting beside his bed. The Dark One would brush Daijen's matted hair aside and stroke his face like a loving father.

"You must bring me what is mine," he would whisper into the night. "They hold my voice in their hearts. Bring them to me so I might reshape the world."

"No!" the Vahlken would cry out, fighting the evil that worked in him.

The more potions he ingested the stronger his will became. So too did the strength in his muscles return, his body quick to remember the gifts of Handuin. And he became more aware of the constant bombardment and the sound of crumbling stone.

Ka'vairn was under siege. It was a fact that helped to root him. As that alarm grew in him, Daijen found rest harder and harder to come by. He *needed* to fight. He needed to protect his *home*.

Finally awake, he was pleased to find his room otherwise unoccupied by persons real or not. He was able to sit on the edge of his cot and maintain his orientation. Moreover, he was able to stand and stay upright, his dizziness having finally abated.

Peering down, his body was beginning to look as it once had, his muscles filled out and well-defined. He squeezed his fist and felt real power there. He discovered another source of strength in the corner of his chamber—his armour and cloak. Feeling the fortress shudder again, he wasted no time donning it all, each piece a welcome part that made him feel whole again.

With no sign of his weapons, the Vahlken made to leave, only to find his new door had been locked from the other side. A precaution, he assumed. The last thing they needed was an unstable Vahlken getting loose in the middle of a siege. Planting his padded shoulder into the wood, however, broke the locking mechanism. Daijen opened the door and passed over the threshold, his feet taking him from Ka'vairn to the depths of Azad-guul.

He froze.

Looking back, his door and room beyond were gone. He was entirely inside the bowels of The Dark One's palace, where his most twisted works could be done without prying eyes.

"Very good." Those two words were short and sharp, delivered by the lips of Skara himself.

Daijen turned to see The Dark One, cloaked and hooded in shadowed robes. He circled a young man, a human of few decades, who stood naked in the gloom of Skara's insidious workshop. He was petrified. That was easy to understand given that the man stood in the shadow of Ahnir. The Golem towered over him, a sentinel whose cloak could swallow the poor soul into the pits of oblivion.

Cutting between them, Skara inspected his subject. He lifted arms, scrutinised fingernails, and even probed the gums about his teeth.

"Yes. Very good," he repeated. "This one will do."

A subtle gesture brought a pair of Skaramangian guards out of the shadows. They grappled with the young man until he was held firm in their grip, his head pulled back by a rough handful of hair.

Ahnir required no verbal instruction to play its part in the experiment. With one sharp nail, the Golem sliced open its own wrist and held the wound over the man's upturned face.

"Yes," The Dark One encouraged, hungry for results.

Daijen rounded the nearest workbench to better see the disturbing event. From the narrow wound, Ahnir parted with some of its unusual blood, a viscid fluid that reflected every colour. It splattered onto the human's face until the guards altered the angle of his head, allowing the blood to enter his mouth.

"That should be more than enough," Skara declared. "Release him."

The guards threw the man down and retreated into the gloom, there to witness The Dark One's machinations from the shadows. Daijen watched on from beside the master himself. Watched as the man writhed and screamed on the damp floor. His muscles contracted, spasming, as he clawed at his own skin.

"Don't fight it," Skara told the poor soul. "Embrace it. You are to be the future. Yes," he drawled, excitement in his eyes.

"He's dying," Skara's new apprentice observed, some concern in her voice.

"A part of him *must* die," The Dark One replied. "The life that follows will be beautiful," he promised.

"Beautiful?" the apprentice questioned. "How is he to strike fear into the hearts of men?"

Skara chuckled to himself. "If there's one thing I learned destroying the wretched Barad-Agin and his works, it's that one should always have a contingency plan."

The Vahlken took a step forwards, desperate to know what exactly he was witnessing, when he heard his own voice cut across the laboratory. His head whipped around to see Ilithranda, the last person he'd expected to see in Azad-guul.

But then again, he wasn't in Azad-guul.

In a blink, Daijen was returned to the hallway outside his room in Ka'vairn. Ilithranda was running towards him at speed until she was thrown from her feet and launched at him with even greater speed. So too was the wall that had been at her back, the stone caved in by the work of a catapult. Amid the debris, Ilithranda skidded and tumbled down the corridor, all the way to Daijen's feet.

"Ilithranda!" She was already rising as he aided her. "What's going on?"

"We're under siege."

Daijen nodded along, his sister having assumed that he'd forgotten that detail. "How long has it been?"

"Three days," Ilithranda told him, fatigue in her voice. "They arrived the same day you... woke up. They've been moving the catapults through The Dain'duil," she went on, returning the way she had come. "Their new angles of attack can reach the towers now."

That was evident enough, Daijen thought as he navigated the blocks of broken stone. Upon reaching the end of the hall, he looked out through the jagged hole to see Ka'vairn and the courtyard below. The sun was beginning to sink in the west, burning the sky orange. From their elevated position in the fortress, he could see the eastern edge of The Dain'duil in the depths of the valley.

Ilithranda stopped before taking to the spiralling staircase, one hand pressed into his cuirass. "Are you with me?" she asked him, her violet eyes holding him firm.

"I am," he said before Ahnir's creeping memory could sway him.

"Good. Because there's no more of The Valtorak's potions. You're all the reserves we have now."

"I'm with you," he reiterated.

Ilithranda nodded once before leading the way back down to the courtyard. Once outside, the Vahlken was reunited with his atori short-sword, shogue, a pair of axium vials, and his slaiken blade, the latter the length of a spear.

"I'll have to get The Valtorak to mix *me* some o' those potions," Yamnomora remarked, passing the Vahlken with a large pitch of oil in her hands. "Ye look half *alive* now!" she added with a barking laugh.

"We can ask him nothing," Aphrandhor was saying to Androma, the two conversing quietly beyond the hearing of an ordinary Andaren. "Not yet," the wizard clarified, believing his words were for the Dragon Rider alone. "He was plunged into untold memory. Who knows how much he has witnessed? Questions will only force his mind to relive the answers."

"Why is that so perilous?" Androma enquired, causing Daijen to slow his preparations.

"You saw what happened in the hall. It isn't just memory—it's *consciousness*. I asked him about the helm, and Ahnir's thoughts and feelings surpassed his own. I have suffered similar effects in the past."

"Then how are we to learn what he has seen?"

"Given the sheer volume of what he's seen?" Aphrandhor mused, a shrug in his tone. "Time," he finally declared. "For now, it is important that he stays grounded in the present. He must know *who he is* before he can go exploring all the foreign memories that now dwell in his mind."

"Daijen," Ilithranda called. "Are you coming?"

The Vahlken coiled the last of the shogue's rope and left his unwieldy slaiken blade where it was. "I'm with you," he said again, adopting it as a mantra.

Just eavesdropping on that conversation had begun to dim the edges of his vision, narrowing his focus to that of Ahnir: *obey The Dark One.*

Daijen shrugged it all off and jogged to catch up with his sister. Androma and The Green Leaf emerged from behind the shattered stable, unaware of how far their words had actually carried. They looked exhausted—the wizard more so. Androma still benefited from her centuries of being bonded to a dragon, gifting her reserves no mere mortal could imagine.

"You have recovered well," Aphrandhor commented, stopping notably short of arm's length. "The Valtorak knows his alchemy."

Androma held out her hand, waiting for Daijen to grasp it. The moment he did, the Rider squeezed, testing his robustness, perhaps, before running her hand up his arm and, eventually, to his face. "You still have some strength to recover," she concluded, never one to hold back. "But it will have to do."

Daijen might have protested, but he knew the Rider spoke the truth. Days of malnourishment and dehydration lingered, even in the face of The Valtorak's magic. Still, his pride would not see him retreat. He would prove that what he did have was enough to repel the invaders.

"Where is Valyra?" he asked of them all.

"I sent her into the mountains with Oaken," Ilithranda reported, moving supplies about the courtyard. "They needed to rest and eat. Neither could be achieved here."

Daijen stared up at the snow-capped mountains—The Hellions—and longed to see his companion. He was sure that her presence alone would return him to full strength, just as it had grounded his mind in reality upon waking.

"And The Valtorak?" he asked.

"He flies with Aramis," Ilithranda replied. "They have gone to scout the forces guarding the catapults. He should be back before nightfall."

"Oi!" Mordrith's blunt call turned all to Ka'vairn's main gates, where the dwarf stood atop the ramparts. "Someone's comin' up the path!"

"How many?" Androma questioned, drawing her silvyr blade.

"Jus' the one!"

"One?" The Green Leaf echoed in disbelief.

"A messenger," Daijen reasoned.

As one, the group ascended the stone steps and joined Mordrith above the gates. Protruding from the mountain, a single path connected the valley floor to the fortress, a road that permitted only five men abreast. It made invading Ka'vairn near impossible, but sighting the battalions amassed below, Daijen could see that his kin intended to give it their best shot.

As reported, a single rider was following the curve of the path astride a war horse. On six powerful legs, the mount carried none other than a grand cleric, his robes of red and white contrasting against the dark rock.

"Why would they send a messenger now?" Yamnomora asked. "They've bombarded us for days."

"Perhaps they have realised the fortress cannot be taken," Aphrandhor posed.

"They come with terms of surrender," Daijen said confidently. "They want us alive," he added, looking directly at Ilithranda.

When, at last, the grand cleric arrived, the group slid the drawbar aside and unlocked the gates, opening them just enough to allow them to depart the courtyard one after another.

As a single unit of hardy warriors, they barred the rider and his mutated mount's path. Remaining astride his horse, the grand cleric looked down on them through the narrow slits in his bronze mask.

"I would treat with The Valtorak," he announced. "Where is your master?"

"Jus' say what ye've come to say an' be on with it," Yamnomora groaned.

The grand cleric regarded the dwarf ever so briefly. "You have allied yourself with dwarves and humans," he stated accusingly. "This will be added to your crimes, Daijen Saeth. And to yours, Ilithranda Lhoris."

"And what crimes would those be?" Daijen enquired, hoping secretly that it would jog memories all of his own.

"There are too many who have suffered the bite of your blade to name, Daijen Saeth. But for the murder of the master cleric alone, you will be executed here on this very stone. You will, of course, first be *punished* for the theft and desecration of the Helm of Ahnir."

"Punished?" he asked, recalling now the moment he had placed the helm on the master cleric's head.

"Like those you murdered fleeing the palace, there are too many punishments to name. Needless to say, you will *suffer* before the end."

"If ye've come to persuade us to surrender," Mordrith pointed out, "ye're doin' a terrible job o' it, laddy."

The grand cleric stiffened. "I live in service of the gods—I will not lower myself to converse with the likes of a dwarf."

"We know who you serve," Ilithranda intoned, drawing the Andaren's gaze.

"As your blood cannot be shed, daughter of House Lhoris, you will be stripped of all your trappings, parting you with the ways of the Vahlken. Subsequently, you will be exiled to The Ice Plains of Isendorn, and your Aegre will be slain. You will come to see that this is a mercy."

"Talk abou' sweetenin' the deal," Yamnomora remarked with a scoff.

"The circumstances of your arrest are yours to choose," the grand cleric continued, ignoring the dwarf altogether. "Should you surrender and return the Helm of Ahnir, we are willing to leave Ka'vairn and its master be, allowing the Vahlken order to continue.

Resist and withhold the helm, and we will tear it from the mountain stone. In the process, your allies will all perish."

The mention of the helm was a real weight upon Daijen's mind, as if Ahnir was trying to reach through his skull and retrieve that which belonged to their master.

Its master, Daijen corrected.

"Ka'vairn has never been taken," Ilithranda reminded the grand cleric. "I see no reason why today should be any different."

"Perhaps not today," the grand cleric accepted, "but tomorrow? The day after? Our victory here is inevitable. The last days of the Vahlken have come and gone. You're all—"

Aramis dropped out of the sky and ensnared the war horse in his powerful beak. The horse didn't even have time to protest, its head and neck crushed inside the Aegre's mouth in a hot spray of blood. One whipping turn threw the mutated mount and its rider over the edge of the path, sending both plummeting to the valley floor.

Given the limited size of the path, Aramis was braced between the road and cliff wall, his talons gouging the rock. With a bloody beak, his yellow eyes found the startled group standing before the gates. So too did the violet eyes of his rider, The Valtorak.

"Seal the gates, and do not open them again!" he bellowed.

Aramis flapped his wings once, twice, and then descended into the fortress courtyard, landing before the last of the group had returned inside. Being the last, Daijen paused on the open threshold, his ears detecting the sharp herald of distant war horns.

"They are coming," he muttered to himself.

Shutting the gates behind him, they moved the drawbar back into place and began moving anything and everything to add weight to the heavy doors. Having jumped down from his three-legged Aegre, The Valtorak issued his companion a single command: retrieve Oaken and Valyra.

As Aramis took flight, The Valtorak strode towards the group, staff in hand. "We do not trade words with these worms," he instructed. "Whoever marches on that gate, they are not our kin.

Make no mistake, we fight our true enemy this day. They are Skara-mangians. Not Andarens."

The name triggered an overlap in memories in Daijen, bringing forth hundreds of soldiers, Skaramangians all, clad in black and draped in green cloaks. Their ranks lined the courtyard, filling it from east to west behind The Valtorak, as if he stood in for The Dark One himself.

The vision was cut short when a flaming missile arced over the courtyard and impacted The Valtorak's personal tower. The top of the tower exploded in a shower of deadly debris before the stair-well and adjoining corridor crumbled under its own weight. Some of it spilled into the courtyard, crushing the stables.

The Valtorak stood, neck craned, the flames reflected in his eyes. How many before him had sat in that office? Ka'vairn had just lost more than a few personal things—its history was in jeopardy.

"Those catapults must fall," he seethed.

"I will bring 'em down," Mordrith vowed, the head of The Anther falling into her open palm.

"No," The Valtorak reported. "I would have such a weapon guard the gates. We will see to the catapults," he asserted, looking to Daijen and Ilithranda. "The rest of you are to keep our foes at bay until we return."

A chorus of squawks cleaved the air, turning all eyes upwards to see a trio of Aegres gliding down from the heights of The Hellions. Following behind The Valtorak and Ilithranda, Daijen claimed his slaiken blade and climbed the steps to the ramparts three at a time.

"There are four catapults," The Valtorak informed them. "They have brought down many a tree moving them."

"How many protect them?" Ilithranda asked.

"A hundred, perhaps more," The Valtorak said, stepping onto the parapet.

One after the other, the Vahlken leaped from the walls of Ka'vairn, their great strength propelling them far from the ancient stone. As they had so many times before, Aegre and rider came together mid-fall, Valyra matching Daijen's descent with practised ease.

It seemed an age since Daijen had felt the power of Valyra. He gripped the familiar handles at the head of the saddle, the tips of his boots slipping into the grooves. The Aegre dipped her left wing and glided away from Ka'vairn, exerting pressure against her rider's chest. Aramis and Oaken were already soaring over The Dain'duil, leading the way.

"Incoming!"

The Valtorak's voice carried back on the wind and found Daijen's ears. By then, of course, all four of the catapults had unleashed their payload. Three of them sent their missiles high, enormous boulders that sailed over the flying Aegres and struck the cliffside that supported Ka'vairn's eastern ramparts. Sheets of rock fell free, plunging into the forest below, threatening the fortress's integrity.

One of the four, however, had been set to a different angle. Its payload unlike the rest, it fired dozens of smaller missiles over The Dain'duil. They scattered before the approaching Aegres and exploded mid-air, spraying acid in every direction.

Valyra squawked in pain and protest, her voice added to Aramis's and Oaken's. Suffering from hundreds of small burns, the Aegres' flight path went wild. Aramis flew up, darting for the freedom of the sky, while Oaken sank below the tree line, his fate and that of Ilithranda unknown. Valyra clipped the tops of several trees before striking a trunk that would not give, sending her spiralling down through the forest.

Splattered by the acid himself, Daijen's cuirass smoked as he was whipped and lashed by the branches. Valyra's skidding impact was enough to free him of the saddle, sending the Vahlken tumbling over the hard ground for several metres.

Pushing through the pain—an all-too-familiar companion in his life—Daijen picked himself up. He rolled his wrists, bent his elbows, and squeezed his fists, checking for any fractures that might hinder him. While he could feel the sting of small burns here and there, his mutations had saved him from any breakages.

"Valyra!" He ran along the deep groove her impact had created and skidded to a stop beside her head.

She was alive, her breathing revealing as much. Many of her feathers were singed, their ends emitting wisps of smoke. As intended, her armour had protected her from the brunt of the attack, the steel plates of her beak tarnished and smoking. One yellow eye fluttered open before closing again.

The sound of charging feet pierced the forest and alerted Daijen to the fight coming his way. He ran one hand down the side of Valyra's face. "Recover quickly, old friend."

With light feet, he scrambled over his companion and found his slaiken blade. A simple twist freed it of the straps holding it firm to the back of his saddle. He jumped down, hardly aware of the weapon in his hand, the silvyr so delicate and near weightless.

Giving his Aegre one last look, the Vahlken strode off towards the east and the catapults that had wounded her. He could only spy the machines of war at a distance, and through the slight gaps between trees, before a wall of Andarens filled his vision.

"*They are Skaramangians,*" The Valtorak had said. "*Not Andarens.*"

Daijen took a breath, his oaths weighing upon him like never before. He was to safeguard Andaren lives. Could his oath still be upheld if that meant taking Andaren lives? His hand tightened around the hilt of his slaiken blade. He had only to think of Valyra at his back, wounded and suffering—because of *them*.

Rage set his blood on fire, disintegrating any thought of oaths and duty. If they had it in their heart to kill an Aegre, then they would find he had it in his to send them all into the Black Abyss.

His charge was twice their speed, a terrifying sight that only lent weight to the legend of every Vahlken. He was upon them before they could have anticipated his first move. Daijen leaped, closing the final gap between them in a single bound. Round came the slaiken blade, six feet of tempered silvyr. It was an unwieldy thing, designed for aerial combat against dragons. Daijen would make it work just fine.

The blade sliced through the trunk of a whole tree before going on to cut two men in half, splitting them from shoulder to groin. As they fell in pieces, so too did the tree. It groaned and protested, something the four Andarens it flattened could not. The rest scattered, diving aside and landing in an armoured heap amidst the snow.

Daijen pivoted swiftly and cleaved through two more foes. With barely any resistance, the slaiken blade went on to maim a third, his lower jaw removed entirely. The Vahlken jumped forwards, a pushing kick launching the wounded soldier into those at his back, his cuirass caved in.

Twisting back the other way, Daijen threw the slaiken blade, releasing it horizontally from both hands. It looked no more than a blur of steel as it crossed the forest. Six more fell to the deadly weapon, their bodies and blood adding to the massacre that stained the snow. Its spinning flight came to an end in the trunk of a large tree some distance away.

Amidst the whimpers and moans of approaching death, the sound of a crunching *thud* could be heard from beside Daijen's boot. There, he had unfurled his shogue, its hooked blade sitting ready in the snow. The fools kept coming, believing blindly that their numbers would be sufficient to overpower him.

How wrong they were.

With two hands, the Vahlken manipulated the rope and sent the blade spinning over his head. Thus began the dance Kastiek had drilled into him decades earlier. The shogue whipped around, lashed out, and buried deep into pale flesh. One Andaren came to a halt when the blade sank into the side of his ribs, where his cuirass could not protect him. Daijen tugged hard, his Vahlken strength taking the man from his feet and into a trio of his kin.

Dropping the shogue, Daijen freed the atori short-sword from his belt and rammed into his enemies. While many attacked him, their scimitars were met every time by the bronze edge of the Weavers' craftsmanship. Their battle rang out, a great clatter in the quiet calm of The Dain'duil. The Vahlken worked furiously to restore that serenity, a deed that saw him leave none alive.

The last of them fled for his life, seeing all too late that his fate had been sealed the moment he obeyed his orders to attack Valyra. His sword abandoned, his boots ploughed desperately through the snow to get him as far away from the killing machine as possible. He couldn't have predicted the distance a Vahlken could cover at a dead sprint.

Like an Aegre pouncing on its prey, Daijen came down on the soldier with all his weight and talons of his own. The atori blade sank through the back of his foe's neck, killing him instantly. The warrior Kastiek had spent so long forging stood up, mentally disconnected from his violent actions, if only for a time. He would relive the fight in his own time, he knew, and come to terms with the anger he had allowed to drive him. Until then, he had a job to finish.

The invaders' camp was already in chaos. Aramis had flown into the side of the most northern catapult, reducing it to useless parts and broken machinery. Astride his Aegre, The Valtorak held firm as his companion wreaked havoc. Soldiers were tossed aside by powerful wings, buried beneath scraping talons, and bitten in half by an unrelenting beak.

On the other side of the camp, Ilithranda had emerged astride Oaken. The Vahlken was as much an author of carnage as her Aegre companion, the two dismembering any and all between them and the southernmost catapult. That left two in the middle, both mostly unguarded thanks to the concurrent attacks at each end. Still, Daijen's arrival caught the attention of those who had remained at their stations.

Breaking into a sprint again, he weaved between the whistling arrows while his fingers nimbly untied the knot on his belt, freeing the axium vials. Before he could clash with anymore soldiers, Daijen threw the volatile liquids far and high. Smashing against the nearest catapult, the vials spilled their contents across the thick beam of the central frame. Combined together, the liquids of purple and gold reacted violently, creating an acid even the grand clerics couldn't concoct.

Within seconds it had eaten through the wood and rendered the catapult unusable. Proving as much, the beam splintered and the taut ropes snapped while the machine was being lowered back into position. As it collapsed into a heap, Daijen fell upon those who had used it against his home and companion.

Swift, yet brutal, was his vengeance. His every action was fuelled by the thought of what the Andarens would have done if they had reached Valyra in her wounded condition. That wrath might have continued had he not been confronted by a cleric. Armed only with potions, the masked Skaramangian ripped off the bronze plate that concealed his face, if only so he could consume a vial of green liquid.

Just as the Vahlken had witnessed in The Tomb—Azad-guul— the ingested potion transformed the Andaren into a monster. His arms and legs disappeared, the bones fused into sharp points and the flesh torn to make way for nightmarish limbs.

Daijen crouched, his battle style changing to meet a different kind of foe. He was not to face it, however, his winged companion never one to let him fight alone.

The Aegre squawked as she reared up, her front talons bristling, as she emerged heroically from the trees. The monster, lacking its former intelligence now, rushed Valyra with a hunger only evil could inspire. The Aegre dropped down and pinned the creature to the ground, all three of her talons piercing its twisted torso. One snap of her beak removed everything above its shoulders, ending the fight.

The last of the catapults unleashed its payload, hammering the cliffside once more. Daijen's keen eyes witnessed some of the hewn stone lose its place and fall with the rest of the debris, but the eastern wall remained standing. For now.

Experiencing rage of her own, Valyra charged the surviving war machine. Utter destruction was achieved in seconds, sending the rest of the soldiers running south, back to the bulk of their forces.

Daijen let them run this time, his attention reserved for Valyra. He was sure to make a noise as he approached from behind, all too aware of an Aegre's instincts while injured. Her yellow eyes snapped to him, and she released a reverberating *coo* from deep in her chest. Head lowered, Valyra allowed him to stroke her feathers and reconnect.

"Nothing can keep *you* down," he whispered, his voice brimming with affection.

Before he could inspect the extent of her wounds and the damage to her armour, something swept over the site, cutting through the air. Looking up, Daijen realised for the first time that night had fallen over the valley, the sky now awash with stars. Sailing through it, obstructing the field of twinkling lights was the familiar shape of an Aegre.

A pit opened inside of Daijen.

Aramis and Oaken were still on the ground, not far from where he stood. While it could have been a wild Aegre come down from the mountains or a Vahlken returning from years protecting the borders, Daijen knew the truth. He tracked the Aegre as it flew west with all haste, climbing ever higher towards Ka'vairn.

Slait had come home.

54

SURVIVE THE DAY

The sound of grinding stone and slamming walls snapped Cob from his slumber. Androma was already rising to her feet, the old Rider having been on watch while he stole a few more hours. Such had been the night, each taking it in turns to grab what rest they could. But the labyrinth had awoken once more, its iron skeleton changing shape with them still lost in its bowels.

"Move!" Androma urged, her free hand reaching out to find the edge of the door.

The Kedradi was already rushing through, pulling her along as he did. The room they had occupied disappeared, blocked by a new wall as the entire area reconfigured itself. The ranger skidded to a stop before another wall shot out and slammed into place.

"This way!" he instructed, grabbing his companion's arm.

Emerging along a low and narrow corridor, Cob could see numerous walls slotting into place, one after the other, and they were getting closer. If they lingered in that corridor their fate would be sealed, sandwiched in a cell with no doors. But there was hope ahead. The soft light of a pale dawn pierced the gloom of Taraktor through an archway.

"Run!" he barked.

Boom!

Boom!

Boom!

The new walls hammered relentlessly into place, the dominoes rushing towards them. Cob was slowed by Androma's pace, his hand always extended behind him to keep hold of hers and ensure she ran in a straight line—there was no time for even the slightest error.

Without knowing what was beyond the archway though with the light shone, Cob took his chances and let Androma barrel into him before throwing his weight through the opening. As they passed over the threshold, the entrance vanished, blocked by a thick wall pushed out from the interior, fitting perfectly into the archway.

An icy wind blew through the ranger's dreadlocks, a welcome chill for his dark skin that glistened with sweat. A quick glance informed him they had leaped out onto a long balcony that lined the eastern wall of Taraktor, just below the cliff's edge.

They had survived the night inside the prison, but the Kedradi knew better than to believe the light of a new day would bring salvation to match its beauty. They were still trapped at some height in a fortress that didn't want them to escape.

"Are you hurt?" Androma enquired, picking herself up.

"I'm fine," he replied, checking her over.

"Where are we now?" she asked hopelessly.

"Outside," Cob informed her, his gaze cast over the waters of The Deep, where the sea sat within the embrace of Erador's western hook. His chestnut eyes were swiftly drawn to a particular patch of water, not far from the shore, where a small dock had been built, granting access to a zig-zagging stairway that ascended the entire face of the cliff.

"What is it?" the old Rider asked, sensing his unease.

"There are boats approaching," he told her. "Six of them—rowboats all."

Androma moved to the rail, her brow furrowed beneath her blindfold. "Approaching Taraktor? From where?"

Cob turned his attention to the east, to the island that sat behind the boats. "Nareene," he declared grimly, aware of his companion's time on that dreaded scrap of land.

Androma's hand gripped the railing, her knuckles paling. "Skaramangians..."

As the name left her lips, Cob heard a voice on the wind, turning him to his right. "We're not alone up here."

Nocking an arrow, he moved cautiously south along the balcony, his aim high enough to take a man in the chest. With Androma close behind, the pair soon came across a jagged wound in Taraktor's iron walls. Like everything else that had been damaged around the prison, the walls were bent outwards, suggesting the source had come from inside.

Hearing that same voice again, a mere drone on the wind, the ranger replaced his arrow and bow to use both hands to climb up and through the angled debris.

"Wait here," he whispered to the old Rider, who would need help navigating the broken walls and partially destroyed ceilings to reach the opening. Slow and deliberate, the Kedradi moved without a sound, his leaps timed with the howl of the wind.

"Cob?"

The ranger stopped, almost at the top, and looked up and to his left. There stood The Green Leaf, staff in hand, dwarfed by the tower above them. His long beard blowing out beside him, relief and concern simultaneously split his expression.

"Where is Androma?"

"Is that you Green Leaf?" the old Rider called up.

On hearing her voice, Aphrandhor gave a broad grin, and together they aided Androma in reaching the base of Taraktor's central tower. "You survived the night," the wizard beamed, truly happy to be reunited with them.

"Gallien?" the Kedradi questioned.

Aphrandhor glanced over one shoulder, leading Cob's gaze to the only cell without a door and considerable damage around the frame. "The spell put upon him is worse than I thought. If we stay here much longer, I fear he will slip between the cracks of his mind. There is madness here."

"What's wrong with him?" Androma asked.

The Green Leaf licked his dry lips, his mouth contorting in thought. "His father's magic is most potent," he began, gesturing at the damage that surrounded them. "So potent, in fact, that it seems he managed to break out of Taraktor using raw magic alone. I can only imagine his abilities with demetrium at his disposal," he muttered, his thoughts taking him adrift.

"Green Leaf," the old Rider prompted.

"I'm only guessing," he caveated, "but I would say our smuggler friend is struggling with the truth he's known and the truth that is. He cannot reconcile the two. His memories appear to be fighting his father's spell. I see him experience absences. Seeing things that aren't there. Here, he's come face to face with the reality that his father was not the man he believed him to be—who his limited memories have informed him to be. And there's more..."

Cob listened intently to Aphrandhor's account and the new weapon of power drawn inside cell twelve amid an ancient script that none but the Pendains could use.

"Gallien's reaction to the necklace would suggest he knows something about it," The Green Leaf went on. "As I said, his memories are fighting the spell. He is unable to grasp neither truth nor lie. Instead, he's slipping between the two."

"Into madness," Androma uttered.

"Indeed."

Cob glanced from the cell to the waves beyond the mighty gash in the wall. "Our troubles do not end there," he reported gravely.

"Skaramangians are coming by boat," Androma said.

The wizard frowned. "Their ilk? Here?"

"They look to hail from Nareene," the Kedradi stated.

"Skaramangians, then," Aphrandhor agreed glumly. "Why would they..." He trailed off, his confusion turning to revelation. "Rogun," he muttered, naming the Jainus they had heard the other inquisitors talk of.

"What happened?" the old Rider demanded.

"We were discovered here by Rogun. Gallien chased him out there—only to talk. He chose death instead. Leaped from the railing."

That jarred with the ranger. "He killed himself? That doesn't sound like a Jainus."

"I suspect now that he never was. Or, if he was, Rogun's true allegiance was with the Skaramangians. His leap from the balcony was strategic. Beyond Taraktor's boundaries, he was able to use magic again. He sent a flare of sorts into the night. It would easily have been seen from Nareene's shores."

"But why send the signal in the first place?" Androma queried.

Aphrandhor's grey eyes shifted to cell twelve and back. "He seemed quite perturbed by Gallien's translation skills."

"Perturbed?" the old Rider echoed. "The man *killed* himself alerting Nareene."

"Perhaps I am understating his response," the wizard conceded. "Either way, it would seem our enemy has been investigating this site as long as the Jainus have. The Skaramangians know there is another weapon, and they want someone who can translate the mad scrawls."

"Then they're searching for Bragen Pendain as well," Cob concluded.

"They won't need to if they can get their hands on Gallien," The Green Leaf pointed out.

"The damage to the main gates would suggest that his father made it beyond the walls," Cob remarked.

"Bragen is long gone from here. I would estimate his escape to have taken place at least twenty years ago, perhaps longer. There might be only one way to find him now." The wizard turned to settle his gaze over cell twelve, where Gallien remained.

"I want to see it," Cob said, his desire bringing him to the threshold of cell twelve.

Gallien was seated on the edge of the rusty cot, his blank stare locked with the adjacent wall while his finger and thumb twisted a small red scale incessantly round and round.

Leaving the smuggler to his reverie for the moment, the ranger took in the cell as a whole. He soon found the necklace Aphrandhor had spoken of, nestled amongst the other weapons of power. Everything else was lost on the Kedradi, from the ancient script to the drawings of places and figures. It was madness made manifest.

"Gallien."

Cob spoke the man's name with a firm tone, though it still took the smuggler an extra second to register his presence in the cell.

"I can't make sense of it," he said, his voice so small. He had no reaction to their reunion, his mind unbalanced in the heart of his father's bloody sanctum.

The ranger looked at the lines and lines of script that Gallien had been staring at. "What does it say?"

The smuggler's expression twitched with bemusement. "They're just names." He gestured at the other walls. "All of them. Names. Men, women. Some are even Andaren names. There's no order to them. Just... hundreds of names."

Cob moved to block his view of the walls and crouched down to meet his eye line. "There's a fight coming our way," he said gently, his unusually soft tone capturing Gallien's attention. "Skaramangians. We'll make sense of all this," he vowed, "but not here and not now. We need to get out."

Gallien was shaking his head. "This is all I have. This is all there is of him. All the clues are here—we can't leave."

Cob paused, sure to keep his tone low and calm. "Is there anything in here that can tell us where your father might have gone?"

Gallien's jaw tensed beneath his thick beard. "No," he admitted.

"But we do know about that now," the ranger replied, looking at the necklace painted on the wall behind the smuggler. "It's a good start," he lied.

"It's nothing," Gallien argued, seeing the truth of it.

"Your father is alive, Gallien. That's *something*," Cob insisted evenly. "Give me a chance to track him down."

The smuggler was shaking his head. "He likely fled Taraktor decades ago. He could be anywhere by now."

"From here," Cob deduced, "it's logical that he would have found his way to Caster Hold. The trail will be cold, but if there's anything to find of him, I swear I will." Seeing the debt in the smuggler's eyes, the ranger added an irrefutable statement to his argument. "I found you and Joran, didn't I?"

Gallien met his gaze. "Yes," he breathed.

The Kedradi nodded, a fine smile cutting his lips. "First we survive the day. Then we find Bragen Pendain." He stood up and offered a hand. "Are you with me?"

Reluctantly, it seemed, Gallien took the hand and stood up.

"The axe?" Cob asked, looking at the hand he had just gripped.

The smuggler scrutinised his palm, his thoughts wandering before he replied, "I haven't seen it since..." He swallowed. "Since Thedaria."

Cob had to wonder if his resentment at the weapon was clouding his need for it. "Take this," he instructed, offering him the curved and slender, curved dagger from his belt, the blade hewn from Wither bone.

Gallien accepted the weapon, tilting it in his grip to see the three feathers attached to the pommel—the colours of House Thayne. "Thank you," he said absently.

The ranger ushered the smuggler from the cell and gave those wretched walls one last look before turning his back on it for good.

———

With naught but torchlight to accompany them in the dark of Taraktor, it was impossible to say how much time passed after they had abandoned the cell block. They weaved through tight spaces and navigated the rise and fall of stairwells that revealed only more of the prison's oil-black walls.

The companions stopped routinely to share food and water from the enchanted satchels of both Aphrandhor and Gallien. In those silences, Cob listened.

He waited for the sound of boots, the *clink* of armour, and the whispers of their enemy. But that was not all. The ranger waited for the inevitable return of the cursed drums. Time was running down. He didn't even have the option to hunt down a monster and bloody his blades. He was trapped in an iron box—and with his friends, no less.

Cob looked at his hand. Steady. It was a sickening thought to imagine what would happen when that was no longer the case. He thought of the manacles his mother took everywhere with her. She had never hesitated to use them on his father, and he had never hesitated to let her. Such had been the case when his father's horse had fallen ill, preventing him from leaving for the hunt and satiating the curse. How many days had he spent chained up in the stables?

A subtle vibration ran through Taraktor's ironwork, a precursor to the distant *booms* of shifting walls.

"Get ready," Androma warned.

"Stay together," the ranger urged.

They had safely navigated half a dozen shifts since departing the cell block, but it would only take a single wall to split them up again.

The reconfiguration rippled across the prison and, inevitably, created chaos in their section. The wall to their left dropped down, while the wall to the right split into three smaller walls so they could all spin and slot into new places. The companions were as light on their feet as their various injuries and fatigue would allow, but it was not fast enough to stop all four of them from being pushed into a different corridor.

At the front of the group, Cob froze, suddenly eye to eye with the old Jainus in charge of the site. Behind him, holding a knife to the wizard's throat, was a Skaramangian clad in brown leathers and a silver helm that concealed most of his face.

Taraktor, in its twisted delights, had brought them together.

The cursed ranger was the first to react, and violently so. His hands snapped into action, bringing bow and arrow into harmony. It was more reflex and instinct that aimed the weapon, and both proved true as the arrow whistled down the corridor and into the Skaramangian's face. The old Jainus made a desperate dash for the companions, another arrow flying an inch past his ear to find the next Skaramangian down the hallway.

With two of their number dead, the remaining enemies charged. Cob killed a third before the bow became useless. He side-stepped a chopping blow and rushed the man, pinning him to the wall while sticking out a leg to trip up another. It gave Aphrandhor time to angle Yalaqin and thrust, driving through the tooled leathers of the man running behind. Gallien dropped to one knee and plunged the Kedradi's dagger into the Skaramangian who had fallen over, giving them an overall tally of five to none.

But there were more.

Cob dragged his foe across the slick wall and threw him into the others, slowing them down. It was impractical, he knew, to keep using his hands, but in such a confined space, he also knew that any sword he might utilise had the potential to catch the wall or ceiling mid-swing. It certainly did for the next Skaramangian, his blade met by the wall to his right. His attack staggered, the Kedradi jabbed his open hand into the man's throat, collapsing his windpipe. He would die shortly and, therefore, required no further attention, but his helm could be of use.

The ranger roughly grabbed at him and forced his head into another grunt, trying to get past him. A swift kick to the outside of his knee robbed him of his ability to walk or even stand—an easy kill for The Green Leaf. A thrusting sword ran along Cob's left arm, just beneath his pauldron of silver and gold. It stung and forced him to pivot his shoulders, exposing his chest to a second attack. The Skaramangian might have landed that blow too, but the man suddenly found it impossible to act at all with a dagger stuck in his face.

Glancing back, Cob saw Gallien's arm still outstretched after throwing the blade of Wither bone. He gave a nod of thanks and returned to the fight, only glimpsing Androma as she weaved and skidded past him. The old Rider popped up, defying her age and lack of sight, and met the Skaramangians with ferocity. The atori short-sword flashed in the torchlight of both groups while she wrought chaos amongst them. Cob could only envy the acuity of her remaining senses and how in tune with them she was.

Then, without warning, Taraktor spasmed again.

The walls reconfigured as always but, worst of all, the floor also dropped at one end, its smooth surface settling into a long set of steps. Along with the Skaramangians, the four companions tumbled down the new stairs and into the light.

Lying flat out on the stone, the Kedradi was keenly aware of the knock to his head, blood oozing from above his right eyebrow and dripping onto his eyelashes. It seemed an age before he made sense of their new surroundings and the people around him.

Some of the Skaramangians were already rising, their footsteps and voices disturbingly distant despite their close proximity. Between them, he determined the shape of the balcony they had been deposited on was circular and perched between the walls of Taraktor, offering a view of the sea under the light of a setting sun.

A pained cry pierced the air, bringing a notch of clarity to the ranger. Androma! He began to rise, pushing through the disorientation. The old Rider was on her knees to one side, her head pulled back by a handful of her short hair. Cob meant to intercede, already visualising how he would slay the man, but before he could, another Skaramangian intervened, ramming into him from his periphery.

Muscle memory moved his limbs and he quickly flipped the man onto his back. A hammering stomp of his boot ended any further fight. Another rushed him, believing his strength alone would be enough to defeat the last son of House Thayne. Cob ducked beneath the swing and twisted mid-evasion, bringing him up behind his enemy. A heel to the back of his leg dropped him just enough for the ranger to grab his helm and jaw. *Crack!*

A dead man at his feet, Cob drew the great scimitar of Draven bone from his hip.

"Enough!" came a sharp command.

Cob turned around, putting his back to the sea. At the base of the steps, all three of his companions were on their knees with a blade held at their necks. Standing in the middle, his sword free to attack any he chose, was the only Skaramangian garbed in a cloak.

He dipped his head and removed his helm, revealing himself to be a man in his late thirties or early forties. His cropped hair was greying, much like his skin, which had a sickly pallor that suggested a long life in the dark.

"The fabled Kedradi," he drawled, a wicked smile parting his lips to display yellow teeth. "We have heard of your exploits on Nareene. You have proven yourself a worthy adversary. I can only thank the Fates that you would cause trouble so close to our shores."

"And you are?" Cob demanded, trying to ignore the fact that his vision was doubling.

"I am one of the many," the Skaramangian replied. "A nameless servant."

"A curator," Aphrandhor grunted, wincing at the steel pressing into his skin.

The cloaked warrior turned to regard the wizard. "Ah yes, The Green Leaf. You met my predecessors. And you dragon witch," he added, looking at Androma. "The Eldan has long sought you all. He would see you answer for your desecration of The Tomb. As would I." The nameless one gestured at the bone sword in Cob's hand. "Drop it and submit," he commanded.

The Kedradi stood fast, his grip tightening while his vision continued to drift.

"Submit," the Skaramangian ordered again. "Or they die."

"Die here or die there," the ranger countered, flicking his head back at Nareene. "What does it matter?"

Up came the Draven sword, the weapon angled to cleave the man's head from his shoulders. By his second step, however, his knees were crashing into the stone, his head rolling. Taraktor and all upon it tilted drastically to one side.

He hardly registered the *clatter* of his scimitar falling away. While he *did* register the sole of the boot coming towards his face, the Kedradi was too slow to do anything about it.

55

NEITHER HERE NOR THERE

0 Years Ago...

4

Leaving the ruined catapults behind, Daijen soared above The Dain'duil, the Vahlken lifted high on Valyra's wings. Like him, she was quick to heal, her blood coursing with Handuin's ancient magic. Still, he could feel a subtle pull to the left, her wing harbouring a source of pain for the Aegre. More time was required to see her return to full strength.

He only hoped she had strength enough to face Slait, who had returned to the valley astride an Aegre of his own—the exile.

The pair could be seen rising to meet Ka'vairn, soon to top the ramparts and fly over the courtyard. Daijen thought of the companions he had left there. Were they any match for the Vahlken-trained killer? Had she her sight, he had no doubt that Androma would run Slait through, but she would face him blind, her eyes taken from her by Daijen's own axium.

The Green Leaf would prove troublesome, his magic not to be

underestimated. And for all his skill, Slait was not immune to the spells of wizards. But was Aphrandhor experienced enough to face a warrior of Slait's calibre? The answer was miserably bleak.

Then there were the dwarves. Their strength was a close rival to a Vahlken's, and they possessed a stubbornness where defeat was concerned. Added to their hearty nature, Mordrith wielded The Anther, a weapon of power that Slait had never been trained to anticipate. Equally, Daijen had to acknowledge, neither Mordrith nor Yamnomora had been trained to battle a Vahlken or an Aegre —the latter would kill them all without any aid from Slait.

As a terrible sinking feeling began to tear through his insides, The Valtorak's words came back to him. "*Let them go while they still can, Daijen. Your recklessness is going to get them all killed.*" Haunted by that warning, Daijen voiced his need to reach Ka'vairn, his words urging Valyra to make haste.

"Look!" Ilithranda yelled over the wind.

Daijen followed her pointing finger to the rising path that connected the forest floor to Ka'vairn's main gates. Rank upon rank of Andarens marched up the slope, their armour of bronze catching in the moonlight. The Vahlken narrowed his eyes, searching for any sign of a battering ram in their midst. At only five men abreast, it would be easily seen and would be absolutely necessary if they were to get through the gates.

"I don't see any ram!" he yelled.

"Nor I!" Ilithranda replied.

"That's because they don't have one!" The Valtorak called out from his saddle. "*He's* the battering ram!"

Daijen followed his master's implication with a fresh revelation of dread in his bones. Slait was going to destroy the gates.

"We have to stop him!" he cried, but there was no going any faster.

Pained by the injury to her wing, Valyra was unable to take the lead, so Oaken topped the ramparts first. Even then, Ilithranda and her Aegre were too late to stop Slait and his own mount. The pale-feathered exile glided over the courtyard at speed, there to deliver a catastrophe from which there was no return.

The axium flew from Slait's hand, the glass vials shattering against the great doors to deliver a blow unlike any Ka'vairn had ever been dealt. The betrayer and his mount were already flying away from the mountains and the fortress before the potent acid could complete its menacing work. Eating away at the doors, it created enough smoke to conceal the entire entrance.

"Slait!" Daijen bellowed, his entire body leaning to direct Valyra into pursuit.

"No!" The Valtorak countered. "I want you where I can see you! We will defend the keep! Ilithranda! Bring him down!"

Ilithranda hesitated—a rarity.

"Bring him down!" The Valtorak barked again.

There was no time to argue, as much as Daijen wished to. Ilithranda managed to shoot him a look of determination before Oaken and Valyra peeled away from each other. It seemed a façade to Daijen, who knew her so well, though he couldn't say why she lacked true determination—they had both wished vengeance upon Slait for years.

"Daijen!" The Valtorak snapped. "Now is not the time to lose yourself! Ka'vairn needs you!"

The Vahlken gave a short, sharp nod. "Let's run them from the path!"

"Take the lead!" came the master's response.

Having circled above the fortress, Valyra was directed down, towards the path. The Aegre needed no such instruction where war was concerned. It had been bred into her blood by Handuin millennia past. She was a machine of war as much as any catapult could be. Valyra also knew who her enemy was.

Her wings, thick sails of muscle and brown feathers, unfurled so she might glide along the path. The advancing soldiers saw what was coming but had no hope of avoiding it, with a handful even falling over the edge of the cliff to their deaths in the mad scramble. Those that remained were flattened when Valyra's right wing cut through their ranks. The Aegre would have continued her glide the entire length of the path, toppling many from a great height, but necessity forced her to barrel roll and fly away.

The ballista bolt missed the swift Aegre and buried deep into Hellion stone, just below the path. It was the first of a volley, each bolt spearing through the air in search of Valyra and Aramis, who had swept in behind Valyra, using his talons to brush many of the survivors over the side.

Angled away from the mountains, Daijen got a clear view of Ilithranda and Oaken in the distance. To any other, they would have vanished amidst the starfield, but his Vahlken eyes spotted them closing in on Slait. It was all he could glimpse before Valyra evaded another bolt, turning them back towards Ka'vairn.

"Return to the keep!" The Valtorak yelled. "Valyra and Aramis can see to the ballistas without us!" The master of Ka'vairn pointed to the ranks of soldiers picking themselves up at the front of the advance. "Let us thin their number all the more!"

Dodging half a dozen more ballista bolts, both Aegres managed to ascend the path, allowing The Valtorak and Daijen to leap from their saddles. A wave of dust plumed in every direction as both Vahlken impacted the ground only feet in front of the recovering soldiers.

With one hand, Daijen drew the sabre Ilithranda had left out for him, and with the other, he freed his atori short-sword. It felt so wrong that both would, again, taste the blood of his kin, but now was not the time for emotion. Now was the time for action.

Yet the Vahlken hesitated.

The soldiers who had survived Valyra's wings were already on their feet, sabres drawn, as they prepared themselves to face not one but two Vahlken. They stared at their foes through the V-shaped gap in their helms—helms that had ever sat upon Andaren heads.

But these were not Andarens.

Daijen looked upon the pink and brown flesh of men—humans! He blinked, sure that Ahnir's memories were playing tricks on him, yet the humans remained, garbed in the black cloaks and bronze armour of his kin. The truth, grim as it may have been, dawned on him.

They were fodder. Whether they had been captured from

battlefields or simply bred on one of the farms, these humans had been armed and given a single instruction: take the keep. It was impossible to say whether they did it out of fear of their captors or blind loyalty to those who had reared them. Either way, they were a threat to Ka'vairn, and so they were all to die in The Hellion Mountains.

Holding firm to that cold hard fact, Daijen embraced the warrior Kastiek had instilled in him. Unencumbered, perhaps, by a conscience such as Daijen's—or simply not one to be taken by surprise—The Valtorak waded in first.

His staff gripped at one end and in both hands, he swung it from right to left, directly across the front line of humans. Daijen was stunned to see the wood explode on impact, splintered and crushed between the soldiers and that which had lain concealed. It was a scabbard!

None could stand against Vahlken strength, especially when that strength was sweeping a *slaiken blade* at speed. The Valtorak cut five men in half with his single strike, the silvyr edge making short work of their chainmail, plate, and all that sat within their flesh.

Gripping the wooden hilt of his six-foot blade, Ka'vairn's ancient master dashed forwards and swung again. Three more were added to the pile of corpses, then another four. With every strike, the slaiken blade delivered death to many, decorating the Hellion stone with blood.

Daijen's disbelief that The Valtorak's silvyr blade had been hiding in plain sight was short-lived, his muscle memory throwing him into battle beside the master. The Valtorak changed his style immediately, ensuring that the great arcs of his slaiken sabre did not bring death to his fellow Vahlken. Thusly, the humans forced to invade Ka'vairn found themselves being skewered two or three at a time before being shoved over the cliff's edge.

Using the sheer face of the cliff to his right, Daijen leaped off the stone and landed in his enemies' midst, putting some distance between him and The Valtorak. How confusing it was for the human soldiers to see someone so big move so swiftly and with acrobatic agility they could never master. They were cut down high and low, their opponent always on the move.

Daijen weaved through their ranks, slashing and slicing at speed. Ramming his way through disturbed their ranks all the more, sending several humans over the cliff to their deaths. Only when he felt the scrape of steel across his cuirass did the Vahlken decide he had delved far enough into their advance.

A powerful push kick sent the man directly in front of him flying back through a number of others. It was there that Daijen Saeth drew his line, content to kill and wait for The Valtorak to meet him.

Coming at him from all sides, the advantage was theirs, and they knew it. Such foolish belief saw them close in without a strategy, sure in their hearts that they had only to thrust out and the Vahlken would succumb to half a dozen swords. If only they didn't move so slowly.

Daijen spun around, his sabre and atori blade deflecting two swords at a time. A jumping kick sent one over the edge of the path and propelled the Vahlken in the opposite direction, where he dropped low and skidded on his knees, both weapons whipped out to cut through a soldier each. Jumping back to his feet in a deft flip, he continued his momentum up the cliff face and came back down amid the soldiers.

Vahlken fury was unleashed upon them, his ferocity delivered with deadly precision. Always the edge of his blades found the gaps in their armour, biting through to split arteries and ensure the quickest death possible.

It wasn't long before the threat at his back was distracted by The Valtorak's relentless advance. His slaiken blade remained further up the path, standing upright in the back of a corpse. The master of Ka'vairn defended his home with a sabre in each hand, the weapons taken from the dead.

"Back to the keep!" he commanded.

As Daijen turned to run up the path, a single sound pierced his heart. The Vahlken had dreaded that particular sound for years, always fearing that, one day, he would live to hear it. Rather than ascend any further, he dashed to the edge of the path and looked over The Dain'duil, searching desperately for the source of the shrill squawk.

"NO!" The Valtorak bellowed, spying the Aegres first.

As Valyra soared over an arcing ballista bolt, Aramis fell from the air beside her. The three-legged Aegre was already dead, his chest punched in by two bolts. There was nothing Daijen or The Valtorak could do but watch Aramis plummet to the ground, never to fly again.

It had all happened so quickly. One moment, the Aegre had been there, alive, fighting alongside Valyra. Then he was gone, brought down by their fellow Andarens no less. It was painful for Daijen to watch the magnificent creature fall from life. He could only imagine what was burning in The Valtorak.

The much older Andaren turned to the soldiers and took a threatening step towards them. A white flame raged behind his eyes, a promise of death to all who had entered the valley. His wild emotions would see the path run with blood, but Daijen knew it would likely get the master killed, his edge dulled by grief and rage.

"No," he said forcefully, one hand pressed hard into The Valtorak's cuirass. "Back to the keep," he urged. "*Now.*"

At the base of the path, where the lush Dain'duil reigned over the valley floor, another great horn blasted up the mountain stone. Daijen spotted masses of Andarens preparing to add their number to the humans. The fight was far from over.

With glassy eyes, each wide with mad ferocity, The Valtorak turned and dashed for the keep, hardly pausing as he reclaimed his slaiken blade. Daijen was close on his heels, only he left his master to pass through the broken doors in favour of rising to the ramparts above. After executing one mighty leap, Daijen scrambled nimbly up the hewn stone and topped the wall to stand beside Yamnomora.

"Were that Aramis or Valyra?" the dwarf asked, her eyes not as good as his.

"Aramis," he confirmed gravely.

"Kuds!" she cursed, hefting one of her axes. "I hope ye left some for us!"

Daijen planted a hand on one of her pauldrons. "You can have the rest," he promised.

"They're still coming," The Green Leaf pointed out, his wizard's staff held close to his chest.

Daijen looked beyond the oncoming forces, where Valyra continued to harass the ballistas. He worried all the more for her now, but she proved her skill as she succeeded in getting past the next salvo and went on to pick up an entire ballista between all four of her talons. Distant though it was, Daijen still witnessed the Andaren who had been operating the weapon fall from a deadly height. Soon after, Valyra let go of the ballista, deliberately dropping it on top of another.

The Valtorak was striding across the courtyard, slaiken blade in hand. "Ready the oil!" he commanded, his voice rasping like gravel rolling over stone.

"Oh it's *ready*," Yamnomora replied hungrily, stirring the vats. "The first to reach the gates are in for a shock!"

"Prepare for battle!" The Valtorak declared, a call to all but those seeing to the vats of boiling oil.

Daijen dropped over the side, landing in front of the smoking doors before The Green Leaf could descend even a single step. Androma and Mordrith were already in the courtyard and making their way towards the keep's master.

Having seen what they were up against, their number felt pitiful as they gathered. They were too few, he feared. Even if Tovun had stood with them, they would still have been fiercely outnumbered. Perhaps, then, it was a good thing that the initiate was with The Weavers, sparing at least one Vahlken for the war.

Looking at the doors—or what remained of them—Daijen didn't need much of an imagination to envision the invaders charging through. Still, the ragged hole that had been carved out by Slait's axium would allow no more than three men abreast and had failed to destroy the drawbar keeping the doors locked together. The soldiers would be funnelled further when trying to enter Ka'vairn, a fact that would work to the defenders' advantage.

Seeing The Valtorak, Daijen could clearly discern the pain behind his eyes. The rage. Yet his centuries of discipline and focus were also on display, keeping him right there in the moment, where he was needed most. Aramis would be grieved when the time was appropriate. Until then, the invaders would have to face his wrath.

"Aramis will be avenged," Daijen vowed.

The Valtorak said nothing, his sharp gaze never shifting from the broken doors.

Without warning, Ahnir's memory swept across the courtyard like a sandstorm, replacing Daijen's reality. The Valtorak vanished, his form replaced by that of another, while Ka'vairn's stonework morphed into that of a looming tower. The courtyard was gone, and in its place, a hard desert ground supported a raging battle, bringing, once again, the red cloaks of the Dragon Riders into conflict with the green-cloaked Skaramangians of ages past.

Daijen quite naturally moved to avoid the clashing soldiers—it all felt so real. He even felt the splatter of blood strike his pale face. Running his fingers over one cheek, his hand came away with that same blood staining his skin. Something was wrong. It wasn't like before. He should only be observing it, not living it.

The experience got dramatically worse.

The war cry of a red cloak turned his attention to a man who fought under the banner of the Riders. He was charging at the Vahlken, sword raised. Daijen retreated, glancing over one shoulder to see who the warrior had targeted. There was no one. And so the sword came down to carve him from head to groin.

Seeing no choice but to defend himself, Daijen stepped forward and intercepted the soldier's arm at the wrist, halting the blow. Without thought, he thrust his other hand forward, plunging his own sword through the man's gut. Had he always been holding that weapon?

Keeping hold of the sword, he let the human soldier slide off the end and crumple at his feet. "No, no, no, no," he muttered.

"This isn't real. This isn't real!" he yelled, his voice lost to the heated battle.

Another red cloak peeled away from his forces to challenge the Vahlken. Daijen shut his eyes and shook his head, waiting for the sound of war to fade from his ears. It wasn't going anywhere. Men who had been dead for untold eons were still fighting each other in every direction.

Opening his eyes, the soldier advancing on him reached out. It took everything Daijen had to just let it happen, hoping against it all that death might see him return to Ka'vairn. At the last second, as the man grabbed the rim of his leather cuirass, the soldier's appearance melted away, leaving The Valtorak standing in his place, gripping the edge of his cuirass.

His violet eyes roamed over Daijen. "Stay behind me," he commanded.

"I can fight," he insisted, his pride feeling the familiar sting.

"Your mind is compromised," The Valtorak told him simply. "Of all the pieces that make you who you are, Daijen Saeth, your mind is your greatest asset. That, above all else, is what your training was for. Now you've thrown it all away. And for what? How is Ka'vairn to be saved by your actions? What did you glean that might repel our attackers? All you've done is bring death to our gates. Death to..." He couldn't say the Aegre's name.

Daijen was shaking his head, feeling himself sinking beneath the weight of so much memory. It was imperative that he remain grounded in that moment lest he recall the ancient past and fall into it.

"Your actions here have been no less foolish than your actions in Aran'saur," The Valtorak continued, his anger running away with him. "I warned you of your pride, Daijen. It makes you reckless. Those around you must now suffer for it."

Talk of Aran'saur helped root Daijen in the present, where events of his own making had taken place. He raised his chin in defiance. "I did only what Kastiek trained me to do. Just as I will today. *That's* how Ka'vairn will be saved."

The Valtorak leaned in. "Stay behind me," he repeated.

Turning his back on the Vahlken, the master of Ka'vairn faced the broken doors, his slaiken blade held over his shoulder in the manner of a spear.

"Here they come!" Yamnomora called out.

Three vats of boiling oil were tipped over the ramparts to the sound of screaming men. Their agony was paralysing, causing all those behind them to crash into the line in front. It created more chaos on the treacherous path, echoing all the way down to the base. Inevitably, those unharmed by the oil stepped over the dead and dying to infiltrate the keep.

"They're human!" The Green Leaf exclaimed in disbelief.

"What?" Androma spat.

"They are extensions of the Skaramangians," The Valtorak reiterated, his slaiken blade launched from his hand. It went on to skewer man after man, casting them back through the jagged hole in the doors. "Nothing more!" the master declared, drawing his sabre.

As more piled in, passing through the entrance, Yamnomora made herself known. The dwarven warrior stepped off the ramparts and landed on two soldiers, crushing one with her bulk and killing the other with one of her large axes. Jumping to her feet, she created pandemonium in seconds. A single spin brought down four soldiers, her axes slicing and hacking through their limbs and midriff.

Mordrith let loose her battlecry and charged into the fray to fight beside her kin. The dwarf would have been the first to reach the entrance had The Valtorak and Daijen not joined her. Their long strides, propelled by Vahlken mutations, saw the pair pierce the ranks a few seconds earlier, creating room for the others to find their place in the melee.

As Daijen had suspected, the invading force was being funnelled through the entrance and could only breach the fortress three at a time. That wasn't nearly enough to push back the eclectic group of defenders, who included a Dragon Rider.

Androma was more reserved than the others, keeping at a distance and waiting for her enemies to come to her. The cacophonous anarchy taking place in front of the doors was no place for the blind, where she might accidentally wound or kill her allies. Still, her form was strict, her blows decisive and devastating. The Rider was soon fighting amidst a growing pile of bodies.

Daijen darted in, saving Mordrith from a sword in the back. He pinned the soldier to the wall by the point of his sabre, holding him there until he ran his atori blade across the man's throat.

"Wizard!" The Valtorak cried, gesturing at the hole in the gate.

Aphrandhor dashed into the available gap and shoved his staff into the torrent of soldiers. All but Androma were momentarily blinded by the branches of lightning that erupted forth. The spell consumed the jagged hole, killing any and all trying to rush through, before spreading beyond to cut through the column of humans.

It gave the defenders some reprieve, though Aphrandhor alone looked to be the only one in need of a rest. Even so, The Green Leaf was the only one who had the power to kill so many at once—his magic would be needed all the more before the end.

Daijen reached out and pulled him back. "Take a breath."

"I'm fine," the wizard assured him, despite looking like he was still suffering from his interaction with the skeleton he had touched in The Tomb...

The Vahlken tried not to follow his own thoughts through, but there was no stopping that black pyramid from coming to life in his mind's eye. *Azad-guul.* His master's palace.

Daijen stumbled away from his companions, shaking his head. "No," he hissed, feeling Ahnir's loyalty becoming his own.

"They're still comin'," Mordrith warned, dragging Daijen back to the present, if only barely. The dwarf instructed them all to stand back, giving her some space inside the entrance. "I've learned a new trick," she said devilishly.

The Anther hammered into the stone at her feet, the magic therein ignited by the mighty blow. The flash was brief as the power of the weapon sucked in the air around the dwarf. Daijen expected to see Mordrith disappear, only she remained where she stood and the littered bodies around her ported away. A moment later, and they heard the crashing impact as those same corpses rained down on the men outside.

While the soldiers with broken bones were filtered back through the ranks, they gained a brief respite. Yet it also gave Daijen's mind more time to spiral. His thoughts lingered on Azadguul. For all he had learned exploring Ahnir's history, he still had no idea why The Tomb—as it was known amongst present-day Skaramangians—housed hundreds, if not thousands, of skeletons. It was the worst time to think about it, but the Vahlken felt like he knew the answer. It was just out of his reach.

The Valtorak bolted forwards, his sabre arcing round to slice through the next wave of invaders. Of those who found their way past him, two came for Daijen, their swords thrusting towards his gut. His atori blade, reversed in his grip, batted two swords aside and returned in a slashing backhand, slaying them both. Yamnomora forced herself into the fight beside him, using one horizontal axe to push them back and one swinging axe to cut them down. She did it all with a grin on her stubbled face.

"They're on the ramparts!" The Green Leaf yelled.

Daijen looked up, as if he could see them through the stone that covered the entrance. "They must have ladders!"

"No!" The Valtorak commanded. "I want you here!"

Where you can see me, Daijen thought. "They'll flank us!" he countered, breaking away.

By the time Daijen had run along the interior wall and ascended the steps, humans attired in Andaren armour were already scattering, finding their own way into the courtyard.

Those who had hoped to get down via the steps were met by the Vahlken. The first suffered an atori blade to the chest, the weapon launched from Daijen's hand and then retrieved as the body fell down the steps. A second and third had their swords deflected before feeling the bite of his sabre.

Beyond the steps were two ladders resting against the ramparts, both of which allowed a seemingly never-ending stream of invaders to get over the walls. From the steps on the other side, Aphrandhor hurled spell after spell, burning, freezing, and paralysing the soldiers. Even then, some of the humans were able to run past him and along the ramparts, where they could descend into the courtyard on the northern side. Like rats, they were finding their way into the keep.

Intending to destroy the ladders, Daijen advanced along the rampart, weaving and attacking as he went. As he came to stand over the entrance, he spotted something between the soldiers on the path below. Clerics, masked in bronze, were pushing through the human fodder, their route carved out by a trio of escorting Andarens.

Fighting for a second look, the Vahlken spied each of the clerics wielding some kind of staff, the end of which had been shaped into a scoop. The light from the braziers reflected off whatever was sat inside those scoops. Too late, Daijen realised that they were glass spheres, made to house whatever alchemical spell the clerics had concocted.

One of them stopped on the path and twisted their hips, the flinger braced behind them in both hands.

"Incoming!" Daijen grabbed the nearest soldier and yanked him round, using him as a shield.

His Vahlken ears only just heard the glass sphere as it shattered against the stone beside him, the sound of it almost immediately drowned out by the resulting explosion. The deafening *boom* was nothing compared to the shockwave that threw Daijen and his human shield from their feet.

Along with several tons of debris, the Vahlken was flung beyond the ramparts and down into the courtyard. His body limp, Daijen rolled over his limbs, tumbling shoulder over shoulder before flipping over his head to skid across the stone on his back.

As the smoke blew over him, he lay there looking up at a blue sky. Dazed, it took the Vahlken more time than it should have to realise it had been night only seconds ago. Even the smell had changed. All too familiar was the scent of Ka'vairn and the mountain stone, but both had been replaced by something else. Acrid blood and the musk of dragons.

Then he heard it—the carnage of battle.

Picking himself up, the black smoke was wafted aside by the flap of bat-like wings. He recognised the silver scales of Orvax, Gelakor's dragon. The hulking creature took off over the battle, leading Daijen's gaze across the warring armies. Dominating the view, Azad-guul towered over the bloodshed, an obsidian observer of the death and destruction.

Standing above the soldiers, Daijen spotted the Golems, draped in their black ethereal robes. They picked up red cloaks, plucking them from the battlefield, and split them in half with all four of their hands. He witnessed a single backhand from Meliax launch three men high into the air.

Daijen was able to place himself then. He had returned to Azad-guul, to the battle that had taken place after Malliath—the Drakalis—had been dragged into The Shadow Realm. He was now witnessing the Riders' retribution and the mayhem that had followed the robbing of their Dragonlord.

Only now he was actually in it.

As before, the soldiers—red cloaks all—came for his life, forcing the Vahlken to defend himself. Locked in memory, he could but fight in the hope that he would find his way back to reality.

In the hope that he wasn't just lying on the stone of Ka'vairn's courtyard, waiting to die.

56
THE CREEPING FOE

Again and again, the day and the night rolled over each other, closing the gap between Valgala and Taraktor. Rest had been a short affair for Joran Pendain, always waking and setting off before the dawn.

He was not alone.

Oaken flew without complaint, his strong wings taking them clear over The Spine of Erador and into the golden lands of the setting sun. They had, eventually, given way to Erador's hook, where Joran was sure to keep the white cliff faces on their left as they advanced further west. To his right, the waves of The Deep stretched on and on, reaching for northern shores beyond his sight.

How much more beautiful the realm was from the heavens! It was all connected in a way that couldn't be comprehended from the ground. Up where only gods might dwell, it seemed the world was sprawled beneath them like a map. Oaken had only to point his head, and their destination would come to *them*.

For a time, it had been the perfect distraction from the revelations that shadowed his thoughts. Alas, even Verda's exquisite face could not keep him from the blood that coursed through his veins. House Lhoris. Blood Etragon. To be both human and Andaren was abomination enough for the world, but to be of two thrones was a complication Joran couldn't wrap his head around.

There were hundreds of thousands of humans and Andarens— millions even. What web of Kaliban could have brought Edris Valayan and Ilithranda Lhoris together? One he would never know, and the other he wasn't sure he even wanted to know. For all the good he had seen in the King of Erador, it was a keen sting to know he had abandoned Joran's pregnant mother when she had needed him most.

It was all so heavy, a weight he could never have imagined bearing. Should he try to escape his reality, his father's voice rang clear in his ears, as if he was still standing in the throne room.

"*You,* Joran Etragon, *stand in the shadow of kings who have come before you,*" he had declared. "*You also stand as a son of the broken circle, of House Lhoris. What will you do?*"

What will you do?

Those four words were like hooks deep in his skin. It was a challenge he couldn't hide from. But that didn't mean he had to face it there and then.

In the distance was a stark reminder that he had left Kassanda and Garganafan for a reason. Joran narrowed his eyes to better see the black behemoth gripping to the edge of the cliff.

Taraktor.

It looked a blight on the land, a black spot on an otherwise lush strip of good earth. Its iron walls contrasted with the white cliffs that lined Erador's hooking arm, as if a volcano had bubbled over and oozed down the pristine face. Keeping Erador on their left and the sea on their right, the pair were soon close enough to see the yellowed grass that surrounded the prison, lending some truth to its effect on the environment.

Joran felt a flutter inside as Oaken steadily descended. It was the niggling brush of doubt. What was he doing there? What was his plan? If Gallien and the others were already inside, how was he to reach them? Somewhere like Taraktor had to be guarded and well—by wizards no less! The word *fool* came to mind more than once as Oaken began to bank over the land.

Joran cast his gaze over the green fields and patches of dense woods below, hoping against it all that they hadn't reached the prison yet. Such hope came to naught. Taraktor was the land's sole occupier, a titan lording over its domain. With no desire to set foot on that yellow grass, Joran shouted the single command to land while they were still some distance from the prison. Oaken squawked and made for a wooded area in the northwest.

Caught in the setting sun, the Aegre's shadow stretched across the grassland behind them. But his was not the only shadow. Oaken growled from deep in his chest and banked hard to the left. Joran yelped, nearly torn from the saddle as the world rotated sideways. With a single hand, the boy managed to keep his grip on the handle, his legs tossed up into the air. A white streak roared past them, spearing towards the ground.

Oaken levelled off and Joran was flung the other way, forcing him to scramble back into the saddle. His sandy cloak billowing out behind him again, he looked beyond the Aegre's horned head to see their quarry. There was no mistaking the creature as it turned on soaring white wings to face them, its long tail rippling behind it.

The Dawn Sword's Aegre.

From beak to tail, the Aegre's feathers were white as snow, though they were interrupted almost everywhere by a tapestry of scars. Of the two horns that branched from its brow, one was broken in half, and the other was missing its tip. Like Oaken, it sported a saddle, various sheets of chainmail, and a plated beak, all of which had been dented or ripped by Oaken himself when the pair had clashed in The Ruins of Gelakor.

How long had the beast stalked them? Had it followed them to Drakanan or discovered them as they flew over The Giant's Throat? Either way, the Aegre had clearly been waiting until Garganafan was out of the picture before making its move.

Caught in those yellow eyes, Joran was paralysed, rooted to his mother's saddle as he envisioned his end. Oaken was not so afraid. Ilithranda's Aegre flapped his wings once and hard, taking him higher than the pale beast as they crossed paths. All four of his legs ran over the top of his enemy's back, his talons stabbing along the way. The Dawn Sword's mount reared its head in pain and dived.

Oaken's bulk shifted once more, and the Aegre banked to the right. Joran tensed every muscle in his body, desperately clinging to the saddle. As Oaken dipped his head, taking him down, The Dawn Sword's Aegre tipped up, its talons bristling. The boy tightened his grip all the more, but he hadn't the strength to hold on when the two collided and spun from their flight path. Flung free, Joran hurtled through nothingness for a few seconds.

Then came the pain.

Swallowed by the tress of a small wood, the finer branches lashed at him, drawing red lines across his hands, neck, and face. The thicker branches were not so forgiving. While they repeatedly slowed his descent, each one was a blow of fresh pain that jarred his bones and pounded his muscles. His chest met the last and lowest of them, flipping him round so he landed awkwardly on his left arm. The *snap* of bone was slightly sharper than those of the breaking twigs and branches.

His cry of agony was distorted by the lack of air in his lungs, the wind having been beaten out of him on the way down. He rolled aside, suffering the shooting pains that ran through his left arm. Looking up, the canopy concealed the sky—and the warring Aegres with it.

For a time, while the setting sun burned the world a deepening orange, Joran lay on his back, waiting for his vision to realign. It didn't. Instead, his vision dimmed and the world closed in on him. While it was a numbing sleep, it was not a lasting sleep. His arm throbbed, demanding he wake up.

Night had settled over the realm, but he had, at least, recovered enough strength to rise. He groaned, stumbling into the same tree that had saved his life and broken his arm.

Staggered steps took him north until he came across a large mound near the edge of the woods. He took a few more steps and realised it wasn't a mound but an Aegre!

"Oaken!" he cried, making for the creature's head.

The Aegre was very still, his breathing shallow. Joran placed one hand on his armoured beak and called softly to his mother's companion. His eyes closed, Oaken didn't so much as stir. He was also coated in blood, his feather matted with it.

Joran scanned the area, searching for the exile between the trees. There was no sign of the beast—only the damage he had wrought. Joran wasn't nearly experienced enough to assess the Aegre's wounds. Would he recover? Would he die?

It was a different type of pain to think Oaken might perish. The Aegre was all that remained of his mother, a tether to her that Joran had come to treasure more than he thought. And what a comfort it had been to have a killing machine for a companion. The latter felt all the more important when he looked through the trees and laid eyes on Taraktor.

Gallien was in there.

"I'm sorry," he whispered, his good hand stroking Oaken's feathers.

Joran blinked, hard, preventing any tears from escaping. He knew he had to go on. There was little he could do for a wounded Aegre and even less defending himself from one should the exile arrive.

"I'm sorry," he said again, moving on.

The stars looked down on Verda as he left the woods, just as they did the lone boy who wandered towards Taraktor. It was even more menacing at night, a fact that Joran was all too aware of in the absence of Oaken.

Alone or not, wounded or not, he *would* find Gallien and the others. He would help them to find the weapon of power they sought and then, finally, impact the war as he was intended to. And so onward he walked, his left arm bruised and limp at his side.

Fear was a creeping foe, a whisper that couldn't quite be heard but its tone a promise of danger. It was incessant in his ear as Taraktor loomed over him. There was no doubt in Joran's mind that pain and death were all that awaited him inside. If that was true, then so too did they await Gallien and the others. Joran held onto that, a vow made to himself that he would not leave them to suffer such a fate.

Then, amidst the gusts of wind and grass blowing in the breeze, there came a new sound. Joran stopped in his tracks, eyes fixed on Taraktor's entrance. He hadn't noticed it on his approach, but the main gates had been blasted open from the inside. It was there that he made out the distinct shapes of people departing the prison.

The boy dashed across the yellow grass and ducked behind what he had believed to be a boulder. Crouched behind it now, he realised it was, in fact, a hulking chunk of iron and stone, a piece of Taraktor that had been thrown clear of the prison. While that begged questions, he crept to the edge and looked beyond.

A dozen men, clad in tooled leathers and iron helms, turned east out of the broken gates and left the path to make for the cliff edge. Shifting his attention to their destination, he spied a platform and railing that protruded from the clifftop—a set of stairs. They were going down to the shore.

There was a jostling in the middle of their group, bringing Joran's gaze back to the men. He narrowed his eyes to see through the dark.

His heart leaped.

Gallien was amongst them!

He saw Androma behind him and The Green Leaf behind her. It was with great concern that he then laid eyes on Cob at the rear, the Kedradi was being dragged by two others, his head sunk to his chest.

They were prisoners.

Led at the point of steel, they were being marched towards the steps. Joran didn't think. How could he when his friends were in peril?

So he acted, and brashly.

The broken sword was in his good hand as he cleared the iron debris, though he winced in severe pain as his injured arm protested against any kind of speed. He sweated through the pain and fell into a meaningful stride, his knuckles paling against the hilt. He soon had their attention.

"Who are you?" the cloaked man in the lead barked.

"Joran?" His name left Gallien's lips with all the smuggler's disbelief behind it. "Joran!" he yelled with realisation. "No! No! Run, Joran! Get away from here!"

There was real fear in his voice, but it wasn't enough to dissuade the boy.

Seeing the weapon in his hand, two of the helmed men peeled away from the group to intercept Joran, their swords at the ready. They hesitated, their gaze darting from the broken sword back to their leader. Joran looked down to see the glyphs and fine splinters of bright orange burning bright inside the steel.

Joran's confidence grew tenfold.

"Take him!" the leader growled.

Aware that he lacked the strength to block any of their attacks, Joran dropped to one knee and bowed under the first sword to swing at him. He was also aware of the power held by the broken blade when he was near other weapons of the same ilk. Pointed down in his grip, he hooked his arm around, running the jagged point across the man's leg—no more than a simple flesh wound.

And yet...

Joran shielded his eyes from the burst of light, his enemy's body igniting into sparks and ash. His comrade was both shocked and blinded, his mouth agape under his helm. Joran sprang through the cloud of ash and plunged the broken sword into the man's chest and had the good sense to turn his head away at the same time. Once again, the dark of night was interrupted by fiery obliteration.

Damned if his arm wasn't torturous now, the pain lancing at his focus. But the fight was far from over. Another of their group broke away to challenge him, crossing Gallien as he did.

His mistake.

The smuggler lunged at him, his grip now filled with the most magnificent axe of silver and bronze. It sank deep into the man's skull, cleaving through steel helm and bone alike. There was a wild look in Gallien's eyes as he started forward, and, for just a moment, it looked like chaos would have its day. But the cloaked leader stepped in, and decisively so.

His pommel hammered the back of Gallien's head. The smuggler dropped like a stone, his fingers resting lightly on the haft of the axe. The leader looked down at it, wonder in his eyes. That wonder turned to bewildered astonishment when the weapon blinked out of existence. His attention then lingered on Gallien, a touch of revelation behind his eyes.

Joran pressed on, the broken sword rising to slash at the man's arm. He had only to scratch the skin and his foe would be ash like the others. But this foe was swifter than his lackeys, pivoting on his heel to face the boy before he could strike. His free hand snatched at Joran's wrist, halting the blow before it could land, while the flat of his blade slapped against his broken arm.

The pain was that of a lightning bolt that left Joran feeling like he was going to be sick. He dropped to his knees, the broken blade dropped and forgotten, while he cradled the top of his arm, not daring to touch anything below the elbow. The blood pounding in his ears was enough to drown out his own wail.

When, at last, he managed to open his eyes again, the cloaked man was holding the shattered sword, his eyes aglow with the orange reflection. What joy there was behind that helm, his glee shining bright in his crooked smile.

Joran looked to the group behind the man, where Andromra and Aphrandhor had been forced to their knees, swords pressed to their throats. They wouldn't be able to help him, just as he couldn't help them.

That was his last thought before a pommel struck him across the face.

57
DUEL OF THE AGES

0 Years Ago...

4

There was only war. There was only the fight. There was only *him*.

It was for the master that Daijen Saeth carved a red path through the battlefield. For Skara. For The Pendain! He was their saviour, their hero. How could they have turned against him? They owed him their very lives, their bloodlines having survived because he had defeated Barad-Agin and his Leviathans.

Their ignorance and outright defiance brought wrath upon them—the wrath of a Vahlken! The red cloaks who fought under the banner of the Dragon Riders were relentless, falling upon him in droves, and so he slaughtered them in droves.

Daijen relished in it. With every body he dropped, his master lost an enemy. Victory would belong to Skara, and his vision for the world would come to be. Was there any cause more worthy than that?

A part of his mind rebelled against that question. Notions of duty and oaths pressed upon him—a duty to another cause and oaths of another time. Caught up in the bloodshed, however, Daijen was unable to follow his thoughts through to any conclusion.

Ever present were the shadows that glided over the conflict. The dragons wreaked havoc, their fiery breath scarring the battle-field with black lines and hundreds of charred bodies. Then there were those who remained on the ground, preferring to crush the Skaramangians under claw, flatten them with hulking tails, and even devour them in mighty jaws.

The Golems kept them at bay, preventing the dragons from overrunning the battle and turning the tide. All four of them leaped from the battlefield, tackling dragons with their many arms. They were a nuisance more than anything, but he spotted Ahnir clambering over the face of a dragon, where his powerful hands were able to claw at the beast's eyes.

Good, Daijen thought. *Drag them out of the sky.*

From the madness, a red cloak leaped at Daijen with abandon, his sword arcing round in a devastating attack. The Vahlken shifted his shoulders and allowed the steel to slice neatly through the air, an inch from his cuirass. Darting forwards, he plunged his atori blade deep into the man's chest, another sent to The Black Abyss.

Even as the body fell at his feet, a new warrior planted himself before the Andaren. The wind blew his muddy blond hair back, revealing the strong features of Gelakor. His scale mail reflected Orvax's blinding silver under the hot sun, but it was his axe that drew the Vahlken's gaze. It wasn't his to wield!

"That doesn't belong to you!" Daijen cried.

A single burst of energy closed the gap between them, the two fighters colliding in a sparking clash of steel. Gelakor was a seasoned warrior, a man who had fought in more campaigns than Daijen had lived years. He moved with a smooth grace, his foot-work impeccable as he navigated the littered corpses. Moreover, his counterattacks were ruinous, always forcing the Vahlken to rethink his strategy and begin a new approach.

Then there were the blows that landed.

Wielding a weapon of power changed everything. Daijen had received no training against such a weapon as that axe, and so he was slow to adapt.

Gelakor would let it fly again and again, making the Vahlken duck and weave, yet it had always returned to his hand by the time they fell back into combat. When he wasn't cutting through the Weavers' magnificent work and actually drawing blood, the Rider would feign his attacks and throw the axe into the ground at Daijen's feet, interrupting his flow and allowing Gelakor to plant a boot in his chest or across his face.

After such a blow, Daijen found himself face down on the blood-soaked sand. Slowly but surely, a plethora of wounds began to make themselves known, from his face down to his legs. Looking up, Gelakor stood out against the chaos that raged about him, his cream cloak billowing beside him. Why did he stand idle? The moment to strike a mortal blow had come and gone.

The Vahlken wouldn't question it for long. Daijen picked himself up, gathering his sabre and atori blade with him. "I will have that axe," he vowed, pointing his short-sword at the Rider.

Gelakor hefted the weapon of power and adopted a battle stance. "You are not yourself," he said forcefully.

The statement struck Daijen as odd, but he wasn't to be distracted by Rider trickery. Gelakor would die, and the axe would be returned to The Dark One.

Again, a part of Daijen's mind rebelled against it all. He knew that Gelakor survived this battle, didn't he? Hadn't he seen him, years on from that moment, fighting Skara—killing him, in fact? The Vahlken couldn't answer his own questions, his anger reaching a new crescendo at the thought of any felling his master.

Again, he launched himself at Gelakor. His determination informed his fighting style, and the Vahlken employed every technique that had ever been imparted to him, be it from Kastiek, The Valtorak, or even his sparring matches with Ilithranda.

Daijen found some success with intermittent speeds, confusing Gelakor by being deliberate and slow before exploding with a flurry of lashes and strikes. In just one encounter, he scored three cuts across his arms and leg, and with a final jab of his sabre, he pierced the soft flesh at the base of the Rider's neck. He recoiled, the back of his hand pressed to his throat. It wasn't to be the end of him, but it felt good to have drawn blood.

"Control yourself!" the Rider yelled at him.

Being told what to do proved only another trigger, bolstering Daijen's fury. He ran one of his blades against the edge of the other and came at Gelakor with a roar. Their duel took them across the battlefield, forcing them to regularly peel away from each other to dispatch opportunistic soldiers who thought to wound them.

Again, Daijen called upon the magic of Handuin that flowed through his veins, using his enhanced strength and speed to kick off a soldier—throwing the man from his feet—and hammer the pommel of his sabre into the side of Gelakor's head. It knocked the Rider from his feet and left Daijen's pommel dull with his blood.

"You're good," the Vahlken stated, watching Gelakor rise on unsteady feet. "I'm *better.*"

"You're stronger than this," the Dragon Rider declared.

"I'm stronger than *you*," Daijen assured him, throwing himself back into combat.

His blades were deflected and blocked by the axe, but Gelakor was ever on the back foot, forced into constant retreat by the Vahlken's relentless advance. They shoved their way through the battle, giving Daijen more opportunities to display his superior skill and slaughter the red cloaks that strayed from the fray.

"You're better than this!" Gelakor yelled in his face, a precursor to the fist he slammed into Daijen's jaw.

In that crack of pain, day turned to night, and, for just an instant, all the heat was sucked from the world in the lashing of heavy rain.

But it was no more than a flash, a blink of the eye. Daijen remained on that battlefield, locked in violence and bloodshed. Face to face with his enemy, the Vahlken darted forwards and skidded on his knees, only to whip his sabre out and slice across Gelakor's waist. Placing his weight against one braced hand,

Daijen then pivoted, his hips swinging his left leg up and round to catch the Rider in the head. It was enough to flip Gelakor over and onto his back.

Still on his knees, the Vahlken went for the kill, his sabre held high where the steel could kiss the light of the sun. A product of immense training, however, Gelakor was quick to recover, intercepting Daijen's wrist before that last blow could be dealt. The point of his fingers stabbed into the Vahlken's forearm, numbing the tendons enough to see him lose his grip on the sabre. It did nothing to affect his other hand.

Face to face and on their knees, the atori blade shot up and *through*.

Gelakor grunted and grabbed Daijen by the pauldron to steady himself. His eyes went wide with shock, as they would when in the cold grasp of Death itself. Tears escaped his eyes before it seemed his entire face and hair were dripping wet. Daijen felt it too, the cool drops of water on his hands and face.

It was raining.

The Vahlken tore his eyes from his victim and looked up at the clear blue sky, bewildered by the rain now falling out of it in horrendous sheets.

A weak voice called to him. "Daijen..."

His attention returned to Gelakor, and with it, grim reality replaced his madness. The Dragon Rider was gone, and the sun-baked battlefield with him. Under ferocious storm clouds and unyielding rain, Daijen was on his knees in Ka'vairn's courtyard. A hand was resting on his pauldron. His own hand remained firmly gripped about the hilt of his atori blade.

He looked at the one who held onto his pauldron.

Into those violet eyes.

"No!" he gasped.

Looking back at him, The Valtorak was positioned just as Gelakor had been. So too did he bear all the cuts and gashes Daijen had mercilessly delivered. Scattered in that same courtyard, two dwarves, a wizard, and a blind Dragon Rider did their best to fend off the invaders. All were Andarens now, their human contingent having perished breaching the fortress. Occupied with their own battles, they could only glimpse now and then at the conclusion to the Vahlkens' duel.

What unthinkable woe that conclusion had come to be.

Daijen examined the atori blade, its angle and depth spelling doom for any, even a Vahlken, even a Valtorak. While it had missed his heart, granting him whatever seconds he had left, it had certainly severed major blood vessels that fed his heart. A wound from which there was no return.

"This... This isn't real," Daijen said to himself, his words a hollow truth. "This... I'm sorry," he groaned, desperately trying to understand what had happened. "I'm so sorry," he said again, his words lost to the rain hammering their cuirasses.

The Valtorak lost more of his strength, requiring Daijen to catch him at the back of the neck and lower him to his lap. He left the atori blade where it was, concerned that removing it would only hasten the master's passing.

"There's no time... for that. What's done... is done." The Valtorak croaked, his face sheltered from the rain by Daijen, who looked down on him. "I warned you," he reminded him, his pale skin highlighted in a flash of the wizard's spell. "Others will always... suffer the price... of your pride." The Valtorak's hand came up to find his cheek. "Accept that what you were... is dead... and that what you are... is who you were always... meant to be."

An Andaren soldier came close to swinging his sword through the middle of the Vahlken, only to be intercepted by Mordrith. Dwarven strength saw The Anther planted in the centre of his chest and threw him back.

Daijen was shaking his head. "I have brought ruin to Ka'vairn," he agonised.

The Valtorak looked to be gathering what little strength he had left. "You always had it in you... to be the best of us. You must see this through... to the end, Daijen. You must... finish this fight."

"I cannot be trusted to," he countered, glimpsing another Andaren soldier being blasted by The Green Leaf's staff, casting him far from the pair.

The Valtorak coughed, splashing his lips with blood. "You have seen... what so many others... have only... guessed. You... are the only one... who can see it through. The only one..."

The master's eyes stopped moving, his gaze so distant as to pierce Daijen and all else behind him to the very edge of the world.

"No," Daijen uttered, cupping The Valtorak's face. "NO!" he bellowed, hating himself more than anything, even more than the Skaramangians and Slait.

The shame that settled over him then was a weight unlike any he had ever endured, a black curtain that concealed all of his achievements.

For a brief moment, the rain failed to reach them in the court-yard. It would have been welcome to believe that it was The Valtorak's soul, finally departing that ancient stone. But it wasn't. It was Death depositing a flying reaper upon Ka'vairn. In Oaken's wake, the rain returned with a vengeance, as did the Aegre's companion, Ilithranda.

The Vahlken landed in the courtyard, an agent of wrath and retribution. The invaders backed off, allowing her all the space she required to swing an uppercut into Daijen's jaw. Lifted bodily from the ground, he was launched high and across the courtyard, parting him from The Valtorak. The pain was sharp, then horribly numb, before it returned with a fury, just in time for his back to slam into the ground.

Ilithranda's boots splashed through the puddles as she strode towards him, her sabre lashing out once, twice, then a third time to remove the Andarens foolish enough to get in her way.

"WHAT HAVE YOU DONE?" she roared.

Upon Daijen again, the Vahlken didn't give him any time to get up, her powerful kick folding him in half at the waist and throwing him further across the courtyard.

Hit by fresh waves of pain, Daijen coughed and groaned as he rose to his hands and knees. Beyond Ilithranda, through the matted strands of his white hair, he saw Valyra glide through the ruins of what had once been Ka'vairn's entrance. Her four talons flexed, snatching soldiers from their feet as she angled towards

Daijen. All four Andarens were crushed in her grip, their armour no match for her strength. They were left scattered on the stone, her sharp eyes fixed on Ilithranda.

"No," Daijen croaked, one hand coming up.

It was enough to warn Ilithranda, though she was still too slow to do anything about the Aegre coming at her. Valyra's front talons came up as she landed on her back legs—she didn't care who Ilithranda was. No one hurt Daijen.

Pushing his pain aside—a lesson that had taken many years to master—Daijen threw himself at the only person he had ever considered to be family. It saved Ilithranda's life, who was no longer standing where Valyra's right talon pierced the air.

A sharp squawk speared the night and the rain, heralding Oaken's arrival. The black-feathered Aegre hurtled into Valyra, sending them scrambling over each other's wings and armoured beaks into the keep wall. It was enough to create an almighty crack in the stone, the gash running up into the south tower, as well as flatten three soldiers between them.

"Stop!" Daijen cried, watching the two rake their talons across the other, but there was no getting through to the Aegres, their wings flapping and beaks snapping.

It took a third Aegre to stop them from killing each other.

The exile thundered into Oaken's side, carelessly hurling him into a mass of Andaren soldiers, before swatting Valyra across the face. Like his kin, the exile was armoured, saddled, and covered in scars, only Slait's Aegre displayed a level of anger not often seen in their kind. He lashed out at Valyra again and again, pinning her to the wall of the keep before Oaken rammed into him, creating more chaos in the courtyard.

Daijen and Ilithranda leaped out of harm's way, but the battling Aegres were erratic and frighteningly fast. The exile's wing flapped hard and struck Daijen's entire body, throwing him up and onto the steps that led to the northern ramparts. Ilithranda was left in the courtyard, faced by a mob of invading soldiers. The odds were against them.

From atop the steps, his right shoulder aching from the impact,

Daijen observed Ilithranda blow through the group below. Her sabre whipped up and out, lashing left and right. She required no more than a single strike to end a life. Valyra, meanwhile, threw herself back into battle, her talons sinking into the exile's back. It gave Oaken some reprieve but forced Ilithranda to dive aside.

The Aegres continued their fight across the courtyard, knocking down or killing any soldiers who got in their way. It was to be the end of Androma, who could not see the calamity coming her way. The Dragon Rider was proving formidable against the Andaren soldiers, her silvyr blade making short work of their defences while her training and discipline allowed her to fight without sight. But there was naught to be done about several tons of Aegre tumbling towards her.

"Androma!" Daijen called out, his warning lost to the rain and the fighting.

Above the Rider, on the eastern ramparts, Mordrith Underborn saw Androma's impending doom. The dwarf beat back her attackers and jumped off the edge, bringing her into the courtyard beside the Dragon Rider.

Only a second before Valyra and the exile crashed into the eastern ramparts, Mordrith landed and struck the stone as she did. The Anther flashed a brilliant blue, distorting the air around the two.

Another flash caught Daijen's eye, turning him back towards the keep, where the pair had been ported to safety. Androma staggered immediately, dazed by the effects of The Anther's magic. While she remained unsteady, Mordrith stood as an impenetrable wall between her and the soldiers who saw an easy kill. Daijen moved to aid them when the sound of discharging magic turned him to the south.

The Green Leaf was in peril.

Exhausted, he was doing his best to push back those still pouring in through the ruined gates. They stumbled and fell as they tried to navigate the debris and large stones that had been blown into the keep. It made them easy targets for the wizard, but it seemed his magic was finally beginning to take its toll. His spells had gone from being devastating, ensuring the soldiers never rose again, to merely painful deterrents as he pushed them back.

Seeing that Yamnomora had slammed into those attacking Mordrith and Androma, her axes chopping and hacking high and low, Daijen stepped off the edge of the northern rampart and broke into a run the moment his feet touched the stone of the courtyard. He would have been at Aphrandhor's side in a few seconds had his path not been blocked by Ilithranda.

The Vahlken skidded to a stop, bringing him within an inch of her sabre's edge. There was such hurt behind her eyes, such betrayal. Reading what he could of her, Daijen knew that Ilithranda's world had been turned upside down.

Just beyond her, he caught sight of The Green Leaf being overwhelmed. One soldier swung his sword, batting the wizard's staff aside, before another stepped in and booted him in the chest. On his back, his green robes soaking in the puddles, he was at the mercy of his enemy.

"There's no time for this!"

"You cannot be trusted!" Ilithranda spat.

Her words sent Daijen's gaze to the body that lay in the very middle of the courtyard. She was right, of course. He was not alone inside his mind anymore. Ahnir's thoughts and sense of purpose were entangled with his own, along with the Golem's loyalty.

But the key to it all was also in there—the weapon they would need to win the war. How to say as much without falling into memory? How to voice all that he had learned without Ahnir's thought patterns assuming control?

It didn't matter then anyway. Their friends were on the verge of dying, a fact that would always be enough to ground him. As his mind calculated the fastest way to get past his sister, the Aegres let loose a chorus of ear-piercing squawks, their fight taking them up into the night.

It was all the distraction Daijen needed. He deflected Ilithranda's sabre with his own and shoulder-barged her. His dead run ended with a leaping attack that brought the Vahlken down on the soldiers standing over Aphrandhor.

They met his arrival with all that they had, with all that The Saible had been able to drill into them. It was not enough. Daijen Saeth was pale death, his sabre and atori short-sword extensions of his arms. His speed, strength, and stamina were magnitudes beyond theirs, and they each fell at his feet, their bodies split, broken, and bleeding.

At his back, The Green Leaf managed to get up and collect his staff. He pointed it at Daijen. "Do you know where you begin and Ahnir ends?" he asked, the rain diluting the blood running from a cut on his forehead.

Daijen recognised the phrase, first spoken by the wizard before he had stolen the vambrace from him. Another warning he had ignored. There was no time to answer, for the Vahlken was already pressed upon by more soldiers. He pivoted and ducked, slicing one across the waist before rising to stab another through the neck.

"Find the others!" Daijen yelled at The Green Leaf. "Get inside the keep! Seal the doors!"

The wizard hesitated.

"Go!" the Vahlken barked, turning his attention to a trio of soldiers.

The Green Leaf finally turned and ran for the keep, where Androma and the dwarves were proving to be a fighting force the Andarens had never trained for. Wondering why Ilithranda had yet to continue their confrontation, Daijen spotted her on the northern ramparts. She had gone to face a large group of Andarens who had circumnavigated the ramparts in the hope of infiltrating the keep without resistance. Their hopes were dashed by the edge of her steel.

Daijen moved to join her, imagining their stand together might be enough to repel what remained of the invaders while their friends sheltered inside. He would have to face her wrath when the dust settled. As he knew he deserved.

But the Vahlken was stopped in his tracks.

Through hammering rain and charging boots, his keen ears detected a sound not heard on battlefields.

Laughter. Joyous, unadulterated laughter.

Amid the soldiers running to aid their kin against Ilithranda, Daijen found the source.

Standing over The Valtorak's body, glee on his face, was the betrayer. Slait placed one boot upon the master's chest and leaned on his knee so he might bend over and speak to the corpse. Daijen could only imagine what the wretch was saying—words he had likely spent years thinking about while he festered in the arms of the Skaramangians.

The sight of him, standing as if victorious over The Valtorak, gripped Daijen's heart, igniting a ferocious storm within him. That very night, the Vahlken decided, one of them was to die at the hands of the other.

His knuckles paling around the hilts of his blades, he charged into a duel long overdue.

58
OLD GROUND

The night's bitter cold was not to be sweetened by the light of dawn, the sun's warmth yet to settle over the waters of The Deep. His breath clouding the air, Gallien squeezed Joran a little tighter as Nareene took shape in the east. Without a sound, a dull mist pushed out from between the trees to float over the shore, where it drifted effortlessly across the lapping water.

"Questions... and monsters." That had been The Green Leaf's only description of the island. It was the last place Joran should be.

Using his only hand, Gallien brushed some of Joran's white hair aside so he could examine the wound on his head. The pommel had cut the skin and left a dark bruise that stretched around his temple and across his brow. It wasn't dissimilar to Cob's head injury, though the Kedradi had come to his senses during their crossing.

He met the ranger's dark eyes across the water. He had awoken before Gallien and with fury in his veins, the man a caged lion inside a rowboat. Their captors had taken precautions, however. His hands bound, Cob also sported an extra length of rope around his neck, attaching him to a weight that could be tossed overboard with ease. That and the sword that never left his shoulder had kept the Kedradi under control.

Looking to his left, Androma and Aphrandhor had been stowed together, similarly bound at the wrists and under constant guard. The nameless cloaked one who had led the Skaramangians at Taraktor was in another boat altogether, accompanied by their weapons, including the broken sword and vambrace snatched from The Green Leaf's forearm.

Shadows began to take shape in the mist, sharpening Gallien's attention on the shore. Those silhouettes soon took shape as men and women, all armed with swords and clad in the same brown leathers and helms as those who had attacked them at Taraktor. They reminded the smuggler of a private militia, the kind of people a Padoshi would employ.

As the boat ground against the shore, Joran woke up for the first time since he had been struck by the leader. His confusion and concern melted away, if briefly, when he realised he was resting against Gallien's chest. The boy's beaming smile was like that first breath upon breaking the water. The smuggler held him a little tighter until he winced, his arm clearly broken.

"What happened?" he asked, aware that Joran had arrived at Taraktor with the injury.

"It's a long story."

"Well it shouldn't be," he chastised in hushed tones. "You shouldn't be here."

Joran's violet eyes shifted from the men on their boat to those on the shore, the two groups working together now as they moved the prisoners. "Where are we?" he asked.

"Nareene," Gallien answered grimly. "Some kind of Skaramangian stronghold," he added with a shrug.

"I'm sorry," Joran blurted. "I just wanted to—"

"Silence!" one of the militiamen snapped.

A rough hand grabbed Joran by his cloak and shoved him forwards, forcing him to step over the side of the boat and onto the muddy beach. Gallien received the same treatment, only his lack of two hands robbed him of balance and he fell face down in the boat.

The helmed Skaramangian growled and thrust a swift kick into his ribs. Somewhere out of sight, Joran protested against his captors, causing a commotion on the shore. After a short tussle, the boy groaned in pain and ceased his objections.

As Gallien was rising, the cloaked leader appeared by the side of the boat. It was impossible to say what he was thinking, for it was as if the man had never been taught expressions or social cues, but he stared at the smuggler for an uncomfortable amount of time. The Skaramangian who had kicked him grasped the back of Gallien's neck and dragged him up, his free hand clenched and poised to land a blow in his gut.

The leader's hand shot out first, his palm slamming into the other Skaramangian's cuirass. He simply shook his head at the man, a silent order that saw the lackey's fist unclench.

"Get them moving!" the leader commanded to the others across the beach, pausing to give Gallien one last look.

Hauled out of the boat, Gallien's bandaged wrist was plain to see, and Joran didn't miss it. His face dropped and his eyes welled with tears. A torrent of questions was about to break forth, his lips shaping into the first word, when the smuggler shook his head. Joran glanced at the wound again before he was ushered into the mist with the rest of them.

The sun was past its apex by the time the tall trees of Nareene revealed anything but more trees. With his exhausted companions at his back, Gallien wiped the sweat from his brow and craned his neck, his eyes drinking in the sight. With cliffs guarding it against light from the east, the black pyramid dominated the clearing, its obsidian surface shining in the afternoon sun.

Azad-guul.

That ancient name came to him again, as it had in cell twelve. What had his father known about the pyramid? Had he been there? Was this where he found the weapon of power? Gallien had to wonder if he had been with him, and Corben too. The more he learned of his father, the more he grew to resent him. What would his life have been had he not spilled magic into his mind and poured out so much of what he knew?

Hands pressed into their backs, pushing the prisoners into the clearing. There were Skaramangians everywhere, dotted between the buildings that littered the base of the pyramid. It was a small army, humans all, and every one of them pledged to the Skaramangian order.

"This is not as it was," The Green Leaf whispered, coming up to the smuggler's side. "I saw into his memories when he took the bracer," he reported, nodding at the cloaked leader in front. "Androma and I were here, some decades ago. It seems our intrusion was not to be repeated."

"They weren't here?" Gallien asked, careful to keep himself from looking at the wizard.

"No. But, like their predecessors, these people were all taken as children and raised here. Skaramangian lore is all they know. *Unlike* their predecessors, they have been trained as a fighting force —a secret army bred solely to protect... what did you call it? *Azadguul.*"

"This Eldan fella you've talked about," Gallien murmured. "Is he here?"

"I think not. As far as I'm aware, The Eldan has always been an Andaren—a high-ranking one at that. He will be safely tucked away behind Andara's lines."

"Then why do they protect this place?"

Aphrandhor dared to glance at him. "It's a tomb."

Gallien frowned, looking at the well-trained militia patrolling every inch of the area. "Whose tomb is it?" he had to ask.

"We never discovered the truth of it," The Green Leaf admitted before his wounded leg gave out.

Gallien extended his hand to help him up, hoping to prevent the brash Skaramangian hands from hurting the old man. Aphrandhor accepted the aid, using the opportunity to pull the smuggler towards him.

"They know of the axe," he breathed in his ear. "He saw it," he reported, looking again at the nameless leader.

Gallien nodded his understanding, hooking his arm under the wizard's to give him some forward momentum. "I won't summon it," he vowed, feeling a Skaramangian hand urge him forward.

"I fear you will not have a choice," Aphrandhor said gravely, his eyes cast beyond the smuggler.

Gallien turned his head to see Joran walking side by side with Androma, the old Rider's hand gripped to the boy's good arm. Fearing for Joran's life at Taraktor had been enough to conjure the axe, the weapon not seen since Thedaria. It had been reflexive, out of his control.

"Get them on the platform!" the leader yelled, cutting through the smuggler's concerns.

One after the other, they were marched across a wooden bridge, over a great hole in the earth, to a square platform in the middle of the clearing. Along with the Skaramangian leader and enough guards to maintain control, they waited while others operated the levers and mechanisms around the edge of the shaft. Foot by foot, the surface disappeared, and the pyramid with it.

At least, Gallien had assumed they were descending beneath the pyramid. In fact, the lift eventually descended through a jagged hole in a sloping wall of black stone, bringing them into a chamber of damaged pillars and flickering torchlight.

"That was just the capstone," Aphrandhor informed him, seeing his confusion. "The pyramid itself is buried beneath the land."

Gallien might have responded, but he got caught in the leader's gaze. He had seen the wizard speak to him and yet he rebuked neither of them, content to simply stare at the smuggler from the platforms edge. It was unnerving.

"This way," the Skaramangian bade them, stepping off the platform.

Joran moved to be close to Gallien, though his arm remained in Androma's grip. Cob was moved on from the rear, his throat laced by more than one rope now, each in the hands of a different militiaman. They weren't taking any chances with the Kedradi.

Passing between the pillars, the smuggler let his attention

wander over the relief that ran their length and the tarnished images that still clung to the ancient walls.

He had walked inside that chamber before.

His memories collided, and painfully so. His only hand came up to cover his eyes but the darkness he found there did nothing to soothe the barbed tentacles that wormed through his mind. Hands came at him from every direction, trying to steady him.

For a time, the smuggler managed no more than left foot, right foot, his direction guided by Joran at his side. The temperature dropped as they took to stairwells and passed through new chambers.

Here and there, he glimpsed the interior between his fingers. It was all so familiar. The more he tried to remember, the more his father's magic pressed upon him, burning through his memories like a purging forest fire. He heard Joran ask again and again what was happening to him, but the answers never came while they were under Skaramangian supervision.

That came to an end, however, when they were unceremoniously deposited beyond a set of towering double doors. Gallien's fall was staggered by Joran, who gently lowered him to the floor. Daring to move his hand from his face, the smuggler observed the Skaramangians retreating back through the doorway, leaving the companions alone but together.

"You will wait here," the nameless leader announced, his eyes still on Gallien.

"For what?" Aphrandhor demanded.

The doors were sealed shut with a resounding *boom*. Indeed, the echo of it made Gallien roll his neck to gauge the chamber's extent. Crafted into a vast circle, it was massive, both wide and exceedingly tall with numerous torches lined from top to bottom. The rounded walls were pockmarked by alcoves and balconies at random intervals, each a tunnel to who knew where. The ground floor boasted a handful of doors, though every one of them was barred by an iron grate screwed into the stone. Judging by the sounds coming from the other side of the double doors, their captors had locked them in.

While one half of his mind considered it to be the strangest cell he had ever occupied, the other half was desperately trying to remind him what that chamber was. The pain swelled behind his eyes and he cried out, hand slapping against the floor.

"What in the hells is happening to him?" Joran begged.

"He's treading over old ground," The Green Leaf replied. "He's been here before."

"What are you talking about?"

Unforgiving and unrelenting was the pain that gripped Gallien's head in an unseen vice. He arched his back and clenched his fist, though he could still feel the fingers and thumb of his missing hand as they knotted into a ball. Through the agony and his own groans, he heard The Green Leaf explaining what he could of the magic that plagued him.

"His father?" Joran questioned. "He never spoke about him."

There was more, their exchange a blur of words that the smuggler couldn't keep up with. He heard of recent events, recognising names like The Silver Trees of Akmar and Thedaria. Mention of the latter turned into a conversation that included Galahart and the Padoshi, but the details were lost on him.

Curled up in a ball, Gallien was barely holding on to consciousness by the time their tale had been recounted in full for the boy. Someone had taken his satchel and placed it under his head as a makeshift pillow.

Cob wandered past his vision at intervals, the ranger testing the strength of every grate that blocked the doors. He also pressed into the stone now and then, reaching for potential points of purchase that might see him ascend the walls. Alas, he remained among them, pacing like a caged animal.

"You should not be here." Androma's stern voice was close, the old Rider seated just behind him.

"And yet I am," Joran responded defiantly, crouched beside Gallien.

"You should never have left Kassanda's side," Androma continued, the name and thread of discussion escaping Gallien somewhat. He could only assume they had conversed previously, on their way to the pyramid. "There is no better Rider to learn from. If any had the right to challenge Rhaymion, it was Kassanda, not Baelon. Under her watch you could have become—"

"A *good warrior*, I know," Joran interjected. "But not a Dragon Rider. I told you: I didn't bond with an egg. And Kassanda told me being a good warrior wasn't enough to make a bond. The dragon has to see some kind... *reflection of themselves*." The boy moved into Gallien's view, shaking his head while gripping his broken arm. "It would have been a waste of time. This is where the fight is—with *you*, here and now. If there's a weapon of power that might turn the tide, then I would help you find it."

"Help?" Androma balked. "You were helping by staying away, training with Kassanda. Now, you have not only abandoned that path but delivered a weapon of power into the hands of the enemy."

"I didn't think—"

"No," the Rider cut in, "you didn't *think*. You acted and hoped for the best." Androma sighed, her voice weighed down by raw emotion. "We're all out of hope, Joran. That's what you were supposed to do. You were to be the hope that inspired others. *Your future was a future for us all.*"

Joran hung his head and closed his eyes. "That future was shattered the moment you learned of it. We're not supposed to know what's to come."

Androma raised her chin. "The days are shadowed by approaching night," she declared. "The war to devour all wars has come again." The old Rider let her words hang in the frigid air for a moment. "Your mother used to say that in her sleep."

Joran perked up. "My mother?"

"Ilithranda was present for the Ankala. She heard the visions herself. The war to devour all wars has come again," Androma repeated. "Without a time of dragons, *that's* what's to come."

With that grim end ringing in his ears, Gallien's mind finally succumbed to the pain that ripped through his skull, and he fell into sweet oblivion.

59
RECKONING

4

Daijen's charge dropped into a skid across the wet stone. Slait had seen him coming and removed his boot from The Valtorak's cuirass. In so doing, he revealed that which had been secured over his back, tied with rope at each end. The betrayer had already infiltrated the keep and stolen Ahnir's femur bone.

His first strike sweeping through naught but air, the Vahlken jumped to his feet and glanced back, seeing the open doors that led into the keep. They remained so for a few seconds more before The Green Leaf ushered the dwarves and Androma inside. As soldiers hacked at the now-sealed doors, Daijen looked up at Ilithranda on the northern ramparts. It required no great feat of deduction to know that she had abandoned her fight with Slait because of him. Because of what he had done to The Valtorak.

Now the enemy possessed the bone, allowing them to complete

Ahnir and the spells that Skara had carved into his precious Golem. Furthermore, if they had unlocked the blood magic The Dark One once used to breathe life into his Golems, they could bring Ahnir back into the world of the living. And The Shadow Realm with it...

It was to be another failing piled upon Daijen's shoulders, a consequence of *his* actions. It wouldn't matter, he decided. Slait and all who had accompanied him would be dead before the dawn. He would see to it himself.

"Your numbers are dwindling, Runt!" Slait sneered. "A pity I didn't get the chance to slay him myself," he added, gesturing at The Valtorak.

"You've taken your last life, Slait," Daijen promised him.

"Impossible. Not while *you're* still breathing. Or the princess." His golden eyes glanced up at Ilithranda. "Even if the gods came back this very moment," he went on, "I don't think I would be satiated until both of your heads sit upon a spike."

Daijen's jaw firmed in determination. Threatening him was one thing, often a spark to his pride, but threatening his sister was the key to unleashing his wrath.

A single push from one foot was enough to see Daijen clear The Valtorak's body and bring him face to face with his foe. How different it was to fight another of his ilk after contending with ordinary soldiers. Slait's footwork was light and effortless, yet it took him from harm's way, seeing him evade first Daijen's sabre and then his atori blade.

Pushing off the eastern wall, the betrayer came back at him with a downward thrust of his own sabre. Daijen pivoted his shoulders and still felt the rough drag of steel slice through his leather pauldron, threatening the silk of the Weavers beneath. Slait touched down and twisted his hips, bringing his elbow up and round into the Vahlken's face.

Slait's strength was another stark reminder that Daijen faced one transformed by Handuin's magic.

Daijen's head snapped back, and he staggered into the eastern wall, a dark bruise swelling under his right eye. He heard the swift cut of steel through the air before he saw it, the sound prompting him to drop beneath the edge of Slait's sabre.

His knees bent, Daijen propelled himself forwards and slammed into his enemy, taking him by the waist. They impacted the ground together and rolled and tumbled, their weapons pressed from their hands. They exchanged blows, hammering their fists and jabbing their elbows. They cut and bruised each other, their blood spilling into the puddles beneath them, until Slait came out on top, his hands gripping Daijen by the collar of his cuirass.

The betrayer roared in his face and thrust his head into the Vahlken's, knocking his head back into the ground. "You owe me an ear," Slait rasped.

Daijen felt a rough grab enclose his right ear while his own free hand felt the Arkalon hanging from his foe's belt by a fine chain. As Slait intensified his grip, preparing to tear the ear from his head, Daijen snatched the Arkalon, snapping the chain. With Vahlken strength behind it, he cracked that holy book into the side of his jaw.

The blow pushed Slait aside, allowing Daijen to pick himself up and backhand him with the Arkalon. The betrayer's blood sprayed from his mouth, mixing with the rain. A third strike was delivered using the top of the book, its hard edges and flat pages shoved directly into Slait's face. Puddles of water splashed in every direction as he landed on his back, his white cuirass thoroughly marred now.

Daijen regarded the book in his hand—Skaramangian propaganda. With no care, he tossed it away and advanced on his opponent. "Everything you believe in is a lie," he told him, swinging his leg up to boot the fool in the face. "The gods you worship are just monsters," he stated, reaching down to grab his enemy, a fist raised and ready to break his nose.

But Daijen faltered.

He had begun to voice Ahnir's memories, opening the dam to the flood that pressed relentlessly against it. Daijen shut his eyes, focusing on the present. He needed to stay grounded. He thought desperately of his own life, recalling all that he could of Slait. There wasn't a single memory of the wretch that didn't boil his blood, though his recent mocking of The Valtorak's body rooted him in the there and then.

It was too late. Slait had recovered from his beating and offered Daijen a wicked grin, the harbinger of an uppercut. It was the second one Daijen had received that night, and, like the first, it took him from his feet.

"There are depths to the Black Abyss, you know? Folds upon folds of darkness where faithless runts like you are bound to dwell for eternity."

Daijen rolled over and started to find his hands and knees when he heard the distinct scrape of steel across stone. Turning his head, he watched Slait stalk towards him, sabre in hand. It seemed so distant, but he heard Ilithranda call out his name, alarm in her voice—she could see his impending execution from atop the ramparts.

"The princess can't save you now," Slait informed him, the edge of his sabre resting against the back of Daijen's neck. "Tell me where the helm is, and I promise to kill her swiftly."

The threat enraged the Vahlken, but Slait's question brought some amusement to his expression. "The helm is lost to us all," he answered, his face angled so one blue eye could see the betrayer towering over him.

Slait snarled. "What have you done with it?" he growled.

His anger flaring, the zealot raised his sabre with the promise of a hammering blow to the back of Daijen's cuirass. It wouldn't kill him, the silk of the Weavers durable enough to withstand even a Vahlken's strike, but it would inflict significant pain. Even so, he had no intention of letting that steel touch him.

Like Daijen, it seemed Slait had spent too long fighting and sparring with ordinary Andarens, those he trained to join the cleric guard. He had forgotten what the children of Handuin were capable of.

Daijen would remind him.

From his hands and knees, the Vahlken pushed up from the ground and twisted his body, maintaining a horizontal lift. As Slait's arm reached the apex of its upswing, Daijen's right fist came round and up. His knuckles collided with the betrayer's face, breaking his nose.

Completing his full twist, the Vahlken landed on his feet and grabbed Slait by the collar, preventing him from falling away. Dragging him back in, Daijen landed another punch to his face. Then another. And another. By the fourth blow, the zealot had dropped his sabre. A jump, spin, and back kick sent the betrayer into the wall, where he crumpled at its base.

The flick of his boot sent a fallen sabre into Daijen's waiting hand. "This is the only way our story was ever going to end."

Slowly, in pain, Slait began to pick himself up. Somehow, he managed a soft laugh. "This isn't our story, Runt. It never was. Like all stories, this one belongs to the gods. At least I am to be named in their tome," he said, now on his feet again, his back resting against the stone. "The Eldan has bestowed upon me a title of the ages. I am *The Dancing Sword of the Dawn*."

Daijen recalled the name from the ancient pages of the Arkalon —the greatest warrior in all of Andaren history, he who fought beside the gods against the Dark Ones. It was all myth, of course. There was only *The* Dark One, and the so-called *gods* were his children. Added to that terrible truth, *The Dancing Sword of the Dawn* had been one of many names given to Skara during his righteous crusade against Barad-Agin, the world's first dark wizard.

Slait was just another poor soul desperate to believe in the divine, to believe that he was part of something bigger, something that had real meaning. That desperation made it so much easier to fool him, to weaponise him.

So too did his pride make him vulnerable to manipulation. Granting him such a title secured his loyalty to the Skaramangian cause without ever, in fact, telling him what that real cause was. It blinded him.

Only twenty feet from The Valtorak's corpse, Daijen was reminded that he was in no position to judge the depths of another's pride.

"Cling to that title if it brings you any kind of peace," Daijen said. "I'm still going to cleave your head from your shoulders."

Following through with his words, the Vahlken gripped the sabre in both hands and brought the blade back behind his head. But the swing was violently interrupted.

The exile—Slait's pale Aegre—descended into the courtyard with terrifying speed, his beak snapping at Daijen. The Vahlken had no choice but to forget his duel with Slait and dive aside. The talons followed him, scraping at the ground and wall. Every Aegre had a fierce look about them, but the exile looked mean, as if it lived only to torment and kill.

Scrambling, rolling, and darting erratically, Daijen evaded certain death again and again. Pushed along the length of the eastern wall, he was coming dangerously close to the corner, where he would have no option but to face the Aegre. It would be his end, Daijen knew. But the Vahlken was not without his own guardian angel, her sharp eyes ever watchful where her companion was concerned.

Valyra's wings fanned, slowing her just enough to bring all four talons to bear. They sank into the side of the exile before her momentum pinned the creature to the eastern wall. That same wall had already taken so much punishment from the catapults. The weight of two Aegres pushing into it sent fresh cracks through the stone.

The exile squirmed under Valyra's pressure, his wings flapping wildly. Still at risk of being killed by the warring Aegres, Daijen dashed to the corner, where the eastern wall met the southern wall. Light of foot, he sprang from wall to wall until he reached the ramparts above.

Slait was already there, waiting for him with sabre in hand.

A feral roar escaped his lips, his bound taking him high before he came crashing down on the Vahlken. Their blades clashed, twisting and rolling as they pivoted and danced across the ramparts. With no Kastiek and no Valtorak, there was finally no one to intervene as there had been during their days as initiates.

Even Ilithranda was too far away, blocked by Andaren soldiers on the northern parapet.

Free to kill each other, they fought ferociously across the battlements.

While Daijen intended to kill Slait, he also intended to reclaim Ahnir's femur bone. It was too important, both for the future of the Vahlken and the potential to make the Golem whole again. Resting over his back, the black fossil was strapped to his cuirass with rope, an easy obstacle to overcome considering the length of steel in the Vahlken's hand.

Feigning an attack to his enemy's head, Daijen reversed his grip at the last second slashed horizontally across Slait's chest. As well as gouging a neat line it gouged through the white armour, it severed the rope. A swift kick pushed The Dancing Sword of the Dawn back and over the fallen bone, allowing Daijen to scoop it up. Without hesitation, he tossed it into the courtyard, far from Slait's reach.

"You will die here,"Daijen told him. "Or you will return to your master a failure."

Slait inhaled loudly through his nose, pinching his brow into a fierce frown. Without a word, he pounced, bringing them back together in combat, their sabres twisting and slashing, always searching for weak points. Beneath their feet, the stone shuddered under the bombardment of the fighting Aegres. It only stopped when they took to the air again, where they were soon joined by Oaken, who speared out of the night to chase the exile off.

Their sudden departure proved a momentary distraction for Daijen, who had ducked to avoid the talons that flew over his head. Slait rushed forwards and dropped to skid on his knees, his sabre flicking across Daijen's thigh. The Vahlken yelled out in pain and staggered to one side so he might still see his foe.

"You can't beat me, Runt! You never could!"

"I think the previous Eldan would disagree," Daijen remarked, a notch of fatigue digging into his lungs like claws. "If he still had his head," he added devilishly.

The zealot bared his teeth and charged, always ruled by his

rage. Having predicted as much, if not orchestrated it with his deliberate choice of words, Daijen had already planned his counterattack.

His feet briefly inverted, allowing him to twist on the spot, while his wrist rolled, spinning his sabre. In one fluid movement, he deflected Slait's thrusting sword, dragged the edge of his sabre across his shoulder to find the unprotected flesh, and, finally, came back around to jam the pommel into the betrayer's head.

Slait was sent stumbling to the floor, his weapon lost, and his shoulder and head bleeding. As he impacted the stone, the ramparts shuddered again, the sound of cracking rock breaching the rain. The subsequent quake was so violent it nearly knocked Daijen from his feet. Still, he was determined to end the murderer once and for all.

The zealot crawled along the ramparts, his skull notably broken at the back of his head. Added to that, the other minor wounds Daijen had inflicted over the course of the fight were now leaving a bloody trail behind him.

"You always sacrificed skill for brutality," Daijen announced, advancing at a walk. "If only you had finished your training. If only all our brothers and sisters had finished their training."

Catching up with him, Daijen planted a heavy boot on Slait's back, halting him in his bloody tracks. Unlike the betrayer, he would employ Kastiek's teaching when it came to executions. The Vahlken repositioned his grip on the hilt, bringing the point of his sabre to hang over the back of his enemy's neck. He had only to plunge now, and The Black Abyss would swallow him whole.

It seemed fitting to do so as the night faded and the rain lightened, heralding the first rays of a new day beyond the peaks of The Morthil Mountains.

"NO!"

The sudden sharp cry lifted Daijen's gaze—just in time to see a blood-soaked Ilithranda as she rammed into him. The wind knocked from him, Daijen was knocked to the battlements beneath them, their impact sending another shockwave through the fragmenting stone. The wall shuddered, threatening to let go of Ka'vairn altogether and fall into the valley below.

Seconds later, while Daijen struggled to make sense of Ilithranda's attack, the eastern ramparts gave up their fight. The stone cracked, the sound drowning out all else. The two Vahlken scrambled to their feet, heading for the keep's interior.

Slait managed to rise unsteadily to his feet. "Uthain!" he bellowed, naming his Aegre. Then he leaped from the rampart as the rampart itself toppled into the valley.

At that same moment, Daijen and Ilithranda jumped, their hands reaching for the jagged edge of the courtyard. They found purchase and held on among the rocks, their bodies slamming into the uneven wall.

Looking over his shoulder, Daijen watched the ramparts fall among sheets of rock face. Fuelling his ire, he also watched as Uthain swooped low and intercepted Slait mid-fall. Oaken and Valyra made to pursue them until it became clear their enemy was departing the region.

The Vahlken pair heaved themselves onto the courtyard stone, where they faced the hundred or so Andarens who had turned to observe the ramparts fall away. Beyond them, it was clear they had failed thus far to penetrate the keep's doors. There was still a victory to be claimed, though, should they defeat the two Vahlken who now stood before them. Those two, however, soon became four when Valyra and Oaken landed beside their companions. The Aegres squawked and reared up, wings unfurled to maximise their size.

A tense moment was shared collectively by the gathered soldiers, ushering them all to silence. Then it ushered them from Ka'vairn, and with all haste. They ran across the courtyard and did their best to navigate the ruined entrance at speed.

In their wake, one of the towers finally succumbed to the damage wrought by the catapults. It collapsed upon itself, spitting stone bricks in every direction. It flattened a dozen of the fleeing soldiers when it found its resting place over the southern ramparts, blocking Ka'vairn's entrance once and for all.

Daijen looked up at Valyra. "Chase them from the valley," he commanded.

Following Valyra's lead, Oaken took off behind her, leaving the Vahlken alone in the courtyard. As the plumes of dust washed over them and the last of the rain rattled against the numerous cuirasses that littered the fortress, Daijen turned to his sister. A great fury burned within him, his vengeance robbed by madness. Yet he could not reveal the extent of his anger, for his shame still weighed heavily on him, pressing all the more with their proximity to The Valtorak's body.

"You cannot hate me so much that you would spare that wretched—"

"He's my *son*," Ilithranda declared, her eyes filled with tears.

Daijen was stunned to silence. Those three words emptied him of thought and reason. He could but stand there, dumbstruck, as Ilithranda walked away.

Her *son*...

60

DUTY-BOUND

The clouds were that of a grey fog, a misted veil to part the heavens from the earth. They were no such barrier to Garganafan. The white dragon dipped his snout and tucked in his wings, a glistening arrow set to pierce that veil. Kassanda held fast to the reins, the straps taut between her belt and the saddle as the world came into view.

While the strip of sea between Erador's hook and Andara's eastern face was narrow on any map, it remained a vast stretch of water by any scale of man or beast. Upon those waves were the king's ships and a handful of private vessels, all carrying soldiers of Blood Etragon.

Joran's blood...

It had been a little over ten days since she had seen the boy outside Valgala's walls, and not a day had gone by without her dwelling on the revelation of his heritage. It seemed an impossibility that she could train and serve the same person, for the latter would upend the dynamic of master and apprentice.

Not that it mattered, was her daily conclusion. Joran had forsaken his potential destiny and abandoned his training. Flying over the royal fleet, those thoughts and more rose to the surface again. They niggled and scratched at the inside of her skull, plaguing her as they had at Caster Hold.

Say it, Garganafan spoke into her mind.

What if I'm the reason his future is off course? the Rider responded. **What if he was always meant to leave for Taraktor and the others, and I was to go after him? Or to have never allowed him to go in the first place?**

You think we should pursue him?

Kassanda could sense the truth of their situation, as if it resonated through her companion's voice. **He is close,** she pointed out, looking to the east, where the hook of land curled around The Deep. **We could fly to Taraktor and rejoin the fleet long before they reach the towers.**

That we could, Garganafan agreed knowingly. **You think we should go after Joran.**

I think we should go after Joran for the right reasons, the dragon replied, bringing out a frown from the Rider.

His future has the potential to bring about a time of dragons. Isn't that reason enough?

For me... yes.

You think it isn't for me?

You would see Joran's fate to its intended end, but your path to that end is one of vengeance. I feel it in you, Kassanda. That hunger. You would claim the weapons of power and use them against Baelon.

Shouldn't we?

Our order has been shattered. Our kin scattered across the realm on two sides of a war born of greed and malcontent. Vengeance won't restore peace or honour the dead. It will only taint both our hearts. That blood will never come off our claws. If the Dragon Riders are to thrive once more, we must inspire.

Kassanda's emotions warred with each other. She wanted to rip and claw and tear at her enemies for what they had done to her, for what they had done to her family. **Isn't that Joran's role in all this?** she posed, having no desire to inspire anyone.

Garganafan tilted his horned head, laying a single eye on her. *Should we let him suffer that burden alone?*

Kassanda sighed, her shoulders sinking as she reached out to rub a patch of gold-speckled scales. Garganafan was unlike any dragon she had ever known or even read about, and not because of his physically rare qualities. Dragons weren't beyond revenge; their hearts were more than capable of burning with hatred. If anything, their hatred for another being could be tenfold anything a human might experience. Yet Garganafan differed from his kin. While capable of wrath, it seldom controlled him.

He sought balance, not power.

The Rider loved that in him and wished the same for herself, an attribute she had worked towards all her long life by his side, but it was eclipsed by pain. Baelon Vos and all who followed him had left a scar on her heart that refused to heal without their blood as a balm. What terrible retribution she could inflict with an arsenal of weapons crafted by beings whose power was comparable to gods. Her victory would be swift.

Every victory comes at a cost, Garganafan spoke into her mind.

Kassanda thought to reduce the flow of their bond for a moment, limiting the dragon's access to her thoughts and feelings, but she chose to stay accountable to him. **Joran has potential that cannot be left to spoil. I would make a Rider of him.** Kassanda glanced at the ships below. **Let them sail north,** she announced. **We make for Taraktor.**

We will make him see sense, Garganafan assured her.

Kassanda let some of her doubt shade their bond. **He's a teenager,** the Rider intoned. **Even your wisdom's in for a fight.**

A ripple of amusement ran out from the dragon's chest and along his neck. Kassanda patted his scales affectionately as he began to bank towards the east, but the moment was ruined by a shard of alarm that saw Garganafan whip his head to the west. The Rider instinctively tensed every muscle, preparing for a sudden change in direction that never came. Instead, she followed her companion's gaze and found the source of his unease.

As it climbed towards midday, the morning sun caught scales of blood red, lending the distant dragon the look of a scarlet star hurtling through the daylight sky.

Herragax...

Vander rides with her, Garganafan reported, his sharp eyes unfailing.

Kassanda looked to the north-west, where the undying city of Harendun sat upon Andara's shores. **He fears for his little fiefdom,** she said venomously.

They will likely accompany the fleet until they're certain it isn't bound for Harendun.

Should we run him off? Kassanda asked.

They are both impulsive, the dragon stated, *but Baelon's leash is tight. Whatever his intentions, he has clearly commanded Vander to hold the city and the forces therein. They will not risk a fight with Harendun in the balance. They will observe the fleet and act only if they pose a real threat. The moment they sail past, Herragax will see them both returned to the undying city.*

Garganafan's logic was irrefutable, if jarring. Kassanda would have enjoyed seeing them bank swiftly westward and flee like cowards.

We should still see the fleet past Harendun, she said reluctantly, aware of the days that had already passed since parting ways with Joran.

Just to be sure, Garganafan replied, his tone mirroring her reluctance.

Kassanda looked to the east again. Joran was out there somewhere. As was Taraktor. Were she a dragon, her chest would have rumbled with a low growl.

"Damn you, Vander," she cursed under the rushing wind.

———

Every minute thereafter had felt an age, her concern for Joran growing exponentially after deciding they should seek him out. Vander and Herragax had flown beside the fleet for several hours and well past Harendun before peeling away. It had delayed their return to the south all the more, the sun having risen twice more.

Now, as the light dipped into the west and the stars reached out from the east, Garganafan soared over Taraktor. It was just as ugly as Kassanda remembered, a collection of towers, buildings, and spires that appeared to have been designed by someone with a fondness for knives. It was Garganafan who noted its state of disrepair, the prison having suffered some kind of attack, though the dragon soon banked away from the prison, taking them further south.

What is it? the Rider asked, trying to see beyond his horns.

Garganafan angled his head down, wings spread so he might glide towards the grassy earth. There, limping along the edge of a small wood, was Oaken. The Aegre had a lifeless deer hanging out of his beak, which he quickly released upon sighting Garganafan's approach. Rearing up on his hind legs, it was clear to see that his front left leg had been severely wounded. Added to that, his feathers were streaked heavily with blood, and there were gouges marring him from head to tail.

Those wounds were inflicted by another Aegre, Garganafan mused.

Another? Kassanda scanned the twilight sky.

The same one who attacked them at the ruins, Garganafan deduced, recalling Joran's description of the battle.

But where is it now?

I can find no trace of it, the dragon reported as his claws sank into the mud, his snaking tail skimming across the ground.

Where's Joran? she asked gravely.

Seeing the state of Oaken didn't fill the Rider with much hope.

"Joran," she said out loud, gaining the Aegre's attention. "Where is Joran?"

Oaken squawked and tilted his head as a dog might, his yellow eyes blinking.

Kassanda sighed. "I thought they were supposed to be intelligent."

Oaken squawked again, and with a notch of aggression this time.

I think he understands you perfectly, Garganafan said. *I think the problem is our inability to understand* him.

I don't speak bird, Kassanda grumbled.

"Joran!" she yelled at the wounded Aegre."Did he survive? Where is he?"

Oaken made a keening sound from deep in his throat and flapped his wings.

"We're wasting time," the Rider decided. "We're going to the tower," she announced. "Come if you wish. If you can," she added quietly, seeing more wounds as the Aegre moved.

Having adopted an aggressive stance, Garganafan and Oaken simultaneously turned to the woods. Kassanda felt her companion's alarm and naturally reached for her sword.

The exile—Uthain. The Aegre had been creeping between the trees and rightly stopped in the sights of Garganafan. It squawked once and clawed at the ground, eliciting the same from Oaken and a rumbling growl from the dragon.

Kassanda kept her weapon where it was, confident it wouldn't be required given the company she was in. That besides, Uthain was severely injured. His wounds were too many to count, his feathers red with so much blood there was barely any white to see.

Uthain squawked one more time before turning around and walking off into the depths of the woods. Kassanda had thought the beast too feral to know when it was beaten.

Like his Rider, Garganafan remarked, *Uthain is a survivor.*

Kassanda glanced Oaken. **As is this one, apparently.**

While the Aegre was slower to take off than Kassanda had previously seen in the Aegre, Oaken did succeed in taking to the sky behind them. He did so with the deer in his beak again, the catch not to be abandoned.

What are the chances, Kassanda said across their bond, **of Joran surviving two warring Aegres?**

If their battle began in the air... almost no chance at all.

With Taraktor in sight again, the dragon began to shake his head, as if he were trying to shrug something from his scaled brow.

What's wrong?

This place, it feels... wrong.

How so?

I can feel it in the air. Smell it. Taste it, even. A raw and powerful magic has been unleashed here. It stains the very fabric of the world.

Kassanda looked over the dark tower. **The Jainus meddle with things they don't understand.**

No, Garganafan disagreed. *This is something else. Something unchecked, unbound. Reckless.*

The dragon's head turned and dipped, their bond informing the Rider that he had seen someone without the need for words. He plummeted without a sound for a time, their presence only made known when his mighty wings unfurled and caught the air.

The Jainus wizard fell to the ground, his sack of supplies spilling across the grass. Petrified, his hands came up to shield his face as all four of Garganafan's feet thundered into the earth, Oaken following beside him.

Kassanda was already unclipped and sliding out of her saddle and down the dragon's ribs. The dying light caught the silvyr as it was freed from her scabbard, the tip whipped down to point at the aged wizard. Propped up on his elbows, his eyes darted from Rider to dragon, his fear palpable. He had likely already come to the conclusion that he didn't know nearly enough spells to protect himself against either of them.

There was a time when we were more revered than feared, Garganafan commented.

Two hundred years of butchering people on battlefields will change that, Kassanda replied dryly.

"What is your name?" she demanded of the wizard.

"Is that... an Aegre?" the man uttered, voice breaking.

"Your *name*," she repeated sternly.

"Willem," he revealed. "I am a Jainus—a friend to the Riders."

I would not call their ilk a friend, Garganafan remarked.

"What happened here?" Kassanda questioned. "Speak!"

The Jainus flinched. "I don't know!" he blurted. "We were attacked by armed men—they came by sea. They slaughtered my colleagues."

"When was this?"

"Over a week ago. They were looking for someone. There were

others inside. Burglars and the like, I imagine. I didn't even know they were inside," he admitted, appearing confused.

"Armed men?" Kassanda echoed. "They did all this?" she enquired, waving her sword over the debris that littered Taraktor's grounds.

The wizard glanced at the broken tower heads and twisted fragments of wall. "No," he answered, as if that should have been obvious. "This was... I am not to speak of it," he said swiftly.

The Rider took a threatening step closer. "You will speak of it to me."

The Jainus looked from the point of her sword to her dark eyes. "There was a prison break, years ago. We kept it a secret, even from the king and his spies."

"The *prisoners* did this?"

"Just *one*," Willem specified. "I have been in charge of the investigation for some time. No one comes here. We've never needed to guard the doors or patrol the area."

Kassanda absorbed the knowledge, not yet sure what to make of it or its importance. "These armed men. What did they look like?"

The Jainus clawed at the grass beneath him as Garganafan's hot breath rolled over his body. He swallowed and looked to be using significant energy to recall all he had seen. "They wore no sigil. Their armour was that of leather, not plate. I've never seen their like before."

"And you couldn't fend them off? A wizard of many years?"

There was a look of reluctance about the Jainus, but it is hard to keep secrets when the breath of a dragon is kissing one's neck. "The prisoner who escaped," he began tentatively. "His magic broke every warding spell in Taraktor. Our investigation suggests that the collision of magic inside those walls has permanently damaged the way magic bleeds into the world. Even demetrium cannot aid us."

He speaks the truth, Garganafan confirmed, the wizard's description matching all that the dragon could feel.

"And these burglars you speak of," Kassanda probed. "You saw them?"

Willem nodded. "There were four of them. Until another arrived," he added, as if the memory had just come to him, "though he was too late to help them—they were captured and bound by then."

The Rider's eyes narrowed. "Another arrived? Tell me, was he young? White hair? He would have been wearing a cloak like mine."

"I only saw from a distance, and it was dark," the Jainus replied apologetically. "He fought some of them, though. I don't know what magic he brought against them, but those he battled burst into... nothingness."

The sword, Garganafan concluded. *He's talking about Joran.*

"What happened next?" she asked urgently.

"He was captured like the rest," he relayed, opening a pit inside Kassanda. "They took them all to the steps." He looked north from his low position, directing them to a wooden platform that protruded over the cliff. "It's a small dock," the wizard informed them. "We haven't used it in some time."

"They came by sea," Kassanda repeated absently, her gaze cast out beyond the cliffs. "Where would they have come..."

Her eyes settled, as Garganafan's did, on the hazy mass of land on the eastern horizon.

Nareene, the dragon growled.

Kassanda recalled well what Androma had reported from that wretched island. "Skaramangians," she said aloud.

Willem's expression creased into confusion. "I don't know what that is."

The Rider glanced at him, content to ignore the witless wizard while she turned to her companion. ***They have been taken by the enemy.***

So it would seem, the dragon agreed.

Kassanda's jaw firmed. "Run to your betters, wizard," she instructed him dismissively.

The Jainus scooped up a handful of supplies and staggered to his feet before running away. As he departed, the Rider's attention was split between Nareene to the east their intended destination to the north.

It is our duty to accompany the king's men, she felt compelled to point out. *That skeleton must be secured.*

The white dragon looked down at her, his eyes dark in the fading light. *It must,* he agreed.

Our presence on the battlefield would save many lives, Kassanda went on, her commitment audibly waning.

It would also end many lives, Garganafan countered.

Her sandy cloak blowing in the wind that swept across from the sea, Kassanda Grey watched as Nareene slowly slipped from view, claimed by the encroaching night.

The same oaths that pledge us to the king also pledge us to the future, that there would be a realm still standing under the rule of Blood Etragon. That future cannot be assured in the north. But there might yet be hope for it in Joran.

Garganafan arched his neck, his huge head coming to loom over her. *Then we are duty-bound for Nareene.*

Kassanda sheathed her blade. "For Nareene."

61

REGRET

0 Years Ago...

4

Ka'vairn was wounded, and mortally so. There would be no putting her back together. The eastern ramparts were gone, leaving a gaping hole in the fortress's defences. The entrance was under several hundred tons of stone. They didn't have the resources to rebuild nor an alliance with The Saible, who had sent forth so many to tear it down in the first place. There was every chance The Saible would issue more soldiers in the coming days, a larger force to ensure that Ka'vairn was cleaved from The Hellion Mountains for good.

Despite the rising sun, a great shadow had fallen over the ancient home of the Vahlken. Henceforth, it would be naught but a ruin upon the land, soon to fall into myth and legend. That and more should have weighed Daijen Saeth down, cracking his foundations, yet he could not dwell on any of it.

"He's my son," Ilithranda had said.

Those three words echoed inside his mind as he entered the keep, the great doors opened by The Green Leaf from the inside. Daijen couldn't make sense of them. What had she meant? She couldn't possibly have meant that Slait was her son.

The Vahlken's attention was momentarily stolen by the others. He might once have considered them friends, but his foolishness—his pride—had nearly cost them their lives and the weapons of power they were responsible for. He didn't deserve to call them friends. They were allies at best, but allies had to be able to rely on others. While Ahnir's long life dwelled within him, mixing with his own memories and emotions, he was far from reliable.

"Are you hurt?" Aphrandhor asked him, his eyes glancing at the black bone in Daijen's hand.

Indeed, it should have been Daijen asking that question of the wizard. He was coated in sweat and ash, his hair more black than its usual blond. His face was marred by cuts and gashes and his green robes were stained with both his blood and those he had bested in battle. More than anything, he looked exhausted—on the point of collapse even.

Daijen didn't answer him, though he could still feel the sting of Slait's sabre across various parts of his body, especially the biting blow dealt to his left thigh. Instead, he looked over the dwarves and Androma. Like The Green Leaf, they were greatly fatigued and covered in sweat and ash. Yamnomora was already dabbing a wet cloth over a wound to Mordrith's hip, unaware, it seemed, of the dagger protruding from her own shoulder.

The Dragon Rider had faired the best, protected inside her form-fitting undersuit of blue scale mail. Even in death, Maegar was protecting her. The Rider's dark leathers showed plenty of signs, however, that she had taken numerous blows. Beneath all her armour, the Vahlken had no doubt that she was sporting a tapestry of bruises.

For the first time, Daijen was glad Androma lacked the eyes to see him. It would have been too much to have her look upon him as the others did in that moment. Suspicion. Betrayal. Scorn, even. He couldn't imagine that any of them had enjoyed The Valtorak's company in the short time they had occupied Ka'vairn, but he had been an ally. Just like them. More than that, they knew of his lengthy history with the keep's master.

He had lost their trust—that much was obvious, seen in their eyes. Good, he thought, thinking on The Valtorak's warning. They would survive longer without him by their side.

Without a word, the Vahlken left them to their wounds in search of Ilithranda. He knew he wouldn't be able to focus on anything until he had confronted her, though there was naught that could truly distract him from his part in The Valtorak's death.

Following his nose, which had already detected his sister's distinct and rare sweat, he ascended the steps and made his way up to The Valtorak's private office—or what was left of it. Half of the tower's head had been blown away by one of the catapults, exposing it to the winds. Still, he could hear Ilithranda rifling through parchments and opening drawers, the desk having been thrown to one side.

Having discarded her black pelt cloak and left her weapons resting against the shattered doorframe, the Vahlken was crouched on the other side of The Valtorak's desk, her violet eyes scrutinising the contents of the top drawer. Looking around at the various scrolls and documents cast about, it seemed impossible that they would find anything.

"What are you looking for?" he asked, his voice hoarse.

She didn't meet his gaze. "Handuin's translation," she replied simply.

"Translation?" he echoed, his thoughts returning to *Linguistics, Dialects, and Allogpraphy*, the dense tome that The Valtorak had mentioned prior to the Ankala. He even spotted the book, still in its slot, saved by no more than chance.

Ilithranda looked up, but only so her eyes could glance over the bone in his hand. "Handuin translated the glyphs. That's how he was able to create the pits that transformed us. It's how every Valtorak has been able to replicate it. That translation is the key to our entire order." The Vahlken growled and slammed the drawer shut. "It's not here!" she fumed.

Daijen said nothing on the matter, his vision occupied by the image of The Valtorak lying dead in his arms. The shame and guilt he felt was locked away inside a knot deep in his gut. It was numbing, his reasoning mind struggling to reconcile with the facts. It prevented him from making sense of it. Too much had happened around the grim event, he decided, crowding his thoughts and emotions.

He was already dreading the moment those feelings made themselves known.

In that moment, however, standing before Ilithranda, Daijen was confounded by one thing and one thing only. He stared at her expectantly, waiting. Ilithranda moved on from the desk and rummaged through a stack of scrolls strewn across the floor. Her frustration was clearly mounting, the process expedited by Daijen's silent presence.

When the next pile of parchments proved to be as useless as the previous one, the Vahlken scattered them and sighed, her head bowing deep to her chest. "If you want to talk about anything," she growled, "we can start with you murdering The Valtorak."

It was the last thing Daijen wanted to be dragged into, but a conversation—even a heated one—was the lightest punishment he deserved.

"It wasn't... I wasn't me," he began.

"It looked like you," Ilithranda retorted. "It's *your* atori blade in his chest."

"It *was* me," he replied, a bite of anger in his voice. "But I wasn't..." Daijen paused, wondering how to describe his experience. "I wasn't there. I wasn't fighting *him*. I thought I was fighting someone else, in a different place, in a different *time!*"

Ilithranda reacted violently, hurling a weighty book at him. "I told you not to use the bracer!" she yelled as he blocked the book with his forearm. "I went to Aran'saur so you wouldn't! I didn't want to go! I didn't want to..." Her rage slipped, replaced with sorrow.

Daijen's investigative mind put the pieces together then. He recalled the conversation with Barris Tanyth, the emperor's spymaster. Barris had spoken of her duty besides those of a Vahlken and would have revealed more had Ilithranda not cut him off.

"*You don't even want to know?*" the spymaster had asked, his question met with silence.

Then there had been the conversation with the emperor himself, during their escape from the palace. Daijen had been instructed to go on while Ilithranda stayed behind to speak with her father.

"*You left something behind the last time you were here,*" Emperor Qeledred had announced boldly.

"*I don't want to know,*" Ilithranda had replied, and with great apprehension.

"*But you must,*" the emperor had intoned.

"Slait," Daijen breathed, hardly able to believe his own deduction. "You left something behind. It was Slait, wasn't it?"

Tears broke free of her violet eyes and streaked down her pale face, running through the ash. "They took him from me," she uttered. "I didn't even get to hold him. I didn't even get to name him."

Daijen stepped further into the room and licked his dry lips. "Who took him?"

"Barris Tanyth and his lackeys," she said with disdain. "I didn't have a choice." Ilithranda stopped and took a breath. "I didn't *feel* like I had a choice. They had offered me a way in, to be a part of the imperial family, if at a distance."

"You had to prove yourself," Daijen said, remembering her explanation from years earlier in The Ruins of Kharis Vhay.

Ilithranda nodded. "Join the war effort. Fight for Andara. Prove the strength of the blood in my veins. Then I could return and live in their perfect world." Her fist knotted and pressed into the surface of The Valtorak's desk, her head shaking from the memory of it. "I was so desperate for that life. I had already lived a human lifetime on the streets of Aran'saur. It was brutal. Unforgiving. I would have done anything to get out, but it was all the harder being pregnant."

Daijen swallowed, unsure if his next question would be met by more violence. "Who was the father?"

Ilithranda's eyes glanced over Daijen and rested on the mountains beyond the jagged wall, as if the past could be seen on the other side. "His name was Tarik. He never knew his house name." She took a calming breath, though it did nothing to stop fresh tears from breaking free from her lashes. "Slait has his eyes," she mused, her expression suggesting the thought had only just occurred to her. "He was sweet. *Too* sweet. He died on the streets like everyone else who lived that life." She paused there, perhaps taking a moment to remember the man. "I was about ready to give birth when Barris Tanyth found me. He made it very clear that my baby would be the death of me and that the child would soon share my fate if I wasn't around to protect them. He made it sound so simple," she said, her voice breaking.

"What happened to him—to Slait?"

"I never knew. Not until my father told me before our escape. He had been aware of my... situation. As with everything else, he did nothing to intervene lest it disturb his little world. He knew Slait had been taken away while I was sent to The Saible. He was moved around a lot, but he spent most of his youth in the clerics' priories. Somewhere along the way, my father stopped checking in. The next he heard of Slait, he was being handpicked to walk the Path of Handuin. That must have been a decade before we did."

Daijen did his best to take it all in, shocked by the revelation. He had always assumed Slait was older than both of them, just because he was ahead of them in their training. It hadn't occurred to him that Slait had simply proved himself a worthy candidate at a younger age, though he was still a couple of centuries older than Daijen.

"Does Slait know any of this?" he asked, thinking of every interaction he had witnessed between the two of them.

"No," Ilithranda answered. "Even after the Skaramangians took him in and he joined the cleric guard, his origins have been kept from him. He would probably hate me all the more if he knew the truth. And he would be right to," she added, her tone dripping with self-loathing.

"You should never have had to go through that," Daijen said, defending her past self. "You shouldn't even have been cast onto the streets to begin with. I'm sorry you were so alone in all that. You never said..."

Ilithranda managed to raise her chin and even look him in the eyes. "Walking away from my responsibility as a mother... I regret nothing more than that. I hoped coming here would end that life and let me start a new one. I thought I could find some freedom from the regret. Even some power to take control of my life so I could never be put in that position again."

Freedom and *power*. It wasn't the first time Daijen had heard his sister speak of such things. She believed that the Vahlken embodied both of those things and that she intended to harness them. He had never imagined the truth that lay behind the need for both.

"I know what The Valtorak said about letting go of our old selves," Ilithranda continued. "That whoever we were before the pits is dead. I have wished more than anything for that to be true. But, in two hundred years, not a day has gone by when I haven't wondered where he is. Who is he? What is he doing? I was just learning to live with it—with not knowing. Then I had to go back there," she said bitterly.

"I'm sorry," Daijen apologised, aware of his part in coercing her to attend the Ankala. "What will you do now? About Slait," he specified.

Ilithranda deflated and turned away from him. "What can I do, Daijen? I cannot kill my son."

He was stumped by her response. "You can't really see him as that?"

"Of course I can," Ilithranda rebuffed, turning back. "I birthed him, Daijen. His flesh was born of mine. His deeds, ill or not, cannot change what he is to me."

Daijen frowned. "By his blade and his actions, Slait butchered our brothers and sisters. He slew Kastiek. He killed Strix. Being your son does not *redeem* him, Ilithranda."

"I'm not saying it does," she argued. "I'm saying I cannot... I *will* not take his life."

"But you will stop others from doing just that," he concluded, and accusingly so.

"I didn't *want* to know," Ilithranda insisted, something in her tone suggesting that Daijen was partly to blame. "I was finally able to leave it in the past, to leave *him* in the past. And if we're talking about irredeemable acts, killing The Valtorak and ending the Vahlken line definitely qualifies. Should I kill you? Should I let others kill you? There are Vahlken out there still, Daijen. What should I do when they discover The Valtorak's fate? Or Ka'vairn's? Should I stop them from killing you?"

"Do not compare me to that monster!" Daijen glowered. "Everything I have done is to further our cause against the Skaramangians. I'm trying to end the war. I'm trying to save lives."

"You're trying to *prove* yourself!" Ilithranda countered. "You're trying to show the world that Daijen Saeth is not to be underestimated. That you, and you alone, have the power to make real change. The truth is, you do have that power. But you'll never change a damned thing as long as you're ruled by your pride."

Daijen was shaking his head, desperate to refute any notion that his pride had become an obstacle, but he had only to look out on the courtyard to see otherwise. His brash actions had brought the wrath of the Andaren army down on Ka'vairn and made the Skaramangians' work all the easier, regardless of whether they possessed the helm or not. Besides the ruin made of their home, The Valtorak lay dead at its heart—the work of his own hands.

And why?

Because he'd thought that he, and he alone, could uncover the secrets of the past and discover the key to victory. He'd just *had* to use the vambrace—and without training. The Vahlken had foolishly overestimated himself, and the price would cost them all for generations to come.

Daijen could see it now. His pride. It stood beside him like a shadow, following his every step. He had let it counsel him again and again, informing his decisions.

Feeling the sheer weight of it all, Daijen drew in on himself, his voice diminished. "I thought I was doing the right thing."

"You were," Ilithranda replied, her agreement surprising him. "But you should have done it another way."

Daijen could only nod, sombrely. He should have done it on his own, he thought. He should have heeded The Valtorak's warning and banished himself from Ka'vairn. But it was too late for any of that. He knew, as ever, that the only way was forward, but, for the first time in his life, the Vahlken had no idea what that first step should be. He doubted himself, fearful that his next decision would be made from a place of pride.

"Where's the helm?"

The question stopped Daijen's thoughts from spiralling any further, though the pivot took his mind to darker places, where the shadow of Ahnir crept ever closer. He could feel the Golem's need to make safe its master's helm. The Vahlken squeezed the black bone in his hand, his will battling to discern where Ahnir ended and he began.

"I threw it into the pit," he finally revealed.

"Truly?"

"It's lost to everyone down there. Even to us," he added, only imagining what sundering their minds and bodies would endure should they be submerged in Handuin's magic for a second time.

"I half expected you to try it on," Ilithranda remarked.

A dark and twisted part of Daijen's mind wondered if he still should, but what remained of his tattered confidence reminded him that he alone possessed so many of the answers they had been searching for. There was still a chance, however narrow, that he might find a way through the tragedies and revelations to end the cycle of war.

"Where do we go from here?" he asked.

Ilithranda gave a subtle shrug. "I don't know. I'm not even sure if I care," she added honestly.

Unsure how to respond to that, Daijen's eyes settled on The

Valtorak below. "We must honour our dead," he declared. "We should build a pyre."

Ilithranda brushed past him, making for the door. "Build it yourself."

———

In the heart of Ka'vairn's courtyard, a great pyre burned bright into the starlit night. Stripped of their armour, body upon body had been stacked upon it, there to burn without ceremony. The flames were reflected in Daijen's eyes as he watched humans and Andarens burn together, their ashes mixing as they blew high with the black smoke.

It had taken the Vahlken all day to build the pyre, remove their armour, and pile the bodies, the exertion proving enough to bring out a sheen of sweat on his brow. Daijen had relished in it, happy to give his hands and muscles something to do while the others tended to their wounds inside the keep

It was not all he had done. To the east, where the ramparts had fallen away, there stood another pyre yet to be set alight. It was significantly smaller, though each piece had been put together with more care. Upon the top, there was just enough room for a single body.

That body was now being carried out from the keep in Ilithranda's strong arms. Still in his traditional armour and bear pelt, The Valtorak lay limp in her grip. Daijen observed his sister's approach and that of their companions, who trailed in her wake. Solemn was the atmosphere that came with them.

Daijen would have shared in it had he not been so alarmed to see his atori blade still protruding from his master's chest. "You haven't removed it," he remarked as Ilithranda came to stand before him.

"You put it there," she stated harshly. "You can be the one to remove it."

The Vahlken accepted her response, deserved as it was. He gripped the familiar hilt with one hand and slowly drew the bronze blade from The Valtorak's body. It felt wrong to sheathe the weapon, so he kept hold of it, stepping aside. He didn't move entirely out of the way, however, his gaze having lingered on The Valtorak's torso. It had been only a glimpse, seen between the master's body and his broken armour.

"Daijen."

Ilithranda's tone was low, his name delivered short and sharp.

"Wait," he muttered, putting himself firmly between her and the pyre again. "Put him down."

Ilithranda frowned. "His place is on the pyre now."

"Please," the Vahlken pleaded.

After glancing over his shoulder and looking at the pyre, Ilithranda relented and carefully placed their master's body on the stone at their feet.

Daijen hesitated, his fingers lingering over the clasps that held The Valtorak's cuirass in place. It felt so disrespectful, but he knew what he had seen.

"Daijen..." Ilithranda protested as the armour was peeled away from The Valtorak's chest.

Her lips clamped shut when Daijen tore open the ragged shirt, exposing their master's bare torso. The Vahlken didn't blink, his icy blue eyes running over every glyph that lined The Valtorak's skin. Written in Andaren, the tattooed script started at his right clavicle and stopped just beneath his navel. The only interruption came from the wound where Daijen's blade had brought an end to their fight.

"What is that?" Aphrandhor enquired, leaning over them.

"Instructions," Daijen answered, the slightest hint of a smile curling his sharp cheeks.

"For what?" the wizard asked.

Ilithranda looked up from The Valtorak to meet Daijen's eyes. "This is Handuin's translation," she said. "This is how we make more Vahlken."

It wasn't required for his mind to commit every word to permanent memory, but Daijen looked over the script one more time before replacing the cuirass.

"Then the line is not ended after all," Androma declared.

"It is for me," Ilithranda stated, picking up the body once more. Without another word, she placed The Valtorak on the pyre and stepped back.

The Green Leaf stepped in and touched his staff to the piled wood. The fire spread quickly, consuming every inch of the pyre until the master could only be seen behind flames.

It reminded Daijen so much of the last time they had performed the tradition, when he had brought Kastiek's body down from the abandoned eyries. Before that, he recalled Elivar's body set to the flames, never having had the chance to see through the eyes of a Vahlken.

He realised then, in that quiet moment, that it was the destiny of every Vahlken to find their final rest in the fire. While terribly morbid, it also seemed quite poetic that their ashes would then float into the sky, where every Vahlken felt so at peace astride their Aegre.

Knowing what he did of the Arkalon's fabrication and the gods who were no more than the creations of a dark wizard, Daijen had lost whatever scraps of his faith still remained. Gone was the notion of the Black Abyss and the promise of reclamation day, when the gods would be restored and the heavens with them. What happened after death was now a mystery to the Vahlken, but he hoped The Valtorak found his way to Aramis again, just as he had hoped for Kastiek and Strix.

One by one, the group departed, leaving Daijen alone in the light of the flames. "You warned me," he said into those flames. "And I did not listen. I'm sorry it was you who had to pay the price for my... *failings*," he continued, unable to list all his mistakes. "Handuin made us strong so we wouldn't need allies. So we could face the enemy and do what others could not. I see what must be done now, the path I alone must follow."

Leaving the pyre to burn, Daijen returned to the keep. He had work to do.

62

FOUND ALL THE SAME

With a strength gifted from the roots of the earth, the dwarven people put mile after mile behind them. Their ancient home, the mountains that had long been those of Morthil, was to fade, a bitter-sweet memory of time now past. Through cold winds and hard lands, they ploughed into a future of their own making.

They did so in the footsteps of Grarfath and Yamnomora.

Those footsteps had been slow in the weeks following their exodus, their numbers bloated with young and old alike. The smith had been content with their pace, however, his strength still recovering from using The Anther so much.

Some of their collective strength was required to keep The Dancing Sword of the Dawn in chains and on the move. He said nothing, receiving his meagre portions of food and water without opinion or remark. He just observed, those golden eyes scrutinising every one of them.

Grarfath tried to give the Andaren as little thought as possible.

While the smith's speech had been galvanising, they had faced branching paths upon reaching the end of The Dorth Road, where they had been presented with a left, taking them deeper into Andara, and a right, bringing them to Erador's borders.

"We should take our chances with the humans!" some insisted.

"We've a better chance formin' an alliance with the Andarens!" others cried out.

"We can't trust either o' 'em!" came the more unhelpful opinions.

The guild lord of the Boldbanes had stepped forth, having been biding his time. "What says the Hammerhold?" he demanded, looking to put Grarfath in another difficult position.

Fortunately, the smith had spent many a night discussing their options with Yamnomora, who knew the lay of the world so much better than he.

"I say we cannot stand idly in the open while we debate our very future!" Grarfath had bellowed, projecting his voice across the masses. "We must find shelter for our elders an' babes! East o' 'ere, along this road," he had shouted, pointing down The Yemmel Path, "are The Ruins o' Tor Valan! There's no settlements between 'ere an' there! The journey would be a peaceful one, if a cold one! The ruins o' that city are large enough for us all. I say we rest there an' decide our next step!"

Damned if that very moment hadn't arrived.

In the blackened ruins of that once fair city, Grarfath Underborn stood atop a rock, the eyes of his kin boring into him. They had rested for two nights, untroubled by the shadows of the Andaren husk.

Still, the stone bones were restless, their world having been upended in a single day. They needed strong leadership, a quality Grarfath would never boast, yet he wielded The Anther. Duun's ancient weapon had made him a hero for many, and so leadership had been thrust upon him.

It had also put a very large target on his back. Whispers had reached him and Yamnomora that the guild lords intended to remove him from the picture. They each had their loyal members, any of whom could be charged with putting a knife in the smith's back. Those he had saved in Khardunar had closed ranks thereafter, ensuring that he had someone watching him at all times. They had even managed to secure a sword from somewhere and put it directly in Yamnomora's hand.

Atop that rock, Grarfath glanced over the cluster of guild lords. They were willing him to fail, to make the wrong decision that would turn all against him. The smith looked to Yamnomora, with whom he had talked long into the night. Their plan was for all, not any one guild. He tightened his grip about The Anther's haft, willing it to lend him the necessary courage.

He swallowed, his first words forgotten in the eyes of so many. His lips parted as a familiar sound drifted to him, a tune he had long known. Looking down, he located the source: a young girl stood with her back pressed to her mother. She was watching him like everyone else, only she was humming one of the oldest songs known to their people.

The Ballad of Sunstrun.

Her mother silenced her with a whisper, but it had already brought a warm smile to Grarfath's dark face. He had heard that ballad all his life, the lyrics and tune never far from his mother's lips. For so long, he had resented his mother for abandoning him and his father. Now he knew the truth. Now he knew the responsibility she had taken upon her shoulders and what lengths she had gone to in order to keep them safe from the Skaramangians.

Now he knew of the *courage* Mordrith Underborn had shown every day of her life.

Such was her courage that Grarfath felt it now in view of his people and those who would kill him. He wasn't living in Duun's shadow. He was the Hammerhold, like his mother before him.

"Like many o' ye, I don' know the names o' the old gods! Such things were replaced by profit, success, industry! But I remember where we came from! Our oldest ancestors emerged from the roots o' the earth, our bodies forged from the same pressures that raised the mountains! Our skin is that o' the hardest stone! Our hearts harness the deep wells o' the world! An' our minds were made to see the world as it could be, not as it is!

"I remind ye all o' this because it feels like we've lost our home!

But I say to ye: we are *home!*" Grarfath beat a solid fist to his chest. "As long as we stick together, dwarves will always be home! Our strength lies in ourselves, not where we work the stone! Like the mountain itself, if we are one people, we will never be moved, never be commanded, and never be broken!"

To the guild lords' chagrin, this was met by a chorus of cheers, the likes of which Tor Valan had not heard in centuries.

"Our journey has not yet come to an end!" Grarfath continued as the roar died down. "We've caught our breath, aye, but we cannot linger! On the surface, it is only inevitable that we will get caught in the middle o' the war! An' for all our warriors, we cannot fight from a place o' strength if we're roamin' the wilds.

"But," he added, offering a note of hope, "there is a place we can go where neither man nor Andaren hold sway over the surface! On the other side o' these mountains," the smith said, pointing at the dark rock that towered over Tor Valan, "is The Unadine! That forest sits north o' The Watchtower of Argunsuun an' White Tower! No man's land!"

The response was that of general dissent, and it was swiftly voiced by the masses.

"A forest?"

"We're dwarves! Not birds!"

"I'll not live in some tree!"

"Nor under the sky!"

Grarfath patted the air with one hand, calling for calm. All the while, the cadre of guild lords and bankers grinned, ushering their underlings to add their disgruntled voices to the others.

"I'm not for makin' a home o' The Unadine!" the smith assured them all. "But the deep halls o' Morthil weren' made in a day! We need somewhere on the surface that cannot be claimed by Erador or Andara!" To the sound of more unrest, Grarfath raised his voice to that of a bellow. "We need time! The Unadine can give us that! We can live off the land an' take fresh water from The Serpent's Tongue in the north! We can *live!* Is that not a good startin' point from which to rebuild?"

While that question silenced most, the Boldbane pivoted to

project his voice up and round. "We should be carvin' out our *own* place in the world—as our ancestors did! They claimed The Morthil Mountains, an' there weren' anythin' the Andarens could do abou' it!"

"Aye!" came a smattering of responses.

"The Andarens 'ave never been so aggressive!" argued Yamnomora, not one to hold her tongue. "They've been on a war footin' for centuries now! Give 'em half a chance an' they'll put every one o' us to work in their war machine! We'll be forgin' weapons an' buildin' 'em forts before ye can slip those fancy jewels from yer fat fingers!"

The guild lord took a threatening step towards the dwarven warrior, and he was quickly backed up by his supporters. Yamnomora wasn't without her own allies, those she had helped to save in the depths of Morthil, but it was Grarfath who brought an end to the potential conflict.

He stepped off, coming down between the two on one knee. The Anther's golden head knocked against the stone, and just the sound of it was enough to pause the Boldbane and all behind him. Slowly rising, the smith was sure to lock eyes with the guild lord, silently reminding him what happened the last time they clashed.

"I'm not for tellin' any o' ye what to do!" he began again, turning on the spot. "Yer lives are yer own! I'm also not for givin' any o' ye guarantees! I don' know what's out there! I only know that if we face it together, we'll get through it! If ye're with me, I set out from Tor Valan this very morn! If ye're not with me, I pray the old gods show ye the way!"

As Grarfath retreated to his makeshift camp, the dwarven population fell into debate, the sound rising up through the ruin's many levels. Yamnomora gave him an approving nod and a pat on the arm while others vowed to follow him to the ends of Verda itself.

Rough was one hand that grabbed him by the arm and forced the son of Thronghir to turn around. The mightiest of Boldbanes stood before him, his eyes islands of white amidst the thick tattoos that covered the skin around them. The guild lord didn't hide his contempt for Grarfath, nor for those he considered fools who damn-near worshipped him.

"Ye've only got their ear because ye're holdin' that," he growled, looking at The Anther. "Without it, ye're jus' a smith. They'll come to see that. I'll make sure o' it," he promised.

Grarfath took back his arm and walked away, humming The Ballad of Sunstrun as he did.

———

In the days that followed, it became clear that not everyone had followed them out of Tor Valan. While that number didn't even amount to a hundred, the smith felt burdened by the loss. There was no hope to be found in those ruins, and they had nowhere to go.

Since the majority had chosen to accompany him ever eastward, the guild lords and members of The Banking Federation had also remained with the enormous caravan. They were like vultures circling him, waiting for him to trip so they might pick him clean to the bone.

Pulling his cloak of white fur close about his neck, Grarfath looked ahead, pleased to see The Watchtower of Argunsuun on the horizon, a dark tower standing tall on the white vista. He also saw Yamnomora, the dwarf standing ahead and to one side of the procession. She stood with one foot upon the root of a tree, her gaze piercing beyond measure. There was great concern in her expression.

"What troubles ye?" he asked, wondering if she too feared any aggression from the Andarens in the tower.

Yamnomora didn't answer him immediately, her green eyes wandering over the dense column of dwarves behind the smith. "Ye're doin' a good thing 'ere. A *great* thing. Hells, it's more than I ever thought ye capable of. Mordrith would be damned proud o' ye."

Grarfath couldn't hide the surprise he felt. The dwarf wasn't one for handing out praise. "This is *us*, Mora. We're doin' this—"

"Ye can't keep The Anther," she declared, bluntly cutting through his words.

The smith's solid brow knotted like broken stone. "What are ye abou'?"

"I mean to say... The Anther can' keep to this course. It's a weapon o' power, an' it's needed elsewhere. Ye heard The Green Leaf, same as me. The enemy are winnin'. They've a victory comin' their way that will make 'em invincible. Our only chance o' beatin' the Skaramangians is with an arsenal o' weapons like that one. The way I see it, ye can either deliver it to the wizard yerself an' even wield it, or ye can give it to me, an' I'll see it used against our enemy."

Grarfath was so taken aback he could only listen in stunned silence. "But... But ye said it yerself. I'm the Hammerhold. Me mother meant for me to wield it, an' *I am*. I'm usin' it to steer our people from extinction. Isn' that a good enough cause?"

"There's nowhere we can go where the war won't find us," Yamnomora countered. "If the Skaramangians win, they'll bring back the Talakin, Grarfath. *The Dark Ones. The Eikor.* Whatever name those monsters hold to, they will be returned to Verda, an' every scrap o' history tells us they 'ave the power to wipe us out. They'll come for us all," she told him, doubling down. "The only real hope our people 'ave is to eradicate that threat." The dwarf looked down at the hammer in Grarfath's hand. "Ye're holdin' one o' the few things ever known to defeat a Talakin. It can't stay 'ere. I'm sorry."

The smith looked to the east again, to the watchtower, and knew why her gaze was fixed on that distant land. "Ye're takin' it into Erador," he concluded.

"With any luck, I'll catch up with The Green Leaf in Caster Hold. They might even 'ave located the missin' weapon by then."

Grarfath ran a hand over his mouth and down through his beard. "Our people are on a knife's edge, Mora. We're exposed out 'ere. We need to get 'em somewhere safe," he insisted.

"And ye *are*," the warrior pointed out, gesturing at the white plains ahead of them.

"How long will that last if I've no Anther? They're only listenin' to me because they want me to be Duun. It's like that *blasted* Boldbane said: without it, I'm jus' a smith. If ye leave with the hammer, I'll be dead before the new day. If I leave with ye, the guild lords will have their power back, an' what's left o' our people will be forced into servin' *them* before each other."

It was a pitying smile that crossed Yamnomora's stubbled face. "Ye're not the same dwarf I met in that workshop," she remarked. "Ye're on the same path yer mother was now. She wasn' born into any great destiny, but it found her all the same."

Rare were any genuine smiles upon her face, so even a pitying one captured Grarfath's attention for just a moment. Beyond all those brash and hard characteristics that made her the warrior he knew, there was another side to Yamnomora. Perhaps it was a part of her that remained untouched by the work of the Skaramangians, a piece of her old self, her true self. Caught in that tender moment, the smith found himself in desperate need to know her better.

What had put her on that path?

Where had she learned to fight so well?

What was her life like before the Skaramangians?

It was with a notch of shame that Grarfath realised how little he knew his closest companion, someone he might have dared to call a friend after all they had been through. And now she was talking of parting ways with him. It crushed his spirit even more than the thought of being parted from The Anther.

"I'll accompany ye into The Unadine," she told him, looking to the east again. "Once everyone's settled, I'll slip away in the night. I'll take the dancin' kud with me an' all. Let 'im face the wrath o' Androma, I say."

Grarfath looked over the long line of his people and found Slait amongst them with ease, his stature putting him several feet above everyone. The mutated Andaren was bound and tethered to a donkey that kept him moving at pace, while a number of armed dwarves escorted from all sides with spears at the ready.

"I don' know how to do this without ye," he blurted, whipping his head back around. "Ye can't leave. Not now. Not then either. There must be another way."

"We're both fightin' for the same thing," she replied. "But our people need us in different places."

Grarfath scoffed. "Me body'll be *scattered* in different places without *ye* by me side."

Yamnomora laughed with a lilt unlike the sound she made while laughing mid-battle. It was almost melodic. "Come on, smith," she bade, slapping his shoulder. "Ye'll see. All will be fine."

With Yamnomora astride Bludgeon once more, they moved alongside their kin at an ambling pace. Despite being so much further south than The Ice Plains of Isendorn, the weather was still bitterly cold, the wind a harsh mistress, and the land deceivingly vast. Given their numbers and the varying abilities amongst the aged and the young, it took most of the day before they found themselves on the edge of Andara's territory.

Even so, there remained enough light to see White Tower in the distance, a grey smudge on the horizon. The last time the smith had seen it, the tower's battlements had been blown away by Andaren catapults and ballistas, its battalions slaughtered by the pale army.

The Watchtower of Argunsuun remained a beacon of Andaren strength in the west, its black stone and thick struts untouched by the humans. By the look of it, it had also been abandoned, the tower's inhabitants having accompanied the marching army. That was a relief to Grarfath, who had feared reprisals for what might have looked like an exodus into Erador and a statement of dwarven allegiance.

That relief, however, was short-lived.

Grarfath halted the column of dwarves beside the watchtower, his eyes wide and set to that which lay distant, beyond no man's land. Others saw as he did, and word soon spread down the thick line. Fear made a mess of their formation, its borders bursting as dwarves spread out to see the eastern horizon for themselves.

And the army that sat upon it.

Grave concern rippled across the dwarven population, whispers of doom passing between thousands of lips. There were louder voices amongst them, those who supported the guild lords above all others.

"He's marched us to ruin!"

"He's killed us all!"

"We should never 'ave trusted 'im!"

Grarfath blocked it all out and stepped away from Yamnomora. He focused his memories on a single point, recalling White Tower in as much detail as possible. Down came The Anther, the top of the head slamming into the ground beside his right boot. To the dwarf's perception, the transition was seamless, absent the blinding flash or the glimmer of an overlay in environments. The next moment, he simply rose from one knee inside the broken walls of White Tower.

With caution, the smith crept to the gaping hole in the top floor of the tower. The army was deafening, their armour and relentless march a cacophony of thundering boots and rattling metal. Peering through the hole, Grarfath looked upon the same army he had observed invading Erador weeks earlier. Just as the wizard had predicted, the Andarens were leaving Erador without further campaign, their objective complete.

That objective could be seen in the middle of that dark sea of bronze and black. With a mobile ballista guarding each of its corners, a single crate rested on a platform being towed by one of the catapults and dozens of mutated horses. By its size, the smith guessed the crate to be large enough to fit a Giant inside. It had to be the skeleton, the one Yamnomora's companions had spoken of.

The Skaramangians were that much closer to the victory The Green Leaf had forewarned. And they were that much closer to rolling over the dwarves. Given how precious their cargo was, the Andarens wouldn't stop for anyone. It was entirely possible they would see the dwarves as a threat, not realising from afar that they weren't an army. Grarfath imagined those catapults at work, decimating his people at a distance.

Then he didn't need to imagine.

He heard the machine straining before spotting it, the great lever moving into position.

"No!" he growled.

Without further delay, the smith plummeted the hammer into the stone and ported back to the dwarven line. A collective gasp met his return, though he still heard some of the louder voices insisting that he had abandoned them.

"Incoming!" he called out.

As one, the dwarves before him looked up to the sky at his back. With dread in his bones, Grarfath turned around. Sailing with a promise of death, the Andarens had hurled their first missile, and it was coming for the son of Thronghir.

63
SELLING THE LIE

0 Years Ago...

4

The Vahlken feared sleep in the days that followed The Valtorak's funeral. It was there, in his dreams, that he walked through halls of memory that were not his own. He would always wake up and require several minutes to collect his thoughts and ground himself in the present.

Daijen had thought to forgo sleep altogether, giving himself a few days without Ahnir's ancient life pressing on him, but he was still exhausted from his interaction with the bone and all the violence that had followed. And so, like an ordinary Andaren, he had taken to his cot every night and slumbered until the dawn.

During his waking hours, however, the Vahlken set himself to a singular task: unravelling Ahnir's memories. They were inside his mind, a web of events that each held their own revelations. There seemed a clear path before him, yet he could not see it through the mess of tangled memories.

After raiding the keep for any and all blank parchments, along with pots of ink and several quills, Daijen had taken over every inch of wall space in his room. Days would go by without word from the others. He wouldn't even glimpse them as he ventured out in need of food and water—both necessities and never a luxury. Using some string he found in a supply cupboard in the armoury, he connected the parchments on his walls, creating a physical timeline.

It all took so long to put together, each memory threatening to rob him of the present. Again and again he was forced to rely on deep meditation to tease out the memory and remain grounded.

"No one wants to look in the shadows," he would say to himself, recalling The Valtorak's words from years earlier when he first learned of the Skaramangian threat. "We alone must tread where others dare not. We alone must bring the light."

It had become a mantra for him, his master's voice a clearing breeze in his mind.

Still, it was all the harder when trying to piece together what he had learned through Ahnir with what he had learned in his own life, but he knew so much of what he had heard during the Ankala now made sense.

"*The days are shadowed by approaching night,*" he said aloud, reading from a parchment he had used to write down one of the many visions. "*The war to devour all wars has come again.*" The Vahlken thought of the war he had witnessed, fought furiously between the Dragon Riders and The Dark One.

"*He who lies entombed in the dark will rise, and the fires with him. Death cannot hold him.*" Daijen naturally thought of Azadguul, a place now referred to as The Tomb. Even so, he could not make sense of the words and all he had seen in that terrible place.

"*He will stand amidst four pillars of his own creation, and with them he will harness the power of the world. Of every world.*" He followed a thread from that parchment to a drawing of the four Golems. He tapped it twice. "*He will stand amidst four pillars of his own creation,*" he repeated, knowing now that the vision had referred to Ahnir and his brothers, who would look like enormous black pillars beside anyone.

Moving across the wall, he stood before another array of parchments, his attention focusing on just one of them. *"Six there were, and six there are. Tempered by magic, they hold his voice in their hearts."*

The Vahlken paced his room, one hand cupping his strong jaw. *"Six there were and six there are,"* he repeated. "Six... tempered by magic." The choice of words made him think of steel, which led him to weapons. The visions, however, would not be talking about any old weapons.

With a new piece of thread, Daijen connected the parchment to another set of drawings on the other side of the room. There he looked upon The Anther, wielded by Duun, Dawnbreaker, the sword once used by Nathara, the nameless axe always in Gelakor's hand, the vambrace, taken from Qirann's lifeless arm, and, finally, the Helm of Ahnir, the only weapon Skara failed to complete.

That was five.

Daijen picked up his latest sketch from where it lay on his small table. He examined the parchment before pinning it to the wall so it slightly overlapped The Anther. Stepping back, he now looked at six drawings, but the last one was not a weapon or a piece of armour.

Based on what he had seen during Skara's final moments and the mould that had sat beside the Helm of Ahnir, the Vahlken had replicated the necklace taken from The Dark One's corpse by his apprentice. He only had black ink, however, so he had been unable to replicate the red ruby or the green stone that sat at its heart.

"What do you do?" he asked, the image consuming his entire view. *"They hold his voice in their hearts,"* he said again, his gaze turning to land on one particular sketch pinned to the wall behind his door. It was the messiest drawing of them all, but it still captured The Dark One robed and hooded in black, the shadows drawn to him.

Looking back at the six sketches, he reminded himself that, for the most part, they were gifted to the Riders when Skara was still counted among them. Ultimately, they were his. It was Skara's voice they held in their stony hearts, each waiting—like his devout followers—for The Dark One's return.

Daijen shook his head, seeing no possible way for Skara to exist in the present day.

Pivoting on the spot, he turned his attention to another parchment. "*Break the crystal, break the world,*" he read aloud.

The writing was connected by a length of thread to another drawing depicting Mount Athan. The Vahlken wasn't convinced he had made the right connection between the two, but the mountain —famous for its coating of impenetrable crystal—was an obvious conclusion. Even even more so when he consulted Ahnir's memories and the events that took place in the bowels of Azad-guul.

"*If it's not malleable,*" Skara had raged, referring to the leaves of red crystal taken from another realm, "*I cannot construct the shell! Without a shell, I cannot contain the heart within! Do you know what happens then?*"

His apprentice had replied, "*I have seen Mount Athan with my own eyes, my lord.*"

"*You have seen nothing,*" The Dark One had assured him. "*Pray that you never do.*"

It seemed a fair deduction in Daijen's eyes that Skara had been referring to his initial attempts at constructing the rubies—made from the mysterious leaves—and the colourful stones that kept being referred to as *hearts*. Why these stones required a shell the Vahlken could not say, but The Dark One certainly implied that something catastrophic might happen if the shell failed to contain it. Why that had led to Mount Athan being imprisoned beneath inches of crystal lay beyond Daijen's apprehension. All he knew for sure was that breaking the crystal had been seen to break the world.

Moving to the patch of wall beside his window, the Vahlken read one of the more obscure visions that, even after all he had seen, made no sense. "*The oldest demon from the oldest world slumbers beneath stone and bone.*" He paused, the last three words jumping out at him for the first time. "The stone bones," he muttered, naming the dwarves by a colloquial term. It stood to reason that the vision was referring to something beneath The Mountains of Morthil, which led him to the skeleton Mordrith had discovered in its depths. It seemed odd to Daijen, however, that the Golem would be called the oldest demon from the oldest world. Still, there was something in there about the dwarves. He just couldn't see it yet.

"*The waters will boil and the seas will rise,*" he continued, reading the rest. "*It cannot be tamed, it cannot be harnessed. It has no master but hunger.*" He stopped again, sure that such a description did not fit any of the Golems. "*The Dawnbreaker will bring about everlasting night,*" he went on. "*Doom to the seas. Doom to the lands. Doom to the skies. The Black Abyss rises.*"

While mention of the Dawnbreaker had meant nothing to those gathered in the imperial throne room during the Ankala, including Daijen at the time, he now knew that Skara's sword had a part to play in unfolding events. If only he could say who would be wielding it and how they were able to use it to doom so much.

Then there was the wording. Something slumbered beneath the earth. The seas would rise. The Black Abyss would rise. Whether the vision spoke literally or metaphorically remained to be seen. Either way, it painted a dark picture.

If that hadn't been made clear after thousands of violent deaths, there was another vision that had repeated throughout those bloody days.

"*The skies will rain with blood,*" Daijen whispered, his eyes following the words along the next piece of parchment. "*Dragons will fall. Aegres will fall. The heavens will fall.*" The Vahlken couldn't help but think of Maegar and the other dragons who had already been slain in the Riders' civil war. And Aramis, of course, whose death would forever sit heavily on Daijen's heart.

Pressing on with his investigation, he read the rest of the vision. "*He will wipe away the lines on the map, and the first empire will rise again.*"

Impossible as it seemed, there was only one *he* who it could be referring to. Only Skara had the scope of vision to wipe away the lines on the map and build an empire from scratch. He could feel his own desires mounting at the thought of it, of such a world. Daijen shut his eyes and clenched his fists while he focused on his breathing.

Daring to open his eyes again, he was relieved to see that he was still standing in his room. Deciding he would come back to the collected visions he felt referred directly to The Dark One, Daijen navigated the crossing threads to another area on the wall, where he had collated anything spoken about the so-called *chosen one*.

"*The broken circle will live up to its blood and break the cycle of war,*" he read. "*One will stand between the two, for the two. Rider, Vahlken. Rider, Vahlken. Rider, Vahlken.*" Those two titles repeated again and again, suggesting that the *one* would be both. Or, he considered, as The Valtorak would, the future had yet to be decided as to which *the one* would be.

Moving along the wall, he voiced the various visions. "*She will ride scales and feathers. He will master talon and claw. Only he can end the war. She stands between two worlds, a saviour and destroyer to both.*"

He recalled The Valtorak's perspective on the matter, that they were trying to interpret a possible future, a future in which the child in question had yet to be born. Had they been born since then? Daijen could only wonder, frustrated that there was still so much he didn't know. It didn't seem fair, given all that had been sacrificed to learn what he had.

Standing before the last vision that had spoken of the chosen one, Daijen read it in his mind before he was set to pacing, repeating the words aloud. "*Only he who stands in the shadow of kings can bridge the broken circle. Only he can usher in a new age of heroes. Only he can bring about a time of dragons.*"

Damned if he could make sense of it.

Daijen sighed and resisted the urge to kick his chair across the room. He was sure it all pointed to something real, something tangible. If only he could understand it all, he might be able to actually locate the child and help to usher them along their destined path.

The sound of boots striding across stone pulled at his attention, drawing his eyes to the closed door. For just a moment, he feared there was no one really there, that he was hearing footsteps from eons past as another memory overwhelmed him.

His fears abated when he recognised that particular stride, his sister's gait all too familiar. Daijen opened the door as she arrived at the threshold, though he was sure to obscure her view of his work.

"Ilithranda," he said after clearing his throat. "Where are the others?" he asked, glancing over her shoulder.

"They weren't sure who they'd find up here, so they sent me."

Daijen couldn't hide his deflation. "They don't trust me," he reasoned.

"They trust *Daijen Saeth*," Ilithranda told him confidently. "We just don't know where he's gone."

"I'm right here," he said.

"Were you *right there* when you killed The Valtorak?" his sister countered.

When he had no reply, Ilithranda tried to push past him. "What are you doing?" he questioned sharply.

"Move, or *be* moved."

Daijen was too exhausted to run through a fight in his mind and, in truth, he wasn't sure who would emerge the victor. Stepping to one side, he allowed Ilithranda to enter his room. She walked to the middle of his room and slowly turned on the spot, taking it all in.

"What is this?"

Daijen's gaze roamed over one of the walls, and he shrugged at the question. "My futile attempt to make sense of everything I saw."

Ilithranda's attention shifted to him. "That's why they sent me," she clarified. "There's no reason to stay here any longer. They want to know where they should go next. They were hoping you saw something in the past that might give them some direction."

Her tone and choice of words struck him. "*They*? What about you?"

His sister said nothing for a time. "I'm tired of this fight. The Skaramangians. The Dark Ones. The war within the war." She sounded as exhausted as he felt. "I'm going south with Oaken. I'll find Tovun and see to it that he completes his training. It's what The Valtorak would have wanted and the last thing I can do for him—for the order."

Daijen was taken aback by her intended course, honourable though it was. "And after that?"

Those violet eyes wandered over his scribbles and drawings, not really seeing any of them. "I don't know," she confessed. "Maybe I'll go back to actually fighting the war everyone thinks we're fighting. It doesn't really matter anymore. None of it does."

Learning she was Slait's mother had undone the Vahlken to an extent, though Daijen was too cautious to voice as much. He couldn't imagine what it would be like to learn he was anyone's father, let alone someone as brutal and sadistic as Slait.

"Do any of them know?" he enquired lightly. "About Slait?"

"No," Ilithranda was quick to reply. "Androma knows that I left a baby behind when I departed Aran'saur the first time. Neither she nor the others will ever know more than that."

Daijen bowed his head, knowing now what Androma had alluded to when she'd spoken of their shared loss. "If I see him again," he began hesitantly, "I can't promise I won't—"

"You will do whatever you deem needs to be done," Ilithranda cut in. "As you always have," she added, her words barbed. "Slait's fate is his own, as it's ever been," the Vahlken went on, her tone clipped, suggesting she was putting the subject to bed. "But you've proved yourself the better warrior, maybe even the best. I hope that will be enough for you."

"It's not about who's the best," Daijen countered, feeling there was an important distinction to be made. "It's about what he deserves."

"I know what he *deserves*," Ilithranda insisted. "Just as I know that you will see to it." When Daijen opened his mouth to speak again, his sister raised her palm and took a breath to collect herself.

"Aphrandhor said to give you time. They've waited. *I've* waited. Now you need to tell me what you learned from the bone. In time, the others might permit you to travel with them again—"

"No," Daijen interjected.

"No?"

"This fight was meant for the Vahlken. I was wrong to bring them into this."

"This fight is for everyone," Ilithranda pointed out, even if she was choosing to exclude herself. "And you didn't bring them in. They were already fighting the Skaramangians."

Daijen wouldn't hear it. "None of them can do what we can do. Handuin made us this way for a reason. I should have seen the truth of that sooner. Maybe then we wouldn't have met Aphrandhor and I would never have used the vambrace and The Valtorak would still be..."

The chain of events was there to see, and it could all be laid at Daijen's feet.

Ilithranda stepped closer. "I'm not staying in this fight, Daijen. Don't rob yourself of allies now."

"Allies who don't trust me? And rightfully so." He shook his head. "The path ahead is my own. They will be safer fighting the Skaramangians their own way. Without me."

"How will they be safer fighting the enemy so blind? You have seen the past, yes? You must know where their weaknesses lie. What blow might cripple their efforts. You must know what needs to be done!"

Daijen had to step away, feeling the weight of Ahnir's life pressing on his mind. It was so much harder to focus with Ilithranda in the room. "If they stay by my side, they will all die. It's that simple."

"It's too late for that."

"No! They were doing just fine before they met us. All of them. Let them fight the Skaramangians their own way."

"What good does it do them if they're fighting in the wrong place? They're more likely to die because they don't know enough,

Daijen. And what good does it do the war if all their efforts are wasted against an insignificant target?"

"What does it matter to you?" Daijen questioned, biting back. "You're running away, remember?"

Ilithranda closed the gap between them with frightening speed, her forearm pinning Daijen to the back wall, making a mess of his numerous threads. In his face, she bared her teeth and revealed a sliver of the fury that burned behind her eyes.

"I have been fighting for over two hundred years," she fumed. "My body has more scar tissue than anything else. So don't talk to me about running away. I've done nothing but charge into battle after battle after battle. You've been a Vahlken most of your life. I've fought in more battles than you've lived in years, and I did so without a scrap of Handuin's power. I am owed. Do you understand? I am owed something of this life that doesn't include so much bloodshed."

Then the Vahlken backed away from her brother as quickly as she had rammed into him.

"What did you see?" she asked again, gesturing at the parchments covering every inch of wall space.

Daijen held that question in his mind for a moment—such a simple thing. Yet the answer was so vast he felt he needed an entire lifetime to tell her everything. And what if he did? What would Ilithranda do with all that knowledge? Like the others, she would get herself killed. Let them keep searching for the Dark Ones and all the other myths the Skaramangians had conjured over the eons, false breadcrumbs to lead their enemies astray. Their ignorance would prevent them from ever becoming a serious threat in The Eldan's eyes.

It wasn't much, but it was all Daijen could do now to give them a chance at life.

"I saw nothing," he lied.

Ilithranda turned on him, disbelief etched across her face. "Nothing? *This* is all nothing?" she spat, tearing one of the parchments from the wall.

"There's nothing on there you don't already know," Daijen told her, aware that she held one of the visions they had both been present for.

Ilithranda snatched at two of the surviving threads. "Then what about this? Or those?" She was pointing at his many drawings. "What did you see, Daijen?"

A spark of anger flared inside him, driving him threateningly towards her. "I saw..." Eye to eye, Daijen immediately lost his bluster, aware that she was infuriating him for a reason. "I saw nothing of any use," he said, deflating.

Ilithranda pressed her finger into his cuirass. "I don't believe you."

Daijen glanced over his days of work. "Look at all this. It looks worse in my head. I have no idea where to start. It could take years to make sense of it all. Decades, even. And that's without..." He trailed off before trying to explain the ways in which Ahnir was influencing him, for it would require him to reveal the truth of the so-called *god*.

"I saw a lot," he admitted. "But I saw nothing that will give them any direction," the Vahlken added, being as sincere as he could with the lie.

A wave of disappointment washed over Ilithranda, her expression as crushing as any blow. "Then it was all for nothing," she whispered.

The temptation to tell her everything surged inside of Daijen, his pride wading through all thought and emotion to see him elevated in her eyes once more. But the Vahlken could still feel the resistance as he plunged his atori blade into The Valtorak's chest. What could be more sobering, more humbling, than that? And so he kept his lips sealed and embraced his sister's sheer disappointment in him.

"I'm sorry," he uttered, the word too small to make a real difference.

Ilithranda turned away, slowly returning to the open doorway. She paused there, as if remembering something, her right hand probing the pouches on her belt.

"Here," she said, removing a small book. "I have no need of it. Maybe you can make all of this mean something."

Daijen caught the book in one hand, recognising it as the journal Emperor Qeledred had given to his daughter. Its edges were frayed, the paper discoloured, and the leather binding rough and scratched at the corners. Its contents, however, were to be a matter of great consideration given the number of emperors who had scribed its pages.

By the time he looked up, Ilithranda was gone. With one hand gripping the doorframe, it took every ounce of strength Daijen had to stay where he was and not go after her. He was keeping them all as safe as he could by letting them go. The Vahlken repeated that to himself—and would for some time.

64

THE PENDAIN

Seconds burned into minutes. Minutes toiled into hours. Hours stretched into days. Untold, they were, in the secret depths of Nareene.

Cob had staggered their rests, ensuring there were always two awake while the others slept in Azad-guul's dark bowels. The ranger had spent almost every waking moment on his feet, searching hopelessly for a way out of that vast and empty chamber.

While he didn't know exactly how the magic worked, the Kedradi had even delved into Gallien's satchel, searching through its seemingly endless depths for anything useful. He discovered years' worth of scrolls, books, and a few items of spare clothing— nothing to help them escape. Ultimately, they had used Gallien's red dragon scale to spark a fire amongst the many pages and loose sheets of parchment. The ranger would have gone on to root through the wizard's enchanted satchel, but it seemed the bag had been lost during their fight in Taraktor.

Nevertheless, their captors brought them food and water, though the great doors never opened without a dozen armed men and women on the other side. Most of them watched the Kedradi for the entire exchange, clearly informed of his skill and the danger he posed. Soon, their stern gaze and pointed spears wouldn't be enough to hold him back. The drums would demand action.

They would demand blood.

His eyes had snapped open to the distant sound of them when last he woke. They were so real he had even searched for them in the alcoves and balconies above. As ever, they originated deep in his soul, where that most ancient of curses had been cast upon every male of House Thayne since the fall of Kanofell, millennia before his birth.

With one hand pressed to the cold, damp wall, he could even *feel* the beat of the drums through the stone. There was no outrunning it, and there was no ending it, not when he was trapped like some animal.

An animal...

That's what he would become. The madness would take him, mind and body, and unleash him upon his companions. He would rip them apart with his bare hands, clawing at them with his fingers if he had to. The ranger clenched his fist against the wall, pressing until his knuckles began to bleed.

"How long do you think we've been down here?" Joran asked in a whisper, cutting through the spiralling well he had fallen into.

Cob turned to face the boy. He had tended to Gallien as much as the ranger had searched in vain for a way out. Having the smuggler to take care of had been a good distraction for him, taking his mind from their isolation and captivity.

The ranger could still see his fear. All that brimming energy couldn't hide it, though it seemed his half-blood physiology had been well used elsewhere. Standing before him now, the cut and bruise to Joran's head were all but gone, and his arm...

The Kedradi had watched in silent amazement over the last few days, observing what he knew to be a broken arm heal almost completely. While mixed with that of a human, his Vahlken blood was hardly watered down, its mutated properties offering the boy abilities beyond the norm.

"Days," he eventually answered. "A week or more, perhaps."

"Why do you think they're just keeping us here?" Joran had voiced that same question to both Androma and Aphrandhor over the last couple of days and found no answers.

"You can never say with the Skaramangians. Secrets are their ways."

Joran nodded along, his apprehension palpable. "Something tells me it isn't for anything good," he remarked.

The ranger managed a tight smile despite the building pressure of his curse. "You have good instincts, Joran Pendain. You should have been born a Kedradi." The boy looked at him intently. "What?" Cob asked.

Joran softened his expression. "It's nothing. It's just... No one's ever called me by my name before. It's a strange thing to hear."

"We don't get to choose our names," the ranger replied before looking at Gallien, curled up between the others. "Whatever your circumstances, that man raised you. He is your father..."

Cob trailed off, stunned to silence by the apparition that stood behind Joran. "Baba?" he breathed, looking at the ghost of his own father.

Adonis Thayne grinned wickedly at his son, his eyes alight with violent glee as he put one finger to his lips, bidding the ranger say nothing while he gripped the boy by his chin and behind his head. The Kedradi started forward, compelled to stop his father, but he was too slow to act.

Snap!

In the same instance that Joran fell to the ground, his neck broken, the waking nightmare ceased altogether. Adonis Thayne was gone, and Joran was left looking at him, confused by the ranger's sudden step forwards. The boy's lips moved, shaping into a question, but his words were so distant as not to be heard at all.

He was running out of time.

Over the sound of the ethereal drums, the great doors ground open, and with a touch of theatricality not seen when their food and water were delivered. The sound awoke Androma and The

Green Leaf, while it appeared Gallien was already awake, his blank stare piercing Azad-guul's walls.

His personal slip into madness had been dramatic compared to the drip-drip of Cob's curse. The boundaries placed inside his mind, as Aphrandhor had explained it, were combating the memories desperate to surface. The wizard took it as proof that the smuggler had visited Azad-guul in his past. His father's spells would be the end of him if his current condition was anything to go by.

With swords already in hand, two rows of Skaramangian soldiers entered the tall chamber, though they were not of those above who safeguarded the island. There was an elegance and grace in their steps, a strength in the way they held themselves. Their faces were hidden within silver helms that revealed no more than their eyes, while their bodies were protected behind white cuirasses and scarlet battle skirts. Hanging from their belts, they each sported a small leather-bound book accented with gold to match the chain that tethered it.

The cleric guard! The Kedradi recalled their ilk chasing them out of Warth upon meeting Gallien and Joran for the first time, and all by the lead of The Dancing Sword of the Dawn.

Cob felt his heart quicken. With Joran at his side, he moved to rejoin his companions as the guards reordered themselves into a new formation. Moving within the safety of their ranks, another Andaren entered the chamber. Unlike the guard, he wore a helm of bronze and gold that flared on each side into the style of a bird's wings. So too did his robes of dark red set him apart from his protectors, identifying him as the master cleric. The ranger knew he went by another name, the title unearthed before his time.

The Eldan came to a stop before reaching the five companions, his golden eyes roaming over them until, at last, they landed on Gallien in their midst, While the others had risen to meet their captors, he remained curled up on the floor. The wizard leaned into Androma's ear, explaining who had entered the chamber while Cob positioned himself at the ready.

The Eldan's bejewelled hand rose up from within his red robes to cup his bronze mask. As he lifted it from his head, white hair, pure as snow, cascaded down past his chest. His features were handsome and sharp, a common characteristic among Andarens. His chalky-white skin and smooth complexion would have put him in his early thirties were he a human. As it was, his actual age could not be calculated by the ranger's eyes.

"I applaud your efforts," The Eldan began, his voice as smooth as his skin and as rich as his attire. "For such a small band, you have proved yourselves to be quite the adversary. The order has not faced a quarry of such calibre since the Vahlken. I suppose it was inevitable that you would follow in their footsteps and fall short."

"Not all the Vahlken are dead," Androma stated flatly.

The Eldan's gaze shifted to the blind Rider. "Are you so sure?" he retorted, a sharp smile cutting through his marble-like face.

"We aren't the only ones out there fighting you," The Green Leaf announced. "Killing us won't save your dark future."

"Kill you?" The Eldan echoed. "You have been troublesome, yes, but I did not travel across land and sea just to kill you. I think it better that you bear witness to the glory that every Skaramangian has ever died fighting for."

Two more Andarens entered the chamber, their strides deliberate and slow, as if they were part of a holy ceremony. Cob looked over The Eldan's shoulder to see that each held a cushion, upon which were the weapons of power taken from Joran and Aphrandhor. The vambrace and broken sword were brought to The Eldan's side, where he could look over them at his leisure.

"Long have my predecessors searched for these," he explained. "One, lost to the depths of the ocean, beyond even the reach of our allies there. And the other," he said, picking up the bracer with delicate fingers. "Well, the other tells a tale unlike any of its cousins. Its story begins in Akmar, found there by the Jainus. I believe you are familiar with this part of its history, wizard.

"Of course, it does not end there," The Eldan went on, enjoying himself by the look of it. "There was a burglar afoot. A man—just a man—walks into The Silver Trees of Akmar and *takes* it. Enter the hunters," he intoned mockingly. "They track the thief down, return the vambrace to the Jainus, and doom the man to torment in the halls of Taraktor. *But!* The bracer's tale does not end there. No, no, no. The bracer's role in all things is to uncover their history, and so it did.

"Enter Aphrandhor of Blood Ganleif, son of Rynold and Diani!" The Eldan declared, holding his free hand out to the wizard. "Don't look so surprised. Is it not prudent to know one's enemy? The Jainus had such hopes for you, Green Leaf. They saw the Magus in your future. They didn't realise how unpredictable you are. Nor did we," he added with a mirthless laugh. "We did not foresee that any would use the bracer and lay bare the minds of our agents in Akmar. But thank goodness you did," he said, beaming with real joy.

"The bracer's tale continues, leaving Akmar in your hands. What adventures it went on. What marvels it has revealed to you. Not everyone can handle the past. Your friend Daijen would attest to that," he quipped, naming the Vahlken Cob had only ever heard of. "How wonderful that you should get embroiled in the life of young Joran here."

The drums weren't enough to rob the ranger of his protective instincts, and he adjusted his stance to put him between The Eldan and the boy that much more.

"You are tied up in events even I do not understand yet," The Eldan said directly to him. "Alas, I digress. Enter, the smuggler!" His pale head tilted to one side so his golden eyes could settle on Gallien behind the group. "I assume you found your way to Taraktor because of him," he continued, looking to Aphrandhor. "Are you with us, Gallien? Gallien *Pendain*. He suffers," the Andaren observed, more curious than concerned.

"You will learn nothing from us," The Green Leaf stated defiantly.

His head still at an angle, The Eldan's bright eyes shifted across to Aphrandhor as a smug grin stretched his lips. "That's where you're wrong. Seize them."

As one, the cleric guard advanced on the companions. By the edge of a blade, Cob was lowered to his knees with the rest of them and forced to watch as The Eldan allowed one of his servants to fit him with the vambrace.

"Knowledge has ever been the greatest weapon at our disposal," he said, marvelling at the armour on his arm. "With knowledge, you can make sense of the truth. It's astonishing how such a thing can be used to confuse the masses, to steer entire civilisations. You can bend it, break it, *withhold* it. But first, you must possess the truth." He looked down at The Green Leaf. "What truth do you possess?"

Without hesitation, he placed his thumb in the centre of Aphrandhor's brow, his fingers cupping the side of his head. The Eldan sucked in a breath and closed his eyes. The transaction took no more than a couple of seconds and left the Andaren stumbling back into his servant's arms. He blinked hard and several times, his mind reconciling past and present. Still, his Andaren mind had the ability to stretch for centuries, allowing him to recover that much quicker.

"I see," he rasped, slow to reassume his full height. Standing over them once more, he laughed to himself, the sound carrying up to the shadows above. "A tale unlike any other," he uttered again, gazing at the bracer on his arm. "Incredible." The Andaren whipped his head around. "Bring it up!" he commanded.

Rough hands grabbed under Cob's arms, as they did with the others, and forced them all away from the heart of the chamber before turning them around. On his knees again, the ranger watched The Eldan stroll around the edge of the circular seam that ringed the centre. And the Andaren was not all he saw.

Again, Adonis of House Thayne walked among them, stalking between the cleric guard. His dark eyes never strayed from Cob as he removed the dagger from one of the Andarens' belts. He put the blade to his mouth and licked the steel until it cut his tongue, the touch of it bringing him delight.

"It would be so easy," he purred in Ked, their native language. "Think what you could do with steel in your hands, son. You would be invincible." His father slaughtered them one after another, plunging the dagger into eyes, throats, and hearts.

The ranger shut his eyes and concentrated on his breathing. He knew full well what would happen if he fought with steel, an act that would only fuel the curse and hasten his descent into madness. When he opened his eyes again, Adonis was gone and the Andarens remained on their feet, intact and still very much armed.

At that moment, the stone beneath their knees began to tremble. Dust rained down from the unseen ceiling. The pyramid groaned like an ancient beast waking from an age of slumber.

"Oh no," The Green Leaf whispered hoarsely beside him.

From depths unknown, a colossal tower of black stone rose from the heart of the chamber. The first forty feet were naught but blank stone, its grooves designed to pair it with those likely in the ceiling. Below that, the gargantuan cylinder was lined with countless alcoves, each matted in cobwebs.

"Stop!" The Eldan's voice boomed.

The would-be pillar came to a slow halt, such that only the first two rows of alcoves rose above the floor. Only then did Cob see the alcoves for what they were—tombs. Each housed a skeleton— most ancient ones by the look of them.

The Eldan walked along the alcoves, his eyes wandering over the numbers above each. "Like the rest of the world, Green Leaf, you had truth without knowledge. And what were you to do with that truth if you didn't have all the facts? You did what everyone else does and followed it through to the wrong conclusion."

The Andaren came to a stop in front of Gallien, who had been left where he lay.

"Leave him alone!" Joran called out. The guard at his back pulled on his hair and pressed his sword up against the flat of his jaw.

The Eldan crouched beside Gallien. "He's been alone for far too long," he muttered pityingly. The Andaren rose once more and looked over the kneeling company before him. He chuckled softly to himself. "All these years we've been fighting each other, always wondering, *fearing*, how much the other really knew." He laughed with zeal this time. "You knew *nothing*. You've been here before, in this very chamber, and you still don't understand its significance. Do you know who they were?" he asked, gesturing to the skeletons. "These men and women of history."

Cob's attention was momentarily pulled away by the voice in his ear. "Get off your knees," his father insisted, right there beside him. "Get off your knees and slaughter them like pigs."

"For the most part," The Eldan explained, "they were ordinary people. Just men and women living their lives on Verda's green earth. But, at some point in their dull and dreary lives, they each exhibited dangerous levels of magic. If it didn't kill them, it killed those around them. Such explosive displays of magic are how we've continued to find them over the millennia. We were always too many steps behind," he lamented.

"Then we hear of a similar display, some years ago. In Taraktor. A prisoner defies every ward, spell, and hunter to break out of an unbreakable prison. Bragen Pendain," he clarified, tapping the side of his head as he looked at Aphrandhor. "*Pendain*," The Eldan repeated. "An old name. A *sacred* name to us. Some of these men and women once called themselves such. Another marker we used to track them down, but always too late.

"How long, I wonder, would you have searched for Bragen Pendain?" he pondered. "How long before you realised... you had already found him?"

Cob retained enough of his wits to know that didn't make any sense. He turned to his companions, seeing their confusion mirrored his own.

The Eldan nodded at the handful of servants lingering by the main doors, and they snapped to attention, rushing over. They began to manhandle Gallien, stripping him down to his trousers and naught else.

"What are you doing?" Joran yelled.

Ignoring the boy, The Eldan removed the bracer from his arm and went about fitting it to Gallien's.

"This is madness!" the wizard barked, fighting against his captor.

"You know what this is," The Eldan replied calmly. "This is where he will remember who he is."

The Andaren stepped aside and indicated for the servants to take the smuggler to the alcove numbered *1*. Masked and nameless, one of the servants took Gallien's only hand and placed it on the skeleton inside. The smuggler gasped, a display of life he hadn't shown in many days. The servants braced him, keeping him connected to the skeleton.

Then he began to groan.

Then he screamed.

Then he *roared*.

The servants were hurled away at terrifying speed, their bodies shattered from the inside out before they skidded across the floor. The stone pillar cracked in every direction, and a handful of skeletons were broken into pieces as an unnatural wind swept through the chamber, wrapping around the great column to disturb the torchlight.

The Eldan was beaming from ear to ear.

Gallien's display of raw magic ended as suddenly as it began. The smuggler crumpled to the stone, his chest heaving rapidly. His skin, slick with sweat, was steaming.

"I can't imagine it," The Eldan said softly, breaking the silence that followed. "All those years, the centuries, the millennia. Even an Andaren mind could not hold so much. How did you describe it?" he asked, glancing at The Green Leaf. "A broken mirror, yes. No two pieces fitting together. An apt description, I'm sure, though your interpretation was a little off."

Gallien began spasming on the floor, his body in the grip of a seizure.

"What's happening to him?" Joran cried, defying the blade against his throat.

"The wizard would have you believe his mind is battling the spells of his father, of Bragen Pendain," The Eldan replied. "I would wager Bragen Pendain is among our friends here," he said, gesturing at the skeletons.

"What's he saying?" Androma questioned, her head tilted towards Aphrandhor.

"Skaramangian lies," the wizard fumed.

The Eldan offered the old man a pitying smile. "I've no need to lie, Green Leaf. We've already won," he insisted, one hand extended towards Gallien. "You brought him back to us. *The Dark One.*"

It was a cold and barbed hand that reached up inside Cob and grabbed him heart and soul. Beside him, both Aphrandhor and Androma were frozen in shock, mouths ajar. With just a handful of words, their world had been turned upside down.

"Ah, yes," the Andaren drawled, seeing their shattering surprise. "You believed our efforts were made in search of the Dark Ones, the beasts who challenged the very gods. A deliberate translation error, I'm afraid. There are no gods. There are no beasts. There is only *him*. And his *children*," he added with a mischievous grin. "Of whom, we now possess three of the four. He will be most pleased," he asserted, looking down at Gallien.

"You lie!" The Green Leaf blurted.

The Eldan ignored the accusation. "You can't fathom the time we've spent searching for him. He's tumbled through time, always moving on, always forgetting where he came from and who he really is."

Crouching by the smuggler's side, The Eldan ran a hand through the air just above his blond head. "The burden of so much *life*. The bodies might change but the mind remains the same, breaking a little bit more with every new body."

Gallien's back arched with the latest spasm, sending The Eldan into retreat before arcing bolts of blue lightning rippled out from his body.

"I should thank you for returning the vambrace as well," The Eldan remarked. "Without it, his oldest memories would have remained beyond his reach." The Andaren pressed one hand to alcove *1*. "His last apprentice," he said affectionately. "He was there when the final blow was struck. He willingly gave up his life and body so The Dark One might live in his flesh."

Aphrandhor was shaking his head. "This... This is impossible."

"Forgive me. I have given you more truth without the knowledge to understand it. It might have all made more sense had you uncovered the last weapon of power—the *necklace*. You must have seen the drawings in his cell, as we did. It's the only relic he's carried with him through the ages. Until now, of course.

"Our best guess is that he hid the necklace when the Jainus began hunting him. Untold years trapped in a time spell, combined with routine questioning and torture, has a way of fragmenting the mind. Add that to a mind already cracking under the weight of his previous lives," he said, gesturing at the many skeletons, "and the weapon remains lost to us all."

"You're wrong!" Joran yelled. "He's Gallien Pendain! He's my father!"

"As we speak, boy, your *father* is dying. Everything that he was—everything you knew of him—is being drowned in memory. And not just any memory. The *purest* memory. Before his mind was diluted by time and hardship," the Eldan detailed, waving one hand at the skeletons. "When he was the closest to his true self, before the Riders destroyed his original body."

"No!" Joran forced the blade from his neck, slicing his hand open, and bolted forwards. He made it no more than two steps before other guards stepped in and detained him.

"Yes," The Eldan countered firmly. "You think his father gave him his name? He hasn't had a father for thousands of years. The man he remembers—even the brother he remembers—is just himself from another time, another life. Don't you get it yet? There's only so much the fragile human mind can hold," he told them again. "Only so much memory before everything... spills over and evaporates. You can cling to years—decades, even. But centuries? Millennia? Impossible. He walked out of Taraktor and started a new life as a soldier with naught but fog in his past. Yet a single trace of his true self has passed down through almost every host. It was his first title. Given to him by the people of Verda."

"The *Pen... Dain.*" The Andaren spread out his arms. "The *First Rider!*"

The Green Leaf physically sagged on his knees, his spirit breaking in front of their eyes. "That's... That can't be."

"Skara Pendain shaped this world long before us. He gave us magic. He gave us dragons. And he would have given us peace, had he not been betrayed by his fellow Riders. That peace is what every Skaramangian fights for. And it begins here, now!"

"I'm getting bored," Adonis Thayne uttered in Cob's ear. "Let's open them up and see what falls out."

"You're not real," the Kedradi stated through clenched teeth.

Gallien roared again, his entire body now levitating off the floor. The magic that tore free of him blasted everything in the chamber, launching all of them, The Eldan included, across the stone. So too did it impact Gallien's satchel left by their makeshift camp. The raw magic broke the spells etched into the rough leather, and the satchel exploded, its uncountable contents scattered in every direction.

Feeling like he'd been struck by a battering ram, Cob rolled over and looked up, drawn to movement.

Gallien was on his feet now, head bowed, body steaming. Fresh blood soaked through the bandage covering his wrist, the droplets amassing on the floor.

He was holding the axe, its copper blade alight with purple runes and bright shards.

"Gallien!" Aphrandhor croaked, stumbling to his feet as he rushed to meet the smuggler. The wizard crashed into him, ensnaring the man in a tight embrace. "You must fight it, my boy. Whatever they're doing, you *must* fight it."

Gallien pulled away, his eyes scrutinising The Green Leaf, as if he were looking for something he might recall in the old man. He smiled, his expression genuine and warm.

"Yes," Aphrandhor said eagerly, hopefully. "Fight it."

"You wanted to see the whole me," Gallien replied, his voice not quite his own.

Then he ran the axe across Aphrandhor's throat, slicing through the paper-thin skin.

It was a silent gasp of sheer disbelief that escaped Cob's lips.

Blood poured out of the wizard, drenching his green robes and splattering across the floor. The Green Leaf fell to his knees at Gallien's feet before death took him and his body crumpled to one side.

All eyes fell on Gallien—on Skara.

On *The Dark One* reborn.

65

BOUND FOR DARKNESS

0 Years Ago…

4

"This is not the end," Androma said. "You're too hard to kill, and I'm too stubborn to die. We *will* meet again, Daijen Saeth."

Even though the Dragon Rider couldn't see him, the Vahlken averted his gaze, his shame somehow amplified when in the presence of a warrior so noble and righteous as Androma. He was only thankful that she hadn't witnessed his murdering of The Valtorak.

"Our meeting at all seems an incalculable chance," he replied softly, thinking of the circumstances that had brought them together. "Perhaps fate will deem to bring us together again. I hope it does," he added, and truthfully so.

"We will meet again," the Rider repeated, as if she had seen the future. "Until then," she continued, fully entering the fortress's library, "I will remain at Ilithranda's side for a time. If I can, I will get her back in the fight. She is a warrior we cannot afford to lose."

Daijen was tempted to stop her from doing as much, thinking

back to what Ilithranda had said to him about being owed some time. But it was not his place to interfere. If Ilithranda was happy for Androma to accompany her, somewhere, deep down, she must want to be convinced as much.

"I could say the same about you, Daijen. Besides dragons, I would say you are the biggest threat to the Skaramangians. Do what you must," she caveated, aware of his problems after using the vambrace, "but see that you don't remain here too long. You're needed out there."

Using a wooden staff Yamnomora had crafted for her after the siege, the Dragon Rider tapped the floor twice. Daijen wished to rise from his seat and embrace her, but he felt he hadn't earned such a thing. Isolation was to be a part of his penance.

The Vahlken waited until Androma had departed the library before returning to the task he had set himself for the day. He had already created numerous piles of books—those that had survived the tower that collapsed in the final moments of the siege. He had done his best to categorise them, but his concerns remained with the hundreds of books trapped or destroyed beneath tons of rubble.

Having read them all, of course, Daijen vowed to, one day, restore the library's wealth of knowledge by scribing them all himself. For now, he could but save and store those that had survived. In truth, he hoped it would take his mind off what was happening beyond the library's shattered walls.

The dwarves had raided Ka'vairn for all they could carry, ensuring they had enough supplies to see them through the last days of winter. Along with The Green Leaf, they would be leaving the valley before they lost the sun. Likewise, Ilithranda had packed Oaken's saddle, preparing to take her and Androma south to find Tovun.

The council they had formed would soon be at an end.

When he went in search of food, Daijen inevitably crossed paths with the dwarves, who were apparently happy to leave him with little. A quick scan of Yamnomora's shoulder informed the Vahlken that the dagger he had seen lodged there after the battle still troubled her. She winced as she picked up a crate of salted pork joints, though the pain didn't stop her from taking what she wanted.

Mordrith was slow to move around the old stone kitchen, her wounded hip biting into her dwarven resolve. She noted Daijen's arrival immediately and looked pleased, almost, for an excuse to stand still for a minute.

"Ye live," she announced sarcastically. "We were startin' to wonder if ye'd died up there."

Daijen responded with a half-hearted, and entirely fake, smile. "I was just looking for some food," he said.

"Don' worry, lad," Yamnomora said, an onion resting between her teeth, "we'll leave ye with a radish or two."

"How generous of you," the Vahlken remarked.

"Abou' as generous as ye've been with whatever ye learned from the past," Yamnomora retorted dryly. "It were us who came to this dump an' told ye abou' The Tomb. The least ye can do in return is give us a headin'! Ye must know somethin', lad! Ye touched a bloody *god*!"

"Easy," Mordrith bade. "Take what ye've got to the hall."

Yamnomora spat the onion into the crate and waited for Daijen to step aside. "If it turns out ye've been holdin' out on us, Vahlken, I'll chop ye down until ye can pass for a dwarf. Understand?"

"Crystal."

"I hope so. 'Cos I'll 'ave no one killin' more Skaramangians than *me*."

"Yamnomora," Mordrith insisted.

"I'm goin', I'm goin'." The fierce dwarf paused one last time on the threshold and turned back. "Ye've a mean swing, Daijen Saeth. It were an honour to fight beside ye."

Taken off guard, Daijen bowed his head before fully absorbing the words. "And you."

Turning back to Mordrith, the Vahlken's sharp eyes caught sight of The Anther propped up in the far corner. He knew he should have shut his eyes, and without delay, but he was seduced by the weapon, by the fact that it had been forged and crafted by

The Dark One's very hands. The Valtorak's words returned to him then, a mantra to remind him of his duty to the light, but it wasn't enough in the presence of the hammer.

He stepped towards it—only to find a dwarf standing in his way.

Mordrith's dark eyes bored into him, her judgement enough to ground him right there in Ka'vairn's kitchen.

"Ye're not the same Andaren I met in the forest all those years ago," she began. "I suppose ye wouldn' be. It's not every day ye mix yer mind with a god." Her gaze was scrutinising, searching for any tell that might lend truth to her words. "Is that what's happened? 'Ave ye been hollowed out as the wizard feared?"

"I'm still me," Daijen assured her.

"Aye," Mordrith drawled, tapping her head, "but ye're not alone up there, are ye? I saw ye kill The Valtorak. They weren' yer eyes. It were like ye were somewhere else. *Someone* else."

"I have a lot of... *years* to make sense of. Years that were never mine. If I lose my focus, though, they begin to feel like mine, as if I actually lived them. As if I actually—"

As if I actually served him, he was going to say. But he stopped himself. It would reveal too much he knew. Better they believe in the Dark Ones or the Talakin, as the dwarves called them. The truth of the Golems would be his alone. His burden.

"There's a touch o' darkness abou' ye now, fella. Whatever ye do next, Daijen, I pray the old gods go with ye. Ye need the light."

"We alone must bring the light," the Vahlken muttered under his breath.

"What were that?"

Daijen shrugged. "Something The Valtorak told me before I earned my place in the order." He had thought to keep it to himself, but he wondered if his mantra might shed some light on his recent choices. "No one wants to look in the shadows," he said, the words crystallised in his memory. "We alone must tread where others dare not. We alone must bring the light."

Mordrith nodded along. "Sounds... *lonely.*"

"The warrior's path often is," he reasoned. "At least I have Valyra."

"I'm no warrior," Mordrith replied. "The path I walk is that o' *victory*. I can tell ye for nothin', that path is paved by *allies*. The scale o' our enemy cannot be comprehended. Ye alone... *me* alone, we cannot hope to beat the darkness. *Together?*" she considered, one finger in the air. "Together, we might jus' find a way."

"You would still have me?" he asked incredulously.

"Hells no!" the dwarf exclaimed. "Ye're a damned liability. Get yer head together an' come find us. Until then, ye'd be doin' the whole realm a favour by stayin' on this mountain."

A pained smile moved Daijen's lips. "I have no doubt the Skaramangians will rue the day Mordrith Underborn took her first breath."

"Aye, an' I'll be damned if they're to take me *last* breath." The dwarf moved away and retrieved The Anther.

The sound of the metal scraping lightly against the floor was almost enough to see Daijen snatch the weapon from her, his hand gripping the corner of the stone island with all his strength. He hadn't realised it, but his eyes had clamped shut at the same time as his mind repeated the mantra. When, at last, he opened them again, Mordrith was looking at him intently, knowingly.

"Aye, ye saw some things, didn' ye? I don' know what yer problem is with weapons o' power, lad, but ye'll 'ave to find yer own. This one belongs with me an' mine."

"You have no idea how true that is," Daijen managed to reply, his jaw still tense.

His dual minds overlapped for a moment, bringing Duun, son of Darl, into the kitchen. The dwarven Rider simply stood in the corner, behind Mordrith, as if he were no more than a harmless observer from another time, just as Daijen had been.

The Vahlken blinked, hard, and the son of Darl was gone from the kitchen.

Mordrith's hand came to rest on his forearm, rooting him to that moment. "Ye've a lot on yer shoulders now, lad. Including murder." She squeezed his arm, holding him fast before his shame saw him turn away. "I don' believe it were yer hand that truly killed The Valtorak, but ye're goin' to 'ave to come to terms with yer part in it."

The dwarf shrugged, unsure, perhaps, of her own advice.

"Ye've more power an' skill than the rest o' us combined— Ilithranda too. Though, ye'd never catch Yamnomora sayin' as much. Be sure to get yer head around... whatever it needs to get around. We need ye out there. The war ain' over, not by a long way. Farewell, Daijen Saeth."

The Vahlken remained as still as the dead, not daring to move while she passed him with The Anther in hand. He wished to return the farewell, but every scrap of discipline he could muster was required to stop him from killing her for the weapon.

It seemed a long time before he moved again, his lips parting to inhale much needed air. He forgot to get any food, setting his feet to wander the halls of Ka'vairn for a while. Every time he glanced back over his shoulder, he laid eyes on Duun, Gelakor, Nathara, and Qirann, the Riders content to follow him in silence. Every now and then, Daijen caught a glimpse of another crossing the end of the hall in his wake. It was Skara, he knew, robed and hooded in shadow black.

The sound of an Aegre's squawk cut through his mindless walking, drawing him to the large balcony above the keep's doors. Only half of it remained intact, where the fallen tower had missed it. Beyond the rubble and debris, Oaken dominated the courtyard. Ilithranda was aiding Androma, moving her hands and feet to show her the proper way to climb up to the saddle. The Vahlken herself was considerably faster.

"Let this not be the last time we meet, Ilithranda Lhoris," The Green Leaf called up.

"Nor the last time we fight together," Yamnomora added.

"It was an honour," Ilithranda replied, speaking of no path that would bring them all back together again.

"As usual, old friend," Androma said, speaking to the wizard, "I shall meet you in Riverwatch, at The Tallow Inn."

"I shall be sure to frequent it every summer," Aphrandhor replied.

Daijen heard it all while he and Ilithranda looked at each other from afar. For years, they had been able to communicate so much by their eyes alone, each possessing an intuitiveness where the other was concerned. He got nothing from her now. Ilithranda had shut herself off from him. Like him, she had so much to make sense of, her emotions battling themselves to come to terms with Slait.

Oaken squawked one last time and flapped his mighty wings. The companions were buffeted and forced back a step as they watched the Aegre take to the late afternoon sky. They were soon a dark smudge against the burned orange of the heavens. Daijen spied Valyra in Oaken's wake. She would follow them, he knew, seeing them out of the valley.

It saddened the Vahlken to know that the Aegres were being split up. While it was common practice for Vahlken and their Aegres to go out into the world alone, rarely encountering others of their kind, Daijen and Ilithranda had been at each other's side since bonding with their feathered companions. In a way, Valyra and Oaken had become a nest of two, Ka'vairn their eyrie.

His contemplation proved distracting enough to miss the approach of the wizard, who had left the courtyard and made his way up to the balcony. "Daijen?"

The young man's voice broke his reverie. "Aphrandhor," he said, greeting him softly.

The Green Leaf came to stand by the broken balustrade, his young eyes cast over the distant mountains in the east, where the realm of Morthil lay as a jagged beast across the land.

"I'm a fraction of your age," the wizard began. "I have not, and will not, live the years you have already. I would not be so arrogant as to offer you platitudes or sage advice. I honestly don't know what will help you to move forwards. What I *do* know," he countered, "is limited, but it's potentially of some use to you now."

Daijen looked at him with a question behind his eyes. At the same time, he noticed the wizard wasn't wearing the bracer. He wondered if it was a deliberate choice.

"I still have much to learn where the vambrace is concerned," The Green Leaf went on. "I'm not sure it was intended for someone like me—someone with limited capacity. A Rider, perhaps, who has the benefit of their dragon's mind," he theorised, no idea how accurate he was. "Or a Vahlken. Ilithranda tells me every Vahlken has the ability to walk through the halls of their life while they sleep."

Daijen nodded in agreement. "We can relive any moment of our lives."

Aphrandhor kept his own counsel for a moment, deep in thought. "You were unconscious for some time, but given the potential age of that bone, I would guess you only saw *some* of the memories it holds. Am I right?"

The Vahlken didn't want to dwell on the specifics, so he nodded again.

The wizard stroked his blond goatee, his thoughts gathering momentum. "Given the capacity of your own memory, we should assume you have absorbed more than the sum of what you witnessed."

"What are you saying?"

"I'm saying there's a high probability that every one of Ahnir's memories is locked away inside your mind, even if you haven't seen them yet. And whether you were subjected to them or not, your mind will hold onto them with a clarity I cannot imagine. While you sleep, you will be able to walk down halls that were never your own—you don't even need the bracer."

"I'm not sure I could handle more," Daijen confessed, his grip tightening around the top of the balustrade.

"While you might be feeling the weight of them right now, I'm confident that, in time, you will find a way to assimilate it all. If and when you do, you must hold to a single belief."

Daijen turned so he was completely facing the wizard. "What belief?"

"That you are in control," Aphrandhor articulated. "There is more than one life inside your mind now. This will seem over-whelming. You will feel carried away by the memory, a slave to the events around you. Do you feel this way when peering into your own life?"

"No," the Vahlken answered.

"Of course you don't. There's a part of your mind that understands it has already lived the events you are witnessing. It knows the past is the past, that you are an observer and not a participant. You must come to accept the same when standing in Ahnir's memories. When you do, you will walk as a god through all that you have seen, able to manipulate the memory to your will."

Daijen couldn't say he fully understood the wizard, but he certainly found the idea of control appealing. "You have done this?"

The Green Leaf shrugged. "Once or twice, on *younger* objects. I will forever be limited by my mind's capacity. Humans weren't meant to remember more than a few years, and even they become hazy. I only hope you come to master it all before my time is over. I should like to know what a god has seen."

Daijen bowed his head, allowing some time to pass and, with it, the urge to tell Aphrandhor the truth. They would all be gone soon, he thought, and the burden of his secrets would lighten.

"I wish you luck in this endeavour," the young wizard eventually said. "Kaliban willing, we will meet again."

Daijen gave what smile he could and gripped The Green Leaf's forearm in farewell. As the stars began to appear in the eastern sky, heavenly eyes looking down on the valley, Aphrandhor regrouped with the dwarves in the courtyard. They regarded Daijen one last time before Mordrith brought The Anther down with all her strength. Along with a portion of the courtyard, the trio vanished in a flash of light and a clap of air.

The Vahlken sighed, his shoulders physically sinking as he leaned down on the balustrade. It was done. Their alliance was at an end.

———

In the days that followed, Daijen delved deeper into his investigation. Only once did he allow himself some reprieve, a break that saw him take to hunting deer in The Dain'duil. While in the forest, he retrieved his slaiken blade, the great weapon still resting horizontally in a tree. So too were the bodies of the fallen still resting on the ground.

Leaving them to nature, the Vahlken had returned to the fortress and set himself to the task of reading the journal of emperors. He might not have put much stock in it, but given that Emperor Qeledred had known more than Daijen would ever have expected, he opened its pages.

Much of it he already knew or had seen the truth of the emperors' assumptions through Ahnir's memories. But there were whole entries from epochs back that spoke of other *things*. Things the Vahlken could never see through the Golem, who had long perished by the time the journal had been started.

There were entries older still that had been scribed in Andara's oldest language by the first of the Lhoris line. Unable to make sense of it, his mind found the answer in recent memory, leading him up to The Valtorak's shattered office.

For days or weeks—he could not say—the Vahlken pored over *Linguistics, Dialects, and Allogpraphy.* Word by word, he built the ancient language in his mind, often voicing it into the empty halls of Ka'vairn.

As his confidence grew and those weeks turned to months, he returned to the imperial journal, applying his newfound knowledge. While his memory required no more than a single readthrough, he read the entries again and again, shocked by the revelations therein.

Again and again, he was drawn back to the sketches he had made of the four Golems in their flowing cloaks of ethereal black. Connections were being made in his mind, his investigation aiding the formation of a new plan. It all sat upon the foundation of a comment Mordrith had made to him.

"*I don' know what yer problem is with weapons o' power, lad,*" she had said, "*but ye'll 'ave to find yer own.*"

He needed his own weapon. Something that could actually challenge The Dark One upon his inevitable return. Consulting all that he had learned and all he had read, he found that there was only one weapon that could beat Skara The Pendain—and only one way to harness it.

With that epiphany, he was reminded of one final vision, a future seen and spoken for him and Ilithranda alone.

"*Cast into the black,*" The Eldan had announced in his final moments, there on his knees and under the thrall of the helm, "*he drowns in shadow. The Drakalis is without sight. He is without voice. He is to suffer for his betrayal, he who should have reigned beside the Pendain. But the darkness cannot hold him. His chains are destined to be broken by the power of Handuin.*"

At the time, it had been another riddle spat forth from the wretched helm, but Daijen had seen the Drakalis with his own eyes now. He knew well the blinding hate Skara held for the dragon, the one whose betrayal stung the most.

It all percolated. Mordrith's comment. The visions. The past. The secrets found in the imperial journal.

While he remained unsure of the future, Daijen knew it would not be found in Ka'vairn. He gathered what meagre supplies had been left by the others and packed Valyra's saddle bags. In the courtyard, he paused over the spot where he had ended The Valtorak's life. He crouched down and touched the darkened stone, vowing to make all his mistakes mean something.

"I think I have seen a way through it all," he said, as if his old master could hear him. "You were right. Without my pride in the way, I see the answer does not lie with me. Our victory lies where others dare not tread. I must walk in shadow if I am to bring the light."

The Vahlken mounted Valyra, his pale eyes rising and falling over the ruins of Ka'vairn. It was a tomb now, there to contain the helm and what secrets their order had amassed. It was bound for myth, destined for legend.

Valyra lifted her head and squawked, one yellow eye spotting him on her back. Daijen patted her thick neck and rubbed the majestic brown feathers that coated her. "It's alright," he assured her, thinking of the weapon they would wield against The Dark One and his Skaramangians. "Our purpose remains the same, old friend."

Every flap of Valyra's wings parted them further from the ancient stone. Ka'vairn was soon small beneath them, its presence diminished as they rose into the sunrise. Together they flew over the mountains and into a future of their own forging, the light of the new day chasing them.

Daijen's thoughts, however, dwelled in shadow, for it was there that he needed to venture.

Only there would he find the weapon Skara so feared above all else.

Only there would he find... *Malliath*.

EPILOGUE

J oran's heart was breaking, his world unravelling before his
violet eyes. Tears streaked his face and blood trickled down
his throat, running free from the edge of the blade that bit
into his flesh. He was hardly aware of his Andaren captor or
even the Andaren who had revealed the dark truth.

He could only watch as his father succumbed to ancient
memories. Everything that made Gallien the man he was, the
father and protector he had been to Joran, was being purged from
existence.

In his despair, something new was born inside of Joran
Pendain. Something primal. Something wretched.

Rage.

Unbridled, it demanded action and banished all thought of
consequence.

With a single burst of energy, he leaped up, thrusting his head
into the Andaren's jaw, just beneath his mask. He might have made
it a step closer to Gallien had his father not cried out and risen
bodily from the floor. The wave of energy that exploded out from
him was powerful enough to lift Joran from his feet and launch
him into the wall.

At the same time, Gallien's satchel burst like a water skin, dispersing trinkets, books, and all manner of sundries across the cold stone. Joran bounced off the wall and slammed into the floor as one of those dispersed items skidded towards him, ejected at speed. His eyes shut and pain lancing through his back, he felt the object pummel his chest and get caught up in his arms.

His gaze drawn to his hands and that which he held, the world and its troubles shrank to a pinhead, as if the chamber and all its peril ceased to exist.

In that moment, there was only Joran... and the *dragon egg*.

His rage was instantly sucked into a void, quashed into nothingness.

Where had it come from? The question led him back to Gallien's satchel—*Androma's* satchel. Had the old Rider been carrying a dragon egg all these years? It seemed an impossibility, considering she had intended for him to bond with one. Yet there it was, hurled from the very same satchel that had been with him all his life, the two only separated by the magic etched into the leather.

Like those he had seen in the heart of Drakanan, its shell was patterned with scales. Dark purple they were, and speckled with the lightest touch of gold. Joran knew right there and then that it was the most beautiful thing he had ever seen. It was also the most precious thing he had ever seen, appearing to him as fragile and vulnerable despite its impenetrable shell.

A whisper slipped into his mind. The words were beyond him, a different language, if not entirely unintelligible. Yet it was soothing, familiar almost, as if he had known that voice all his life.

While the circumstances surrounding its presence in Gallien's satchel remained a mystery to him, he knew he had to keep it safe. That was more important than anything else.

"Gallien!" Aphrandhor called, the wizard rising.

That name meant something to Joran. It was important to him. Gallien was important to him. Regardless, the boy could only spare a glance as The Green Leaf embraced the man he knew to be his father. Why was it so hard to concentrate? He looked down at the egg again, feeling the scales in his hands, and knew he was *home*.

"You must fight it, my boy," Aphrandhor was pleading. "Whatever they're doing, you *must* fight it."

It almost hurt to look away from the purple egg, but Joran managed to lay his eyes on the two men. Something was wrong. Gallien was wrong. It was so hard to focus, his instincts talking to him more than anything else.

That wasn't his father.

"Yes," Aphrandhor said, cupping Gallien's face. "Fight it."

Gallien removed the hands from his cheeks, offering the wizard a warm smile. "You wanted to see the whole me."

What horror Joran then witnessed, sure that his eyes must be deceiving him. There was no deception in death, however. The Green Leaf fell to his knees, his blood spilling unrestrained across the stone.

Joran brought the dragon egg to his chest and held it a little tighter. He stared at the man that had been Gallien Pendain. The Dark One. Splattered in Aphrandhor's blood, he crouched down, the axe placed beside him so his fingers could pick something from the growing pool of red. It was the single dragon scale Gallien had taken from Harendun all those years ago. Skara, as he had been so named, was transfixed by it.

Chaos followed.

The pyramid quaked, groaning and cracking. Dust fell from the ceiling in sheets, and one of the balconies lost its place on the wall and plummeted in pieces, killing one of the Andarens. The impact was almost drowned out by a thunderous roar so terrible it managed to pierce the wretched depths of Azad-guul. The next tremor was worse, knocking everyone from their feet.

Almost everyone.

Cob leaped like an animal, pouncing atop one of the Andarens with feral glee. He bashed his head into the stone again and again until the *crunch* became a wet *thud*. Steel dragged across the floor, the guard's sword scooped up by the incensed Kedradi. Two more died before they could pick themselves up, while the first to challenge him was sliced from throat to groin.

The Eldan dashed towards Skara, their exchange concealed by falling debris and a horn that resounded from somewhere beyond Azad-guul. Narrowly avoiding a chunk of falling rock that would have ended them there and then, the two dashed away, surrounded by Andaren guards who escorted them away from the crumbling chamber with all haste.

"Joran!" Androma shouted over the clash of steel and cries of death.

One of the Andarens turned on the old Rider, inhaling sharply as he raised his sword to cut her down. Androma slid on her knees, pivoting as she did, and came up to lock his arm in a vice-like grip. *Snap!* The bone shot through the guard's arm, eliciting a shriek of agony. The Rider back-handed him, ending the fight before it could go any further.

"Joran!" she yelled again, blindly crashing into him.

Her hands probed his arms and face before finding that which he held. Her fingers ran over the scales, taking in the item's its shape and texture. The old Rider knew exactly what it was, her mouth agape with utter shock.

"It came out of the satchel," he said absently, removing the egg from her touch.

"The satchel?" Androma echoed incredulously, her words almost lost to Cob's wild fighting and the slabs of stone falling about them. "*Daijen,*" she breathed with an air of revelation about her. "He fell... He fell! It must have landed in the satchel! All this time..."

Another Andaren came barrelling towards them, sword swinging. Androma pushed Joran back and dived into the rushing guard, taking him by the waist. She coiled around him like a snake, snatching at his limbs with her legs until he was immobilised and she could crack his neck in her hands.

Joran was stumbling away from the bloody scene, one hand blindly guiding him along the wall towards the main doors. He watched Cob hack and chop, laughing as he slaughtered Andaren after Andaren. Beyond him, Aphrandhor lay in a pool of his own blood, eyes gazing into an abyss only the dead could see.

Androma had claimed her victim's sword, bringing the weapon against any who got in her way. She called for Joran repeatedly, her voice laden with real fear. He couldn't answer her. He had to get out of there—he had to get the *egg* out of there. It was his responsibility. His *life*. Taking the egg into such a bloodbath would doom them both.

Help them! his head cried.

Get out! his instincts screamed.

Help them!

Get out!

To the sound of Cob's manic laughter, Joran ran from the chamber, pausing only to investigate the metallic object that nearly tripped him up.

The broken sword.

His mind so occupied by the egg, he picked the weapon up without thought and made his escape. The pyramid trembled all the while, its interior collapsing under its own weight.

Again, he heard the terrifying roar as it reverberated throughout Azad-guul. He could only run, so he did, taking every turn and stairwell until he was returned to the chamber that housed the pulley system and platform.

It was still there, as if it had been waiting for him. There was no sign of his father—of Skara—or The Eldan, their escape having taken them down a different path.

Joran didn't hesitate to kick the lever and jump onto the platform. His neck craned, he looked up at the stars beyond the lift shaft, the sky alight with those heavenly jewels. So too was it alight with fire. The flames blew over the opening in a narrow jet, scorching men and women, judging by the sounds of their screams. Added to the cacophony was the ringing of steel and the distinct discharge of magic.

It was everything Joran imagined a war to sound like.

As his head broke the surface, he saw the truth of all he had heard, and it was so much more terrifying than it had sounded.

Men and women, Skaramangians all, were running in every direction. Fleeing. Even the most fanatical lost their resolve in the face of a dragon, and Nareene had been set upon by *three* of them.

They torched everything, burning the buildings and surrounding trees and filling the air with thick ash. Men and women were crushed underfoot, clubbed by tails as thick as the strongest trunks, and devoured whole by maws of sharp teeth.

Stepping off the platform, Joran cradled the egg close to his chest, his sandy cloak blown out by the swish of a dragon's tail. Charging through the debris and broken bodies, the earth was churned and thrown high into the air. Their roars piled upon each other, chilling the boy to his bones. He had to get the egg to safety, an imperative that filled every fibre of his being, yet there was nowhere to go. Every direction spelled annihilation.

A Skaramangian ran past him, his entire body in the grip of flames. Such was his pain that the man threw himself over the edge of the pit, where death was assured. Fearing for the egg, Joran broke into a run, weaving between the Skaramangians fleeing for their lives and the hulking dragons that stomped and clawed at anything that moved.

One of them exhaled a sharp breath of fire, the heat so intense it forced Joran to change his direction. Then he saw her, the last person he had expected to see on Nareene.

Kassanda Grey was locked in battle, her silvyr sword spinning, thrusting, and slashing with deadly precision. But it wasn't enough to ensure the Rider's victory, her opponent deflecting her every strike with fluid ease and countering with blows of his own. His obsidian cloak billowed out behind him, exposing the bronze cuirass and pauldrons of dragon scales, each a dark honey like those on his vambraces. His face was aged, his older appearance amplified by his short grey hair and full beard, though he held himself with a core that spoke volumes about his strength.

There was no doubt in Joran's mind that he looked upon the Dragonlord—Baelon Vos.

He didn't move nearly as much as Kassanda, his sword always

moving to control the flow of their duel. It made his fighting style look effortless, as if he were merely toying with the Rider.

Kassanda, however, was relentless. She came at him from every angle, her form always perfect, her attacks executed with matchless skill. Sparks arced into the air when her blade ran up his cuirass, scoring a neat line through the steel. Following through, she leaped high and twisted her hips to launch a boot into his chest, throwing him from his feet.

Her dark eyes found the boy. "Joran? Joran!" The Rider's gaze fell on the purple egg in his hands. "Run!" she urged, having no time to ask him questions.

Baelon's spell slammed into her, kicking up dirt and snow along with the Rider. Kassanda was contorted and flung into the wreckage of a building, her body buried by the debris.

The world shook with the roar that followed. It gripped both earth and air, carrying a message of violent retribution.

Joran turned just in time to see the edge of the forest explode, the trees snapped and brought down like twigs, as Garganafan burst into the clearing. There was another dragon with him, its claws scrambling beneath him, teeth gnashing. Garganafan put one foot on his foe's chest, suppressing the dragon's attacks, and raised his head to deliver another mighty ear-splitting roar. Without warning, his colossal head whipped down and his jaws extended, but it was not fire he unleashed.

The dragon beneath him was powerless to stop the *ice* that filled its mouth and hardened inside its throat. Its tail thrashed and wings spasmed beneath Garganafan, but the white dragon did not relent. Only when his opponent was still, its head a frozen block of steaming scales and bone, did he look up with fury in his eyes. Stepping over his kill, he barely advanced before two more dragons descended on him, their brawl killing a dozen Skaramangians.

And the dragon did not fight alone.

Oaken!

The Aegre fell upon them, a killing machine born of the night, his talons and sharp beak added to the fray.

Joran looked back at the debris, his fear abating on seeing Kassanda slowly digging her way out. But there was something enormous in his periphery. Battling his dread, Joran turned, his violet eyes rising to meet reptilian eyes of vivid green. The dragon exhaled a cloud of hot air over the boy before its nostrils explored his scent... and that of the egg.

Baelon Vos stepped in front of him, a pillar of black and bronze, his shoulders all the broader for his pauldrons and his expression unyieldingly stern. He managed to eclipse the dragon at his back, dominating Joran's world. His cold eyes fell on the egg.

The Dragonlord planted a heavy hand on the boy's shoulder, his lips curling into a hungry smile. "Long have I searched for you, Joran Pendain. Fate has brought us together, at last." His grip tightened all the more. "You have my word—when I am done with you, there will be no greater legend than yours... *Dragon Rider.*"

A Time of Dragons

OF

Dragons

BOOK 3

THE SAGA CONTINUES IN 2025

PHILIP C. QUAINTRELL

---

*Hear more from Philip C. Quaintrell including
book releases and exclusive content:*

 PHILIPCQUAINTRELL.COM

 FACEBOOK.COM/PHILIPCQUAINTRELL

 @PHILIPCQUAINTRELL.AUTHOR

 @PCQUAINTRELL

ABOUT THE AUTHOR

Philip C. Quaintrell is the author of the epic fantasy series, The Echoes Saga, as well as the Torran Cycle sci-fi series. He was born in Cheshire in 1989 and started his career as an emergency nurse.

Having always been a fan of fantasy and sci-fi fiction, Philip started to find himself feeling frustrated as he read books, wanting to delve into the writing himself to tweak characters and story-lines. He decided to write his first novel as a hobby to escape from nursing and found himself swept away into the world he'd created. Even now, he talks about how the characters tell him what they're going to do next, rather than the other way around.

With his first book written, and a good few rejected agency submissions under his belt, he decided to throw himself in at the deep end and self-publish. 2 months and £60 worth of sales in, he took his wife out to dinner to celebrate an achievement ticked off his bucket list - blissfully unaware this was just the beginning.

Fast forward 12 months and he was self-publishing book 1 of his fantasy series (The Echoes Saga; written purely as a means to combat his sci-fi writers' block). With no discernible marketing except the 'Amazon algorithm', the book was in the amazon best-sellers list in at least 4 countries within a month. The Echoes Saga has now surpassed 700k copies sold worldwide, has an option agreement for a potential TV-series in the pipeline and Amazon now puts Philip's sales figures in the top 1.8% of self-published authors worldwide.

Philip lives in Cheshire, England with his wife and two children. He still finds time between naps and wiping snot off his clothes to remain a movie aficionado and comic book connoisseur, and is hoping this is still just the beginning.

AUTHOR NOTES

We're in it now! A Time of Dragons has two books under its belt and the villain has arrived in dramatic fashion.

This one was a mammoth from the writing side of things. It clocked in at 245,000 words, beating out a Clash of Fates by 7,000 words and making it my longest book to date. I think it might also have the most twists and turns of any Verda book to date. A lot took place In The Shadow of Kings and I'm probably going to use this section to waffle on about it and talk a little about my process and how the story unfolded for me.

Before that though: a little about where I'm at right now. It's always nice to share something of my own life with you all since most of what you see of me is between thee pages.

Life has been busy—which I love! My three year-old daughter is *very* three and thinks that boundaries are for babies. Thankfully, my five year-old son is a great big brother and is teaching her so much (mostly good things).

School is a thing that's now back in my life as my son is in his first year. This has brought some change to our rhythm and my writing routine. On the whole, I love change, it keeps life interesting, but I'm still getting used to school just ending in the middle of the day!

That said, my years working as a nurse before I became a full time writer taught me how to be adaptable. I've retrained all my writing muscles now, and I get 2,000 words written between 09:30 and 14:45 Monday-Friday.

I've said it before and I'll say it again, I'm not a writer who goes looking for inspiration. If I did, I'd likely never write a damn thing. Instead, I keep to my routine and use the methods I know (soundtracks) will flex my imagination. If I do this, inspiration knows where to find me.

Depending on when you're reading this, you might already know that Book 2 isn't the end of this series. Normally, I would take a break between books and recharge a bit, but I've already dived straight into book 3. Again, this change in routine is due to family life (school).

I've six weeks ahead of me this summer in which my son will be on his holidays. So, rather than take time between books this year, I'm saving it up for his school break. While I'm looking forward to that time with my kids, I can tell you, my brain is a little fried.

Thankfully, book 3 is awesome and going places I didn't anticipate, so it's keeping me extremely entertained. If you follow me on social media or sign up to my mailing list, you can keep up to date on all my releases and news (no spam, I promise).

So... In The Shadow Of Kings!

I'm actually writing this the very same day I finished the epilogue, so the ending is super fresh in my mind—seems like a good place to start!

Huzzah! Joran has bonded with a dragon egg! I'm sure we can all think of a book in which the young man, a stable boy or some such, wanders out from his sleepy village and bonds with an egg that's just sitting there, waiting for him. And I like those stories. It's a good trope. It's just not the trope I wanted to go with for Joran.

I've enjoyed the graft that's gone into bringing him and the right egg together, even if it took two books to get there. It feels deserved and, by the end, probably not what people were expecting for him, given all that transpired in this book. Of course, Oaken is still on the scene, so there's still that complication...

I also enjoyed the way in which the egg found its way to him. The idea that it had actually been with him since he was born felt important to me, helping to distinguish between this bonding story and all the others out there.

I'm very excited to get stuck into book three and see where Joran's journey goes next. Baelon Vos will certainly make it interesting, I'm sure.

I have to talk about the ones we lost, of course. The Green Leaf! I enjoyed writing the talkative wizard and he will be missed in the present-day story line. I didn't see his death coming exactly; it was more a feeling that 'someone' would likely die with the big reveal —besides Gallien I mean. Losing the two of them will change the dynamics going forward, and even more so since Gallien is still around physically.

Obviously, I can't go into much detail on Gallien/Skara right now as he will have a bigger part in the next book. I've been super excited about his storyline for a long time actually.

I don't know why, but I've been fascinated with *memory* and our inability to contain so much of our life with any clarity. The idea of a man—an ordinary human—moving from body to body, living for thousands of years struck me as interesting, but I became obsessed with the idea when I realised he wouldn't be able to remember much beyond the decades.

Enter, the villain!

I could probably write an entirely new series just moving through the centuries as Skara, his consciousness inhabiting body after body in order to stay alive. I'm sure there would be some vey exciting parts of his life—especially in those years closer to his death at Gelakor's hands.

I fear it would get boring eventually, when his human mind began to collapse under the weight of lifetimes. How many thousands of lives did he experience as just an ordinary person or a wanderer who couldn't recall where he came from or where he was going?

Bringing Skara as he was during his reign into the present day is going to be very interesting. The world has changed since the days of his earliest lives. He has a lot of work to do.

As do I, now that I think about. I'm waffling away when there's editing to be done! I better get on with—busy, busy, busy.

As always, I would encourage you to leave a review on Amazon and the usual places. I'm a self-publisher (by choice these days) and your support with reviews and word of mouth goes a long way to keeping my dream alive.

Until the next time...

VERDA TIMELINE

A TIME OF DRAGONS

12,000 YEARS

THE RANGER ARCHIVES

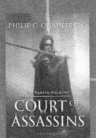

12 DAYS

THE ECHOES SAGA

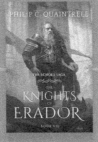

Printed in the USA
CPSIA information can be obtained
at www.ICGtesting.com
CBHW021933080824
12905CB00023B/298/J

9 781916 610361